PENGUIN CLASSICS

THE PORTABLE DANTE

DANTE ALIGHIERI was born in Florence in 1265 and belonged to a noble but impoverished family. He followed a normal course of studies, possibly attending University in Bologna, and when he was about twenty he married Gemma Donati, by whom he had several children. He had first met Bice Portinati, whom he called Beatrice, in 1274, and when she died in 1290, he sought distraction by studying philosophy and theology and by writing the *Vita nuova*. During this time he became involved in the strife between the Guelfs and the Ghibellines; he became a prominent White Guelf, and when the Black Guelfs came to power in 1302, Dante, during an absence from Florence, was condemned to exile. He took refuge first in Verona, and after wandering from place to place—as far as Paris and even, some have said, to Oxford—he settled in Ravenna. While there he completed *The Divine Comedy*, which he began in about 1308. Dante died in Ravenna in 1321.

MARK MUSA is a graduate of Rutgers University, the University of Florence, and The John Hopkins University. A former Guggenheim Fellow, he is the author of a number of books and articles. Best known for his translations of the Italian classics (Dante, Petrarch, Boccaccio, Machiavelli, and the poetry of the Middle Ages) as well as his Dante criticism, he holds the title of Distinguished Professor of Italian at Indiana University.

The Portable Dante

Translated, Edited and with an
Introduction and Notes by
MARK MUSA

PENGUIN BOOKS

PENGUIN BOOKS

Published by the Penguin Group

Penguin Group (USA) Inc., 375 Hudson Street, New York, New York 10014, U.S.A.

Penguin Books Ltd, 80 Strand, London WC2R 0RL, England

Penguin Books Australia Ltd, 250 Camberwell Road, Camberwell, Victoria 3124, Australia

Penguin Books Canada Ltd, 10 Alcorn Avenue, Toronto, Ontario, Canada M4V 3B2

Penguin Books India (P) Ltd, 11 Community Centre, Panchsheel Park, New Delhi – 110 017, India

Penguin Books (N.Z.) Ltd, Cnr Rosedale and Airborne Roads, Albany, Auckland, New Zealand

Penguin Books (South Africa) (Pty) Ltd, 24 Sturdee Avenue, Rosebank, Johannesburg 2196, South Africa

Penguin Books Ltd, Registered Offices: 80 Strand, London WC2R 0RL, England

First published in the United States of America by Penguin Books 1995
This edition published 2003

5   7   9   10   8   6

The Divine Comedy: Inferno
This translation first published in the United States of America by Indiana University Press 1971
Published in Penguin Books 1984
Copyright © Indiana University Press, 1971
Copyright © Mark Musa, 1984

The Divine Comedy: Purgatory
This translation first published in the United States of America by Indiana University Press 1981
Published in Penguin Books 1984
Copyright © Mark Musa, 1981

The Divine Comedy: Paradise
This translation first published in the United States of America by Indiana University Press 1984
Published in Penguin Books 1986
Copyright © Mark Musa, 1984

Vita Nuova
This translation first published in the United States of America by Indiana University Press 1973
Published in Great Britain in different format by Oxford University Press
Reprinted by arrangement with Indiana University Press
Copyright © Indiana University Press, 1973

LIBRARY OF CONGRESS CATALOGING IN PUBLICATION DATA
Dante Alighieri, 1265–1321
[Selections. English. 1995]
The portable Dante / edited and with an introduction and notes by Mark Musa.
p.   cm.
"A Penguin original".
Includes bibliographical references.
ISBN 0 14 24.3754 9
1. Dante Alighieri, 1265–1321.   Translations into English.   I. Musa, Mark.   II. Title.
PQ4315.A3M87   1995
851'.1—dc20   94–15988

Printed in the United States of America
Set in Sabon

FOR
ISABELLA
WITH
LOVE

CONTENTS

INTRODUCTION

LIFE

DANTE ALIGHIERI WAS BORN in Florence in May 1265 in the district of San Martino, the son of Alighiero di Bellincione d'Alighiero. His mother died when he was young; his father, whom he seems to avoid mentioning as much as possible, remarried and produced two more children. The Alighieri family may be considered noble by reason of the titles and dignities bestowed upon its members, although by Dante's time it seems to have been reduced to modest economic and social circumstances. According to Dante himself, the family descended from the noble seed of the Roman founders of the city (*Inferno* XV.73–78). This claim remains largely unsubstantiated, as nothing is known of Dante's ancestors before his great-great-grandfather, Cacciaguida, who was knighted by Emperor Conrad III and died, as Dante tells us, during the Second Crusade, about 1147 (*Paradiso* XV.139–148).

Like most of the city's lesser nobility and artisans, Dante's family was affiliated with the Guelf party, as opposed to the Ghibellines, whose adherents tended to belong to the feudal aristocracy. These two parties came into Italy from Germany, and their names represent italianized forms of those attached to the two quarreling houses of Germany, Welf and Waiblingen. In Italy the parties were at first identified with broad allegiances: to papal authority for the Guelfs, and to imperial authority in the case of the Ghibellines. Eventually, however, this church-empire distinction disappeared, and the two parties became less clearly defined in outlook and purpose. The local connotations of the parties became much more important as their issues and activities became tied to geographical situation, rivalries of neighborhoods in the same city, family feuds, and private interests. Thus the Guelfs and Ghibellines of Florence were factions peculiar to that region alone.

As far as one can tell from his writings, Dante's recollections of family life were pleasant ones. It is fairly certain that he received a careful education, although little of it is known precisely. He may have attended the Franciscan lower schools and, later, their schools of philosophy. The family's modest social standing did not prevent him from pursuing his studies, nor was he hindered in his effort to lead the life of a gentleman. His writings indicate that he was familiar with the ways of the country as well as with city life. Dante probably studied rhetoric with the scholar and statesman Brunetto Latini (ca. 1220–1294), from whom he says that he learned "how man makes himself eternal" (*Inferno* XV.85), during a period when he was driven by a desire to master the techniques of style. It seems that Brunetto fed his keenness for study and learning, and this may account for a trip in about 1287 to Bologna, where Dante elected to pursue his study of rhetoric in the highly renowned school there.

Dante tells us that as a young man he taught himself the art of writing verse (*Vita nuova* III.9). In time he became acquainted with the best-known troubadours of Florence, corresponding with them and circulating his own love lyrics. For the youthful Dante, writing poetry gradually became an important occupation, nourished by his sincere love for art and learning, and his interest in the nature of genuine love. Equally significant at this time was his friendship with the wealthy, aristocratic poet Guido Cavalcanti (ca. 1255–1300). Guido exerted a strong influence on his early poetic endeavors. This period was also marked by the death of Dante's father (ca. 1283), and by his marriage to Gemma, a gentlewoman of the Donati family. The marriage had been arranged by Dante's father in 1277, well before his death. Gemma and Dante had two sons, Pietro and Jacopo, and at least one daughter. (There exist the names of two daughters, Antonia and Beatrice, but they could refer to the same person, the second, Beatrice, being a monastic name.) Dante's marriage and children seem to have had little influence on him as a poet; nowhere in his works does he make direct reference to his wife.

Besides his associations with Guido Cavalcanti and Brunetto Latini, Dante knew well the notary Lapo Gianni and became acquainted later on with the youthful Cino da Pistoia. Both of these men were poets. Dante was also on friendly terms with the musician Casella (*Purgatorio* II.76–114), about whom there exists little information. The artists Oderisi da Gubbio and Giotto may also have been among his acquaintances. A comrade chosen with far less discrimination, perhaps, was Forese Donati (*Purgatorio* XXIII), a kinsman of Dante's wife and a regular rogue, with whom Dante had an exchange of reproaches and coarse insults in sonnet form. The exchange may have begun only as a joke in a moment of good humor.

Along with Guido, Dante refined and developed his poetic skill in Latin and began to distinguish himself in his art from the other writers of the time. In their poetry Dante and Guido presented their ideas on the nature of love and its ability to contribute to the inner perfection of man. Guido, however, was more interested in natural philosophy than was Dante, who, because of his more artistic orientation, favored the study and emulation of the Latin poets. He particularly admired Virgil, from whom he learned so much about matters of style. Though Dante was deeply influenced in his writing by the example of his friend Guido, he eventually responded to his own artistic temperament, to his study of Virgil, and to the example provided by a more recent poetic master, Guido Guinizzelli (ca. 1230–1276). The result was a shift to composition in the vernacular, a poetic innovation that is praised by Bonagiunta Orbicianni in the *Purgatorio* (XXIV.49–62).

Dante's life and writings were also influenced by his acquaintance with a noble Florentine woman of outstanding grace and beauty. He had named her among the sixty fairest women of Florence, but it was not until later that the poet truly "discovered" her. This revelation proved to be an extremely powerful force in his artistic development. According to the testimony of Boccaccio and others, the woman, called Bice, was the daughter of Folco Portinari of Florence. She later became the wife of the banker Simone de' Bardi. Dante called her Beatrice, "the bringer of blessings," the one who brought bliss to all who looked upon her.

Dante claims to have met Beatrice for the first time when he was nine years old. Theirs was not an easy relationship, for Beatrice took offense at the attention he paid other women. The resulting rebuff caused Dante great sorrow. His emotional attachment to Beatrice brought him to idealize her more and more as the guide of his thoughts and feelings, as the one who would lead him toward the inner perfection that is the ideal of every noble mind. In his poems Dante praises his lady as a model of virtue and courtesy, a miraculous gift given to earth by God to ennoble and enrich all those who appreciated her qualities. Such an exalted view of this woman was bound to carry with it the fear that she would not remain long in this life; in fact, premature death did befall her. Beatrice's father died first, and then she died on June 8, 1290. Dante was overcome with grief at his loss. There followed a period of contemplating Beatrice's significance after her death. After the first anniversary of her death, another woman, who is never mentioned by name, succeeded in winning Dante's affection for a brief time. However, Beatrice soon came vividly to mind again, and while feeling guilt and remorse for having neglected the memory of her, Dante reaffirmed his fidelity to her. This experience prompted him to gather together all the poems he had written in her honor, in an attempt to celebrate her virtue. This collection, to which Dante added a commentary on the meaning and occasion of each poem, became the little volume that he called the *Vita nuova* (*New Life*), about which I shall have more to say later on in this essay.

During all of this time Dante's passion for study had continued unabated. His vision had been broadened by the reading of Boethius and Cicero. The dissemination of Aristotle's works on physical and metaphysical subjects brought recognition of the need to harmonize the ideas of the great guide of human reason with the truths and teachings of the faith. Dante, by now a grown man, was attracted to many of the new schools and universities that were operating under the tutelage of the new religious orders. Among the Franciscans, Dominicans, and Augustinians were many eminent teachers and scholars. In this brisk intellectual environment of around 1290 Dante applied his energies to philosophy with such fervor that "in a short time, perhaps thirty months," he began "to be so keenly aware of her sweetness that the love of her drove away and destroyed every other thought" (*Convivio* II.2.7). Dante read so much, it seems, that his eyes were weakened considerably because of it. Among Christian scholars and theologians, he certainly read Saint Thomas Aquinas, Albertus Magnus, Saint Augustine, Hugh and Richard of Saint Victor, Saint Bonaventura, Saint Bernard, and Peter Lombard. In the area of history he took up Livy and Paulus Orosius, among others. Evidence of this extensive course of study found its way into his poetry as he became interested in the glorification of philosophy as mistress of the mind. Dante also treated questions of moral philosophy, such as nobility and courtship, in a number of beautifully composed *canzoni*, or odes. Nevertheless, in spite of this ardent pursuit of philosophical matters he retained his view of love as the most important force behind noble actions and lofty endeavors. To his appreciation of the Latin poets he added an admiration for the Provençal troubadours, and this encouraged him to attempt new poetic techniques that would serve him well in his later writings.

Along with his spiritual and intellectual activities Dante engaged in civic enterprises as well. In 1289 he had fought on the Guelf side at the battle of Campaldino. In 1295 he began an active public life, and within a few years he became an important figure in Florentine politics. He had joined the Guild of Physicians and Apothecaries in order to participate in government (except for certain offices, government was closed to those without guild affiliation), and there is evidence that he served as a member of the People's Council of the Commune of Florence (1295), on the Council for Election of the Priors of the City (1295), and on the Council of the Hundred (1296), a body that dealt with finance and other important civic matters.

This was a time of political ferment and instability. Between 1215 and 1278 the Guelfs and Ghibellines of Florence had engaged in a bitter struggle for power, with numerous reversals of fortune for both sides, countless plots and conspiracies, and frequent expulsion orders issued against whoever was on the losing side. The Guelfs finally prevailed. Around 1300, however, there occurred a split in the Guelf party into two very hostile factions: the Blacks and the Whites. The Blacks, staunch Guelfs, remained in control of the commune. The Whites eventually associated themselves with the Ghibellines. Dante, meanwhile, fought to preserve the independence of Florence, and repeatedly opposed the schemes of Pope Boniface VIII, who wanted to place Florence and all of Tuscany under the control of the Church. Boniface attempted to take advantage of the unrest in the city and undermine his opponents by promising protection to those who displayed some sympathy with his cause. He met with firm opposition from the six priors (magistrates) of Florence, of whom Dante was one, in the summer of 1300. To show his displeasure Boniface moved to excommunicate the members of the priorate. Dante was spared this fate only because his term of office was soon due to expire. Obviously, none of this served to improve Dante's opinion of the pontiff. He made no secret of his opposition to the pope's ambitious policy; he regarded Boniface as an enemy of peace.

In 1301 Boniface summoned Charles of Valois and his army to Italy in an attempt to neutralize anti-Church forces in Florence. It was at this time, as Charles approached the city, that Dante was sent as one of three envoys on behalf of the commune to the pope, in order to request a change in papal policy toward the city and to protest the intrigues of the Blacks. After the initial talks the other envoys were dismissed, but Dante was retained. During his absence Charles of Valois entered Florence, and the Blacks staged a revolution and gained complete control of the commune. Dante found himself sentenced to exile on trumped-up charges of graft, embezzlement, opposition to the pope and his forces, disturbance of the peace of Florence, and a number of other transgressions. Dante always felt that his difficulties had been brought on by the trickery of Boniface, and this only aggravated his already pronounced hatred for the pontiff and his methods. When Dante failed to appear to answer the charges against him, and when he did not pay the fine levied against him for his "crimes," a second sentence was imposed: should he ever return to the commune, he would be seized and burned alive. There is no evidence that Dante saw his beloved Florence again.

In 1302, shortly after his banishment, Dante conspired with his fellow exiles, most of them Whites, to regain admission to Florence. However, disapproving of their machinations and possibly in danger of his life because of their violence, he abandoned them and set off on his own to lead the life of an exiled courtier. It appears that he first took refuge with the Scala family at Verona. He is believed to have visited the university at Bologna, where he had been known since 1287. This visit probably occurred after the death in 1304 of his generous patron, Bartolommeo della Scala. It is generally thought that Dante traveled extensively in Italy, particularly in the north. He may have been in Padua in 1306. During that same year he appeared in Lunigiana with the Malaspina family, and it was probably then that he went to the mountains of Casentino, on the upper Arno. It is also thought that he went to Paris sometime between 1307 and 1309.

In 1310 Henry VII of Luxembourg, Holy Roman emperor from 1312 to 1313, entered Italy in an effort to reunite Church and state, restore order, and force various rebellious cities to submit to his authority. His coming caused a great deal of excitement and conflict. Florence generally opposed him, but Dante, who attributed the woes of Florence and all of Italy to the absence of imperial guidance, welcomed Henry as a savior. Dante's state of great exaltation is documented in three letters that he wrote in 1310 and 1311. However, Henry's invasion proved fruitless; he met opposition from all sides, including Pope Clement V, who had sent for him in the first place. Just as the situation for Henry and his supporters began to improve, the emperor died near Siena in 1313. With him went Dante's every hope of restoring himself to an honorable position in his city. Thus in 1314 he took shelter with the Ghibelline captain Can Grande della Scala in Verona.

Dante did not totally abandon his quest to return to his native city. He wrote letters to individual members of the government, attempting to appease those who ruled. He even sent a *canzone* to the city of Florence, praising her love for justice and asking that she work with her citizens on his behalf. Dante strove to be acceptable to the Florentines, but for many reasons the public associated him with the Ghibellines; no matter how Dante tried to free himself of suspicion, he did not succeed. He also tried to appeal to them on the grounds of his poetic ability, and sought to show that if he had cultivated poetry in the vernacular it was not for lack of skill or study. He was compelled to display his love for learning and his great respect for philosophy and matters having to do with civic education. He therefore composed two treatises (both left incomplete), the *De vulgari eloquentia* (*On Eloquence in the Vernacular*) and the *Convivio* (*Banquet*), sometime between 1304 and 1307. In them can be seen his longing to reestablish himself in the good graces of his city and to find consolation for his wretchedness in the study of matters useful to man's well-being and his art. Thus in the ten years or so between the *Vita nuova* and the *Commedia* (*Divine Comedy*), Dante's studies were essentially of a philosophical and artistic nature. The *Convivio* is often acknowledged as the key to his philosophical researches, while the *De vulgari eloquentia* is viewed as the key to his artistic inquiries.

Though he desperately hoped to restore his reputation as a Florentine and resume his life in the city that had turned against him, Dante refused to compromise his principles and turned down more than one opportunity to return to Florence, because such opportunities involved answering the false charges made against him. Such unwillingness to dishonor himself brought him yet another sentence of death, this one extending to his sons as well.

The last years of the poet's life were spent at Ravenna, where he was offered asylum by Guido Nevella da Polenta, the nephew of the famous Francesca da Rimini, the only woman sinner who actually speaks in the *Inferno*. These years seem to have been serene ones. In Ravenna he was greatly esteemed, and he enjoyed a very pleasant social life and an eager following of pupils, for he was already well known for his lyrics, and especially the *Convivio, Inferno,* and *Purgatorio.* Shortly before his death he was sent by Guido on a mission to Venice. Although Florence still rejected him, other cities very much valued his presence. Dante's friendship with Can Grande della Scala remained intact, and Dante placed great store in him; it is to him that he dedicated the *Paradiso*. Ravenna was Dante's home until his death on September 13 or 14, 1321.

WORKS

The *Vita nuova*, one of Dante's earliest works, is a combination of prose and poetry (thirty-one poems accompanied by a prose text). It is one of the first important examples of Italian literary prose and probably the first work of fiction that has come down to us in which the prose serves the purpose not only of offering a continuous narrative but also of explaining the occasion for the composition of each of the poems included. The originality of the *Vita nuova* consists of the functional relationship between the poetry and the prose.

In recent years the critics of the *Divine Comedy* have come to see more clearly the necessity of distinguishing between Dante the poet, the historical figure who wrote the poem in his own voice, and Dante the pilgrim, who is the poet's creation and who moves in a world of the poet's invention. In the case of the *Vita nuova* it is more difficult to distinguish between Dante the poet and Dante the lover, because in this book the lover, the protagonist, is himself a poet. More important, however, is the fact that the events of the *Vita nuova*, unlike those of the *Divine Comedy*, are surely not to be taken as pure fiction, and the protagonist himself is no fictional character: he is the historical character Dante at an earlier age. But we must attempt, just as we must in the case of any first-person novel, to distinguish between the point of view of the one who has already lived through the experiences recorded and has had time to reflect upon them in retrospect, and the point of view of the one undergoing the experiences at the time. What we have in the *Vita nuova* is a more mature Dante, reevoking his youthful experiences in a way that points up the folly of his younger self.

Also significant is the chronological relationship between the composition of the poems and that of the prose narrative, which reflects the way in which the author has adapted to a new purpose some of his earlier writings. In general scholars agree that when Dante, sometime between 1292 (that is, two years after the death of Beatrice) and 1300, composed the *Vita nuova*, most, if not all, of the poems that were to appear in the text had already been written. The architecture of the work, as has been said, consists of selected poems arranged in a certain order, with bridges of prose that serve primarily a narrative function: to describe those events in the life of the protagonist that supposedly inspired the poems included in the text. By giving the poems a narrative background, Dante was able to make their meaning clearer or even to change their original meaning or purpose.

For example, though the beauty of the first *canzone* in the book, *Donne ch'avete intelletto d'amore* ("Ladies who have intelligence of love") (chapter XIX), is independent of its position in the work, the poem owes entirely to the preceding narrative its dramatic significance as the proclamation of a totally new attitude adopted by the young poet-lover at this time in the story. This is also true, though from a different point of view, of what is probably the most famous sonnet in the *Vita nuova*, *Tanto gentile e tanto onesta pare* ("Such sweet decorum and such gentle grace") (chapter XXVI).

Just how much of the narrative prose is fiction we shall never know. We can never be sure that a given poem actually arose from the circumstances related in the prose preceding it. A few critics believe that all of the events of the narrative reflect biographical truth; most, fortunately, are more skeptical. But it goes without saying that to enjoy reading the *Vita nuova* we must suspend our skepticism and accept as "true" the events of the narrative. For only by doing so can we perceive the significance that Dante attributed to his poems by placing them where he did. And most critics of the *Vita nuova* seem to be agreed that in interpreting this work as a piece of literature, in seeking to find its message, the reader must try to forget the biographical fact that any given poem may have been written before Dante could know the use he would make of it later on.

In the opening chapter or preface (for it is so short) of his little book the author states that his purpose is to copy from his "book of memory" only those past experiences that belong to the period beginning his "new life"—a life made new by the poet's first meeting with Beatrice and the God of Love, who together with the poet-protagonist are the three main characters in the story. And by the end of chapter II all of the motifs that are important for the story that is about to unfold step by step have been introduced.

The first word of the opening sentence is "Nine": "Nine times already since my birth the heaven of light had circled back to almost the same point, when there appeared before my eyes the now glorious lady of my mind, who was called Beatrice even by those who did not know what her name was." The number nine will be repeated twice more in the next sentence (and it will appear another twenty times before the book comes to an end). In this opening sentence the reader not only finds a reference to the number nine of symbolic significance, but he also sees the emphasis on mathematical precision that will appear at frequent intervals throughout the *Vita nuova*.

In the opening sentence also the child Beatrice is presented as already enjoying the veneration of the people of her city, including strangers who did not know her name. With the words "the now glorious lady of my mind" (the first of two time shifts, in which the figure of the living Beatrice at a given moment is described in such a way as to remind us of Beatrice dead) the theme of death is delicately foreshadowed at the beginning of the story. As for the figure of Beatrice, when she appears for the first time in this chapter she wears a garment of blood-red color—the same color as her shroud will be in the next chapter.

In the next three sentences the three main spirits are introduced: the "vital" (in the heart), the "animal" (in the brain), and the "natural" (in the liver). They rule the body of the nine-year-old protagonist, and they speak in Latin, as will the God of Love in the chapter that follows (and once again later on). The words of the first spirit describing Beatrice anticipate the first coming of Love in the next chapter and suggest something of the same mood of terror. The words of the second spirit suggest rapturous bliss to come (that bliss rhapsodically described in chapter XI), while in the words of the third spirit there is the first of the many references to tears to be found in the *Vita nuova*. It is the spirit of the liver that weeps. It is only after this reference to the organ of digestion that Love is mentioned. He is mentioned first of all as a ruler, but we learn immediately that much of his power is derived from the protagonist's imagination—this faculty of which there will be so many reminders in the form of visions throughout the book.

We are also told that Love's power was restricted by reason, and later in the book the relation between Love and reason becomes an important problem. Two more themes are posited in this beginning chapter, to be woven into the narrative: the godlike nature of Beatrice and the strong "praise of the lady" motif. Both sound throughout the chapter as the protagonist's admiration for Beatrice keeps growing during the nine years after her first appearance.

Thus the opening chapter prepares for the rest of the book not only in the obvious way of presenting a background situation, an established continuity out of which single events will emerge in time, but also by setting in motion certain forces that will propel the *Vita nuova* forward—forces with which Dante's reader will gradually become more and more familiar.

In chapter XLII, the final chapter of the *Vita nuova*, the poet expresses his dissatisfaction with his work: "After I wrote this sonnet there appeared to me a miraculous vision in which I saw things that made me resolve to say no more about this blessèd one until I should be capable of writing about her in a nobler way." As the result of a final vision, which is not revealed to the reader, he decides to stop writing about Beatrice until he can do so more worthily. The preceding vision he had in the course of the story had made him decide to keep on writing; this one made him decide to stop. If the main action of the book is to be seen, as some critics believe, as the development of Dante's love from his preoccupation with his own feelings to his enjoyment of Beatrice's excellence and, finally, to his exclusive concern with her heavenly attributes and with spiritual matters, then this action, and the *Vita nuova* itself, ends in an important sense in failure.

To understand the message of the book, to understand how it succeeds through failure, we must go back in time and imagine the poet Dante, somewhere between the ages of twenty-seven and thirty-five, having already glimpsed the possibility of what was to be his terrible and grandiose masterpiece, the *Divine Comedy*. We must imagine him rereading the love poems of his earlier years and feeling shame for a number of them. He would have come to view Beatrice as she was destined to appear in the *Divine Comedy*, and indeed as she does appear briefly in the *Vita nuova*, specifically in that essay (chapter XXIX) on the miraculous quality of the number nine (the square of the number three, the symbol of the Blessed Trinity)—that is, as an agent of divine salvation.

Having arrived at this point, he would have chosen from among his earlier love poems many that exhibit his younger self at his worst, in order to offer a warning example to other young lovers and especially to other love poets. This would imply on Dante's part, as he is approaching the midmost part of life (the "*mezzo del cammin di nostra vita*" of the *Divine Comedy*), a criticism of most of the love poetry in Italian literature, for which his century was famous, and also that for which Provençal poetry was famous in the preceding century.

One might even say that the *Vita nuova* is a cruel book; cruel, that is, in the treatment of the human type represented by the protagonist. In the picture of the lover there is offered a condemnation of the vice of emotional self-indulgence and an exposure of its destructive effects on a man's integrity. The "tender feelings" that move the lover to hope or despair, to rejoice or to grieve (and perhaps even to enjoy his grief), spring from his vulnerability and instability and self-love; however idealistically inspired, these feelings cannot, except spasmodically, lead him ahead and above as long as he continues to be at their mercy. In short, he must always fall back into the helplessness of his self-centeredness. The man who would realize a man's destiny must ruthlessly cut out of his heart the canker at its center, the canker that the heart instinctively tends to cultivate. This is, I am convinced, the main message of the *Vita nuova*. And the consistent, uncompromising indictment it levels has no parallel in the literature of Dante's time. But of course the *Vita nuova* offers more than a picture of the misguided lover: there is also the glory of Beatrice and the slowly increasing ability of the lover to understand it, although he must nevertheless confess at the end that he has not truly succeeded.

Both in the treatment of the lover and in that of Beatrice, Dante has gone far beyond what he found at hand in the love poetry of the troubadours and their followers. He has taken up two of their preoccupations (one might almost say obsessions) and developed each of them in a most original way: the lover's glorification of his own feelings, and his glorification of the beloved. Of the first he has made a caricature. Unlike his friend Guido Cavalcanti, also highly critical of the havoc wrought by the emotions within a man's soul, who makes of the distraught lover a macabre portrait of doom, Dante has presented his protagonist mainly as an object of derision.

As to the glorification of the lady, all critics of the *Vita nuova* admit that Dante has carried this idealization to a degree never before reached by any poet, and one that no poet after him will ever quite attempt to reach. However blurred may be the lover's vision of the gracious, pure, feminine Beatrice, Dante the poet, in chapter XXIX, probes to the essence of her being and presents the coldness of her sublimity. Thus the tender foolishness of the lover is intensified by contrast with the icy perfection of the beloved.

With a few exceptions, Dante's lyrical poems (and not only those contained in the *Vita nuova*) are inferior as works of art to those of Cavalcanti and Guinizelli, or, for that matter, to those of Bernart de

Ventadorn and Arnaut Daniel. The greatness of the *Vita nuova* lies not in the poems but in the purpose that Dante made them serve. Certainly the book is the most original form of recantation in medieval literature—a recantation that takes the form of a reenactment, seen from a new perspective, of the sin recanted.

The *Convivio*, or *Banquet*, which Dante wrote in Italian sometime between 1304 and 1308, is an unfinished piece of work (it would be difficult to call it a work of art). His purpose in writing it is explained in the opening sentence, which is a quotation from Aristotle's *Metaphysics*: "All men by nature desire to know." Dante invites his reader to a feast consisting of fourteen courses (only three were completed), of which the "meat" of each is a *canzone* concerning love and virtue, while the "bread" is the exposition of it. Dante invites to his *Banquet* all those worthy people who, because of public duties, family responsibilities, and the like, have not been introduced to the science of philosophy. It is the laymen whom Dante invites to his feast, for it is through philosophy, he believes, that they can attain the temporal goal of happiness.

While the *Vita nuova* is Dante's monument to his first love, the lady Beatrice, the *Convivio* is a monument to his "second love," the lady Philosophy. That the lady who offers to console Dante a year after the death of Beatrice in the *Vita nuova* is that same lady Philosophy of the *Convivio* is revealed in book II, chapter II.

> To begin with, then, let me say that the star of Venus had already revolved twice in that circle of hers that makes her appear at evening or in the morning, according to the two different periods, since the passing away of that blessed Beatrice who dwells in heaven with the angels and on earth with my soul, when that gentle lady, of whom I made mention at the end of the *Vita nuova*, first appeared to my eyes, accompanied by love, and occupied a place in my mind.

What attracted the poet-protagonist to this lady was her offer of consolation. In the *Vita nuova* his love for the lady at the window lasts for a short time, and he refers to this love as "the adversary of reason" and "most base," but in the *Convivio* he calls this love "most noble." It should be remembered, however, that Philosophy in the *Vita nuova* tries to make the young protagonist forget the fact that he has lost Beatrice —something of this earth (such as Philosophy) cannot replace the love of Beatrice. After the vision in chapter XXXIX of the *Vita nuova*, after grasping the true significance of his lady, he returns to Beatrice and vows to never again stray. In doing this he is to be thought of not as rejecting Philosophy, but rather as rejecting the ideal of replacing Beatrice with Philosophy. Never in the *Convivio* does he consider such a replacement.

Here Dante exalts learning and the use of reason to the highest, for only through knowledge can man hope to attain virtue and God. The *Convivio* seems to be the connecting link between the *Vita nuova* and the *Divine Comedy*, since a love that at first has earthly associations turns out to have religious significance. Furthermore, just as Dante praises reason in this work, we know that in the *Divine Comedy*, reason in the pursuit of knowledge and wisdom is man's sole guide on earth, except for the intervention of divine grace.

One might say that the *Convivio* is the philosophical counterpart of the *Vita nuova*. Even from a quick reading of the *canzone* that opens book II, "*Voi che 'ntendendo*" ("You who by understanding"), the reader easily sees that, given the appropriate prose background, it might well have fitted into the *Vita nuova*. But when Dante begins the exposition of this ode it is "the sail of reason" that bears him on.

In the preamble to the *Convivio* Dante suggests reform in his declaring the vernacular suitable for ethical subjects as well as amorous ones. He was a leader in considering the vernacular a potential medium for all forms of expression, and his impassioned defense and praise of it manifest his awareness of its value in scientific interpretation as he comments at length on its uses.

He tells his reader that writings should be expounded in four senses. The first is the literal level. The second is the allegorical; for example, when Ovid tells his reader that Orpheus moved both animals and stones with his music he is signifying the power of eloquence over what is not rational. In this case the literal level of the story or poem need not be true. If it is not true, it is known as the allegory of poets; if the literal level is taken to be the truth, it is known as the allegory of theologians, because the literal level of the Scriptures was considered to be true. The third is the moral level, and this has a didactic purpose: when Christ took only three of his disciples with him on the occasion of the Transfiguration, it was another way of saying that for those things that are most secret we should have little company. The fourth sense is the anagogical, as when Scripture signifies certain spiritual or mystical truths. When we read, for example, that the people of Israel came out of Egypt and that Judea was made free, we must take this to be literally true, but the statement also signifies the spiritual truth that when a soul turns away from sin it becomes holy and free.

The literal level of a writing must always be exposed first, for it is impossible to delve into the "form" of anything without first preparing the "subject" upon which the form is to be stamped—you must prepare the wood before you build the table. Dante, in book II, chapter I of the *Convivio*, proposes to expound the literal level of his *canzone* first and then the allegorical, bringing into play the other levels or senses when it seems appropriate. There are very few passages in Dante's work where all four senses are at work; in fact, of the three *canzoni* expounded in the *Convivio* he manages to treat only the first two poems on two levels, while the third he discusses only on the literal level. And when Dante talks about the literal sense he means, of course, not the words but what the words mean. We must bear in mind that the literal sense contains all the other meanings.

In the third book Dante expounds the *canzone* "*Amor che ne la mente mi ragiona*" ("Love that converses with me in my mind"), which Casella in the *Divine Comedy* will sing to the newly arrived souls on the shores of Purgatory. In discussing the literal level of this ode he gives most of his attention to the meaning of *amor* (love).

Dante begins the fourth book, which treats the third and final *canzone*, "*Le dolci rime d'amor ch'i'solìa*" ("Those sweet rhymes of love that I was wont"), by stressing the fact that his love of philosophy has led him to love all those who pursue the truth and despise those who follow error. He also tells us in chapter 1 of this book that in order to have the utmost clarity he will discuss the poem only on the literal level. The lady involved, however, is still Philosophy.

Critics have proposed a number of theories on why Dante completed only four of the projected fourteen books of the *Convivio*. Thomas Bergin goes as far as to suggest that the *Convivio* might be thought of as the *selva oscura* (dark wood) of the *Divine Comedy*, from which the poet's lady, Beatrice, in a more graceful and harmonious work of art, felt obliged to rescue her poet-lover. I tend to agree with Rocco Montano, who suspects that it was some kind of personal crisis or "conversion" that made Dante stop working on this project. Montano assigns such a conversion and the writing of the *Divine Comedy* to the insight that resulted from Dante the poet's great disappointment at the failure of Henry VII's expedition into Italy. In any case, whatever Dante's reason for cutting short his work on the *Convivio*, whether it was personal or political, if this meant he could get on with the *Divine Comedy* and complete his masterpiece, we should be grateful that he did.

In all his works Dante shows his concern for words and the structure of language. In chapter XXV of the *Vita nuova* he takes time to explain and illustrate the use of personification, as he does in the early chapters of the *Convivio*, where he defends the use of Italian rather than Latin. But this concern is most evident in his Latin treatise *De vulgari eloquentia*. Before it there was no such scholarly treatment of a language. Dante completed only the first and second books, but he refers to a fourth; it is not known if that one was to be the last.

In book I Dante deals with the origin and history of the Italian language. The first five chapters cover the basic definitions of human speech while a good deal of the rest is given over to a discussion of dialects and the principles of poetic composition in the vulgar tongue, which he calls the "illustrious" vulgar tongue—the language of Guido Guinizzelli and, most perfectly, of Guido Cavalcanti, Cino da Pistoia, and Dante himself.

The second book of the *De vulgari eloquentia* is devoted to a more thorough discussion of Italian, which, Dante asserts, is just as appropriate for works of prose as for poetry. Early in this book (chapter II) he discusses what kind of subject is worthy of this vernacular and concludes that it is suited for only the most elevated subjects. And they are three: war (or prowess of arms), love, and virtue (or direction of the will). He states that the greatest writers using a vulgar tongue wrote only on these three subjects. Among Provençal poets, Dante cites Bertran de Born, who wrote about war, Arnaut Daniel on love, and Guiraut de Bornelh on virtue; he also mentions that in Italian Cino da Pistoia wrote about love and "his friend" (Dante), about virtue, citing an example of verse from each poet and including one of his own. Then he admits that he can find no Italian poet who has written on the topic of war. In chapter III of this book we learn that while poets have used a variety of forms (*canzoni*, *ballate*, sonnets, and other irregular types), the most excellent form remains the *canzone*, and it is this form that is most suited to lofty subjects. In the remaining chapters of book II the author goes on to discuss style and the rules and form of the *canzone*; the work ends abruptly with the incomplete chapter XIV, in which he intended to treat the number of lines and syllables in the stanza.

Most scholars agree that the *De vulgari eloquentia* is not a finished work, but is rather an unfinished first draft. There are three basic reasons for this belief: the paucity of manuscripts (there are only three), the way the work breaks off in chapter XIV, and the fact that references to points the author promises to discuss in coming chapters are never followed up. Perhaps Dante stopped writing the work, as Aristide Marigo suggests, because he was not certain of the direction he was taking. There is an obvious difference between the wide, humanistic scope of book I and the dry, manual-like approach of book II. Or could Dante simply have become bored with it?

The date of composition of the *De vulgari eloquentia* has not been definitively resolved. Boccaccio claims that it was written in Dante's old age. Marigo, who has done the standard edition of the work (Florence, 1938), dates it between the spring of 1303 and the end of 1304. And because in the *Convivio* Dante makes an allusion to this work in progress we must assume, at least, that he had the project in mind during this time.

It is also difficult to assign a date of composition to Dante's *De monarchia* (*On Monarchy*), primarily because it contains no references to the author's contemporaries or to events taking place at the time. Some say that it was written before Dante's exile because the work contains no mention of it; others tend to think that it was written even later than the *Convivio*, because a number of ideas appearing in an embryonic stage in that work are fully developed in the *De monarchia*. Nevertheless, it was probably written between 1312 and 1313 (sometime before or after the coronation of Henry VII) to commemorate Henry's advent into Italy.

The treatise is divided into three books. In the first book Dante attempts to prove that temporal monarchy is necessary for the welfare of the world. Temporal monarchy, or the empire, means a single command exercised over all persons; that is, in those things that are subject to time as opposed to eternal matters. In the opening sentence of the *De monarchia* the author pays tribute to both God and Aristotle while he establishes the reason for undertaking the present work: "All men whom the higher nature has imbued with a love of truth should feel impelled to work for the benefit of future generations, whom they will thereby enrich, just as they themselves have been enriched by the labors of their ancestors." According to Dante (and we find the idea throughout his writings), the man who does not contribute to the common good fails sadly in his duty.

Clearly Dante is convinced that he is doing something new in his treatise. There is nothing new, however, in his ideas of justice, freedom, and law—they are very much in line with the medieval philosophy of

his day. The idea so elaborately set forth in book I, that a higher juris-
diction is necessary whenever there is a possibility of discord or strife,
was an argument that had already been used by Pope Boniface VIII and
his followers. The originality of the *De monarchia*, the new element that
Dante brings to the old idea of empire, rests precisely in its main prem-
ise, upon which and around which the treatise is constructed: Dante's
justification from a philosophical point of view of a single ruler for all
the human race. It is in his concern with founding a "universal com-
munity of the human race" ("*universalis civilitas humani generis*") that
he is new and even daring—daring because in Dante's day this idea of
a universal community existed only as a religious one, in the form of
the church. His new idea, then, took its shape from universal Christen-
dom; it is, in a sense, an imitation of it elaborated from a philosophical
point of view. Working from the Averroistic concept of the "possible
intellect," Dante affirms that the particular goal of mankind as a whole
is to realize to the fullest all the potentialities of this intellect (to have
all the intellectual knowledge it is capable of having); this can happen
only under the direction of a single ruler, under one world government.
And the most important essential, if we are to secure our happiness and
if the human race is to fulfill its proper role, is universal peace.

Dante considers the monarch to be the purest incarnation of justice,
for there is nothing for him to desire, nothing more to be greedy about.
He is a man who has everything, having authority over all territories.
Dante also tells us that the human race is at its best when it is most
free—meaning self-dependent. Under the monarch the citizens do not
exist for his sake; on the contrary, it is the monarch who exists for his
citizens.

In the closing paragraph of the first book we hear the desperate voice
of Dante the poet warning all humanity. Rarely do we hear this voice
in the poet's Italian or Latin prose works, where his intention is to
remain as objective as possible. It is a preview of what is to come, for
Dante makes frequent and effective use of this device of authorial in-
tervention in the *Divine Comedy*. After presenting his case for the ne-
cessity of a monarch in a logical and scholastic fashion, as Saint Thomas
Aquinas or Aristotle might have done, Dante the poet bursts forth:

> O humanity, in how many storms must you be tossed, how many
> shipwrecks must you endure, so long as you turn yourself into a
> many-headed beast lusting after a multiplicity of things! You are
> ailing in both your intellectual powers and heart. You pay no heed

to the unshakable principles of your higher intellect, nor tune your heart to the sweetness of divine counsel when it is breathed into you through the trumpet of the Holy Spirit: "Behold how good and pleasant it is for brethren to dwell together in unity."

In book II Dante is primarily concerned with showing that the Romans were justified in assuming imperial power. He attempts to prove his thesis first by a number of arguments based on rational principles, then by the principles of the Christian faith.

In book III the poet proposes the question he has from the start wanted to ask and can ask only now that he has prepared the way in books I and II: whether the authority of the Holy Roman emperor is directly dependent on God or whether his authority comes indirectly from another, a vicar or minister of God, meaning the pope. Dante ignores the vast historical distance between the Roman Empire and the Holy Roman Empire, preferring to see the two governments joined by historical and political continuity. First Dante must refute those scriptural arguments (based on Genesis 1:16: "And God made two great lights: the greater light to rule the day and the lesser light to rule the night") used by his opponents to show the dependence of the emperor on the pope. Having done this, he turns to those historical arguments that must be refuted. The main one he must deal with is the very one that up to this point in his treatise he has been able to cope with only in a rather subjective, emotional, and even poetic way: the painful reality of the Donation of Constantine, a document that purported to prove that the emperor Constantine had invested Pope Sylvester with temporal authority. Dante proceeds by means of his two preferred sources: Scripture and philosophy (from Matthew and, on this occasion, Aristotle).

Man, who participates in two natures—one corrupt (the body), the other incorruptible (the soul)—has a twofold goal, and since he is the only being who participates in both corruptibility and incorruptibility, he has a goal for his body and a goal for his soul. God, who never errs, has, then, given man two goals: happiness in this life and happiness in the eternal life. The pope leads mankind to eternal life in accordance with revelation, while the emperor leads mankind to temporal happiness in accordance with philosophical teaching. The temporal monarch, who must devote his energies to providing freedom and peace for men as they pass through the "testing time" of this world, receives his authority directly from God.

Intellectual perfection, the happiness of this world, can therefore be attained without the Church. With proper guidance from the universal monarch, man can regain the happiness of the earthly paradise—this is a dangerous conclusion that can easily follow from Dante's arguments in his treatise, and one that Dante himself does not draw. Not surprisingly, the book was placed on the *Index of Forbidden Books*. Unfortunately for Dante, what he wished and wrote for in the *De monarchia* did not come about. It is for this reason that the poet's main political focus shifted from the empire to the Church when he wrote the *Divine Comedy*. With the death of Henry VII, Dante's hopes for the empire and the universal monarch began to fade; he was forced to put aside his ideal and face facts: a monarch and an empire would not overcome the power of the pope and the Church.

While Dante divides temporal and spiritual authority in the *De monarchia* by means of ingenious logic and scholastic arguments (and in the *Divine Comedy* by its larger allegorical structure), his masterpiece reveals the sad truth that temporal and spiritual authority are often in the same hands. There are many passages that lament this fact. In the *Purgatorio* (canto XVI), to cite one of the more famous passages, Marco Lombardo tells the pilgrim why the world has gone bad ("*la cagion che 'l mondo ha fatto reo*": 106–112):

> On Rome, that brought the world to know the good,
> once shone two suns that lighted up two ways:
> the road of this world and the road of God.
>
> The one sun has put out the other's light,
> the sword is now one with the crook—and fused
> together thus, must bring about misrule,
>
> since joined, now neither fears the other one.

No one is quite sure if Dante is the author of a pedantic little essay written in Latin with the title *Questio de aqua et terra* (*Discourse on the Nature of Water and Earth*). According to a statement attached to the original manuscript, the essay is in essence a lecture delivered at Verona in 1320. It consists of twenty-four brief chapters that debate in detail the question of whether or not the water of the sea anywhere rises higher than land emerging from it. The document was first published in 1508 by G. B. Moncetti, who claimed that he had copied it from an autograph manuscript of Dante's; the manuscript, however, was never found.

Among Dante's other minor works we find his two pastoral odes in Latin, addressed to Giovanni del Virgilio, who was a professor of Latin at the University of Bologna, where Dante at one time had probably studied. The exchange of Latin hexameters between the two men took place when Dante was staying in Ravenna some two years before his death. In his verses Giovanni del Virgilio reprimands Dante for writing his great poem in Italian rather than Latin. The eclogues are interesting insofar as they reveal Dante's mood toward the end of his life: he seems to be playful, happy, and at peace with himself. Also evident in these verses is the poet's pathetic wish to return to his fair city to receive the laurel crown, as well as his feelings and hopes for the *Divine Comedy*.

A brief mention should be made of *Il fiore* (*The Flower*), the authenticity of which has been questioned by many scholars. It is a sequence of 232 sonnets based on the French *Roman de la Rose*. Those few who are sure that this allegorical story of a successful seduction was written by Dante give two reasons: first, the author is referred to as Durante, which is a form of Dante; second, it is much too well composed to have been written by anyone else but Dante. *Il fiore*, which is worth reading in its own right, is to be found in one manuscript of the late thirteenth century (first published in 1881 in Paris by Ferdinand Castets).

There are approximately fifty-four (and a possible twenty-six more) short poems (not included in the *Vita nuova* or *Convivio*) that Dante did not group together or organize in any way, but that modern editors have collected and called the *Canzoniere* or *Rime* (*Songbook* or *Rhymes*). They consist of scattered lyrics written over a long period of the poet's life, many of which he probably tried to, but could not, fit into the structure of the *Vita nuova* or *Convivio*. Many, of course, were inspired by Beatrice, but there are some written for other women; some done as exercises, as part of his correspondence with other poets; and some composed simply to please ladies and gentlemen who were fond of poetry.

Dante undoubtedly wrote many letters. Unfortunately, only ten letters considered authentic have come down to us; all ten are written in Latin, and none is of a personal or intimate nature. There are also three other letters that Dante may have written on behalf of the countess of Battifolle, but they do not reflect his own thoughts.

To the student of the *Divine Comedy* the most interesting of Dante's letters is the one addressed to Can Grande della Scala in which the author sets forth his purpose and method in writing his poem. The letter is extant in six manuscripts, three of which (all sixteenth-century) contain the letter in its entirety. He talks about the different meanings contained in the *Divine Comedy*: the first is called literal, the second allegorical or mystical. We learn that on the literal level the poem is about the state of souls after death; on the allegorical level, "The subject is man, liable to the reward or punishment of Justice, according to the use he has made of his free will."

In his letter he also discusses why he has called his poem a "comedy." The word, he says, is derived from *comus* and *oda* and means a "rustic song." Unlike tragedy, which begins in tranquillity but comes to a sad end, comedy may begin under adverse circumstances, but it always comes to a happy end. The style or language of comedy is humble while that of tragedy is lofty. Therefore, because his poem begins in Hell and has a happy ending in Paradise, and because it is written in a most humble language, which is the Italian vernacular, it is called the *Commedia*. The letter goes on with a meticulous, almost word-by-word examination of the beginning verses of the opening canto of the *Paradiso* up to the invocation to Apollo. The letter is thought by many to be an important piece of literary criticism seen in the framework of Dante's time and tradition, and as such it certainly is worth reading in its own right.

THE DIVINE COMEDY

Dante's masterpiece is, of course, the *Divine Comedy* (the word *divina* was added to *commedia* by posterity). It is to some degree a result of his determination to fulfill the promise he made at the close of the *Vita nuova*: "If it be the wish of Him in whom all things flourish that my life continue for a few years, I hope to write of her that which has never been written of any lady."

No one knows when Dante began composing his great poem; some say perhaps as early as 1307. In any case the *Inferno* was completed in 1314, and it is probable that the final touches to the *Paradiso* were, as Boccaccio states, not made until 1321, the year of Dante's death. The purpose of the poem, which has moved readers through the centuries, is, as Dante reveals in his epistle to Can Grande, "to remove those living in this life from the state of misery and lead them to the state of felicity."

The poem is divided into three major sections: *Inferno* (Hell), *Purgatorio* (Purgatory), and *Paradiso* (Heaven). Each section contains thirty-three cantos, with the exception of Hell, which has thirty-four—the opening canto serving as an introduction to the work as a whole. For the *Commedia* Dante invented a rhyme scheme known as *terza rima* (tertiary rhyme: *aba bcb cdc*), thus continuing to display his fascination with the number three, which was so much on his mind when he was composing the *Vita nuova* many years earlier. And each canto is divided into three-line stanzas called *terzine*, or tercets, in which the first and third lines rhyme, while the middle or second lines rhyme with the first and third of the next *terzina*. The basic metrical unit of the verse is the hendecasyllabic line, quite common in Italian poetry: it is an eleven-syllable line in which the accent falls on the tenth syllable.

The drama or main action of the poem centers on one man's journey to God. It tells how God through the agency of Beatrice drew the poet to salvation; and the moral that Dante wishes his reader to keep in mind is that what God has done for one man he will do for every man, if every man is willing to make this journey. The reader of the poem would do well to distinguish from the very beginning of the *Commedia* between the two uses of the first-person singular: one designates Dante the pilgrim, the other Dante the poet. The first is a character in a story invented by the second. The events in the narrative are represented as having taken place in the past; the writing of the poem and the memory of these events, however, are represented as taking place in the present. For example, we find references to both past and present, and to both pilgrim and poet, in line 10 of the introductory canto of the *Inferno*: "How *I entered* there I *cannot* truly say" (italics added).

There are times in the poem when the fictional pilgrim (Dante the pilgrim) embodies many of the characteristics of his inventor (Dante the poet); for the *Commedia*, though it is above all the journey of Everyman to God, is in many ways a personal, autobiographical journey. It is often difficult, most times impossible, to say whether what is happening in the poem belongs to the real-life biography of the poet or the fictional biography of the pilgrim. For instance, at the beginning of canto XIX of the *Inferno* the pilgrim alludes to having broken a baptismal font in the church of his "lovely San Giovanni" (line 17). Now, Dante the poet may well have broken the font to save someone who was drowning within, but it is highly unlikely (and most inartistic) that he would mention the incident for the sole purpose of clearing his name in connection with an act that some of his contemporaries would have thought sinful. The breaking of the font is an event that took place in the life of the pilgrim, and the pilgrim is not trying to "clear his name," as critics have suggested. Rather the poet is giving an example to the reader of the true nature of the sin of simony (the sin punished in canto XIX), which "breaks" the holy purposes of the church by perverting them.

The poet is the poet, but he is not the pilgrim, and the story traced in the *Commedia* is the story of Dante the pilgrim, who is at once himself and Everyman. We must keep in mind the allegory of the opening verse of the poem: "*Nel mezzo del cammin di nostra vita / mi ritrovai . . .*" ("Midway along the journey of our life / I found myself . . ."). Dante begins to construct his allegory of the double journey: that is, his personal experience in the world beyond ("I found myself"), open to Everyman in his own journey through this life ("of our life"). The poet finds himself wandering in a dark wood (the worldly life). He tries to escape by climbing a mountain that is lit from behind by the rays of the sun (God). His journey upward is impeded by the sudden appearance of three beasts: a leopard, a lion, and a she-wolf (the three major divisions of sin, signifying the three major divisions of Hell: fraud, violence, and concupiscence). The poet is about to be driven back when, just as suddenly, Virgil (reason or human understanding) appears. He has been sent by Beatrice (divine revelation) to aid Dante, to guide him on this journey that cannot fail. The only way to escape from the dark wood is to descend into Hell (man must first descend into humility before he can raise himself to salvation or God). The way up the mountain, then, is to go down: before man can hope to climb the mountain of salvation, he must first know what sin is. The purpose of Dante's journey through Hell is precisely this: to learn all there is to know about sin as a necessary preparation for the ascent to God. In fact, from the opening canto of the *Inferno* to the closing one of the *Paradiso*, Dante the poet presents his pilgrim as continuously learning, his spiritual development being the main theme of the entire poem. His progress is slow, and there are even occasional backslidings.

In *Inferno* IV the pilgrim and his guide, Virgil, who are now in Limbo, see a hemisphere of light glowing in the distance, and as they move toward it they are met by four great pagan poets. Virgil explains to his ward:

"Observe the one who comes with sword in hand,
    leading the three as if he were their master.

It is the shade of Homer, sovereign poet,
  and coming second, Horace, the satirist;
  Ovid is the third, and last comes Lucan.

(86–90)

Together with Virgil these four non-Christians form the group of those classical poets whom Dante most admired and from whom he drew much of the material for his poem. It must be said, however, that while Homer was known in the Middle Ages as the first of the great epic poets, the author of the *Iliad* and *Odyssey*, few people—and Dante was not among them—could read Greek; thus Homer's great epics were known almost entirely second-hand through the revised versions of Dares and Dictys, who told the tale of the Trojan war in a way that exalted the Trojans and often disparaged the Greeks. Dante admired Homer more for his reputation than for any intimate knowledge that he had of his works. The second of the four is Horace, whom Dante calls the "satirist" but whom he must have thought of mainly as a moralist since Dante was familiar only with the *Ars poetica*. Ovid, who comes next, was the most widely read Roman poet in the Middle Ages, and he was Dante's main source of mythology in the *Commedia*. Dante, however, seems to have been acquainted with only the *Metamorphoses*. Coming last is Lucan, author of the *Pharsalia*, which deals with the Roman civil war between the legions of Pompey and those of Caesar. The book was one of Dante's important historical sources.

When the pilgrim and his guide have seen all there is to see of sin (canto XXXIV) they find they must exit from Hell by climbing down Lucifer's monstrous, hairy body. Only by grappling with sin itself, by knowing the foundation of all sin, which is pride, personified in the hideous figure of Lucifer frozen in the ice at the very center of the universe, can they hope to make their way out "to see again the stars."

The island-mountain of Purgatory, invented by Dante, is divided into three parts. At the very top is the Earthly Paradise; the upper part of the mountain is sealed off from the lower by a gate that a resplendent angel guards, equipped with St. Peter's keys. This upper half, with its seven cornices corresponding to the seven deadly sins, is reserved for those who have been permitted to enter the gate from below in order to begin the self-willed torments of their purgation; after its accomplishment they pass to the Earthly Paradise, from which they ascend to Heaven. In the lower half, the "Antepurgatory," dwell those souls who are not yet ready to begin their purgation. As for the reason why certain souls are forced to put off the experience they all desire, the pilgrim is told by a number of individuals he meets that, while alive, they had put off repentance until the end (thus their delay is in the nature of a *contrapasso*, or retribution); it is generally accepted that all of the inhabitants of the Antepurgatory are to be considered as "late repentants." (The Antepurgatory is dealt with in the first nine cantos.) This mountain (whose creation was the miraculous result of Lucifer's fall) keeps not only those assigned to Purgatory but also those destined for immediate passage to Heaven.

The middle portion of the mountain of Purgatory is surrounded by seven concentric ledges, each separated from the other by a steep cliff. On each ledge, or terrace, one of the seven capital sins is purged: Pride, Envy, Wrath, Sloth, Avarice (and Prodigality), Gluttony, Lust. The setup of the First Terrace (cantos IX–XII), where souls are being punished for the sin of Pride, establishes the pattern of purgation that is followed throughout Purgatory proper.

Each group of souls on its particular terrace is assigned a prayer. When a soul has finished purging his sin on one level, he climbs to the next via a stairway, where there is an angel-sentry who performs a final cleansing gesture. A beatitude appropriate to the sin that has been cleansed is assigned to each ledge. In addition, on each terrace of Purgatory, representations of the sin being purged there are found, as well as examples of the virtue which is opposed to that sin. The representation of the sin is intended to incite disdain for the sin, while that of the virtue is designed to inspire souls to the emulation of virtuous behavior. These representations take on various forms—on the First Terrace they appear as carvings in the stone of the mountain—and both "disdain for the sin" and "inspiration for virtuous behavior" are drawn from examples of Christian and pagan love. But the first example of every virtue is always taken from the life of the Virgin Mary.

In the first canto of the *Purgatorio* Dante and Virgil are at the foot of a mountain again, and the reader is naturally reminded of the first canto of the *Inferno*: it is the same mountain, the one they could not climb then, because Dante was not spiritually prepared. But now, having investigated all sin, having shaken off pride during his perilous descent into humility, Dante will be able to climb the mountain.

Purgatory is a place of repentance, regeneration, conversion. Though the punishments inflicted on the penitents here are often more severe than in Hell, the atmosphere is totally different: it is one of sweet encounters, culminating in Dante's reunion with Beatrice in the Earthly

Paradise and Virgil's elegant disappearance. Brotherly love and humility reign here, necessary qualities for the successful journey of man's mind to God. Everyone here is destined to see God eventually; the predominant image is one of homesickness (especially in the Antepurgatory), a yearning to return to man's real home in Heaven. Toward the close of the *Purgatorio* the time comes for Beatrice (divine revelation) to take charge of the pilgrim; human reason (Virgil) can take man only so far; it cannot show him God or explain his many mysteries.

The *Paradiso* is an attempt to describe the religious life, one in which man centers his attention wholly on God, divine truth, and ultimate happiness. Only in perfect knowledge of the true God can man have perfect happiness.

Unlike Hell and Purgatory, Heaven in Dante's poem does not exist in a physical sense. The celestial spheres through which the pilgrim and his guide, Beatrice, ascend and in which the souls of the blessed appear to the wayfarer are not part of the real Paradise. That place is beyond the spheres and beyond space and time; it is the Empyrean, and Beatrice takes pains to explain this early in the *Paradiso*, while they are in the first sphere of the moon:

> Not the most godlike of the Seraphim,
>   not Moses, Samuel, whichever John
>   you choose—I tell you—not Mary herself
>
> has been assigned to any other heaven
>   than that of these shades you have just seen here,
>   and each one's bliss is equally eternal;
>
> all lend their beauty to the Highest Sphere,
>   sharing one same sweet life to the degree
>   that they can feel the eternal breath of God.
>
>   (IV.28–36)

The dominant image in this realm is light. God is light, and the pilgrim's goal from the very start was to reach the light (we are reminded of the casual mention of the rays of the sun behind the mountain in the opening canto).

The word "stars," the last word of the poem, glows with a number of meanings which *The Divine Comedy* itself has given it in the course of the journey. The sun is another star, as the last verse surely implies through the use of the word "other," and we know that the sun is the symbol for God—this is clear from the first canto of the *Inferno*, and the stars stand for all the heavens. It is through the sphere of the Fixed Stars, immediately below the Primum Mobile, that God's grace is filtered down through the lower spheres, finally reaching the material universe—that is what canto II concerning the spots on the moon is all about. The stars, then, are the link between God and His creation. They are His eyes set in the outermost limits of the physical universe:

> O Triune Light which sparkles in one star
>   upon their sight, Fulfiller of full joy!
>   look down upon us in our tempest here!
>
> (XXXI, 28–30)

They are the constant reminder to mankind of his connection to his Maker. Through them we see God from our earth. Through them God touches us. Through them Dante connects the three distinct parts of his miraculous poem, the *Inferno*, the *Purgatory*, and the *Paradise*, into a single unity which is *The Divine Comedy*.

The formal beauty of the *Commedia* should not be dissociated from its spiritual message. The universal appeal of the poem comes precisely from a combination of the two: poetry and philosophy. For Dante, though not for the majority of poets of the Renaissance, ultimate truth was known—in principle it was contained in the *Summa* of Saint Thomas Aquinas, and the doctrine of the *Commedia* comes largely from the writings of Aquinas and the other church fathers.

Dante was in accord with Hugh of Saint Victor, who, in his *Didascalia* (VI.5), says: "Contemplating what God has done, we learn what is for us to do. All nature speaks God. All nature teaches man." Dante, then, with his special kind of allegory, tries to imitate God: the symbolic world he creates in his poem is in principle a mirror of the actual world created by God himself.

TRANSLATOR'S NOTE:
ON BEING A GOOD LOVER

To WHAT extent should the translator of Dante's *Comedy* strive to be faithful to the original? Ezra Pound distinguishes between what he calls "interpretative translation," which is what most translators are after, and a more creative, original type of paraphrase—the translator using the original mainly as an inspiration for writing his own poem. But even those who attempt an interpretive rendering differ greatly in the degree and manner of their faithfulness to the original. The question has been raised and debated: should it be the poet's voice that is heard, or the voice of the one who is making the poet accessible in another language? This is obviously a delicate, sophisticated, and complicated problem.

Surely much depends on what it is that is being translated. A principle that might apply to a sonnet or perhaps any short poem, especially a lyrical one, would not be appropriate to a lengthy narrative with theological and encyclopedic underpinnings such as *The Divine Comedy*. I should say that anyone who attempts to translate this massive poem must try, with humility and flexibility, to be as faithful as possible. He should do what Jackson Mathews recommends to the guild of translators in general—"be faithful without seeming to be"—and he adds in regard to this type of faithfulness: "a translator should make a good lover."

Perhaps it must always be the voice of Dante's translator that we hear (if we have to hear an intervening voice at all), but he should have listened most carefully to Dante's voice before he lets us hear his own. He should not only read and reread what he is translating, in order to

know what it is about (know a whole canto thoroughly before trans-
lating a line), but he should also read Dante aloud, listening to the
rhythm and movement within the lines and the movement from line to
line. Consider, for example, line 63 of the famous canto V of the *Inferno*
(Paolo and Francesca's canto), where Virgil points out to the Pilgrim
the figure of Cleopatra among the lustful souls of Dido's band, and
characterizes her with one word that caps the line:

> *Poi è Cleopatràs lussurïosa*
> (And there is Cleopatra, who loved men's lusting)

This epithet, epitomizing the whole career of the imperial wanton, serves
to remind us of the technical nature of the sin being punished in the
second circle, the circle of the lustful: *i lussuriosi.* And in the movement
of the word *lus-su-ri-o-sa* (Dante forces us to linger over the word this
way; otherwise the verse would be a syllable short) there is an important
anticipation of a movement in the second part of the canto: the dovelike
movement that starts with the actual descent of Francesca and Paolo, a
gentle movement that becomes the movement of the entire second half
of this canto and offers such a contrast to the wild buffetings of the
winds we hear in the first half, where we see the damned dashed along
by the tempestuous storm. The sensitive translator must stop to question
(then to understand) the rhythm of *lussuriosa* at this point in the canto:
to sense how this diaphanous word in this melodious line stands out
against the howling noises in the background. This seductive rhythm
applied to Cleopatra's sin anticipates not only the gentle movements but
the seductive atmosphere of the second half of the canto, when Fran-
cesca is on stage and melting the Pilgrim's heart. No translator I have
read seems to have made any attempt to reproduce the effect intended
by the line in the original: the simplicity of the first half of the line (*Poi
è Cleopatràs . . .*) and the mellifluous quality of the epithet (*lussuriosa*)
in final position, with its tapering-off effect.

Again, the translator should study Dante's use of poetic devices such
as enjambment and alliteration. This does not mean that the translator
should always use such devices when Dante does and only when he
does, but that he should study the effects Dante has achieved with these
devices—and his economical use of them. Dante is a greater poet than
any of his translators have been or are likely to be. A translator using
the English iambic pentameter may even learn from Dante's flowing
lines to use better the meter he has chosen. It is true that Dante's hen-

decasyllabic verse is quantitative and not accentual; still, the words of the Italian language have their own natural accent. In reading aloud Dante's lines with their gentle stress, one can hear the implicit iambs and trochees and dactyls and anapaests. And one may learn to achieve the same effect of "implicitness" to counterbalance the natural tendency of English meters to have too insistent a stress.

Finally, there is the matter of diction. Here the translator must be *absolutely* faithful, choosing words and phrases that have the same tone as those of the poet. They must obviously suggest solemnity when he is solemn, lightness when he is light; they must be colloquial or formal as he is colloquial or formal. But, most of all, the diction should be simple when Dante's is. And this is where the translators have sinned the most. There are two ways to sin against simplicity of diction: one concerns only the matter of word material and syntax—for instance the use of stilted or overflowery language and of archaic phraseology. Most translators would not agree with me; some feel free to use any word listed in the *O.E.D.* after A.D. 1000: *to girn, to birl, to skirr, scaling the scaur, to abye the fell arraign*—to say nothing of syntactical archaisms.

A more subtle sin against the simplicity of Dante's diction is the creation of original striking rhetorical or imagistic effects where Dante has intended none. Dante himself saves spectacular effects for very special occasions. Most of his narrative, if we make an exception of the elaborate similes, is composed in simple, straightforward style. Occasionally one finds an immediately striking effect in a line or phrase, and when this does happen, it is magnificent. Consider line 4 of canto V (so different from line 63, quoted earlier, with its muted, inconspicuous effect):

> *Stavvi Minòs orribilmente e ringhia*
> (There stands Minòs grotesquely, and he snarls)

Surely Dante meant to startle his reader with this sudden presentation (after the sober explanation of the opening three lines) of the monster-judge. The line ends with the resounding impact of the verb *ringhia*— it ends with a snarl that sounds like the lash of a whip (or tail). And we are made to feel the horror of Minòs by the key word in the middle of the line, the slow-moving *orribilmente*, which points both backward and ahead: *Stavvi orribilmente, ringhia orribilmente.* Grammatically, of course, the adverb modifies the opening word, the static verb, *stavvi.*

This construction, in which an adverb of manner modifies a verb of presence, is most unusual: Minòs was present horribly!

Usually, however, one comes to realize only at the end of several tercets that a certain effect has been achieved by the passage as a whole, one to which each single line has been quietly contributing. Dante's effects, then, are mainly of a cumulative nature. And often there are no "effects," only simple, factual, narrative details. In fact, sometimes Dante's style (and not unfortunately!) is purely prosaic. An adventurous, imaginative translator is easily tempted to speed up the movement of Dante's tranquil lines, to inject fire and color into a passage of neutral tone. Even if he carries it off successfully, I would tend to question his goal. And when the translator fails, when he falls, great is the fall thereof.

If the translator had to choose in general between a style that strives for striking effects, sometimes succeeding and sometimes failing, and one less colorful but more consistent, the choice could be merely a matter of personal taste. But when it is a question of translating a poet who himself is so economical in his use of conspicuous effects, then, I believe, it is no longer a wide-open choice. I have set as my goal simplicity and quiet, even, sober flow—except when I feel that the moment has come to let myself go, to pull out the stops: to be flamboyant or complicated instead of simple, to be noisy instead of quiet, to be rough instead of smooth—or to be deliberately mellifluous. Except for those rare occasions, I have consistently tried to find a style that does not call attention to itself. And I might add that, in translating, this requires a great deal of effort. To the extent that I have succeeded, those readers who admire the fireworks of some recent translations of the *Inferno* will find my own less exciting—as little exciting as Dante himself often is.

My desire to be faithful to Dante, however, has not led me to adopt his metrical scheme. I do not use *terza rima*, as, for example, Dorothy Sayers does, or even the "dummy" *terza rima* of John Ciardi. My medium is rhymeless iambic pentameter, that is, blank verse. I have chosen this, first, because blank verse has been the preferred form for long narrative poetry from the time of Milton on. It cannot be proved that rhyme necessarily makes verse better: Milton declared rhyme to be a barbaric device, and many modern poets resolutely avoid it. Karl Shapiro, an enthusiast for rhyme, is considering only shorter poems when he speaks of the five main qualities that rhyme gives to verse: the musical, the emphatic, the architectural, the sense of direction one feels in a well-turned stanza, and, finally, the effect of the rests that come between the stanzas. Three of these qualities could apply only to stanzaic poetry, where rhyme is much more necessary in establishing structure than in a poem with the dimensions of *The Divine Comedy*, whose only large subdivision is the canto. Only two of the qualities of rhyme he mentions might apply to Dante's poem: the musical and the emphatic.

But my main reason for avoiding rhyme has been the results achieved by all those who have used rhyme in translating *The Divine Comedy*: they have shown that the price paid was disastrously high. I believe that all those who have offered rhymed translations of Dante could have produced far better poems if they had not used rhyme. There are two reasons for the crippling effects of rhyme in translating a lengthy poem. First of all it is apparently impossible always to find perfect rhymes in English for a long stretch of lines—and if good rhyme gives a musical effect, bad rhyme is cacophonous; it is a reminder (and with some translators we are being constantly reminded) that the search for rhyme has failed. I have found at least six kinds of bad rhyme in translations of Dante: vowels that do not match, consonants that do not match, stresses that do not match, plus combinations of these. Especially when there is a pause at the end of a line or the line ends with a stressed syllable, so that the cacophonous element is put into relief, the result can be most painful. One can be more faithful to Dante (without seeming to be) by avoiding rhyme than by introducing imperfect rhyme into the rendition of his lines, whose rhymes are always acoustically perfect.

Shapiro, speaking of the power of rhyme to draw us into the movement of a poem, says that our expectation is thereby being continually raised and then satisfied; ideally, rhyme helps pull us through, and pull us in deep, as we anticipate the scheme. But, when the translator uses a mixture of perfect and imperfect rhyme—when, that is, we never know whether our expectation will be satisfied—the effect is quite different. In every tercet the reader with a sensitive ear will always be wondering "Will he make it this time?" and may often look ahead to see the result, thus breaking the movement of the poem.

But the rhymed translations of the *Comedy* reveal, all of them, a second disadvantage, and a far greater one than the difficulty of matching sounds. Because of the difficulty imposed by the continuous mechanical necessity of finding rhyme, good or bad, the translator is often forced to use a diction that is aesthetically unacceptable, or even contrary to the spirit of the language (and once a translator has agreed to distort the English language for the sake of rhyme, the result could well be an increasing insensitivity to the requirements of natural diction). To be forced to think, with every line, in terms of the sound of the final stressed syllable has resulted, far too often, in lines that sound like a translation. And the first of the Capital Sins in translating is for a translation to sound like one!

For the poet creating original verse in his own language, the search for rhyme also, of course, imposes limitations, but these limitations themselves may be a help in the creative process, and the rhyme, when found, as Shapiro says, may bring an image or idea that will suggest a new line of development. At its best, rhyme leads the poet into discoveries. And since he is in the process of creation, he can afford at any moment to change the course of his poetic fluidity. But for the translator, who is faced from the beginning with an existing structure whose shape has been forever fixed, rhyme constitutes a crippling burden.

But if I feel such horror at the paralyzing potentiality of rhyme when used to translate *The Divine Comedy*, why have I chosen to bind myself to the mechanical device of meter? Five beats in every line—no more and no less. Why not choose free verse? Free verse, I feel, is more appropriate for purely creative composition than for translation; and it is more suitable for verse deeply charged with emotion than for narrative. The irregular rhythms, the modulations, of free verse must be determined by the writer's own moods, which will direct the ebbing and flowing of his verse. For this he needs space; as a translator such a writer would need to get as far away as possible from the original!

Moreover, the requirements of iambic pentameter can be very flexible if one is ready to avail oneself of the alternations possible. One need not limit oneself continually to the sequence: ˇ´/ˇ´/ˇ´/ˇ´/ˇ´/. The last foot, for example, may be given, when desired, an extra unstressed syllable (feminine ending; in Italian this is the norm):

Whĕn thóse / ŏffén / dĕd soúls / hăd tóld / *thĕir stórў* . . .

For an iamb one may substitute its opposite, a trochee (´ˇ):

Hátefŭl / tŏ Gód / ănd tó / Hĭs eń / ĕ / miés . . .

Or a further extension of itself, the anapaest (ˇˇ´):

Iň thĕ wořld / thĭs mán / wăs fílled / wĭth ař / rŏgańce . . .

(The reader sensitive to rhythm should be on the alert for such opening anapaests.)

Or the opposite of this, the dactyl (´ ˘ ˘):

Ĭ saíd / tŏ hím, / bówĭng / mў heád / *módeštlў* . . .

And I have often used a substitution that some translators seem to avoid, the amphibrach (˘ ´ ˘; the final foot is always an amphibrach when there is a feminine ending):

Ĭ saíd, / "*Frăncéscă,* / t̆he tór / mĕnt thát / yŏu súffĕr . . ."

(Compare this with Dorothy Sayers's and John Ciardi's translations of the same line, in which the natural rhythm of the name *Francesca* is not echoed in an amphibrach foot: "[*Thy dreadful fate,*] Frăncés / că, mákes / mĕ wéep, / ĭt só / iňspíres [*pity*]"; "Ĭ sáid: / 'Frăncés / că whát / yŏu súf / fĕr heŕe . . .' ")

Finally, one may let just one syllable count as a foot when the stress is very heavy:

Loŕe, / thăt kín / dlĕs quíck / ĭn t̆he gén / t̆le heárt . . .

And there may be gradation in degrees of stress. Iambic pentameter is a beautiful, flexible instrument, but only when the translator is freed from preoccupation with rhyme.

Because I am free of this tyranny I have had time to listen carefully to Dante's voice, and though the result is far from being a miracle of perfect translation, still, I believe I can promise that my reader seldom, if ever, will wince or have his teeth set on edge by an overambitious attempt to force the language into the unnatural tensions almost never felt in poetry other than translations.

CANTO I

Halfway through his life, Dante the Pilgrim wakes to find himself lost in a dark wood. Terrified at being alone in so dismal a valley, he wanders until he comes to a hill bathed in sunlight, and his fear begins to leave him. But when he starts to climb the hill his path is blocked by three fierce beasts: first a Leopard, then a Lion, and finally a She-Wolf. They fill him with fear and drive him back down to the sunless wood. At that moment the figure of a man appears before him; it is the shade of Virgil, and the Pilgrim begs for help. Virgil tells him that he cannot overcome the beasts which obstruct his path; they must remain until a "Greyhound" comes who will drive them back to Hell. Rather by another path will the Pilgrim reach the sunlight, and Virgil promises to guide him on that path through Hell and Purgatory, after which another spirit, more fit than Virgil, will lead him to Paradise. The Pilgrim begs Virgil to lead on, and the Guide starts ahead. The Pilgrim follows.

Midway along the journey of our life
   I woke to find myself in a dark wood,
   for I had wandered off from the straight path.   3

How hard it is to tell what it was like,
   this wood of wilderness, savage and stubborn
   (the thought of it brings back all my old fears),   6

a bitter place! Death could scarce be bitterer.
   But if I would show the good that came of it
   I must talk about things other than the good.   9

How I entered there I cannot truly say,
   I had become so sleepy at the moment
   when I first strayed, leaving the path of truth;   12

1. The imaginary date of the poem's beginning is the night before Good Friday in 1300, the year of the papal jubilee proclaimed by Boniface VIII. Born in 1265, Dante would be thirty-five years old, which is half the seventy years allotted to man in the Bible.

but when I found myself at the foot of a hill,
    at the edge of the wood's beginning, down in the valley,
    where I first felt my heart plunged deep in fear,   15

I raised my head and saw the hilltop shawled
    in morning rays of light sent from the planet
    that leads men straight ahead on every road.   18

And then only did terror start subsiding
    in my heart's lake, which rose to heights of fear
    that night I spent in deepest desperation.   21

Just as a swimmer, still with panting breath,
    now safe upon the shore, out of the deep,
    might turn for one last look at the dangerous waters,   24

so I, although my mind was turned to flee,
    turned round to gaze once more upon the pass
    that never let a living soul escape.   27

I rested my tired body there awhile
    and then began to climb the barren slope
    (I dragged my stronger foot and limped along).   30

Beyond the point the slope begins to rise
    sprang up a leopard, trim and very swift!
    It was covered by a pelt of many spots.   33

And, everywhere I looked, the beast was there
    blocking my way, so time and time again
    I was about to turn and go back down.   36

The hour was early in the morning then,
    the sun was climbing up with those same stars
    that had accompanied it on the world's first day,   39

31–51. The three beasts that block the Pilgrim's path could symbolize the three major divisions of Hell. The spotted Leopard (32) represents Fraud (cf. Canto XVI, 106–108) and reigns over the Eighth and Ninth Circles where the Fraudulent are punished (Cantos XVIII–XXXIV). The Lion (45) symbolizes all forms of Violence that are punished in the Seventh Circle (XII–XVII). The She-Wolf (49) represents the different types of Concupisence or Incontinence that are punished in Circles Two to Five (V–VIII).

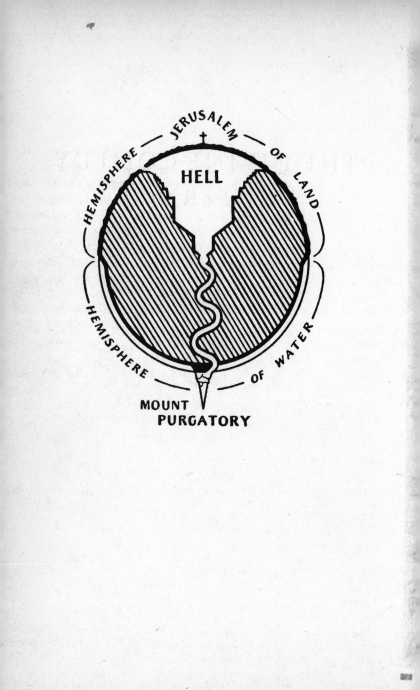

THE DIVINE COMEDY:
INFERNO

the day Divine Love set their beauty turning;
   so the hour and sweet season of creation
   encouraged me to think I could get past   42

that gaudy beast, wild in its spotted pelt,
   but then good hope gave way and fear returned
   when the figure of a lion loomed up before me,   45

and he was coming straight toward me, it seemed,
   with head raised high, and furious with hunger—
   the air around him seemed to fear his presence.   48

And now a she-wolf came, that in her leanness
   seemed racked with every kind of greediness
   (how many people she has brought to grief!).   51

This last beast brought my spirit down so low
   with fear that seized me at the sight of her,
   I lost all hope of going up the hill.   54

As a man who, rejoicing in his gains,
   suddenly seeing his gain turn into loss,
   will grieve as he compares his then and now,   57

so she made me do, that relentless beast;
   coming toward me, slowly, step by step,
   she forced me back to where the sun is mute.   60

While I was rushing down to that low place,
   my eyes made out a figure coming toward me
   of one grown faint, perhaps from too much silence.   63

And when I saw him standing in this wasteland,
   "Have pity on my soul," I cried to him,
   "whichever you are, shade or living man!"   66

62. The approaching figure represents (though not exclusively, for he has other meanings) Reason or Natural Philosophy. The Pilgrim cannot proceed to the light of Divine Love (the mountaintop) until he has overcome the three beasts of his sin; and because it is impossible for man to cope with the beasts unaided, Virgil has been summoned to guide the Pilgrim.

63. The voice of Reason has been silent in the Pilgrim's ear for a long time.

"No longer living man, though once I was,"
   he said, "and my parents were from Lombardy,
   both of them were Mantuans by birth.   69

I was born, though somewhat late, *sub Julio*,
   and lived in Rome when good Augustus reigned,
   when still the false and lying gods were worshipped.   72

I was a poet and sang of that just man,
   son of Anchises, who sailed off from Troy
   after the burning of proud Ilium.   75

But why retreat to so much misery?
   Why not climb up this blissful mountain here,
   the beginning and the source of all man's joy?"   78

"Are you then Virgil, are you then that fount
   from which pours forth so rich a stream of words?"
   I said to him, bowing my head modestly.   81

"O light and honor of the other poets,
   may my long years of study, and that deep love
   that made me search your verses, help me now!   84

You are my teacher, the first of all my authors,
   and you alone the one from whom I took
   the noble style that was to bring me honor.   87

You see the beast that forced me to retreat;
   save me from her, I beg you, famous sage,
   she makes me tremble, the blood throbs in my veins."   90

"But you must journey down another road,"
   he answered, when he saw me lost in tears,
   "if ever you hope to leave this wilderness;   93

this beast, the one you cry about in fear,
   allows no soul to succeed along her path,
   she blocks his way and puts an end to him.   96

91. Dante must choose another road because, in order to arrive at the Divine Light, it is necessary first to recognize the true nature of sin, renounce it, and pay penance for it.

She is by nature so perverse and vicious,
    her craving belly is never satisfied,
    still hungering for food the more she eats.   99

She mates with many creatures, and will go on
    mating with more until the greyhound comes
    and tracks her down to make her die in anguish.   102

He will not feed on either land or money:
    his wisdom, love, and virtue shall sustain him;
    he will be born between Feltro and Feltro.   105

He comes to save that fallen Italy
    for which the maid Camilla gave her life
    and Turnus, Nisus, Euryalus died of wounds.   108

And he will hunt for her through every city
    until he drives her back to Hell once more,
    whence Envy first unleashed her on mankind.   111

And so, I think it best you follow me
    for your own good, and I shall be your guide
    and lead you out through an eternal place   114

where you will hear desperate cries, and see
    tormented shades, some old as Hell itself,
    and know what second death is, from their screams.   117

And later you will see those who rejoice
    while they are burning, for they have hope of coming,
    whenever it may be, to join the blessèd—   120

101–111. The Greyhound has been identified with Henry VII, Charles Martel, and even Dante himself. It seems more plausible that the Greyhound represents Can Grande della Scala, the ruler of Verona from 1308 to 1329, whose "wisdom, love, and virtue" (104) were certainly well-known to Dante. Whoever the Greyhound may be, the prophecy would seem to indicate in a larger sense the establishment of a spiritual kingdom on earth in which "wisdom, love, and virtue" will replace the bestial sins of the world. Perhaps Dante had no specific person in mind.

107. Camilla was the valiant daughter of King Metabus, who was slain while fighting against the Trojans (*Aeneid* XI).

108. Turnus was the king of the Rutulians. Nisus and Euryalus were young Trojan warriors slain during a nocturnal raid on the camp of the Rutulians.

117. The "second" death is that of the soul, which occurs when the soul is damned.

to whom, if you too wish to make the climb,
    a spirit, worthier than I, must take you;
    I shall go back, leaving you in her care,   123

because that Emperor dwelling on high
    will not let me lead any to His city,
    since I in life rebelled against His law.   126

Everywhere He reigns, and there He rules;
    there is His city, there is His high throne.
    Oh, happy the one He makes His citizen!"   129

And I to him: "Poet, I beg of you,
    in the name of God, that God you never knew,
    save me from this evil place and worse,   132

lead me there to the place you spoke about
    that I may see the gate Saint Peter guards
    and those whose anguish you have told me of."   135

Then he moved on, and I moved close behind him.

CANTO II

*BUT THE PILGRIM begins to waver; he expresses to Virgil his misgivings
about his ability to undertake the journey proposed by Virgil. His pred-
ecessors have been Aeneas and Saint Paul, and he feels unworthy to
take his place in their company. But Virgil rebukes his cowardice, and
relates the chain of events that led him to come to Dante. The Virgin*

122. Just as Virgil, the pagan Roman poet, cannot enter the Christian Paradise be-
cause he lived before the birth of Christ and lacks knowledge of Christian salvation,
so Reason can only guide the Pilgrim to a certain point: In order to enter Paradise,
the Pilgrim's guide must be Christian Grace or Revelation (Theology) in the figure of
Beatrice.

124. Note the pagan terminology of Virgil's reference to God: It expresses, as best
it can, his unenlightened conception of the Supreme Authority.

Mary took pity on the Pilgrim in his despair and instructed Saint Lucia
to aid him. The Saint turned to Beatrice because of Dante's great love
for her, and Beatrice in turn went down to Hell, into Limbo, and asked
Virgil to guide her friend until that time when she herself would become
his guide. The Pilgrim takes heart at Virgil's explanation and agrees to
follow him.

The day was fading and the darkening air
   was releasing all the creatures on our earth
   from their daily tasks, and I, one man alone,   3

was making ready to endure the battle
   of the journey, and of the pity it involved,
   which my memory, unerring, shall now retrace.   6

O Muses! O high genius! Help me now!
   O memory that wrote down what I saw,
   here your true excellence shall be revealed!   9

Then I began: "O poet come to guide me,
   tell me if you think my worth sufficient
   before you trust me to this arduous road.   12

You wrote about young Sylvius's father,
   who went beyond, with flesh corruptible,
   with all his senses, to the immortal realm;   15

but if the Adversary of all evil
   was kind to him, considering who he was,
   and the consequence that was to come from him,   18

this cannot seem, to thoughtful men, unfitting,
   for in the highest heaven he was chosen
   father of glorious Rome and of her empire,   ·   21

and both the city and her lands, in truth,
   were established as the place of holiness
   where the successors of great Peter sit.   24

And from this journey you celebrate in verse,
   Aeneas learned those things that were to bring
   victory for him, and for Rome, the Papal seat;   27

then later the Chosen Vessel, Paul, ascended
   to ring back confirmation of that faith
   which is the first step on salvation's road.   30

But why am I to go? Who allows me to?
   I am not Aeneas, I am not Paul,
   neither I nor any man would think me worthy;   33

and so, if I should undertake the journey,
   I fear it might turn out an act of folly—
   you are wise, you see more than my words express."   36

As one who unwills what he willed, will change
   his purpose with some new second thought,
   completely quitting what he first had started,   39

so I did, standing there on that dark slope,
   thinking, ending the beginning of that venture
   I was so quick to take up at the start.   42

"If I have truly understood your words,"
   that shade of magnanimity replied,
   "your soul is burdened with that cowardice   45

which often weighs so heavily on man,
   it turns him from a noble enterprise
   like a frightened beast that shies at its own shadow.   48

To free you from this fear, let me explain
   the reason I came here, the words I heard
   that first time I felt pity for your soul: 51

I was among those dead who are suspended,
   when a lady summoned me. She was so blessed
   and beautiful, I implored her to command me.   54

With eyes of light more bright than any star,
   in low, soft tones she started to address me
   in her own language, with an angel's voice: 57

28–30. In his Second Epistle to the Corinthians (12:2–4), the apostle Paul alludes to his mystical elevation to the third heaven and to the arcane messages pronounced there.

'O noble soul, courteous Mantuan,
   whose fame the world continues to preserve
   and will preserve as long as world there is,   60

my friend, who is no friend of Fortune's, strays
   on a desert slope; so many obstacles
   have crossed his path, his fright has turned him back   63

I fear he may have gone so far astray,
   from what report has come to me in Heaven,
   that I may have started to his aid too late.   66

Now go, and with your elegance of speech,
   with whatever may be needed for his freedom,
   give him your help, and thereby bring me solace.   69

I am Beatrice, who urges you to go;
   I come from the place I am longing to return to;
   love moved me, as it moves me now to speak.   72

When I return to stand before my Lord,
   often I shall sing your praises to Him.'
   And then she spoke no more. And I began,   75

'O Lady of Grace, through whom alone mankind
   may go beyond all worldly things contained
   within the sphere that makes the smallest round,   78

your plea fills me with happy eagerness—
   to have obeyed already would still seem late!
   You needed only to express your wish.   81

But tell me how you dared to make this journey
   all the way down to this point of spacelessness,
   away from your spacious home that calls you back.'   84

'Because your question searches for deep meaning,
   I shall explain in simple words,' she said,
   'just why I have no fear of coming here.   87

A man must stand in fear of just those things
   that truly have the power to do us harm,
   of nothing else, for nothing else is fearsome.   90

God gave me such a nature through His Grace,
   the torments you must bear cannot affect me,
   nor are the fires of Hell a threat to me.   93

A gracious lady sits in Heaven grieving
   for what happened to the one I send you to,
   and her compassion breaks Heaven's stern decree.   96

She called Lucia and making her request,
   she said, "Your faithful one is now in need
   of you, and to you I now commend his soul."   99

Lucia, the enemy of cruelty,
   hastened to make her way to where I was,
   sitting by the side of ancient Rachel,   102

and said to me: "Beatrice, God's true praise,
   will you not help the one whose love was such
   it made him leave the vulgar crowd for you?   105

Do you not hear the pity of his weeping,
   do you not see what death it is that threatens him
   along that river the sea shall never conquer?"   108

There never was a wordly person living
   more anxious to promote his selfish gains
   than I was at the sound of words like these—   111

to leave my holy seat and come down here
   and place my trust in you, in your noble speech
   that honors you and all those who have heard it!' 114

When she had finished reasoning, she turned
   her shining eyes away, and there were tears.
   How eager then I was to come to you!   117

And I have come to you just as she wished,
   and I have freed you from the beast that stood
   blocking the quick way up the mount of bliss.   120

94. The lady is the Virgin Mary.

102. In the Dantean Paradise Rachel is seated by Beatrice.

So what is wrong? Why, why do you delay?
   Why are you such a coward in your heart,
   why aren't you bold and free of all your fear,   123

when three such gracious ladies, who are blessed,
   watch out for you up there in Heaven's court,
   and my words, too, bring promise of such good?"   126

As little flowers from the frosty night
   are closed and limp, and when the sun shines down
   on them, they rise to open on their stem,   129

my wilted strength began to bloom within me,
   and such warm courage flowed into my heart
   that I spoke like a man set free of fear.   132

"O she, compassionate, who moved to help me!
   And you, all kindness, in obeying quick
   those words of truth she brought with her for you—   135

you and the words you spoke have moved my heart
   with such desire to continue onward
   that now I have returned to my first purpose.   138

Let us start, for both our wills, joined now, are one.
   You are my guide, you are my lord and teacher."
   These were my words to him and, when he moved,   141

I entered on that deep and rugged road.

CANTO III

*As the two poets enter the vestibule that leads to Hell itself, Dante
sees the inscription above the gate, and he hears the screams of anguish
from the damned souls. Rejected by God and not accepted by the pow-
ers of Hell, the first group of souls are "nowhere," because of their
cowardly refusal to make a choice in life. Their punishment is to follow
a banner at a furious pace forever, and to be tormented by flies and
hornets. The Pilgrim recognizes several of these shades but mentions*

none by name. Next they come to the River Acheron, where they are
greeted by the infernal boatman, Charon. Among those doomed souls
who are to be ferried across the river, Charon sees the living man and
challenges him, but Virgil lets it be known that his companion must
pass. Then across the landscape rushes a howling wind, which blasts
the Pilgrim out of his senses, and he falls to the ground.

I AM THE WAY INTO THE DOLEFUL CITY,
   I AM THE WAY INTO ETERNAL GRIEF,
   I AM THE WAY TO A FORSAKEN RACE.   3

JUSTICE IT WAS THAT MOVED MY GREAT CREATOR;
   DIVINE OMNIPOTENCE CREATED ME,
   AND HIGHEST WISDOM JOINED WITH PRIMAL LOVE.   6

BEFORE ME NOTHING BUT ETERNAL THINGS
   WERE MADE, AND I SHALL LAST ETERNALLY.
   ABANDON EVERY HOPE, ALL YOU WHO ENTER.   9

I saw these words spelled out in somber colors
   inscribed along the ledge above a gate;
   "Master," I said, "these words I see are cruel."   12

He answered me, speaking with experience:
   "Now here you must leave all distrust behind;
   let all your cowardice die on this spot.   15

We are at the place where earlier I said
   you could expect to see the suffering race
   of souls who lost the good of intellect."   18

Placing his hand on mine, smiling at me
   in such a way that I was reassured,
   he led me in, into those mysteries.   21

Here sighs and cries and shrieks of lamentation
   echoed throughout the starless air of Hell;
   at first these sounds resounding made me weep: 24

5–6. Divine Omnipotence, Highest Wisdom, and Primal Love are, respectively, the
Father, the Son, and the Holy Ghost. Thus, the gate of Hell was created by the Trinity
moved by Justice.

18. Souls who have lost sight of God.

tongues confused, a language strained in anguish
    with cadences of anger, shrill outcries
    and raucous groans that joined with sounds of hands,   27

raising a whirling storm that turns itself
    forever through that air of endless black,
    like grains of sand swirling when a whirlwind blows.   30

And I, in the midst of all this circling horror,
    began, "Teacher, what are these sounds I hear?
    What souls are these so overwhelmed by grief?"   33

And he to me: "This wretched state of being
    is the fate of those sad souls who lived a life
    but lived it with no blame and with no praise.   36

They are mixed with that repulsive choir of angels
    neither faithful nor unfaithful to their God,
    who undecided stood but for themselves.   39

Heaven, to keep its beauty, cast them out,
    but even Hell itself would not receive them,
    for fear the damned might glory over them."   42

And I. "Master, what torments do they suffer
    that force them to lament so bitterly?"
    He answered: "I will tell you in few words: 45

these wretches have no hope of truly dying,
    and this blind life they lead is so abject
    it makes them envy every other fate.   48

The world will not record their having been there;
    Heaven's mercy and its justice turn from them.
    Let's not discuss them; look and pass them by."   51

And so I looked and saw a kind of banner
    rushing ahead, whirling with aimless speed
    as though it would not ever take a stand;   54

52–69. In the *Inferno* divine retribution assumes the form of the *contrapasso*, i.e., the just punishment of sin, effected by a process either resembling or contrasting to the sin itself. In this canto the *contrapasso* opposes the sin of neutrality, or inactivity: The souls who in their early lives had no banner, no leader to follow, now run forever after one.

behind it an interminable train
   of souls pressed on, so many that I wondered
   how death could have undone so great a number.   57

When I had recognized a few of them,
   I saw the shade of the one who must have been
   the coward who had made the great refusal.   60

At once I understood, and I was sure
   this was that sect of evil souls who were
   hateful to God and to His enemies.   63

These wretches, who had never truly lived,
   went naked, and were stung and stung again
   by the hornets and the wasps that circled them   66

and made their faces run with blood in streaks;
   their blood, mixed with their tears, dripped to their feet,
   and disgusting maggots collected in the pus.   69

And when I looked beyond this crowd I saw
   a throng upon the shore of a wide river,
   which made me ask, "Master, I would like to know: 72

who are these people, and what law is this
   that makes those souls so eager for the crossing—
   as I can see, even in this dim light?"   75

And he: "All this will be made plain to you
   as soon as we shall come to stop awhile
   upon the sorrowful shore of Acheron."   78

And I, with eyes cast down in shame, for fear
   that I perhaps had spoken out of turn,
   said nothing more until we reached the river.   81

And suddenly, coming toward us in a boat,
   a man of years whose ancient hair was white
   shouted at us, "Woe to you, perverted souls!   84

Give up all hope of ever seeing Heaven:
   I come to lead you to the other shore,
   into eternal darkness, ice, and fire.   87

60. The coward could be Pontius Pilate, who refused to pass sentence on Christ.

And you, the living soul, you over there,
   get away from all these people who are dead."
   But when he saw I did not move aside,   90

he said, "Another way, by other ports,
   not here, shall you pass to reach the other shore;
   a lighter skiff than this must carry you."   93

And my guide, "Charon, this is no time for anger!
   It is so willed, there where the power is
   for what is willed; that's all you need to know."   96

These words brought silence to the woolly cheeks
   of the ancient steersman of the livid marsh,
   whose eyes were set in glowing wheels of fire.   99

But all those souls there, naked, in despair,
   changed color and their teeth began to chatter
   at the sound of his announcement of their doom.   102

They were cursing God, cursing their own parents,
   the human race, the time, the place, the seed
   of their beginning, and their day of birth.   105

Then all together, weeping bitterly,
   they packed themselves along the wicked shore
   that waits for every man who fears not God.   108

The devil, Charon, with eyes of glowing coals,
   summons them all together with a signal,
   and with an oar he strikes the laggard sinner.   111

As in autumn when the leaves begin to fall,
   one after the other (until the branch
   is witness to the spoils spread on the ground),   114

so did the evil seed of Adam's Fall
   drop from that shore to the boat, one at a time,
   at the signal, like the falcon to its lure.   117

Away they go across the darkened waters,
   and before they reach the other side to land,
   a new throng starts collecting on this side.   120

"My son," the gentle master said to me,
  "all those who perish in the wrath of God
  assemble here from all parts of the earth;   123

they want to cross the river, they are eager;
  it is Divine Justice that spurs them on,
  turning the fear they have into desire.   126

A good soul never comes to make this crossing,
  so, if Charon grumbles at the sight of you,
  you see now what his words are really saying."   129

He finished speaking, and the grim terrain
  shook violently; and the fright it gave me
  even now in recollection makes me sweat.   132

Out of the tear-drenched land a wind arose
  which blasted forth into a reddish light,
  knocking my senses out of me completely,   135

and I fell as one falls tired into sleep.

CANTO IV

WAKING FROM HIS SWOON, *the Pilgrim is led by Virgil to the First
Circle of Hell, known as Limbo, where the sad shades of the vir-
tuous non-Christians dwell. The souls here, including Virgil, suffer
no physical torment, but they must live, in desire, without hope of
seeing God. Virgil tells about Christ's descent into Hell and His sal-
vation of several Old Testament figures. The poets see a light glowing*

124–126. It is perhaps a part of the punishment that the souls of all the damned are
eager for their punishment to begin; those who were so willing to sin on earth, are
in hell damned with a willingness to receive their just retribution.

*in the darkness, and as they proceed toward it, they are met by the
four greatest (other than Virgil) pagan poets: Homer, Horace, Ovid,
and Lucan, who take the Pilgrim into their group. As they come closer
to the light, the Pilgrim perceives a splendid castle, where the greatest
non-Christian thinkers dwell together with other famous historical
figures. Once within the castle, the Pilgrim sees, among others, Elec-
tra, Aeneas, Caesar, Saladin, Aristotle, Plato, Orpheus, Cicero, Avi-
cenna, and Averroës. But soon they must leave; and the poets move
from the radiance of the castle toward the fearful encompassing
darkness.*

A heavy clap of thunder! I awoke
    from the deep sleep that drugged my mind—startled,
    the way one is when shaken out of sleep.   3

I turned my rested eyes from side to side,
    already on my feet and, staring hard,
    I tried my best to find out where I was,   6

and this is what I saw: I found myself
    upon the brink of grief's abysmal valley
    that collects the thunderings of endless cries.   9

So dark and deep and nebulous it was,
    try as I might to force my sight below,
    I could not see the shape of anything.   12

"Let us descend into the sightless world,"
    began the poet (his face was deathly pale):
    "I will go first, and you will follow me."   15

And I, aware of his changed color, said:
    "But how can I go on if you are frightened?
    You are my constant strength when I lose heart."   18

And he to me: "The anguish of the souls
    that are down here paints my face with pity—
    which you have wrongly taken to be fear.   21

Let us go, the long road urges us."
    He entered then, leading the way for me
    down to the first circle of the abyss.   24

Down there, to judge only by what I heard,
   there were no wails but just the sounds of sighs
   rising and trembling through the timeless air,   27

the sounds of sighs of untormented grief
   burdening these groups, diverse and teeming,
   made up of men and women and of infants.   30

Then the good master said, "You do not ask
   what sort of souls are these you see around you.
   Now you should know before we go on farther,   33

they have not sinned. But their great worth alone
   was not enough, for they did not know Baptism,
   which is the gateway to the faith you follow,   36

and if they came before the birth of Christ,
   they did not worship God the way one should;
   I myself am a member of this group.   39

For this defect, and for no other guilt,
   we here are lost. In this alone we suffer:
   cut off from hope, we live on in desire."   42

The words I heard weighed heavy on my heart;
   to think that souls as virtuous as these
   were suspended in that limbo, and forever!   45

"Tell me, my teacher, tell me, O my master,"
   I began (wishing to have confirmed by him
   the teachings of unerring Christian doctrine),   48

"did any ever leave here, through his merit
   or with another's help, and go to bliss?"
   And he, who understood my hidden question,   51

answered: "I was a novice in this place
   when I saw a mighty lord descend to us
   who wore the sign of victory as his crown.   54

He took from us the shade of our first parent,
   of Abel, his good son, of Noah, too,
   and of obedient Moses, who made the laws;   57

Abram, the Patriarch, David the King,
   Israel with his father and his children,
   with Rachel, whom he worked so hard to win;   60

and many more he chose for blessedness;
   and you should know, before these souls were taken,
   no human soul had ever reached salvation."   63

We did not stop our journey while he spoke,
   but continued on our way along the woods—
   I say the woods, for souls were thick as trees.   66

We had not gone too far from where I woke
   when I made out a fire up ahead,
   a hemisphere of light that lit the dark.   69

We were still at some distance from that place,
   but close enough for me vaguely to see
   that honorable souls possessed that spot.   72

"O glory of the sciences and arts,
   who are these souls enjoying special honor,
   dwelling apart from all the others here?"   75

And he to me: "The honored name they bear
   that still resounds above in your own world
   wins Heaven's favor for them in this place."   78

And as he spoke I heard a voice announce:
   "Now let us honor our illustrious poet,
   his shade that left is now returned to us."   81

And when the voice was silent and all was quiet
   I saw four mighty shades approaching us,
   their faces showing neither joy nor sorrow.   84

---

69. The "hemisphere of light" emanates from a "splendid castle" (106), the dwelling place of the virtuous men of wisdom in Limbo. The light is the illumination of human intellect, which those who dwell in the castle had in such high measure on earth.

Then my good master started to explain:
   "Observe the one who comes with sword in hand,
   leading the three as if he were their master.   87

It is the shade of Homer, sovereign poet,
   and coming second, Horace, the satirist;
   Ovid is the third, and last comes Lucan.   90

Since they all share one name with me, the name
   you heard resounding in that single voice,
   they honor me and do well doing so."   93

So I saw gathered there the noble school
   of the master singer of sublimest verse,
   who soars above all others like the eagle.   96

And after they had talked awhile together,
   they turned and with a gesture welcomed me,
   and at that sign I saw my master smile.   99

Greater honor still they deigned to grant me:
   they welcomed me as one of their own group,
   so that I numbered sixth among such minds.   102

We walked together toward the shining light,
   discussing things that here are best kept silent,
   as there they were most fitting for discussion.   105

We reached the boundaries of a splendid castle
   that seven times was circled by high walls
   defended by a sweetly flowing stream.   108

86–88. Because his name was inseparably linked with the Trojan War, Homer is portrayed by Dante as a sword-bearing poet, one who sang of arms and martial heroes.

106–111. The allegorical construction of the castle is open to question. It may represent natural philosophy unilluminated by divine wisdom, in which case the seven walls serving to protect the castle would be the seven moral and speculative virtues (prudence, justice, fortitude, temperance, intellect, science, and knowledge); and the seven gates that provide access to the castle would be the seven liberal arts that

We walked right over it as on hard ground;
    through seven gates I passed with those wise spirits,
    and then we reached a meadow fresh in bloom.   111

There people were whose eyes were calm and grave,
    whose bearing told of great authority;
    seldom they spoke and always quietly.   114

Then moving to one side we reached a place
    spread out and luminous, higher than before,
    allowing us to view all who were there.   117

And right before us on the lustrous green
    the mighty shades were pointed out to me
    (my heart felt glory when I looked at them).   120

There was Electra standing with a group,
    among whom I saw Hector and Aeneas,
    and Caesar, falcon-eyed and fully armed.   123

---

formed the medieval school curriculum (music, arithmetic, geometry, astronomy—
the *quadrivium*; and grammar, logic, and rhetoric—the *trivium*). The symbolic value
of the stream also remains uncertain; it could signify eloquence, a "stream" that the
eloquent Virgil and Dante should have no trouble crossing—and indeed, they
"walked right over it as on hard ground" (109).

112–144. The inhabitants of the great castle are important pagan philosophers and
poets, as well as famous writers. Three of the shades named (Saladin, Avicenna,
Averroës) lived only one hundred or two hundred years before Dante. Modern readers
might wonder at the inclusion of medieval non-Christians among the virtuous pagans
of antiquity, but the three just mentioned were among the non-Christians respected,
particularly during the Middle Ages.

121. Electra was the daughter of Atlas, the mother of Dardanus, and the founder of
Troy; thus, her followers include all members of the Trojan race. She should not be
confused with Electra, daughter of Agamemnon, the character in plays by Aeschylus,
Sophocles, and Euripides.

122. Among Electra's descendants are Hector, the eldest son of Priam, king of Troy,
and Aeneas (cf. Canto I, 73–75; and Canto II, 13–24).

123. Julius Caesar proclaimed himself the first emperor of Rome after defeating nu-
merous opponents in civil conflicts.

I saw Camilla and Penthesilea;
   across the way I saw the Latian King,
   with Lavinia, his daughter, by his side.   126

I saw the Brutus who drove out the Tarquin;
   Lucretia, Julia, Marcia, and Cornelia;
   off, by himself, I noticed Saladin,   129

and when I raised my eyes a little higher
   I saw the master sage of those who know,
   sitting with his philosophic family.   132

All gaze at him, all pay their homage to him;
   and there I saw both Socrates and Plato,
   each closer to his side than any other;   135

Democritus, who said the world was chance,
   Diogenes, Thales, Anaxagoras,
   Empedocles, Zeno, and Heraclitus;   138

124–126. For Camilla see Canto I, note on line 107. Penthesilea was the glamorous queen of the Amazons who aided the Trojans against the Greeks and was slain by Achilles during the conflict. King Latinus commanded the central region of the Italian peninsula, the site where Aeneas founded Rome. He gave Lavinia to the Trojan conqueror in marriage.

127–129. Outraged by the murder of his brother and the rape (and subsequent suicide) of his sister (Lucretia), Lucius Brutus incited the Roman populace to expel the Tarquins, the perpetrators of the offenses. This accomplished, he was elected first consul and consequently became the founder of the Roman Republic. The four women were famous Roman wives and mothers. Lucretia was the wife of Collatinus; Julia the daughter of Julius Caesar and wife of Pompey; Marcia the second wife of Cato of Utica (in the *Convivio* Dante makes her the symbol of the noble soul); and Cornelia the daughter of Scipio Africanus Major and mother of the Gracchi, the tribunes Tiberius and Caius. A distinguished soldier, Saladin became sultan of Egypt in 1174. Medieval opinion of Saladin was favorable; he was lauded for his generosity and his magnanimity.

131. To Dante, Aristotle represented the summit of human reason, that point which man could reach on his own without the benefit of Christian revelation.

137. Diogenes was the Cynic philosopher who believed that the only good lies in virtue secured through self-control and abstinence. Anaxagoras was a Greek philosopher of the Ionian school (500–428 B.C.). Among his famous students were Pericles and Euripides. Thales (ca. 635–ca. 545 B.C.), an early Greek philosopher born at Miletus, founded the Ionian school of philosophy and in his main doctrine maintained that water is the elemental principle of all things.

I saw the one who classified our herbs:
  Dioscorides I mean. And I saw Orpheus,
  Tully, Linus, Seneca the moralist,   141

Euclid the geometer, and Ptolemy,
  Hippocrates, Galen, Avicenna,
  and Averroës, who made the Commentary.   144

I cannot tell about them all in full;
  my theme is long and urges me ahead,
  often I must omit things I have seen.   147

The company of six becomes just two;
  my wise guide leads me by another way
  out of the quiet into tempestuous air.   150

I come into a place where no light is.

---

140. Dioscorides was a Greek natural scientist and physician of the first century A.D. Orpheus was a mythical Greek poet and musician whose lyrical talent was such that it moved rocks and trees and tamed wild beasts.

141. Tully was Marcus Tullius Cicero, celebrated Roman orator, writer, and philosopher (106–43 B.C.). Linus was a mythical Greek poet and musician who is credited with inventing the dirge. Lucius Annaeus Seneca (4 B.C.–A.D. 65) followed the philosophy of the Stoics in his moral treatises. Dante calls him "the moralist" to distinguish him from Seneca the tragedian, who was thought (erroneously) during the Middle Ages to be another person.

142. Euclid was a Greek mathematician (ca. 300 B.C.) who wrote a treatise on geometry that was the first codification and exposition of mathematical principles. Ptolemy was a Greek mathematician, astronomer, and geographer. The universe, according to the Ptolemaic system (which was accepted by the Middle Ages), so named although he did not invent it, had the earth as its fixed center encircled by nine spheres.

143. Hippocrates was a Greek physician (ca. 460–377 B.C.) who founded the medical profession and introduced the scientific art of healing. Galen was a celebrated physician (ca. A.D. 130–ca. 200) who practiced his art in Greece, Egypt, and Rome. Avicenna (or Ibn-Sina) was an Arabian philosopher and physician (A.D. 980–1037) who was a prolific writer.

144. Ibn-Rushd, called Averroës (ca. A.D. 1126–ca. 1198), was a celebrated Arabian scholar born in Spain. He was widely known in the Middle Ages for his commentary on Aristotle, which served as the basis for the work of St. Thomas Aquinas.

CANTO V

FROM LIMBO Virgil leads his ward down to the threshold of the Second Circle of Hell, where for the first time he will see the damned in Hell being punished for their sins. There, barring their way, is the hideous figure of Minòs, the bestial judge of Dante's underworld; but after strong words from Virgil, the poets are allowed to pass into the dark space of this circle, where can be heard the wailing voices of the Lustful, whose punishment consists in being forever whirled about in a dark, stormy wind. After seeing a thousand or more famous lovers— including Semiramis, Dido, Helen, Achilles, and Paris—the Pilgrim asks to speak to two figures he sees together. They are Francesca da Rimini and her lover, Paolo, and the scene in which they appear is probably the most famous episode of the Inferno. At the end of the scene, the Pilgrim, who has been overcome by pity for the lovers, faints to the ground.

This way I went, descending from the first
    into the second round, that holds less space
    but much more pain—stinging the soul to wailing.   3

There stands Minòs grotesquely, and he snarls,
    examining the guilty at the entrance;
    he judges and dispatches, tail in coils.   6

By this I mean that when the evil soul
    appears before him, it confesses all,
    and he, who is the expert judge of sins,   9

knows to what place in Hell the soul belongs;
    the times he wraps his tail around himself
    tell just how far the sinner must go down.   12

4. Minòs was the son of Zeus and Europa. As king of Crete he was revered for his wisdom and judicial gifts. For these qualities he became chief magistrate of the underworld in classical literature. (See Virgil, *Aeneid* VI, 432–433.) Although Dante did not alter Minòs' official function, he transformed him into a demonic figure, both in his physical characteristics and in his bestial activity.

The damned keep crowding up in front of him:
    they pass along to judgment one by one;
    they speak, they hear, and then are hurled below.   15

"O you who come to the place where pain is host,"
    Minòs spoke out when he caught sight of me,
    putting aside the duties of his office,   18

"be careful how you enter and whom you trust
    it's easy to get in, but don't be fooled!"
    And my guide said to him: "Why keep on shouting?   21

Do not attempt to stop his fated journey;
    it is so willed there where the power is
    for what is willed; that's all you need to know."   24

And now the notes of anguish start to play
    upon my ears; and now I find myself
    where sounds on sounds of weeping pound at me.   27

I came to a place where no light shone at all,
    bellowing like the sea racked by a tempest,
    when warring winds attack it from both sides.   30

The infernal storm, eternal in its rage,
    sweeps and drives the spirits with its blast:
    it whirls them, lashing them with punishment.   33

When they are swept back past their place of judgment,
    then come the shrieks, laments, and anguished cries;
    there they blaspheme God's almighty power.   36

I learned that to this place of punishment
    all those who sin in lust have been condemned,
    those who make reason slave to appetite;   39

31–32. The *contrapasso* or punishment suggests that lust (the "infernal storm") is
pursued without the light of reason (in the darkness).

and as the wings of starlings in the winter
   bear them along in wide-spread, crowded flocks,
     so does that wind propel the evil spirits: 42

now here, then there, and up and down, it drives them
   with never any hope to comfort them—
     hope not of rest but even of suffering less.   45

And just like cranes in flight, chanting their lays,
   stretching an endless line in their formation,
     I saw approaching, crying their laments,   48

spirits carried along by the battling winds.
   And so I asked, "Teacher, tell me, what souls
     are these punished in the sweep of the black wind?"   51

"The first of those whose story you should know,"
   my master wasted no time answering,
     "was empress over lands of many tongues;   54

her vicious tastes had so corrupted her
   she licensed every form of lust with laws
     to cleanse the stain of scandal she had spread;   57

she is Semiramis, who, legend says,
   was Ninus' wife as well as his successor;
     she governed all the land the Sultan rules.   60

The next is she who killed herself for love
   and broke faith with the ashes of Sichaeus;
     and there is Cleopatra, who loved men's lusting.   63

See Helen there, the root of evil woe
   lasting long years, and see the great Achilles,
     who lost his life to love, in final combat;   66

64. Helen of Troy.

65–66. Enticed by the beauty of Polyxena, a daughter of the Trojan king, Achilles desired her to be his wife, but Hecuba, Polyxena's mother, arranged a counterplot with Paris so that when Achilles entered the temple for his presumed marriage, he was treacherously slain by Paris.

see Paris, Tristan"—then, more than a thousand
   he pointed out to me, and named them all,
   those shades whom love cut off from life on earth.   69

After I heard my teacher call the names
   of all these knights and ladies of ancient times,
   pity confused my senses, and I was dazed.   72

I began: "Poet, I would like, with all my heart,
   to speak to those two there who move together
   and seem to be so light upon the winds."   75

And he: "You'll see when they are closer to us;
   if you entreat them by that love of theirs
   that carries them along, they'll come to you."   78

When the winds bent their course in our direction
   I raised my voice to them, "O wearied souls,
   come speak with us if it be not forbidden."   81

As doves, called by desire to return
   to their sweet nest, with wings raised high and poised,
   float downward through the air, guided by will,   84

so these two left the flock where Dido is
   and came toward us through the malignant air,
   such was the tender power of my call.   87

67. Paris was the son of Priam, king of Troy, whose abduction of Helen ignited the Trojan War. Tristan was the central figure of numerous medieval French, German, and Italian romances. Sent as a messenger by his uncle, King Mark of Cornwall, to obtain Isolt for him in marriage, Tristan became enamored of her, and she of him. After Isolt's marriage to Mark, the lovers continued their love affair, and in order to maintain its secrecy they necessarily employed many deceits and ruses. According to one version, Mark, increasingly suspicious of their attachment, finally discovered them together and ended the incestuous relationship by mortally wounding Tristan with a lance.

74. The two are Francesca, daughter of Guido Vecchio da Polenta, lord of Ravenna; and Paolo Malatesta, third son of Malatesta da Verrucchio, lord of Rimini. Around 1275 the aristocratic Francesca was married for political reasons to Gianciotto, the physically deformed second son of Malatesta da Verrucchio. In time a love affair developed between Francesca and Gianciotto's younger brother, Paolo. One day the betrayed husband discovered them in an amorous embrace and slew them both.

"O living creature, gracious and so kind,
  who makes your way here through this dingy air
  to visit us who stained the world with blood,   90

if we could claim as friend the King of Kings,
  we would beseech him that he grant you peace,
  you who show pity for our atrocious plight.   93

Whatever pleases you to hear or speak
  we will hear and we will speak about with you
  as long as the wind, here where we are, is silent.   96

The place where I was born lies on the shore
  where the river Po with its attendant streams
  descends to seek its final resting place.   99

Love, quick to kindle in the gentle heart,
  seized this one for the beauty of my body,
  torn from me. (How it happened still offends me!)   102

Love, that excuses no one loved from loving,
  seized me so strongly with delight in him
  that, as you see, he never leaves my side.   105

Love led us straight to sudden death together.
  Caïna awaits the one who quenched our lives."
  These were the words that came from them to us.   108

When those offended souls had told their story,
  I bowed my head and kept it bowed until
  the poet said, "What are you thinking of?"   111

When finally I spoke, I sighed, "Alas,
  all those sweet thoughts, and oh, how much desiring
  brought these two down into this agony."   114

And then I turned to them and tried to speak;
  I said, "Francesca, the torment that you suffer
  brings painful tears of pity to my eyes.   117

107. Caïna was one of the four divisions of Cocytus, the lower part of Hell, wherein those souls who treacherously betrayed their kin are tormented.

But tell me, in that time of your sweet sighing
    how, and by what signs, did love allow you
    to recognize your dubious desires?"   120

And she to me: "There is no greater pain
    than to remember, in our present grief,
    . past happiness (as well your teacher knows)!   123

But if your great desire is to learn
    the very root of such a love as ours,
    I shall tell you, but in words of flowing tears.   126

One day we read, to pass the time away,
    of Lancelot, of how he fell in love;
    we were alone, innocent of suspicion.   129

Time and again our eyes were brought together
    by the book we read; our faces flushed and paled.
    To the moment of one line alone we yielded: 132

it was when we read about those longed-for lips
    now being kissed by such a famous lover,
    that this one (who shall never leave my side)   135

then kissed my mouth, and trembled as he did.
    Our Galehot was that book and he who wrote it.
    That day we read no further." And all the while   138

the one of the two spirits spoke these words,
    the other wept, in such a way that pity
    blurred my senses; I swooned as though to die,   141

and fell to Hell's floor as a body, dead, falls.

CANTO VI

ON RECOVERING consciousness the Pilgrim finds himself with Virgil in
the Third Circle, where the Gluttons are punished. These shades are
mired in filthy muck and are eternally battered by cold and dirty hail,

rain, and snow. Soon the travelers come upon Cerberus, the three-
headed, doglike beast who guards the Gluttons, but Virgil pacifies him
with fistfuls of slime and the two poets pass on. One of the shades
recognizes Dante the Pilgrim and hails him. It is Ciacco, a Florentine
who, before they leave, makes a prophecy concerning the political future
of Florence. As the poets move away, the Pilgrim questions Virgil about
the Last Judgment and other matters until the two arrive at the next
circle.

Regaining now my senses, which had fainted
    at the sight of these two who were kinsmen lovers,
    a piteous sight confusing me to tears,   3

new suffering and new sinners suffering
    appeared to me, no matter where I moved
    or turned my eyes, no matter where I gazed.   6

I am in the third circle, in the round of rain
    eternal, cursed, cold, and falling heavy,
    unchanging beat, unchanging quality.   9

Thick hail and dirty water mixed with snow
    come down in torrents through the murky air,
    and the earth is stinking from this soaking rain.   12

Cerberus, a ruthless and fantastic beast,
    with all three throats howls out his doglike sounds
    above the drowning sinners of this place.   15

His eyes are red, his beard is slobbered black,
    his belly swollen, and he has claws for hands;
    he rips the spirits, flays and mangles them.   18

Under the rain they howl like dogs, lying
    now on one side with the other as a screen,
    now on the other turning, these wretched sinners.   21

13–22. In classical mythology Cerberus is a fierce three-headed dog that guards the
entrance to the Underworld, permitting admittance to all and escape to none. He is
the prototype of the Gluttons, with his three howling, voracious throats that gulp
down huge handfuls of muck. He has become Appetite and as such he flays and
mangles the spirits who reduced their lives to a satisfaction of appetite. With his three
heads, he appears to be a prefiguration of Lucifer and thus another infernal distortion
of the Trinity.

When the slimy Cerberus caught sight of us,
   he opened up his mouths and showed his fangs;
   his body was one mass of twitching muscles.   24

My master stooped and, spreading wide his fingers,
   he grabbed up heaping fistfuls of the mud
   and flung it down into those greedy gullets.   27

As a howling cur, hungering to get fed,
   quiets down with the first mouthful of his food,
   busy with eating, wrestling with that alone,   30

so it was with all three filthy heads
   of the demon Cerberus, used to barking thunder
   on these dead souls, who wished that they were deaf.   33

We walked across this marsh of shades beaten
   down by the heavy rain, our feet pressing
   on their emptiness that looked like human form.   36

Each sinner there was stretched out on the ground
   except for one who quickly sat up straight,
   the moment that he saw us pass him by.   39

"O you there being led through this inferno,"
   he said, "try to remember who I am,
   for you had life before I gave up mine."   42

I said: "The pain you suffer here perhaps
   disfigures you beyond all recognition:
   I can't remember seeing you before.   45

But tell me who you are, assigned to grieve
   in this sad place, afflicted by such torture
   that—worse there well may be, but none more foul."   48

"Your own city," he said, "so filled with envy
   its cup already overflows the brim,
   once held me in the brighter life above.   51

36. The shades in Hell bear only the *appearance* of their corporeal forms, although they can be ripped and torn and otherwise suffer physical torture—just as here they are able to bear the Pilgrim's weight. Yet they themselves evidently are airy shapes without weight (cf. Canto VIII, 27), which will, after the Day of Judgment, be possessed of their actual bodies once more (see Canto XIII, 103).

You citizens gave me the name of Ciacco;
    and for my sin of gluttony I am damned,
    as you can see, to rain that beats me weak.   54

And my sad sunken soul is not alone,
    for all these sinners here share in my pain
    and in my sin." And that was his last word.   57

"Ciacco," I said to him, "your grievous state
    weighs down on me, it makes me want to weep;
    but tell me what will happen, if you know,   60

to the citizens of that divided state?
    And are there any honest men among them?
    And tell me, why is it so plagued with strife?"   63

And he replied: "After much contention
    they will come to bloodshed; the rustic party
    will drive the other out by brutal means.   66

Then it will come to pass, this side will fall
    within three suns, and the other rise to power
    with the help of one now listing toward both sides.   69

52. The only Glutton whom the Pilgrim actually talks to is Ciacco, one of his Flor-
entine contemporaries, whose true identity has never been determined. Several com-
mentators believe him to be Ciacco dell'Anguillaia, a minor poet of the time and
presumably the Ciacco of one of Boccaccio's stories (*Decameron* IX, 8). However,
more than a proper name, *ciacco* is a derogatory Italian word for "pig," or "hog,"
and is also an adjective, "filthy," or "of a swinish nature."

65–75. Ciacco's political prophecy reveals the fact that the shades in Hell are able
to see the future; they also know the past, but they know nothing of the present (see
Canto X, 100–108). The Guelph party, having gained complete control over Florence
by defeating the Ghibellines (1289), was divided into factions: the Whites (the "rustic
party," 65), headed by the Cerchi family; and the Blacks (the "other," 66), led by
the Donatis. These two groups finally came into direct conflict on May 1, 1300, which
resulted in the expulsion of the Blacks from the city (1301). However, they returned
in 1302 ("within three suns," 68, i.e., within three years), and with the help of Pope
Boniface VIII, sent the Whites (including Dante) into exile. Boniface VIII, the "one
now listing toward both sides" (69), for a time did not reveal his designs on Florence,
but rather steered a wavering course between the two factions, planning to aid the
ultimate victor.

"Pape Satàn, pape Satàn aleppe!"
    the voice of Plutus clucked these words at us,
    and that kind sage, to whom all things were known,   3

said reassuringly: "Do not let fear
    defeat you, for whatever be his power,
    he cannot stop our journey down this rock."   6

Then he turned toward that swollen face of rage,
    crying, "Be quiet, cursèd wolf of Hell:
    feed on the burning bile that rots your guts.   9

This journey to the depths does have a reason,
    for it is willed on high, where Michael wrought
    a just revenge for the bold assault on God."   12

As sails swollen by wind, when the ship's mast breaks,
    collapse, deflated, tangled in a heap,
    just so the savage beast fell to the ground.   15

And then we started down a fourth abyss,
    making our way along the dismal slope
    where all the evil of the world is dumped.   18

Ah, God's avenging justice! Who could heap up
    suffering and pain as strange as I saw here?
    How can we let our guilt bring us to this?   21

As every wave Charybdis whirls to sea
    comes crashing against its counter-current wave,
    so these folks here must dance their roundelay.   24

More shades were here than anywhere above,
    and from both sides, to the sound of their own screams,
    straining their chests, they rolled enormous weights.   27

1. This is simple gibberish (cf. Nimrod's speech in Canto XXXI, 67).

22–66. The Miserly and the Prodigal, linked together as those who misused their wealth, suffer a joint punishment. Their material wealth has become a heavy weight that each group must shove against the other, since their attitudes toward wealth on earth were opposed to each other. Part of their punishment is to complete the turn of the Wheel (circle) of Fortune against which they had rebelled during their short space of life on earth.

And when they met and clashed against each other
    they turned to push the other way, one side
    screaming, "Why hoard?," the other side, "Why waste?"   30

And so they moved back round the gloomy circle,
    returning on both sides to opposite poles
    to scream their shameful tune another time;   33

again they came to clash and turn and roll
    forever in their semicircle joust.
    And I, my heart pierced through by such a sight,   36

spoke out, "My master, please explain to me
    who are these people here? Were they all priests,
    these tonsured souls I see there to our left?"   39

He said, "In their first life all you see here
    had such myopic minds they could not judge
    with moderation when it came to spending;   42

their barking voices make this clear enough,
    when they arrive at the two points on the circle
    where opposing guilts divide them into two.   45

The ones who have the bald spot on their heads
    were priests and popes and cardinals, in whom
    avarice is most likely to prevail."   48

And I: "Master, in such a group as this
    I should be able to recognize a few
    who dirtied themselves by such crimes as these."   51

And he replied, "Yours is an empty hope:
    their undistinguished life that made them foul
    now makes it harder to distinguish them.   54

Eternally the two will come to blows;
    then from the tomb they will be resurrected:
    these with tight fists, those without any hair.   57

It was squandering and hoarding that have robbed them
    of the lovely world, and got them in this brawl:
    I will not waste choice words describing it!   60

You see, my son, the short-lived mockery
 of all the wealth that is in Fortune's keep,
  over which the human race is bickering;   63

for all the gold that is or ever was
 beneath the moon won't buy a moment's rest
  for even one among these weary souls."   66

"Master, now tell me what this Fortune is
 you touched upon before. What is she like
  who holds all worldly wealth within her fists?"   69

And he to me, "O foolish race of man,
 how overwhelming is your ignorance!
  Now listen while I tell you what she means: 72

that One, whose wisdom knows infinity,
 made all the heavens and gave each one a guide,
  and each sphere shining shines on all the others, 75

so light is spread with equal distribution:
 for worldly splendors He decreed the same
  and ordained a guide and general ministress   78

who would at her discretion shift the world's
 vain wealth from nation to nation, house to house,
  with no chance of interference from mankind;   81

so while one nation rules, another falls,
 according to whatever she decrees
  (her sentence hidden like a snake in grass).   84

Your knowledge has no influence on her;
 for she foresees, she judges, and she rules
  her kingdom as the other gods do theirs.   87

Her changing changes never take a rest;
 necessity keeps her in constant motion,
  as men come and go to take their turn with her. 90

And this is she so crucified and cursed;
 even those in luck, who should be praising her,
  instead revile her and condemn her acts.   93

But she is blest and in her bliss hears nothing;
    with all God's joyful first-created creatures
    she turns her sphere and, blest, turns it with joy.   96

Now let's move down to greater wretchedness;
    the stars that rose when I set out for you
    are going down—we cannot stay too long."   99

We crossed the circle to its other bank,
    passing a spring that boils and overflows
    into a ditch the spring itself cut out.   102

The water was a deeper dark than perse,
    and we, with its gray waves for company,
    made our way down along a rough, strange path.   105

This dingy little stream, when it has reached
    the bottom of the gray malignant slopes,
    becomes a swamp that has the name of Styx.   108

And I, intent on looking as we passed,
    saw muddy people moving in that marsh,
    all naked, with their faces scarred by rage.   111

They fought each other, not with hands alone,
    but struck with head and chest and feet as well,
    with teeth they tore each other limb from limb.   114

And the good teacher said: "My son, now see
    the souls of those that anger overcame;
    and I ask you to believe me when I say,   117

beneath the slimy top are sighing souls
    who make these waters bubble at the surface;
    your eyes will tell you this—just look around.   120

Bogged in this slime they say, 'Sluggish we were
    in the sweet air made happy by the sun,
    and the smoke of sloth was smoldering in our hearts;   123

98–99. The time is past midnight. The stars setting in the west were rising in the
east when Virgil first met Dante on the evening of Good Friday in the "dark wood."

108. The river Styx is the second of the rivers of Hell; Dante, following the *Aeneid*,
refers to it here as a marsh or quagmire.

now we lie sluggish here in this black muck!'
    This is the hymn they gurgle in their throats
    but cannot sing in words that truly sound."   126

Then making a wide arc, we walked around
    the pond between the dry bank and the slime,
    our eyes still fixed on those who gobbled mud.   129

We came, in time, to the foot of a high tower.

CANTO VIII

BUT BEFORE *they had reached the foot of the tower, the Pilgrim had noticed two signal flames at the tower's top, and another flame answering from a distance; soon he realizes that the flames are signals to and from Phlegyas, the boatman of the Styx, who suddenly appears in a small boat speeding across the river. Wrathful and irritated though he is, the steersman must grant the poets passage, but during the crossing an angry shade rises from the slime to question the Pilgrim. After a brief exchange of words, scornful on the part of the Pilgrim, who has recognized this sinner, the spirit grabs hold of the boat. Virgil pushes him away, praising his ward for his just scorn, while a group of the wrathful attack the wretched soul, whose name is Filippo Argenti. At the far shore the poets debark and find themselves before the gates of the infernal City of Dis, where howling figures threaten them from the walls. Virgil speaks with them privately, but they slam the gate shut in his face. His ward is terrified, and Virgil too is shaken, but he insists that help from Heaven is already on the way.*

I must explain, however, that before
    we finally reached the foot of that high tower,
    our eyes had been attracted to its summit   3

by two small flames we saw flare up just there;
    and, so far off the eye could hardly see,
    another burning torch flashed back a sign.   6

I turned to that vast sea of human knowledge:
  "What signal is this? And the other flame,
  what does it answer? And who's doing this?"   9

And he replied: "You should already see
  across the filthy waves what has been summoned,
  unless the marsh's vapors hide it from you."   12

A bowstring never shot an arrow off
  that cut the thin air any faster than
  a little boat I saw that very second   15

skimming along the water in our direction,
  with a solitary steersman, who was shouting,
  "Aha, I've got you now, you wretched soul!"   18

"Phlegyas, Phlegyas, this time you shout in vain,"
  my lord responded, "you will have us with you
  no longer than it takes to cross the muck."   21

As one who learns of some incredible trick
  just played on him flares up resentfully—
  so, Phlegyas there was seething in his anger.   24

My leader calmly stepped into the skiff
  and when he was inside, he had me enter,
  and only then it seemed to carry weight.   27

Soon as my guide and I were in the boat
  the ancient prow began to plough the water,
  more deeply, now, than any time before.   30

And as we sailed the course of this dead channel,
  before me there rose up a slimy shape
  that said: "Who are you, who come before your time?"   33

And I spoke back, "Though I come, I do not stay;
  but who are you, in all your ugliness?"
  "You see that I am one who weeps," he answered.   36

---

18. Phlegyas, the son of Mars, set fire to Apollo's temple at Delphi, furiously enraged because Apollo had raped his daughter Coronis. For this Apollo killed him and sent him to Tartarus. Dante makes Phlegyas the demonic guardian of the Styx.

32. The "slimy shape" is Filippo Argenti (61), a member of the Adimari family.

And then I said to him: "May you weep and wail,
   stuck here in this place forever, you damned soul,
   for, filthy as you are, I recognize you." 39

With that he stretched both hands out toward the boat
   but, on his guard, my teacher pushed him back:
   "Away, get down there with the other curs!" 42

And then he put his arms around my neck
   and kissed my face and said, "Indignant soul,
   blessèd is she in whose womb you were conceived. 45

In the world this man was filled with arrogance,
   and nothing good about him decks his memory;
   for this, his shade is filled with fury here. 48

Many in life esteem themselves great men
   who then will wallow here like pigs in mud,
   leaving behind them their repulsive fame." 51

"Master, it certainly would make me happy
   to see him dunked deep in this slop just once
   before we leave this lake—it truly would." 54

And he to me, "Before the other shore
   comes into sight, you will be satisfied:
   a wish like that is worthy of fulfillment." 57

Soon afterward, I saw the wretch so mangled
   by a gang of muddy souls that, to this day,
   I thank my Lord and praise Him for that sight: 60

"Get Filippo Argenti!" they all cried.
   And at those shouts the Florentine, gone mad,
   turned on himself and bit his body fiercely. 63

We left him there, I'll say no more about him.
   A wailing noise began to pound my ears
   and made me strain my eyes to see ahead. 66

"And now, my son," the gentle teacher said,
   "coming closer is the city we call Dis,
   with its great walls and its fierce citizens." 69

And I, "Master, already I can see
   the clear glow of its mosques above the valley,
   burning bright red, as though just forged, and left   72

to smolder." And he to me: "Eternal fire
   burns within, giving off the reddish glow
   you see diffused throughout this lower Hell."   75

And then at last we entered those deep moats
   that circled all of this unhappy city
   whose walls, it seemed to me, were made of iron.   78

For quite a while we sailed around, until
   we reached a place and heard our boatsman shout
   with all his might, "Get out! Here is the entrance."   81

I saw more than a thousand fiendish angels
   perching above the gates enraged, screaming:
   "Who is the one approaching? Who, without death,   84

dares walk into the kingdom of the dead?"
   And my wise teacher made some kind of signal
   announcing he would speak to them in secret.   87

They managed to suppress their great resentment
   enough to say: "You come, but he must go
   who thought to walk so boldly through this realm.   90

Let him retrace his foolish way alone,
   just let him try. And you who led him here
   through this dark land, you'll stay right where you are."   93

And now, my reader, consider how I felt
   when those foreboding words came to my ears!
   I thought I'd never see our world again!   96

"O my dear guide, who more than seven times
   restored my confidence, and rescued me
   from the many dangers that blocked my going on,   99

don't leave me, please," I cried in my distress,
   "and if the journey onward is denied us,
   let's turn our footsteps back together quickly."   102

Then that lord who had brought me all this way
    said, "Do not fear, the journey we are making
    none can prevent: such power did decree it.   105

Wait here for me and feed your weary spirit
    with comfort and good hope; you can be sure
    I will not leave you in this underworld."   108

With this he walks away. He leaves me here,
    that gentle father, and I stay, doubting,
    and battling with my thoughts of "yes"—but "no."   111

I could not hear what he proposed to them,
    but they did not remain with him for long;
    I saw them race each other back for home.   114

Our adversaries slammed the heavy gates
    in my lord's face, and he stood there outside,
    then turned toward me and walked back very slowly   117

with eyes downcast, all self-assurance now
    erased from his forehead—sighing, "Who are these
    to forbid my entrance to the halls of grief!"   120

He spoke to me: "You need not be disturbed
    by my vexation, for I shall win the contest,
    no matter how they plot to keep us out!   123

This insolence of theirs is nothing new;
    they used it once at a less secret gate,
    which is, and will forever be, unlocked;   126

you saw the deadly words inscribed above it;
    and now, already past it, and descending,
    across the circles, down the slope, alone,   129

comes one by whom the city will be opened."

CANTO IX

THE HELP FROM Heaven has not yet arrived; the Pilgrim is afraid and Virgil is obviously worried. He reassures his ward by telling him that, soon after his own death, he was forced by the Sorceress Erichtho to resume mortal shape and go to the very bottom of Hell in order to bring up the soul of a traitor; thus Virgil knows the way well. But no sooner is the Pilgrim comforted than the Three Furies appear before him, on top of the tower, shrieking and tearing their breasts with their nails. They call for Medusa, whose horrible face has the power of turning anyone who looks on her to stone. Virgil turns his ward around and covers his eyes. After an "address to the reader" calling attention to the coming allegory, a strident blast splits the air, and the poets perceive an Angel coming through the murky darkness to open the gates of the City for them. Then the angel returns on the path whence he had come, and the two travelers enter the gate. Within are great open burning sarcophagi, from which groans of torment issue. Virgil explains that these are Arch-Heretics and their lesser counterparts.

The color of the coward on my face,
    when I realized my guide was turning back,
    made him quickly change the color of his own.   3

He stood alert, like one who strains to hear;
    his eyes could not see far enough ahead
    to cut the heavy fog of that black air.   6

"But surely we were meant to win this fight,"
    he said, "or else . . . but no, such help was promised!
    Oh, how much time it's taking him to come!"   9

I saw too well how quickly he amended
    his opening words with what he added on!
    They were different from the ones he first pronounced;   12

but nonetheless his words made me afraid,
    perhaps because the phrase he left unfinished
    I finished with worse meaning than he meant.   15

"Has anyone before ever descended
    to this sad hollow's depths from that first circle
    whose pain is all in having hope cut off?"   18

I put this question to him. He replied,
    "It is not usual for one of us
    to make the journey I am making now.   21

But it happens I was down here once before,
    conjured by that heartless witch, Erichtho
    (who could recall the spirit to its body).   24

Soon after I had left my flesh in death
    she sent me through these walls, and down as far
    as the pit of Judas to bring a spirit out;   27

and that place is the lowest and the darkest
    and the farthest from the sphere that circles all;
    I know the road, and well, you can be sure.   30

This swamp that breathes with a prodigious stink
    lies in a circle round the doleful city
    that now we cannot enter without strife."   33

And he said other things, but I forget them,
    for suddenly my eyes were drawn above,
    up to the fiery top of that high tower   36

where in no time at all and all at once
    sprang up three hellish Furies stained with blood,
    their bodies and their gestures those of females;   39

their waists were bound in cords of wild green hydras,
    horned snakes and little serpents grew as hair,
    and twined themselves around the savage temples.   42

And he who had occasion to know well
    the handmaids of the queen of timeless woe
    cried out to me "Look there! The fierce Erinyes!   45

22–30. Having no literary or legendary source, the story of Virgil's descent into Hell
was probably Dante's invention.

That is Megaera, the one there to the left,
   and that one raving on the right, Alecto,
   Tisiphone, in the middle." He said no more.   48

With flailing palms the three would beat their breasts,
   then tear them with their nails, shrieking so loud,
   I drew close to the poet, confused with fear.   51

"Medusa, come, we'll turn him into stone,"
   they shouted all together glaring down,
   "how wrong we were to let off Theseus lightly!"   54

"Now turn your back and cover up your eyes,
   for if the Gorgon comes and you should see her,
   there would be no returning to the world!"   57

These were my master's words. He turned me round
   and did not trust my hands to hide my eyes
   but placed his own on mine and kept them covered.   60

O all of you whose intellects are sound,
   look now and see the meaning that is hidden
   beneath the veil that covers my strange verses: 63

and then, above the filthy swell, approaching,
   a blast of sound, shot through with fear, exploded,
   making both shores of Hell begin to tremble;   66

it sounded like one of those violent winds,
   born from the clash of counter-temperatures,
   that tear through forests; raging on unchecked,   69

52. Medusa, in classical mythology, is one of the three Gorgons. Minerva, furious at Medusa for giving birth to two children in one of the former's temples, changed her beautiful hair into serpents, so that whoever gazed on her terrifying aspect was turned to stone.

54. Theseus, the greatest Athenian hero, descended to Hades with his friend Pirithous, king of the Lapithae, in order to kidnap Proserpina for him. Pluto slew Pirithous, however, and kept Theseus a prisoner in Hades by having him sit on the Chair of Forgetfulness, which made his mind blank and thereby kept him from moving. Dante chooses a less common version of the myth, which has Theseus set free by Hercules. (See note on lines 98–99.)

it splits and rips and carries off the branches
　　and proudly whips the dust up in its path
　　and makes the beasts and shepherds flee its course! 72

He freed my eyes and said, "Now turn around
　　and set your sight along the ancient scum,
　　there where the marsh's mist is hovering thickest." 75

As frogs before their enemy, the snake,
　　all scatter through the pond and then dive down
　　until each one is squatting on the bottom, 78

so I saw more than a thousand fear-shocked souls
　　in flight, clearing the path of one who came
　　walking the Styx, his feet dry on the water. 81

From time to time with his left hand he fanned
　　his face to push the putrid air away,
　　and this was all that seemed to weary him. 84

I was certain now that he was sent from Heaven.
　　I turned to my guide, but he made me a sign
　　to keep my silence and bow low to this one. 87

Ah, the scorn that filled his holy presence!
　　He reached the gate and touched it with a wand;
　　it opened without resistance from inside. 90

"O Heaven's outcasts, despicable souls,"
　　he started, standing on the dreadful threshold,
　　"what insolence is this that breeds in you? 93

Why do you stubbornly resist that will
　　whose end can never be denied and which,
　　more than one time, increased your suffering? 96

What do you gain by locking horns with fate?
　　If you remember well, your Cerberus
　　still bears his chin and throat peeled clean for that!" 99

94. The will of God.

98–99. When Hercules descended into Hell to rescue Theseus, he chained the three-headed dog Cerberus and dragged him around and outside Hell so that the skin around his neck was ripped away.

He turned then and retraced the squalid path
   without one word to us, and on his face
   the look of one concerned and spurred by things   102

that were not those he found surrounding him.
   And then we started moving toward the city
   in the safety of the holy words pronounced.   105

We entered there, and with no opposition.
   And I, so anxious to investigate
   the state of souls locked up in such a fortress,   108

once in the place, allowed my eyes to wander,
   and saw, in all directions spreading out,
   a countryside of pain and ugly anguish.   111

As at Arles where the Rhône turns to stagnant waters
   or as at Pola near Quarnero's Gulf
   that closes Italy and bathes her confines,   114

the sepulchers make all the land uneven,
   so they did here, strewn in all directions,
   except the graves here served a crueler purpose: 117

for scattered everywhere among the tombs
   were flames that kept them glowing far more hot
   than any iron an artisan might use.   120

Each tomb had its lid loose, pushed to one side,
   and from within came forth such fierce laments
   that I was sure inside were tortured souls.   123

I asked, "Master, what kind of shades are these
   lying down here, buried in the graves of stone,
   speaking their presence in such dolorous sighs?"   126

And he replied: "There lie arch-heretics
   of every sect, with all of their disciples;
   more than you think are packed within these tombs.   129

127–131. The Heretics are in a circle in Hell that is outside of the three main divisions of Incontinence, Violence, and Fraud. Heresy is not due to weaknesses of the flesh or mind (Incontinence), nor is it a form of violence.

Like heretics lie buried with their like
   and the graves burn more, or less, accordingly."
   Then turning to the right, we moved ahead   132

between the torments there and those high walls.

CANTO X

*THEY COME to the tombs containing the Epicurean heretics, and as they
are walking by them, a shade suddenly rises to full height in one tomb,
having recognized the Pilgrim's Tuscan dialect. It is the proud Farinata,
who, in life, opposed Dante's party; while he and the Pilgrim are con-
versing, another figure suddenly rises out of the same tomb. It is the
shade of Cavalcante de' Cavalcanti, who interrupts the conversation
with questions about his son Guido. Misinterpreting the Pilgrim's con-
fused silence as evidence of his son's death, Cavalcante falls back into
his sepulcher and Farinata resumes the conversation exactly where it
had been broken off. He defends his political actions in regard to Flor-
ence and prophesies that Dante, like himself, will soon know the pain
of exile. But the Pilgrim is also interested to know how it is that the
damned can see the future but not the present. When his curiosity is
satisfied, he asks Farinata to tell Cavalcante that his son is still alive,
and that his silence was caused only by his confusion about the shade's
inability to know the present.*

Now onward down a narrow path, between
   the city's ramparts and the suffering,
   my master walks, I following close behind.   3

"O lofty power who through these impious gyres
   lead me around as you see fit," I said,
   "I want to know, I want to understand: 6

the people buried there in sepulchers,
   can they be seen? I mean, since all the lids
   are off the tombs and no one stands on guard."   9

And he: "They will forever be locked up,
   when they return here from Jehoshaphat
   with the bodies that they left up in the world.   12

The private cemetery on this side
   serves Epicurus and his followers,
   who make the soul die when the body dies.   15

As for the question you just put to me,
   it will be answered soon, while we are here;
   and the wish you are keeping from me will be granted."   18

And I: "O my good guide, I do not hide
   my heart; I'm trying not to talk too much,
   as you have told me more than once to do."   21

"O Tuscan walking through our flaming city,
   alive, and speaking with such elegance,
   be kind enough to stop here for a while.   24

Your mode of speech identifies you clearly
   as one whose birthplace is that noble city
   with which in my time, perhaps, I was too harsh."   27

One of the vaults resounded suddenly
   with these clear words, and I, intimidated,
   drew up a little closer to my guide,   30

who said, "What are you doing? Turn around
   and look at Farinata, who has risen,
   you will see him from the waist up standing straight."   33

I already had my eyes fixed on his face,
   and there he stood out tall, with his chest and brow
   proclaiming his disdain for all this Hell.   36

14–15. The philosophy of the Epicureans taught that the highest good is temporal happiness, which is to be achieved by the practice of the virtues. In Dante's time Epicureans were considered heretics because they exalted temporal happiness and therefore denied the immortality of the soul and the afterlife. Epicurus is among the heretics even though he was a pagan, because he denied the immortality of the soul, a truth known even to the ancients.

My guide, with a gentle push, encouraged me
  to move among the sepulchers toward him:
  "Be sure you choose your words with care," he said.   39

And when I reached the margin of his tomb
  he looked at me, and half-contemptuously
  he asked, "And *who* would *your* ancestors be?"   42

And I who wanted only to oblige him
  held nothing back but told him everything.
  At this he lifted up his brows a little,   45

then said, "Bitter enemies of mine they were
  and of my ancestors and of my party;
  I had to scatter them not once but twice."   48

"They were expelled, but only to return
  from everywhere," I said, "not once but twice—
  an art your men, however, never mastered!"   51

Just then along that same tomb's open ledge
  a shade appeared, but just down to his chin,
  beside this other; I think he got up kneeling.   54

He looked around as though he hoped to see
  if someone else, perhaps, had come with me
  and, when his expectation was deceived,   57

he started weeping: "If it be great genius
  that carries you along through this blind jail,
  where is my son? Why is he not with you?"   60

"I do not come alone," I said to him,
  "that one waiting over there guides me through here,
  the one, perhaps, your Guido held in scorn."   63

(The place of pain assigned him, and what he asked,
  already had revealed his name to me
  and made my pointed answer possible.)   66

53. The shade is Cavalcante de' Cavalcanti, a member of an important Florentine
family. His son Guido, born about 1255, was one of the major poets of the day and
was Dante's "first friend," as he says in the *Vita nuova*.

Instantly, he sprang to his full height and cried,
 "What did you say? He *held*? Is he not living?
 The day's sweet light no longer strikes his eyes?" 69

And when he heard the silence of my delay
 responding to his question, he collapsed
 into his tomb, not to be seen again. 72

That other stately shade, at whose request
 I had first stopped to talk, showed no concern
 nor moved his head nor turned to see what happened; 75

he merely picked up where we had left off:
 "If that art they did not master," he went on,
 "that gives me greater pain than does this bed. 78

But the face of the queen who reigns down here will glow
 not more than fifty times before you learn
 how hard it is to master such an art; 81

and as I hope that you may once more know
 the sweet world, tell me, why should your party be
 so harsh to my clan in every law they make?" 84

I answered: "The massacre and butchery
 that stained the waters of the Arbia red
 now cause such laws to issue from our councils." 87

He sighed, shaking his head. "It was not I
 alone took part," he said, "nor certainly
 would I have joined the rest without good cause. 90

But I alone stood up when all of them
 were ready to have Florence razed. It was *I*
 who openly stood up in her defense." 93

"And now, as I would have your seed find peace,"
 I said, "I beg you to resolve a problem
 that has kept my reason tangled in a knot: 96

79–81. The face is that of Hecate or Proserpina, the moon goddess, queen of the Underworld (cf. Canto IX, 44). Farinata makes the prophecy that Dante will know how difficult the art of returning from exile is before fifty months have passed.

if I have heard correctly, all of you
    can see ahead to what the future holds
    but your knowledge of the present is not clear." 99

"Down here we see like those with faulty vision
    who only see," he said, "what's at a distance;
    this much the sovereign lord grants us here. 102

When events are close to us, or when they happen,
    our mind is blank, and were it not for others
    we would know nothing of your living state. 105

Thus you can understand how all our knowledge
    will be completely dead at that time when
    the door to future things is closed forever." 108

Then I, moved by regret for what I'd done
    said, "Now, will you please tell the fallen one
    his son is still on earth among the living; 111

and if, when he asked, silence was my answer,
    tell him: while he was speaking, all my thoughts
    were struggling with that point you solved for me." 114

My teacher had begun to call me back,
    so I quickly asked that spirit to reveal
    the names of those who shared the tomb with him. 117

He said, "More than a thousand lie with me,
    the Second Frederick is here and the Cardinal
    is with us. And the rest I shall not mention." 120

His figure disappeared. I made my way
    to the ancient poet, reflecting on those words,
    those words which were prophetic enemies. 123

He moved, and as we went along he said,
    "What troubles you? Why are you so distraught?"
    And I told him all the thoughts that filled my mind. 126

"Be sure your mind retains," the sage commanded,
    "those words you heard pronounced against yourself,
    and listen carefully now." He raised a finger: 129

"When at last you stand in the glow of her sweet ray,
　　the one whose splendid eyes see everything,
　　from her you'll learn your life's itinerary."   132

Then to the left he turned. Leaving the walls,
　　he headed toward the center by a path
　　that strikes into a vale, whose stench arose,   135

disgusting us as high up as we were.

CANTO XI

CONTINUING THEIR WAY *within the Sixth Circle, where the heretics are
punished, the poets are assailed by a stench rising from the abyss ahead
of them which is so strong that they must stop in order to accustom
themselves to the odor. They pause beside a tomb whose inscription
declares that within is Pope Anastasius. When the Pilgrim expresses his
desire to pass the time of waiting profitably, Virgil proceeds to instruct
him about the plan of punishments in Hell. Then, seeing that dawn is
only two hours away, he urges the Pilgrim on.*

We reached the curving brink of a steep bank
　　constructed of enormous broken rocks;
　　below us was a crueler den of pain.   3

And the disgusting overflow of stench
　　the deep abyss was vomiting forced us
　　back from the edge. Crouched underneath the lid   6

of some great tomb, I saw it was inscribed:
　　"Within lies Anastasius, the pope
　　Photinus lured away from the straight path."   9

131. The "one" is Beatrice.

8–9. Anastasius II, pope from 496 to 498, was popularly believed for many centuries
to be a heretic because, supposedly, he allowed Photinus, a deacon of Thessalonica
who followed the heresy of Acacius, to take communion.

"Our descent will have to be delayed somewhat
   so that our sense of smell may grow accustomed
   to these vile fumes; then we will not mind them,"   12

my master said. And I: "You will have to find
   some way to keep our time from being wasted."
   "That is precisely what I had in mind,"   15

he said, and then began the lesson: "My son,
   within these boulders' bounds are three more circles,
   concentrically arranged like those above,   18

all tightly packed with souls; and so that, later,
   the sight of them alone will be enough,
   I'll tell you how and why they are imprisoned.   21

All malice has injustice as its end,
   an end achieved by violence or by fraud;
   while both are sins that earn the hate of Heaven,   24

since fraud belongs exclusively to man,
   God hates it more and, therefore, far below,
   the fraudulent are placed and suffer most.   27

In the first of the circles below are all the violent;
   since violence can be used against three persons,
   into three concentric rounds it is divided: 30

violence can be done to God, to self,
   or to one's neighbor—to him or to his goods,
   as my reasoned explanation will make clear.   33

By violent means a man can kill his neighbor
   or wound him grievously; his goods may suffer
   violence by arson, theft, and devastation;   36

so, homicides and those who strike with malice,
   those who destroy and plunder, are all punished
   in the first round, but all in different groups.   39

Man can raise violent hands against himself
   and his own goods; so in the second round,
   paying the debt that never can be paid,   42

are suicides, self-robbers of your world,
    or those who gamble all their wealth away
    and weep up there when they should have rejoiced.   45

One can use violence against the deity
    by heartfelt disbelief and cursing Him,
    or by despising Nature and God's bounty;   48

therefore, the smallest round stamps with its seal
    both Sodom and Cahors and all those souls
    who hate God in their hearts and curse His name.   51

Fraud, that gnaws the conscience of its servants,
    can be used on one who puts his trust in you
    or else on one who has no trust invested.   54

This latter sort seems only to destroy
    the bond of love that Nature gives to man;
    so in the second circle there are nests   57

of hypocrites, flatterers, dabblers in sorcery,
    falsifiers, thieves, and simonists,
    panders, seducers, grafters, and like filth.   60

The former kind of fraud both disregards
    the love Nature enjoys and that extra bond
    between men which creates a special trust;   63

thus, it is in the smallest of the circles,
    at the earth's center, around the throne of Dis,
    that traitors suffer their eternal pain."   66

And I, "Master, your reasoning runs smooth,
    and your explanation certainly makes clear
    the nature of this pit and of its inmates,   69

50. Sodom was the biblical city (Genesis 18–19) destroyed by God for its vicious
sexual offenses. Cahors was a city in the south of France that was widely known in
the Middle Ages as a thriving seat of usury. Dante uses the city names to indicate
the sodomites and usurers who are punished in the smallest round of Circle Seven.

65. Here the name Dis refers to Lucifer.

but what about those in the slimy swamp,
   those driven by the wind, those beat by rain,
   and those who come to blows with harsh refrains?   72

Why are they, too, not punished here inside
   the city of flame, if they have earned God's wrath?
   If they have not, why are they suffering?"   75

And he to me, "Why do you let your thoughts
   stray from the path they are accustomed to?
   Or have I missed the point you have in mind?   78

Have you forgotten how your *Ethics* reads,
   those terms it explicates in such detail:
   the three conditions that the heavens hate,   81

incontinence, malice, and bestiality?
   Do you not remember how incontinence
   offends God least, and merits the least blame?   84

If you will reconsider well this doctrine
   and then recall to mind who those souls were
   suffering pain above, outside the walls,   87

you will clearly see why they are separated
   from these malicious ones, and why God's vengeance
   beats down upon their souls less heavily."   90

"O sun that shines to clear a misty vision,
   such joy is mine when you resolve my doubts
   that doubting pleases me no less than knowing!   93

70–75. The sinners are those guilty of Incontinence. Virgil's answer (76–90) is that
the Incontinent suffer a lighter punishment because their sins, being without malice,
are less offensive to God.

79–84. Virgil says "your *Ethics*" in referring to Aristotle's *Ethica Nicomanchea* be-
cause he realizes how thoroughly the Pilgrim studied this work.

   While the distinction here offered between Incontinence and Malice is based on
Aristotle, it should be clear that the overall classification of sins in the *Inferno* is not.
Dante's is a twofold system, the main divisions of which may be illustrated as follows:

Sins of   Incontinence
             Malice   through violence
                               through Fraud

Go back a little bit once more," I said
   "to where you say that usury offends
   God's goodness, and untie that knot for me."   96

"Philosophy," he said, "and more than once,
   points out to one who reads with understanding
   how Nature takes her course from the Divine   99

Intellect, from its artistic workmanship;
   and if you have your *Physics* well in mind
   you will find, not many pages from the start,   102

how your art too, as best it can, imitates
   Nature, the way an apprentice does his master;
   so your art may be said to be God's grandchild.   105

From Art and Nature man was meant to take
   his daily bread to live—if you recall
   the book of Genesis near the beginning;   108

but the usurer, adopting other means,
   scorns Nature in herself and in her pupil,
   Art—he invests his hope in something else.   111

Now follow me, we should be getting on;
   the Fish are shimmering over the horizon,
   the Wain is now exactly over Caurus,   114

and the passage down the bank is farther on."

101–105. Aristotle's *Physics* (II, ii) concerns the doctrine that Art imitates Nature. Art, or human industry, is the child of Nature in the sense that it is the use to which man puts nature, and thus is the grandchild of God. Usurers, who are in the third round of Circle Seven, by doing violence to human industry are, in effect, doing violence to God.

113–115. Each sign of the Zodiac covers about two hours; thus it must be nearly two hours before sunrise. Caurus is the Northwest Wind.

CANTO XII

THEY DESCEND the steep slope into the Seventh Circle by means of a great landslide, which was caused when Christ descended into Hell. At the edge of the abyss is the Minotaur, who presides over the circle of the Violent and whose own bestial rage sends him into such a paroxysm of violence that the two travelers are able to run past him without his interference. At the base of the precipice, they see a river of boiling blood, which contains those who have inflicted violence upon others. But before they can reach the river they are intercepted by three fierce Centaurs, whose task it is to keep those who are in the river at their proper depth by shooting arrows at them if they attempt to rise. Virgil explains to one of the centaurs (Chiron) that this journey of the Pilgrim and himself is ordained by God; and he requests him to assign someone to guide the two of them to the ford in the river and carry the Pilgrim across it to the other bank. Chiron gives the task to Nessus, one of the centaurs, who, as he leads them to the river's ford, points out many of the sinners there in the boiling blood.

Not only was that place, where we had come
    to descend, craggy, but there was something there
    that made the scene appalling to the eye.   3

Like the ruins this side of Trent left by the landslide
    (an earthquake or erosion must have caused it)
    that hit the Adige on its left bank,   6

when, from the mountain's top where the slide began
    to the plain below, the shattered rocks slipped down,
    shaping a path for a difficult descent—   9

so was the slope of our ravine's formation.
    And at the edge, along the shattered chasm,
    there lay stretched out the infamy of Crete: 12

4–10. The steep, shattered terrain was caused by the earthquake that shook Hell just before Christ descended there.

the son conceived in the pretended cow.
   When he saw us he bit into his flesh,
   gone crazy with the fever of his rage.   15

My wise guide cried to him: "Perhaps you think
   you see the Duke of Athens come again,
   who came once in the world to bring your death?   18

Begone, you beast, for this one is not led
   down here by means of clues your sister gave him;
   he comes here only to observe your torments."   21

The way a bull breaks loose the very moment
   he knows he has been dealt the mortal blow,
   and cannot run but jumps and twists and turns,   24

just so I saw the Minotaur perform,
   and my guide, alert, cried out: "Run to the pass!
   While he still writhes with rage, get started down."   27

And so we made our way down through the ruins
   of rocks, which often I felt shift and tilt
   beneath my feet from weight they were not used to.   30

I was deep in thought when he began: "Are you,
   perhaps, thinking about these ruins protected
   by the furious beast I quenched in its own rage?   33

Now let me tell you that the other time
   I came down to the lower part of Hell,
   this rock had not then fallen into ruins;   36

but certainly, if I remember well,
   it was just before the coming of that One
   who took from Hell's first circle the great spoil,   39

that this abyss of stench, from top to bottom
   began to shake, so I thought the universe
   felt love—whereby, some have maintained, the world   42

38. The "One" was Christ, who, in the Harrowing of Hell, removed to Heaven the souls of the Elect.

41–43. According to Empedoclean doctrine, Hate, by destroying pristine harmony (i.e., original chaos), occasions the creation of all things, and Love, by reunifying these disparate elements, reestablishes concord in the universe.

has more than once renewed itself in chaos.
     That was the moment when this ancient rock
     was split this way—here, and in other places.   45

But now look down the valley. Coming closer
     you will see the river of blood that boils the souls
     of those who through their violence injured others."   48

(Oh, blind cupidity and insane wrath,
     spurring us on through our short life on earth
     to steep us then forever in such misery!)   51

I saw a river—wide, curved like a bow—
     that stretched embracing all the flatland there,
     just as my guide had told me to expect.   54

Between the river and the steep came centaurs,
     galloping in single file, equipped with arrows,
     off hunting as they used to in the world;   57

then, seeing us descend, they all stopped short
     and three of them departed from the ranks
     with bows and arrows ready from their quivers.   60

One of them cried from his distant post: "You there,
     on your way down here, what torture are you seeking?
     Speak where you stand, if not, I draw my bow."   63

And then my master shouted back: "Our answer
     we will give to Chiron when we're at his side;
     as for you, I see you are as rash as ever!"   66

47–48. The river is Phlegethon, the Virgilian river of fire, here one of boiling blood,
in which are punished those shades who committed violence against their fellow men.

56. Like the Minotaur, the centaurs who guard the murderers and tyrants are men-
beasts (half-horse, half-man) and thus appropriate to the sins of violence or bestiality.

65. Chiron, represented by the ancient poets as chief of the centaurs, was particularly
noted for his wisdom. In mythology he was the son of Saturn (who temporarily
changed himself into a horse to avoid the notice and anger of his wife) and Philyra.

He nudged me, saying: "That one there is Nessus,
    who died from loving lovely Dejanira,
    and made of himself, of his blood, his own revenge.					69

The middle one, who contemplates his chest,
    is great Chiron, who reared and taught Achilles;
    the last is Pholus, known for his drunken wrath.					72

They gallop by the thousands round the ditch,
    shooting at any daring soul emerging
    above the bloody level of his guilt."					75

When we came closer to those agile beasts,
    Chiron drew an arrow, and with its notch
    he parted his beard to both sides of his jaws,					78

and when he had uncovered his great mouth
    he spoke to his companions: "Have you noticed,
    how the one behind moves everything he touches?					81

This is not what a dead man's feet would do!"
    And my good guide, now standing by the torso
    at the point the beast's two natures joined, replied:					84

"He is indeed alive, and so alone
    that I must show him through this dismal valley;
    he travels by necessity, not pleasure.					87

A spirit came, from singing Alleluia,
    to give me this extraordinary mission;
    he is no rogue nor I a criminal spirit.					90

67–69. Nessus is the centaur who is the first to speak to the two travelers. He is later appointed by Chiron (lines 98–99) to accompany them; he does so, pointing out various sinners along the way. Virgil refers to Dejanira, Hercules' wife, whom Nessus desired. In attempting to rape her, Nessus was shot by Hercules, but as he died he gave Dejanira a robe soaked in his blood, which he said would preserve Hercules' love. Dejanira took it to her husband, whose death it caused, whereupon the distraught woman hanged herself.

72. During the wedding of Pirithous and Hippodamia, when the drunken centaurs tried to rape the Lapithaen women, Pholus attempted to rape the bride herself.

88. The spirit is Beatrice.

Now, in the name of that power by which I move
    my steps along so difficult a road,
    give us one of your troop to be our guide: 93

to lead us to the ford and, once we are there,
    to carry this one over on his back,
    for he is not a spirit who can fly."   96

Chiron looked over his right breast and said
    to Nessus, "You go, guide them as they ask,
    and if another troop protests, disperse them!"   99

So with this trusted escort we moved on
    along the boiling crimson river's bank,
    where piercing shrieks rose from the boiling souls.   102

There I saw people sunken to their eyelids,
    and the huge centaur explained, "These are the tyrants
    who dealt in bloodshed and plundered wealth.   105

Their tears are paying for their heartless crimes:
    here stand Alexander and fierce Dionysius,
    who weighed down Sicily with years of pain;   108

and there, that forehead smeared with coal-black hair,
    is Azzolino; the other one, the blond,
    Opizzo d'Esti, who, and this is true,   111

was killed by his own stepson in your world."
    With that I looked to Virgil, but he said
    "Let him instruct you now, don't look to me."   114

107–108. Dante could possibly have meant Alexander the Great (356–323 B.C.), who is constantly referred to as a cruel and violent man by Orosius, Dante's chief source of ancient history. But many modern scholars believe this figure to be Alexander, tyrant of Pherae (368–359 B.C.), whose extreme cruelty is recorded by Cicero and Valerius Maximus. Both of these authors link Alexander of Pherae with the tyrant Dionysius of Syracuse, mentioned here.

110. Azzolino was Ezzelino III da Romano (1194–1259), a Ghibelline chief and tyrant of the March of Treviso. He was notoriously cruel and committed such inhuman atrocities that he was called a "son of Satan."

111–114. Obizzo d'Esti, a cruel tyrant, was marquis of Ferrara and the March of Ancona (1264–1293).

A little farther on, the centaur stopped
 above some people peering from the blood
 that came up to their throats. He pointed out   117

a shade off to one side, alone, and said:
 "There stands the one who, in God's keep, murdered
 the heart still dripping blood above the Thames."   120

Then I saw other souls stuck in the river
 who had their heads and chests above the blood,
 and I knew the names of many who were there.   123

The river's blood began decreasing slowly
 until it cooked the feet and nothing more,
 and here we found the ford where we could cross.   126

"Just as you see the boiling river here
 on this side getting shallow gradually,"
 the centaur said, "I would also have you know   129

that on the other side the riverbed
 sinks deeper more and more until it reaches
 the deepest meeting place where tyrants moan: 132

it is there that Heaven's justice strikes its blow
 against Attila, known as the scourge of earth,
 against Pyrrhus and Sextus; and forever   135

120. In 1272 during Holy Mass at the church ("in God's keep") in Veterbo, Guy de Montfort (one of Charles d'Anjou's emissaries), in order to avenge his father's death at the hands of Edward I, king of England, stabbed to death the latter's cousin, Prince Henry, son of Richard, Earl of Cornwall. According to Giovanni Villani, the thirteenth-century chronicler, Henry's heart was placed in "a golden cup . . . above a column at the head of London bridge" where it still drips blood above the Thames (*Cronica* VII, xxxix). The dripping blood signifies that the murder has not yet been avenged.

124–126. The sinners are sunk in the river to a degree commensurate with the gravity of their crimes; tyrants, whose crimes of violence are directed against both man and his possessions, are sunk deeper than murderers, whose crimes are against men alone. The river is at its shallowest at the point where the poets cross; from this ford, in both directions of its circle, it grows deeper.

134. Attila, king of the huns, was called the "scourge of God."

135. Pyrrhus is probably Pyrrhus (318–272 B.C.), king of Epirus, who fought the Romans three times between 280 and 276 B.C. before they finally defeated him.

extracts the tears the scalding blood produces
   from Rinier da Corneto and Rinier Pazzo,
     whose battlefields were highways where they robbed."   138

Then he turned round and crossed the ford again.

CANTO XIII

NO SOONER are the poets across the Phlegethon than they encounter a dense forest, from which come wails and moans, and which is presided over by the hideous harpies—half-woman, half-beast, birdlike creatures. Virgil tells his ward to break off a branch of one of the trees; when he does, the tree weeps blood and speaks. In life he was Pier Delle Vigne, chief counselor of Frederick II of Sicily; but he fell out of favor, was accused unjustly of treachery, and was imprisoned, whereupon he killed himself. The Pilgrim is overwhelmed by pity. The sinner also explains how the souls of the suicides come to this punishment and what will happen to them after the Last Judgment. Suddenly they are interrupted by the wild sounds of the hunt, and two naked figures, Lano of Siena and Giacomo da Sant' Andrea, dash across the landscape, shouting at each other, until one of them hides himself in a thorny bush; immediately a pack of fierce, black dogs rush in, pounce on the hidden sinner, and rip his body, carrying away mouthfuls of flesh. The bush, which has been torn in the process, begins to lament. The two learn that the cries are those of a Florentine who had hanged himself in his own home.

Not yet had Nessus reached the other side
   when we were on our way into a forest
     that was not marked by any path at all.   3

Sextus is probably the younger son of Pompey the Great. After the murder of Caesar he turned to piracy, causing near famine in Rome by cutting off the grain supply from Africa. He is condemned by Lucan (*Pharsalia* VI, 420–422) as being unworthy of his father. A few commentators believe that Dante is referring to Sextus Tarquinius Superbus, who raped and caused the death of Lucretia, the wife of his cousin.

137–138. Rinier da Corneto and Rinier Pazzo were two highway robbers famous in Dante's day.

No green leaves, but rather black in color,
     no smooth branches, but twisted and entangled,
     no fruit, but thorns of poison bloomed instead.   6

No thick, rough, scrubby home like this exists—
     not even between Cecina and Corneto—
     for those wild beasts that hate the run of farmlands.   9

Here the repulsive Harpies twine their nests,
     who drove the Trojans from the Strophades
     with filthy forecasts of their close disaster.   12

Wide-winged they are, with human necks and faces,
     their feet are clawed, their bellies fat and feathered;
     perched in the trees they shriek their strange laments.   15

"Before we go on farther," my guide began,
     "remember, you are in the second round
     and shall be till we reach the dreadful sand;   18

now look around you carefully and see
     with your own eyes what I will not describe,
     for if I did, you wouldn't believe my words."   21

Around me wails of grief were echoing,
     and I saw no one there to make those sounds;
     bewildered by all this, I had to stop.   24

I think perhaps he thought I might be thinking
     that all the voices coming from those stumps
     belonged to people hiding there from us,   27

and so my teacher said, "If you break off
     a little branch of any of these plants,
     what you are thinking now will break off too."   30

Then slowly raising up my hand a bit
     I snapped the tiny branch of a great thornbush,
     and its trunk cried: "Why are you tearing me?"   33

8–9. The vast swampland known as the "Maremma toscana" lies between the towns
of Cecina and Corneto, which mark its northern and southern boundaries.

And when its blood turned dark around the wound,
  it started saying more: "Why do you rip me?
  Have you no sense of pity whatsoever?   36

Men were we once, now we are changed to scrub;
  but even if we had been souls of serpents,
  your hand should have shown more pity than it did."   39

Like a green log burning at one end only,
  sputtering at the other, oozing sap,
  and hissing with the air it forces out,   42

so from that splintered trunk a mixture poured
  of words and blood. I let the branch I held
  fall from my hand and stood there stiff with fear.   45

"O wounded soul," my sage replied to him,
  "if he had only let himself believe
  what he had read in verses I once wrote,   48

he never would have raised his hand against you,
  but the truth itself was so incredible,
  I urged him on to do the thing that grieves me.   51

But tell him who you were; he can make amends,
  and will, by making bloom again your fame
  in the world above, where his return is sure."   54

And the trunk: "So appealing are your lovely words,
  I must reply. Be not displeased if I
  am lured into a little conversation.   57

I am that one who held both of the keys
  that fitted Frederick's heart; I turned them both,
  locking and unlocking, with such finesse   60

that I let few into his confidence.
  I was so faithful to my glorious office,
  I lost not only sleep but life itself.   63

47–49. Virgil is referring to that section of the *Aeneid* (III, 22–43) where Aeneas breaks a branch from a shrub, which then begins to pour forth blood; at the same time a voice issues from the ground beneath the shrub where Polydorus is buried. (See Canto XXX, 18.)

That courtesan who constantly surveyed
    Caesar's household with her adulterous eyes,
    mankind's undoing, the special vice of courts,   66

inflamed the hearts of everyone against me,
    and these, inflamed, inflamed in turn Augustus,
    and my happy honors turned to sad laments.   69

My mind, moved by scornful satisfaction,
    believing death would free me from all scorn,
    made me unjust to me, who was all just.   72

By these strange roots of my own tree I swear
    to you that never once did I break faith
    with my lord, who was so worthy of all honor.   75

If one of you should go back to the world,
    restore the memory of me, who here
    remain cut down by the blow that Envy gave."   78

My poet paused awhile, then said to me,
    "Since he is silent now, don't lose your chance,
    ask him, if there is more you wish to know."   81

"Why don't you keep on questioning," I said,
    "and ask him, for my part, what I would ask,
    for I cannot, such pity chokes my heart."   84

He began again: "That this man may fulfill
    generously what your words cry out for,
    imprisoned soul, may it please you to continue   87

by telling us just how a soul gets bound
    into these knots, and tell us, if you know,
    whether any soul might someday leave his branches."   90

At that the trunk breathed heavily, and then
    the breath changed to a voice that spoke these words:
    "Your question will be answered very briefly.   93

68–72. Pier was also a renowned poet of the Sicilian School, which flourished under Frederick's patronage and which is noted for its love of complex conceits and convoluted wordplay.

The moment that the violent soul departs
  the body it has torn itself away from,
  Minòs sends it down to the seventh hole;   96

it drops to the wood, not in a place allotted,
  but anywhere that fortune tosses it.
  There, like a grain of spelt, it germinates,   99

soon springs into a sapling, then a wild tree;
  at last the Harpies, feasting on its leaves,
  create its pain, and for the pain an outlet.   102

Like the rest, we shall return to claim our bodies,
  but never again to wear them—wrong it is
  for a man to have again what he once cast off.   105

We shall drag them here and, all along the mournful
  forest, our bodies shall hang forever more,
  each one on a thorn of its own alien shade."   108

We were standing still attentive to the trunk,
  thinking perhaps it might have more to say,
  when we were startled by a rushing sound,   111

such as the hunter hears from where he stands:
  first the boar, then all the chase approaching,
  the crash of hunting dogs and branches smashing,   114

then, to the left of us appeared two shapes
  naked and gashed, fleeing with such rough speed
  they tore away with them the bushes' branches.   117

The one ahead: "Come on, come quickly, Death!"
  The other, who could not keep up the pace,
  screamed, "Lano, your legs were not so nimble   120

115–121. The second group of souls punished here are the Profligates, who did vi-
olence to their earthly goods by not valuing them as they should have, just as the
Suicides did not value their bodies. The "tournament of Toppo" (121) recalls the
disastrous defeat of the Sienese troops at the hands of the Aretines in 1287 at a river
ford near Arezzo. Lano went into this battle to die because he had squandered his
fortune: as legend has it, he remained to fight rather than escape on foot (hence
Giacomo's reference to his "legs," 120), and was killed.

when you jousted in the tournament of Toppo!"
    And then, from lack of breath perhaps, he slipped
    into a bush and wrapped himself in thorns.   123

Behind these two the wood was overrun
    by packs of black bitches ravenous and ready,
    like hunting dogs just broken from their chains;   126

they sank their fangs in that poor wretch who hid,
    they ripped him open piece by piece, and then
    ran off with mouthfuls of his wretched limbs.   129

Quickly my escort took me by the hand
    and led me over to the bush that wept
    its vain laments from every bleeding sore: 132

"O Giacomo da Sant' Andrea," it said,
    "what good was it for you to hide in me?
    What fault have I if you led an evil life?"   135

My master, standing over it, inquired:
    "Who were you once that now through many wounds
    breathes a grieving sermon with your blood?"   138

He answered us: "O souls who have just come
    in time to see this unjust mutilation
    that has separated me from all my leaves,   141

gather them round the foot of this sad bush.
    I was from the city that took the Baptist
    in exchange for her first patron, who, for this,   144

swears by his art she will have endless sorrow;
    and were it not that on the Arno's bridge
    some vestige of his image still remains,   147

143–150. The identity of this Florentine Suicide remains unknown. The "first pa-
tron" of Florence was Mars, god of war; a fragment of his statue was to be found
on the Ponte Vecchio until 1333. The second patron of the city was John the Baptist
(143), whose image appeared on the florin, the principal monetary unit of the time.
Florence's change of patron indicates its transformation from stronghold of martial
excellence (under Mars) to one of servile money-making (under the Baptist).

those citizens who built anew the city
    on the ashes that Attila left behind
        would have accomplished such a task in vain;   150

I turned my home into my hanging place."

CANTO XIV

THEY COME to the edge of the Wood of the Suicides, where they see before them a stretch of burning sand upon which flames rain eternally and through which a stream of boiling blood is carried in a raised channel formed of rock. There, many groups of tortured souls are on the burning sand; Virgil explains that those lying supine on the ground are the Blasphemers, those crouching are the Usurers, and those wandering aimlessly, never stopping, are the Sodomites. Representative of the blasphemers is Capaneus, who died cursing his god. The Pilgrim questions his guide about the source of the river of boiling blood; Virgil's reply contains the most elaborate symbol in the Inferno, *that of the Old Man of Crete, whose tears are the source of all the rivers in Hell.*

The love we both shared for our native city
    moved me to gather up the scattered leaves
        and give them back to the voice that now had faded.   3

We reached the confines of the woods that separate
    the second from the third round. There I saw
        God's justice in its dreadful operation.   6

Now to picture clearly these unheard-of things:
    we arrived to face an open stretch of flatland
        whose soil refused the roots of any plant;   9

151. The Florentine's anonymity corroborates his symbolic value as a representative of his city. Like the suicides condemned to this round, the city of Florence was killing itself, in Dante's opinion, through its internecine struggles.

the grieving forest made a wreath around it,
   as the sad river of blood enclosed the woods.
   We stopped right here, right at the border line.   12

This wasteland was a dry expanse of sand,
   thick, burning sand, no different from the kind
   that Cato's feet packed down in other times.   15

O just revenge of God! how awesomely
   you should be feared by everyone who reads
   these truths that were revealed to my own eyes!   18

Many separate herds of naked souls I saw,
   all weeping desperately; it seemed each group
   had been assigned a different penalty: 21

some souls were stretched out flat upon their backs,
   others were crouching there all tightly hunched,
   some wandered, never stopping, round and round.   24

Far more there were of those who roamed the sand
   and fewer were the souls stretched out to suffer,
   but their tongues were looser, for the pain was greater.   27

And over all that sandland, a fall of slowly
   raining broad flakes of fire showered steadily
   (a mountain snowstorm on a windless day),   30

like those that Alexander saw descending
   on his troops while crossing India's torrid lands:
   flames falling, floating solid to the ground,   33

and he with all his men began to tread
   the sand so that the burning flames might be
   extinguished one by one before they joined.   36

---

15. Cato sided with Pompey in the Roman civil war. After Pompey was defeated at Pharsalia, and when it became apparent that he was about to be captured by Caesar, he killed himself (46 B.C.). The year before his death he led a march across the desert of Libya.

22–24. The shades in this third round of the Seventh Circle are divided into three groups: the Blasphemers lie supine on the ground, the Usurers are "crouching," and the Sodomites wander "never stopping." The sand they lie on perhaps suggests the sterility of their acts.

Here too a never-ending blaze descended,
    kindling the sand like tinder under flint-sparks,
    and in this way the torment there was doubled.   39

Without a moment's rest the rhythmic dance
    of wretched hands went on, this side, that side,
    brushing away the freshly fallen flames.   42

And I: "My master, you who overcome
    all opposition (except for those tough demons
    who came to meet us at the gate of Dis),   45

who is that mighty one that seems unbothered
    by burning, stretched sullen and disdainful there,
    looking as if the rainfall could not tame him?"   48

And that very one, who was quick to notice me
    inquiring of my guide about him, answered:
    "What I was once, alive, I still am, dead!   51

Let Jupiter wear out his smith, from whom
    he seized in anger that sharp thunderbolt
    he hurled, to strike me down, my final day;   54

let him wear out those others, one by one,
    who work the soot-black forge of Mongibello
    (as he shouts, 'Help me, good Vulcan, I need your help,'   57

the way he cried that time at Phlegra's battle),
    and with all his force let him hurl his bolts at me,
    no joy of satisfaction would I give him!"   60

My guide spoke back at him with cutting force,
    (I never heard his voice so strong before):
    "O Capaneus, since your blustering pride   63

44–45. The "tough demons" were the rebel angels of Canto IX who barred the travelers' entrance to the city of Dis.

51–60. The representative of the Blasphemers is Capaneus, who, as Virgil will explain, was one of the seven kings who assaulted Thebes. Statius describes how Capaneus, when scaling the walls of Thebes, blasphemed against Jove, who then struck him with a thunderbolt. Capaneus died with blasphemy on his lips, and now, even in Hell, he is able to defy Jove's thunderbolts.

will not be stilled, you are made to suffer more:
   no torment other than your rage itself
   could punish your gnawing pride more perfectly."   66

And then he turned a calmer face to me,
   saying, "That was a king, one of the seven
   besieging Thebes; he scorned, and would seem still   69

to go on scorning God and treat him lightly,
   but, as I said to him, he decks his chest
   with ornaments of lavish words that prick him.   72

Now follow me and also pay attention
   not to put your feet upon the burning sand,
   but to keep them well within the wooded line."   75

Without exchanging words we reached a place
   where a narrow stream came gushing from the woods
   (its reddish water still runs fear through me!);   78

like the one that issues from the Bulicame,
   whose waters are shared by prostitutes downstream,
   it wore its way across the desert sand.   81

This river's bed and banks were made of stone,
   so were the tops on both its sides; and then
   I understood this was our way across.   84

"Among the other marvels I have shown you,
   from the time we made our entrance through the gate
   whose threshold welcomes every evil soul,   87

your eyes have not discovered anything
   as remarkable as this stream you see here
   extinguishing the flames above its path."   90

These were my master's words, and I at once
   implored him to provide me with the food
   for which he had given me the appetite.   93

79–80. Near Viterbo there was a hot spring called the Bulicame, whose sulphurous waters transformed the area into a watering place. Among the inhabitants were many prostitutes who were required to live in a separate quarter. A special stream channeled the hot spring water through their section, since they were denied use of public baths.

"In the middle of the sea there lies a wasteland,"
    he immediately began, "that is known as Crete,
    under whose king the world knew innocence.   96

There is a mountain there that was called Ida;
    then happy in its verdure and its streams,
    now deserted like an old, discarded thing;   99

Rhea chose it once as a safe cradle
    for her son, and, to conceal his presence better,
    she had her servants scream loud when he cried.   102

In the mountain's core an ancient man stands tall;
    he has his shoulders turned toward Damietta
    and faces Rome as though it were his mirror.   105

His head is fashioned of the finest gold;
    pure silver are his arms and hands and chest;
    from there to where his legs spread, he is brass;   108

the rest of him is all of chosen iron,
    except his right foot which is terra cotta;
    he puts more weight on this foot than the other.   111

Every part of him, except the gold, is broken
    by a fissure dripping tears down to his feet,
    where they collect to erode the cavern's rock;   114

94–119. The island of Crete is given as the source of Acheron, Styx, and Phlegethon, the joined rivers of Hell whose course eventually leads to the "pool," Cocytus, at the bottom of Hell (116–119). According to mythology, Mount Ida on Crete was the place chosen by Rhea to protect her infant son, Jupiter, from his father, Saturn, who usually devoured his sons when they were born. Rhea, to keep him from finding Jupiter, "had her servants scream loud when he cried" (102) to drown out the infant's screams.

    Within Mount Ida Dante places the statue of the Old Man of Crete with his back to Damietta and gazing toward Rome (104–105). Damietta, an important Egyptian seaport, represents the East, the pagan world; Rome, of course, represents the modern, Christian world. The figure of the old man is drawn from the book of Daniel (2:32–35), but the symbolism is different and more nearly reflects a poetic symbol utilized by Ovid (*Metamorphoses* I). The head of gold represents the Golden Age of man (that is, in Christian terms, before the Fall). The arms and breast of silver, the trunk of brass, and the legs of iron represent the three declining ages of man. The clay foot (the one made of terra cotta) may symbolize the Church, weakened and corrupted by temporal concerns and political power struggles.

from stone to stone they drain down here, becoming
   rivers: the Acheron, Styx, and Phlegethon,
   then overflow down through this tight canal   117

until they fall to where all falling ends:
   they form Cocytus. What that pool is like
   I need not tell you. You will see, yourself."   120

And I to him: "If this small stream beside us
   has its source, as you have told me, in our world,
   why have we seen it only on this ledge?"   123

And he to me: "You know this place is round,
   and though your journey has been long, circling
   toward the bottom, turning only to the left,   126

you still have not completed a full circle;
   so you should never look surprised, as now,
   if you see something you have not seen before."   129

And I again: "Where, Master, shall we find
   Lethe and Phlegethon? You omit the first
   and say the other forms from the rain of tears."   132

"I am very happy when you question me,"
   he said, "but that the blood-red water boiled
   should answer certainly one of your questions.   135

And Lethe you shall see, but beyond this valley,
   at a place where souls collect to wash themselves
   when penitence has freed them of their guilt.   138

Now it is time to leave this edge of woods,"
   he added. "Be sure you follow close behind me:
   the margins are our road, they do not burn,   141

and all the flames above them are extinguished."

CANTO XV

THEY MOVE OUT across the plain of burning sand, walking along the ditchlike edge of the conduit through which the Phlegethon flows, and after they have come some distance from the wood they see a group of souls running toward them. One, Brunetto Latini, a famous Florentine intellectual and Dante's former teacher, recognizes the Pilgrim and leaves his band to walk and talk with him. Brunetto learns the reason for the Pilgrim's journey and offers him a prophecy of the troubles lying in wait for him—an echo of Ciacco's words in Canto VI. Brunetto names some of the others being punished with him (Priscian, Francesco d'Accorso, Andrea de' Mozzi); but soon, in the distance, he sees a cloud of smoke approaching, which presages a new group, and because he must not associate with them, like a foot-racer Brunetto speeds away to catch up with his own band.

Now one of those stone margins bears us on
   and the river's vapors hover like a shade,
   sheltering the banks and the water from the flames.   3

As the Flemings, living with the constant threat
   of flood tides rushing in between Wissant
   and Bruges, build their dikes to force the sea back;   6

as the Paduans build theirs on the shores of Brenta
   to protect their town and homes before warm weather
   turns Chiarentana's snow to rushing water—   9

so were these walls we walked upon constructed,
   though the engineer, whoever he may have been,
   did not make them as high or thick as those.   12

We had left the wood behind (so far behind,
   by now, that if I had stopped to turn around,
   I am sure it could no longer have been seen)   15

when we saw a troop of souls come hurrying
   toward us beside the bank, and each of them
   looked us up and down, as some men look   18

11. The engineer is God.

at other men, at night, when the moon is new.
    They strained their eyebrows, squinting hard at us,
    as an old tailor might at his needle's eye.   21

Eyed in such a way by this strange crew,
    I was recognized by one of them, who grabbed
    my garment's hem and shouted: "How marvelous!"   24

And I, when he reached out his arm toward me,
    straining my eyes, saw through his face's crust,
    through his burned features that could not prevent   27

my memory from bringing back his name;
    and bending my face down to meet with his,
    I said: "Is this really you, here, Ser Brunetto?"   30

And he: "O my son, may it not displease you
    if Brunetto Latini lets his troop file on
    while he walks at your side for a little while."   33

And I: "With all my heart I beg you to,
    and if you wish me to sit here with you,
    I will, if my companion does not mind."   36

"My son," he said, "a member of this herd
    who stops one moment lies one hundred years
    unable to brush off the wounding flames,   39

so, move on; I shall follow at your hem
    and then rejoin my family that moves
    along, lamenting their eternal pain."   42

I did not dare step off the margin-path
    to walk at his own level but, with head
    bent low in reverence, I moved along.   45

He began: "What fortune or what destiny
    leads you down here before your final hour?
    And who is this one showing you the way?"   48

"Up there above in the bright living life
    before I reached the end of all my years,
    I lost myself in a valley," I replied;   51

"just yesterday at dawn I turned from it.
    This spirit here appeared as I turned back,
    and by this road he guides me home again."   54

He said to me: "Follow your constellation
    and you cannot fail to reach your port of glory,
    not if I saw clearly in the happy life;   57

and if I had not died just when I did,
    I would have cheered you on in all your work,
    seeing how favorable Heaven was to you.   60

But that ungrateful and malignant race
    which descended from the Fiesole of old,
    and still have rock and mountain in their blood,   63

will become, for your good deeds, your enemy—
    and right they are: among the bitter berries
    there's no fit place for the sweet fig to bloom.   66

They have always had the fame of being blind,
    an envious race, proud and avaricious;
    you must not let their ways contaminate you.   69

Your destiny reserves such honors for you:
    both parties shall be hungry to devour you,
    but the grass will not be growing where the goat is.   72

Let the wild beasts of Fiesole make fodder
    of each other, and let them leave the plant untouched
    (so rare it is that one grows in their dung-heap)   75

in which there lives again the holy seed
    of those remaining Romans who survived there
    when this new nest of malice was constructed."   78

67. During a Roman power struggle, Cataline fled Rome and found sanctuary for himself and his troops in the originally Etruscan town of Fiesole. After Caesar's successful siege of that city, the survivors of both camps founded Florence, where those of the Roman camp were the elite.

The prophesy with its condemnation of the current state of Florence (and Italy) and its implied hope of a renascent empire continues the political theme begun with the speech of the anonymous Suicide in Canto XIII and continued in the symbol of the Old Man of Crete in Canto XIV.

"Oh, if all I wished for had been granted,"
   I answered him, "you certainly would not,
   not yet, be banished from our life on earth;   81

my mind is etched (and now my heart is pierced)
   with your kind image, loving and paternal,
   when, living in the world, hour after hour   84

you taught me how man makes himself eternal.
   And while I live my tongue shall always speak
   of my debt to you, and of my gratitude.   87

I will write down what you tell me of my future
   and save it, with another text, to show
   a lady who can interpret, if I can reach her.   90

This much, at least, let me make clear to you:
   if my conscience continues not to blame me,
   I am ready for whatever Fortune wants.   93

This prophecy is not new to my ears,
   and so let Fortune turn her wheel, spinning it
   as she pleases, and the peasant turn his spade."   96

My master, hearing this, looked to the right,
   then, turning round and facing me, he said:
   "He listens well who notes well what he hears."   99

But I did not answer him; I went on talking,
   walking with Ser Brunetto, asking him
   who of his company were most distinguished.   102

And he: "It might be good to know who some are,
   about the rest I feel I should be silent,
   for the time would be too short, there are so many.   105

In brief, let me tell you, all here were clerics
   and respected men of letters of great fame,
   all befouled in the world by one same sin: 108

89–90. Again (as in Canto X, 130–132), Beatrice is referred to as the one who will reveal to the Pilgrim his future course. However, in the *Paradiso* this role is given to Dante's ancestor, Cacciaguida.

95–96. It is as right for Fortune to spin her wheel as it is for the peasant to turn his spade; and the Pilgrim will be as indifferent to the first as to the second.

Priscian is traveling with that wretched crowd
    and Franceso d'Accorso too; and also there,
      if you could have stomached such repugnancy,   111

you might have seen the one the Servant of Servants
    transferred to the Bacchiglione from the Arno
      where his sinfully erected nerves were buried.   114

I would say more, but my walk and conversation
    with you cannot go on, for over there
      I see a new smoke rising from the sand: 117

people approach with whom I must not mingle.
    Remember my *Trésor*, where I live on,
      this is the only thing I ask of you."   120

Then he turned back, and he seemed like one of those
    who run Verona's race across its fields
      to win the green cloth prize, and he was like   123

the winner of the group, not the last one in.

CANTO XVI

CONTINUING *through the third round of the Circle of Violence, the Pilgrim hears the distant roar of a waterfall, which grows louder as he and his guide proceed. Suddenly three shades, having recognized him as*

112–114. Andrea de Mozzi was Bishop of Florence from 1287 to 1295, when, by order of Pope Boniface VIII (the "Servant of Servants," i.e., the servant of the servants of God), he was transferred to Vicenza (on the Bacchiglione River), where he died that same year or the next. The early commentators make reference to his naïve and inept preaching and to his general stupidity. Dante, by mentioning his "sinfully erected nerves" calls attention to his major weakness: unnatural lust or sodomy.

119–120. The "*Trésor*" is the *Livres dou Trésor*, Brunetto's most significant composition, an encyclopedic work in French prose written during his exile in France.

123–124. The first prize for the footrace held annually on the first Sunday of Lent in Verona during the thirteenth century was a green cloth.

a Florentine, break from their company and converse with him, all the while circling like a turning wheel. Their spokesman, Jacopo Rusticucci, identifies himself and his companions (Guido Guerra and Tegghiaio Aldobrandini) as well-known and honored citizens of Florence, and begs for news of their native city. The three ask to be remembered in the world and then rush off. By this time the sound of the waterfall is so deafening that it almost drowns out speech, and when the poets reach the edge of the precipice, Virgil takes a cord which had been bound around his pupil's waist and tosses it into the abyss. It is a signal, and in response a monstrous form looms up from below, swimming through the air. On this note of suspense, the canto ends.

Already we were where I could hear the rumbling
   of the water plunging down to the next circle,
   something like the sound of beehives humming,   3

when three shades with one impulse broke away,
   running, from a group of spirits passing us
   beneath the rain of bitter suffering.   6

They were coming toward us shouting with one voice:
   "O you there, stop! From the clothes you wear, you seem
   to be a man from our perverted city."   9

Ah, the wounds I saw covering their limbs,
   some old, some freshly branded by the flames!
   Even now, when I think back to them, I grieve.   12

Their shouts caught the attention of my guide,
   and then he turned to face me, saying, "Wait,
   for these are shades that merit your respect.   15

And were it not the nature of this place
   to rain with piercing flames, I would suggest
   you run toward *them*, for it would be more fitting."   18

When we stopped, they resumed their normal pace
   and when they reached us, then they started circling;
   the three together formed a turning wheel,   21

9. The "perverted city" is Florence.

just like professional wrestlers stripped and oiled,
    eyeing one another for the first, best grip
    before the actual blows and thrusts begin.   24

And circling in this way each kept his face
    pointed up at me, so that their necks and feet
    moved constantly in opposite directions.   27

"And if the misery along these sterile sands,"
    one of them said, "and our charred and peeling flesh
    make us, and what we ask, repulsive to you,   30

let our great worldly fame persuade your heart
    to tell us who you are, how you can walk
    safely with living feet through Hell itself.   33

This one in front, whose footsteps I am treading,
    even though he runs his round naked and skinned,
    was of noble station, more than you may think: 36

he was the grandson of the good Gualdrada;
    his name was Guido Guerra, and in his life
    he accomplished much with counsel and with sword.   39

This other one, who pounds the sand behind me,
    is Tegghiaio Aldobrandi, whose wise voice
    the world would have done well to listen to.   42

And I, who share this post of pain with them,
    was Jacopo Rusticucci, and for sure
    my reluctant wife first drove me to my sin."   45

37–39. Gualdrada is the daughter of Bellincione Berti of Florence. Her grandson was the Guido Guerra (1220–1272), mentioned here. This Guido was a Guelph leader in several battles, hence his nickname (*guerra*, "war"). His wisdom ("counsel," 39) is exemplified by his advice to the Florentine Guelphs not to undertake the campaign against Siena in 1260; they ignored his words, and that battle destroyed the Guelph party in Florence.

41–42. Tegghiaio Aldobrandi, like Guido Guerra, was a leader of the Guelph party in Florence. He died before 1266.

44–45. Little is known of Jacopo Rusticucci, the spokesman for the three Sodomites. He is occasionally mentioned in Florentine records between 1235 and 1266 and was probably a rich merchant.

If I could have been sheltered from the fire,
    I would have thrown myself below with them,
    and I think my guide would have allowed me to;   48

but, as I knew I would be burned and seared,
    my fear won over my first good intention
    that made me want to put my arms around them.   51

And then I spoke: "Repulsion, no, but grief
    for your condition spread throughout my heart
    (and years will pass before it fades away),   54

as soon as my lord here began to speak
    in terms that led me to believe a group
    of such men as yourselves might be approaching.   57

I am from your city, and your honored names
    and your accomplishments I have always heard
    rehearsed, and have rehearsed, myself, with fondness.   60

I leave the bitter gall, and journey toward
    those sweet fruits promised me by my true guide,
    but first I must go down to the very center."   63

"So may your soul remain to guide your body
    for years to come," that same one spoke again,
    "and your fame's light shine after you are gone,   66

tell us if courtesy and valor dwell
    within our city as they used to do,
    or have they both been banished from the place?   69

Guglielmo Borsiere, who joined our painful ranks
    of late, and travels there with our companions,
    has given us reports that make us grieve."   72

"A new breed of people with their sudden wealth
    have stimulated pride and unrestraint
    in you, O Florence, made to weep so soon."   75

70–72. Little is known of Guglielmo Borsiere except that he must have died about 1300, as is evident from lines 70–71. Boccaccio says that he was a knight of the court, a matchmaker, and a peacemaker.

These words I shouted with my head strained high,
  and the three below took this to be my answer
  and looked, as if on truth, at one another.   78

"If you always answer questions with such ease,"
  they all spoke up at once, "O happy you,
  to have this gift of ready, open speech;   81

therefore, if you survive these unlit regions
  and return to gaze upon the lovely stars,
  when it pleases you to say 'I was down there,'   84

do not fail to speak of us to living men."
  They broke their man-made wheel and ran away,
  their nimble legs were more like wings in flight.   87

"Amen" could not have been pronounced as quick
  as they were off, and vanished from our sight;
  and then my teacher thought it time to leave.   90

I followed him, and we had not gone far
  before the sound of water was so close
  that if we spoke we hardly heard each other.   93

As that river on the Apennines' left slope,
  first springing from its source at Monte Veso,
  then flowing eastward holding its own course   96

(called Acquacheta at its start above
  before descending to its lower bed
  where, at Forlì, it has another name),   99

reverberates there near San Benedetto
  dell'Alpe (plunging in a single bound),
  where at least a thousand vassals could be housed,   102

so down a single rocky precipice
  we found the tainted waters falling, roaring
  sound loud enough to deafen us in seconds.   105

---

102. According to Boccaccio, one of the conti Guidi, who ruled over this region, had planned to construct, near the waterfall, lodgings for a large number of his vassals; he died, however, before his plan could be put into effect.

I wore a cord that fastened round my waist,
   with which I once had thought I might be able
   to catch the leopard with the gaudy skin.   108

As soon as I removed it from my body
   just as my guide commanded me to do,
   I gave it to him looped into a coil.   111

Then taking it and turning to the right,
   he flung it quite a distance past the bank
   and down into the deepness of the pit.   114

"Now surely something strange is going to happen,"
   I thought to myself, "to answer the strange signal
   whose course my master follows with his eyes."   117

How cautious a man must be in company
   with one who can not only see his actions
   but read his mind and understand his thoughts!   120

He spoke: "Soon will rise up what I expect;
   and what you are trying to imagine now
   soon must reveal itself before your eyes."   123

It is always better to hold one's tongue than speak
   a truth that seems a bold-faced lie when uttered,
   since to tell this truth could be embarrassing;   126

but I shall not keep quiet; and by the verses
   of my *Comedy*—so may they be received
   with lasting favor, Reader—I swear to you   129

I saw a figure coming, it was swimming
   through the thick and murky air, up to the top
   (a thing to startle even stalwart hearts),   132

like one returning who has swum below
   to free the anchor that has caught its hooks
   on a reef or something else the sea conceals,   135

spreading out his arms, and doubling up his legs.

106–108. This may be evidence that Dante the Poet became a Franciscan friar, the
cord being a sign of that order.

CANTO XVII

THE BEAST *that had been seen approaching at the end of the last canto is the horrible monster Geryon; his face is appealing like that of an honest man, but his body ends in a scorpionlike stinger. He perches on the edge of the abyss and Virgil advises his ward, who has noticed new groups of sinners squatting on the fiery sand, to learn who they are, while he makes arrangements with Geryon for the descent. The sinners are the Usurers, unrecognizable except by the crests on the moneybags hanging about their necks, which identify them as members of the Gian-figliazzi, Ubriachi, and Scrovegni families. The Pilgrim listens to one of them briefly but soon returns to find his master sitting on Geryon's back. After he conquers his fear and mounts, too, the monster begins the slow, spiraling descent into the Eighth Circle.*

"And now, behold the beast with pointed tail
    that passes mountains, annulling walls and weapons,
    behold the one that makes the whole world stink!"   3

These were the words I heard my master say
    as he signaled for the beast to come ashore,
    up close to where the rocky levee ends.   6

And that repulsive spectacle of fraud
    floated close, maneuvering head and chest
    on to the shore, but his tail he let hang free.   9

His face was the face of any honest man,
    it shone with such a look of benediction;
    and all the rest of him was serpentine;   12

his two clawed paws were hairy to the armpits,
    his back and all his belly and both flanks
    were painted arabesques and curlicues: 15

1. In classical mythology Geryon was a three-bodied giant who ruled Spain and was slain by Hercules in the course of his Twelve Labors. Here in the *Inferno* he is the personification of Fraud.

the Turks and Tartars never made a fabric
    with richer colors intricately woven,
    nor were such complex webs spun by Arachne.   18

As sometimes fishing boats are seen ashore,
    part fixed in sand and part still in the water;
    and as the beaver, living in the land   21

of drunken Germans, squats to catch his prey,
    just so that beast, the worst of beasts, hung waiting
    on the bank that bounds the stretch of sand in stone.   24

In the void beyond he exercised his tail,
    twitching and twisting-up the venomed fork
    that armed its tip just like a scorpion's stinger.   27

My leader said: "Now we must turn aside
    a little from our path, in the direction
    of that malignant beast that lies in wait."   30

Then we stepped off our path down to the right
    and moved ten paces straight across the brink
    to keep the sand and flames at a safe distance.   33

And when we stood by Geryon's side, I noticed,
    a little farther on, some people crouched
    in the sand quite close to the edge of emptiness.   36

Just then my master spoke: "So you may have
    a knowledge of this round that is complete,"
    he said, "go and see their torment for yourself.   39

---

18. Arachne was a legendary Lydian maiden who was so skilled in the art of weaving that she challenged the goddess Minerva to a contest. Minerva, furious because her opponent's cloth was perfect, tore it to shreds; Arachne hanged herself, but Minerva loosened the rope, turning it into a web and Arachne into a spider.

21–22. According to medieval bestiaries, the beaver, squatting on the ground at the edge of the water, catches fish with its tail hanging in the water. Geryon assumes a similar pose.

35–36. The Usurers, described in Canto XI as those who scorn "Nature in herself and in her pupil / Art" (110–111), are the last group in the third round of the Seventh Circle.

But let your conversation there be brief;
   while you are gone I shall speak to this one
   and ask him for the loan of his strong back."   42

So I continued walking, all alone,
   along the seventh circle's outer edge
   to where the group of sufferers were sitting.   45

The pain was bursting from their eyes; their hands
   went scurrying up and down to give protection
   here from the flames, there from the burning sands.   48

They were, in fact, like a dog in summertime
   busy, now with his paw, now with his snout,
   tormented by the fleas and flies that bite him.   51

I carefully examined several faces
   among this group caught in the raining flames
   and did not know a soul, but I observed   54

that around each sinner's neck a pouch was hung,
   each of a different color, with a coat of arms,
   and fixed on these they seemed to feast their eyes.   57

And while I looked about among the crowd,
   I saw something in blue on a yellow purse
   that had the face and bearing of a lion;   60

and while my eyes continued their inspection
   I saw another purse as red as blood
   exhibiting a goose more white than butter.   63

And one who had a blue sow, pregnant-looking,
   stamped on the whiteness of his moneybag
   asked me: "What are you doing in this pit?   66

55–56. The identity (or rather the family connection) of the usurers, who "feast their
eyes" (57) on the purses dangling from their necks, is revealed to the Pilgrim by the
different coats of arms visible on the pouches. Apparently the usurers are unrecog-
nizable through facial characteristics because their total concern with their material
goods has caused them to lose their individuality. The yellow purse with the blue lion
(59–60) indicates the Gianfigliazzi family of Florence; the red purse with the "goose
more white than butter" (62–63), the Ubriachi family, also of Florence; the one with
the "blue sow, pregnant-looking" (64–65), the Scrovegni family of Padua.

Get out of here! And since you're still alive,
    I'll tell you that my neighbor Vitaliano
    will come to take his seat on my left side.   69

Among these Florentines I sit, one Paduan:
    time after time they fill my ears with blasts
    of shouting: 'Send us down the sovereign knight   72

who will come bearing three goats on his pouch.' "
    As final comment he stuck out his tongue—
    as far out as an ox licking its nose.   75

And I, afraid my staying there much longer
    might anger the one who warned me to be brief,
    turned my back on these frustrated sinners.   78

I found my guide already sitting high
    upon the back of that fierce animal;
    he said: "And now, take courage and be strong.   81

From now on we descend by stairs like these.
    Get on up front. I want to ride behind,
    to be between you and the dangerous tail."   84

A man who feels the shivers of a fever
    coming on, his nails already dead of color,
    will tremble at the mere sight of cool shade;   87

I was that man when I had heard his words.
    But then I felt those stabs of shame that make
    a servant brave before his valorous master.   90

As I squirmed around on those enormous shoulders,
    I wanted to cry out, "Hold on to me,"
    but I had no voice to second my desire.   93

68–69. Referred to as "my neighbor" by one of the Scrovegni family, the Vitaliano who will join the company of usurers is undoubtedly from Padua, but beyond this nothing certain is known.

72–73. The "sovereign knight" is generally considered to be Giovanni Buiamonte, one of the Florentine Becchi family. He took part in public affairs and was named an honorific knight in 1298. His business, moneylending, made his family one of the wealthiest in Florence; however, after going bankrupt he died in abject poverty in 1310.

Then he who once before had helped me out
    when I was threatened put his arms around me
    as soon as I was settled, and held me tight;   96

and then he cried: "Now Geryon, start moving,
    descend with gentle motion, circling wide:
    remember you are carrying living weight."   99

Just as a boat slips back away from shore,
    back slowly, more and more, he left that pier;
    and when he felt himself all clear in space,   102

to where his breast had been he swung his tail
    and stretched it undulating like an eel,
    as with his paws he gathered in the air.   105

I doubt if Phaëthon feared more—that time
    he dropped the sun-reins of his father's chariot
    and burned the streak of sky we see today—   108

or if poor Icarus did—feeling his sides
    unfeathering as the wax began to melt,
    his father shouting: "Wrong, your course is wrong"—   111

than I had when I felt myself in air
    and saw on every side nothing but air;
    only the beast I sat upon was there.   114

He moves along slowly, and swimming slowly,
    descends a spiral path—but I know this
    only from a breeze ahead and one below;   117

I hear now on my right the whirlpool roar
    with hideous sound beneath us on the ground;
    at this I stretch my neck to look below,   120

but leaning out soon made me more afraid,
    for I heard moaning there and saw the flames;
    trembling, I cowered back, tightening my legs,   123

109–111. The stories of Phaëthon and Icarus were often used in the Middle Ages as examples of pride, thus giving more support to the theory that Pride and Envy underlie the sins punished in Lower Hell.

and I saw then what I had not before:
   the spiral path of our descent to torment
   closing in on us, it seemed, from every side.   126

As the falcon on the wing for many hours,
   having found no prey, and having seen no signal
   (so that his falconer sighs: "Oh, he falls already"),   129

descends, worn out, circling a hundred times
   (instead of swooping down), settling at some distance
   from his master, perched in anger and disdain,   132

so Geryon brought us down to the bottom
   at the foot of the jagged cliff, almost against it,
   and once he got our bodies off his back,   135

he shot off like a shaft shot from a bowstring.

CANTO XVIII

THE PILGRIM *describes the view he had of the Eighth Circle of Hell while descending through the air on Geryon's back. It consists of ten stone ravines called* Malebolge *(Evil Pockets), and across each* bolgia *is an arching bridge. When the poets find themselves on the edge of the first ravine they see two lines of naked sinners, walking in opposite directions. In one are the Pimps or Panderers, and among them the Pilgrim recognizes Venedico Caccianemico; in the other are the Seducers, among whom Virgil points out Jason. As the two move toward the next* bolgia, *they are assailed by a terrible stench, for here the Flatterers are immersed in excrement. Among them are Alessio Interminei and Thaïs the whore.*

There is a place in Hell called Malebolge,
   cut out of stone the color of iron ore,
   just like the circling cliff that walls it in.   3

Right at the center of this evil plain
    there yawns a very wide, deep well, whose structure
    I will talk of when the place itself is reached.   6

That belt of land remaining, then, runs round
    between the well and cliff, and all this space
    is divided into ten descending valleys,   9

just like a ground-plan for successive moats
    that in concentric circles bind their center
    and serve to protect the ramparts of the castle.   12

This was the surface image they presented;
    and as bridges from a castle's portal stretch
    from moat to moat to reach the farthest bank,   15

so, from the great cliff's base, jut spokes of rock,
    crossing from bank to bank, intersecting ditches
    until the pit's hub cuts them off from meeting.   18

This is the place in which we found ourselves,
    once shaken from the back of Geryon.
    The poet turned to the left, I walked behind him.   21

There, on our right, I saw new suffering souls,
    new means of torture, and new torturers,
    crammed into the depths of the first ditch.   24

Two files of naked souls walked on the bottom,
    the ones on our side faced us as they passed,
    the others moved as we did but more quickly.   27

The Romans, too, in the year of the Jubilee
    took measures to accommodate the throngs
    that had to come and go across their bridge: 30

26–27. The first *bolgia* accommodates two classes of sinners, each filing by rapidly, but in separate directions. The Pimps are those walking toward the Pilgrim and his guide; the Seducers go in the same direction with them.

28–33. Dante compares the movement of the sinners in the first *bolgia* to that of the many pilgrims who, having come to Rome for the Jubilee in 1300, were herded across the bridge, half going toward the Castel Sant'Angelo and St. Peter's and the other half going toward Monte Giordano ("the mount," 33), a small knoll on the opposite side of the Tiber River.

they fixed it so on one side all were looking
   at the castle, and were walking to St. Peter's;
   on the other, they were moving toward the mount.   33

On both sides, up along the deadly rock,
   I saw horned devils with enormous whips
   lashing the backs of shades with cruel delight.   36

Ah, how they made them skip and lift their heels
   at the very first crack of the whip! Not one of them
   dared pause to take a second or a third!   39

As I walked on my eyes met with the glance
   of one down there; I murmured to myself:
   "I know this face from somewhere, I am sure."   42

And so I stopped to study him more closely;
   my leader also stopped, and was so kind
   as to allow me to retrace my steps;   45

and that whipped soul thought he would hide from me
   by lowering his face—which did no good.
   I said, "O you, there, with your head bent low,   48

if the features of your shade do not deceive me,
   you are Venedico Caccianemico, I'm sure.
   How did you get yourself in such a pickle?"   51

"I'm not so keen on answering," he said,
   "but I feel I must; your plain talk is compelling,
   it makes me think of old times in the world.   54

I was the one who coaxed Ghisolabella
   to serve the lusty wishes of the Marquis,
   no matter how the sordid tale is told;   57

50–57. Venedico Caccianemico, born ca. 1228, was head of the Guelphs in Bologna
from 1250 to 1297; he was at various times *podestà* ("mayor") of Pistoia, Modena,
Imola, and Milan. He was accused, among other things, of murdering his cousin, but
he is placed in this *bolgia* because, according to popular report, he acted as a pro-
curer, turning his own sister, Ghisolabella, over to the Marquis of Este (either Obizzo
II or his son, Azzo VIII) to curry favor.

I'm not the only Bolognese who weeps here—
    hardly! This place is packed with us; in fact,
    there are more of us here than there are living tongues,   60

between Savena and Reno, saying 'Sipa';
    I call on your own memory as witness:
    remember we have avaricious hearts."   63

Just at that point a devil let him have
    the feel of his tailed whip and cried: "Move on,
    you pimp, you can't cash in on women here!"   66

I turned and hurried to rejoin my guide;
    we walked a few more steps and then we reached
    the rocky bridge that juts out from the bank.   69

We had no difficulty climbing up,
    and turning right, along the jagged ridge,
    we left those shades to their eternal circlings.   72

When we were where the ditch yawned wide below
    the ridge, to make a passage for the scourged,
    my guide said: "Stop and stand where you can see   75

these other misbegotten souls, whose faces
    you could not see before, for they were moving
    in the same direction we were, over there."   78

So from the ancient bridge we viewed the train
    that hurried toward us along the other tract—
    kept moving, like the first, by stinging whips.   81

And the good master, without my asking him,
    said, "Look at that imposing one approaching,
    who does not shed a single tear of pain: 84

what majesty he still maintains down there!
    He is Jason, who by courage and sharp wits,
    fleeced the Colchians of their golden ram.   87

86–96. Jason, leader of the Argonauts, had been deprived, when a child, of the throne
of Iolcus by his half-brother Pelias. When Jason grew up, Pelias promised him the
kingdom if he could secure the golden fleece of King Aeëtes of Colchis. Jason agreed
to make the attempt, and on the way to Colchis stopped at Lemnos, where he seduced
and abandoned Hypsipyle (92), the daughter of the king of Lemnos. At Colchis, King
Aeëtes agreed to give Jason the fleece if he would yoke two fire-breathing oxen to a

He later journeyed through the isle of Lemnos,
    whose bold and heartless females, earlier,
    had slaughtered every male upon the island;   90

there with his words of love, and loving looks,
    he succeeded in deceiving young Hypsipyle,
    who had in turn deceived the other women.   93

He left her there, with child, and all alone:
    such sin condemns him to such punishment,
    and Medea, too, gets her revenge on him.   96

With him go all deceivers of this type,
    and let this be enough to know concerning
    the first valley and the souls locked in its jaws."   99

We were already where the narrow ridge
    begins to cross the second bank, to make it
    an abutment for another ditch's arch.   102

Now we could hear the shades in the next pouch
    whimpering, making snorting grunting sounds
    and sounds of blows, slapping with open palms.   105

From a steaming stench below, the banks were coated
    with a slimy mold that stuck to them like glue,
    disgusting to behold and worse to smell.   108

The bottom was so hollowed out of sight,
    we saw it only when we climbed the arch
    and looked down from the bridge's highest point: 111

---

plow and sow the teeth of the dragon that guarded the fleece. Medea (96), who was a sorceress and the daughter of the king, fell in love with Jason and with magic helped him fulfill her father's conditions and obtain the fleece. The two returned to Greece where Jason married her, but later he fell in love with Creusa, daughter of Creon, king of Corinth, and deserted Medea to marry her. Medea, mad with rage, killed Creusa by sending her a poisoned coat as a wedding gift, and then murdered her own children; Jason himself died of grief.

    Hypsipyle "deceived the other women" (93) of Lemnos by swearing that she had slain her father Thoas, the king, when the Lemnian women massacred all the males on that island. Instead she hid him, saving his life.

104–105. The sinners found in the excrement of the second *bolgia* are the Flatterers. Note the teeming nature of the language, different from that of the first *bolgia*, a change indicative of the sin of flattery and its punishment.

there we were, and from where I stood I saw
   souls in the ditch plunged into excrement
   that might well have been flushed from our latrines;   114

my eyes were searching hard along the bottom,
   and I saw somebody's head so smirched with shit,
   you could not tell if he were priest or layman.   117

He shouted up: "Why do you feast your eyes
   on me more than these other dirty beasts?"
   And I replied: "Because, remembering well,   120

I've seen you with your hair dry once or twice.
   You are Alessio Interminei from Lucca;
   that's why I stare at you more than the rest."   123

He beat his slimy forehead as he answered:
   "I am stuck down here by all those flatteries
   that rolled unceasing off my tongue up there."   126

He finished speaking, and my guide began:
   "Lean out a little more, look hard down there
   so you can get a good look at the face   129

of that repulsive and disheveled tramp
   scratching herself with shitty fingernails,
   spreading her legs while squatting up and down: 132

it is Thaïs the whore, who gave this answer
   to her lover when he asked: 'Am I very worthy
   of your thanks?': 'Very? Nay, incredibly so!'   135

I think our eyes have had their fill of this."

---

122. The Interminei family was prominent in the White party at Lucca. But of Alessio almost nothing is known save that his name is recorded in several documents of the second half of the thirteenth century.

133. This Thaïs is not the historical person of the same name (the most famous courtesan of all time) but a character in a play by the Roman dramatist Terence (186–159 B.C.) titled *Eunuchus*.

CANTO XIX

FROM THE BRIDGE *above the Third* Bolgia *can be seen a rocky landscape below filled with holes, from each of which protrude a sinner's legs and feet; flames dance across their soles. When the Pilgrim expresses curiosity about a particular pair of twitching legs, Virgil carries him down into the* bolgia *so that the Pilgrim himself may question the sinner. The legs belong to Pope Nicholas III, who astounds the Pilgrim by mistaking him for Boniface VIII, the next pope, who, as soon as he dies, will fall to the same hole, thereby pushing Nicholas farther down. He predicts that soon after Boniface, Pope Clement V will come, stuffing both himself and Boniface still deeper. To Nicholas's rather rhetoric-filled speech the Pilgrim responds with equally high language, inveighing against the Simonists, the evil churchmen who are punished here. Virgil is much pleased with his pupil and, lifting him in an affectionate embrace, he carries him to the top of the arch above the next* bolgia.*

O Simon Magus! O scum that followed him!
   Those things of God that rightly should be wed
   to holiness, you, rapacious creatures,   3

for the price of gold and silver, prostitute.
   Now, in your honor, I must sound my trumpet
   for here in the third pouch is where you dwell.   6

We had already climbed to see this tomb,
   and were standing high above it on the bridge,
   exactly at the mid-point of the ditch.   9

O Highest Wisdom, how you demonstrate
   your art in Heaven, on earth, and here in Hell!
   How justly does your power make awards!   12

1–6. As related in Acts (8:9–24), Simon the magician, having observed the descent of the Holy Spirit upon the apostles John and Peter, desired to purchase this power for himself, whereupon Peter harshly admonished him for even thinking that the gift of God might be bought. Derived from this sorcerer's name, the word "simony" (74) refers to those offenses involving the sale or fraudulent possession of ecclesiastical offices.

I saw along the sides and on the bottom
   the livid-colored rock all full of holes;
     all were the same in size, and each was round.   15

To me they seemed no wider and no deeper
   than those inside my lovely San Giovanni,
     in which the priest would stand or baptize from;   18

and one of these, not many years ago,
   I smashed for someone who was drowning in it:
     let this be mankind's picture of the truth!   21

From the mouth of every hole were sticking out
   a single sinner's feet, and then the legs
     up to the calf—the rest was stuffed inside.   24

The soles of every sinner's feet were flaming;
   their naked legs were twitching frenziedly—
     they would have broken any chain or rope.   27

Just as a flame will only move along
   an object's oily outer peel, so here
     the fire slid from heel to toe and back.   30

"Who is that one, Master, that angry wretch,
   who is writhing more than any of his comrades,"
     I asked, "the one licked by a redder flame?"   33

And he to me, "If you want to be carried down
   along that lower bank to where he is,
     you can ask him who he is and why he's here."   36

And I, "My pleasure is what pleases you:
   you are my lord, you know that from your will
     I would not swerve. You even know my thoughts."   39

When we reached the fourth bank, we began to turn
   and, keeping to the left, made our way down
     to the bottom of the holed and narrow ditch.   42

25. Just as the Simonists' perversion of the Church is symbolized by their "perverted" immersion in holes resembling baptismal fonts, so their "baptism" is perverted: instead of the head being moistened with water, the feet are "baptized" with oil and fire.

The good guide did not drop me from his side
  until he brought me to the broken rock
  of that one who was fretting with his shanks.   45

"Whatever you are, holding your upside down,
  O wretched soul, stuck like a stake in ground,
  make a sound or something," I said, "if you can."   48

I stood there like a priest who is confessing
  some vile assassin who, fixed in his ditch,
  has called him back again to put off dying.   51

He cried: "Is that *you*, here, already, upright?
  Is that you here already upright, Boniface?
  By many years the book has lied to me!   54

Are you fed up so soon with all that wealth
  for which you did not fear to take by guile
  the Lovely Lady, then tear her asunder?"   57

I stood there like a person just made fun of,
  dumbfounded by a question for an answer,
  not knowing how to answer the reply.   60

Then Virgil said: "Quick, hurry up and tell him:
  'I'm not the one, I'm not the one you think!' "
  And I answered just the way he told me to.   63

The spirit heard, and twisted both his feet,
  then, sighing with a grieving, tearful voice,
  he said: "Well then, what do you want of me?   66

53. From the foreknowledge granted to the infernal shades, the speaker shows that Pope Boniface VIII, upon his death in 1303, will take his place in that very receptacle wherein he himself is now being tormented. The Pilgrim's voice, so close at hand, has caused the sinner to believe that his successor has arrived unexpectedly before his time (three years, in fact) and, consequently, that the Divine Plan of Events, the Book of Fate (54), has lied to him.

Having obtained the abdication of Pope Celestine V, Boniface gained the support of Charles II of Nantes and thus was assured of his election to the papacy (1294). In addition to misusing the Church's influence in his dealings with Charles, Boniface VIII freely distributed ecclesiastical offices among his family and confidants. As early as 1300 he was plotting the destruction of the Whites, the Florentine political faction to which Dante belonged.

57. The "Lovely Lady" is the Church.

If it concerns you so to learn my name
   that for this reason you came down the bank,
   know that I once was dressed in the great mantle.   69

But actually I was the she-bear's son,
   so greedy to advance my cubs, that wealth
   I pocketed in life, and here, myself.   72

Beneath my head are pushed down all the others
   who came, sinning in simony, before me,
   squeezed tightly in the fissures of the rock.   75

I, in my turn, shall join the rest below
   as soon as *he* comes, the one I thought you were
   when, all too quick, I put my question to you.   78

But already my feet have baked a longer time
   (and I have been stuck upside-down like this)
   than he will stay here planted with feet aflame: 81

soon after him shall come one from the West,
   a lawless shepherd, one whose fouler deeds
   make him a fitting cover for us both.   84

He shall be another Jason, like the one
   in Maccabees: just as his king was pliant,
   so France's king shall soften to this priest."   87

67–72. Gian Gaetano degli Orsini (lit. "of the little bears," hence the designation "she-bear's son" and the reference to "my cubs") became Pope Nicholas III in 1277. As a cardinal he won renown for his integrity; however, in the short three years between ascent to the papal throne and his death he became notorious for his simoniacal practices.

77. The man still to come is Boniface VIII. (See above, note on line 53.)

82–84. The "lawless shepherd" is Pope Clement V of Gascony, who, upon his death in 1314, will join Nicholas and Boniface in eternal torment.

85–87. Having obtained the high priesthood of the Jews by bribing King Antiochus of Syria, Jason neglected the sacrifices and sanctuary of the temple and introduced Greek modes of life into his community. As Jason had fraudulently acquired his position, so had Menelaus, who offered more money to the king, supplanted Jason (2 Maccabees 47:7–27). As Jason obtained his office from King Antiochus fraudulently, so shall Clement acquire his from Philip.

I do not know, perhaps I was too bold here,
    but I answered him in tune with his own words:
      "Well, tell me now: what was the sum of money   90

that holy Peter had to pay our Lord
    before He gave the keys into his keeping?
      Certainly He asked no more than 'Follow me.'   93

Nor did Peter or the rest extort gold coins
    or silver from Matthias when he was picked
      to fill the place the evil one had lost.   96

So stay stuck there, for you are rightly punished,
    and guard with care the money wrongly gained
      that made you stand courageous against Charles.   99

And were it not for the reverence I have
    for those highest of all keys that you once held
      in the happy life—if this did not restrain me,   102

I would use even harsher words than these,
    for your avarice brings grief upon the world,
      crushing the good, exalting the depraved.   105

You shepherds it was the Evangelist had in mind
    when the vision came to him of her who sits
      upon the waters playing whore with kings: 108

that one who with the seven heads was born
    and from her ten horns managed to draw strength
      so long as virtue was her bridegroom's joy.   111

You have built yourselves a God of gold and silver!
    How do you differ from the idolator,
      except he worships one, you worship hundreds?   114

94–96. After the treachery and subsequent expulsion of Judas, the apostles cast lots in order to replenish their number. Thus, by the will of God, not through monetary payment, was Matthias elected to the vacated post (Acts 1:15–26).

106–111. St. John the Evangelist relates his vision of the dissolute Imperial City of Rome. To Dante, she "who sits / upon the waters" represents the Church, which has been corrupted by the simoniacal activities of many popes (the "shepherds" of the Church). The seven heads symbolize the seven Holy Sacraments; the ten horns represent the Ten Commandments.

O Constantine, what evil did you sire,
   not by your conversion, but by the dower
   that the first wealthy Father got from you!" 117

And while I sang these very notes to him,
   his big flat feet kicked fiercely out of anger,
   —or perhaps it was his conscience gnawing him. 120

I think my master liked what I was saying,
   for all the while he smiled and was intent
   on hearing the ring of truly spoken words. 123

Then he took hold of me with both his arms,
   and when he had me firm against his breast,
   he climbed back up the path he had come down. 126

He did not tire of the weight clasped tight to him,
   but brought me to the top of the bridge's arch,
   the one that joins the fourth bank to the fifth. 129

And here he gently set his burden down—
   gently, for the ridge, so steep and rugged,
   would have been hard even for goats to cross. 132

From there another valley opened to me.

115–117. Constantine the Great, emperor of Rome (306–387), was converted to Christianity in the year 312. Having conquered the eastern Mediterranean lands, he transferred the capital of the Roman Empire to Constantinople (360). This move, according to tradition, stemmed from Constantine's decision to place the western part of the empire under the jurisdiction of the Church in order to repay Pope Sylvester ("the first wealthy Father") for healing him of leprosy. The so-called "Donation of Constantine," though it was proved in the fifteenth century to be a complete fabrication on the part of the clergy, was universally accepted as the truth in the Middle Ages. Dante the Pilgrim reflects this tradition in his sad apostrophe to the individual who first would have introduced wealth to the Church and who, unknowingly, would be ultimately responsible for its present corruption.

CANTO XX

In the Fourth Bolgia they see a group of shades weeping as they walk slowly along the valley; they are the Soothsayers and their heads are twisted completely around so that their hair flows down their fronts and their tears flow down to their buttocks. Virgil points out many of them, including Amphiaraus, Tiresias, Aruns, and Manto. It was Manto who first inhabited the site of Virgil's home city of Mantua, and the poet gives a long description of the city's founding, after which he names more of the condemned soothsayers: Eurypylus, Michael Scot, Guido Bonatti, and Asdente.

Now I must turn strange torments into verse
    to form the matter of the twentieth canto
    of the first chant, the one about the damned.   3

Already I was where I could look down
    into the depths of the ditch: I saw its floor
    was wet with anguished tears shed by the sinners,   6

and I saw people in the valley's circle,
    silent, weeping, walking at a litany pace
    the way processions push along in our world.   9

And when my gaze moved down below their faces,
    I saw all were incredibly distorted,
    the chin was not above the chest, the neck   12

was twisted—their faces looked down on their backs;
    they had to move ahead by moving backward,
    for they never saw what was ahead of them.   15

Perhaps there was a case of someone once
    in a palsy fit becoming so distorted,
    but none that *I* know of! I doubt there could be!   18

So may God grant you, Reader, benefit
    from reading of my poem, just ask yourself
    how I could keep my eyes dry when, close by,   21

I saw the image of our human form
    so twisted—the tears their eyes were shedding
    streamed down to wet their buttocks at the cleft.   24

Indeed I did weep, as I leaned my body
    against a jut of rugged rock. My guide:
    "So you are still like all the other fools?   27

In this place piety lives when pity is dead,
    for who could be more wicked than that man
    who tries to bend divine will to his own!   30

Lift your head up, lift it, see him for whom
    the earth split wide before the Thebans' eyes,
    while they all shouted, 'Where are you rushing off to,   33

Amphiaraus? Why do you quit the war?'
    He kept on rushing downward through the gap
    until Minòs, who gets them all, got him.   36

You see how he has made his back his chest:
    because he wished to see too far ahead,
    he sees behind and walks a backward track.   39

Behold Tiresias, who changed his looks:
    from a man he turned himself into a woman,
    transforming all his body, part for part;   42

then later on he had to take the wand
    and strike once more those two snakes making love
    before he could get back his virile parts.   45

34–36. Amphiaraus was a seer and one of the seven kings who led the expedition against Thebes (see Canto XIV, 68–69). He foresaw that he would die during the siege, and to avoid his fate he hid himself so that he would not have to fight. But his wife Eriphyle revealed his hiding place to Polynices, and Amphiaraus was forced to go to battle. He met his death when the earth opened up and swallowed him.

40–45. Tiresias was the famous soothsayer of Thebes. According to Ovid, Tiresias with his rod once separated two serpents that were coupled together, whereupon he was transformed into a woman. Seven years later he found the same two serpents, struck them again, and became a man once more. Later Jupiter and Juno asked Tiresias, who had the experience of belonging to both sexes, which sex enjoyed love-making more. When Tiresias answered "woman," Juno struck him blind. However, Jupiter in compensation gave him the gift of prophesy.

Backing up to this one's chest comes Aruns,
　　who, in the hills of Luni, worked by peasants
　　of Carrara dwelling in the valley's plain,   48

lived in white marble cut into a cave,
　　and from this site, where nothing blocked his view,
　　he could observe the sea and stars with ease.   51

And that one, with her hair loose, flowing back
　　to cover both her breasts you cannot see,
　　and with her hairy parts in front behind her,   54

was Manto, who had searched through many lands
　　before she came to dwell where I was born;
　　now let me tell you something of her story.   57

When her father had departed from the living,
　　and Bacchus' sacred city fell enslaved,
　　she wandered through the world for many years.   60

High in fair Italy there spreads a lake,
　　beneath the mountains bounding Germany
　　beyond the Tyrol, known as Lake Benaco;   63

by a thousand streams and more, I think, the Alps
　　are bathed from Garda to the Val Camonica
　　with the waters flowing down into that lake;   66

46–51. Aruns was the Etruscan diviner who forecast the Roman civil war and its outcome. He made his home "in the hills of Luni" (47), the area now known as Carrara and renowned for its white marble.

52–60. Manto, upon the death of her father, Tiresias, fled Thebes ("Bacchus' sacred city," 59) and its tyrant Creon. She finally arrived in Italy and there founded the city of Mantua, Virgil's birthplace (56).

63. Lake Benaco, today Lake Garda, lies in northern Italy at the center of the triangle formed by the cities of Trent, Brescia, and Verona.

64–66. Here, the "Alps" refers to that range between the Camonica valley, west of Lake Garda, and the city of Garda, on the lake's eastern shore, that is watered by many streams, which ultimately flow into Lake Garda.

at its center is a place where all three bishops
   of Trent and Brescia and Verona could,
      if they would ever visit there, say Mass;   69

Peschiera sits, a handsome well-built fortress,
   to ward off Brescians and the Bergamese,
      along the lowest point of that lake's shore,   72

where all the water that Benaco's basin
   cannot hold must overflow to make a stream
      that winds its way through countrysides of green;   75

but when the water starts to flow, its name
   is not Benaco but Mencio, all the way
      to Governol, where it falls into the Po;   78

but before its course is run it strikes a lowland,
   on which it spreads and turns into a marsh
      that can become unbearable in summer.   81

Passing this place one day the savage virgin
   saw land that lay in the center of the mire,
      untilled and empty of inhabitants.   84

There, to escape all human intercourse,
   she stopped to practice magic with her servants;
      there she lived, and there she left her corpse.   87

Later on, the men who lived around there gathered
   on that very spot, for it was well protected
      by the bog that girded it on every side.   90

67–69. On an island in Lake Garda (Benaco) the boundaries of the dioceses of Trent, Brescia, and Verona met, thereby making it possible for all three bishops to hold services or "say Mass" there.

70–72. The fortress of Peschiera and the town of the same name are on the southeast shore of Lake Garda.

78. Governol, now called Governolo, is twelve miles from Mantua and situated at the junction of the Mincio and the Po rivers.

They built a city over her dead bones,
    and for her, the first to choose that place, they named it
    Mantua, without recourse to sorcery.   93

Once, there were far more people living there,
    before the foolish Casalodi listened
    to the fraudulent advice of Pinamonte.   96

And so, I warn you, should you ever hear
    my city's origin told otherwise,
    let no false tales adulterate the truth."   99

And I replied: "Master, your explanations
    are truth for me, winning my faith entirely;
    any others would be just like burned-out coals.   102

But speak to me of these shades passing by,
    if you see anyone that is worth noting;
    for now my mind is set on only that."   105

He said: "That one, whose beard flows from his cheeks
    and settles on his back and makes it dark,
    was (when the war stripped Greece of all its males,   108

so that the few there were still rocked in cradles)
    an augur who, with Calchas, called the moment
    to cut the first ship's cable free at Aulis: 111

he is Eurypylus. I sang his story
    this way, somewhere in my high tragedy:
    you should know where—you know it, every line.   114

That other one, whose thighs are scarcely fleshed,
    was Michael Scot, who most assuredly
    knew every trick of magic fraudulence.   117

93. The customs of ancient peoples dictated that the name of a newly founded city be obtained through sorcery. Such was not the case with Mantua.

113. The "high tragedy" is the *Aeneid* (II, 114–119). In this work, however, Eurypylus is not an augur, but a soldier sent to the oracle to discover Apollo's predictions as to the best time to set sail from Troy.

116–117. Michael Scot was a Scottish philosopher attached to Frederick II's court at Palermo (see Canto X, 119), who translated the works of Aristotle from the Arabic of his commentator, Avicenna (see Canto IV, 143). By reputation he was a magician and augur. (Cf. Boccaccio, *Decameron*, VIII, 9.)

See there Guido Bonatti; see Asdente,
    who wishes now he had been more devoted
    to making shoes—too late now for repentance.   120

And see those wretched hags who traded in
    needle, spindle, shuttle, for fortune-telling,
    and cast their spells with image-dolls and potions.   123

Now come along. Cain with his thorn-bush straddles
    the confines of both hemispheres already
    and dips into the waves below Seville;   126

and the moon last night already was at full;
    and you should well remember that at times
    when you were lost in the dark wood she helped you."   129

And we were moving all the time he spoke.

CANTO XXI

WHEN THE TWO *reach the summit of the arch over the Fifth* Bolgia, *they see in the ditch below the bubbling of boiling pitch. Virgil's sudden warning of danger frightens the Pilgrim even before he sees a black devil rushing toward them, with a sinner slung over his shoulder. From the bridge the devil flings the sinner into the pitch, where he is poked at and tormented by the family of Malebranche devils. Virgil, advising his ward to hide behind a rock, crosses the bridge to face the devils alone. They threaten him with their pitchforks, but when he announces*

118–120. Guido Bonatti, a native of Forlì, was a well-known astrologer and diviner. Benvenuto (or Asdente, "toothless," as he was called) was a cobbler from Parma who supposedly possessed certain magic powers.

124–126. By some mysterious power Virgil is able to reckon time in the depths of Hell. The moon (referred to as "Cain with his thorn-bush," 124, the medieval Italian counterpart of our "Man in the Moon") is directly over the line of demarcation between the Northern (land) and the Southern (water) hemispheres and is setting on the western horizon (the "waves below Seville," 126). The time is approximately six A.M.

to their leader, Malacoda, that Heaven has willed that he lead another through Hell, the devil's arrogance collapses. Virgil calls the Pilgrim back to him. Scarmiglione, who tries to take a poke at him, is rebuked by his leader, who tells the travelers that the sixth arch is broken here but farther on they will find another bridge to cross. He chooses a squad of his devils to escort them there: Alichino, Calcabrina, Cagnazzo, Barbariccia, Libicocco, Draghignazzo, Ciriatto, Graffiacane, Farfarello, and Rubicante. The Pilgrim's suspicion about their unsavory escorts is brushed aside by his guide, and the squad starts off, giving an obscene salute to their captain, who returns their salute with a fart.

From this bridge to the next we walked and talked
   of things my Comedy does not care to tell;
   and when we reached the summit of the arch,   3

we stopped to see the next fosse of Malebolge
   and to hear more lamentation voiced in vain:
   I saw that it was very strangely dark!   6

In the vast and busy shipyard of the Venetians
   there boils all winter long a tough, thick pitch
   that is used to caulk the ribs of unsound ships.   9

Since winter will not let them sail, they toil:
   some build new ships, others repair the old ones,
   plugging the planks come loose from many sailings;   12

some hammer at the bow, some at the stern,
   one carves the oars while others twine the ropes,
   one mends the jib, one patches up the mainsail;   15

here, too, but heated by God's art, not fire,
   a sticky tar was boiling in the ditch
   that smeared the banks with viscous residue.   18

I saw it there, but I saw nothing in it,
   except the rising of the boiling bubbles
   breathing in air to burst and sink again.   21

7–15. During the Middle Ages the shipyard at Venice, built in 1104, was one of the most active and productive in all Europe. The image of the busy shipyard with its activity revolving around a vat of viscous pitch establishes the tone for this canto (and the next) as one of tense and excited movement.

I stood intently gazing there below,
   my guide, shouting to me: "Watch out, watch out!"
   took hold of me and drew me to his side.   24

I turned my head like one who can't resist
   looking to see what makes him run away
   (his body's strength draining with sudden fear),   27

but, looking back, does not delay his flight;
   and I saw coming right behind our backs,
   rushing along the ridge, a devil, black!   30

His face, his look, how frightening it was!
   With outstretched wings he skimmed along the rock,
   and every single move he made was cruel;   33

on one of his high-hunched and pointed shoulders
   he had a sinner slung by both his thighs,
   held tightly clawed at the tendons of his heels.   36

He shouted from our bridge: "Hey, Malebranche,
   here's one of Santa Zita's elders for you!
   You stick him under—I'll go back for more;   39

I've got that city stocked with the likes of him,
   they're all a bunch of grafters, save Bonturo!
   You can change a 'no' to 'yes' for cash in Lucca." 42

He flung him in, then from the flinty cliff
   sprang off. No hound unleashed to chase a thief
   could have taken off with greater speed than he. 45

That sinner plunged, then floated up stretched out,
   and the devils underneath the bridge all shouted:
   "You shouldn't imitate the Holy Face!   48

The swimming's different here from in the Serchio!
   We have our grappling-hooks along with us—
   don't show yourself above the pitch, or else!"   51

46–51. The "Holy Face" was a wooden crucifix at Lucca. The sinner surfaces
stretched out (46) on his back with arms flung wide like the figure on a crucifix—
and this gives rise to the devil's remark that here in Hell one does not swim the same
way as in the Serchio (a river near Lucca). In other words, in the Serchio people
swim for pleasure, often floating on their backs (in the position of a crucifix).

With a hundred prongs or more they pricked him, shrieking:
   "You've got to do your squirming under cover,
   try learning how to cheat beneath the surface."   54

They were like cooks who make their scullery boys
   poke down into the caldron with their forks
   to keep the meat from floating to the top.   57

My master said: "We'd best not let them know
   that you are here with me; crouch down behind
   some jutting rock so that they cannot see you;   60

whatever insults they may hurl at me,
   you must not fear, I know how things are run here;
   I have been caught in as bad a fix before."   63

He crossed the bridge and walked on past the end;
   as soon as he set foot on the sixth bank
   he forced himself to look as bold as possible.   66

With all the sound and fury that breaks loose
   when dogs rush out at some poor begging tramp,
   making him stop and beg from where he stands,   69

the ones who hid beneath the bridge sprang out
   and blocked him with a flourish of their pitchforks,
   but he shouted: "All of you behave yourselves!   72

Before you start to jab me with your forks,
   let one of you step forth to hear me out,
   and then decide if you still care to grapple."   75

They all cried out: "Let Malacoda go!"
   One stepped forward—the others stood their ground—
   and moving, said, "What good will this do him?"   78

"Do you think, Malacoda," said my master,
   "that you would see me here, come all this way,
   against all opposition, and still safe,   81

---

76. Malacoda is the leader of the devils in this *bolgia*. It is significant that a devil
whose name means "evil tail" ends this canto with a fart (139).

without propitious fate and God's permission?
  Now let us pass, for it is willed in Heaven
  that I lead another by this savage path."   84

With this the devil's arrogance collapsed,
  his pitchfork, too, dropped right down to his feet,
  as he announced to all: "Don't touch this man!"   87

"You, hiding over there," my guide called me,
  "behind the bridge's rocks, curled up and quiet,
  come back to me, you may return in safety."   90

At his words I rose and then I ran to him
  and all the devils made a movement forward;
  I feared they would not really keep their pact.   93

(I remember seeing soldiers under truce,
  as they left the castle of Caprona, frightened
  to be passing in the midst of such an enemy.)   96

I drew up close to him, as close as possible,
  and did not take my eyes from all those faces
  that certainly had nothing good about them.   99

Their prongs were aimed at me, and one was saying:
  "Now do I let him have it in the rump?"
  They answered all for one: "Sure, stick him good!"   102

But the devil who had spoken with my guide
  was quick to spin around and scream an order:
  "At ease there, take it easy, Scarmiglione!"   105

Then he said to us: "You cannot travel straight
  across this string of bridges, for the sixth arch
  lies broken at the bottom of its ditch;   108

if you have made your mind up to proceed,
  you must continue on along this ridge;
  not far, you'll find a bridge that crosses it.   111

94–96. Dante's personal recollection concerns the siege of Caprona (a fortress on the
Arno River near Pisa) by Guelph troops from Lucca and Florence in 1289.

Five hours more and it will be one thousand,
    two hundred sixty-six years and a day
    since the bridge-way here fell crumbling to the ground.   114

I plan to send a squad of mine that way
    to see that no one airs himself down there;
    go along with them, they will not misbehave.   117

Front and center, Alichino, Calcabrina,"
    he shouted his commands, "you too, Cagnazzo;
    Barbariccia, you be captain of the squad.   120

Take Libicocco with you and Draghignazzo,
    toothy Ciriatto and Graffiacane,
    Farfarello and our crazy Rubicante.   123

Now tour the ditch, inspect the boiling tar;
    these two shall have safe passage to the bridge
    connecting den to den without a break."   126

"O master, I don't like the looks of this,"
    I said, "let's go, just you and me, no escort,
    you know the way. I want no part of them!   129

If you're observant, as you usually are,
    why is it you don't see them grind their teeth
    and wink at one another?—we're in danger!"   132

And he to me: "I will not have you frightened;
    let them do all the grinding that they want,
    they do it for the boiling souls, not us."   135

Before they turned left-face along the bank
    each one gave their good captain a salute
    with farting tongue pressed tightly to his teeth,   138

and he blew back with his bugle of an ass-hole.

112–114. Christ's death on Good Friday, A.D. 34, would in five hours, according to
Malacoda, have occurred 1266 years ago yesterday—"today" being the morning of
Holy Saturday, 1300. Although the bridge across the next *bolgia* was shattered by
the earthquake following Christ's crucifixion, Malacoda tells Virgil and the Pilgrim
that there is another bridge that crosses this *bolgia*. This lie, carefully contrived by
the spokesman for the devils, sets the trap for the overly confident, trusting Virgil
and his wary charge.

CANTO XXII

THE NOTE of grotesque comedy in the bolgia of the Malebranche continues, with a comparison between Malacoda's salute to his soldiers and different kinds of military signals the Pilgrim has witnessed in his lifetime. He sees many Grafters squatting in the pitch, but as soon as the Malebranche draw near, they dive below the surface. One unidentified Navarrese, however, fails to escape and is hoisted up on Graffiacane's hooks; Rubicante and the other Malebranche start to tear into him, but Virgil, at his ward's request, manages to question him between torments. The sinner briefly tells his story, and then relates that he has left below in the pitch an Italian, Fra Gomita, a particularly adept grafter, who spends his time talking to Michel Zanche.

The Navarrese sinner promises to lure some of his colleagues to the surface for the devils' amusement, if the tormentors will hide themselves for a moment. Cagnazzo is skeptical but Alichino agrees, and no sooner do the Malebranche turn away than the crafty grafter dives below the pitch. Alichino flies after him, but too late; now Calcabrina rushes after Alichino and both struggle above the boiling pitch, and then fall in. Barbariccia directs the rescue operation as the two poets steal away.

I have seen troops of horsemen breaking camp,
    opening the attack, or passing in review,
    I have even seen them fleeing for their lives;   3

I have seen scouts ride, exploring your terrain,
    O Aretines, and I have seen raiding-parties
    and the clash of tournaments, the run of jousts—   6

to the tune of trumpets, to the ring of clanging bells,
    to the roll of drums, to the flash of flares on ramparts,
    to the accompaniment of every known device;   9

but I never saw cavalry or infantry
    or ships that sail by landmarks or by stars
    signaled to set off by such strange bugling!   12

1–12. The reference to the Aretines (5) recalls Dante's presence at their defeat in the battle of Campaldino (1289) at the hands of the Florentine and Luccan troops.

So, on our way we went with those ten fiends.
    What savage company! But—in church, with saints—
    with rowdy good-for-nothings, in the tavern!   15

My attention now was fixed upon the pitch
    to see the operations of this *bolgia*,
    and how the cooking souls got on down there.   18

Much like the dolphins that are said to surface
    with their backs arched to warn all men at sea
    to rig their ships for stormy seas ahead,   21

so now and then a sinner's back would surface
    in order to alleviate his pain,
    then dive to hide as quick as lightning strikes.   24

Like squatting frogs along the ditch's edge,
    with just their muzzles sticking out of water,
    their legs and all the rest concealed below,   27

these sinners squatted all around their pond;
    but as soon as Barbariccia would approach
    they quickly ducked beneath the boiling pitch.   30

I saw (my heart still shudders at the thought)
    one lingering behind—as it sometimes happens
    one frog remains while all the rest dive down—   33

and Graffiacan, standing in front of him,
    hooked and twirled him by his pitchy hair
    and hoisted him. He looked just like an otter!   36

By then I knew the names of all the fiends:
    I had listened carefully when they were chosen,
    each of them stepping forth to match his name.   39

"Hey, Rubicante, dig your claws down deep
    into his back and peel the skin off him,"
    this fiendish chorus egged him on with screams.   42

I said: "Master, will you, if you can, find out
    the name of that poor wretch who has just fallen
    into the cruel hands of his adversaries?"   45

My guide walked right up to the sinner's side
    and asked where he was from, and he replied:
    "I was born and bred in the kingdom of Navarre;   48

my mother gave me to a lord to serve,
    for she had me by some dishonest spendthrift
    who ran through all he owned and killed himself.   51

Then I became a servant in the household
    of good King Thibault. There I learned my graft,
    and now I pay my bill by boiling here."   54

Ciriatto, who had two tusks sticking out
    on both sides of his mouth, just like a boar's,
    let him feel how just one tusk could rip him open.   57

The mouse had fallen prey to evil cats,
    but Barbariccia locked him with his arms,
    shouting: "Get back while I've got hold of him!"   60

Then toward my guide he turned his face and said:
    "If you want more from him, keep questioning
    before he's torn to pieces by the others."   63

My guide went on: "Then tell me, do you know
    of some Italian stuck among these sinners
    beneath the pitch?" And he, "A second ago   66

I was with one who lived around those parts.
    Oh, I wish I were undercover with him now!
    I wouldn't have these hooks or claws to fear."   69

Libicocco cried: "We've waited long enough,"
    then with his fork he hooked the sinner's arm
    and, tearing at it, he pulled out a piece.   72

48–54. Early commentators have given the name of Ciampolo or Giampolo to this native of Navarre who, after being placed in the service of a Spanish nobleman, later served in the court of Thibault II. Exploiting the court duties with which he was entrusted, he took to barratry. One commentator suggests that were it not for the tradition which attributes the name of Ciampolo to this man, one might identify him with the seneschal Goffredo di Beaumont, who took over the government of Navarre during Thibault's absence.

53. Thibault II, the son-in-law of Louis IX of France, was count of Champagne and later king of Navarre during the mid–thirteenth century.

Draghignazzo, too, was anxious for some fun;
   he tried the wretch's leg, but their captain quickly
   spun around and gave them all a dirty look.   75

As soon as they calmed down a bit, my master
   began again to interrogate the wretch,
   who still was contemplating his new wound: 78

"Who was it, you were saying, that unluckily
   you left behind you when you came ashore?"
   "Gomita," he said, "the friar from Gallura,   81

receptacle for every kind of fraud:
   when his lord's enemies were in his hands,
   the treatment they received delighted them: 84

he took their cash, and as he says, hushed up
   the case and let them off; none of his acts
   was petty grafting, all were of sovereign order.   87

He spends his time with don Michele Zanche
   of Logodoro, talking on and on
   about Sardinia—their tongues no worse for wear!   90

Oh, but look how that one grins and grinds his teeth;
   I could tell you so much more, but I am afraid
   he is going to grate my scabby hide for me."   93

But their master-sergeant turned to Farfarello,
   whose wild eyes warned he was about to strike,
   shouting, "Get away, you filthy bird of prey."   96

81–87. Fra Gomita was a Sardinian friar, chancellor of Nino Visconti, governor of Pisa, whom Dante places in *Purgatory* (Canto VIII, 53). From 1275–1296, Nino Visconti was judge of Gallura, one of the four districts into which Sardinia, a Pisan possession during the thirteenth century, was divided. Profiting by his position and the good faith of Nino Visconti, who refused to listen to complaints raised against him, Fra Gomita indulged in the sale of public offices. When Nino learned, however, that he had accepted bribes to let prisoners escape, he promptly had him hanged.

88–89. Although no documents mentioning the name of Michele Zanche have been found, he is believed to have been the governor of Logodoro, another of the four districts into which Sardinia was divided in the thirteenth century during the period when King Enzo of Sardinia, the son of Frederick II, was engaged in war.

"If you would like to see Tuscans or Lombards,"
   the frightened shade took up where he left off,
   "and have a talk with them, I'll bring some here;   99

but the Malebranche must back up a bit,
   or else those shades won't risk a surfacing;
   I, by myself, will bring you up a catch   102

of seven, without moving from this spot,
   just by whistling—that's our signal to the rest
   when one peers out and sees the coast is clear."   105

Cagnazzo raised his snout at such a story,
   then shook his head and said: "Listen to the trick
   he's cooked up to get off the hook by jumping!"   108

And he, full of the tricks his trade had taught him,
   said: "Tricky, I surely am, especially
   when it comes to getting friends into worse trouble."   111

But Alichin could not resist the challenge,
   and in spite of what the others thought, cried out:
   "If you jump, I won't come galloping for you,   114

I've got my wings to beat you to the pitch.
   We'll clear this ledge and wait behind that slope.
   Let's see if one of you can outmatch us!"   117

Now listen, Reader, here's a game that's strange:
   they all turned toward the slope, and first to turn
   was the fiend who from the start opposed the game.   120

The Navarrese had perfect sense of timing:
   feet planted on the ground, in a flash he jumped,
   the devil's plan was foiled, and he was free.   123

The squad was stung with shame but most of all
   the one who brought this blunder to perfection;
   he swooped down, howling, "Now I've got you caught!"   126

Little good it did, for wings could not outstrip
   the flight of terror: down the sinner dived
   and up the fiend was forced to strain his chest   129

like a falcon swooping down on a wild duck:
   the duck dives quickly out of sight, the falcon
   must fly back up dejected and defeated.   132

In the meantime, Calcabrina, furious,
   also took off, hoping the shade would make it,
   so he could pick a fight with his companion.   135

And when he saw the grafter hit the pitch,
   he turned his claws to grapple with his brother,
   and they tangled in mid-air above the ditch;   138

but the other was a full-fledged hawk as well
   and used his claws on him, and both of them
   went plunging straight into the boiling pond.   141

The heat was quick to make them separate,
   but there seemed no way of getting out of there;
   their wings were clogged and could not lift them up.   144

Barbariccia, no less peeved than all his men,
   sent four fiends flying to the other shore
   with their equipment at top speed; instantly,   147

some here, some there, they took the posts assigned them.
   They stretched their hooks to reach the pitch-dipped pair,
   who were by now deep-fried within their crusts.   150

And there we left them, all messed up that way.

CANTO XXIII

THE ANTICS of CIAMPOLO, the Navarrese, and the Malebranche *bring to the Pilgrim's mind the fable of the frog, the mouse, and the hawk—and that in turn reminds him of the immediate danger he and Virgil are in from the angry* Malebranche. *Virgil senses the danger too, and grabbing his ward as a mother would her child, he dashes to the edge of the bank and slides down the rocky slope into the Sixth* Bolgia—*not a*

moment too soon, for at the top of the slope they see the angry Male-
branche. When the Pilgrim looks around him he sees weeping shades
slowly marching in single file, each one covered from head to foot with
a golden cloak lined with lead, which weights them down. These are
the Hypocrites. Two in this group identify themselves as Catalano de'
Malavolti and Loderingo degli Andalò, two Jovial Friars. The Pilgrim
is about to address them when he sees the shade of Caiaphas (the evil
counselor who advised Pontius Pilate to crucify Christ), crucified and
transfixed by three stakes to the ground. Virgil discovers from the two
friars that in order to leave this bolgia *they must climb up a rockslide;*
he also learns that this is the only bolgia *over which the bridge is bro-*
ken. Virgil is angry with himself for having believed Malacoda's lie
about the bridge over the Sixth Bolgia *(Canto XXI, 106–111).*

In silence, all alone, without an escort,
   we moved along, one behind the other,
   like minor friars bent upon a journey. 3

I was thinking over one of Aesop's fables
   that this recent skirmish had brought back to mind,
   where he tells the story of the frog and mouse; 6

for "yon" and "there" could not be more alike
   than the fable and the fact, if one compares
   the start and finish of both incidents. 9

As from one thought another often rises,
   so this thought gave quick birth to still another,
   and then the fear I first had felt was doubled. 12

I was thinking: "Since these fiends, on our account,
   were tricked and mortified by mockery,
   they certainly will be more than resentful; 15

with rage now added to their evil instincts,
   they will hunt us down with all the savagery
   of dogs about to pounce upon the hare." 18

I felt my body's skin begin to tighten—
   I was so frightened!—and I kept looking back:
   "O master," I said, "if you do not hide 21

both of us, and very quick, I am afraid
   of the Malebranche—right now they're on our trail—
   I feel they're there, I think I hear them now."   24

And he replied: "Even if I were a mirror
   I could not reflect your outward image faster
   than your inner thoughts transmit themselves to me.   27

In fact, just now they joined themselves with mine,
   and since they were alike in birth and form,
   I decided to unite them toward one goal: 30

if the right-hand bank should slope in such a way
   as to allow us to descend to the next *bolgia*,
   we could escape that chase we have imagined."   33

He had hardly finished telling me his plan
   when I saw them coming with their wings wide open
   not too far off, and now they meant to get us!   36

My guide instinctively caught hold of me,
   like a mother waking to some warning sound,
   who sees the rising flames are getting close   39

and grabs her son and runs—she does not wait
   the short time it would take to put on something;
   she cares not for herself, only for him.   42

And over the edge, then down the stony bank
   he slid, on his back, along the sloping rock
   that walls the higher side of the next *bolgia*.   45

Water that turns a mill wheel never ran
   the narrow sluice at greater speed, not even
   at the point before it hits the paddle-blades,   48

than down that sloping border my guide slid,
   bearing me with him, clasping me to his chest
   as though I were his child, not his companion.   51

His feet had hardly touched rock bottom, when
   there they were, the ten of them, above us
   on the height; but now there was no need to fear: 54

High Providence that willed for them to be
   the ministers in charge of the fifth ditch
   also willed them powerless to leave their realm.   57

And now, down there, we found a painted people,
   slow-motioned: step by step, they walked their round
   in tears, and seeming wasted by fatigue.   60

All were wearing cloaks with hoods pulled low
   covering the eyes (the style was much the same
   as those the Benedictines wear at Cluny),   63

dazzling, gilded cloaks outside, but inside
   they were lined with lead, so heavy that the capes
   King Frederick used, compared to these, were straw.   66

O cloak of everlasting weariness!
   We turned again, as usual, to the left
   and moved with them, those souls lost in their mourning;   69

but with their weight that tired-out race of shades
   paced on so slowly that we found ourselves
   in new company with every step we took;   72

and so I asked my guide: "Please look around
   and see, as we keep walking, if you find
   someone whose name or deeds are known to me."   75

And one who overheard me speaking Tuscan
   cried out somewhere behind us: "Not so fast,
   you there, rushing ahead through this heavy air,   78

perhaps from me you can obtain an answer."
   At this my guide turned toward me saying, "Stop,
   and wait for him, then match your pace with his."   81

I paused and saw two shades with straining faces
   revealing their mind's haste to join my side,
   but the weight they bore and the crowded road delayed them.   84

61–63. The vestments of the monks at Cluny were particularly famous for their fullness and elegance.

When they arrived, they looked at me sideways
    and for some time, without exchanging words;
    then they turned to one another and were saying: 87

"He seems alive, the way his throat is moving,
    and if both are dead, what privilege allows them
    to walk uncovered by the heavy cloak?"   90

Then they spoke to me: "O Tuscan who has come
    to visit the college of the sullen hypocrites,
    do not disdain to tell us who you are."   93

I answered them: "I was born and I grew up
    in the great city on the lovely Arno's shore,
    and I have the body I have always had.   96

But who are you, distilling tears of grief,
    so many I see running down your cheeks?
    And what kind of pain is this that it can glitter?"   99

One of them answered: "The orange-gilded cloaks
    are thick with lead so heavy that it makes us,
    who are the scales it hangs on, creak as we walk.   102

Jovial Friars we were, both from Bologna.
    My name was Catalano, his, Loderingo,
    and both of us were chosen by your city,   105

that usually would choose one man alone,
    to keep the peace. Evidence of what we were
    may still be seen around Gardingo's parts."   108

I began: "O Friars, all your wretchedness . . ."
    but said no more; I couldn't, for I saw
    one crucified with three stakes on the ground.   111

103–108. The Order of the *Cavalieri di Beata Santa Maria*, or "Jovial Friars" (*frati gaudenti*) as they were called, was founded at Bologna in 1261 and was dedicated to the maintenance of peace between political factions and families, and to the defense of the weak and poor. However, because of its rather liberal rules, this high-principled organization gained the nickname of Jovial Friars—which, no doubt, impaired its serious function to some degree.

And when he saw me all his body writhed,
   and through his beard he heaved out sighs of pain;
   then Friar Catalano, who watched the scene,   114

remarked: "That impaled figure you see there
   advised the Pharisees it was expedient
   to sacrifice one man for all the people.   117

Naked he lies stretched out across the road,
   as you can see, and he must feel the load
   of every weight that steps on him to cross.   120

His father-in-law and the other council members,
   who were the seed of evil for all Jews,
   are racked the same way all along this ditch."   123

And I saw Virgil staring down amazed
   at this body stretching out in crucifixion,
   so vilely punished in the eternal exile.   126

Then he looked up and asked one of the friars:
   "Could you please tell us, if your rule permits:
   is there a passage-way on the right, somewhere,   129

by which the two of us may leave this place
   without summoning one of those black angels
   to come down here and raise us from this pit?"   132

He answered: "Closer than you might expect,
   a ridge jutting out from the base of the great circle
   extends, and bridges every hideous ditch   135

except this one, whose arch is totally smashed
   and crosses nowhere; but you can climb up
   its massive ruins that slope against this bank."   138

115–123. The "impaled figure" is Caiaphas, the high priest of the Jews, who main-
tained that it was better that one man (Jesus) die than for the Hebrew nation to be
lost (John 11:49–50). Annas, Caiaphas's father-in-law (121), delivered Jesus to him
for judgment. For their act against God these men and the other evil counselors who
judged Christ were the "seed of evil for all Jews" (122); in retaliation God caused
Jerusalem to be destroyed and the Hebrew people dispersed to all parts of the world.

124–127. Virgil's amazement at seeing the crucified Caiaphas is due to the fact that
he was not there when Virgil first descended into Hell.

My guide stood there awhile, his head bent low,
    then said: "He told a lie about this business,
    that one who hooks the sinners over there."   141

And the friar: "Once, in Bologna, I heard discussed
    the devil's many vices; one of them is
    that he tells lies and is father of all lies."   144

In haste, taking great strides, my guide walked off,
    his face revealing traces of his anger.
    I turned and left the heavy-weighted souls   147

to make my way behind those cherished footprints.

CANTO XXIV

AFTER AN ELABORATE simile describing Virgil's anger and the return of his composure, the two begin the difficult, steep ascent up the rocks of the fallen bridge. The Pilgrim can barely make it to the top even with Virgil's help, and after the climb he sits down to catch his breath; but his guide urges him on, and they make their way back to the bridge over the Seventh Bolgia. From the bridge confused sounds can be heard rising from the darkness below. Virgil agrees to take his pupil down to the edge of the eighth encircling bank, and once they are there, the scene reveals a terrible confusion of serpents, and Thieves madly running.

Suddenly a snake darts out and strikes a sinner's neck, whereupon he flares up, turning into a heap of crumbling ashes; then the ashes gather together into the shape of a man. The metamorphosed sinner reveals himself to be Vanni Fucci, a Pistoiese condemned for stealing the treasure of the sacristy of the church of San Zeno at Pistoia. He makes a prophecy about the coming strife in Florence.

In the season of the newborn year, when the sun
    renews its rays beneath Aquarius
    and nights begin to last as long as days,   3

at the time the hoarfrost paints upon the ground
    the outward semblance of his snow-white sister
    (but the color from his brush soon fades away),   6

the peasant wakes, gets up, goes out and sees
    the fields all white. No fodder for his sheep!
    He smites his thighs in anger and goes back   9

into his shack and, pacing up and down,
    complains, poor wretch, not knowing what to do;
    once more he goes outdoors, and hope fills him   12

again when he sees the world has changed its face
    in so little time, and he picks up his crook
    and out to pasture drives his sheep to graze—   15

just so I felt myself lose heart to see
    my master's face wearing a troubled look,
    and as quickly came the salve to heal my sore: 18

for when we reached the shattered heap of bridge,
    my leader turned to me with that sweet look
    of warmth I first saw at the mountain's foot.   21

He opened up his arms (but not before
    he had carefully studied how the ruins lay
    and found some sort of plan) to pick me up.   24

Like one who works and thinks things out ahead,
    always ready for the next move he will make,
    so, while he raised me up toward one great rock,   27

he had already singled out another,
    saying, "Now get a grip on that rock there,
    but test it first to see it holds your weight."   30

It was no road for one who wore a cloak!
    Even though I had his help and he weighed nothing,
    we could hardly lift ourselves from crag to crag.   33

21. The reference to the mountain of Canto I reminds the reader of the entire journey.

31. Such as the Hypocrites of the previous *bolgia*.

And had it not been that the bank we climbed
  was lower than the one we had slid down—
  I cannot speak for him—but I for one   36

surely would have quit. But since the Evil Pits
  slope toward the yawning well that is the lowest,
  each valley is laid out in such a way   39

that one bank rises higher than the next.
  We somehow finally reached the point above
  where the last of all that rock was shaken loose.   42

My lungs were so pumped out of breath by the time
  I reached the top, I could not go on farther,
  and instantly I sat down where I was.   45

"Come on, shake off the covers of this sloth,"
  the master said, "for sitting softly cushioned,
  or tucked in bed, is no way to win fame;   48

and without it man must waste his life away,
  leaving such traces of what he was on earth
  as smoke in wind and foam upon the water.   51

Stand up! Dominate this weariness of yours
  with the strength of soul that wins in every battle
  if it does not sink beneath the body's weight.   54

Much steeper stairs than these we'll have to climb;
  we have not seen enough of sinners yet!
  If you understand me, act, learn from my words."   57

At this I stood up straight and made it seem
  I had more breath than I began to breathe,
  and said: "Move on, for I am strong and ready."   60

We climbed and made our way along the bridge,
  which was jagged, tight and difficult to cross,
  and steep—far more than any we had climbed.   63

55. Virgil is referring to the ascent up Lucifer's legs and beyond. (See Canto XXXIV, 82–84.)

Not to seem faint, I spoke while I was climbing;
   then came a voice from the depths of the next chasm,
   a voice unable to articulate.   66

I don't know what it said, even though I stood
   at the very top of the arch that crosses there;
   to me it seemed whoever spoke, spoke running.   69

I was bending over, but no living eyes
   could penetrate the bottom of that darkness;
   therefore I said: "Master, why not go down   72

this bridge onto the next encircling bank,
   for I hear sounds I cannot understand,
   and I look down but cannot see a thing."   75

"No other answer," he replied, "I give you
   than doing what you ask, for a fit request
   is answered best in silence and in deed."   78

From the bridge's height we came down to the point
   where it ends and joins the edge of the eighth bank,
   and then the *bolgia* opened up to me: 81

down there I saw a terrible confusion
   of serpents, all of such a monstrous kind
   the thought of them still makes my blood run cold.   84

Let all the sands of Libya boast no longer,
   for though she breeds chelydri and jaculi,
   phareans, cenchres, and head-tailed amphisbenes,   87

she never bred so great a plague of venom,
   not even if combined with Ethiopia
   or all the sands that lie by the Red Sea.   90

Within this cruel and bitterest abundance
   people ran terrified and naked, hopeless
   of finding hiding-holes or heliotrope.   93

85–90. Libya and the other lands near the Red Sea (Ethiopia and Arabia) were renowned for producing several types of dreadful reptiles.

93. According to folk tradition, heliotrope was believed to be a stone of many virtues. It could cure snakebites and make the man who carried it on his person invisible.

Their hands were tied behind their backs with serpents,
   which pushed their tails and heads around the loins
   and coiled themselves in knots around the front.   96

And then—at a sinner running by our bank
   a snake shot out and, striking, hit his mark:
   right where the neck attaches to the shoulder.   99

No *o* or *i* was ever quicker put
   by pen to paper than he flared up and burned,
   and turned into a heap of crumbled ash;   102

and then, these ashes scattered on the ground
   began to come together on their own
   and quickly take the form they had before: 105

precisely so, philosophers declare,
   the phoenix dies to be reborn again
   as she approaches her five-hundredth year;   108

alive, she does not feed on herbs or grain,
   but on teardrops of frankincense and balm,
   and wraps herself to die in nard and myrrh.   111

As a man in a fit will fall, not knowing why
   (perhaps some hidden demon pulls him down,
   or some oppilation chokes his vital spirits),   114

then, struggling to his feet, will look around,
   confused and overwhelmed by the great anguish
   he has suffered, moaning as he stares about—   117

so did this sinner when he finally rose.
   Oh, how harsh the power of the Lord can be,
   raining in its vengeance blows like these!   120

My guide asked him to tell us who he was,
   and he replied: "It's not too long ago
   I rained from Tuscany to this fierce gullet.   123

I loved the bestial life more than the human,
  like the bastard that I was; I'm Vanni Fucci,
  the beast! Pistoia was my fitting den."

I told my guide: "Tell him not to run away;
  ask him what sin has driven him down here,
  for I knew him as a man of bloody rage."

The sinner heard and did not try to feign;
  directing straight at me his mind and face,
  he reddened with a look of ugly shame,

and said: "That you have caught me by surprise
  here in this wretched *bolgia*, makes me grieve
  more than the day I lost my other life.

Now I am forced to answer what you ask:
  I am stuck so far down here because of theft:
  I stole the treasure of the sacristy—

a crime falsely attributed to another.
  I don't want you to rejoice at having seen me,
  if ever you escape from these dark pits,

so open your ears and hear my prophecy:
  Pistoia first shall be stripped of all its Blacks,
  and Florence then shall change its men and laws;

from Valdimagra Mars shall thrust a bolt
  of lightning wrapped in thick, foreboding clouds,
  then bolt and clouds will battle bitterly

in a violent storm above Piceno's fields,
  where rapidly the bolt will burst the cloud,
  and no White will escape without his wounds.

And I have told you this so you will suffer!"

126

129

132

135

138

141

144

147

150

125–129. Vanni Fucci, the illegitimate son of Fuccio de' Lazzari, was a militant leader of the Blacks in Pistoia. His notoriety "as a man of bloody rage" (129) was widespread; in fact, the Pilgrim is surprised to find him here and not immersed in the Phlegethon together with the other shades of the Violent (Canto XII).

CANTO XXV

THE WRATHFUL Vanni Fucci directs an obscene gesture to God, whereupon he is attacked by several snakes, which coil about him, tying him so tight that he cannot move a muscle. As soon as he flees, the centaur Cacus gallops by with a fire-breathing dragon on his back, and following close behind are three shades, concerned because they cannot find Cianfa—who soon appears as a snake and attacks Agnèl; the two merge into one hideous monster, which then steals off. Next, Guercio, in the form of a snake, strikes Buoso, and the two exchange shapes. Only Puccio Sciancato is left unchanged.

When he had finished saying this, the thief
   shaped his fists into figs and raised them high
   and cried: "Here, God, I've shaped them just for you!"   3

From then on all those snakes became my friends,
   for one of them at once coiled round his neck
   as if to say, "That's all you're going to say,"   6

while another twisted round his arms in front;
   it tied itself into so tight a knot,
   between the two he could not move a muscle.   9

Pistoia, ah, Pistoia! why not resolve
   to burn yourself to ashes, ending all,
   since you have done more evil than your founders?   12

Throughout the circles of this dark inferno
   I saw no shade so haughty toward his God,
   not even he who fell from Thebes' high walls.   15

Without another word he fled, and then
   I saw a raging centaur gallop up
   roaring: "Where is he, where is that untamed beast?"   18

2. The gesture described, still current in Italy, is equivalent to "Fuck you!" The gesture is made by closing the hand to form a fist with the thumb inserted between the first and second fingers.

15. The one "who fell" is Capaneus, whom Dante placed among the Blasphemers in the Seventh Circle.

I think that all Maremma does not have
   as many snakes as he had on his back,
   right up to where his human form begins.   21

Upon his shoulders, just behind the nape,
   a dragon with its wings spread wide was crouching
   and spitting fire at whoever came its way.   24

My master said to me: "That one is Cacus,
   who more than once in the grotto far beneath
   Mount Aventine spilled blood to fill a lake.   27

He does not go the same road as his brothers
   because of the cunning way he committed theft
   when he stole his neighbor's famous cattle-herd;   30

and then his evil deeds came to an end
   beneath the club of Hercules, who struck
   a hundred blows, and he, perhaps, felt ten."   33

While he was speaking Cacus galloped off;
   at the same time three shades appeared below us;
   my guide and I would not have seen them there   36

if they had not cried out: "Who are you two?"
   At this we cut our conversation short
   to give our full attention to these three.   39

I didn't know who they were, but then it happened,
   as often it will happen just by chance,
   that one of them was forced to name another: 42

"Where did Cianfa go off to?" he asked. And then,
   to keep my guide from saying anything,
   I put my finger tight against my lips.   45

19–20. Maremma was a swampy area along the Tuscan coast which was infested with snakes.

25–33. Cacus was a centaur, the son of Vulcan; he was a fire-belching monster who lived in a cave beneath Mount Aventine and pillaged the inhabitants of the area. But when he stole several cattle of Hercules', the latter went to Cacus's cave and killed him. His brothers (28) are the centaurs who serve as guardians in the first round of the Seventh Circle.

43. Cianfa was a member of the Florentine Donati family. He makes his appearance in line 50 in the form of a serpent.

Now if, my reader, you should hesitate
    to believe what I shall say, there's little wonder,
    for I, the witness, scarcely can believe it.   48

While I was watching them, all of a sudden
    a serpent—and it had six feet—shot up
    and hooked one of these wretches with all six.   51

With the middle feet it hugged the sinner's stomach
    and, with the front ones, grabbed him by the arms,
    and bit him first through one cheek, then the other;   54

the serpent spread its hind feet round both thighs,
    then stuck its tail between the sinner's legs,
    and up against his back the tail slid stiff.   57

No ivy ever grew to any tree
    so tight entwined, as the way that hideous beast
    had woven in and out its limbs with his;   60

and then both started melting like hot wax
    and, fusing, they began to mix their colors
    (so neither one seemed what he was before),   63

just as a brownish tint, ahead of flame,
    creeps up a burning page that is not black
    completely, even though the white is dying.   66

The other two who watched began to shout:
    "O Agnèl! If you could see how you are changing!
    You're not yourself, and you're not both of you!"   69

The two heads had already fused to one
    and features from each flowed and blended into
    one face where two were lost in one another;   72

two arms of each were four blurred strips of flesh;
    and thighs with legs, then stomach and the chest
    sprouted limbs that human eyes have never seen.   75

68. Besides the indication that Agnèl is Florentine (except for Vanni Fucci, the thieves in this canto are all Florentines), and possibly is one of the Brunelleschi family, nothing more is known of him.

Each former likeness now was blotted out:
  both, and neither one it seemed—this picture
  of deformity. And then it sneaked off slowly.   78

Just as a lizard darting from hedge to hedge,
  under the stinging lash of the dog-days' heat,
  zips across the road, like a flash of lightning,   81

so, rushing toward the two remaining thieves,
  aiming at their guts, a little serpent,
  fiery with rage and black as pepper-corn,   84

shot up and sank its teeth in one of them,
  right where the embryo receives its food,
  then back it fell and lay stretched out before him.   87

The wounded thief stared speechless at the beast,
  and standing motionless began to yawn
  as though he needed sleep, or had a fever.   90

The snake and he were staring at each other;
  one from his wound, the other from its mouth
  fumed violently, and smoke with smoke was mingling.   93

Let Lucan from this moment on be silent,
  who tells of poor Nasidius and Sabellus,
  and wait to hear what I still have in store;   96

and Ovid, too, with his Cadmus and Arethusa—
  though he metamorphosed one into a snake,
  the other to a fountain, I feel no envy,   99

for never did he interchange two beings
  face to face so that both forms were ready
  to exchange their substance, each one for the other's,   102

an interchange of perfect symmetry:
  the serpent split its tail into a fork,
  and the wounded sinner drew his feet together;   105

86. The navel is described here.

94–102. In the *Pharsalia* Lucan tells of the physical transformations undergone by Sabellus and Nasidius, both soldiers in Cato's army, who, being bitten by snakes, turned respectively into ashes and into a formless mass. Ovid relates how Cadmus took the form of a serpent and how Arethusa became a fountain.

the legs, with both the thighs, closed in to join
   and in a short time fused, so that the juncture
   didn't show signs of ever having been there,   108

the while the cloven tail assumed the features
   that the other one was losing, and its skin
   was growing soft, the other's getting scaly;   111

I saw his arms retreating to the armpits,
   and the reptile's two front feet, that had been short,
   began to stretch the length the man's had shortened;   114

the beast's hind feet then twisted round each other
   and turned into the member man conceals,
   while from the wretch's member grew two legs.   117

The smoke from each was swirling round the other,
   exchanging colors, bringing out the hair
   where there was none, and stripping off the other's.   120

The one rose up, the other sank, but neither
   dissolved the bond between their evil stares,
   fixed eye to eye, exchanging face for face;   123

the standing creature's face began receding
   toward the temples; from the excess stuff pulled back,
   the ears were growing out of flattened cheeks,   126

while from the excess flesh that did not flee
   the front, a nose was fashioned for the face,
   and lips puffed out to just the normal size.   129

The prostrate creature strains his face out long
   and makes his ears withdraw into his head,
   the way a snail pulls in its horns. The tongue,   132

that once had been one piece and capable
   of forming words, divides into a fork,
   while the other's fork heals up. The smoke subsides.   135

The soul that had been changed into a beast
   went hissing off along the valley's floor,
   the other close behind him, spitting words.   138

Then he turned his new-formed back on him and said
　　to the shade left standing there: "Let Buoso run
　　the valley on all fours, the way I did."   141

Thus I saw the cargo of the seventh hold
　　exchange and interchange; and let the strangeness
　　of it all excuse me, if my pen has failed.   144

And though this spectacle confused my eyes
　　and stunned my mind, the two thieves could not flee
　　so secretly I did not recognize   147

that one was certainly Puccio Sciancato
　　(and he alone, of that company of three
　　that first appeared, did not change to something else),   150

the other, he who made you mourn, Gaville.

CANTO XXVI

FROM THE RIDGE *high above the Eighth* Bolgia *can be perceived a myriad of flames flickering far below, and Virgil explains that within each flame is the suffering soul of a Deceiver. One flame, divided at the top, catches the Pilgrim's eye and he is told that within it are jointly punished Ulysses and Diomed. Virgil questions the pair for the benefit of the Pilgrim. Ulysses responds with the famous narrative of his last voyage, during which he passed the Pillars of Hercules and sailed the*

140–141. The identity of Buoso, the newly formed serpent, is uncertain; some commentators think him to be Buoso degli Abati and others, Buoso Donati (see Canto XXX, 44).

148. Puccio Sciancato (the only one of the original three Florentine thieves who does not assume a new shape) was a member of the Galigai family and a supporter of the Ghibellines. He was exiled from Florence in 1268.

151. Francesco Cavalcanti, known as Guercio, was slain by the inhabitants of Gaville, a small town near Florence in Valdarno (Arno Valley). The Cavalcanti family avenged his death by decimating the populace; thus, he was Gaville's reason to mourn.

forbidden sea until he saw a mountain shape, from which came sud-
denly a whirlwind that spun his ship around three times and sank it.

Be joyful, Florence, since you are so great
    that your outstretched wings beat over land and sea,
    and your name is spread throughout the realm of Hell!   3

I was ashamed to find among the thieves
    five of your most eminent citizens,
    a fact which does you very little honor   6

But if early morning dreams have any truth,
    you will have the fate, in not too long a time,
    that Prato and the others crave for you.   9

And were this the day, it would not be too soon!
    Would it had come to pass, since pass it must!
    The longer the delay, the more my grief.   12

We started climbing up the stairs of boulders
    that had brought us to the place from where we watched;
    my guide went first and pulled me up behind him.   15

We went along our solitary way
    among the rocks, among the ridge's crags,
    where the foot could not advance without the hand.   18

I know that I grieved then, and now again
    I grieve when I remember what I saw,
    and more than ever I restrain my talent   21

lest it run a course that virtue has not set;
    for if a lucky star or something better
    has given me this good, I must not misuse it.   24

As many fireflies (in the season when
    the one who lights the world hides his face least,
    in the hour when the flies yield to mosquitoes)   27

7. According to the ancient and medieval popular tradition, the dreams that men
have in the early morning hours before daybreak will come true.

as the peasant on the hillside at his ease
   sees, flickering in the valley down below,
   where perhaps he gathers grapes or tills the soil—   30

with just so many flames all the eighth *bolgia*
   shone brilliantly, as I became aware
   when at last I stood where the depths were visible.   33

As he who was avenged by bears beheld
   Elijah's chariot at its departure,
   when the rearing horses took to flight toward Heaven,   36

and though he tried to follow with his eyes,
   he could not see more than the flame alone
   like a small cloud once it had risen high—   39

so each flame moves itself along the throat
   of the abyss, none showing what it steals
   but each one stealing nonetheless a sinner.   42

I was on the bridge, leaning far over—so far
   that if I had not grabbed some jut of rock
   I could easily have fallen to the bottom.   45

And my guide, who saw me so absorbed, explained:
   "There are souls concealed within these moving fires,
   each one swathed in his burning punishment."   48

"O master," I replied, "from what you say
   I know now I was right; I had guessed already
   it might be so, and I was about to ask you: 51

Who's in that flame with its tip split in two,
   like that one which once sprang up from the pyre
   where Eteocles was placed beside his brother?"   54

34–39. The prophet Elisha saw Elijah transported to Heaven in a fiery chariot. When Elisha on another occasion cursed, in the name of the lord, a group of children who were mocking him, two bears came out of the forest and devoured them. (4 Kings, 2:9–12, 23–24).

52–54. Dante compares this flame with that which rose from the funeral pyre of Eteocles and Polynices, twin sons of Oedipus and Jocasta, who, contesting the throne of Thebes, caused a major conflict known as the Seven against Thebes (see Canto XIV, 68–69). The two brothers met in single combat and slew each other. They were placed together on the pyre, but because of their mutual hatred, the flame split.

He said: "Within, Ulysses and Diomed
    are suffering in anger with each other,
    just vengeance makes them march together now.   57

And they lament inside one flame the ambush
    of the horse become the gateway that allowed
    the Romans' noble seed to issue forth.   60

Therein they mourn the trick that caused the grief
    of Deïdamia, who still weeps for Achilles;
    and there they pay for the Palladium."   63

"If it is possible for them to speak
    from within those flames," I said, "master, I pray
    and repray you—let my prayer be like a thousand—   66

that you do not forbid me to remain
    until the two-horned flame comes close to us;
    you see how I bend toward it with desire!"   69

"Your prayer indeed is worthy of highest praise,"
    he said to me, "and therefore I shall grant it;
    but see to it your tongue refrains from speaking.   72

55–57. Ulysses, the son of Laertes, was a central figure in the Trojan War. Although his deeds are recounted by Homer, Dictys of Crete, and many others, the story of his last voyage presented here by Dante (90–142) has no literary or historical precedent. His story, being an invention of Dante's, is unique in the *Divine Comedy*.

Diomed, the son of Tydeus and Deipyle, ruled Argos. He was a major Greek figure in the Trojan War, and was frequently associated with Ulysses in his exploits.

58–60. The Trojans mistakenly believed the mammoth wooden horse, left outside the city's walls, to be a sign of Greek capitulation. They brought it through the gates of the city amid great rejoicing. Later that evening the Greek soldiers hidden in the horse emerged and sacked the city. The Fall of Troy occasioned the journey of Aeneas and his followers ("noble seed") to establish a new nation on the shores of Italy, which would become the heart of the Roman Empire.

61–62. Thetis brought her son Achilles, disguised as a girl, to the court of King Lycomedes on the island of Scyros, so that he would not have to fight in the Trojan War. There Achilles seduced the king's daughter Deïdamia, who bore him a child and whom he later abandoned, encouraged by Ulysses (who in company with Diomed had come in search of him) to join the war.

63. The sacred Palladium, a statue of the goddess Pallas Athena, guaranteed the integrity of Troy as long as it remained in the citadel. Ulysses and Diomed stole it and carried it off to Argos, thereby securing victory for the Greeks over the Trojans.

Leave it to me to speak, for I know well
   what you would ask; perhaps, since they were Greeks,
   they might not pay attention to your words."   75

So when the flame had reached us, and my guide
   decided that the time and place were right,
   he addressed them and I listened to him speaking: 78

"O you who are two souls within one fire,
   if I have deserved from you when I was living,
   if I have deserved from you much praise or little,   81

when in the world I wrote my lofty verses,
   do not move on; let one of you tell where
   he lost himself through his own fault, and died."   84

The greater of the ancient flame's two horns
   began to sway and quiver, murmuring
   just like a flame that strains against the wind;   87

then, while its tip was moving back and forth,
   as if it were the tongue itself that spoke,
   the flame took on a voice and said: "When I   90

set sail from Circe, who, more than a year,
   had kept me occupied close to Gaëta
   (before Aeneas called it by that name),   93

not sweetness of a son, not reverence
   for an aging father, not the debt of love
   I owed Penelope to make her happy,   96

could quench deep in myself the burning wish
   to know the world and have experience
   of all man's vices, of all human worth.   99

So I set out on the deep and open sea
   with just one ship and with that group of men,
   not many, who had not deserted me.   102

90–92. Along the coast of southern Italy above Naples there is a promontory then
called Gaëta, and now on it there is a city by the same name. Aeneas named it to
honor his nurse who had died there.

I saw as far as Spain, far as Morocco,
   both shores; I had left behind Sardinia,
   and the other islands which that sea encloses.   105

I and my mates were old and tired men.
   Then finally we reached the narrow neck
   where Hercules put up his signal-pillars   108

to warn men not to go beyond that point.
   On my right I saw Seville, and passed beyond;
   on my left, Ceüta had already sunk behind me.   111

'Brothers,' I said, 'who through a hundred thousand
   perils have made your way to reach the West,
   during this so brief vigil of our senses   114

that is still reserved for us, do not deny
   yourself experience of what there is beyond,
   behind the sun, in the world they call unpeopled.   117

Consider what you came from: you are Greeks!
   You were not born to live like mindless brutes
   but to follow paths of excellence and knowledge.'   120

With this brief exhortation I made my crew
   so anxious for the way that lay ahead,
   that then I hardly could have held them back;   123

and with our stern turned toward the morning light,
   we made our oars our wings for that mad flight,
   gaining distance, always sailing to the left.   126

The night already had surveyed the stars
   the other pole contains; it saw ours so low
   it did not show above the ocean floor.   129

Five times we saw the splendor of the moon
   grow full and five times wane away again
   since we had entered through the narrow pass—   132

---

108. The "signal-pillars" refer to the Strait of Gibraltar, called in ancient times the Pillars of Hercules. The two pillars were separated by Hercules to designate the farthest reach of the inhabited world, beyond which no man was permitted to venture.

130–131. Five months had passed since they began their voyage.

when there appeared a mountain shape, darkened
   by distance, that arose to endless heights.
   I had never seen another mountain like it.   135

Our celebrations soon turned into grief:
   from the new land there rose a whirling wind
   that beat against the forepart of the ship   138

and whirled us round three times in churning waters;
   the fourth blast raised the stern up high, and sent
   the bow down deep, as pleased Another's will.   141

And then the sea was closed again, above us."

CANTO XXVII

As soon as Ulysses has finished his narrative, another flame—its soul within having recognized Virgil's Lombard accent—comes forward asking the travelers to pause and answer questions about the state of affairs in the region of Italy from which he came. The Pilgrim responds by outlining the strife in Romagna and ends by asking the flame who he is. The flame, although he insists he does not want his story to be known among the living, answers because he is supposedly convinced that the Pilgrim will never return to earth. He is another famous deceiver, Guido da Montefeltro, a soldier who became a friar in his old age; but he was untrue to his vows when, at the urging of Pope Boniface VIII, he counseled the use of fraud in the pope's campaign against the Colonna family. He was damned to Hell because he failed to repent his sins, trusting instead in the pope's fraudulent absolution.

By now the flame was standing straight and still,
   it said no more and had already turned
   from us, with sanction of the gentle poet,   3

133. In Dante's time the Southern Hemisphere was believed to be composed entirely of water; the mountain that Ulysses and his men see from afar is the Mount of Purgatory that rises from the sea in the Southern Hemisphere, the polar opposite of Jerusalem.

when another, coming right behind it,
     attracted our attention to its tip,
     where a roaring of confusing sounds had started.   6

As the Sicilian bull—that bellowed first
     with cries of that one (and it served him right)
     who with his file had fashioned such a beast—   9

would bellow with the victim's voice inside,
     so that, although the bull was only brass,
     the effigy itself seemed pierced with pain: 12

so, lacking any outlet to escape
     from the burning soul that was inside the flame,
     the suffering words became the fire's language.   15

But after they had made their journey upward
     to reach the tip, giving it that same quiver
     the sinner's tongue inside had given them,   18

we heard the words: "O you to whom I point
     my voice, who spoke just now in Lombard, saying:
     'you may move on, I won't ask more of you.'   21

although I have been slow in coming to you,
     be willing, please, to pause and speak with me.
     You see how willing I am—and I burn!   24

If you have just now fallen to this world
     of blindness, from that sweet Italian land
     where I took on the burden of my guilt,   27

tell me, are the Romagnols at war or peace?
     For I come from the hills between Urbino
     and the mountain chain that lets the Tiber loose."   30

7–15. Phalaris, despotic ruler of Agrigentum in Sicily, commissioned Perillus to con-
struct a bronze bull intended to be used as an instrument of torture; it was fashioned
so that, once it was heated, the victim roasting within would emit cries that sounded
without like those of a bellowing bull. To test the device, Phalaris made the artisan
himself its first victim, and thus he received his just reward for creating such a cruel
instrument.

29–30. The speaker is Guido da Montefeltro, the Ghibelline captain whose wisdom
and skill in military strategy won him fame.

I was still bending forward listening
　　when my master touched my side and said to me:
　　"*You* speak to him; *this* one is Italian."   33

And I, who was prepared to answer him,
　　began without delaying my response:
　　"O soul who stands concealed from me down there,   36

your Romagna is not now and never was
　　without war in her tyrants' hearts, although
　　there was no open warfare when I came here.   39

Ravenna's situation has not changed:
　　the eagle of Polenta broods up there,
　　covering all of Cervia with its pinions;   42

the land that stood the test of long endurance
　　and left the French piled in a bloody heap
　　is once again beneath the verdant claws.   45

Verrucchio's Old Mastiff and its New One,
　　who both were bad custodians of Montagna,
　　still sink their fangs into their people's flesh;   48

the cities by Lamone and Santerno
　　are governed by the Lion of the White Lair,
　　who changes parties every change of season.   51

As for the town whose side the Savio bathes:
　　just as it lies between the hills and plains,
　　it lives between freedom and tyranny.   54

And now I beg you tell us who you are—
　　grant me my wish as yours was granted you—
　　so that your fame may hold its own on earth."   57

And when the fire, in its own way, had roared
　　awhile, the flame's sharp tip began to sway
　　to and fro, then released a blow of words: 60

"If I thought that I were speaking to a soul
　　who someday might return to see the world,
　　most certainly this flame would cease to flicker;   63

but since no one, if I have heard the truth,
    ever returns alive from this deep pit,
    with no fear of dishonor I answer you: 66

I was a man of arms and then a friar,
    believing with the cord to make amends;
    and surely my belief would have come true   69

were it not for that High Priest (his soul be damned!)
    who put me back among my early sins;
    I want to tell you why and how it happened.   72

While I still had the form of the bones and flesh
    my mother gave me, all my actions were
    not those of a lion, but those of a fox;   75

the wiles and covert paths, I knew them all,
    and so employed my art that rumor of me
    spread to the farthest limits of the earth.   78

When I saw that the time of life had come
    for me, as it must come for every man,
    to lower the sails and gather in the lines,   81

things I once found pleasure in then grieved me;
    repentant and confessed, I took the vows
    a monk takes. And, oh, to think it could have worked!   84

And then the Prince of the New Pharisees
    chose to wage war upon the Lateran
    instead of fighting Saracens or Jews,   87

67–71. In 1296 Guido joined the Franciscan order. The reason for his harsh condemnation of Pope Boniface VIII ("that High Priest") is found in lines 85–111.

85–90. In 1297 the struggle between Boniface VIII ("the Prince of the New Pharisees") and the Colonna family (who lived near the Lateran palace, the pope's residence, and who did not consider the resignation of Celestine V valid) erupted into open conflict. Boniface did not launch his crusade against the traditional rivals—Saracens and Jews (87)—but rather against his fellow Christians, faithful warriors of the Church who neither aided the Saracens during the conquest of Acre (Acri) in 1291 (the last Christian stronghold in the Holy Land), nor disobeyed the interdict on commerce with Mohammedan lands (89–90).

for all his enemies were Christian souls
    (none among the ones who conquered Acri,
    none a trader in the Sultan's kingdom).   90

His lofty papal seat, his sacred vows
    were no concern to him, nor was the cord
    I wore (that once made those it girded leaner).   93

As Constantine once had Silvestro brought
    from Mount Soracte to cure his leprosy,
    so this one sought me out as his physician   96

to cure his burning fever caused by pride.
    He asked me to advise him. I was silent,
    for his words were drunken. Then he spoke again: 99

'Fear not, I tell you: the sin you will commit,
    it is forgiven. Now you will teach me how
    I can level Palestrina to the ground.   102

Mine is the power, as you cannot deny,
    to lock and unlock Heaven. Two keys I have,
    those keys my predecessor did not cherish.'   105

And when his weighty arguments had forced me
    to the point that silence seemed the poorer choice,
    I said: 'Father, since you grant me absolution   108

for the sin I find I must fall into now:
    ample promise with a scant fulfillment
    will bring you triumph on your lofty throne.'   111

---

102. The Colonna family, excommunicated by Boniface, took refuge in their fortress at Palestrina (twenty-five miles east of Rome), which was able to withstand the onslaughts of papal troops. Acting on Guido's counsel (110–111), Boniface promised (but without serious intentions) to grant complete pardon to the Colonna family, who then surrendered and, consequently, lost everything.

104–105. Deceived by Boniface, who was to be his successor, Celestine V renounced the papacy ("those keys") in 1294.

Saint Francis came to get me when I died,
    but one of the black Cherubim cried out:
    'Don't touch him, don't cheat me of what is mine!   114

He must come down to join my other servants
    for the false counsel he gave. From then to now
    I have been ready at his hair, because   117

one cannot be absolved unless repentant,
    nor can one both repent and will a thing
    at once—the one is canceled by the other!'   120

O wretched me! How I shook when he took me,
    saying: 'Perhaps you never stopped to think
    that I might be somewhat of a logician!'   123

He took me down to Minòs, who eight times
    twisted his tail around his hardened back,
    then in his rage he bit it, and announced: 126

'He goes with those the thievish fire burns.'
    And here you see me now, lost, wrapped this way,
    moving, as I do, with my resentment."   129

When he had brought his story to a close,
    the flame, in grievous pain, departed from us
    gnarling and flickering its pointed horn.   132

My guide and I moved farther on; we climbed
    the ridge until we stood on the next arch
    that spans the fosse where penalties are paid   135

by those who, sowing discord, earned Hell's wages.

---

113. Some of the Cherubim (the *eighth* order of angels) were transformed into demons for their rebellion against God; appropriately they appear in the *Eighth* Circle and the *Eighth Bolgia* of Hell.

CANTO XXVIII

IN THE NINTH Bolgia *the Pilgrim is overwhelmed by the sight of mutilated, bloody shades, many of whom are ripped open, with entrails spilling out. They are the Sowers of Scandal and Schism, and among them are Mahomet, Ali, Pier da Medicina, Gaius Scribonius Curio, Mosca de' Lamberti, and Bertran de Born. All bemoan their painful lot, and Mahomet and Pier da Medicina relay warnings through the Pilgrim to certain living Italians who are soon to meet terrible ends. Bertran de Born, who comes carrying his head in his hand like a lantern, is a particularly arresting example of a Dantean* contrapasso.

Who could, even in the simplest kind of prose
   describe in full the scene of blood and wounds
   that I saw now—no matter how he tried!   3

Certainly any tongue would have to fail:
   man's memory and man's vocabulary
   are not enough to comprehend such pain.   6

If one could bring together all the wounded
   who once upon the fateful soil of Puglia
   grieved for their life's blood spilled by the Romans,   9

and spilled again in the long years of the war
   that ended in great spoils of golden rings
   (as Livy's history tells, that does not err),   12

and pile them with the ones who felt the blows
   when they stood up against great Robert Guiscard,
   and with those others whose bones are still in heaps   15

14. In the eleventh century Robert Guiscard (ca. 1015–1085), a noble Norman adventurer, gained control of most of southern Italy and became duke of Apulia and Calabria, as well as gonfalonier of the Church (1059). For the next two decades he battled the schismatic Greeks and the Saracens for the Church in the south of Italy. Later he fought for the Church in the east, raised a siege against Pope Gregory VII (1084), and died at the age of seventy, still engaged in warfare.

15–18. A further comparison between bloody battles in Puglia and the ninth *bolgia*. In 1266 Charles of Anjou marched against the armies of Manfred, king of Sicily. The final example in the lengthy series of battles was a continuation of the hostilities between Charles of Anjou and the followers of Manfred.

at Ceprano (there where every Puglian
    turned traitor), and add those from Tagliacozzo,
    where old Alardo conquered, weaponless—   18

if all these maimed with limbs lopped off or pierced
    were brought together, the scene would be nothing
    to compare with the foul ninth *bolgia's* bloody sight.   21

No wine cask with its stave or cant-bar sprung
    was ever split the way I saw someone
    ripped open from his chin to where we fart.   24

Between his legs his guts spilled out, with the heart
    and other vital parts, and the dirty sack
    that turns to shit whatever the mouth gulps down.   27

While I stood staring into his misery,
    he looked at me and with both hands he opened
    his chest and said: "See how I tear myself!   30

See how Mahomet is deformed and torn!
    In front of me, and weeping, Ali walks,
    his face cleft from his chin up to the crown.   33

The souls that you see passing in this ditch
    were all sowers of scandal and schism in life,
    and so in death you see them torn asunder.   36

A devil stands back there who trims us all
    in this cruel way, and each one of this mob
    receives anew the blade of the devil's sword   39

each time we make one round of this sad road,
    because the wounds have all healed up again
    by the time each one presents himself once more.   42

But who are you there, gawking from the bridge
    and trying to put off, perhaps, fulfillment
    of the sentence passed on you when you confessed?"   45

31. Mahomet is split open from the crotch to the chin, together with the comple-
mentary punishment of Ali, representing Dante's belief that they were initiators of
the great schism between the Christian Church and Mohammedanism.

32. Ali (ca. 600–661) was the first of Mahomet's followers, who married the proph-
et's daughter Fatima. Mahomet died in 632, and Ali assumed the caliphate in 656.

"Death does not have him yet, he is not here
    to suffer for his guilt," my master answered;
    "but that he may have full experience,   48

I, who am dead, must lead him through this Hell
    from round to round, down to the very bottom,
    and this is as true as my presence speaking here."   51

More than a hundred in that ditch stopped short
    to look at me when they had heard his words,
    forgetting in their stupor what they suffered.   54

"And you, who will behold the sun, perhaps
    quite soon, tell Fra Dolcino that unless
    he wants to follow me here quick, he'd better   57

stock up on food, or else the binding snows
    will give the Novarese their victory,
    a conquest not won easily otherwise."   60

With the heel of one foot raised to take a step,
    Mahomet said these words to me, and then
    stretched out and down his foot and moved away.   63

Another, with his throat slit, and his nose
    cut off as far as where the eyebrows start
    (and he only had a single ear to show),   66

who had stopped like all the rest to stare in wonder,
    stepped out from the group and opened up his throat,
    which ran with red from all sides of his wound,   69

and spoke: "O you whom guilt does not condemn,
    whom I have seen in Italy up there,
    unless I am deceived by similarity,   72

56–60. Fra Dolcino (died 1307), though not a monk as his name would seem to indicate, was the leader of a religious sect banned as heretical by Pope Clement V in 1305. Dolcino's sect, the Apostolic Brothers, preached the return of religion to the simplicity of apostolic times, and among their tenets was community of property and sharing of women. When Clement V ordered the eradication of the Brothers, Dolcino and his followers retreated to the hills near Novara, where they withstood the papal forces for over a year until starvation conquered them. Dolcino and his companion, Margaret of Trent, were burned at the stake in 1307.

recall to mind Pier da Medicina,
    should you return to see the gentle plain
    declining from Vercelli to Marcabò,   75

and inform the two best citizens of Fano—
    tell Messer Guido and tell Angiolello—
    that, if our foresight here is no deception,   78

from their ship they shall be hurled bound in a sack
    to drown in the water near Cattolica,
    the victims of a tyrant's treachery;   81

between the isles of Cyprus and Mallorca
    so great a crime Neptune never witnessed
    among the deeds of pirates or the Argives.   84

That traitor, who sees only with one eye
    and rules the land that someone with me here
    wishes he'd never fed his eyes upon,   87

will have them come to join him in a parley,
    then see to it they do not waste their breath
    on vows or prayers to escape Focara's wind."   90

And I to him: "If you want me to bring back
    to those on earth your message—who is the one
    sated with the bitter sight? Show him to me."   93

At once he grabbed the jaws of a companion
    standing near by, and squeezed his mouth half open,
    announcing, "Here he is, and he is mute.   96

73. Although nothing certain is known about the life of Pier da Medicina, we do
know that his home was in Medicina, a town in the Po River valley ("the gentle
plain," which lies between the towns of Vercelli and Marcabò, 74) near Bologna.
According to the early commentator Benvenuto da Imola, Pier da Medicina was the
instigator of strife between the Polenta and Malatesta families.

92–93. The Pilgrim refers to what Pier da Medicina said earlier about "someone"
who "wishes he'd never fed his eyes upon" Rimini (86–87).

This man, in exile, drowned all Caesar's doubts
    and helped him cast the die, when he insisted:
    'A man prepared, who hesitates, is lost.' "   99

How helpless and bewildered he appeared,
    his tongue hacked off as far down as the throat,
    this Curio, once so bold and quick to speak!   102

And one who had both arms but had no hands,
    raising the gory stumps in the filthy air
    so that the blood dripped down and smeared his face,   105

cried: "You, no doubt, also remember Mosca,
    who said, alas, 'What's done is over with,'
    and sowed the seed of discord for the Tuscans."   108

"And of death for all your clan," I quickly said,
    and he, this fresh wound added to his wound,
    turned and went off like one gone mad from pain.   111

But I remained to watch the multitude,
    and saw a thing that I would be afraid
    to tell about without more evidence,   114

were I not reassured by my own conscience—
    that good companion enheartening a man
    beneath the breastplate of its purity.   117

I saw it, I'm sure, and I seem to see it still:
    a body with no head that moved along,
    moving no differently from all the rest;   120

97–102. Caius Cribonius Curio wishes he had never seen Rimini, the city near which the Rubicon River empties into the Adriatic. Once a Roman tribune under Pompey, Curio defected to Caesar's side, and, when the Roman general hesitated to cross the Rubicon, Curio convinced him to cross and march on Rome. At that time the Rubicon formed the boundary between Gaul and the Roman Republic; Caesar's decision to cross it precipitated the Roman Civil War.

106–108. Mosca, about whom the Pilgrim earlier had asked Ciacco (Canto VI, 80), was a member of the Lamberti family of Florence. His counsel ("What's done is over with," 107) was the cause of the division of Florence into the feuding Guelph and Ghibelline parties.

he held his severed head up by its hair,
　　swinging it in one hand just like a lantern,
　　and as it looked at us it said: "Alas!"   123

Of his own self he made himself a light
　　and they were two in one and one in two.
　　How could this be? He who ordained it knows.   126

And when he had arrived below our bridge,
　　he raised the arm that held the head up high
　　to let it speak to us at closer range.   129

It spoke: "Now see the monstrous punishment,
　　you there still breathing, looking at the dead,
　　see if you find suffering to equal mine!   132

And that you may report on me up there,
　　know that I am Bertran de Born, the one
　　who evilly encouraged the young king.   135

Father and son I set against each other:
　　Achitophel with his wicked instigations
　　did not do more with Absalom and David.   138

Because I cut the bonds of those so joined,
　　I bear my head cut off from its life-source,
　　which is back there, alas, within its trunk.   141

In me you see the perfect *contrapasso*!"

CANTO XXIX

WHEN THE PILGRIM is rebuked by his mentor for his inappropriate
interest in these wretched shades, he replies that he was looking for

134–136. One of the greatest of the Provençal troubadours, Bertran de Born lived
in the second half of the twelfth century. He suffers here in Hell for having caused
the rebellion of Prince Henry (the "young king," 135) against his father, Henry II,
king of England.

someone. Virgil tells the Pilgrim that he saw the person he was looking
for, Geri del Bello, pointing a finger at him. They discuss Geri until they
reach the edge of the next bolgia, *where all types of Falsifiers are pun-*
ished. There miserable, shrieking shades are afflicted with diseases of
various kinds and are arranged in various positions. Sitting back to
back, madly scratching their leprous sores, are the shades of Griffolino
da Arezzo and one Capocchio, who talk to the Pilgrim, the latter shade
making wisecracks about the Sienese.

The crowds, the countless, different mutilations,
   had stunned my eyes and left them so confused
   they wanted to keep looking and to weep,   3

but Virgil said: "What are you staring at?
   Why do your eyes insist on drowning there
   below, among those wretched, broken shades?   6

You did not act this way in other *bolge.*
   If you hope to count them one by one, remember,
   the valley winds some twenty-two miles around;   9

and already the moon is underneath our feet;
   the time remaining to us now is short—
   and there is more to see than you see here."   12

"If you had taken time to find out what
   I was looking for," I started telling him,
   "perhaps you would have let me stay there longer."   15

My guide was moving on, with me behind him,
   answering as I did while we went on,
   and adding: "Somewhere down along this ditch   18

that I was staring at a while ago,
   I think there is a spirit of my family
   mourning the guilt that's paid so dear down there."   21

And then my master said: "From this time on
   you should not waste another thought on him;
   think on ahead, and let him stay behind,   24

10. The sun, then, is directly overhead, indicating that it is midday in Jerusalem.

for I saw him standing underneath the bridge
  pointing at you, and threatening with his gesture,
  and I heard his name called out: Geri del Bello.   27

That was the moment you were so absorbed
  with him who was the lord of Altaforte
  that you did not look his way before he left."   30

"Alas, my guide," I answered him, "his death
  by violence, which has not yet been avenged
  by anyone who shares in his disgrace,   33

made him resentful, and I suppose for this
  he went away without a word to me,
  and because he did I feel great piety."   36

We spoke of this until we reached the start
  of the bridge across the next *bolgia*, from which
  the bottom, with more light, might have been seen.   39

Having come to stand above the final cloister
  of Malebolge, we saw it spreading out,
  revealing to our eyes its congregation.   42

Weird shrieks of lamentation pierced through me
  like arrow-shafts whose tips are barbed with pity,
  so that my hands were covering my ears.   45

Imagine all the sick in the hospitals
  of Maremma, Valdichiana, and Sardinia
  between the months of July and September,   48

crammed all together rotting in one ditch—
  such was the misery here; and such a stench
  was pouring out as comes from flesh decaying.   51

27. Geri del Bello was a first cousin of Dante's father. Little is known about him
except that he was among those to whom reparation was made in 1269 for damages
suffered at the hands of the Ghibellines in 1260, and that he was involved in a blood
feud with the Sacchetti family. It was probably one of the Sacchetti who murdered
him. Vengeance by kinsmen for a slaying was considered obligatory at the time, and
apparently Geri's murder was still unavenged by the Alighieri in 1300.

29. The lord of Altaforte was Bertran de Born. (See Canto XXVIII, 130–142.)

Still keeping to our left, we made our way
    down the long bridge onto the final bank,
    and now my sight was clear enough to find   54

the bottom where the High Lord's ministress,
    Justice infallible, metes out her punishment
    to falsifiers she registers on earth.   57

I doubt if all those dying in Aegina
    when the air was blowing sick with pestilence
    and the animals, down to the smallest worm,   60

all perished (later on this ancient race,
    according to what the poets tell as true,
    was born again from families of ants)   63

offered a scene of greater agony
    than was the sight spread out in that dark valley
    of heaped-up spirits languishing in clumps.   66

Some sprawled out on others' bellies, some
    on others' backs, and some, on hands and knees,
    dragged themselves along that squalid alley.   69

Slowly, in silence, slowly we moved along,
    looking, listening to the words of all those sick,
    who had no strength to raise their bodies up.   72

I saw two sitting, leaning against each other
    like pans propped back to back against a fire,
    and they were blotched from head to foot with scabs.   75

I never saw a curry-comb applied
    by a stable-boy who is harried by his master,
    or simply wants to finish and go to bed,   78

the way those two applied their nails and dug
    and dug into their flesh, crazy to ease
    the itching that can never find relief.   81

58–66. This comparison with the sufferers of the Tenth *Bolgia* concerns the island
of Aegina in the Saronic Gulf. Juno sent a plague to the island which killed all the
inhabitants except Aeacus. Aeacus prayed to Jupiter to repopulate the island, and
Jupiter did so by turning ants into men.

They worked their nails down, scraping off the scabs
   the way one works a knife to scale a bream
   or some other fish with larger, tougher scales.   84

"O you there scraping off your scabs of mail
   and even making pincers of your fingers,"
   my guide began to speak to one of them,   87

"so may your fingernails eternally
   suffice their task, tell us: among the many
   packed in this place is anyone Italian?"   90

"Both of us whom you see disfigured here,"
   one answered through his tears, "we are Italians.
   But you, who ask about us, who are you?"   93

"I am one accompanying this living man
   descending bank from bank," my leader said,
   "and I intend to show him all of Hell."   96

With that each lost the other back's support
   and each one, shaky, turned to look at me,
   as others did who overheard these words.   99

My gentle master came up close to me
   and said: "Now ask them what you want to know,"
   and since he wanted me to speak, I started: 102

"So may the memory of you not fade
   from the minds of men up there in the first world,
   but rather live on under many suns,   105

tell me your names and where it was you lived;
   do not let your dreadful, loathsome punishment
   discourage you from speaking openly."   108

"I'm from Arezzo," one of them replied,
   "and Albert of Siena had me burned,
   but I'm not here for what I died for there;   111

109–117. This man is Griffolino d'Arezzo. He supposedly led the doltish Alberto da
Siena to believe that he could teach him how to fly. Alberto paid him well but, upon
discovering the fraud, he denounced Griffolino to the bishop of Siena as a magician,
and the bishop had him burned.

it's true I told him, jokingly, of course:
   'I know the trick of flying through the air,'
   and he, eager to learn and not too bright,   114

asked me to demonstrate my art; and only
   just because I didn't make him Daedalus,
   he had me burned by one whose child he was.   117

But here, to the last *bolgia* of the ten,
   for the alchemy I practiced in the world
   I was condemned by Minòs, who cannot err."   120

I said to my poet: "Have you ever known
   people as silly as the Sienese?
   Even the French cannot compare with them!"   123

With that the other leper who was listening
   feigned exception to my quip: "Excluding,
   of course, Stricca, who lived so frugally,   126

and Niccolo, the first to introduce
   the luxury of the clove for condiment
   into that choice garden where the seed took root,   129

and surely not that fashionable club
   where Caccia squandered all his woods and vineyards
   and Abbagliato flaunted his great wit!   132

That you may know who this is backing you
   against the Sienese, look sharply at me
   so that my face will give you its own answer,   135

122. The Florentines made the citizens of rival Siena the butt of many jokes.

124–126. Capocchio (see below, line 136) makes several ironic comments here about the foolishness of the Sienese. Stricca (probably Stricca di Giovanni del Salimbeni of Siena) was evidently renowned as a spendthrift. The old commentators hold that he was a member of the Spendthrifts' Brigade (see line 130), a group of young Sienese who wasted their fortunes carelessly.

127–129. Capocchio is referring to Niccolò de' Salimbeni's careless extravagance as another example of the silliness of the Sienese. The "choice garden" is Siena itself, where any fashionable custom, no matter how foolish, could gain acceptance.

and you will recognize Capocchio's shade,
   betrayer of metals with his alchemy;
     you'll surely recall—if you're the one I think—   138

how fine an ape of nature I once was."

CANTO XXX

CAPOCCHIO'S REMARKS *are interrupted by two mad, naked shades who*
dash up, and one of them sinks his teeth into Capocchio's neck and
drags him off; he is Gianni Schicchi and the other is Myrrha of Cyprus.
When they have gone, the Pilgrim sees the ill-proportioned and immo-
bile shade of Master Adamo, a counterfeiter, who explains how mem-
bers of the Guidi family had persuaded him to practice his evil art in
Romena. He points out the fever-stricken shades of two infamous liars,
Potiphar's Wife and Sinon the Greek, whereupon the latter engages
Master Adamo in a verbal battle. Virgil rebukes the Pilgrim for his
absorption in such futile wrangling, but his immediate shame wins Vir-
gil's immediate forgiveness.

In ancient times when Juno was enraged
   against the Thebans because of Semele
     (she showed her wrath on more than one occasion),   3

she made King Athamas go raving mad:
   so mad that one day when he saw his wife
     coming with his two sons in either arm,   6

---

136. Capocchio is the name (or nickname) of a man who in 1293 was burned alive
in Siena for alchemy. Apparently Dante had known him; according to the early com-
mentators, it was in their student days.

1–12. Jupiter's predilection for mortal women always enraged Juno, his wife. In this
case her ire was provoked by her husband's dalliance with Semele, the daughter of
Cadmus, king of Thebes, who bore him Bacchus. Having vowed to wreak revenge
on her and her family, Juno not only had Semele struck by lightning, but also caused
King Athamas, the husband of Ino (Semele's sister), to go insane. In his demented
state he killed his son Learchus. Ino drowned herself and her other son, Melicertes.

he cried: "Let's spread the nets, so I can catch
   the lioness with her lion cubs at the pass!"
   Then he spread out his insane hands, like talons,   9

and, seizing one of his two sons, Learchus,
   he whirled him round and smashed him on a rock.
   She drowned herself with the other in her arms.   12

And when the wheel of Fortune brought down low
   the immeasurable haughtiness of Trojans,
   destroying in their downfall king and kingdom,   15

Hecuba sad, in misery, a slave
   (after she saw Polyxena lie slain,
   after this grieving mother found her son   18

Polydorus left unburied on the shore),
   now gone quite mad, went barking like a dog—
   it was the weight of grief that snapped her mind.   21

But never in Thebes or Troy were madmen seen
   driven to acts of such ferocity
   against their victims, animal or human,   24

as two shades I saw, white with rage and naked,
   running, snapping crazily at things in sight,
   like pigs, directionless, broken from their pen.   27

One, landing on Capocchio, sank his teeth
   into his neck, and started dragging him
   along, scraping his belly on the rocky ground.   30

The Aretine spoke, shaking where he sat:
   "You see that batty shade? He's Gianni Schicchi!
   He's rabid and he treats us all that way."   33

31. The "Aretine" is Griffolino d'Arezzo. (See Canto XXIX, 109–120.)

32. Gianni Schicchi, a member of the Florentine Cavalcanti family, was well known for his mimetic virtuosity. Simone Donati, keeping his father's death a secret in order that he might change the will to his advantage, engaged Gianni to impersonate his dead father (Buoso Donati, 44) and alter the latter's will. The plan was carried out to perfection, and in the process Gianni willed himself, among other things, a prize mare (the "queen of studs," 43).

"Oh," I answered, "so may that other shade
    never sink its teeth in you—if you don't mind,
    please tell me who it is before it's gone."   36

And he to me: "That is the ancient shade
    of Myrrha, the depraved one, who became,
    against love's laws, too much her father's friend.   39

She went to him, and there she sinned in love,
    pretending that her body was another's—
    just as the other there fleeing in the distance,   42

contrived to make his own the 'queen of studs,'
    pretending that he was Buoso Donati,
    making his will and giving it due form."   45

Now that the rabid pair had come and gone
    (from whom I never took my eyes away),
    I turned to watch the other evil shades.   48

And there I saw a soul shaped like a lute,
    if only he'd been cut off from his legs
    below the belly, where they divide in two.   51

The bloating dropsy, disproportioning
    the body's parts with unconverted humors,
    so that the face, matched with the paunch, was puny,   54

forced him to keep his parched lips wide apart,
    as a man who suffers thirst from raging fever
    has one lip curling up, the other sagging.   57

"O you who bear no punishment at all
    (I can't think why) within this world of sorrow,"
    he said to us, "pause here and look upon   60

the misery of one Master Adamo:
    in life I had all that I could desire,
    and now, alas, I crave a drop of water.   63

37–41. The other self-falsifier darting about the *bolgia* with Gianni Schicchi is Myrrha, who, overpowered by an incestuous desire for her father, King Cinyras of Cyprus, went incognito to his bed where they made love.

The little streams that flow from the green hills
   of Casentino, descending to the Arno,
     keeping their banks so cool and soft with moisture, 66

forever flow before me, haunting me;
   and the image of them leaves me far more parched
     than the sickness that has dried my shriveled face. 69

Relentless Justice, tantalizing me,
   exploits the countryside that knew my sin,
     to draw from me ever new sighs of pain: 72

I still can see Romena, where I learned
   to falsify the coin stamped with the Baptist,
     for which I paid with my burned body there; 75

but if I could see down here the wretched souls
   of Guido or Alexander or their brother,
     I would not exchange the sight for Branda's fountain. 78

One is here already, if those maniacs
   running around this place have told the truth,
     but what good is it, with my useless legs? 81

If only I were lighter, just enough
   to move one inch in every hundred years,
     I would have started on my way by now 84

to find him somewhere in this gruesome lot,
   although this ditch winds round eleven miles
     and is at least a half a mile across. 87

It's their fault I am here with this choice family:
   they encouraged me to turn out florins
     whose gold contained three carats' worth of alloy." 90

And I to him: "Who are those two poor souls
   lying to the right, close to your body's boundary,
     steaming like wet hands in wintertime?" 93

---

90. The florin was supposed to contain twenty-four-carat gold; those of Master
Adamo had twenty-one carats.

"When I poured into this ditch, I found them here,"
  he answered, "and they haven't budged since then,
  and I doubt they'll move through all eternity.   96

One is the false accuser of young Joseph;
  the other is false Sinon, the Greek in Troy:
  it's their burning fever makes them smell so bad."   99

And one of them, perhaps somewhat offended
  at the kind of introduction he received,
  with his fist struck out at the distended belly,   102

which responded like a drum reverberating;
  and Master Adam struck him in the face
  with an arm as strong as the fist he had received,   105

and he said to him: "Although I am not free
  to move around, with swollen legs like these,
  I have a ready arm for such occasions."   108

"*But* it was *not* as free and ready, was it,"
  the other answered, "when you went to the stake?
  Of course, when you were coining, it was readier!"   111

And he with the dropsy: "*Now* you tell the truth,
  but you were not as full of truth that time
  when you were asked to tell the truth at Troy!"   114

"My words were false—so were the coins you made,"
  said Sinon, "and *I* am here for one false act
  but *you* for more than any fiend in hell!"   117

"The horse, recall the horse, you falsifier,"
  the bloated paunch was quick to answer back,
  "may it burn your guts that all the world remembers!"   120

"May your guts burn with thirst that cracks your tongue,"
  the Greek said, "may they burn with rotting humors
  that swell your hedge of a paunch to block your eyes!"   123

97. Potiphar's wife falsely accused Joseph, son of Jacob and Rachel, of trying to
seduce her, while in reality it was she who made improper amorous advances.

98. Sinon was left behind by his fellow Greek soldiers in accordance with the master
plan for the capture of Troy. Taken prisoner by the Trojans, and misrepresenting his
position with the Greeks, he persuaded them to bring the wooden horse into the city.

And then the money-man: "So there you go,
   your evil mouth pours out its filth as usual;
   for if *I* thirst, and humors swell me up,   126

you burn more, and your head is fit to split,
   and it wouldn't take much coaxing to convince you
   to lap the mirror of Narcissus dry!"   129

I was listening, all absorbed in this debate,
   when the master said to me: "Keep right on looking,
   a little more, and I shall lose my patience."   132

I heard the note of anger in his voice
   and turned to him; I was so full of shame
   that it still haunts my memory today.   135

Like one asleep who dreams himself in trouble
   and in his dream he wishes he were dreaming,
   longing for that which is, as if it were not,   138

just so I found myself: unable to speak,
   longing to beg for pardon and already
   begging for pardon, not knowing that I did.   141

"Less shame than yours would wash away a fault
   greater than yours has been," my master said,
   "and so forget about it, do not be sad.   144

If ever again you should meet up with men
   engaging in this kind of futile wrangling,
   remember I am always at your side;   147

to have a taste for talk like this is vulgar!"

---

129. The "mirror" is water. According to the myth, Narcissus, enamored with his
own reflection in a pond, continued to gaze at it until he died.

CANTO XXXI

THROUGH THE MURKY AIR they move, up across the bank that separates
the Malebolge *from the pit of Hell, the Ninth (and last) Circle of the*
Inferno. *From a distance is heard the blast of a mighty horn, which*
turns out to have been that of the giant Nimrod. He and other giants,
including Ephialtes, are fixed eternally in the pit of Hell; all are chained
except Antaeus, who, at Virgil's request, lifts the two poets in his mon-
strous hand and deposits them below him, on the lake of ice known as
Cocytus.

The very tongue that first spoke—stinging me,
    making the blood rush up to both my cheeks—
    then gave the remedy to ease the pain,   3

just as, so I have heard, Achilles' lance,
    belonging to his father, was the source
    of pain, and then of balm, to him it struck.   6

Turning our backs on that trench of misery
    gaining the bank again that walls it in,
    we cut across, walking in dead silence.   9

Here it was less than night and less than day,
    so that my eyes could not see far ahead;
    but then I heard the blast of some high horn   12

which would have made a thunder-clap sound dim;
    it drew my eyes directly to one place,
    as they retraced the sound's path to its source.   15

After the tragic rout when Charlemagne
    lost all his faithful, holy paladins,
    the sound of Roland's horn was not as ominous.   18

16–18. In the medieval French epic *La Chanson de Roland*, the title character, one
of Charlemagne's "holy paladins" (17), was assigned to the rear guard on the return
from an expedition in Spain. At Roncesvalles in the Pyrenees the Saracens attacked,
and Roland, proud to the point of foolishness, refused to sound his horn until total
extermination was imminent.

Keeping my eyes still turned that way, I soon
    made out what seemed to be high, clustered towers.
    "Master," I said, "what city lies ahead?"   21

"Because you try to penetrate the shadows,"
    he said to me, "from much too far away,
    you confuse the truth with your imagination.   24

You will see clearly when you reach that place
    how much the eyes may be deceived by distance,
    and so, just push ahead a little more."   27

Then lovingly he took me by the hand
    and said: "But now, before we go on farther,
    to prepare you for the truth that could seem strange, 30

I'll tell you these aren't towers, they are giants;
    they're standing in the well around the bank—
    all of them hidden from their navels down."   33

As, when the fog begins to thin and clear,
    the sight can slowly make out more and more
    what is hidden in the mist that clogs the air,   36

so, as I pierced the thick and murky air,
    approaching slowly, closer to the well,
    confusion cleared and my fear took on more shape.   39

For just as Montereggion is crowned with towers
    soaring high above its curving ramparts,
    so, on the bank that runs around the well,   42

towering with only half their bodies out,
    stood the terrible giants, forever threatened
    by Jupiter in the heavens when he thunders.   45

And now I could make out one of the faces,
    the shoulders, the chest and a good part of the belly
    and, down along the sides, the two great arms.   48

40–41. In 1213 the Sienese constructed Montereggioni, a fortress on the crest of a
hill eight miles from their city. The specific allusion here is to the fourteen high towers
that stood on its perimeter like giant sentries.

Nature, when she cast away the mold
    for shaping beasts like these, without a doubt
    did well, depriving Mars of more such agents.   51

And if she never did repent of whales
    and elephants, we must consider her,
    on sober thought, all the more just and wary: 54

for when the faculty of intellect
    is joined with brute force and with evil will,
    no man can win against such an alliance.   57

His face, it seemed to me, was about as long
    and just as wide as St. Peter's cone in Rome,
    and all his body's bones were in proportion,   60

so that the bank which served to cover him
    from his waist down showed so much height above
    that three tall Frisians on each other's shoulders   63

could never boast of stretching to his hair,
    for downward from the place men clasp their cloaks
    I saw a generous thirty hand-spans of him.   66

"Raphel may amech zabi almi!"
    He played these sputtering notes with prideful lips
    for which no sweeter psalm was suitable.   69

My guide called up to him: "Blathering idiot,
    stick to your horn and take it out on that
    when you feel a fit of anger coming on;   72

search round your neck and you will find the strap
    it's tied to, you poor muddle-headed soul,
    and there's the horn so pretty on your chest."   75

59. This bronze pine cone measuring over seven feet in height, which now stands in
an inner courtyard of the Vatican, was, at Dante's time, in the courtyard of St. Peter's.

63. The inhabitants of Friesland, a northern province of the Netherlands, were re-
nowned for their height.

67. These words are gibberish—the perfect representation of Nimrod's role in the
confusion of languages caused by his construction of the Tower of Babel (the "in-
famous device," 77).

And then he turned to me: "His words accuse him.
　　He is Nimrod, through whose infamous device
　　the world no longer speaks a common language.   78

But let's leave him alone and not waste breath,
　　for he can no more understand our words
　　than anyone can understand his language."   81

We had to walk still farther than before,
　　continuing to the left, a full bow's-shot,
　　to find another giant, huger and more fierce.   84

What engineer it took to bind this brute
　　I cannot say, but there he was, one arm
　　pinned to his back, the other locked in front,   87

with a giant chain winding around him tight,
　　which, starting from his neck, made five great coils—
　　and that was counting only to his waist.   90

"This beast of pride decided he would try
　　to pit his strength against almighty Jove,"
　　my leader said, "and he has won this prize.   93

He's Ephialtes, who made his great attempt
　　when the giants arose to fill the Gods with panic;
　　the arms he lifted then, he moves no more."   96

And I to him: "If it were possible,
　　I would really like to have the chance to see
　　the fantastic figure of Briareus."   99

His answer was: "Not far from here you'll see
　　Antaeus, who can speak and is not chained;
　　he will set us down in the very pit of sin.   102

The one you want to see is farther off;
　　he too is bound and looks just like this one,
　　except for his expression, which is fiercer."   105

78. Before the construction of the Tower of Babel all men spoke a common language.

99. The Titan Briareus, son of Uranus and Gaea (Earth), joined the rebellion against the Olympian deities.

No earthquake of the most outrageous force
    ever shook a tower with such violence
    as, suddenly, Ephialtes shook himself.   108

I never feared to die as much as then,
    and my fear might have been enough to kill me,
    if I had not already seen those chains.   111

We left him and continued moving on
    and came to where Antaeus stood, extending
    from the well a good five ells up to his head.   114

"O you who in the celebrated valley
    (that saw Scipio become the heir of glory,
    when Hannibal with all his men retreated)   117

once captured a thousand lions as your quarry
    (and with whose aid, had you chosen to take part
    in the great war with your brothers, the sons of earth   120

would, as many still think, have been the victors),
    do not disdain this modest wish: take us,
    and put us down where ice locks in Cocytus.   123

Don't make us go to Tityus or Typhon;
    this man can give you what all long for here,
    and so bend down, and do not scowl at us.   126

He still can spread your legend in the world,
    for he yet lives, and long life lies before him,
    unless Grace summons him before his time."   129

Thus spoke my master, and the giant in haste
    stretched out the hands whose formidable grip
    great Hercules once felt, and took my guide.   132

And Virgil, when he felt the grasping hands,
    called out: "Now come and I'll take hold of you."
    Clasped together, we made a single burden.   135

124. Tityus and Typhon were members of the race of Titans.

As the Garisenda looks from underneath
    its leaning side, at the moment when a cloud
    comes drifting over against the tower's slant,   138

just so the bending giant Antaeus seemed
    as I looked up, expecting him to topple.
    I wished then I had gone another way.   141

But he, most carefully, handed us down
    to the pit that swallows Lucifer with Judas.
    And then, the leaning giant immediately   144

drew himself up as tall as a ship's mast.

CANTO XXXII

*THEY DESCEND FARTHER down into the darkness of the immense plain
of ice in which shades of Traitors are frozen. In the outer region of the
ice-lake, Caïna, are those who betrayed their kin in murder; among
them, locked in a frozen embrace, are Napoleone and Alessandro of
Mangona, and others are Mordred, Focaccia, Sassol Mascheroni, and
Camicion de'pazzi. Then the two travelers enter the area of ice called
Antenora, and suddenly the Pilgrim kicks one of the faces sticking out
of the ice. He tries to force the sinner to reveal his name by pulling out
his hair, and when another shade identifies him as Bocca degli Abati,
the Pilgrim's fury mounts still higher. Bocca, himself furious, names
several other sinners in Antenora, including Buoso da Durea, Tesauro
dei Beccheria, Gianni de' Soldanier, Ganelon, and Tibbald. Going far-
ther on, the Pilgrim sees two heads frozen in one hole, the mouth of
one gnawing at the brain of the other.*

136–138. Of the two leaning towers in Bologna, the Garisenda, built ca. 1110, is
the shorter. The passage of a cloud "against the tower's slant" (138) would make
the tower appear to be falling.

If I had words grating and crude enough
   that really could describe this horrid hole
   supporting the converging weight of Hell,   3

I could squeeze out the juice of my memories
   to the last drop. But I don't have these words,
   and so I am reluctant to begin.   6

To talk about the bottom of the universe
   the way it truly is, is no child's play,
   no task for tongues that gurgle baby-talk.   9

But may those heavenly ladies aid my verse
   who aided Amphion to wall-in Thebes,
   that my words may tell exactly what I saw.   12

O misbegotten rabble of all rabble,
   who crowd this realm, hard even to describe,
   it were better you had lived as sheep or goats!   15

When we reached a point of darkness in the well
   below the giant's feet, farther down the slope,
   and I was gazing still at the high wall,   18

I heard somebody say: "Watch where you step!
   Be careful that you do not kick the heads
   of this brotherhood of miserable souls."   21

At that I turned around and saw before me
   a lake of ice stretching beneath my feet,
   more like a sheet of glass than frozen water.   24

In the depths of Austria's wintertime, the Danube
   never in all its course showed ice so thick,
   nor did the Don beneath its frigid sky,   27

as this crust here; for if Mount Tambernic
   or Pietrapana would crash down upon it,
   not even at its edges would a crack creak.   30

The way the frogs (in the season when the harvest
   will often haunt the dreams of the peasant girl)
   sit croaking with their muzzles out of water,   33

so these frigid, livid shades were stuck in ice
   up to where a person's shame appears;
     their teeth clicked notes like storks' beaks snapping shut.   36

And each one kept his face bowed toward the ice:
   the mouth bore testimony to the cold,
     the eyes, to sadness welling in the heart.   39

I gazed around awhile and then looked down,
   and by my feet I saw two figures clasped
     so tight that one's hair could have been the other's.   42

"Tell me, you two, pressing your chests together,"
   I asked them, "who are you?" Both stretched their necks
     and when they had their faces raised toward me,   45

their eyes, which had before been only glazed,
   dripped tears down to their lips, and the cold froze
     the tears between them, locking the pair more tightly.   48

Wood to wood with iron was never clamped
   so firm! And the two of them like billy-goats
     were butting at each other, mad with anger.   51

Another one with both ears frozen off,
   and head still bowed over his icy mirror,
     cried out: "What makes you look at us so hard?   54

If you're interested to know who these two are:
   the valley where Bisenzio's waters flow
     belonged to them and to their father, Albert;   57

the same womb bore them both, and if you scour
   all of Caïna, you will not turn up one
     who's more deserving of this frozen aspic—   60

55–58. The two brothers were Napoleone and Alessandro, sons of Count Alberto of
Mangona, who owned part of the valley of the Bisenzio near Florence. The two
quarreled often and eventually killed each other in a fight concerning their in-
heritance.

59. The icy ring of Cocytus is named Caïna after Cain, who slew his brother Abel.
Thus, in the first division of this, the Ninth Circle, are punished those treacherous
shades who murderously violated family bonds.

not him who had his breast and shadow pierced
  with one thrust of the lance from Arthur's hand;
  not Focaccia; not even this one here, 63

whose head gets in my way and blocks my view,
  known in the world as Sassol Mascheroni,
  and if you're Tuscan you must know who he was. 66

To save me from your asking for more news:
  I was Camicion de' Pazzi, and I await
  Carlin, whose guilt will make my own seem less." 69

Farther on I saw a thousand doglike faces,
  purple from the cold. That's why I shudder,
  and always will, when I see a frozen pond. 72

While we were getting closer to the center
  of the universe, where all weights must converge,
  and I was shivering in the eternal chill— 75

by fate or chance or willfully perhaps,
  I do not know—but stepping among the heads,
  my foot kicked hard against one of those faces. 78

Weeping, he screamed: "Why are you kicking me?
  You have not come to take revenge on me
  for Montaperti, have you? Why bother me?" 81

61–62. Mordred, the wicked nephew of King Arthur, tried to kill the king and take his kingdom. But Arthur pierced him with such a mighty blow that when the lance was pulled from the dying traitor a ray of sunlight traversed his body and interrupted Mordred's shadow. The story is told in the Old French romance *Lancelot du Lac*, the book that Francesca claims led her astray with Paolo in Canto V, 127.

63. Focaccia was one of the Cancellieri family of Pistoia and a member of the White party. His treacherous murder of his cousin, Detto de' Cancellieri (a Black), was possibly the act that led to the Florentine intervention in Pistoian affairs.

65. The early commentators say that Sassol Mascheroni was a member of the Toschi family in Florence who murdered his nephew in order to gain his inheritance.

68–69. Nothing is known of Camicion de' Pazzi except that he murdered one Umbertino, a relative. Another of Camicion's kin, Carlino de' Pazzi (69) from Valdarno, was still alive when the Pilgrim's conversation with Camicion was taking place. But Camicion already knew that Carlino, in July 1302, would accept a bribe to surrender the castle of Piantravigne to the Blacks of Florence.

And I: "My master, please wait here for me,
   let me clear up a doubt concerning this one,
   then I shall be as rapid as you wish."   84

My leader stopped, and to that wretch, who still
   had not let up in his barrage of curses,
   I said: "Who are you, insulting other people?"   87

"And you, who are *you* who march through Antenora
   kicking other people in their faces?
   No living man could kick as hard!" he answered.   90

"I am a living man," was my reply,
   "and it might serve you well, if you seek fame,
   for me to put your name down in my notes."   93

And he said: "That's the last thing I would want!
   That's not the way to flatter in these lowlands!
   Stop pestering me like this—get out of here!"   96

At that I grabbed him by his hair in back
   and said: "You'd better tell me who you are
   or else I'll not leave one hair on your head."   99

And he to me: "Go on and strip me bald
   and pound and stamp my head a thousand times,
   you'll never hear my name or see my face."   102

I had my fingers twisted in his hair
   and already I'd pulled out more than one fistful,
   while he yelped like a cur with eyes shut tight,   105

when someone else yelled: "What's the matter, Bocca?
   It's bad enough to hear your shivering teeth;
   now you bark! What the devil's wrong with you?"   108

---

88. Dante and Virgil have passed into the second division of Cocytus, named Antenora after the Trojan warrior who, according to one legend, betrayed his city to the Greeks. In this round are tormented those who committed acts of treachery against country, city, or political party.

106. Bocca degli Abati was a Ghibelline who appeared to side with the Florentine Guelphs. However, while fighting on the side of the Guelphs at the battle of Montaperti in 1260, he is said to have cut off the hand of the standard bearer. The disappearance of the standard led to panic among the Florentine Guelphs, who were then decisively defeated by the Sienese Ghibellines and their German allies under Manfred.

"There's no need now for you to speak," I said,
     "you vicious traitor! Now I know your name
     and I'll bring back the shameful truth about you."   111

"Go away!" he answered. "Tell them what you want;
     but if you do get out of here, be sure
     you also tell about that blabbermouth,   114

who's paying here what the French silver cost him:
     'I saw,' you can tell the world, 'the one from Duera
     stuck in with all the sinners keeping cool.'   117

And if you should be asked: 'Who else was there?'
     Right by your side is the one from Beccheria
     whose head was chopped off by the Florentines.   120

As for Gianni Soldanier, I think you'll find him
     farther along with Ganelon and Tibbald,
     who opened up Faenza while it slept."   123

Soon after leaving him I saw two souls
     frozen together in a single hole,
     so that one head used the other for a cap.   126

As a man with hungry teeth tears into bread,
     the soul with capping head had sunk his teeth
     into the other's neck, just beneath the skull.   129

116–117. The "one from Duera" is Buoso da Duera, a chief of the Ghibelline party
of Cremona, who was a well-known traitor.

119–120. The "one from Beccheria" is Tesauro dei Beccheria of Pavia, an abbot of
Vallombrosa and a papal legate to Alexander IV in Tuscany. He was tortured and
finally beheaded in 1258 by the Guelphs of Florence for carrying on secret intercourse
with Ghibellines who had been exiled.

121. Gianni de' Soldanier was an important Ghibelline of Florence who, when the
Florentines (mostly Guelph) began to chafe under Ghibelline rule, deserted his party
and went over to the Guelphs.

122–123. Ganelon was the treacherous knight who betrayed Roland (and the rear
guard of Charlemagne's army) to the Saracens.
     Tibbald was one of the Zambrasi family of Faenza. In order to avenge himself
on the Ghibelline Lambertazzi family (who had been exiled from Bologna in 1274
and had taken refuge in Faenza) he opened his city to their Bolognese Guelph enemies
on the morning of November 13, 1280.

Tydeus in his fury did not gnaw
   the head of Menalippus with more relish
   than this one chewed that head of meat and bones.   132

"O you who show with every bestial bite
   your hatred for the head you are devouring,"
   I said, "tell me your reason, and I promise,   135

if you are justified in your revenge,
   once I know who you are and this one's sin,
   I'll repay your confidence in the world above   138

unless my tongue dry up before I die."

CANTO XXXIII

COUNT UGOLINO *is the shade gnawing at the brain of his onetime associate Archbishop Ruggieri, and Ugolino interrupts his gruesome meal long enough to tell the story of his imprisonment and cruel death, which his innocent offspring shared with him. Moving farther into the area of Cocytus known as Tolomea, where those who betrayed their guests and associates are condemned, the Pilgrim sees sinners with their faces raised high above the ice, whose tears freeze and lock their eyes. One of the shades agrees to identify himself on condition that the ice be removed from his eyes. The Pilgrim agrees, and learns that this sinner is Friar Alberigo and that his soul is dead and damned even though his body is still alive on earth, inhabited by a devil. Alberigo also names a fellow sinner with him in the ice, Branca d'Oria, whose body is still functioning up on earth. But the Pilgrim does not honor his promise to break the ice from Alberigo's eyes.*

Lifting his mouth from his horrendous meal,
   this sinner first wiped off his messy lips
   in the hair remaining on the chewed-up skull,   3

130–131. Tydeus, one of the Seven against Thebes, in combat slew Menalippus—who, however, managed to wound him fatally. Tydeus called for his enemy's head, which, when brought to him by Amphiaraus, he proceeded to gnaw in rage.

then spoke: "You want me to renew a grief
   so desperate that just the thought of it,
   much less the telling, grips my heart with pain;   6

but if my words can be the seed to bear
   the fruit of infamy for this betrayer,
   who feeds my hunger, then I shall speak—in tears.   9

I do not know your name, nor do I know
   how you have come down here, but Florentine
   you surely seem to be, to hear you speak.   12

First you should know I was Count Ugolino
   and my neighbor here, Ruggieri the Archbishop;
   now I'll tell you why I'm so unneighborly.   15

That I, trusting in him, was put in prison
   through his evil machinations, where I died,
   this much I surely do not have to tell you.   18

What you could not have known, however, is
   the inhuman circumstances of my death.
   Now listen, then decide if he has wronged me!   21

Through a narrow slit of window high in that mew
   (which is called the tower of hunger, after me,
   and I'll not be the last to know that place)   24

I had watched moon after moon after moon go by,
   when finally I dreamed the evil dream
   which ripped away the veil that hid my future.   27

13–14. Ugolino della Gherardesca, the Count of Donoratico, belonged to a noble Tuscan family whose political affiliations were Ghibelline. In 1275 he conspired with his son-in-law, Giovanni Visconti, to raise the Guelphs to power in Pisa. Although exiled for this subversive activity, Ugolino (Nino) Visconti took over the Guelph government of the city. Three years later (1288) he plotted with Archbishop Ruggieri degli Ubaldini to rid Pisa of the Visconti. Ruggieri, however, had other plans, and with the aid of the Ghibellines, he seized control of the city and imprisoned Ugolino, together with his sons and grandsons, in the "tower of hunger" (23). The two were evidently just at the boundary between Antenora and Ptolomea, for Ugolino is being punished for betraying his country (in Antenora), and Ruggieri for betraying his associate, Ugolino (in Ptolomea).

I dreamed of this one here as lord and huntsman,
   pursuing the wolf and the wolf cubs up the mountain
   (which blocks the sight of Lucca from the Pisans)   30

with skinny bitches, well trained and obedient;
   he had out front as leaders of the pack
   Gualandi with Sismondi and Lanfranchi.   33

A short run, and the father with his sons
   seemed to grow tired, and then I thought I saw
   long fangs sunk deep into their sides, ripped open.   36

When I awoke before the light of dawn,
   I heard my children sobbing in their sleep
   (you see they, too, were there), asking for bread.   39

If the thought of what my heart was telling me
   does not fill you with grief, how cruel you are!
   If you are not weeping now—do you ever weep?   42

And then they awoke. It was around the time
   they usually brought our food to us. But now
   each one of us was full of dread from dreaming;   45

then from below I heard them driving nails
   into the dreadful tower's door; with that,
   I stared in silence at my flesh and blood.   48

I did not weep, I turned to stone inside;
   they wept, and my little Anselmuccio spoke:
   'What is it, father? Why do you look that way?'   51

For them I held my tears back, saying nothing,
   all of that day, and then all of that night,
   until another sun shone on the world.   54

28–36. Ugolino's dream was indeed prophetic. The "lord and huntsman" (28) is Archbishop Ruggieri, who with the leading Ghibelline families of Pisa ("Gualandi . . . Sismondi and Lanfranchi," 33) and the populace ("skinny bitches," 31), runs down Ugolino and his offspring ("the wolf and the wolf cubs," 29) and finally kills them.

50. Anselmuccio was the younger of Ugolino's grandsons, who, according to official documents, must have been fifteen at the time.

A meager ray of sunlight found its way
   to the misery of our cell, and I could see
   myself reflected four times in their faces;   57

I bit my hands in anguish. And my children,
   who thought that hunger made me bite my hands,
   were quick to draw up closer to me, saying: 60

'O father, you would make us suffer less,
   if you would feed on us: you were the one
   who gave us this sad flesh; you take it from us!'   63

I calmed myself to make them less unhappy.
   That day we sat in silence, and the next day.
   O pitiless earth! You should have swallowed us!   66

The fourth day came, and it was on that day
   my Gaddo fell prostrate before my feet,
   crying: 'Why don't you help me? Why, my father?'   69

There he died. Just as you see me here,
   I saw the other three fall one by one,
   as the fifth day and the sixth day passed. And I,   72

by then gone blind, groped over their dead bodies.
   Though they were dead, two days I called their names.
   Then hunger proved more powerful than grief."   75

He spoke these words; then, glaring down in rage,
   attacked again the wretched skull with his teeth
   sharp as a dog's, and as fit for grinding bones.   78

O Pisa, blot of shame upon the people
   of that fair land where the sound of "sì" is heard!
   Since your neighbors hesitate to punish you,   81

let Capraia and Gorgona move and join,
   damming up the River Arno at its mouth,
   and let every Pisan perish in its flood!   84

68. Gaddo was one of Ugolino's sons.

80. The "fair land" is Italy. It was customary in Dante's time to indicate a language area by the word signifying "yes."

For if Count Ugolino was accused
   of turning traitor, trading-in your castles,
   you had no right to make his children suffer.   87

Their newborn years (O newborn Thebes!) made them
   all innocents: Brigata, Uguiccione,
   and the other two soft names my canto sings.   90

We moved ahead to where the frozen water
   wraps in harsh wrinkles another sinful race,
   with faces not turned down but looking up.   93

Here, the weeping puts an end to weeping,
   and the grief that finds no outlet from the eyes
   turns inward to intensify the anguish: 96

for the tears they first wept knotted in a cluster
   and like a visor made for them in crystal,
   filled all the hollow part around their eyes.   99

Although the bitter coldness of the dark
   had driven all sensation from my face,
   as though it were not tender skin but callous,   102

I thought I felt the air begin to blow,
   and I: "What causes such a wind, my master?
   I thought no heat could reach into these depths."   105

And he to me: "Before long you will be
   where your own eyes can answer for themselves,
   when they will see what keeps this wind in motion."   108

And one of the wretches with the frozen crust
   screamed out at us: "O wicked souls, so wicked
   that you have been assigned the ultimate post,   111

89–90. Brigata was Ugolino's second grandson; Uguiccione was his fifth son.

91–93. Virgil and the Pilgrim have now entered the third division of Cocytus, called Tolomea (124) after Ptolemy, the captain of Jericho, who had Simon, his father-in-law, and two of his sons killed while dining (see 1 Macabees 16:11–17). Or possibly this zone of Cocytus is named after Ptolemy XII, the Egyptian king who, having welcomed Pompey to his realm, slew him. In Tolomea are punished those who have betrayed their guests.

break off these hard veils covering my eyes
    and give relief from the pain that swells my heart—
    at least until the new tears freeze again."   114

I answered him: "If this is what you want,
    tell me your name; and if I do not help you,
    may I be forced to drop beneath this ice!"   117

He answered then: "I am Friar Alberigo,
    I am he who offered fruit from the evil orchard:
    here dates are served me for the figs I gave."   120

"Oh, then!" I said. "Are you already dead?"
    And he to me: "Just how my body is
    in the world above, I have no way of knowing.   123

This zone of Tolomea is very special,
    for it often happens that a soul falls here
    before the time that Atropos should send it.   126

And that you may more willingly scrape off
    my cluster of glass tears, let me tell you:
    whenever a soul betrays the way I did,   129

a demon takes possession of the body,
    controlling its maneuvers from then on,
    for all the years it has to live up there,   132

while the soul falls straight into this cistern here;
    and the shade in winter quarters just behind me
    may well have left his body up on earth.   135

115–117. The Pilgrim, fully aware that his journey will indeed take him below the ice, carefully phrases his treacherous promise to the treacherous shade, and successfully deceives him (149–150). The Pilgrim betrays a sinner in this circle, as the latter does one of his companions there with him in the ice (by naming him).

118–120. Friar Alberigo is one of the Jovial Friars (see Canto XXIII, 103–108).

124–135. According to Church doctrine, under certain circumstances a living person may, through acts of treachery, lose possession of his soul before he dies ("before the time that Atropos [the Fate who cuts man's thread of life] should send it," 126). Then, on earth, a devil inhabits the body until its natural death.

But you should know, if you've just come from there:
  he is Ser Branca D'Oria; and many years
  have passed since he first joined us here, icebound."   138

"I think you're telling me a lie," I said,
  "for Branca D'Oria is not dead at all;
  he eats and drinks, he sleeps and wears out clothes."   141

"The ditch the Malebranche watch above,"
  he said, "the ditch of clinging, boiling pitch,
  had not yet caught the soul of Michel Zanche,   144

when Branca left a devil in his body
  to take his place, and so did his close kinsman,
  his accomplice in this act of treachery.   147

But now, at last, give me the hand you promised.
  Open my eyes." I did not open them.
  To be mean to him was a generous reward.   150

O all you Genovese, you men estranged
  from every good, at home with every vice,
  why can't the world be wiped clean of your race?   153

For in company with Romagna's rankest soul
  I found one of your men, whose deeds were such
  that his soul bathes already in Cocytus   156

but his body seems alive and walks among you.

137–147. Ser Branca D'Oria, a prominent resident of Genoa, murdered his father-in-law, Michel Zanche (see Canto XXII, 88), after having invited him to dine with him.

154. The soul is Friar Alberigo, and Faenza, his hometown, was in the region of Romagna (now part of Emilia-Romagna).

155. The man is Branca D'Oria.

CANTO XXXIV

FAR ACROSS the frozen ice can be seen the gigantic figure of Lucifer, who appears from this distance like a windmill seen through fog; and as the two travelers walk on toward that terrifying sight, they see the shades of sinners totally buried in the frozen water. At the center of the earth Lucifer stands frozen from the chest downward, and his horrible ugliness (he has three faces) is made more fearful by the fact that in each of his three mouths he chews on one of the three worst sinners of all mankind, the worst of those who betrayed their benefactors: Judas Iscariot, Brutus, and Cassius. Virgil, with the Pilgrim on his back, begins the descent down the shaggy body of Lucifer. They climb down through a crack in the ice, and when they reach the Evil One's thighs, Virgil turns and begins to struggle upward (because they have passed the center of the earth), still holding on to the hairy body of Lucifer, until they reach a cavern, where they stop for a short rest. Then a winding path brings them eventually to the earth's surface, where they see the stars.

"Vexilla regis prodeunt Inferni,"
　　my master said, "closer to us, so now
　　look ahead and see if you can make him out."   3

A far-off windmill turning its huge sails
　　when a thick fog begins to settle in,
　　or when the light of day begins to fade,   6

that is what I thought I saw appearing.
　　And the gusts of wind it stirred made me shrink back
　　behind my guide, my only means of cover.   9

1. The opening lines of the hymn "*Vexilla regis prodeunt*"—"The banners of the King advance"—(written by Venantius Fortunatus, sixth-century bishop of Poitiers; this hymn belongs to the liturgy of the Church) are here parodied by the addition of the word *Inferni*, "of Hell," to the word *regis*, "of the King." Sung on Good Friday, the hymn anticipates the unveiling of the Cross; Dante, who began his journey on the evening of Good Friday, is prepared by Virgil's words for the sight of Lucifer, who will appear like a "windmill" in a "thick fog." The banners referred to are Lucifer's wings.

Down here, I stood on souls fixed under ice
    (I tremble as I put this into verse);
    to me they looked like straws worked into glass.   12

Some lying flat, some perpendicular,
    either with their heads up or their feet,
    and some bent head to foot, shaped like a bow.   15

When we had moved far enough along the way
    that my master thought the time had come to show me
    the creature who was once so beautiful,   18

he stepped aside, and stopping me, announced:
    "This is he, this is Dis; this is the place
    that calls for all the courage you have in you."   21

How chilled and nerveless, Reader, I felt then;
    do not ask me—I cannot write about it—
    there are no words to tell you how I felt.   24

I did not die—I was not living either!
    Try to imagine, if you can imagine,
    me there, deprived of life and death at once.   27

The king of the vast kingdom of all grief
    stuck out with half his chest above the ice;
    my height is closer to the height of giants   30

than theirs is to the length of his great arms;
    consider now how large all of him was:
    this body in proportion to his arms.   33

If once he was as fair as now he's foul
    and dared to raise his brows against his Maker,
    it is fitting that all grief should spring from him.   36

Oh, how amazed I was when I looked up
    and saw a head—one head wearing three faces!
    One was in front (and that was a bright red),   39

38–45. Dante presents Lucifer's head as a perverted parallel of the Trinity. The colors
of the three single faces (red, yellow, black) are probably antithetically analogous to
the qualities attributed to the Trinity (see Canto III, 5–6). Therefore, Highest Wisdom
would be opposed by ignorance (black), Divine Omnipotence by impotence (yellow),
Primal Love by hatred or envy (red).

the other two attached themselves to this one
    just above the middle of each shoulder,
    and at the crown all three were joined in one: 42

The right face was a blend of white and yellow,
    the left the color of those people's skin
    who live along the river Nile's descent.   45

Beneath each face two mighty wings stretched out,
    the size you might expect of this huge bird
    (I never saw a ship with larger sails):   48

not feathered wings but rather like the ones
    a bat would have. He flapped them constantly,
    keeping three winds continuously in motion   51

to lock Cocytus eternally in ice.
    He wept from his six eyes, and down three chins
    were dripping tears all mixed with bloody slaver.   54

In each of his three mouths he crunched a sinner,
    with teeth like those that rake the hemp and flax,
    keeping three sinners constantly in pain;   57

the one in front—the biting he endured
    was nothing like the clawing that he took:
    sometimes his back was raked clean of its skin.   60

"That soul up there who suffers most of all,"
    my guide explained, "is Judas Iscariot:
    the one with head inside and legs out kicking.   63

As for the other two whose heads stick out,
    the one who hangs from that black face is Brutus—
    see how he squirms in silent desperation;   66

61–63. Having betrayed Christ for thirty pieces of silver, Judas endures greater punishment than the other two souls.

65. Marcus Brutus, who was deceitfully persuaded by Cassius (67) to join the conspiracy, aided in the assassination of Julius Caesar. It is fitting that in his final vision of the Inferno the Pilgrim should see those shades who committed treacherous acts against Divine and worldly authorities: the Church and the Roman Empire. This provides the culmination, at least in this canticle, of these basic themes: Church and Empire.

the other one is Cassius, he still looks sturdy.
  But soon it will be night. Now is the time
  to leave this place, for we have seen it all." 69

I held on to his neck, as he told me to,
  while he watched and waited for the time and place,
  and when the wings were stretched out just enough, 72

he grabbed on to the shaggy sides of Satan;
  then downward, tuft by tuft, he made his way
  between the tangled hair and frozen crust. 75

When we had reached the point exactly where
  the thigh begins, right at the haunch's curve,
  my guide, with strain and force of every muscle, 78

turned his head toward the shaggy shanks of Dis
  and grabbed the hair as if about to climb—
  I thought that we were heading back to Hell. 81

"Hold tight, there is no other way," he said,
  panting, exhausted, "only by these stairs
  can we leave behind the evil we have seen." 84

When he had got me through the rocky crevice,
  he raised me to its edge and set me down,
  then carefully he climbed and joined me there. 87

I raised my eyes, expecting I would see
  the half of Lucifer I saw before.
  Instead I saw his two legs stretching upward. 90

If at that sight I found myself confused,
  so will those simple-minded folk who still
  don't see what point it was I must have passed. 93

---

67. Caius Cassius Longinus was another member of the conspiracy against Caesar.
By describing Cassius as "still look[ing] sturdy," Dante shows he has evidently con-
fused him with Lucius Cassius, whom Cicero calls *adeps*, "corpulent."

"Get up," my master said, "get to your feet,
    the way is long, the road a rough climb up,
    already the sun approaches middle tierce!"   96

It was no palace promenade we came to,
    but rather like some dungeon Nature built:
    it was paved with broken stone and poorly lit.   99

"Before we start to struggle out of here,
    O master," I said when I was on my feet,
    "I wish you would explain some things to me.   102

Where is the ice? And how can he be lodged
    upside-down? And how, in so little time,
    could the sun go all the way from night to day?"   105

"You think you're still on the center's other side,"
    he said, "where I first grabbed the hairy worm
    of rottenness that pierces the earth's core;   108

and you *were* there as long as I moved downward
    but, when I turned myself, you passed the point
    to which all weight from every part is drawn.   111

Now you are standing beneath the hemisphere
    which is opposite the side covered by land,
    where at the central point was sacrificed   114

the Man whose birth and life were free of sin.
    You have both feet upon a little sphere
    whose other side Judecca occupies;   117

when it is morning here, there it is evening.
    And he whose hairs were stairs for our descent
    has not changed his position since his fall.   120

When he fell from the heavens on this side,
    all of the land that once was spread out here,
    alarmed by his plunge, took cover beneath the sea   123

96. The time is approximately halfway between the canonical hours of Prime and Tierce, i.e., 7:30 A.M. The rapid change from night ("But soon it will be night," 68) to day (96) is the result of the travelers' having passed the earth's center, thus moving into the Southern Hemisphere, which is twelve hours ahead of the Northern.

and moved to our hemisphere; with equal fear
   the mountain-land, piled up on this side, fled
   and made this cavern here when it rushed upward.   126

Below somewhere there is a space, as far
   from Beelzebub as the limit of his tomb,
   known not by sight but only by the sound   129

of a little stream that makes its way down here
   through the hollow of a rock that it has worn,
   gently winding in gradual descent."   132

My guide and I entered that hidden road
   to make our way back up to the bright world.
   We never thought of resting while we climbed.   135

We climbed, he first and I behind, until,
   through a small round opening ahead of us
   I saw the lovely things the heavens hold,   138

and we came out to see once more the stars.

127–132. Somewhere below the land that rushed upward to form the Mount of Purgatory "there is a space" (127) through which a stream runs, and it is through this space that Virgil and Dante will climb to reach the base of the Mount. The "space" is at the edge of the natural dungeon that constitutes Lucifer's "tomb," and serves as the entrance to the passage from the earth's center to its circumference, created by Lucifer in his fall from Heaven to Hell.

THE DIVINE COMEDY:
PURGATORY

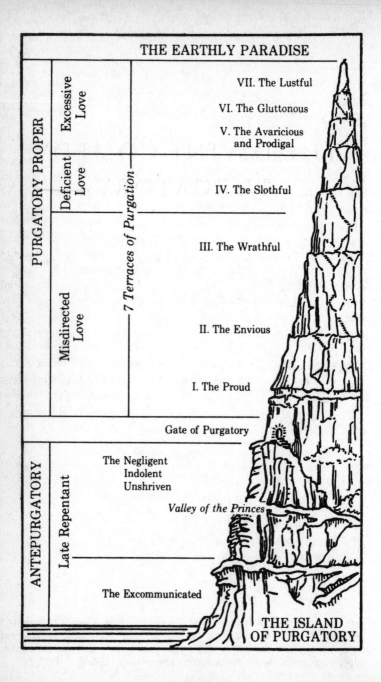

THE EARTHLY PARADISE

PURGATORY PROPER

Excessive Love
VII. The Lustful
VI. The Gluttonous
V. The Avaricious and Prodigal

Deficient Love
IV. The Slothful

Misdirected Love
III. The Wrathful
II. The Envious
I. The Proud

7 Terraces of Purgation

Gate of Purgatory

ANTEPURGATORY

Late Repentant
The Negligent
Indolent
Unshriven

Valley of the Princes

The Excommunicated

THE ISLAND OF PURGATORY

CANTO I

HAVING LEFT THE Inferno behind, Dante announces his intention to sing of the second kingdom, Purgatory, and calls upon the Muses, in particular Calliope, to accompany his song. As the dawn approaches, he feels a sense of renewal, and, looking up into the heavens, he sees four stars. Turning his gaze earthward again, he discovers standing near him a dignified old man: Cato of Utica. Cato thinks Dante and Virgil are refugees from Hell, and he questions them as to how they managed to escape. Virgil explains that Dante is still a living man, and that, at the command of a lady from Heaven, he, Virgil, has been sent to guide this man on a journey for the purpose of his salvation. Already this journey has taken them through Hell, and now it is their intention to see the souls of Purgatory. Cato assents to their passage. He then instructs Virgil to bind a reed around the Pilgrim's waist and to be sure to cleanse him of every trace of stain from the infernal regions. The two poets descend to the shore of the island on which they've found themselves after leaving Hell, where they proceed to carry out Cato's instructions. The purgation is marked by a miracle: when Virgil pulls a reed from the ground, another springs up immediately to take its place.

For better waters, now, the little bark
    of my poetic powers hoists its sails,
    and leaves behind that cruelest of the seas.   3

And I shall sing about that second realm
    where man's soul goes to purify itself
    and become worthy to ascend to Heaven.   6

1–6. The first tercet introduces the theme of the sea voyage, a metaphor both for the journey undertaken by Dante the Pilgrim and for the process of composition in which the genius of Dante the Poet is involved. The same image with the same twofold implication is found in the *Paradise* at the beginning of Canto II.

Here let death's poetry arise to life,
 O Muses sacrosanct whose liege I am!
 And let Calliope rise up and play   9

her sweet accompaniment in the same strain
 that pierced the wretched magpies with the truth
 of unforgivable presumptuousness.   12

The tender tint of orient sapphire,
 suffusing the still reaches of the sky,
 as far as the horizon deeply clear,   15

renewed my eyes' delight, now that I found
 myself free of the deathly atmosphere
 that had weighed heavy on my eyes and heart. 18

The lovely planet kindling love in man
 made all the eastern sky smile with her light,
 veiling the Fish that shimmered in her train. 21

Then to my right I turned to contemplate
 the other pole, and there saw those four stars
 the first man saw, and no man after him.   24

7. The poetry of the *Inferno* is dead in that it treated of souls dead to God and to His grace. But note also the suggestion of resurrection contained in this line.

9. Calliope is the greatest of the Muses, who, in Greek mythology, presides over heroic or epic poetry.

11–12. Pierus, king of Emathia in Macedonia, had nine daughters, to whom he unwisely gave the names of the nine Muses. In their presumption they challenged the Muses to a contest in song, in which they sang the praises of the Titans who waged war against Jupiter (cf. *Inferno* XXXI). Defeated by Calliope, who was chosen to represent all the Muses, they were punished by being transformed into magpies (cf. Ovid, *Metamorphoses* V, 294–678).

23. No living man since the time of Adam and Eve has seen the four stars that the Pilgrim now sees. These stars would have been visible to Adam and Eve because the Garden of Eden, in which they were placed after their creation, was located atop the mountain of Purgatory (the Pilgrim is now at the bottom of this same mountain). After the Fall, Adam and Eve were driven from the garden, and they and their offspring—the whole human race—were consigned to inhabit the lands opposite the Earthly Paradise, that is, according to Dante's geography, the Northern Hemisphere. Hence, the stars of the southern sky would be invisible in the inhabited northern part of the globe.
 Allegorically, the four stars represent the four cardinal virtues: Prudence, Temperance, Justice, and Fortitude.

The heavens seemed to revel in their flames.
   O widowed Northern Hemisphere, deprived
   forever of the vision of their light!   27

And when I looked away from those four stars,
   turning a little toward the other pole,
   where no sign of the Wain was visible,   30

I saw near me an ancient man, alone,
   whose face commanded all the reverence
   that any son could offer to his sire.   33

Long-flowing was his beard and streaked with white,
   as was his hair, which in two tresses fell
   to rest upon his chest on either side.   36

The rays of light from those four sacred stars
   struck with such radiance upon his face,
   it was as if the sun were shining there.   39

"Who are you two who challenged the blind stream
   and have escaped from the eternal prison?"
   he said, moving his venerable locks.   42

"Who guided you? What served you as a lamp
   to light your way out of the heavy night
   that keeps the pit of Hell forever black?   45

Are all the laws of God's Abyss destroyed?
   Have new decisions now been made in Heaven
   so that, though damned, you come up to my cliff?"   48

My leader quickly seized me by the arm;
   his words, his touch, the way he looked at me,
   compelled my knees and brow to reverence.   51

Then he addressed him: "Not on my behalf
   have I come here; a lady sent from Heaven
   asked me to guide this man along his way.   54

30. The constellation of the Wain (or Big Bear, Ursa Major), since it is near the North Pole, is not visible in the Southern Hemisphere.

40. This is the "little stream" that comes from Lethe and flows into Cocytus. The Pilgrim and his guide had followed the course of this stream out of Hell, through the earth, to the lower slope of the mountain of Purgatory (cf. *Inferno* XXXIV, 127–34).

But since it is your will that we reveal
   the circumstances of our presence here,
   how can my will deny yours what it asks?   57

This man has not yet seen his final hour,
   although so close to it his folly brought him
   that little time was left to change his ways.   60

So I was sent to help him, as I said;
   there was no other way to save his soul
   than by my guiding him along this road.   63

Already I have shown him all the Damned;
   I want to show him now the souls of those
   who purge themselves of guilt in your domain.   66

How we came here would take too long to tell;
   from Heaven comes the power that has served
   to lead him here to see and hear you now.   69

May it please you to welcome him—he goes
   in search of freedom, and how dear that is,
   the man who gives up life for it well knows.   72

You know, you found death sweet in Utica
   for freedom's sake; there you put off that robe
   which will be radiant on the Great Day.   75

We have not broken Heaven's timeless laws.
   This man still lives; Minòs does not bind *me*;
   I come from that same Round where the chaste eyes   78

of your dear Marcia still plead with your soul,
   O blessed heart, to hold her as your own;
   for love of her, then, bend your will to ours,   81

---

73. Utica was the scene of the last stand of Pompey against Caesar, as well as the place where Cato subsequently took his life.

79. In 56 B.C. Cato gave his second wife, Marcia, to his friend Hortentius. When Hortentius died, Marcia asked Cato to take her back. The episode was seen by Dante in the *Convivio* as an allegory of the soul's tardy return to God at the onset of old age.

allow us to go through your seven realms,
    and I shall tell her how you have been kind—
        if you will let me speak your name below."   84

"Marcia was so enchanting to my eyes,"
    he answered then, "that while I was alive,
        there was no wish of hers I would not grant.   87

She dwells beyond the evil river now,
    and can no longer move me by that law
        decreed upon the day I issued forth.   90

But if a heavenly lady, as you say,
    moves and directs you, why your flattery?
        Ask in her name, there is no need for more.   93

Go with this man, see that you gird his waist
    with a smooth reed; take care to bathe his face
        till every trace of filth has disappeared,   96

for it would not be fitting that he go
    with vision clouded by the mists of Hell,
        to face the first of Heaven's ministers.   99

Around this little island at its base,
    down there, just where the waves break on the shore,
        you will find rushes growing in soft sand.   102

No other plant producing leaves or stalk
    that hardens could survive in such a place—
        only the reeds that yield to buffeting.   105

When you are ready to begin to scale
    the mountainside, do not come back this way;
        the rising sun will show you where to climb."   108

89. The law is one representing the absolute distinction between the Damned and the Blessed, made forever on that day of the Harrowing of Hell, when the elect souls were rescued from Limbo. Cato's allusion to it here would explain his estrangement from Marcia.

95. The reed will now replace the cord that the Pilgrim wore fastened round his waist while going through the Inferno (*Inferno* XVI, 100–108). In order to ascend the Mount of Purgatory, he must be girded with a reed, clearly symbolizing humility, the opposite of his former self-confidence.

With that he vanished. From my knees I rose,
  and silent, drawing closer to my guide,
  I looked into his eyes. He said to me: 111

"Follow my footsteps; now we must turn back,
  for over there the plain begins to slope,
  descending gently to the shore below."   114

The dawn was gaining ground, putting to flight
  the last hour of the night; I recognized,
  far off, the rippling waters of the sea.   117

We made our way along that lonely plain
  like men who seek the right path they have lost,
  counting each step a loss till it is found.   120

When we had reached a place where the cool shade
  allowed the dew to linger on the slope,
  resisting a while longer the sun's rays,   123

my master placed both of his widespread hands
  gently upon the tender grass, and I,
  who understood what his intention was,   126

offered my tear-stained face to him, and he
  made my face clean, restoring its true color,
  once buried underneath the dirt of Hell.   129

At last we touched upon the lonely shore
  that never yet has seen its waters sailed
  by one who then returned to tell the tale.   132

There, as another willed, he girded me.
  Oh, miracle! When he pulled out the reed,
  immediately a second humble plant   135

sprang up from where the first one had been picked.

134–36. The springing back of the reed is modeled on an episode in the sixth book
of the *Aeneid*. In preparation for his descent into the underworld, Aeneas must pluck
a golden bough to carry with him as a kind of a passport; no sooner is the bough
pulled out than another springs up to take its place. Similarly, here, the reed (of
humility) is the Pilgrim's necessary passport to the mountain of Purgatory.

CANTO II

*As the sun rises, Dante and Virgil are still standing at the water's edge
and wondering which road to take in order to ascend the mountain of
Purgatory, when the Pilgrim sees a reddish glow moving across the
water. The light approaches at an incredible speed, and eventually they
are able to discern the wings of an angel. The angel is the miraculous
pilot of a ship containing souls of the Redeemed, who are singing the
psalm* In exitu Israël de Aegypto. *At a sign from the angel boatsman,
these souls disembark, only to roam about on the shore. Apparently,
they are strangers, and, mistaking Virgil and Dante for familiars of the
place, they ask them which road leads up the mountainside. Virgil an-
swers that they, too, are pilgrims, only recently arrived. At this point
some of the souls realize that the Pilgrim is still alive, and they stare at
him in fascination. Recognizing a face that he knows in this crowd of
souls, Dante tries three times in vain to embrace the shade of his old
friend Casella, a musician; then he asks Casella for a song and, as he
sings, all the souls are held spellbound. Suddenly the Just Old Man,
Cato, appears to disperse the rapt crowd, sternly rebuking them for their
negligence and exhorting them to run to the mountain to begin their
ascent.*

The sun was touching the horizon now,
    the highest point of whose meridian arc
    was just above Jerusalem; and Night,   3

revolving always opposite to him,
    rose from the Ganges with the Scales that fall
    out of her hand when she outweighs the day.   6

Thus, where we were, Aurora's lovely face
    with a vermilion flush on her white cheeks
    was aging in a glow of golden light.   9

We were still standing at the water's edge,
    wondering about the road ahead, like men
    whose thoughts go forward while their bodies stay,   12

1–6. At the time the canto opens, it is midnight at the Ganges, sunset at Jerusalem,
noon at the Pillars of Hercules, and dawn at Purgatory.

when, suddenly, I saw, low in the west
  (like the red glow of Mars that burns at dawn
  through the thick haze that hovers on the sea),   15

a light—I hope to see it come again!—
  moving across the waters at a speed
  faster than any earthly flight could be.   18

I turned in wonder to my guide, and then,
  when I looked back at it again, the light
  was larger and more brilliant than before,   21

and there appeared, on both sides of this light,
  a whiteness indefinable, and then,
  another whiteness grew beneath the shape.   24

My guide was silent all the while, but when
  the first two whitenesses turned into wings,
  and he saw who the steersman was, he cried: 27

"Fall to your knees, fall to your knees! Behold
  the angel of the Lord! And fold your hands.
  Expect to see more ministers like him.   30

See how he scorns to use man's instruments;
  he needs no oars, no sails, only his wings
  to navigate between such distant shores.   33

See how he has them pointing up to Heaven:
  he fans the air with these immortal plumes
  that do not moult as mortal feathers do."   36

Closer and closer to our shore he came,
  brighter and brighter shone the bird of God,
  until I could no longer bear the light,   39

and bowed my head. He steered straight to the shore,
  his boat so swift and light upon the wave,
  it left no sign of truly sailing there;   42

and the celestial pilot stood astern
  with blessedness inscribed upon his face.
  More than a hundred souls were in his ship: 45

42. The boat draws no water because the souls of the Saved have no weight.

In exitu Israël de Aegypto,
    they all were singing with a single voice,
    chanting it verse by verse until the end.   48

The angel signed them with the holy cross,
    and they rushed from the ship onto the shore;
    he disappeared, swiftly, as he had come.   51

The souls left there seemed strangers to this place:
    they roamed about, while looking all around,
    endeavoring to understand new things.   54

The sun, which with its shafts of light had chased
    the Goat out of the heavens' highest field,
    was shooting rays of day throughout the sky,   57

when those new souls looked up to where we were,
    and called to us: "If you should know the road
    that leads up to the mountainside, show us."   60

And Virgil answered them: "You seem to think
    that we are souls familiar with this place,
    but we, like all of you, are pilgrims here;   63

we just arrived, not much ahead of you,
    but by a road which was so rough and hard—
    to climb this mountain now will be like play."   66

Those souls who noticed that my body breathed,
    and realized that I was still alive,
    in their amazement turned a deathly pale.   69

46. *"In exitu Israël de Aegypto"*—"When Israel came out of Egypt" (Psalm 113)—
is a song of thanksgiving to God for freeing the nation of Israel from the bondage
of Egypt. For Christians the Exodus, or liberation of the Jews, prefigures Christ's
Resurrection from the dead. In turn, his death and Resurrection served to free each
individual Christian soul from the slavery of sin. Since at this point in the action of
the poem it is Easter Sunday morning, the very day of the Resurrection, the singing
of this psalm is particularly appropriate, and the connection between the Exodus and
Resurrection is thus reinforced.

55–57. At dawn the constellation Capricorn lies on the meridian, ninety degrees from
the horizon. Because of the sun's ever-increasing light, Capricorn is now invisible. In
other words, the daylight is getting stronger.

Just as a crowd, greedy for news, surrounds
   the messenger who bears the olive branch,
   and none too shy to elbow-in his way,   72

so all the happy souls of these Redeemed
   stared at my face, forgetting, as it were,
   the way to go to make their beauty whole.   75

One of these souls pushed forward, arms outstretched,
   and he appeared so eager to embrace me
   that his affection moved me to show mine.   78

O empty shades, whose human forms seem real!
   Three times I clasped my hands around his form,
   as many times they came back to my breast.   81

I must have been the picture of surprise,
   for he was smiling as he drew away,
   and I plunged forward still in search of him.   84

Then, gently, he suggested I not try,
   and by his voice I knew who this shade was;
   I begged him stay and speak to me awhile.   87

"As once I loved you in my mortal flesh,
   without it now I love you still," he said.
   "Of course I'll stay. But tell me why you're here."   90

"I make this journey now, O my Casella,
   hoping one day to come back here again,"
   I said. "But how did you lose so much time?"   93

He answered: "I cannot complain if he
   who, as he pleases, picks his passengers,
   often refused to take me in his boat,   96

for that Just Will is always guiding his.
   But for the last three months, indulgently,
   he has been taking all who wish to cross;   99

---

91. Casella, a musician and singer, was a friend of Dante's and very likely set to
music Dante's *canzone* "Amor che ne la mente mi ragiona," if not others as well.

so, when I went to seek the shore again,
   where Tiber's waters turn to salty sea,
   benignly, he accepted me aboard.   102

Now, back again he flies to Tiber's mouth,
   which is the meeting place of all the dead,
   except for those who sink to Acheron's shore."   105

"If no new law prevents remembering
   or practicing those love songs that once brought
   peace to my restless longings in the world,"   108

I said, "pray sing, and give a little rest
   to my poor soul which, burdened by my flesh,
   has climbed this far and is exhausted now."   111

Amor che ne la mente mi ragiona.
   began the words of his sweet melody—
   their sweetness still is sounding in my soul.   114

My master and myself and all those souls
   that came with him were deeply lost in joy,
   as if that sound were all that did exist.   117

And while we stood enraptured by the sound
   of those sweet notes—a sudden cry: "What's this,
   you lazy souls?" It was the Just Old Man.   120

"What negligence to stand around like this!
   Run to the mountain, shed that slough which still
   does not let God be manifest to you!"   123

Just as a flock of pigeons in a field
   peacefully feeding on the grain and tares,
   no longer strutting proud of how they look,   126

immediately abandon all their food,
   flying away, seized by a greater need—
   if something should occur that startles them—   129

101. Ostia, where the Tiber River enters the sea, is the place where souls departing for Purgatory gather to await transport.

112. "*Amor che ne la mente mi ragiona*" ("Love that speaks to me in my mind") is the first verse of the second *canzone*, which Dante comments on in the third book of his *Convivio*.

so did that new-formed flock of souls give up
    their feast of song, and seek the mountainside,
    rushing to find a place they hoped was there.   132

And we were just as quick to take to flight.

CANTO III

As THE CROWD of souls breaks up, Virgil seems ashamed of having permitted the Pilgrim's self-indulgence. But they resume their journey and Dante raises his eyes to take in the enormous height of the mountain that stretches up toward Heaven. Then, looking down, he sees his own shadow on the ground in front of him and becomes alarmed when he fails to see the shadow of his guide, thinking, for one brief second, that he has been deserted. This leads to an explanation by Virgil of the diaphanous bodies of the dead: though a shade casts no shadow, it is yet sensitive to pain and heat and cold; such is the mysterious will of the Creator, which cannot be understood by human reason. In the meantime, they have reached the foot of the mountain but find the slope impossible to scale because it is too steep. They then see a band of souls moving toward them with unbelievable slowness, and they set out to meet them in order to ask directions. The souls are amazed to see the Pilgrim's shadow; their spokesman, Manfred, explains that, despite his excommunication by the church, he has been saved through everlasting love by repenting at the very end of his life. Because of this delay, however, he is required to wait in the Antepurgatory thirty times as long as he waited on earth to repent—though this period can be shortened by the good prayers of the faithful in the world.

In sudden flight those souls were scattering,
    rushing across the plain and toward the hill
    where Reason spurs the probing of the soul,   3

but I drew closer to my faithful friend.
    And where could I have run without his help?
    Who else but he could take me up the mount?   6

He looked as if he suffered from remorse—
   O dignity of conscience, noble, chaste,
   how one slight fault can sting you into shame!   9

Now when he had resumed his normal stride,
   free of the haste that mars man's dignity,
   my mind, confined till then to what took place,   12

broke free, and now was eager to explore:
   I raised my eyes to marvel at the mount
   that grew out of the sea toward Heaven's height.   15

The sun behind us blazing red with light
   outlined my human form upon the ground
   before me, as my body blocked its rays.   18

I quickly turned around, seized by the fear
   that I had been abandoned, for I saw
   the ground was dark only in front of me;   21

and then my Comfort turned to me and said:
   "Why are you so uneasy—do you think
   that I am not here with you, guiding you?   24

Evening has fallen on the tomb where lies
   my body that could cast a shadow once;
   from Brindisi to Naples it was moved.   27

If now I cast no shadow on the ground,
   you should not be surprised. Think of the spheres:
   not one of them obstructs the others' light.   30

Yet bodies such as ours are sensitive
   to pain and cold and heat—willed by that Power
   which wills its secret not to be revealed;   33

madness it is to hope that human minds
   can ever understand the Infinite
   that comprehends Three Persons in One Being.   36

16. The two poets have begun their journey on the eastern side of the island; the recently risen sun lies behind them as they turn to face the mountain.

Be satisfied with *quia* unexplained,
   O human race! If you knew everything,
   no need for Mary to have borne a son.   39

You saw the hopeless longing of those souls
   whose thirst, were this not so, would have been quenched,
   but which, instead, endures as endless pain: 42

I speak of Plato and of Aristotle,
   and many others." Then he bent his head,
   remaining silent with his anguished thoughts.   45

By now we had come to the mountain's foot,
   and there we found a rocky slope so steep
   the nimblest legs would not have served you there.   48

The craggiest, the cruelest precipice
   between Turbia and Lerici would seem,
   compared with this, inviting stairs to climb.   51

"How can we tell," my guide said, stopping short,
   "just where this mountain face might slope enough
   to let someone who has no wings ascend?"   54

While he was standing there, his head bent low,
   searching his mind to find some helpful way,
   and I was looking up at all that rock—   57

along the cliffside to my left, a crowd
   of souls was coming toward us, moving slow,
   so slowly that they did not seem to move.   60

"Master," I said, "look over there! You'll see
   some people coming who should know the way—
   if you have not yet found it by yourself."   63

---

50. Lerici lies south of Genoa near La Spezia; Turbia between Monaco and Nice. Between these two towns along the coast, the mountains descend abruptly—indeed, perpendicularly—into the sea, making passage all but impossible.

He looked up then, and said with great relief:
  "Let us go meet them, for they move so slow;
  and you, dear son, be steadfast in your hopes."   66

We were as yet as far from that long crowd
  (even after we had gone a thousand steps),
  as a good slingsman's hand could throw a stone,   69

when they all pressed together suddenly
  and huddled up against the towering rock;
  too stunned to move, they stared in disbelief.   72

"O you elect who ended well your lives,"
  Virgil began, "I ask you, in the name
  of that same peace I know awaits you all,   75

to tell us where the mountain slopes enough
  for us to start our climb: the more one learns,
  the more one comes to hate the waste of time."   78

As sheep will often start to leave the fold,
  first one, then two, then three—then, hesitantly,
  the rest will move, with muzzles to the ground,   81

and what the first sheep does, the others do:
  if it should stop, they all push up against it,
  resigned to huddle quiet in ignorance—   84

just so I saw the leaders of that flock
  of chosen souls take their first steps toward us,
  their faces meek, their movements dignified.   87

But when the souls in front saw the sun's light
  was broken on the ground to my right side,
  my shadow stretching to the rising cliff,   90

they stopped, and started slowly shrinking back;
  all of the rest that followed on their heels
  did as they did, not knowing why they did.   93

"Before you ask me I will answer you:
  this form you see breaking the sunlight here
  upon the ground is a man's body. But,   96

this should not startle you; you can be sure
   that not without the power coming from Heaven
   does he come here seeking to scale this wall."   99

Thus spoke my master. And that worthy group,
   with gesturing hands that urged us to turn round,
   replied: "Go lead the way ahead of us."   102

Then one soul cried: "Whoever you may be,
   look back as you walk on and ask yourself
   if you have ever seen me down on earth."   105

I turned to him and looked hard at his face:
   a handsomely patrician blond he was,
   although a sword wound cut through one eyebrow.   108

When I, in all humility, confessed
   I did not recognize him, he said: "Look,"
   as he revealed a gash above his breast.   111

Then with a smile he said, "Manfred I am,
   grandson of Empress Constance, and I beg you,
   when you are with the living once again,   114

go to my lovely child, mother of kings
   who honor Sicily and Aragon;
   whatever may be rumored, tell her this: 117

As I lay there, my body torn by these
   two mortal wounds, weeping, I gave my soul
   to Him Who grants forgiveness willingly.   120

112. Manfred (1232–1266) was the natural son of Frederick II, who legitimized him and stipulated that he should be regent during the reign of his half-brother, Conrad IV.

113. Constance (1154–1198), wife of Henry VI, was the mother of Frederick II of Sicily. Since Manfred is the natural son of Frederick, he identifies himself with reference to his paternal grandmother.

115–116. Manfred's daughter and grandmother had the same name, Constance. His daughter's two sons became, respectively, the King of Aragon and the King of Sicily.

Horrible was the nature of my sins,
    but boundless mercy stretches out its arms
    to any man who comes in search of it,   123

and if the Pastor of Cosenza, sent
    by Clement in his rage to hunt me out,
    had understood those words in God's own book,   126

my body's bones would still be where they were:
    by the bridgehead near Benevento trenched
    under the guard of a heavy mound of stones.   129

Now they are swept by wind and drenched by rain
    outside my kingdom, by the Verde's banks,
    where they were brought by him with tapers quenched.   132

The church's curse is not the final word,
    for Everlasting Love may still return,
    if hope reveals the slightest hint of green.   135

True, he who dies scorning the Holy Church,
    although he turns repentant at life's end,
    must stay outside, a wanderer on this bank,   138

for thirty times as long as he has lived
    in his presumptuousness—although good prayers
    may shorten the duration of his term.   141

124. This particular Archbishop of Cosenza has been identified as either Bartolomeo
Pignatelli or his successor, Tommaso d'Agni. The archbishop referred to here had
Manfred's body disinterred on the order of Pope Clement IV and cast outside Church
territory (see note to Canto III, 112).

132. When the bodies of the Excommunicated were taken to their graves, the mor-
tuary candles were first extinguished, then carried upside down.

135. Green is the color of hope. Manfred's hope and faith at the end of his life have
brought him to Purgatory and allow him to smile as he tells the gruesome story of
his death and the vindictiveness of the pope. There is even a glimmer of hopefulness
in the ignominious disposition of Manfred's body on the banks of the Verde, which
is Italian for "green." (During his life, according to contemporary accounts, Manfred
always dressed in green.)

You see how you can make me happy now
   by telling my good Constance I am here;
   explain to her this law that holds me back,   144

for those down there can help us much up here.

CANTO IV

AFTER LISTENING TO Manfred for some time (the Pilgrim being deeply absorbed), the two poets are shown a gap in the rock through which they may begin their ascent. The climb is arduous, and they must use both hands and feet in making their way. When they finally reach a ledge, the Pilgrim is exhausted and they stop to rest. He is puzzled by the fact that the sun is on their left, and Virgil explains that this phenomenon is due to the geographical location of the mountain of Purgatory. Furthermore, he adds, the mountain is such that it is most difficult to climb at the beginning but becomes easier and easier, until at last it requires no effort. Their conversation, however, has been overheard and is interrupted by a sarcastic remark from behind a massive rock. The speaker is Belacqua, an old friend of the Poet's, who, together with the other souls on this level, belongs to the second class of the Late Repentant: the Indolent. They must wait outside the gates of Purgatory proper for as many years as they put off repentance on earth. Belacqua repeats the doctrine that prayer can shorten their period of waiting, adding the qualification that it must be prayer from a heart in the state of grace.

When any of our senses is aroused
   to intensity of pleasure or of pain,
   the soul gives itself up to that one sense,   3

---

143. Constance was Manfred's daughter, who died in 1302, at Barcelona. Her mother was Beatrice of Savoy. In 1262 Constance married Peter III of Aragon, who thereupon claimed the sovereignty of Sicily.

oblivious to all its other powers.
    This fact serves to refute the false belief
    that in our bodies more than one soul burns.   6

And so it is that when we see or hear
    something which wholly captivates the soul,
    we easily can lose all sense of time.   9

The sense aware of time is different
    from that which dominates all of the soul:
    the first is free to roam, the other, bound.   12

And I was now experiencing this truth,
    listening to that soul and marvelling.
    The sun had climbed a good fifty degrees,   15

and I had not been conscious of the fact,
    when at some point along the way, those souls
    cried out in one voice: "Here is what you seek."   18

A peasant, at the time the grapes grow ripe,
    with one small forkful of his thorns could seal
    an opening within his hedge more wide   21

than was the gap through which my guide and I
    were forced to climb, the two of us alone,
    once we had parted company with that flock.   24

Up to San Leo, down to Noli, climb,
    climb to the top of Mount Bismantova
    on your two feet, but here a man must fly: 27

yes, fly—that is to say, with the swift wings
    of strong desire, and following that guide
    who gave me hope, spreading his light before me.   30

Squeezed in between the tight walls of the pass,
    we struggled upward through that broken rock,
    using our hands and feet to climb the ground.   33

15. One degree of the sun's arc is equal to four minutes; therefore, fifteen degrees equal one hour. If the sun has risen fifty degrees, then three hours and twenty minutes have passed since sunrise.

25–26. San Leo and Noli are names of towns that are accessible only with great difficulty.

Once we were through that narrow passageway
   up the high cliff and on an open slope,
      "Master," I said, "where must we go from here?"   36

And he replied: "Now, do not change your course,
   keep climbing up the mountain, close to me,
      until we find a more experienced guide."   39

The peak rose higher than my sight could reach,
   the slope soared upright, steeper than a line
      drawn from mid-quadrant to the center's point.   42

I felt my strength drain from me, and I cried:
   "O my sweet father, turn and look at me;
      unless you slow your pace, you'll lose me here."   45

"My son," he said, "keep climbing, just to there,"
   and pointed to a ledge, not far above,
      that made its way around the mountain slope.   48

His words were like a goad, and I strained on
   behind him, climbing with my hands and knees
      until I felt the ledge beneath my feet.   51

And here we both sat down to face the east,
   to rest, as we surveyed all we had climbed—
      a backward glance can often lift the heart.   54

I looked down at the shoreline far below,
   and then looked up: the sun, amazingly,
      was shining to the left of us. The Poet   57

was well aware that I was stupefied
   as I observed the chariot of light
      making its course between us and the north.   60

"Now, were Castor and Pollux," he began,
   "to take that mirror in their company,
      whose light is shed below and heavenward,   63

42. That is, the mountain slopes at an angle even steeper than forty-five degrees.

61. Castor and Pollux are the twins represented in the constellation of Gemini.

you would perceive the flaming Zodiac
   revolving even closer to the Bears—
     unless the sun strayed from its ancient path.   66

If you would understand how this may be,
   try to imagine Zion and this Mount
     located on the earth in such a way   69

that while each lies in different hemispheres,
   the two of them share one horizon; then,
     the lofty path, which Phaëton's chariot   72

could not hold fast to, had to pass this height
   on one side here, but on the other there—
     as you must see, if you think carefully."   75

"Oh, master, you are right!" I answered him;
   "Now, finally, I clearly understand
     this point that always baffled me before: 78

of Heaven's moving circles, the mid-one
   (called the Equator by astronomers),
     which always lies between winter and sun,   81

is, for the very reason you set forth,
   as far north from this place where we now stand
     as once the Hebrews saw it to the south.   84

But would you kindly tell me, if you please,
   how much more climbing we must do: this peak
     soars higher than my eyes can see." And he: 87

"This Mount is not like others: at the start
   it is most difficult to climb, but then,
     the more one climbs the easier it becomes;   90

and when the slope feels gentle to the point
   that climbing up would be as effortless
     as floating down a river in a boat—   93

---

72. The "lofty path" is that of the sun. Having gained permission from his father, Apollo, to guide the chariot of the sun, Phaëton lost control of the horses. To prevent a catastrophe, Jupiter struck down Phaëton with a thunderbolt.

well then, you have arrived at the road's end,
    and there you can expect, at last, to rest.
    I say no more, and what I said is true."   96

Hardly had he stopped speaking when we heard
    a voice not far away: "But, probably,
    you'll feel like sitting down before you do!"   99

Both of us turned to where the voice had come
    and to our left we saw a massive rock
    that neither one of us had noticed there.   102

We went up to the boulder and, behind,
    there were some people hidden in its shade:
    so many sprawling shapes of indolence.   105

There was one there who, you could tell, was tired,
    for he sat with his arms hugging his knees,
    letting his head droop down between his legs.   108

"O my dear master, look at him!" I said,
    "See that man? Lazier he could not look,
    not even if 'Lazy' were his middle name."   111

That shape then turned to look at us, and said,
    raising his face no higher than his thigh:
    "If you're so energetic, run on up."   114

And then I knew who this soul had to be!
    Exhausted, out of breath, nevertheless,
    I struggled toward him. Finally, when I   117

stood by his side, he raised his head a bit
    and said: "Is it quite clear to you by now
    just why the sun drives past you on the left?"   120

His lazy ways and his sarcastic words
    made me half smile, and I replied to him:
    "Belacqua! I'll not have to worry now   123

123. Belacqua was a Florentine lute-maker and friend of Dante's, famous for his indolence.

about your fate! But tell me why are you
   just sitting like this? Waiting for a guide?
   Or simply being your old self again?" 126

"Brother, what good will climbing do?" he said.
   "God's angel sitting at the gate will not
   let me begin my penitence inside. 129

Before I start, the heavens must revolve
   as many times as while I was alive,
   for I put off repenting till the end. 132

Prayers could, of course, make my time shorter here:
   prayers from a heart that lives in grace—the rest
   are worthless, for they go unheard in Heaven!" 135

The Poet had by now begun to climb;
   he said, "Come now, see how the sun has touched
   Heaven's highest point, while on the western shore 138

Night sets her foot upon Morocco's sands."

CANTO V

*THE PILGRIM LEAVES behind the souls of the Indolent and is following
in his guide's footsteps when, suddenly, he turns to look back: one of
the group has discovered the Pilgrim's shadow and is calling it to the
attention of the others. Virgil upbraids him for lagging behind and
warns him against losing sight of his true goal. As they continue up-
ward, they encounter a group of souls chanting the* Miserere. *They are
the third class of the Late Repentant: those who died a violent death
but managed to repent in their final moments. The first soul to come
forward and speak is Jacopo del Cassero of Fano, who tells how he was*

138–139. Since the beginning of the canto, the sun has reached the meridian of Pur-
gatory, which would make the time there noon. Morocco, for Dante part of the
westernmost area of human habitation, would be experiencing dusk (6:00 P.M.), so
that night would just be setting foot there (see note to Canto II, 1–6).

ambushed and left to bleed to death in a swamp. Next comes Buonconte
of Montefeltro. At his death there ensued a struggle between the powers
of good and evil for his soul; since he had uttered the name of Mary
with his dying breath and shed a tear of true repentance, the heavenly
faction prevailed and bore his soul off to Paradise. But a demon took
possession of his corpse and played havoc with it: he conjured up a
storm and sent the mortal remains plummeting down the raging and
swollen river channels. Finally La Pia steps forth and gently asks Dante
to remember her.

I had already parted from those shades,
    following in the footsteps of my guide,
    when one of them back there pointed and called: 3

"That soul climbing behind the other one!
    Look! To his left no light is shining through!
    He seems to walk as if he were alive!"   6

Hearing these words, I turned around and saw
    souls staring in amazement at my form,
    at me alone—and at the broken light.   9

"What is it that has caught your interest so
    and makes you lag behind?" my master asked.
    "What do you care, if they are whispering?   12

Keep up with me and let the people talk!
    Be like a solid tower whose brave height
    remains unmoved by all the winds that blow;   15

the man who lets his thoughts be turned aside
    by one thing or another, will lose sight
    of his true goal, his mind sapped of its strength."   18

What could I say except: "I'm coming now"?
    I said it, and my face took on the color
    that makes a man deserve to be excused.   21

Meanwhile, across the slope ahead of us,
    people were passing, chanting *Miserere*,
    singing the psalm in alternating parts.   24

But when they noticed that the rays of light
   did not shine through my human form, they changed
   their chanting to a drawn-out, breathless "Ohhh!"   27

Then two of them, dispatched as messengers,
   came running up and started to implore:
   "We pray you, please tell us about yourselves."   30

My master answered them: "You may return,
   bearing the news to those who sent you here
   that this man's body is true flesh and blood;   33

if they were stunned, as I suppose they were,
   because he casts a shadow—now they know,
   and it could profit them to honor him."   36

I never saw a meteor at night
   cut through the tranquil air, or bolts of light
   flash through the cloudy August sky at dusk,   39

as quickly as they rushed back to their group;
   then all together they wheeled round and rushed
   toward us like a full-charging cavalry.   42

"Oh look at all those souls pressing toward us,"
   the Poet said; "each one will have his plea;
   listen to them, but move on as you do."   45

"O soul," they cried, "you there, moving toward bliss
   clothed in the body you were born with, stop,
   just for a moment, look at us and see   48

if you know anyone among us here,
   so as to bring back news of him to earth.
   Oh, wait! Where are you going? Oh, please stop!   51

We are all souls who met a violent death,
   and we were sinners to our final hour;
   but then the light of Heaven lit our minds,   54

and penitent and pardoning, we left
   that life at peace with God, Who left our hearts
   with longing for the holy sight of Him."   57

I said: "I see your faces, but cannot
    recognize one. But, O souls, born for bliss,
    if there is some way I can please you now,   60

tell me, and I will do so—by that peace
    which I go searching for while following
    from world to world so great a guide as this."   63

One soul replied: "We need no oath from you;
    all of us here know you will keep your word,
    unless some lack of power thwarts your will.   66

Now, speaking for myself, I will plead first:
    if ever you should travel to the land
    between Romagna and the realm of Charles,   69

I beg you, be so gracious as to ask
    the souls in Fano to say prayers for me,
    that I may soon begin to purge my guilt.   72

I came from Fano, but the deep-cut wounds
    from which I saw my life's blood spilling out,
    were dealt me in the Antenori's land—   75

the land where I believed I was most safe.
    Azzo of Este had me killed (his hatred
    for me reached far beyond all reason's bounds).   78

If only I had fled toward Mira when
    at Oriaco they took me by surprise,
    I still would be with men who live and breathe;   81

instead, I ran into the swampy mire:
    the reeds entangled me; I fell, and there
    I watched a pool of blood fill from my veins."   84

64. The soul, who is not named in the canto, is Jacopo del Cassero. In 1296, as podestà of Bologna, he opposed the designs of the powerful and ruthless Azzo VIII of Este. In 1298, while en route to Milan to assume the office of podestà there, Jacopo was set upon and brutally murdered by Azzo's henchmen at Oriago, a town on the river Brenta between Venice and Padova. He is the first of the three speakers in this canto who died a violent death.

75–76. The Antenori's land is Padova, where Jacopo thought he would be safe.

77. Azzo VIII of Este was the Marquis of Este and Lord of Ferrara, Modena, and Reggio. He died in 1308.

Another soul said: "Oh, may the desire
   that draws you up the mountain be fulfilled;
   and you, please help me satisfy my own.   87

I am Buonconte, once from Montefeltro;
   no one, not even Giovanna, cares for me,
   and so, I walk ashamed among these souls."   90

I said: "What violence—or was it chance?—
   swept you so far away from Campaldin
   that no one ever found your burial place?"   93

He said: "Below the Casentino flows
   the river Archiano, which arises
   above the convent in the Apennines.   96

Beyond, it takes another name, and there
   I made my way, my throat an open wound,
   fleeing on foot, and bloodying the plain.   99

There I went blind. I could no longer speak,
   but as I died, I murmured Mary's name,
   and there I fell and left my empty flesh.   102

Now hear the truth. Tell it to living men:
   God's angel took me up, and Hell's fiend cried:
   'O you from Heaven, why steal what is mine?   105

You may be getting his immortal part—
   and won it for a measly tear, at that,
   but for his body I have other plans!'   108

---

88. Buonconte was the son of Guido of Montefeltro (*Inferno* XXVII). In 1289 he led the forces of the Ghibellines of Arezzo against the Florentine Guelphs in the battle of Campaldino. Guido's side suffered defeat and he was slain. His body was never found.

89. The widow of Buonconte was named Giovanna, and "no one" probably refers to the daughter and brother who survived him.

95. The river Archiano is a tributary of the Arno.

You know how vapor gathers in the air,
    then turns to water when it has returned
    to where the cold condenses it as rain.   111

To that ill will, intent on evilness,
    he joined intelligence and, by that power
    within his nature, stirred up mist and wind,   114

until the valley, by the end of day,
    from Pratomagno to the mountain chain,
    was fogbound. With dense clouds he charged the sky: 117

the saturated air turned into rain;
    water poured down, and what the sodden ground
    rejected filled and overflowed the deepest   120

gullies, whose spilling waters came to join
    and form great torrents rushing violently,
    relentlessly, to reach the royal stream.   123

Close to its mouth the raging Archiano
    discovered my cold body—sweeping it
    into the Arno, loosening the cross   126

I'd made upon my breast in final pain;
    it dragged me to its banks, along its bed,
    then swathed me in the shroud of all its spoils."   129

"Oh, please, when you are in the world again,
    and are quite rested from your journey here,"
    a third soul, following on the second, said,   132

"Oh, please remember me! I am called Pia.
    Siena gave me life, Maremma death,
    as he knows who began it when he put   135

his gem upon my finger, pledging faith."

---

116. Pratomagno was a locale near Arezzo on the Arno, now called Pratovecchio.

CANTO VI

THE SOULS OF those who have died by violence continue to press eagerly upon the Pilgrim. Among them Dante recognizes Benincasa of Laterina; Guccio Tarlati of Pietramala; Federigo Novello; Farinata, son of Marzucco degli Scornigiani; Count Orso of Mangona; and Pierre de la Brosse of Turenne. As he frees himself from this encumbering crowd of shades, the Pilgrim asks Virgil about the power of prayer to affect the will of Heaven. Virgil gives a partial explanation and tells the Pilgrim that he will have to wait until Beatrice gives him a more comprehensive elucidation of the matter. Noting a figure seated in silence not far away, Virgil and the Pilgrim go up to him to ask directions; upon learning that Virgil is a Mantuan by birth, the stranger embraces him. It is the shade of Sordello. At this point there is a break in the action of the poem, and Dante inveighs at length against the evil and corruption of Italy.

The loser, when a game of dice breaks up,
   despondent, often lingers there as he,
   learning the hard way, replays all his throws.   3

The crowd leaves with the winner: some in front,
   some tugging at him from behind, the rest
   close to his side beg to be recognized.   6

He keeps on going, listening to them all;
   the ones who get a handout will not push,
   and this is his protection from the crowd.   9

I was that man caught in a begging throng,
   turning my face toward one and then the next,
   buying my way out with my promises.   12

I saw the Aretine who met his death
   at the revengeful hand of Ghin di Tacco;
   I saw that soul who drowned giving pursuit.   15

I saw with hands outstretched, imploring me,
   Federigo Novello, and the Pisan, too,
   whose death inspired good Marzucco's strength.   18

I saw Count Orso, and I saw that soul
   torn from its body, so he said, by hate
   and envy—not for any wrong he did: 21

Pierre de la Brosse, I mean. And while still here
   on earth, the Lady of Brabant might well
   take care lest she end up in fouler flock.   24

Once I had freed myself from all those shades
   who prayed only that others pray for them
   and thus quicken their way to bliss, I said: 27

"It seems to me that somewhere in your verse,
   you, O my Light, deny explicitly
   the power of prayer to bend the laws of Heaven; 30

---

13. The Aretine was Benincasa da Laterina, a jurist from Arezzo. Ghin di Tacco (14), motivated by a desire to vindicate the death sentence given to a close relative, perhaps his father or brother, entered Benincasa's courtroom in disguise, murdered him, and escaped, carrying with him the judge's head.

15. Guccio Tarlati da Pietramala drowned in the Arno following the battle of either Campaldino or Montaperti.

17. Son of Count Guido Novello, Federigo was killed in 1291 by one of the Guelphs, Bostoli d'Arezzo, in a battle that took place in the Casentino. The Pisan is Farinata, a doctor of law and son of Messer Marzucco degli Scornigiani of Pisa.

18. This line is supposedly a reference to the fortitude of a Francescan Friar Minor (Marzucco), who demonstrated his "strength" by forgiving the murderer of his son, Farinata, "the Pisan" mentioned in the preceding line (17).

19. Count Orso, the son of Napoleone dell'Acerbaia, was viciously murdered by his cousin Alberto di Mangona. Alberto's father, Alessandro, and Napoleone were brothers who killed each other. Both are punished among the traitors in Caina (*Inferno* XXXII, 55–58).

22–24. Pierre de la Brosse, surgeon and chancellor to Philip III of France, was falsely accused of treachery by Philip's second wife, Mary of Brabant (23), and was hanged in 1278.

yet these souls ask precisely for such prayers.
    Does this, then, mean their hopes are all in vain?
    Or have I failed to understand your words?"   33

And he: "What I once wrote means what it says;
    yet, if you think about it carefully,
    you must see that their hopes are not deceived.   36

High justice would in no way be debased
    if ardent love should cancel instantly
    the debt these penitents must satisfy.   39

The words of mine you cite apply alone
    to those whose sins could not be purged by prayer,
    because their prayers had no access to God.   42

Do not try to resolve so deep a doubt;
    wait until she shall make it clearer—she,
    the light between truth and intelligence.   45

You understand me: I mean Beatrice,
    she will appear upon this mountain top;
    you will behold her smiling in her bliss."   48

I said: "My lord, let us make greater haste:
    I'm not as tired as I was before;
    and look! The mountain casts a shadow now."   51

"As long as daylight lasts we shall move on,
    climbing as far as possible," he said,
    "but things are not the way you think they are.   54

Before you reach the top you'll see the sun
    come out from where the slope is hiding him,
    preventing you from casting any shade.   57

---

45. Beatrice, standing, as it were, "between" Truth (the meaning of prayer) and Intellect (the Pilgrim's mind), will be able to illuminate fully for him the true meaning of prayer. The matter involves grace, which goes beyond Virgil's understanding.

But see that spirit stationed over there,
   all by himself, the one who looks at us;
   he will show us the quickest way to go."   60

We made our way toward him. (O Lombard soul,
   how stately and disdainful you appeared,
   what majesty was in your steady gaze!)   63

He did not say a word to us, but let
   us keep on moving up toward him, while he
   was watching like a couchant lion on guard.   66

But Virgil went straight up to him and asked
   directions for the best way to ascend.
   The shade ignored the question put to him,   69

asking of us, instead, where we were born
   and who we were. My gentle guide began:
   "Mantua . . ." And the other, until then   72

all self-absorbed, sprang to his feet and came
   toward him: "O Mantuan, I am Sordello
   of your own town"—and the two shades embraced.   75

(Ah, slavish Italy, the home of grief,
   ship without pilot caught in a raging storm,
   no queen of provinces—whorehouse of shame!   78

How quick that noble soul was to respond
   to the mere sound of his sweet city's name,
   by welcoming his fellow citizen—   81

while, now, no one within your bounds knows rest
   from war, and those enclosed by the same wall
   and moat, even they are at each other's throats!   84

O wretched Italy, search all your coasts,
   probe to your very center: can you find
   within you any part that is at peace?   87

58. This is the spirit of Sordello of Goito. An adventurer and a poet, Sordello was born in the town of Goito, near Mantua, about 1200. Although relatively little is known about his life, it is likely that the wrath he incurred as a result of several episodes with women necessitated his leaving Italy.

What matter if Justinian repaired
   the bridle—if the saddle's empty now!
   The shame would have been less if he had not.   90

You priests who should pursue your holiness,
   remembering what God prescribes for you,
   let Caesar take the saddle as he should—   93

see how this beast has grown viciously wild,
   without the rider's spurs to set her straight,
   since you dared take the reins into your hands!   96

O German Albert, you abandon her,
   allowing her, ungoverned, to run wild.
   You should have been astride her saddle-bow!   99

Let a just judgment fall down from the stars
   upon your house: one unmistakable
   and strange enough to terrify your heir!   102

You and your sire, whom greed for greater wealth
   holds back up there, have let this come to pass:
   the garden of the Empire is laid waste.   105

Come see the Cappelletti, callous heart,
   see the Monaldi, the Montecchi ruined,
   the Filippeschi fearful of their fate.   108

Come, heartless one, come see your noblemen
   who suffer; help them heal their wounds; come see
   how safe it is to dwell in Santafior.   111

Come see your city, Rome, in mourning now,
   widowed, alone, lamenting night and day:
   "My Caesar, why have you abandoned me?"   114

Come see how people love each other now!
   If you cannot be moved to pity us,
   then come and feel the shame your name has earned!   117

O Jove Supreme, crucified here on earth
   for all mankind, have I the right to ask
   if Your just eyes no longer look on us?   120

Or is this part of a great plan conceived
  in Your deep intellect, to some good end
  that we are powerless to understand?   123

For all the towns of Italy are filled
  with tyrants: any dolt who plays the role
  of partisan can pass for a Marcellus.   126

Florence, my Florence! How happy you must be
  with this digression, for you're not involved—
  thank your resourceful citizens for that!   129

Some men have justice in their hearts; they *think*
  before they shoot their judgments from the bow—
  your people merely shoot off words about it!   132

Some men think twice when offered public post;
  your citizens accept before they're asked,
  shouting, "I'll gladly sacrifice myself!"   135

Rejoice, I say to you, you have good cause,
  rich as you are, so wise, knowing such peace!
  The facts bear out the truth of what I say.   138

Athens and Lacedaemon, still well known
  for ancient laws and civil discipline,
  showed but the faintest signs of order then   141

compared to you, who plan so cleverly
  that by the time November is half done
  the laws spun in October are in shreds.   144

How often within memory have you changed
  coinage and customs, laws and offices,
  and members of your body politic!   147

Think back, and if you see the truth, you'll see
  that you are like a woman, very sick,
  who finds no rest on her soft, sumptuous bed,   150

but turns and tosses to escape her pain.)

CANTO VII

THE ACTION IS renewed as Virgil and Sordello conclude their elaborate embrace. Upon learning that he has embraced not merely a fellow Mantuan but Virgil, the very glory of the Latin race, Sordello does him further homage. Virgil explains to Sordello the nature and scope of his journey with the Pilgrim and asks to be shown the quickest way up the mountain. Sordello volunteers his services as guide but remarks that it is almost nightfall and that it is the law of Purgatory that no one may ascend the mountain at night: the darkness of the shadows afflicts the will with impotence. However, Sordello knows of a good place to rest and suggests that they might spend the night there. He leads the two poets to a ledge above the Valley of the Princes, where they see the so-called Negligent Rulers, who are singing the Salve Regina. *From this vantage above the valley, Sordello points out a number of the souls below: Rudolf of Hapsburg; Henry VII of Luxembourg; Ottokar II, king of Bohemia; Philip III of France; Henry the Fat of Navarre; Peter III of Aragon; his son, Charles of Anjou; Henry III of England; and William VII (Longsword).*

When this glad, ceremonious embrace
    had been repeated several times, Sordello,
    stepping back, said, "Tell me, who are you two?"   3

"Before those souls worthy to climb to God
    were taken to this mountain by His grace,
    my bones were buried by Octavian.   6

I am Virgil. The reason I lost Heaven
    was through no other fault than lack of faith."
    This was the answer my guide gave that shade.   9

As one who suddenly beholds a thing
    incredible will first believe and then
    misdoubt and say: "It is—it cannot be!"   12

---

6. Octavian was the emperor Augustus, the first of the Roman emperors (63 B.C.–A.D. 14).

so seemed Sordello. Then he bent his head
   and, this time, reverently, turned to embrace
   my master as a vassal does his lord.   15

"O glory of the Latin race," he said,
   "you who did prove the power of our tongue,
   O deathless excellence of my own land,   18

what merit or what grace grants me this sight?
   Tell me, if I am worthy of your words,
   are you from Hell and, if so, from what ward?"   21

"Through all the circles of the realm of grief
   have I come here," he said. "A heavenly power
   showed me this road, and with its aid I come.   24

Not what I did, but what I did not do
   cost me the sight of that high Sun you seek
   whose meaning was revealed to me too late.   27

There is a place down there made sorrowful
   by darkness of its untormented grief:
   no shrieks of pain are heard, but hopeless sighs.   30

I dwell with infant souls of innocence
   bit off from life by death before the sin
   that they were born with could be washed away;   33

I dwell with those who could not clothe themselves
   in the three holy virtues but, unstained,
   knew all the rest, and practiced all of them.   36

But if you know, and are allowed to tell,
   how can we find the quickest way to reach
   the place where Purgatory truly starts?"   39

"Since we are not restricted to one spot,
   being free to roam around and up," he said,
   "I'll be your guide as far as I may climb.   42

---

16. "Latin race" (*Latini,* "Latins") is the general term for ancient, and modern, Italians who considered Latin their language.

But, see, the day is coming to an end;
   at night it is forbidden to ascend,
   so we should think of some good place to rest.   45

Off to the right here is a group of souls;
   if you allow me, I shall take you there;
   I think you will take pleasure meeting them."   48

"What do you mean?" my guide said, "If a soul
   started to climb at night, would he be stopped,
   or would he simply find he could not move?"   51

Sordello drew his finger along the ground
   answering, "Look! After the sun has set
   you could not go a step beyond this line.   54

There's nothing that prevents our going up
   except the darkness of the shadows: this,
   alone, afflicts the will with impotence.   57

We can, indeed, go *down* the slope and roam
   as far around the mountain as we wish,
   as long as the horizon locks out day."   60

My lord, amazed by what he heard, replied:
   "In that case, take us to the place you said,
   where we would find a pleasurable rest."   63

We started on our way, and soon I saw
   a hollow in the mountain slope, just like
   the hollow that a valley makes on earth.   66

"Now we will go," the shade announced to us,
   "to where the mountain folds into a lap;
   there we will wait until the new day comes."   69

A winding path that was not very steep
   led to a point upon the hollow's rim
   where the side sloped to less than half its height.   72

Think of fine silver, gold, cochineal, white lead,
   Indian wood, glowing and deeply clear,
   fresh emerald the instant it is split—   75

the brilliant colors of the grass and flowers
within that dale would outshine all of these,
as nature naturally surpasses art. 78

But nature had not only painted there:
the sweetness of a thousand odors fused
in one unknown, unrecognizable. 81

I heard *Salve Regina;* sitting there
upon the grass and flowers I saw souls
hidden till then below the valley's rim. 84

"Please do not ask me," said our Mantuan guide,
"to lead you down to where you see those souls,
until the sinking sun has found its nest; 87

from here it is much easier to see
the faces and the movements of them all
than if you were among them there below. 90

The one who sits the highest and who looks
as if he left undone what was to do,
and does not join the others in their song, 93

was Rudolf, Emperor, who could have cured
the wounds that were the death of Italy—
it will be long before she lives again! 96

The one who seems to comfort him once ruled
over that land whose waters flow into
the Moldau to the Elbe to the sea: 99

Ottokar—more respected as a babe
than Wenceslaus, his bearded son, is now,
feasting on lechery and idleness. 102

94. Rudolf of Hapsburg (1218–1291), the first emperor of the House of Austria, gave priority to the internal affairs of Germany and neglected Italy, allowing it to remain outside the unifying influence of the empire.

100. In a spirit of reconciliation, Ottokar II, king of Bohemia from 1253 to 1278, a valiant warrior, comforts Rudolf of Hapsburg, formerly his bitterest enemy.

101. Wenceslaus IV (1270–1305) succeeded his father, Ottokar II, as king of Bohemia in 1278.

That snub-nosed figure in close conference
   with the kind-looking person at his side,
   dishonoring the lily, died in flight. 105

Look at him there, see how he beats his breast;
   look at the other soul, cradling his cheek
   within his palm, sighing. Father-in-law 108

and father of the Plague of France they are;
   they know about his dissolute, foul life,
   and that is why they feel such piercing grief. 111

That sturdy-looking soul seated beside
   the big-nosed one, singing in tune with him,
   was girded with the cord of every good. 114

103. The figure, Philip III the Bold, king of France (1245–1285), called *le Camus* because of his nose, was defeated by Peter of Aragon in 1285 during the massacre of the French in Sicily. Philip was the son of Louis IX, whom he succeeded, and the nephew of Charles of Anjou. In 1262 he married Isabella, the daughter of James I of Aragon. From this marriage was born his son, Philip, who succeeded him as Philip IV the Fair, whom Dante dubs "the Plague of France" (109).

104. Henry the Fat of Navarre, contrary to his kindly appearance, was reputed to have had a harsh temperament. He died in 1274, suffocated by his fat. Henry was king of Navarre from 1270 to 1274, succeeding Thibaut II, his brother. His daughter Jeanne married Philip the Fair.

105. The lily (*fleur de lis*) was the emblem of the kings of France.

109. The "Plague of France" is Philip IV the Fair, son of Philip III the Bold and son-in-law of Henry the Fat. His reign was characterized by tyranny, corruption, and viciousness. Though never mentioned by name, he is the frequent object of Dante's scorn in the *Comedy* (*Purgatory* XX, 85–96; XXXII, 148–60; XXXIII, 34–45; *Paradise* XIX, 118). Philip died in 1314.

112. The soul is that of Peter III of Aragon (1236–1285), the husband of Manfred's daughter, Constance, who became king of Sicily in 1282, succeeding Charles of Anjou, after the massacre of the Sicilian Vespers.

113. The "big-nosed one" is Charles I of Anjou (1226–1285), champion of the Guelphs in Italy. He defeated Manfred at Benevento in 1266 to become king of Sicily and Naples, later losing the throne to Peter III. Though these two were bitter rivals, here they are presented as singing in harmony. Charles married Beatrix, daughter of Count Raymond Berenger IV of Provence, in 1246, thus becoming count of Provence. After Beatrix's death in 1267, he married Margaret of Burgundy in 1268.

If only that young man behind him there
    had lived to rule a longer time, indeed,
    true merit would have flowed from cup to cup—   117

as did not happen with the other heirs.
    Now James and Frederick possess his realms,
    but neither got the better heritage.   120

Not often does the sap of virtue rise
    to all the branches. This is His own gift,
    and we can only beg that He bestow it.   123

My words apply to him with the big nose
    as well as Peter there, who sings with him
    on whose account Provence and Puglia grieve.   126

As much as this seed's plant is less than he,
    just so much more than Margaret and Beatrix
    can Constance boast her husband's excellence.   129

And see Henry of England sitting there
    all by himself, king of the simple life
    whose branches bear him better fruit by far.   132

115. The man is most likely Alfonso III of Aragon, who was Peter III's eldest son and who reigned less than six years (1285–1291).

119. James II of Aragon and Frederick II of Sicily, the second and third sons of Peter III of Aragon, were involved in a lengthy dispute over a claim to the kingdom of Sicily.

127. This seed, the father, is Charles I; his plant, the son, is Charles II. Here we have a recapitulation of what had been hinted at in the lines immediately preceding: Charles I, like Peter III, was unfortunate in his progeny.

128–129. Margaret of Burgundy and Beatrix of Provence were both wives of Charles I of Anjou; Constance, daughter of Manfred, was the wife of Peter III of Aragon. Thus Dante is really saying in lines 127–129 that Charles II is as much inferior to Charles I as Charles I is to Peter III.

130–131. Henry III (1216–1272), whose son, Edward I, is credited with an enduring reform of English law, is reproached in Sordello's lament for Blacatz (see note to Canto VI, 74) for his sloth and cowardice. His contemporaries frequently referred to his piety.

The one who sits below them on the ground
   and who looks up at them is Marquis William,
   whose war with Alessandria has made   135

all Montferrat and Canavese weep.

CANTO VIII

*AS THE PILGRIM looks on, one of the souls in the valley below rises and
begins singing the* Te lucis ante. *The rest of the inhabitants of the valley
join in and sing the hymn through to the end, keeping their eyes fixed
on the sky. As they continue to stare upward, two angels are seen to
descend from Heaven. These angels take up positions on either side of
the group of souls, and Sordello explains that they have come to guard
the valley against the serpent who will appear at any moment; he then
announces that it is time to go down among the great shades of the
valley. Having descended only a few steps, Dante recognizes the shade
of Nino Visconti. Nino, righteously indignant, discusses with Dante the
infidelity of widows who remarry. Virgil is explaining certain stellar
phenomena of the Southern Hemisphere, when suddenly Sordello an-
nounces the coming of the serpent. No sooner does the beast appear,
however, than it is put to flight by the two angel guardians. The Pilgrim
then speaks to Conrad Malaspina, lavishly praising the reputation of
the Malaspina family, and Conrad prophesies that Dante will one day
have cause from his own experience to praise this family.*

It was the hour when a sailor's thoughts,
   the first day out, turn homeward, and his heart
   yearns for the loved ones he has left behind,   3

134. William VII, surnamed "Longsword," was Marquis of Montferrat from 1254
to 1292. Failing in his attempt to quell a revolt in the city of Alessandria in Piedmont,
William was locked in an iron cage by his enemies and put on display until his death
in 1292.

the hour when the novice pilgrim aches
    with love: the far-off tolling of a bell
    now seems to him to mourn the dying day—   6

I was no longer listening to words
    but looking at a soul who had stood up,
    requesting, with a gesture, to be heard.   9

He raised his hands, joining his palms in prayer,
    his gaze fixed toward the east, as if to say:
    "I have no other thought but Thee, dear Lord."   12

Te lucis ante, with such reverence,
    and so melodiously, came from his lips,
    that I was lost to any sense of self;   15

the rest then, reverently, in harmony,
    joined in to sing the hymn through to the end,
    keeping their eyes fixed on the heavenly spheres.   18

Sharpen your sight, Reader: the truth, this time,
    is covered by a thinner veil, and so,
    the meaning should be easy to perceive.   21

I saw that noble host of souls, who now
    in silence kept their eyes raised to the heavens,
    as if expectant, faces pale and meek,   24

and then I saw descending from on high
    two angels with two flaming swords, and these
    were broken short and blunted at the end.   27

Their garments, green as tender new-born leaves
    unfurling, billowed out behind each one,
    fanned by the greenness of their streaming wings.   30

One took his stand above us on our side,
    and one alighted on the other bank;
    thus, all the souls were held between the two.   33

26. The flaming swords of the angels recall the *flammeum gladium* of the Cherubim placed at the entrance to Eden as guardians after the Fall (Genesis 3:24).

28. The green color of the angels is, of course, the symbol of hope.

My eyes could see with ease their golden hair,
  but could not bear the radiance of their faces:
  light that makes visible can also blind.   36

"From Mary's bosom both of them descend
  to guard us from the serpent in the vale,"
  Sordello said. "He'll be here soon, you'll see."   39

Not knowing from what point he would appear,
  I turned around and, frozen by my fear,
  I pressed close to those shoulders I could trust.   42

Sordello spoke again: "Now it is time
  for us to join the noble shades below
  and speak with them—I know they will be pleased."   45

I only had to take three steps, I think,
  before I reached the bottom. I saw a shade
  peering at me, trying to know my face.   48

By now, the air had started turning dark,
  but not so dark that we could not see clear
  (so close we were) what was concealed before.   51

He made his way toward me, and I toward him—
  Noble Judge Nino, how I did rejoice
  to see that you were not among the Damned!   54

No loving words of welcome did we spare;
  then he: "How long since you have come across
  the boundless waters to the mountain's base?"   57

"Oh," I replied, "I left the realm of grief
  this morning; I am still in my first life,
  but hope to gain the other by this road."   60

When Nino and Sordello heard my words,
  both of them backed away from me, amazed,
  unable to believe what they had heard.   63

53. Nino Visconti (died 1296) was the son of Giovanni Visconti and (on his mother's side) the grandson of Count Ugolino della Gherardesca (see *Inferno* XXXIII).

One turned to Virgil, and the other one
  turned to a soul nearby. "Corrado, rise!"
  he cried: "Come here! See what God's grace has willed!"   66

He turned to me: "I beg you in the name
  of that grace shown to you by Him who hides
  His primal cause too deep for man to delve—   69

when you have crossed the enormous gulf once more,
  tell my Giovanna she should plead for me,
  for prayers from guiltless hearts are listened to.   72

I think her mother has stopped loving me,
  for she has put aside those bands of white
  which she, poor soul, will soon be longing for.   75

From her it is not difficult to learn
  how long love's flame burns in a woman's heart,
  if sight and touch do not rekindle it.   78

The snake that leads the Milanese to war
  will not provide an emblem for her tomb
  as splendid as Gallura's cock would be."   81

These were his words, and his whole countenance
  displayed the signs of righteous zeal, the kind
  which flares up when it should within the heart.   84

My eyes kept looking at the sky just where
  the stars move slowest—as, within a wheel,
  the axle moves more slowly than the rest.   87

My guide said: "Son, what are you staring at?"
  I answered him: "At those three brilliant torches
  lighting up all the polar region here."   90

71. Giovanna, born around 1291, was Nino's daughter by Beatrice d'Este.

73. Giovanna's mother was Beatrice d'Este, daughter of Obizzo II d'Este and sister of Azzo VIII.

89. The torches are the theological virtues, Faith, Hope, and Charity. These virtues supersede the cardinal virtues symbolized by the four stars, in the sense that they are necessary to direct human actions toward God, and they are given to men through Christ.

And he to me: "Those four bright stars you saw
   this morning, now are underneath the mount,
   and these have risen here to take their place."   93

But then Sordello clutched his arm and said:
   "Behold our adversary over there!"—
   he pointed to the place where we should look.   96

Along the little valley's open side
   a serpent moved—the very one, perhaps,
   that offered Eve the bitter fruit to eat.   99

Through grass and flowers slid the vicious streak,
   stopping from time to time to turn its head
   and lick its back to make its body sleek.   102

I did not see, so I cannot describe,
   how the two holy falcons took to flight,
   but I saw clearly both of them fly down.   105

Hearing those green wings cutting through the air,
   the serpent fled, the angels wheeled around,
   flying in perfect time back to their posts.   108

The shade who had drawn close to Nino's side,
   when called by him, did not at any time
   during the skirmish take his eyes from me.   111

"So may the lamp that lights your upward path
   find in your will enough sustaining fuel
   to take you to the enamelled mountaintop,"   114

he then began, "if you have recent news
   of Val di Magra or parts thereabout,
   tell me, for in that land I once was great.   117

Corrado Malaspina was my name—
   but not the elder, though I sprang from him;
   and here I cleanse the love I bore my own."   120

118. Corrado II was the son of Federigo I, Marquis of Villafranca, and the grandson
of Corrado I, the "elder" (119). He was a Ghibelline, according to Boccaccio, who
mentions him and his daughter, Spina, in *The Decameron* (II, 6). Corrado died
around 1294.

"Oh," I replied, "I've never visited
     the lands you ruled; the whole of Europe, though,
     has heard about your glorious domain.   123

The fame that honors your great family
     proclaims resoundingly its lords and lands,
     even to those who never travelled there.   126

And, as I hope to reach the top, I swear
     that your great lineage maintains intact
     the glorious honor of the purse and sword.   129

Habit and virtue have so shaped your race
     that while the Wicked Head perverts the world,
     they shun the path of evil, they alone."   132

He said: "Know that the sun will not repose
     a seventh time on the large bed the Ram
     spreads over and bestrides with all four feet,   135

before the kind opinion you just gave
     shall be nailed hard into your brain with nails
     truer than words you may have heard of us—   138

unless God's course of justice be cut short!"

CANTO IX

*THE PILGRIM FALLS asleep and, near dawn, dreams that he is being
snatched up into the sphere of fire by an eagle. The imaginary heat of
his dream wakes him, and he is dazed and terrified until he discovers
that Virgil is sitting close by. Virgil explains that they have now come
to the gates of Purgatory proper and that while the Pilgrim slept, a lady
named Lucia came and bore him up there in her arms. As they draw
near the gates, the Pilgrim discerns three steps of different colors leading
up to them. The first is white as marble; the second is darker than
purple-black, and rough and crumbling; the third is red as flaming por-
phyry. On the threshold of the gate, above this last step, sits a guardian*

angel with a naked sword, clothed in garments the color of ashes. With
the tip of the sword, he traces seven P's on the Pilgrim's forehead and
instructs him to be sure to "wash away" these wounds during his stay
in the place of purgation. The guardian then takes two keys—one gold
and one silver—with which he was entrusted by St. Peter, and unlocks
the gateway to Purgatory. He warns the Pilgrim that, once inside, he is
not to look back again, or he will be expelled; then the hinges of the
heavy, sacred doors make a strange sound as they swing open. As the
Pilgrim passes through, he hears the faint and distant strains of what
seems to be the Te Deum laudamus.

Now, pale upon the eastern balcony,
   appeared the concubine of old Tithonus,
   arisen now from her sweet lover's arms;   3

her brow was glittering with precious stones
   set in the shape of that cold-blooded beast
   that strikes and poisons people with its tail;   6

and of the hour-steps that Night ascends,
   already, where we were, two had been climbed,
   and now the third was folding down its wings,   9

when I, who carried with me Adam's weight,
   conquered by sleep, stretched out upon the grass
   on which all five of us were sitting then.   12

At the hour when the swallow, close to dawn,
   begins to sing her melancholy lays,
   perhaps remembering her ancient woes,   15

and when our mind, far straying from the flesh,
   less tangled in the network of its thoughts,
   becomes somehow prophetic in its dreams,   18

dreaming, I seemed to see hovering above,
   a golden-feathered eagle in the sky,
   with wings outspread, and ready to swoop down;   21

2. The concubine is Aurora, daughter of the sun, goddess of the dawn, who became
enamored of Tithonus, brother of Priam, and married him. She obtained for him
from the gods the gift of immortality but neglected to ask for that of eternal youth.

12. The five are the Pilgrim, Virgil, Sordello, Nino, and Corrado.

I seemed to find myself in that same place
    where Ganymede was forced to leave his friends,
    caught up to serve the conclave of the gods.   24

I wondered: "Could this be the only place
    the eagle strikes? Perhaps he does not deign
    to snatch his prey from anywhere but here."   27

Dreaming, I saw him circle for a while,
    then terrible as lightning, he struck down,
    swooping me up, up to the sphere of fire.   30

And there it seemed the bird and I both burned;
    the heat of that imaginary blaze
    was so intense it woke me from my sleep.   33

Just as Achilles woke up in a daze,
    glancing around himself with startled eyes,
    not knowing where he was or whence he came,   36

when he, asleep, was taken by his mother,
    borne in her arms, from Chiron's care to Skyros
    from where the Greeks would lure him finally—   39

so I was dazed, when sleep had fled my face;
    I turned the deathly color of a man
    feeling the freezing grip of fright on him.   42

Beside me was my Comfort, all alone.
    Now it was day, the sun two hours high,
    and what I saw before me was the sea.   45

"You must not be afraid," my leader said,
    "take heart, for we are well along our way;
    do not hold back, push on with all your strength,   48

you have arrived at Purgatory now.
    You see the rampart that surrounds it all
    and, where you see the cleft, that is the gate.   51

23. Ganymede, the son of Tros, the mythical founder of Troy, was reported to be
the most beautiful of all mortals. While hunting on Mount Ida, he was snatched up
by Jove disguised as an eagle, to become the cup-bearer to the gods.

Before the break of day, while your soul slept
  within your body, still at rest below
  upon the flowers of that painted glen, 54

a lady came. She said 'I am Lucia.
  Come, let me take this man who lies asleep;
  I wish to speed him on his journey up.' 57

Sordello and the other shades remained.
  She took you in her arms at break of day
  and brought you here. I followed after her. 60

Before she set you down, her lovely eyes
  showed me the open entrance; then she left,
  and as she went, she took away your sleep." 63

As one who, first perplexed, is reassured,
  and feels his fear replaced by confidence,
  once what is true has been revealed to him— 66

such was the change in me. And when he saw
  me free of care, my leader made his way
  up and along the bank with me behind. 69

Reader, you see how lofty is my theme!
  You should not be surprised if now I try
  to match its grandeur with more subtle art. 72

Close to the top, we reached a point from where
  I saw a gate (it first appeared to be
  merely a gap, a break within the wall) 75

and, leading up to it, there were three steps,
  each one a different color; and I saw
  the silent figure of someone on guard. 78

I slowly raised my eyes: I saw that he
  was sitting on the highest step, his face
  too splendid for my eyes—I looked away! 81

78–84. The guardian holds a naked sword, the symbol of divine authority. The sword
brilliantly reflects the rays of the sun, which is the symbol of God.

And in his hand he held a naked sword;
  so dazzling were the rays reflected thence,
  each time I tried to look I could not see.   84

He said to us: "Speak up from where you are.
  What is it that you want? Where is your guide?
  Beware, you may regret your coming here."   87

"A while ago, a lady sent from Heaven
  acquainted with such matters," said my guide,
  "told me: 'Behold the gate. You must go there.' "   90

"May she continue guiding you to good,"
  the courteous keeper of the gate replied,
  "and so, come forward now up to our stairs."   93

We reached the steps. White marble was the first,
  and polished to the glaze of a looking glass:
  I saw myself reflected as I was.   96

The second one was deeper dark than perse,
  of rough and crumbling, fire-corroded stone,
  with cracks across its surface—length and breadth.   99

The third one, lying heavy at the top,
  appeared to be of flaming porphyry,
  red as the blood that spurts out from a vein;   102

upon this step the angel of the Lord
  rested his feet; he sat upon the sill
  which seemed to be of adamantine rock.   105

Up the three steps my master guided me
  benevolently, saying: "Ask him now,
  in all humility, to turn the key."   108

Falling devoutly at his holy feet,
  in mercy's name I begged to be let in;
  but, first of all, three times I smote my breast.   111

94–102. The three steps are generally taken to represent the three stages of repen-
tance: the first step, which is white and mirrorlike, stands for self-examination; the
second, black, rough step stands for sorrow for sin, or contrition; the third, flaming-
red step signifies satisfaction of the sinner's debt, or penance.

Then with his sword he traced upon my brow
 the scars of seven *P*'s. "Once entered here,
 be sure you cleanse away these wounds," he said.   114

Ashes, or earth when it is dug up dry—
 this was the color of the robes he wore;
 he reached beneath them and drew out two keys.   117

One key was silver and the other gold;
 first he applied the white one, then the yellow—
 with that the gate responded to my wish.   120

"Whenever either one of these two keys
 fails to turn properly inside the lock,"
 the angel said, "the road ahead stays closed.   123

One is more precious, but the other needs
 wisdom and skill before it will unlock,
 for it is that one which unties the knot.   126

I hold these keys from Peter, who advised:
 'Admit too many, rather than too few,
 if they but cast themselves before your feet.' "   129

Then, pushing back the portal's holy door,
 "Enter," he said to us, "but first be warned:
 to look back means to go back out again."   132

And then the pivots of that sacred gate,
 fashioned of heavy metal, resonant,
 turned slow inside their sockets. The rolling roar   135

113. The letter *P* stands for the Latin *peccatum*, "sin." The seven *P*'s carved on the Pilgrim's forehead represent the stains of the seven Capital Sins that the Penitents must purge by their suffering on the mountain of Purgatory before their souls are ready to enter the Kingdom of Heaven.

135–138. The tribune Metellus attempted in vain to prevent Julius Caesar, after the crossing of the Rubicon in 49 B.C., from entering the temple of Saturn at the foot of the Tarpeian Rock, where the treasury was located. Lucan is describing the loud grating sound that echoed in the rock when the doors to the vault were opened (*Pharsalia* III, 153–57, 167–68).

was louder and more stubborn than Tarpeia's,
  when it was robbed of vigilant Metellus—
  its treasury made lean from that time on.   138

And as the grating pivots rolled, I turned,
  for I heard chanting: *Te Deum laudamus*—
  accompanied by the sweet notes of that door.   141

This harmony of sounds made me recall
  just how it seems in church when we attend
  to people singing as the organ plays: 144

sometimes the words are heard, and sometimes lost.

CANTO X

VIRGIL AND THE Pilgrim *pass through the gate, and it shuts resoundingly behind them as they make their way along a narrow path through a rocky cleft. They finally emerge from this "needle's eye" to find themselves on a deserted ledge. The wall of the cliff that rises to one side of the ledge is adorned with carvings in white marble, all of them offering examples of the virtue of humility. The first example is the scene of the Annunciation. The second carving represents David, who has put aside his kingly splendor to dance in humility before the Lord. The third shows the Emperor Trajan halting his mighty array of warriors on horseback to listen to a poor widow's plea for justice. As the Pilgrim stands marvelling at these august humilities, Virgil directs his attention to a group of souls that is moving toward them. These are the Proud, who, beating their breasts, make their way around the ledge under the crushing weight of tremendous slabs of stone that they carry on their backs.*

140. *Te Deum laudamus* ("We praise Thee, O God"), a famous Ambrosian hymn of gratitude to God, here appears to be sung somewhat mysteriously, on the occasion of the gates' opening to admit the Pilgrim into Purgatory.

When we had passed the threshold of the gate
    forever closed to souls whose loves are bad
    and make the crooked road seem like the straight,   3

I heard it close again, resoundingly;
    if I had turned to look back at the gate,
    how could I have explained this fault of mine?   6

Then we were climbing through a narrow cleft
    along a path that zigzagged through the rock
    the way a wave swells up and then pulls back.   9

"Now, we are at the point," my guide began,
    "where we must use our wits: when the path bends,
    we keep close to the far side of the curve."   12

This forced us into taking smaller steps,
    so that the waning moon had made its way
    to rest already in its bed, before   15

we finally squeezed through that needle's eye.
    When we were free, once more out on the mount,
    where this recedes enough to form a ledge,   18

we stopped there on the level space that stretched
    lonelier than a desert path—I, tired,
    and both of us uncertain of the way.   21

From the plain's edge, verging on empty space,
    to where the cliff-face soars again, was room
    for three men's bodies laid out end to end;   24

as far as I could take in with my eyes,
    measuring carefully from left to right,
    this terrace did not vary in its width.   27

And standing there, before we took a step,
    I realized that all the inner cliff,
    which, rising sheer, offered no means to climb,   30

was pure white marble; on its flawless face
    were carvings that would surely put to shame
    not only Polyclete but Nature too.   33

The angel who came down to announce on earth
    the peace longed for by weeping centuries,
    which broke the ancient ban and opened Heaven,   36

appeared before our eyes: a shape alive,
    carved in an attitude of marble grace,
    an effigy that could have spoken words.   39

One would have sworn that he was saying "Ave!"
    for she who turned the key, opening for us
    the Highest Love, was also figured there;   42

the outlines of her image carved the words
    Ecce ancilla Dei, as clearly cut
    as is the imprint of a seal on wax.   45

"Why don't you look at other parts as well?"
    my gentle master said, the while I stood
    close by his side, the side that holds the heart.   48

And so I turned my eyes and looked ahead
    past Mary's figure to that point where he
    who prompted me now stood, and there I saw   51

another story cut into the stone;
    crossing in front of Virgil, I drew near,
    so that my eyes could take in all of it.   54

Carved in the spread of marble there, I saw
    the cart and oxen with the holy Ark:
    a warning not to exceed one's competence.   57

31–32. The carvings here illustrate examples of the virtue of Humility; they will be
followed two cantos later by "carved examples" of the vice of Pride. Thus on the
first cornice, Dante has chosen to represent the relevant pair of contrasts on the visual
plane, imagining illustrative scenes carved with consummate art.

33. Polyclete, or Polycletus, was a celebrated Greek sculptor (ca. 452–412 B.C.) and
a contemporary of Phidias. Just as Phidias was thought to be unsurpassed in carving
images of the gods, so Polycletus was thought to execute perfect carvings of men.

41. The Virgin Mary in conceiving Christ "unlocked" for mankind the love of God.

57. This line refers to the presumptuous act of Uzzah, who accompanied the Ark
during the first stage of its journey.

Ahead of it moved seven separate choirs
    testing my senses: one of these said, "No,"
    the other one said, "Yes, they truly sing!"   60

With equal art, the smoke which censers poured
    was traced so faithfully that eyes and nose
    could not decide between a "yes" or "no."   63

Ahead, and far beyond the sacred Ark,
    his robes girt up, the humble Psalmist danced,
    showing himself both more and less than king.   66

Depicted on the other side was Michal,
    as from a palace window she looked on,
    her face revealed her sadness and her scorn.   69

I moved away from that place to observe
    at closer range another story told
    in whiteness just beyond the face of Michal.   72

Here was retold the magnanimity
    of that great Prince of Rome whose excellence
    moved Gregory to win his greatest fight: 75

there rode the noble Trajan, Emperor,
    and clinging to his bridle as she wept
    a wretched widow, carved in lines of grief.   78

The trampled space surrounding him was packed
    with knights on horseback—eagles, flying high,
    threaded in gold of banners in the wind.   81

That poor widow amid the mass of shapes
    seemed to be saying: "Lord, avenge my son
    who has been killed; my heart is cut with grief."   84

---

67. Michal, David's first wife, daughter of King Saul, observed with disdain and reproach her husband's humble dance of joy. For her arrogant attitude she was punished with sterility (cf. 2 Kings 6:23).

He seemed to answer: "You will have to wait
   for my return." And she, like one impelled
   by frantic grief: "But, oh, my lord, if you   87

should not return?" And he: "Who takes my place
   will do it for me." She: "How can you let
   another's virtue take the place of yours?"   90

Then he: "Take comfort, for I see I must
   perform my duty, now, before I leave:
   Justice so wills, and pity holds me here."   93

That One for Whom no new thing can exist
   fashioned this art of visible speech—so strange
   to us who do not know it here on earth.   96

As I stood there delighting in the sight
   of these august humilities displayed,
   dear to behold for their own Craftsman's sake,   99

"See, over there, how slowly they approach,
   that crowd of souls," the Poet whispered to me,
   "they will direct us to the lofty stairs."   102

My eyes, intent on their admiring,
   were, nonetheless, not slow to turn toward him,
   for they are always eager for new sights.   105

But, Reader, when I tell you how God wills
   His penitents should pay their debts, do not
   abandon your intention to repent.   108

You must not think about the punishment,
   think but of what will come of it—at worst
   it cannot last beyond the Final Day.   111

"Master, what I see moving toward us there,"
   I said, "do not seem to be shades at all;
   I don't know what they are, my sight's confused."   114

"The grievous nature of their punishment,"
   he answered, "bends their bodies toward the ground;
   my own eyes were not sure of what they saw.   117

---

94. The "One" is God (cf. *Inferno* XV, 11).

Try hard to disentangle all the parts
 of what you see moving beneath those stones.
 Can you see now how each one beats his breast?"   120

O haughty Christians, wretched, sluggish souls,
 all you whose inner vision is diseased,
 putting your trust in things that pull you back,   123

do you not understand that we are worms,
 each born to form the angelic butterfly,
 that flies defenseless to the Final Judge?   126

Why do your souls' pretensions rise so high,
 since you are but defective insects still,
 worms as yet imperfectly evolved?   129

Sometimes one sees a corbel, holding the weight
 of roof or ceiling, carved in human shape
 with chest pressed tightly down against its knees,   132

so that this unreality gives real
 anguish to one who sees it—this is how
 these souls appeared, and how they made me feel.   135

True, some of them were more compressed, some less,
 as more or less weight pressed on each one's back,
 but even the most patient of them all   138

seemed through his tears to say: "I can't go on!"

CANTO XI

THE CANTO OPENS with the prayer of the Proud—an expanded version of the Lord's Prayer. Virgil then asks the penitents to tell him the quickest way up the mountain, and one of the souls replies that he will show them an opening through which they may ascend. This is the soul of Omberto Aldobrandesco, who acknowledges that the sin of pride in family has ruined not only himself but his entire house. The Pilgrim is then recognized by another soul, Oderisi of Gubbio, who proclaims

against the empty glory of human talent. And Oderisi points to still
another of the souls of the Proud—Provenzan Salvani, the presumptu-
ous dictator of Siena.

"Our Father Who in Heaven dost abide,
    not there constrained but dwelling there because
    Thou lovest more Thy lofty first effects,   3

hallowed be Thy name, hallowed Thy Power,
    by Thy creatures as it behooves us all
    to render thanks for Thy sweet effluence.   6

Thy kingdom come to us with all its peace;
    if it come not, we of ourselves cannot
    attain to it, no matter how we strive.   9

And as Thine angels offer up their wills
    to Thee in sacrifice, singing Hosannah,
    let all men offer up to Thee their own.   12

Give us this day our daily manna, Lord:
    without it, those most eager to advance
    go backwards through this wild wasteland of ours.   15

As we forgive our trespassers, do Thou,
    forgive our trespasses, merciful Lord,
    look not upon our undeserving worth.   18

Our strength is only weakness, lead us not
    into temptation by our ancient foe:
    deliver us from him who urges evil.   21

This last request, beloved Lord, we make
    not for ourselves, who know we have no need,
    but for those souls who still remain behind."   24

4–5. The phrase "by Thy creatures," added to the original "hallowed be Thy name,"
is reminiscent of the *Laudes creatururum* of Saint Francis, who was perhaps the
greatest example of humility in the Middle Ages.

13–15. The replacement of the original "daily bread" by a "daily manna," as well
as the reference to the desert, recalls the Exodus theme of the Antepurgatory (in
particular see *Purgatory* II, 45).

24. The souls are those still living on earth, who need protection from temptation.

Thus, praying for their welfare and for ours,
    those souls moved slowly bent beneath their weights—
    the slowness that oppresses us in dreams—   27

unequally tormented by their loads,
    making their tired way on the First Round,
    purging away the filth of worldliness.   30

If they, up there, pray always for our good,
    think of what we down here can do for them,
    when praying hearts are rooted in good will!   33

We ought, indeed, to help them wash away
    the stains they bring from earth, that they may rise,
    weightless and pure, into the wheeling stars.   36

"Ah, so may justice joined with pity free
    you from your load, that you may spread your wings
    and fly up to the goal of your desire,   39

show us how we may find the shortest way
    to reach the stairs; if there are many paths,
    direct us to the one least steep to climb: 42

this man who comes here with me bears a weight;
    he is invested still with Adam's flesh,
    and so, against his will, is slow to climb."   45

Some words then came in answer to the ones
    that had been spoken by my leader, but
    it was not clear to me from whom they came;   48

someone, however, said: "Follow this bank
    along the right with us, and you will find
    the road a living man can surely climb.   51

If I were not prevented by this stone
    that curbs the movement of my haughty neck,
    and makes me keep my face bent to the ground,   54

I would look up to see if I might know
    this unnamed living man, and hope to move
    him to compassion for my burdened back.   57

28. Each soul is tormented according to the gravity and extent of his own sin.

I was Italian, born of a great Tuscan:
    Guglielmo Aldobrandesco was my sire.
    Perhaps you never heard the name before.   60

My ancient lineage, the gallant deeds
    of my forebears had made me arrogant:
    forgetful of our common Mother Earth,   63

I held all men in such superb disdain,
    I died for it, as all Siena knows
    and every child in Compagnatico.   66

I am Omberto. And the sin of Pride
    has ruined not only me but all my house,
    dragging them with it to calamity.   69

This weight which I refused while I still lived,
    I now am forced to bear among the dead,
    until the day that God is satisfied."   72

I had my head bent low, to hear his words,
    and someone—not the one who spoke just now—
    twisted around beneath his punishment,   75

and saw my face, and knew me, and called out,
    straining to keep his eyes on me, as I
    moved with those souls, keeping my body bent.   78

"Oh!" I said, "*you* must be that Oderisi,
    honor of Gubbio, honor of the art
    which men in Paris call 'Illuminating.' "   81

"The pages Franco Bolognese paints,"
    he said, "my brother, smile more radiantly;
    his is the honor now—mine is far less.   84

59. The name Guglielmo Aldobrandesco, which occupies almost the entire line, seems to echo the grandiose qualities of Omberto's father, the mighty Tuscan.

67. Omberto was the second son of Guglielmo Aldobrandesco (59), Count of Santafiora, whose hatred of the Sienese led him to abandon the Ghibelline cause and ally himself with the Guelphs of Florence and Tuscany.

79. Oderisi (ca. 1240–1299?) was an illuminator of manuscripts.

Less courteous would I have been to him,
   I must admit, while I was still alive
   and my desire was only to excel. 87

For pride like that the price is paid up here;
   I would not even be here, were it not
   that, while I still could sin, I turned to God. 90

Oh, empty glory of all human power!
   How soon the green fades from the topmost bough,
   unless the following season shows no growth! 93

Once Cimabue thought to hold the field
   as painter; Giotto now is all the rage,
   dimming the lustre of the other's fame. 96

So, one Guido takes from the other one
   poetic glory; and, already born,
   perhaps, is he who'll drive both from fame's nest. 99

Your earthly fame is but a gust of wind
   that blows about, shifting this way and that,
   and as it changes quarter, changes name. 102

Were you to reach the ripe old age of death,
   instead of dying prattling in your crib,
   would you have more fame in a thousand years? 105

What are ten centuries to eternity?
   Less than the blinking of an eye compared
   to the turning of the slowest of the spheres. 108

94. Cenni de Pepo, known as Giovanni Cimabue (1240?–1302?), was considered in the Florence of his day a great master. He broke from the Byzantine tradition of art to develop a more natural style.

95. Giotto of Bondone (1266 or 1267–1337) was a pupil of Cimabue's who went on to surpass his master. Giotto appears to have been a personal friend of Dante's (one or two years his junior), and is most likely responsible for the famous portrait of Dante in the Bargello at Florence.

97–99. The first Guido is Guido Cavalcanti (1259–1300), and the other is Guido Guinizelli (ca. 1230–ca. 1276), a Bolognese poet whom Dante refers to as his "father" and the father of "all those who wrote poetry of love in a sweet and graceful style" (*Purgatory* XXVI, 97–99).

You see that soul ahead crawling along?
   All Tuscany resounded with his name;
   now hardly is it whispered in Siena,   111

where once he ruled, and managed to destroy
   the mad attack of Florence—once, so proud
   but, now, become as venal as a whore.   114

Your earthly fame is like the green in grass:
   it comes and goes, and He who makes it grow
   green from the earth will make it fade again."   117

And I to him: "Your words of truth have humbled
   my heart; they have reduced my swollen pride.
   But who is he you spoke about just now?"   120

"That's Provenzan Salvani," he replied,
   "and he is here because presumptuously
   he sought to gain control of all Siena.   123

So he crawls on, and has crawled since he died,
   knowing no rest. And such coin is paid here
   by those who were presumptuous down there."   126

And I: "If it is true that any soul
   who has delayed repentance till the last
   must wait down there before he can ascend,   129

the same amount of time he lived on earth
   (unless he's helped by efficacious prayer)—
   then how has he arrived so fast up here?"   132

He said: "While at the apex of his glory,
   in Siena's marketplace, of his free will,
   putting aside all shame, he took his stand,   135

---

109. In line 121 this soul "crawling along" is identified as Provenzan Salvani (ca. 1220–1269), Ghibelline chief of Siena. Provenzan's sins are an example of pride in temporal power.

and there, to ransom from his suffering
    a friend who was immured in Charles's jail,
    he brought himself to do what chilled his veins!   138

(I say no more. My words, I know, are vague,
    but your own neighbors not too long from now
    will help you to interpret what I've said.)   141

It was this deed of his that sped him here."

CANTO XII

As THEY LEAVE *the souls of the Proud, Virgil calls the Pilgrim's attention to a series of carvings in the bed of rock beneath their feet. These are the examples of the vice of Pride, of the haughty who have been brought low. Depicted in the carvings are Satan, the giant Briareus, Nimrod, Niobe, Saul, Arachne, Rehoboam, the slaying of Eriphyle by her son Alcmeon, Sennacherib's murder by his sons, the slaughter of Cyrus by Tomyris, the destruction of Holofernes and the rout of the Assyrians, and finally the fall of Troy. As they continue circling the ledge, Virgil admonishes the Pilgrim to lift his head in anticipation of the angel of Humility. With a brush of his wings, the angel removes the first P from the Pilgrim's forehead, and, as the two poets make their way through the pass to the next terrace, they hear a sweetly resounding song—the beatitude "Blessed are the Poor in Spirit." The Pilgrim now feels himself to be lighter, since one of the P's has been removed, and is able to climb with considerably less effort.*

Like oxen keeping step beneath their yoke,
    we moved along, that burdened soul and I,
    as long as my kind teacher would allow;   3

137. The jailer is probably Charles of Anjou.

138. This line is a most indirect way of saying "he forced himself to beg in the public square."

2. The soul is that of Oderisi.

but when he said: "Now leave him and move on,
    for each one here must drive his boat ahead
    with sail and oar, and all the might he has,"   6

I stood up straight to walk the way man should,
    but, though my body was erect, my thoughts
    were bowed and shrunken to humility.   9

Now I was moving, happily following
    the footsteps of my master, both of us
    showing how light of foot we had become,   12

when, "Now look down," he said. "You will be pleased,
    and it will make your journey easier,
    to see this bed of stone beneath your feet."   15

As tombs set in a church floor often bear
    carved indications of the dead man's life,
    in preservation of his memory   18

(pierced by such recollection of the dead,
    a man is very often brought to tears—
    though only those with piety are moved):   21

just so, I saw—but far more true to life,
    being divinely wrought—stone carvings there
    covering the path that juts out from the mount.   24

I saw, on one side, him who was supposed
    to be the noblest creature of creation,
    plunge swift as lightning from the height of Heaven.   27

I saw Briareus on the other side,
    pierced through by the celestial thunderbolt,
    heavy upon the ground, frozen in death.   30

13–15. The examples illustrating the vice of Pride are cut into the floor: thus they must be viewed with head bent low, in humility.

28. Briareus was one of the giants (*Inferno* XXXI, 98) who challenged Jupiter; he was slain by a thunderbolt and buried beneath Mount Etna.

I saw Thymbraeus, saw Pallas and Mars
　　still armed, close to their father, looking down
　　at severed, scattered members of the giants.　　　　　33

I saw the mighty Nimrod by his tower,
　　standing there stunned and gazing at the men
　　who shared at Shinar his bold fantasy.　　　　　36

O Niobe, I saw your grieving eyes:
　　they wept from your carved image on the road,
　　between your seven and seven children slain.　　　　　39

O Saul, transfixed by your own sword, how dead
　　you seemed to lie on Mount Gilboa's plain—
　　which since that time has known no rain or dew.　　　　　42

O mad Arachne, I could see you there,
　　half-turned to spider, sad above the shreds
　　of your own work of art that sentenced you.　　　　　45

O Rehoboam, the image of you here
　　no longer threatens: in a chariot,
　　it flees fear-stricken, though no man pursues.　　　　　48

Depicted, too, in that hard pavement stone
　　was Alcmeon, who made his mother pay
　　so dearly for the accursèd ornament.　　　　　51

31. Thymbraeus is another name for Apollo.

33. The giants, armed with boulders and tree trunks, presumed to attack Mount Olympus, home of the gods, only to be destroyed.

34. Nimrod was the giant who built the Tower of Babel on the plain of Shinar (Genesis 10:10). (Cf. *Inferno* XXXI, 77–78; *Paradise* XXVI, 126.)

37. Niobe was the daughter of Tantalus and Dione, and the wife of Amphion, king of Thebes.

40. Saul was the son of Kish of the tribe of Benjamin and first king of Israel.

43. Arachne was the daughter of Idmon of Colophon, who challenged Minerva to a weaving contest.

46. Rehoboam, the son of Solomon, succeeded his father as king of Israel.

50. Alcmeon was the son of Amphiaraus the Soothsayer and Eriphyle.

Depicted were Sennacherib's own sons
    assaulting him at prayer within the temple,
    and their departure, as he lay there dead.   54

Depicted was Tomyris with the ruin
    and slaughter that she wrought, her words to Cyrus:
    "Blood you have thirsted for—now, drink your own!"   57

Depicted was the rout of the Assyrians
    who fled at Holofernes' death—it showed
    the remnants of his mutilated corpse.   60

I saw Troy gaping from its ashes there:
    O Ilium, how you were fallen low,
    depicted on the sculptured road of stone.   63

What master artist with his brush or pen
    could reproduce these shapes and shadings here?
    Such art must overwhelm the subtlest mind!   66

The dead seemed dead, the living seemed alive;
    no witness to the scene itself saw better
    than I who trod upon it, head bent low.   69

Be proud, then! Onward, haughty heads held high,
    you sons of Eve! Yes, never bow your head
    to see how evil is the road you tread!   72

We had, by now, gone farther round the mount,
    and much more of the sun's course had been traced,
    than I, preoccupied, could have conceived—   75

when he who always kept a watchful eye
    as he moved on said: "Raise your head up now,
    you have spent time enough lost in your thoughts.   78

52. Sennacherib was the king of Assyria from 705 to 681 B.C., who arrogantly made war upon King Hezekiah of Judah and the Israelites.

55–56. Tomyris (or Thamyris), the queen of the Massagetae (a Scythian people), sought revenge for the treacherous murder of her son at the hands of Cyrus (560–529 B.C.), emperor of the Persians.

59. Holofernes was the general of the armies of Nebuchadnezzar, king of the Assyrians.

Look over there, and see. The angel comes!
   And, see—the sixth handmaiden has returned
   already from her service to the day.   81

Show reverence in your face and attitude,
   so that he will be glad to help us up;
   think that this day will never dawn again!"   84

I was well used to his admonishments
   not to waste time, so, anything he said
   to that effect could never be obscure.   87

Still closer to us, clothed in white, he came,
   the radiantly fair creature, and his face
   was shining like a trembling star at dawn.   90

He spread his arms out wide, and then his wings.
   He said: "Come, now, the steps are very close;
   henceforth, the climbing will be easier."   93

To such an invitation few respond:
   O race of men, born to fly heavenward,
   how can a breath of wind make you fall back? 96

He led us straight to where the rock was cleft.
   Once there, he brushed his wings against my brow,
   then he assured me of a safe ascent.   99

As, on the way up to the mountaintop
   crowned by the church, beyond the Rubaconte,
   set high, above that so well-governed town, 102

the steepness of the bold ascent is cut
   on the right hand by steps carved in the rock
   in times when one could trust ledgers and staves— 105

80. The sixth handmaiden is the sixth hour of the day, or noon.

98. With this gesture of his wings, the angel removes the first *P*, which stands for the sin of Pride, from the Pilgrim's forehead.

102. The town is Florence, of course, and the reference is a bitterly ironic one in view of the incidents alluded to in line 105.

so here, the bank that from the second round
    falls steep has been made easier with steps
    though, on both sides, the high rock presses close.   108

While we were walking toward those steps, the song
    Beati pauperes spiritu! rang out
    more sweetly than could ever be described.   111

How different are these passageways from those
    of Hell! One enters here to music—there,
    below, to sounds of violent laments.   114

As we were climbing up the sacred steps,
    I seemed to feel myself much lighter now
    than I had been before on level ground.   117

"Master," I said, "tell me, what heavy thing
    has been removed from me? I feel as if
    to keep on climbing would be effortless."   120

He answered: "When the *P*'s that still remain
    (though they have almost faded) on your brow
    shall be erased completely like the first,   123

then will your feet be light with good desire;
    they will no longer feel the heavy road
    but will rejoice as they are urged to climb."   126

Then I did something anyone might do,
    made conscious by the way men looked at him
    that he must have some strange thing on his head: 129

his hand will try hard to investigate,
    feeling around to find, fulfilling thus
    the duty that the eyes cannot perform;   132

so, my right hand with fingers spread found just
    six of the seven letters that were carved
    upon my brow by him who keeps the keys.   135

Observing this, my master smiled at me.

CANTO XIII

THE PILGRIM AND *Virgil reach the second cornice, which is the livid color of stone. Since there are no souls in sight of whom to ask directions, Virgil turns to the sun for guidance. When he and Dante have walked about a mile along the ledge, they hear a disembodied voice crying out the examples of Generosity, the virtue opposed to the vice of Envy. The first of the virtuous examples that it cites is the Virgin Mary's solicitude at the wedding feast of Cana when she tells her son, "They have no wine." The second is the attempt of Pylades to save the life of his friend by claiming, "I am Orestes," and the third is the commandment from the gospels "Love your enemy." Virgil explains that on this terrace, the sin of Envy is punished, and he indicates the souls of the Envious sitting huddled together against the face of the cliff. They can be heard reciting the Litany of the Saints, and as the Pilgrim approaches them he remarks their piteous condition. They are dressed in the coarsest of haircloth, and their eyelids have been stitched shut with iron thread. The Pilgrim has a long conversation with Sapìa of Siena, who confesses that she rejoiced in the defeat of her own townsmen at the battle of Colle.*

Now we are standing on the highest step,
    where, for a second time, we saw a ledge
    cut in the mount that heals all those who climb.   3

This terrace stretches all around the hill,
    exactly like the one below, although
    the arc of this one makes a sharper curve.   6

No sign of any souls or carvings here.
    The cliff face is all bare, the roadway bare—
    save for the livid color of the stone.   9

"If we wait here until somebody comes
    to give directions," said the Poet, "our choice,
    I am afraid, will be too long delayed."   12

6. This circle, being higher up the mountain, is smaller.

Then, looking up, and staring at the sun,
   he made of his right side a pivot point,
   bringing the left side of his body round.   15

"O cherished light in whom I place my trust,
   please guide us on this unfamiliar road,"
   he said, "for in this place guidance we need.   18

You warm the world; you shed your light on it;
   unless there be some reason that opposes,
   your radiant light should always show the way."   21

We had already gone along that ledge
   as far as what is called a mile on earth—
   and quickly, too, because of our good will—   24

when spirits, who could not be seen, were heard,
   as they came flying towards us, speaking words
   of courteous invitation to love's board.   27

The first voice that came flying past us sang
   out loud and clear the words *Vinum non habent*;
   then we could hear them echoing behind.   30

Before the notes had faded quietly
   into distance, another voice cried out:
   "I am Orestes!" And that voice too swept by.   33

"Oh," I said, "Father, what voices are these?"
   And just as I was asking this, a third
   said, passing by: "Love those who do you harm!" 36

Then my good master said: "The Envious
   this circle scourges—that is why the whip
   used here is fashioned from the cords of love.   39

29. *"Vinum non habent"* ("They have no wine") is the first example of charitable concern for others. Mary, acting out of concern for the happiness of others, lovingly solicits her son's first miracle: the changing of water into wine.

33. The second example of the virtue opposed to Envy is from antiquity; the one who claims the name Orestes is doing so out of generosity and friendship.

36. The third voice expresses an evangelical precept taken from the Sermon on the Mount (Matthew 5:44).

The curb must sound the opposite of love;
   you will most likely hear it, I should think,
   before the pass of pardon has been reached.   42

Now look in front of you, look carefully
   and you will see some people over there,
   all of them with their backs against the cliff."   45

I looked ahead of me, straining my eyes:
   I saw a mass of spirits wrapped in cloaks
   the color of the stone they leaned against.   48

And then as we came closer to these souls,
   I heard the cry: "O Mary, pray for us";
   then "Michael, Peter, and All Saints," they cried.   51

I do not think there is a man on earth
   with heart so hard that it would not be pierced
   with pity if he saw what I saw then: 54

when I had come up close enough to see
   the nature of the penance they endured,
   the sight squeezed bitter tears out of my eyes.   57

Their cloaks seemed to be made of coarsest cloth,
   and one's head on another's shoulder lay,
   the inner cliff supporting all of them.   60

They brought to mind blind beggars at church doors
   during Indulgences begging their bread:
   the one leaning his head upon the next   63

to stir up pity in their fellow man,
   not only by the sound of begging cries,
   but by the looks that plead no less than words.   66

---

42. This pass is at the entrance to the next terrace, at which point the angel will remove the second *P* of envy from the Pilgrim's brow and admit him to the Third Terrace.

50–51. The souls are reciting the Litany of the Saints.

63. The penitent Envious, who once wished the worst for their neighbors, are now, like so many blind beggars, sustaining and supporting each other.

Just as the blind cannot enjoy the sun,
    so, to the shades I saw before me here,
    the light of Heaven denies its radiance: 69

the eyelids of these shades had been sewn shut
    with iron threads, like falcons newly caught,
    whose eyes we stitch to tame their restlessness.   72

I felt that I was doing something wrong,
    walking along, staring at people who
    could not stare back. I turned to my wise guide,   75

who knew quite well what his mute ward would ask,
    and waiting not for me to speak, said, "Yes,
    but let your words be brief and to the point."   78

Virgil was walking on one side of me,
    along the terrace edge where one could fall
    (for there was no protective parapet),   81

while on the other side of me were massed
    those supplicating souls whose cheeks were wet
    with tears that seeped out through the horrid seams.   84

I turned to them and said: "O souls assured
    that someday you will see the light of Heaven
    which is the only goal that you desire,   87

so may God's grace soon wash away the film
    clouding your consciousness, and thus allow
    the stream of memory to flow through pure,   90

please let me know—I would be very grateful—
    is someone here, perhaps, Italian?
    I could be very helpful if he were."   93

"My brother, all of us are citizens
    of one true city. You mean is there a soul
    who was a pilgrim once in Italy?"   96

---

70. This image is taken from falconry: the eyes of these birds, which were captured
when they were no longer fledglings, were sewn shut (with waxed silk thread, how-
ever, not with iron wire) to facilitate domestication and training.

This answer to my question seemed to come
   from somewhere up ahead, so I moved on
   to where those souls could clearly hear my words.   99

Among them I discerned one shade that looked
   expectant. How could I tell? The chin was raised—
   that searching gesture of the blind. I said: 102

"O soul, learning to dominate yourself
   for the ascent—if it was you who spoke—
   tell me your name, or where you lived." She said: 105

"I was a Sienese; here with the rest
   I mend my evil life with tears and beg
   of Him that He reveal Himself to us.   108

Though named Sapìa, sapient I was not:
   I always reveled in another's grief,
   enjoying that more than my own welfare.   111

If you do not believe me, listen now
   and you will see how far my folly went.
   In the declining arc of my long years,   114

it happened that my townsmen were engaged
   in battle just outside of Colle; I
   prayed God for what already He had willed.   117

Our men were scattered on the plain and forced
   to take the bitter course of flight. I watched
   the chase, seized with a surge of joy so fierce   120

I raised my shameless face to God and cried
   "I have lost all my fear of Thee!" I was
   the blackbird when the sun comes out awhile.   123

109. Sapìa of Siena was the paternal aunt of Provenzan Salvani (*Purgatory* XI, 121) and the wife of Ghinibaldo Saracini. She hated her fellow Sienese and resented her nephew's rise to power.

116. The present Colle di Val d'Elsa in Tuscany was where, in 1269, the Sienese Ghibellines, under Provenzan Salvani and Count Guido Novello, were defeated in battle by the Florentine Guelphs, aided by the French troops of Charles d'Anjou.

120. This line, together with 110–111 ("I always reveled . . ."), indicates that Envy may involve not only resentment of the good fortune of others but positive enjoyment of their misfortunes.

I did not seek my peace with God, not till
    my final hour came—and even then,
    penance would not yet have reduced my debt   126

had it not been for one Pier Pettinaio,
    who, moved by charity to grieve for me,
    remembered me in all his holy prayers.   129

But who are you, so eager to inquire
    about us here—you with your eyes unsewn,
    so I would guess, and breathing out your words?"   132

"My sight one day shall be sewn up," I said,
    "but not for long; my eyes have seldom sinned
    in casting envious looks on other folk.   135

It is a greater fear that shakes my soul:
    that of the penance done below—already
    I feel on me the weight those souls must bear."   138

And she: "Then who has led you here to us,
    if you count on returning down below?"
    And I: "This man with me who does not speak.   141

I am alive. And if you want me to,
    O chosen soul, I would be glad to move
    my mortal feet on earth on your behalf."   144

"Oh, what a miracle this is!" she said.
    "What evidence of God's great love for you!
    Yes, help me with a prayer from time to time.   147

By what you hold most dear, I beg of you,
    if ever you set foot on Tuscan soil,
    restore my name among my kinsfolk there.   150

127. Pier Pettinaio, "Peter the Combseller," was supposedly a member of the Franciscan order who dwelt close to Siena and was known for his piety, the miracles he performed, and his honesty (he refused to sell a defective comb).

147. In the Antepurgatory a number of souls had asked of the Pilgrim that when he returned to earth he solicit prayers for them from their loved ones. This is probably what Dante had in mind when he offered to "move" his "mortal feet" (144) on Sapìa's behalf.

They live with those who dream of Talamone,
    whose foolish hopes will make them lose much more
    than they lost looking for Diana's bed—   153

but, still, the admirals will lose the most."

CANTO XIV

THE CANTO OPENS *with the gossip of two blind souls excited by their awareness of the unprecedented presence before them of a man who is still alive; they finally ask the Pilgrim who he is and where he is from. Dante's reference to his place of origin—the valley of the Arno—touches off a lengthy outburst of anti-Tuscan sentiment from one of his interlocutors. The Pilgrim then asks their names; the speaker identifies himself as Guido del Duca and his fellow shade as Rinier da Calboli—and immediately launches into another invective, this time against the recent degeneracy of Romagna. As the Pilgrim and Virgil are leaving the souls of the Envious, they hear the sharp crack of voices—screaming out exempla of Envy. The first voice is that of Cain, and the second, that of the Athenian princess Aglauros, who was turned to stone because she envied her sister, who was loved by the god Mercury.*

"Who is this roaming round our mountainside
    before his soul is given wings by Death—
    opening his eyes and closing them at will?"   3

"Who knows? All I know is he's not alone.
    Why don't you ask him, you are nearer him;
    speak nicely to him so he'll answer you."   6

---

1. This dramatic opening is a dialogue between two unknown speakers concerning a person standing before them whom they cannot see.

There to my right, I overheard two souls
   talking about me, huddled head to head;
   they raised their faces then, as if to speak.   9

And one said: "O soul, living prisoner
   within the flesh, but moving up to Heaven,
   console us in the name of love: please tell   12

where you are from and who you are. The grace
   that God has given you fills us with awe,
   for this is something never seen before."   15

And I said: "Through the heart of Tuscany
   a little river, born in Falterona,
   winds in its course more than a hundred miles,   18

and from its banks I bring this body here;
   there is no point in telling you my name,
   for I have not as yet won fame on earth."   21

"If I have clearly understood the gist
   of what you have just said," replied the shade,
   "it is the Arno you are speaking of."   24

The other said to him: "Why would he want
   to keep the real name of that river hid,
   as if it were too horrible to say?"   27

The shade who had been questioned answered back:
   "I don't know why, but it could only be
   a blessing for that valley's name to die.   30

For from its source, where the steep mountain chain
   from which Pelorus is cut off is rich
   with waters that no other place can claim,   33

down to the very point where it restores
   that which the sky has taken from the sea,
   thereby supplying rivers with their flow—   36

virtue is loathed. Men run away from it
   as from a snake! Either the place is cursed,
   or else it's old corruption guiding them.   39

The dwellers in that miserable vale
   have let their nature be transformed—it is
   as if they lived on food from Circe's sty.   42

Past hoggish brutes who should be eating acorns
   rather than food prepared for human use,
   this river first directs its puny course;   45

it keeps on dropping down, to run among
   packs of small curs who snarl more than they bite;
   disdainfully, it turns away its snout.   48

Still farther down it falls; the more this damned
   and God-forsaken sewer-ditch expands
   the more the dogs give way to wolves; and then,   51

through many deep-cut gorges it descends
   to run among those foxes steeped in fraud,
   who fear no trap contrived by human skill.   54

I will not stop, though this man hears my words;
   in fact, it would be good for him to know
   what inspiration has revealed to me: 57

I see your grandson now leading the chase,
   hunting down wolves, the ones that pack the banks
   of that wild stream—they live in terror there.   60

He sells their flesh while they are still alive,
   and then, like worn-out cattle, slaughters them.
   Himself he robs of honor, them of life.   63

He comes forth bloody from the wretched woods,
   which even in a thousand years from now
   could not re-wood itself as once it was."   66

---

42. Circe was the daughter of Helios, god of the sun. She was an enchantress who had the power of turning men into beasts.

55. When the speaker here, Guido del Duca (whose name is withheld until line 81), says the words "this man," he is referring to the other penitent soul sitting beside him, who is Rinieri da Calbolì (whose name is not revealed until verses 88–89).

58. Rinieri's grandson, Fulcieri da Calboli, infamously cruel and a perpetrator of atrocities against the White Guelphs (Dante's party) as well as the Ghibellines, was podestà of Florence in 1303.

As at the news of some impending doom
   the face that listens shows the shock received,
   no matter from what side the danger looms—   69

just so that shade, intent on listening,
   revealed his consternation and his grief,
   as he took in the meaning of those words.   72

The words of one of them, the other's face,
   made me so curious to know the pair,
   I asked them, begged them, to reveal their names.   75

At this the shade who spoke to me at first
   replied: "And you want me to bring myself
   to do what you refused to do for me?   78

But since God wills His grace to shine in you
   so generously, stingy I shall not be:
   Guido del Duca used to be my name.   81

Envy was quick to fire up my blood:
   whenever I would see someone rejoice,
   you'd see me turning livid at his joy.   84

I sowed this envy, now I reap this straw!
   O human race, why do you place your hopes
   where partnership must always be denied?   87

This is Rinier; this is the pride and joy
   of Calboli—a house without an heir
   who might inherit any of his worth.   90

From Po to mountains, Reno to the sea,
   their house is not the only one stripped bare
   of all that's good in life and chivalry;   93

for all the land within these boundaries
   is choked by poisonous weeds which would resist
   all efforts to prepare the soil for seeds.   96

81. Little is known about Guido del Duca. Possibly he was the son of Giovanni del Duca of the Onesti family of Ravenna, who settled in Bertinoro.

88. Rinier, Rinieri de' Paolucci da Calboli, was a Guelph from the city of Forlì and podestà of Faenza (1247), Parma (1252), and Ravenna (1265). He was defeated by Guido da Montefeltro in 1276 and died at Forlì in 1296.

Where is Mainardi? Where is the good Lizio?
   Pier Traversaro? Guido di Carpigna?
   O Romagnols, bastard descendents, false!   99

When in Bologna will there grow again
   a Fabbro? When, a Fosco in Faenza,
   that noble scion of a lowly plant?   102

O Tuscan, I must weep when I recall
   Ugolin d'Azzo, Guido da Prata, too,
   who lived among us once. And what about   105

Federigo di Tignoso and his friends,
   the Traversaro clan, the Anastagi,
   both families without an heir? And those   108

97. Mainardi, "the good Lizio," was a contemporary of Guido del Duca and Pier Traversaro and was taken prisoner with the latter by the Faentines in 1170. He was reputed to be a virtuous man with knightly qualities.

   Lizio da Valbona was born in the first half of the thirteenth century, a nobleman of Romagna and a contemporary of Rinieri.

98. Pier (ca. 1145–1225) belonged to the powerful Traversaro family of Ravenna. He was a staunch supporter of the Ghibellines and a close friend of the emperor Frederick II.

   Guido di Carpigna's family seems to have been established in the district of Montefeltro in Ravenna as early as the tenth century. Dante is probably alluding to Guido the younger, who was podestà of Ravenna 1251. He was dead before 1283.

101. Fabbro de' Lambertazzi was a Ghibelline leader of Bologna, whose family was said to have descended from the dukes of Ravenna in the twelfth century.

   Bernardo di Fosco was reputed by early commentators to have been of humble origin, but through his own merits, he distinguished himself to the point of being accepted by the nobility of his city of Faenza on their own level.

104. Ugolino of Azzo was a member of the powerful Ubaldini family. He seems to have been a wealthy landholder who was well known in Romagna; he died in January of 1293.

   Guido da Prata also appears to have been a landholder of some importance in the vicinity of Ravenna. He died before 1245.

106. Federigo di Tignoso was a nobleman of Rimini noted for his wealth and hospitality.

107. The Traversaro clan was a powerful Ghibelline house of Ravenna, whose most distinguished member was Pier Traversaro (see note to Canto XIV, 98).

   The Anastagi were another powerful Ghibelline family in Ravenna, who were most active in politics and antagonistic toward the Church.

ladies and knights, those feats, that courtly play
   which love and courtesy did once inspire
   in that domain where all hearts now grow vile?   111

O, Bretinoro, why don't you disappear!
   Your noble families and others, too,
   have fled from the corruption in your midst!   114

Bagnacaval does well to have no sons;
   and Castrocaro's wrong, and Conio more,
   in bothering to breed such counts as theirs.   117

When the Pagani's demon finally
   drops dead, they will be better off—although
   the record of their evil deeds remains.   120

O Ugolin de' Fantolin, your name
   is safe—since there's no chance it will be stained
   by the degeneracy of future heirs.   123

But now, go, Tuscan, I would rather weep,
   much rather weep, than say another word—
   our discourse has so wrung my sorrowing mind."   126

We knew those good souls heard us move away;
   thus, by their silence we could be assured
   of having taken the right path to climb.   129

---

112. Bretinoro was a small town in Romagna (now Bertinoro), located between Forlì and Cesena.

115. The town of Bagnacavallo in Romagna was a stronghold of the Malvicini, a Ghibelline family that expelled Guido da Polenta and the Guelphs from Ravenna in 1249.

116. Castrocaro, now a village, was once a castle in Romagna belonging to the counts of Castrocaro, who, though Ghibellines, submitted to the Church in 1282.
   The castle of Cunio in Romagna (near Imola), once owned by the counts of Conio, who were for the most part Guelphs, was totally destroyed soon after 1295.

118. The Pagani were a noble Ghibelline family of Faenza and Imola. The "demon" among them was Maghinardo Pagano da Susinana, who ruled Faenza (1290), Forlì (1291), and Imola (1296) and died at Imola in 1302. Guido da Montefeltro refers to him (*Inferno* XXVII, 50) as "the Lion of the White Lair" (his coat of arms).

121-123. Ugolino de' Fantolini, a Guelph, was podestà of Faenza (1253); he died in 1278.

As we were walking on our lonely road
  there came, like lightning ripping through the air,
  a voice, shot out at us from up ahead: 132

"I shall be slain by all who find me!"—Then
  it rolled past us like thunder dying down
  after the sudden bursting of a cloud.   135

Our ears had just begun recovering,
  when came the rumbling of a second voice—
  one clap of thunder thundering on the other: 138

"I am Aglauros, who was turned to stone!"
  With that, instead of going on, I moved
  a little closer to my Poet. By now   141

the air around us was serene once more.
  Then Virgil said: "That was the iron curb
  devised to keep a man within due bounds.   144

But you men take the bait, swallow the hook,
  and let the Adversary reel you in—
  and neither rein nor spur avails for you.   147

The heavens wheeling round you call to you,
  revealing their eternal beauties—yet,
  you keep your eyes fixed on the ground alone,   150

and He, the All-Discerning, strikes you down."

CANTO XV

THE PILGRIM IS *stunned by the light emanating from the Angel of Gen-*
erosity, and Virgil explains that soon such a sight will not be a burden
to his eyes but a great joy. As they climb past the angel, they hear from

---

133. The first voice is that of Cain, who, facing the punishment that God has visited
upon him, cries out "I shall be a fugitive and a wanderer on the earth, and whoever
finds me will kill me" (Genesis 4:13–14).

*below the singing of the beatitude "Blessed are the Merciful." At the
Pilgrim's prompting, Virgil delivers a discourse on the difference be-
tween earthly and heavenly possessions. When he has finished, the two
poets find themselves on the Third Terrace. Here, the exempla of Meek-
ness, the opposite of the sin of Wrath, present themselves in the form
of ecstatic visions. The first vision is of the Virgin meekly questioning
the Christ child as to why he has remained behind in the temple, causing
his parents so much distress. The second vision is of Pisistratus, who,
despite the imprecations of his wife, refused to take revenge on the
young man who had embraced his daughter. The final example of Meek-
ness is taken from the life of St. Stephen, the first martyr. The canto
ends ominously with the menacing appearance of a thick black cloud
of smoke, which envelops the Pilgrim and his guide.*

The same amount of time it takes that sphere
   (which, like a child at play, is never still)
   to go from break of day to the third hour,   3

was left now for the sun to run its course
   toward night: mid-afternoon it was up there
   (and midnight here, where I am writing this).   6

Now, its late rays struck full upon our faces,
   for we had gone so far around the mount
   that we were walking due west toward the sun.   9

But suddenly I felt my brow forced down
   by light far brighter than I sensed before;
   my mind was stunned by what it did not know.   12

I placed both of my hands above my eyes
   and used them as a visor for my face
   to temper the intensity of light.   15

A ray leaps back from water or from glass,
   reflecting back the other way as it
   ascends in the same way it first came down,   18

forming an angle with the plummet-line
   exactly equal to the incidence—
   as theory and experiment both show;   21

in just this way it seemed I had been struck
   by light reflected just in front of me:
   and that is why I quickly looked aside.   24

"Dear father, what is this? There is no way
   for me to shield my eyes from such bright light;
   it's moving toward us, isn't it?" I asked.   27

"Don't be surprised if you can still be dazed
   by members of the Heavenly Court," he said.
   "This is our invitation to ascend.   30

Not long from now, a sight like this will prove
   to be no burden, but a joy as great
   as Nature has prepared your soul to feel."   33

Before the blessed angel now we stood.
   He joyfully announced: "Enter this way
   to stairs less steep by far than those below."   36

Past him we went, already climbing when
   Beati misericordes from behind
   came ringing, and "Conqueror, rejoice."   39

And while my guide and I in solitude
   were moving upward, I, hoping to learn
   from his wise words with every step we took,   42

turned toward him and began to question him:
   "What did that spirit from Romagna mean
   who spoke of 'partnership' and of 'denial'?"   45

"Knowing the price he pays for his worst fault,"
   he answered, "naturally he censures it,
   hoping that others will have less to bear.   48

---

38. Having passed beyond the Terrace of the Envious, the Pilgrim hears from behind him the beatitude (*Beati misericordes,* "Blessed are the Merciful") praising the opposing virtue of Mercy of Generosity. This is from the fifth beatitude (see Matthew 5:7).

39. There is no exact biblical or liturgical source for the words "Conqueror, rejoice."

44–45. The Pilgrim is referring to the words of Guido del Duca (*Purgatory* XIV, 86–87), who reproached mankind for placing its hopes "where partnership must always be denied."

Because you make things of this world your goal,
   which are diminished as each shares in them,
   Envy pumps hard the bellows for your sighs.   51

But if your love were for the lofty sphere,
   your cravings would aspire for the heights,
   and fear of loss would not oppress your heart;   54

the more there are up there who speak of 'ours,'
   the more each one possesses and the more
   Charity burns intensely in that realm."   57

"I hunger more for satisfaction now,"
   I said, "than when I held my tongue before,
   and new perplexities come to my mind.   60

How can one good that's shared by many souls
   make all those who possess it wealthier
   than if it were possessed by just a few?"   63

And he: "Since you insist on limiting
   your mind to thoughts of worldly things alone,
   from the true light you reap only the dark.   66

That infinite, ineffable true Good
   that dwells in Heaven speeds instantly to love,
   as light rays to a shining surface would;   69

just as much ardor as it finds, it gives:
   the greater the proportion of our love,
   the more eternal goodness we receive;   72

the more souls there above who are in love
   the more there are worth loving; love grows more,
   each soul a mirror mutually mirroring.   75

And if my words have not appeased your thirst,
   when you see Beatrice you will see
   all of your longings truly satisfied.   78

Strive hard for the quick disappearance now
   of the five wounds that suffering will heal,
   just as the other two have left no trace."   81

I was about to say "I'm satisfied,"
  but seeing that we had reached the next round,
    my eager eyes forgot about my tongue.   84

And, there, it seemed to me that suddenly
  I was caught up in an ecstatic trance:
    a temple filled with people I could see;   87

a lady at the entrance whispering,
  tenderly as a mother would, "My son,
    why hast Thou dealt with us this way? You see,   90

Thy father and I, both of us in tears,
  have searched for Thee." Silence. The vision then,
    quick to appear, as quickly disappeared.   93

And then, another lady I could see:
  her cheeks were streaked with tears distilled by grief—
    a grief born from the spirit of revenge.   96

She spoke: "If you are master of this town
  whose naming caused such strife among the gods,
    and which shines as the source of all the arts,   99

take vengeance on those wanton arms that dared
  embrace our daughter, O Pisistratus!"
    And then, it seemed, that lord replied to her,   102

his face serene, his words gentle and calm:
  "What shall we do to those who wish us harm
    if we condemn the ones who show us love?"   105

89–90. The first example of Meekness, the virtue opposed to the vice of Wrath (taken, as always, from the life of Mary) is the episode in which Mary and Joseph, having left Jerusalem and traveled an entire day, discover that the boy Jesus is not in their company.

97. The town alluded to here is Athens. Legend has it that both Neptune and Athena desired to give their name to this newly founded capital. A contest ensued, and from it the city came to be called Athens.

103. The second example of Meekness is Pisistratus, the benevolent tyrant of Athens (560–527 B.C.); he was famous for his ability to turn away wrath with a soft answer.

And then I saw a mob, raging with hate,
   stoning a boy to death, as all of them
   kept screaming to each other, "Kill him, kill!"   108

I saw him sinking slowly to his knees,
   the weight of death forcing him to the earth;
   but still his eyes were open gates to Heaven,   111

while he, in agony, prayed to his Lord
   for the forgiveness of his murderers,
   his face showing compassion for them all.   114

When finally my soul became aware
   of the reality that lay beyond,
   I recognized my error and its truth.   117

My leader, who saw I was in the plight
   of someone trying hard to wake from sleep,
   said: "What is wrong? Have you lost all control?   120

You have been walking for a good half-league
   like someone half-asleep or drunk on wine:
   your eyes about to close, unsteady legs."   123

"O my sweet father, listen: I will tell you
   all of the things that did appear to me
   while I could scarcely move my legs," I said.   126

And he: "Were you to put a hundred masks
   upon your face, still you could never hide
   from me the slightest thought that comes to you.   129

The things you saw were shown that you might learn
   to let your heart be flooded by the peace
   that flows eternally from that High Fount.   132

I did not ask, 'What's wrong?' as one who looks
   with eyes that have no gift of insight might,
   eyes doomed to blindness once the body dies;   135

106–114. The third example of Meekness is from the life of St. Stephen, the first
Christian martyr. Stephen was stoned to death by an angry crowd, but, even in his
final agony, he asked the Lord to forgive his persecutors (Acts 7:54–60).

I asked you this to give strength to your limbs;
   so must the lazy man be spurred to put
   the time of his reawakening to best use."   138

We walked along, with evening coming on,
   into the splendor of the setting sun,
   looking ahead as far as we could see.   141

Then gradually a cloud of smoke took shape;
   slowly it drifted toward us, dark as night;
   we were not able to escape its grip: 144

it took away our sight, and the pure air.

CANTO XVI

THE PILGRIM IS blinded by the smoke and clings tenaciously to his guide. He hears the voices of the Wrathful singing the Agnus Dei *in perfect concord. One of the souls, Marco the Lombard, comes forward to speak with the Pilgrim and, at his invitation, accompanies him (and Virgil) to the end of the smoke-filled space, discussing the problems connected with the present-day corruption of society. He belittles the influence of the stars on human affairs, affirms the existence of Free Will, and laments the lack of good leadership in church and state.*

The gloom of Hell or of a night bereft
   of all its planets, under barren skies,
   and totally obscured by dark, dense clouds,   3

never had wrapped my face within a veil
   so thick, made of such harsh and stinging stuff,
   as was that smoke that poured around us there.   6

It was too much for open eyes to bear,
   and so my wise and faithful guide drew near,
   offering me his shoulder for support.   9

Just as the blind man walks close to his guide
   in order not to stray, or to collide
   with something that could hurt or even kill him,   12

so I moved through that foul and acrid air,
   hearing my guide keep telling me: "Watch out!
   Be very careful not to lose me here."   15

I could hear voices, which all seemed to pray
   the Lamb of God Who takes away our sins
   that He be merciful and grant them peace.   18

Each prayer they sang began with *Agnus Dei;*
   the same words, sung in unison, produced
   an atmosphere of perfect harmony.   21

"Master, those voices—are they shades I hear?"
   I asked. And he to me, "Yes, you are right,
   and they are loosening the knot of Wrath."   24

"And who are you whose body cleaves our smoke?
   You speak of us as though you still belonged
   with those who measure time by calendars."   27

I heard a voice, somewhere, that spoke these words.
   My master said: "Answer his question, first,
   then ask him if this is the right way up."   30

And I: "O creature, you who cleanse your soul
   to give it back, made beautiful, to God,
   you will hear wonders if you come with me."   33

"I'll come as far as I'm allowed," he said,
   "and if we cannot see each other's face,
   we can at least hear one another's words."   36

Then I began: "Still wrapped in mortal bonds
   that death has yet to loose, I climb to Heaven;
   and through the pains of Hell I have come here.   39

---

19. *"Agnus Dei"* ("Lamb of God") is a prayer opener taken from the canon of the
Mass. It is significant that the Wrathful are singing to the *Lamb of God,* to Jesus,
the meek One.

Since God has given me the special grace
   of His desire that I should see His court
   by means unknown to men of our own day,   42

please tell me who you were before you died,
   and tell me, too: is this the way to reach
   the passage up? Your words shall be our guide."   45

"I was a Lombard, Marco was my name;
   I knew about the world, I loved that good
   at which men now no longer aim their bows.   48

The path you're on will lead you to the stairs."
   Thus he replied, then added: "Now, I pray
   that you will pray for me when you're above."   51

"I promise you to do what you have asked,"
   I said. "But there's a problem haunting me:
   I can no longer keep it to myself.   54

I first was made aware of it below,
   and now it plagues my mind a second time,
   for your words second what I first heard there: 57

the world, indeed, as you have just declared,
   is destitute of every virtue known,
   swarming with evils, ever breeding more.   60

What is the cause of this? Please make it clear
   that I may teach the truth to other men;
   some see it in the stars, some on the earth."   63

A deep sigh, wrung by grief into "Alas!"
   came first, and then: "The world, brother, is blind,
   and obviously the world is where you're from!"   66

You men on earth attribute everything
   to the spheres' influence alone, as if
   with some predestined plan they moved all things.   69

If this were true, then our Free Will would be
   annihilated: it would not be just
   to render bliss for good or pain for evil.   72

The spheres initiate your tendencies:
    not all of them—but even if they did,
    you have the light that shows you right from wrong,   75

and your Free Will, which, though it may grow faint
    in its first struggles with the heavens, can still
    surmount all obstacles if nurtured well.   78

You are free subjects of a greater power,
    a nobler nature that creates your mind,
    and over this the spheres have no control.   81

So, if the world today has gone astray,
    the cause lies in yourselves and only there!
    Now I shall carefully explain that cause.   84

From the fond hands of God, Who loves her even
    before He gives her being, there issues forth
    just like a child, all smiles and tears at play,   87

the simple soul, pure in its ignorance,
    which, having sprung from her Creator's joy,
    will turn to anything it likes. At first   90

she is attracted to a trivial toy,
    and though beguiled, she will run after it,
    if guide or curb do not divert her love.   93

Men, therefore, needed the restraint of laws,
    needed a ruler able to at least
    discern the towers of the True city. True,   96

the laws there are, but who enforces them?
    No one. The shepherd who is leading you
    can chew the cud but lacks the cloven hoof.   99

And so the flock, that see their shepherd's greed
    for the same worldly goods that they have craved,
    are quite content to feed on what he feeds.   102

As you can see, bad leadership has caused
    the present state of evil in the world,
    not Nature that has grown corrupt in you.   105

On Rome, that brought the world to know the good,
  once shone two suns that lighted up two ways:
  the road of this world and the road of God.   108

The one sun has put out the other's light;
  the sword is now one with the crook—and fused
  together thus, must bring about misrule,   111

since joined, now neither fears the other one.
  If you still doubt, think of the grain when ripe—
  each plant is judged according to its seed.   114

The region of the Po and Adige
  flowed with true worth, with honest courtesy,
  until the time of Frederick's campaign;   117

but now, the kind of man who is ashamed
  to talk with, even meet with, honest folk,
  may travel there completely reassured!   120

There, three old men still live in whom the past
  rebukes the present. How those three must yearn
  for God to call them to a better life!—   123

Currado da Palazzo, good Gherardo,
  and Guido da Castel—who's better named
  'the simple Lombard,' as the French would say.   126

Tell the world this: The church of Rome, which fused
  two powers into one, has sunk in muck,
  defiling both herself and her true role."   129

112. With these words Marco brings to an end the second of his two main topics.

124. Currado was a Guelph from Brescia and acted as vicar to Charles of Anjou in Florence in 1276; he was podestà of Piacenza in 1288.

   Gherardo da Camino, born ca. 1240, was the captain-general of Treviso from 1283 to 1306, the year he died.

125. Guido da Castel was a nobleman of Reggio Emilia, born in 1235 and still living in 1315.

"Well argued, my dear Marco," I replied,
  "and now I understand why Levi's sons
  were not permitted to inherit wealth.   132

But who is this Gherardo whom you give
  as an example of a race extinct,
  whose life rebukes this barbarous age of ours?"   135

"Your words are meant to trick me or to test me!"
  he said. "How can you speak the Tuscan tongue
  and not know who the good Gherardo is?   138

I know him by no other name than this,
  unless he's known as Gaia's father, too.
  God be with you! And now I must go back: 141

see how the rays of light through the thick smoke
  grow brighter now? The angel's near, and I
  must leave before he sees me." And he turned,   144

not giving me a chance to ask him more.

CANTO XVII

*As the Pilgrim emerges from the cloud of smoke that surrounds the
Wrathful, the sun is about to set. He experiences three more visions that
offer exempla of Wrath. They center on the stories of Procne, Haman,
and Amata, the wife of King Latinus. The angel of Meekness then ap-
pears and points to the way by which the two poets may continue their
ascent. As they move toward the indicated stairway, they hear the words
of the beatitude "Blessed are the Peacemakers." Upon reaching the*

131. "Levi's sons" the Levites, members of the tribe of Levi, were designated to serve
the Temple, and, in order to prevent corruption and distraction in the performance
of their sacred function, Jewish law prohibited them from owning property.

140. Gaia was Gherardo's daughter by his second wife, Chiara della Torre of Milan.
She married Tolberto da Camino, a relative, and she died in 1311.

*Fourth Terrace, the Pilgrim feels that all strength has left his limbs, and
both he and his guide rest from their journey: they have reached the
Terrace of the Slothful, and night is about to fall. Virgil takes advantage
of this pause to discourse on the nature of love, showing that all the
sins purged in Purgatory spring from one of three perversions of love.
His words bring the canto to a close.*

Reader, if ever you have found yourself
   caught in a mountain fog, trying to see
   your way through it, as sightless as a mole,   3

remember how at last the damp, dense air
   starts to dissolve, and how the sun's pale disc
   feebly begins to penetrate the mist,   6

and you will find it easy to recall
   what it was like when finally I saw
   the sun again, the sun about to set.   9

Matching the faithful footsteps of my guide,
   I walked out of that cloud into the light
   whose rays had died out on the shore below.   12

O power of fantasy that steals our minds
   from things outside, to leave us unaware,
   although a thousand trumpets may blow loud—   15

what stirs you if the senses show you nothing?
   Light stirs you, formed in Heaven, by itself,
   or by His will Who sends it down to us: 18

In my imagination there took shape
   the impious deed committed by that being
   transformed into the bird that lives to sing;   21

my mind became, at this point, so withdrawn
   into itself that the reality
   of things outside could not have entered there.   24

9. The Pilgrim's second day on Mount Purgatory, Easter Monday, is drawing to a
close.

Then poured into my soaring fantasy,
   a figure crucified, whose face revealed
   contempt and fury even as he died.   27

By him the great Ahasuerus stood,
   Esther his wife, and the just Mordecai,
   integrity in word and deed was his.   30

Then, when this image of its own accord
   burst like a bubble when the watery film
   around it breaks—another vision rose   33

in my imagination: a young girl
   bitterly weeping, saying: "O my queen,
   why did you let your rage destroy your life?   36

You killed yourself rather than lose Lavinia?
   Now you have lost me! I am she who mourns
   your death, Mother, before another's ruin!"   39

When suddenly closed eyes are struck by light,
   our sleep is broken, though it lingers on
   a little while before it fully dies,   42

just so my vision slipped away from me
   when I was struck by light across my eyes,
   a light far brighter than is known on earth.   45

Looking around to find out where I was,
   I heard a voice: "Here is the place to climb."
   This drove all other thoughts out of my mind   48

and left me burning with desire to see
   the one who spoke—a wish that will not cease
   till it comes face to face with its desire;   51

but, as if looking at the burning sun
   whose brilliance overwhelms the sight and veils
   its very form, I felt my powers fail.   54

26. Haman was a minister of Ahasuerus, the king of Persia. Enraged that the Jew Mordecai refused to do him homage, Haman persuaded the king to decree the death of all the Jews in the land; a cross was constructed especially for Mordecai.

35. The queen is Amata, wife of Latinus and mother of Lavinia.

"This is an angel of the Lord who comes
    to show us the ascent before we ask,
    and hides himself in his own radiance.   57

He treats us as a man would treat himself:
    who sees the need but waits for the request,
    already is half-guilty of denial;   60

so, let our feet obey his call, and climb
    as far as possible while there is light,
    for we may not ascend once it grows dark."   63

These were my leader's words; and then, as one,
    the two of us went over to the stairs.
    As soon as I had taken one step up,   66

I felt what seemed to be a wing that moved
    and fanned my face; I heard the words: "*Beati
    pacifici,* who feel no sinful wrath."   69

The day's last rays, which night would follow soon,
    already were so high above us now
    that stars began to show through, here and there.   72

"Why is my strength fading away like this?"
    I kept repeating to myself, as I
    felt all my forces draining from my legs.   75

We had just reached the last step of the stairs,
    and there we found ourselves immobilized,
    just like a vessel having run ashore.   78

I waited for a moment, listening
    to hear some sound come from this unknown round;
    then, turning to my master, I inquired: 81

"O my sweet father, what offense is purged
    here on this terrace? Though our steps have stopped,
    don't you stop speaking to me." So he said: 84

---

67. The angel, with his wing, has removed another *P*, leaving four more to be erased.

68–69. *Beati pacifici* ("Blessed are the Peacemakers") is the Beatitude for the Terrace of the Wrathful. "Who feel no sinful wrath" is a gloss added by Dante to the biblical text.

"That love of good which failed to satisfy
  the call of duty, here is fortified:
  the oar once sluggish now is plied with zeal.   87

But if you want to better understand,
  give me your full attention: you will reap
  excellent fruit from this delay of ours.   90

Neither Creator nor his creatures ever,
  my son, lacked love. There are, as you well know,
  two kinds: the natural love, the rational.   93

Natural love may never be at fault;
  the other may: by choosing the wrong goal,
  by insufficient or excessive zeal.   96

While it is fixed on the Eternal Good,
  and observes temperance loving worldly goods,
  it cannot be the cause of sinful joys;   99

but when it turns toward evil or pursues
  some good with not enough or too much zeal—
  the creature turns on his Creator then.   102

So, you can understand how love must be
  the seed of every virtue growing in you,
  and every deed that merits punishment.   105

Now, since it is a fact that love cannot
  ignore the welfare of its loving self,
  there's nothing in the world can hate itself;   108

and since no being can be conceived as being
  all in itself, severed from the First Being,
  no creature has the power to hate his God.   111

And so it follows, if I argue well,
  the evil that man loves must be his neighbor's.
  This love springs up three ways in mortal clay: 114

There is the man who sees his own success
  connected to his neighbor's downfall; thus,
  he longs to see him fall from eminence.   117

Next, he who fears to lose honor and fame,
    power and favor, if his neighbor rise:
    vexed by this good, he wishes for the worst.   120

Finally, he who, wronged, flares up in rage:
    with his great passion for revenge, he thinks
    only of how to harm his fellow man.   123

This threefold love is purged by those below.
    Now, I would have you know the other kind:
    love that without measure pursues its good.   126

All of you, vaguely, apprehend and crave
    a good with which your heart may be at rest;
    and so, each of you strives to reach that goal.   129

If you aspire to it or grasp at it
    with only lukewarm love, then on this ledge
    you will be punished, once you have confessed.   132

Another good there is: it brings not joy,
    not perfect joy, for it is not the True
    Essence, the fruit and root of every good;   135

the love that yields excessively to this
    is purged above us on three terraces,
    but how the nature of such love is threefold,   138

I would have you discover for yourself."

CANTO XVIII

IN RESPONSE TO the Pilgrim's request, Virgil continues his lecture on love. More than satisfied with the explanations of his guide, the Pilgrim lets his thoughts wander aimlessly and sleepily, when, suddenly, a group

128. This good is, of course, God. These words reflect the famous Augustinian formulation that is never far from the thematic surface of the *Divine Comedy*: "Our hearts are restless till they rest in Thee" (*Confessions* I, i).

of souls rushes upon them from behind. These are the Slothful. Two
souls out in front of the frenzied pack shout out two exempla of the
virtue of Zeal, one involving the Virgin Mary, the other, Julius Caesar.
As the crowd rushes by, one soul, the Abbott of San Zeno, exchanges
a few hasty words with Virgil. The exempla of Sloth are proclaimed by
two souls at the rear of the rapidly moving group: they involve the
recalcitrant Israelites wandering with Moses in the desert, and certain
companions of Aeneas who refused to continue the voyage to Latium
with him.

When he had brought his lecture to an end,
    the lofty scholar looked into my face,
    searching to see if I seemed satisfied;   3

and I, already thirsting for more drink,
    kept silent, wondering: "Could he, perhaps,
    be tired of all this questioning of mine?"   6

But that true father, sensing my desire,
    which was too timid to express itself,
    spoke first, and thus encouraged me to speak.   9

I said: "Master, the light you shed has made
    my sight so keen that now I clearly see
    all that your words mean or what they imply.   12

So I beseech you, father, kind and dear,
    define love for me, please, which is, you say
    the source of every virtue, every vice."   15

"Now focus your mind's eye on what I say,"
    he said, "and you will clearly understand
    the error of the blind who lead the blind.   18

The soul at birth, created quick to love,
    will move toward anything that pleases it,
    as soon as pleasure causes it to move.   21

From what is real your apprehensive power
    extracts an image it displays within you,
    forcing your mind to be attentive to it;   24

and if, attentive, it inclines toward this,
  that inclination is love: Nature it is
  which is through pleasure bound anew in you.   27

Just as a fire's flames always rise up,
  inspired by its own nature to ascend,
  seeking to be in its own element,   30

just so, the captive soul begins its quest,
  the spiritual movement of its love,
  not resting till the thing loved is enjoyed.   33

It should be clear to you by now how blind
  to truth those people are who make the claims
  that every love is, in itself, good love.   36

They think this, for love's substance, probably,
  seems always good, but though the wax is good,
  the impression made upon it may be bad."   39

"Thanks to your words and my keen interest,
  I know what love is now," I answered him,
  "but knowing this brings more uncertainty: 42

if love comes from a source outside of us,
  the soul having no choice, how can you praise
  or blame it for its love of good or bad?"   45

And he to me: "I can explain to you
  as much as reason sees; for the rest, wait
  for Beatrice—it is the work of faith.   48

Every substantial form, being distinct
  from matter, yet somehow conjoined with it,
  contains within itself a certain power   51

---

35. The people are the philosophers, particularly the Epicureans, and their followers
(the "blind" of line 18), who maintain that every kind of love is praiseworthy because
it is a natural tending to the good.

38–39. As a poor seal may stamp on good wax a bad imprint, so may some object
that is unworthy kindle the good instinct of love to a wrongful passion.

49. In scholastic terminology, substantial form is that which gives to anything its
own particular essence. The substantial form in man is, of course, his intellectual
soul.

not visible except as it is made
   manifest through its workings and effects:
      as life in plants is proved by their green leaves.   54

So, man cannot know where his cognizance
   of primal concepts comes from—or his bent
      for those primary objects of desire;   57

these are a part of you, just like the zeal
   of bees for making honey; the primal will
      is neither laudable nor blamable.   60

That other wills conform to this first one,
   you have the innate faculty of reason,
      which should defend the threshold of consent.   63

This is the principle on which is based
   the judgment of your merit—according as
      it winnows out the good love from the bad.   66

Those men who with their reason probed the depths,
   perceived this liberty innate in man,
      thereby bequeathing ethics to the world.   69

Let us assume that every love that burns
   in you arises through necessity;
      you still have power to restrain such love.   72

This noble power Beatrice knows
   as Freedom of the Will: remember that,
      if ever she should mention it to you."   75

The moon was shining close to midnight now,
   like a brass bucket burnished bright as fire,
      and, thinning out the stars that we could see,   78

61. The "other wills," on a more intellective plane, should have the innocence of the primal instinctive will.

67. "Those men" are the philosophers Plato and Aristotle, who, using their reason, perceived the free will innate in man and founded the study of ethics or the science of morality.

72. Just as Marco Lombardo in Canto XVI had assured the Pilgrim that free will could protect him from exterior forces (e.g., astral influences), so Virgil points out that, possessing free will, man need not be the victim of inner forces (e.g., his own temperament).

was following that course against the sky
    made fiery by the sun, when Romans see
        it set between the Sards and Corsicans.   81

That noble shade, who had made Pietola
    renowned above all Mantuan towns, was now
        free of the burden I had laid on him,   84

and I, having been privileged to reap
    such clear, plain answers to my questioning,
        let my thoughts wander vaguely, sleepily;   87

but this somnolent mood did not last long,
    for suddenly we heard a rush of souls
        coming around the mount behind our backs: 90

And as Ismenus and Asopus saw
    in ancient times at night along their banks
        the rush and rage of Theban bacchanalia,   93

just such a frenzied urge I thought I saw
    when that thick rush of souls curved round the bank
        spurred in their race by good will and just love.   96

And then they were upon us—that entire,
    enormous mass of spirits on the run;
        two out in front were shouting as they wept: 99

"Mary in haste ran to the hills," cried one,
    the other: "Caesar, Ilerda to subdue,
        thrust at Marseilles, and then rushed down to Spain."   102

79. The moon is following its monthly course in the direction from west to east.

82–83. The "noble shade" is Virgil, who, according to legend, was born at Pietola, a village near Mantua. The fame and glory of the poet has caused his birthplace to outshine all the other surrounding Mantuan towns.

91. Ismenus and Asopus were two rivers of Bretia near Thebes, along which the orgiastic rites of the god Bacchus were observed.

100. This biblical exemplum refers to Mary's visit to Elizabeth, wife of Zachariah (who lived in the hill country), soon after the angel of the Annunciation had appeared to her.

101. On his way to Ilerda (today Lerida) in Spain, Caesar began the siege of Marseilles; then, leaving part of his army there under Brutus to complete the task, he hurried on to his main goal.

"Faster! faster, we have no time to waste,
    for time is love," cried others from behind,
    "strive to do good, that grace may bloom again."   105

"O souls in whom keen eagerness atones,
    perhaps, for past delay and negligence,
    induced by lukewarm love of doing good—   108

this man, who is, I swear to you, alive,
    would like to climb above when day returns;
    show us the nearest way to reach the cleft."   111

These were my leader's words. One of the shades
    called out as he rushed by: "Follow our path,
    and you will find the passage by yourself.   114

We cannot stop; desire to race keeps on
    running through us; we beg your pardon, then,
    if penance seems to be discourtesy.   117

I was San Zeno's abbott in Verona,
    when the good emperor Barbarossa reigned—
    of him Milan still speaks with bitterness.   120

There is a man with one foot in the grave
    who soon will have good cause to rue the power
    he wielded once over that monastery: 123

in place of its true pastor he has put
    as head a bastardly born son of his,
    deformed in body and maimed worse in mind."   126

118. This abbot was probably a certain Gherardo II, who died in 1187 and was abbot of the church of San Zeno in Verona during the time of Emperor Frederick I.

119. Barbarossa was Emperor Frederick I, who ruled from 1152 to 1190 and was in conflict with Pope Alexander III, by whom he was excommunicated.

121. The man is Alberto della Scala, Lord of Verona, who died in 1301, and hence, in 1300, had one foot in the grave.

124–126. Alberto's illegitimate son, Giuseppe (1263–1313), despite being mentally retarded, crippled, and a bastard, served as the abbot of San Zeno from 1292 to 1313.

If he said more, I did not hear the words,
   the two of us were left so far behind;
   but I was glad to hear as much as this.   129

And he who always was my help in need
   said: "Turn around, look at those racing souls
   straining themselves to put the curb on Sloth."   132

Two at the end were shouting: "All of those
   for whom the Red Sea's waters opened wide
   were dead before the Jordan saw their heirs;   135

and those who found the task too difficult
   to keep on striving with Anchises' son,
   gave themselves up to an inglorious life."   138

Then, when those souls had sped so far ahead
   that they were now completely out of sight,
   a new thought started forming in my mind,   141

creating others, many different ones:
   from one to another to another thought
   I wandered sleepily, then closed my eyes,   144

letting my floating thoughts melt into dreams.

CANTO XIX

JUST BEFORE DAWN the Pilgrim dreams of a hideous female, stuttering, cross-eyed, maimed, and with sallow skin. But as he stares intently at her, she loses all her deformity and takes on a very desirable aspect. She

133–135. The first exemplum of Sloth, taken from the Bible (Numbers 14:1–39), is that of the Israelites, who were sluggish in crossing the desert with Moses after the Lord had opened up the Red Sea so that they could escape from Egypt.

136–138. The second exemplum, from classical lore, indicts the followers of Aeneas, who, instead of following him to Latium, stopped and settled with Akestes in Sicily, thus giving up their share of the glory of founding Rome (*Aeneid* V, 605–640).

is a Siren, and her singing captivates the Pilgrim and holds him en-
tranced, until a saintly lady appears and rouses Virgil to go to the aid
of his charge. Virgil rips open the Siren's garment, to reveal her belly,
the stench from which startles the Pilgrim from his dream. As the two
poets begin to climb again, the angel of Zeal appears to show them the
way and pronounces the beatitude "Blessed are they who mourn."
When the two pilgrims reach the next terrace, they see souls everywhere
stretched out upon the ground, weeping and sighing as they recite the
psalm Adhaesit pavimento anima mea. *This group is the Avaricious.*
The Pilgrim's attention is attracted by one of the souls, and, with Virgil's
consent, he goes over to speak to him. It is the shade of the former
Pope Adrian V, who explains that since the Avaricious turned their
backs on Heaven and fixed their eyes on earthly goods, so Justice has
here bound them face down to the ground. He rebukes the Pilgrim for
kneeling to him, citing a verse from the gospels to indicate that earthly
relationships no longer hold in the spiritual realm, and finally expresses
the desire that his niece Alagia be preserved from the corruption sur-
rounding her.

It was the hour when the heat of day,
    quenched by Earth's cold (at times by Saturn's too),
    cannot prevail against the lunar chill—   3

when geomancers see far in the east
    Fortuna Major rise before the dawn
    along a path soon to be bathed in light.   6

There came into my dream a woman, stuttering,
    cross-eyed, stumbling along on her maimed feet,
    with ugly yellow skin and hands deformed.   9

I stared at her. And as the sun revives
    a body numbed by the night's cold, just so
    my eyes upon her worked to free her tongue   12

4. Geomancers were those who foretold the future by reading random arrangements
of points on a surface and attempting to match them with certain configurations of
stars.

7. This loathsome female, as we shall learn later, symbolizes the vices of Avarice,
Gluttony, and Lust, which the Pilgrim will see being purged on the upper three
terraces.

and straighten out all her deformities,
    gradually suffusing her wan face
    with just the color Love would have desired.   15

And once her tongue was loosened by my gaze,
    she started singing, and the way she sang
    captured my mind—it could not free itself.   18

"I am," she sang, "the sweet Siren, I am,
    whose song beguiles the sailors in mid-sea,
    enticing them, inviting them to joy!   21

My singing made Ulysses turn away
    from his desired course; who dwells with me
    seldom departs, I satisfy so well."   24

Her lips had not yet closed when there appeared
    a saintly lady standing at my side,
    ready to foil the Siren's stratagem.   27

"Virgil, O Virgil, who is this?" she cried
    with indignation. Virgil moved toward her,
    keeping his gaze fixed on that noble one.   30

He seized the other, ripped her garment off,
    exposing her as far down as the paunch!
    The stench pouring from her woke me from sleep.   33

I looked at my good master, and he said:
    "Three times at least I called you. Get up,
    come, let us find the passageway for you."   36

So, I stood up. Daylight had now spread out
    through all the circles of the sacred mount
    as we moved on, the new sun at our back.   39

Following in his footsteps, brow bent low,
    so heavy with my thoughts (I must have looked
    like half a bridge's arch), I suddenly   42

heard a voice say, "Come here, here is the pass,"
    words spoken in soft tones of graciousness,
    tones never heard within our mortal bounds.   45

Then angel's wings, that could have been a swan's
    outstretched, invited us to make our way
    upward between the two high hard stone walls,   48

and then he moved his wings and fanned us both,
    declaring those *qui lugent* to be blest,
    for consolation shall be theirs in Heaven.   51

"What is it that disturbs you?" said my guide,
    "what causes you to stare so at the ground?"
    (By then we had climbed past the angel's post.)   54

I said: "It is that strange dream which I had,
    a vision that still fills me full of dread—
    I cannot get the thought out of my mind."   57

"You saw," he said, "that ageless sorceress
    for whom alone the souls above must weep;
    you also saw how men escape from her.   60

Let these words be enough. Move faster, now,
    and look up at the lure of mighty spheres
    that the Eternal King forever spins."   63

The hawk who has been staring at its feet
    will, when he hears the cry, stretch wide his wings
    ready to soar toward food he knows is there;   66

I did the same: I strained to reach the end
    of the ascending passage in the rock,
    and enter on another circling ledge.   69

When I came out and stood on the Fifth Round,
    I saw spirits stretched out upon the dust,
    lying face downward, all of them in tears.   72

49. With the fanning gesture, the angel removes another *P* from the Pilgrim's forehead.

50. The beatitude chosen for the Fourth Terrace is "Blessed are they who mourn [*qui lugent*], for they shall be comforted" (Matthew 5:4). It is not entirely clear why this beatitude should be appropriate to the purgation of the particular sin of Sloth.

Adhaesit pavimento anima mea.
　　I heard, accompanied with heavy sighs
　　that almost made the words inaudible. 75

"O souls elect of God, whose sufferings
　　Justice and Hope make easier to bear,
　　tell us the way to reach the higher stairs." 78

"If you have been exempt from lying prone,
　　and wish to find the quickest way to go,
　　be sure to keep your right side to the edge." 81

Thus did the poet ask, and thus I heard,
　　from somewhere close in front of us—so close,
　　I could make out the hidden face that spoke. 84

I fixed my eyes upon my master's eyes,
　　and there I saw the joy of his consent
　　to the desire he saw in mine. And then, 87

once free to do exactly as I wished,
　　I walked ahead and stood above that soul
　　whose voice caught my attention earlier; 90

I said, "Spirit in whom weeping makes ripe
　　that without which no one returns to God,
　　I beg you, interrupt your greater task 93

a moment: tell me who you were and why
　　you all lie prone. Is there some way that I
　　can help you in the world I left alive?" 96

"Why Heaven has made us turn our backs to Heaven,"
　　the spirit said, "you soon shall know, but first:
　　scias quod ego fui successor Petri. 99

73. "My soul cleaveth unto the dust": The Fifth Terrace opens with a prayer taken from Psalm 119:25.

99. "Know that I was a successor of Peter": The speaker is Pope Adrian V (Ottobuono de' Fieschi of Genoa), a nephew of Innocent IV, who succeeded Innocent V on July 11, 1276, and died thirty-eight days later, on August 18.

Between Sestri and Chiaveri descends
   a lovely stream, and from its name derives
   the noble title of my family.   102

In hardly more than one month's time I learned
   how the Great Mantle weighs on him who wants
   to keep it clean—all else is feather weight!   105

I was, alas, converted very late:
   only when I became Shepherd of Rome,
   did I perceive the falseness of the world.   108

Man's heart, I saw, could never rest down there;
   nor in that life could greater heights be reached,
   and so, I came to love the other life.   111

Until that time I was a wretched soul,
   servant of Avarice, cut off from God;
   here, I am punished for it, as you see.   114

What Avarice does is declared in this
   purgation as conversion to the ground—
   the mountain knows no harsher penalty.   117

Just as our eyes, attached to worldly goods,
   would never leave the earth to look above,
   so Justice, here, has forced them to the ground.   120

Since Avarice quenched all our love of good,
   without which all our labors were in vain,
   so here the force of Justice holds us fast,   123

our feet and hands bound tight within its grip;
   as long as it shall please the righteous Lord,
   so long shall we lie stretched out, motionless."   126

I was by then already on my knees;
   I started speaking; he, at my first words,
   guessed from their tone the form of my respect.   129

---

101. The "stream" is the river Lavagna, flowing between Sestri and Chiavari, coastal
towns near Genoa. Adrian was of the line of the counts of Lavagna.

"Why are you kneeling at my side?" he asked,
  and I replied, "Your dignity commands.
  My conscience would not let me stand up straight." 132

"Up on your feet, my brother," he replied.
  "You should not kneel: I am a servant, too,
  with you and all the others, of One Power. 135

If you have ever understood the words
  sounded by holy gospel: *Neque nubent.*
  you will know why I answer as I do. 138

Do not stay any longer. Leave me now;
  your presence here prevents the flow of tears
  that ripens what you spoke about before. 141

I have a niece on earth, by name Alagia,
  a good girl—may she not be led astray
  by all the bad examples of our house— 144

and she is all I have left in the world."

CANTO XX

*AS THE PILGRIM and Virgil pick their way through the prostrate souls
of the Avaricious, someone ahead of them begins to call out the exempla
of the virtue opposed to Avarice. He proclaims the poverty of Mary,
evidenced by the place where she gave birth to her son; he then cites
the Roman consul Fabricius, who preferred virtuous poverty to the lux-
ury of vice, and finally, St. Nicholas, whose generosity saved the three
maidens from lives of shame. The speaker is Hugh Capet, who estab-*

137. The words "*Neque nubent*" begin the quotation "They neither marry nor are
given in marriage," which can be found in the gospels of Matthew (22:23–30), Mark
(12:18–25), and Luke (20:27–35).

142. Adrian's niece is Alagia de' Fieschi, daughter of Niccolò de' Fieschi, the imperial
vicar in Italy, and the wife of Morello Malaspina, Dante's friend, by whom she had
three sons.

lished the Capetian dynasty. Addressed by the Pilgrim, he identifies him-
self and goes on to denounce his descendants for their avarice. Hugh
explains that as long as daylight lasts, all the souls, with greater or lesser
force, recite the exempla of virtue, and that during the night, they cry
out condemnations of Avarice: they cite the greed of Pygmalion, Midas,
Achan, Sapphira, Heliodorus, Polymnestor, and Crassus. As the Pilgrim
and his guide take leave of Hugh, they suddenly feel the entire mountain
tremble, and they hear shouts of Gloria in excelsis Deo. *Anxious to*
know what has happened, and puzzled, they continue their journey in
silence.

The lesser will yields to the greater will:
    to satisfy him, I, unsatisfied,
    withdrew my sponge unfilled, and turned away.   3

My master moved ahead close to the cliff,
    wherever there was space—as one who walks
    along the ramparts hugs the battlements: 6

the mass of souls whose eyes were, drop by drop,
    shedding the sin which occupies our world
    left little room along the terrace edge.   9

God damn you, ageless She-Wolf, you whose greed,
    whose never-sated appetite, has claimed
    more victims than all other beasts of prey!   12

You heavens, whose revolutions, some men think,
    determine human fate—when will he come,
    he before whom that beast shall have to flee?   15

Slowly we moved along with cautious steps,
    and I could think of nothing but those shades
    who grieved and sobbed so piteously there.   18

Then, somewhere up ahead of us, I heard
    a voice wailing, "Sweet Mary!" and the cry
    was like that of a woman giving birth;   21

20–21. The soul who calls out in praise of the Virgin is none other than the Hugh
who gave birth to the Capetian line of kings, famous for their avarice.

the voice went on: "How very poor you were
    is clear to all men from the place you found
    to lay your holy burden down." And then   24

I heard: "O good Fabricius, you who chose
    to live with virtue in your poverty,
    rather than live in luxury with vice."   27

Those words pleased me so much I rushed ahead
    to where I thought the voice was coming from,
    eager to know that spirit who just spoke;   30

he kept on speaking—now, of the largesse
    bestowed by Nicholas on the three girls
    that they might live their young lives virtuously.   33

"O soul," I said, "who speaks of so much good,
    tell me who you were, and why no one else
    joins in to praise the praiseworthy with you.   36

Your answer will not go without reward,
    if I return to finish the short road
    of life that races on to its quick end."   39

"I'll answer you," he said, "not out of hope
    for any help from your world, but because
    God's grace shines in your living presence here.   42

22–24. The first example of a virtue opposed to the sin of Avarice apparently extols poverty—the poverty that Mary accepted without complaint when she gave birth to her glorious son in a stable.

25. The second example of the virtue opposing Avarice has to do with poverty as the result of asceticism, deliberate self-denial. Fabricius Caius Luscinus, consul of Rome in 282 and 278 B.C., censor in 275 B.C., refused throughout his public career to accept bribes, as was the custom of his day. He also resisted the greed and luxury of the Romans, so much so that he died a pauper and had to be buried by the state.

32. Here the virtue praised is that of generosity. St. Nicholas, bishop of Myra in Lycia, Asia Minor, who lived under Constantine and was present at the Council of Nicaea in A.D. 325, is venerated. Dante alludes to the legend in which Nicholas, to prevent an impoverished local nobleman from prostituting his daughters, threw a bag of gold, on three different nights, through the nobleman's window as dowries for the girls.

I was the root of that malignant tree
   which overshadows all of Christendom,
     so that good fruit is seldom gathered there;   45

but if Douai and Lille and Ghent and Bruges
   were strong enough, vengeance would soon be theirs—
     and that it may, I beg of God the Judge!   48

On earth beyond I was called Hugh Capet;
   from me have sprung the Louises and Philips,
     rulers of France up to the present day.   51

My father was a Paris cattle man.
   When the old line of kings had all died out,
     except for him who wore a monk's gray robe,   54

I found I held the reins of government
   in my firm grip, and that all my new wealth
     gave me such power, made me so rich in friends,   57

that for the widowed crown of France my own
   son's head was chosen, and it was from him
     that those anointed bones were to descend.   60

43. The "malignant tree" is the Capetian monarchy. Dante confused Hugh I with Hugh II in this passage, or combined the history of both.

46. Douai, Lille, Ghent, and Bruges are the foremost cities of Flanders and are meant here to represent that region as a whole. The revenge that Hugh seems to long for so eagerly will take place in the year 1302, when the Flemish will defeat the French at the battle of Courtrai.

50. From the year 1060 to the fictional date of the *Comedy* (and even beyond), all the Capetian kings were named either Louis or Philip.

54. When Louis V died in 987, after a brief reign, the only living representative of the Carolingian line was Charles, Duke of Lorraine, son of Louis IV, brother of Lothair and uncle of Louis V. But he did not become a monk. He was put in prison by Hugh, against whom he had armed himself. Many scholars believe that Dante is confusing the last of the Carolingians with the last of the Merovingians, Childeric III, who did become a monk after his deposition in 752.

While my descendants kept their sense of shame,
>   they, though worth little, did no harm. Then came
>   their scheme to get the dowry of Provence.   63

With this bloomed their rapacity, their use
>   of force and fraud. Later, to make amends,
>   they seized Ponthieu, Normandy, Gascony.   66

Charles came to Italy; to make amends
>   he made of Conradin his victim; then,
>   sent Thomas off to Heaven, to make amends.   69

I see a time, and not too far away,
>   when there shall come a second Charles from France,
>   and men shall see what he and his are like.   72

He comes bearing no arms, save for the lance
>   that Judas jousted with and, taking aim,
>   he bursts the guts of Florence with one thrust.   75

From this he gains not land but sin and shame!
>   And worse is that he makes light of the weight
>   of all his crimes, refusing all the blame.   78

63. The kingdom of Provence was annexed to the French crown through the marriage of Charles of Anjou (brother of Louis IX of France) to Beatrice, daughter and heiress of Raymond Berenger IV of Provence. Berenger, in giving his daughter to Charles, was breaking his promise to Count Raymond of Toulouse, to whom she had first been betrothed.

66. Normandy was taken from England in 1202 by Philip II; both Ponthieu and Gascony were taken from England in 1295 by Philip the Fair.

67–68. Charles of Anjou, invited by Urban IV to assume the crown of Naples and Sicily, came into Italy in 1265; in 1266 he defeated Manfred at Benevento and was crowned in the same year.

Conradin, the rightful heir (see *Purgatory* III, 112), attempted to wrest the throne from Charles but was defeated at Tagliacozzo in 1268 and executed in Naples in October of the same year.

69. The legend, current in Dante's time, that Charles had poisoned St. Thomas Aquinas is unfounded. Thomas died in 1274 during a journey to the Council of Lyons, to which he had been summoned by Gregory X.

71. This is Charles of Valois (1270–1325), who was called to Italy by Boniface VIII as a peacemaker (i.e., to destroy those who opposed the papacy).

The third, once hauled a captive from his ship,
   I see selling his daughter, haggling the price,
   as pirates do, over their female slaves.   81

O Avarice, what more harm can you do?
   You have so fascinated all my heirs,
   they have no care for their own flesh and blood.   84

That past and future crimes may seem as naught,
   I see the *fleur-de-lis* enter Alagna
   and in His vicar Christ made prisoner.   87

I see the gall and vinegar renewed;
   I see Him being mocked a second time,
   killed once again between the living thieves.   90

I see this second Pilate so full of spite
   that, still unsatisfied, his greedy sails
   he drives, unchartered, into Holy Temple.   93

O Lord, when shall I have the joy to see
   that retribution which, now lying hid,
   makes sweet Thy wrath within Thy secret will?   96

The words that I recited earlier
   about the one Bride of the Holy Ghost
   (which brought you to me that I might explain)   99

make up the prayers that we here must recite
   as long as daylight lasts; when night comes, though,
   our litany is just the opposite: 102

79. This is a reference to the "third Charles." Charles II, king of Naples (1248–1309), son of Charles of Anjou, was defeated in a naval battle by Peter III of Aragon in 1284 and was taken from his own ship.

87. The vicar of Christ here mentioned is Pope Boniface VIII.

92–93. This strange mixed metaphor refers to the persecution and destruction by Philip the Fair of the Knights Templar.

100. For the first and only time the exempla are referred to as "prayers." The single prayer assigned to this terrace is *Adhaesit pavimento anima mea* (XIX, 73), which the Pilgrim heard before his meeting with Adrian.

then, we cry out against Pygmalion,
  how he turned traitor, thief, and parricide
  through his unsated appetite for gold;   105

and avaricious Midas, whose request,
  moved by his greed, made him a starveling wretch,
  the butt of ridicule through centuries;   108

then we recall the foolishness of Achan,
  who stole the spoils, and stirred Joshua's wrath—
  which seems, as we recite, to sting him still.   111

Next we accuse Sapphira with her mate;
  we hail the hoofs that kicked Heliodorus;
  and, all around the mount, echoes the shame   114

of Polymnestor slaying Polydorus;
  the last cry heard is 'Crassus, tell us, now,
  what does gold taste like? *You* should surely know!'   117

At times we cry out loud, at times speak soft,
  according as our feelings spur us on,
  sometimes with greater, sometimes lesser force.   120

103. Not to be confused with the sculptor of Greek legend who fell in love with one of his own statues, this Pygmalion, king of Tyre, was the brother of Dido.

106. Midas was king of Phrygia, to whom Bacchus granted one request in exchange for his kindness to Silenus, Bacchus's instructor. Midas, in his greed, asked that all he touched be turned to gold.

109. Achan was the son of Carmi, who stole and hid some of the Spoils of Jericho, which Joshua had ordered to be consecrated to the Lord.

112. Sapphira and her husband, Ananias, sold some property held in common by the apostles but returned to them only part of the price they had received.

113. Heliodorus, sent by the king of Syria to steal treasures from the temple in Jerusalem, was driven away and nearly kicked to death by a horse who appeared mysteriously, ridden by a man in golden armor.

115. Before the fall of Troy, Priam entrusted Polymnestor, a king of Thrace, with his son Polydorus and a large sum of money. After Troy fell, Polymnestor killed the boy and took the money for himself.

116. The greedy Marcus Licinius Crassus, consul with Pompey in 70 B.C. and later triumvir with Pompey and Caesar, was defeated and beheaded by the Parthians in 53 B.C.

So, I was not the only one to cry
   the good we praise by day; it was by chance
   no other spirit nearby raised his voice."   123

We had already taken leave of him
   and we were striving to cover as much
   ground as those prostrate souls allowed us to,   126

when, suddenly, I felt the mountain shake
   as if about to crumble, and I felt
   my body numb, seized by the chill of death.   129

Delos, before Latona nested there,
   in order to give birth to those two eyes
   that shine in Heaven, was never shaken more.   132

Then on all sides a shout rose up, so loud
   my master drew close to my side and said:
   "You need not fear while I am still your guide."   135

Gloria in excelsis, all sang, *Deo*—
   at least, this is what those close by sang out,
   whose words I could hear clearly as they cried.   138

As had the shepherds who first heard that song,
   we stood fixed with our souls suspended there
   until the hymn ended, the tremor ceased.   141

Then we continued on our sacred road:
   beneath our eyes the prostrate souls once more
   were wholly given up to their laments.   144

Never before, unless my memory errs,
   had my blind ignorance stirred up in me
   so violent a desire for the truth   147

130. Delos is an island in the Cyclades, where Latona went to escape the wrath of
Juno and to bring forth her two children by Jupiter: Apollo and Diana.

136. The song "Glory to God in the Highest" was sung by the angels on the eve of
the Nativity and heard by the shepherds (139) in the fields.

as I felt now, racking my brain to know.
  I dared not slow our pace with questioning,
  and I could see no explanation there.   150

I walked along, timid, deep in my thoughts.

CANTO XXI

As the Pilgrim and Virgil walk along the Terrace of the Avaricious, a shade appears and speaks to them. Virgil explains that the Pilgrim is still alive, and he relates the nature and purpose of their journey, finally asking the shade why the mountain has just trembled. The shade explains that the mountain of Purgatory is not subject to the vicissitudes of Nature such as rain, wind, and lightning, but that when a soul feels that the time of its purification has come to an end and it is ready to ascend to Heaven, then the mountain shakes and voices shout praises to God. The shade speaking is the one who has just experienced this release after more than five hundred years of purgation. He identifies himself as Statius, the author of the Thebaid *and the unfinished* Achilleid. *Statius claims that he has derived his poetic inspiration from the* Aeneid, *and he expresses his ardent wish to have lived when Virgil was alive, and to have met the great poet. At these words the Pilgrim smiles knowingly, and with his guide's permission, reveals to Statius that he is standing in the presence of his mentor. Forgetting himself, Statius bends down to embrace Virgil's knees, but is gently reminded by that prince of poets that they are only empty shades.*

The natural thirst which nothing satisfies
  except that water begged for long ago
  by the poor woman of Samaria   3

tormented me, and haste was urging me
  along the crowded path, and I was still
  grieving at the just pain those souls must pay,   6

---

3. The story of Jesus and the Samaritan woman at the well is told in John 4:5–15.

when suddenly—just as we read in Luke
　　that Christ, new-risen from the tomb, appeared
　　to the two men on the Emmaus road—　　　　　　9

a shade appeared! He had come from behind
　　while we were trying not to step on shades,
　　quite unaware of him until he spoke:　　　　　12

"May God, my brothers, give you peace." At that,
　　we quickly turned around, and Virgil then
　　responded to his words appropriately,　　　　15

and said: "May God's True Court which sentenced me
　　to eternal banishment, lead you in peace
　　into the Congregation of the Blest."　　　　18

"What's that?" he said as we kept forging on.
　　"If you are souls whom God will not receive,
　　who let you climb His stairway this far up?"　　21

And then my teacher said: "If you observe
　　those marks the angel has traced on his brow,
　　you'll see that he must dwell among the Just.　24

But she who labors spinning day and night,
　　had not spun out for him the flax which Clotho
　　packs on her distaff for each one of us;　　　27

therefore, his soul, sister to yours and mine,
　　in coming up, could not come by itself,
　　because it does not see as our eyes do.　　　30

And so I was brought up from Hell's wide throat
　　to serve him as a guide, and guide I shall
　　as far as my own knowledge will permit.　　33

But can you tell me why the mountain shook
　　so hard just now, and why all of the souls
　　down to its marshy base, cried out as one?"　　36

15. In the liturgy, the proper response to *Pax vobis* (Statius's greeting or salutation of peace in line 13) is the kiss of peace.

25–27. The spinner is Lachesis, one of the three Fates. She spins the thread of a man's life from a certain quantity of wool, which her sister, Clotho, has loaded onto the distaff.

My leader's question pierced the needle's eye
   of my desire, and with the eager hope
   that this aroused, I felt my thirst relieved.   39

The shade said: "Sacred laws that rule this mount
   will not let anything take place that is
   uncustomary or irregular.   42

This place is not subject to any change:
   what Heaven takes from itself into itself,
   and nothing else, can serve as cause up here;   45

therefore no rain, no hail, no snow can fall,
   nor dew nor hoarfrost form at any point
   beyond the three-step stairway down below.   48

There are no clouds, misty or dense, no sign
   of lightning or of Thaumas' daughter, she
   who often moves from place to place below;   51

nor can dry vapors rise beyond the height
   of those three steps of which I just now spoke,
   whereon Saint Peter's vicar rests his feet.   54

Quakes may occur below, slight or severe,
   but tremors caused by winds hid in the earth
   (I know not why) have never reached this high.   57

Up here the mountain trembles when some soul
   feels itself pure enough to stand erect
   or start at once to climb—then, comes the shout.   60

The will to rise, alone, proves purity:
   once freed, it takes possession of the soul
   and wills the soul to change its company.   63

It willed to climb before, but the desire
   High Justice set against it, inspired it
   to wish to suffer—as once it wished to sin.   66

And I, who for five hundred years and more,
   have lain here in my pain, felt only now
   will free to raise me to a higher sill.   69

That's why you felt the quake and why you heard
    the pious dwellers on the mount praise God.
    May He soon call them up to be with Him."   72

This was his explanation. And my joy
    was inexpressible: the more the thirst,
    the more enjoyable becomes the drink.   75

And my wise leader: "Now I see what net
    holds you bound here, and how the mesh is torn,
    why the mount shakes, why you rejoice as one.   78

Now, if it please you, I would like to know
    who you once were, and learn from your own words
    why you have lain so many centuries here."   81

"During the rule of the good Titus, who,
    assisted by the King of Kings, avenged
    the wounds that poured forth blood which Judas sold,   84

I bore the title that endures the most
    and which is honored most," that soul replied;
    "renown I had, not yet the Christian faith.   87

The spirit of my verses was so sweet
    that from Toulouse, Rome called me to herself,
    and judged me worthy of the myrtle crown.   90

My name is Statius, still well known on earth.
    I sang of Thebes, then of Achilles' might,
    but found that second weight too great to bear.   93

The spark that kindled my poetic ardor
    came from the sacred flame that set on fire
    more than a thousand poets: I mean the *Aeneid*.   96

That was the mother of my poetry,
    the nurse that gave it suck. Without that poem,
    my verses would have not been worth a thing.   99

82. Titus, son and successor of Vespasian, served as Roman emperor from A.D. 79 to 81.

91. Publius Papinus Statius was born in Naples ca. A.D. 45 and died in 96. He was the major poet of the Silver Age of Latin literature and spent most of his life in Rome.

And if only I could have been alive
    when Virgil lived, I would consent to spend
    an extra year of exile on the mount."   102

At these words Virgil turned to me. His look
    told me in silence: "Silence!" But the power
    of a man's will is often powerless: 105

laughter and tears follow so close upon
    the passions that provoke them that the more
    sincere the man, the less they obey his will.   108

I smiled and unsmiled quicker than a blink,
    but he stopped speaking; staring straight at me,
    into the eyes, where secrets are betrayed: 111

"So may your toiling win you grace," he said,
    "tell me the reason for your smile just now—
    that smile that quickly came and quickly went."   114

Here I am caught between opposing sides:
    the one tells me be quiet, the other bids
    me to speak up. And so, I sigh. My guide   117

perfectly understood: "Don't be afraid
    to speak," he said: "speak to him, answer now
    the question he has asked so earnestly."   120

"You seem to find my smiling very strange,"
    I said to him, "O ancient spirit, but
    I have to tell you something stranger still: 123

This shade here who directs my eyes to Heaven
    is the poet Virgil, who bequeathed to you
    the power to sing the deeds of men and gods.   126

In truth, the only reason for my smile,
    is that you chose to mention Virgil here:
    your very words are guilty of my smile."   129

Already he was bending to embrace
     my teacher's feet, but Virgil: "Brother, no!
     You are a shade; it is a shade you see."   132

And Statius, rising: "Now you understand
     how much my love for you burns deep in me,
     when I forget about our emptiness   135

and deal with shadows as with solid things."

CANTO XXII

Leaving the Fifth Terrace, *the Pilgrim and Virgil, now accompanied
by Statius, are directed to the next ledge by an angel who removes
another* P *from the Pilgrim's forehead and pronounces those blessed
who thirst for righteousness. Virgil tells Statius that he has felt a great
deal of good will toward him ever since Juvenal had come down to
Limbo with the report of Statius's love and admiration for Virgil. But
he is puzzled as to how such a magnanimous spirit could find room in
its heart for avarice. Statius explains that his sin was not Avarice, but
Prodigality, and that whenever two sins are the immediate opposite of
one another, they are purged together on the same terrace of the moun-
tain of Purgatory. Virgil then asks Statius how he came to be a Chris-
tian, and Statius replies that it was Virgil's* Fourth Eclogue *that
eventually led him to give ear to the Christian preachers. Once con-
verted, however, he kept his faith a secret, and for this lack of zeal was
consigned to spend four hundred years on the Terrace of the Slothful.
As the poets finish their conversation, they step out onto the Sixth Ter-
race, where they encounter a tree with sweet-smelling fruit in the middle
of the road. A cascade of clear water rains down on its uppermost
leaves. As they draw closer to the tree, a voice from within the branches
shouts the exempla of the virtue opposed to gluttony.*

By now we had already left behind
     the angel who directs to the Sixth Round
     and from my brow erased another scar,   3

saying that all who looked for righteousness
    are blest—omitting the *esuriunt*,
    and predicating only *sitiunt*.   6

And I, lighter than I had felt before
    at any other stairs, moved easily
    upward, behind those swiftly climbing shades.   9

Now, Virgil was already speaking: "Love,
    kindled by virtue, always kindles love,
    if the first flame is clearly visible;   12

thus, ever since the day that Juvenal
    came down to Hell's Limbo to be with us,
    and told me of the love you felt for me,   15

I have felt more good will toward you, more than
    was felt toward any person not yet seen;
    and so, these stairs will seem much shorter now.   18

But tell me—speak to me as to a friend,
    and as a friend, forgive me if I seem
    too bold in slackening decorum's reins—   21

how could your heart find room for avarice,
    with that abundant store of sound, good sense
    which you acquired with such diligence?"   24

These words of Virgil brought to Statius' lips
    a briefly lingering smile; then he replied:
    "All you have said reveals your love for me.   27

Appearances will often, it is true,
    give rise to false assumptions, when the truth
    to be revealed is hidden from our eyes.   30

---

5. The angel, as always, recites a beatitude. The entire beatitude is "Blessed are they who hunger and thirst after righteousness, for they shall be satisfied" (Vulgate: *Beati qui* esuriunt *et* sitiunt *justitiam* . . .). Here the verse is recited only with *sitiunt* ("thirst"), the other word, *esuriunt* ("hunger"), being omitted: "Blessed are they who thirst after righteousness." "Hunger" is saved for use on the Terrace of the Gluttons.

13. Juvenal (Decimus Junius Juvenalis, ca. A.D. 60–ca. 140) was the Roman satirical poet and author of the *Satires*. He mentions in his *Seventh Satire* the poverty of Statius, his contemporary.

Your question makes it clear to me that you
   believe my sin on earth was Avarice—
   perhaps because you found me where you did.   33

In truth, I had no part of Avarice;
   in fact, too little! The sin I purged below,
   thousands of months, was Prodigality.   36

And if I had not come to change my ways
   while meditating on those lines you wrote,
   where you, enraged by human nature, cry: 39

'To what extremes, O cursèd lust for gold
   will you not drive man's appetite?'—I would
   be rolling weights now in the dismal jousts.   42

But when I understood how hands could spread
   their wings too wide in spending, then that sin,
   and all my others, I repented of.   45

How many shall rise bald the Final Day
   through ignorance of this vice, forbidding them
   repentance during life or on death's bed?   48

And know that when the vice of any sin
   is the rebuttal of its opposite,
   the two of them wither together here.   51

So, though to purge myself I spent my time
   among those souls who weep for Avarice,
   my sin was just the opposite of theirs."   54

"Now, when you sang about the bitter strife
   of the twin sources of Jocasta's grief,"
   the bard of the *Bucolics* said to him,   57

56. Jocasta was the mother of Oedipus, whom she later unwittingly married, giving
birth to Eteocles and Polynices. In the struggle for the throne of Thebes, these two
brothers killed one another, thus producing the twin sorrows of their mother. This
fratricidal conflict was the subject of Statius's *Thebaid*.

57. The *Bucolics* of Virgil contain the *Eclogues,* from which there is a quotation in
line 70.

"from what you wrote in Clio's company,
   it does not seem that you were faithful then
   to that faith without which virtue is vain.   60

If this be so, tell me what heavenly sun
   or earthly beam lit up your course so that
   you could set sail behind the Fisherman."   63

Statius said: "It was you directed me
   to drink Parnassus' waters—it was you
   whose radiance revealed the way to God.   66

You were the lonely traveller in the dark
   who holds his lamp behind him, shedding light
   not for himself but to make others wise;   69

for you once wrote: 'The world is born again;
   Justice returns, and the first age of man,
   and a new progeny descends from heaven.'   72

Through you I was a poet, through you, a Christian.
   And now, to show you better what I mean,
   I shall fill in my outline with more color.   75

By then, the world was laboring in the birth
   of the true faith, sown by the messengers
   of the Eternal Kingdom; and your words,   78

which I just quoted now, so harmonized
   with what the new preachers were saying then,
   that I would often go to hear them speak.   81

These men became so holy in my eyes
   that when Domitian persecuted them,
   I wept, as they wept in their suffering,   84

and, for as long as I remained alive,
   I helped them, and their righteous way of life
   taught me to scorn all other faiths but theirs.   87

58. Clio is the Muse of history, whom Statius invokes at the beginning of the *Thebaid*.

83. Domitian (Titus Flavius Domitianus Augustus) succeeded his brother Titus as emperor of Rome in A.D. 81 and was murdered in 96. Statius's *Thebaid* is dedicated to him.

Before I brought the Greeks to Theban streams
    with my poetic art, I was baptized,
    but was a secret Christian out of fear,   90

pretending to be pagan many years;
    and for this lack of zeal, I had to run
    four hundred years on the Fourth Circle. Now,   93

please tell me, you who did remove the veil
    that once concealed from me the good I praise,
    tell me, while there is still some time to climb,   96

where is our ancient Terence, do you know?
    And Plautus, and Caecilius and Varius?
    Have they been damned? If so, where are they lodged?"   99

"They all, along with Persius and me
    and others," said my guide, "are with that Greek
    the Muses suckled more than all the rest,   102

in the First Round of Hell's unlighted jail.
    We often talk about the mountain slope
    where our nine nurses dwell eternally.   105

Euripides walks with us; Antiphon,
    Simonides, and Agathon are there,
    and other Greeks who wear the laurel crown.   108

88. The Greeks draw near the Theban rivers, the Ismenus and the Asopus, in the seventh book of the *Thebaid*; it was before Statius had reached that point in writing his first epic that he was baptized.

100. Aulus Persius Flaccus was a Roman satirist (A.D. 34–62).

101. The Greek is Homer.

105. The nurses are the nine Muses.

106–107. Virgil proceeds to mention four Greek poets that are with him in Limbo. Euripides (485?–406 B.C.) was a Greek playwright, eighteen of whose tragedies have survived in more or less completed form. Antiphon was a Greek tragic poet, whom Plutarch mentions among the great tragic authors; only fragments of three of his tragedies survive. Simonides, a Greek lyric poet, was born ca. 556 B.C. and died 467 B.C. None of the works of Agathon (ca. 448–ca. 402 B.C.), a Greek tragic poet, has survived.

With us are many of your people too:
   Antigone, Deïphyle, Argia,
   Ismene, sad as she has ever been,   111

and she who showed Langia to the Greeks,
   and Thetis, and the daughter of Tiresias,
   Deïdamia with her sisters, too."   114

The poets now were free of walls and stairs,
   both of them standing silent on the ledge,
   eager again to gaze at everything.   117

Already the four handmaids of the day
   were left behind, and at the chariot-pole,
   the fifth was tilting up the blazing tip,   120

when my guide said: "I think we ought to move
   with our right shoulders to the outer edge,
   the way we always have gone round this mount."   123

So, habit was our guide there, and we went
   our way with much less hesitation now,
   since worthy Statius gave us his assent.   126

They walked ahead and I, behind, alone,
   was paying close attention to their words,
   which taught me things about the art of verse.   129

But then, right in the road a tree appeared,
   laden with fruit whose fragrance filled the air,
   and instantly that pleasant talk was stopped!   132

Just as a fir tree tapers toward the top
   from branch to branch, so this one tapered down,
   to keep the souls from climbing, I suppose.   135

On that side where our way was bounded, poured
   clear water from the high rock to the tree,
   sprinkling the topmost leaves in its cascade.   138

118–120. Since the fifth handmaid is at her post, and the sun rises at 6:00, it is now
between 10:00 and 11:00 A.M.

As the two poets drew close, there came a voice
　　that shouted at us from within the tree:
　　　"This fruit and water is denied to you."   141

Then the voice said: "Mary was more intent
　　on gracing the wedding feast with plenitude
　　than on her own mouth, which now pleads for you!   144

In ancient Rome the women were content
　　with water as their drink! And Daniel, too,
　　acquired wisdom by despising food!   147

Mankind's first age was beautiful as gold,
　　and hunger made the acorns savory,
　　and thirst made nectar run in every stream!   150

Locusts and honey were the only foods
　　that fed the Baptist in the wilderness;
　　to that he owes his glory and his fame,   153

which in the Gospel is revealed to you!"

CANTO XXIII

As THE THREE *poets turn from the tree, they hear the tones of the psalm*
Labia mea Domine. *Soon a quickly moving band of emaciated spirits
with famished faces comes from behind them. These are the Gluttonous.
The Pilgrim recognizes one of these souls by his voice—his features have
been so altered by starvation—as his old friend Forese Donati. Although
a late repentant and dead only five years, Forese has been able to ad-*

142–144. This is the second example from the wedding feast at Cana. *Purgatory*
XIII, 29, shows the generosity of Mary; here we see her temperance.

146–147. Daniel (Daniel 1:3–20) spurned the meat and drink of the king's table and
was given by God the gift of interpreting visions and dreams.

154. The Gospel states "Amen, I say unto you, among those born of women there
has not risen a greater than John the Baptist" (Matthew 11:11).

vance so far up the mountain on account of the prayers of his widow,
Nella. The thought of the virtuous Nella provokes from Forese a dia-
tribe against the shameless women of Florence. The canto ends with the
Pilgrim describing to his old friend the nature of the journey he has
undertaken.

While I peered up through that green foliage,
 trying to see what might be hidden there,
 like one who wastes his lifetime hunting birds,   3

my more than father called to me: "Dear son,
 come with me now; the time allotted us
 ought to be spent more profitably." So,   6

I quickly turned and, just as quickly, moved
 to follow the two poets whose talk was such
 that every step I took cost me no strain.   9

Then suddenly we heard the tearful chant
 of *Labia mea Domine,* in tones
 inspiring a sweet blend of joy and pain.   12

"Dear father, tell me, what is this I hear?"
 I asked, and he replied: "They may be shades
 loosing the knot of their great debt to God."   15

As pilgrims wrapped in meditation pass
 someone they do not know along the road
 and turn to stare and then go quickly on,   18

so, from behind us, moving swiftly, came
 and passed us by with a quick look of doubt,
 a band of spirits, silent and devout,   21

their eyes dark-shadowed, sunken in their heads,
 their faces pale, their bodies worn so thin
 that every bone was molded to their skin.   24

11. "*Labia mea Domine*" is the prayer of the Gluttonous, who are punished on the
Sixth Terrace of Purgatory. It is taken from the *Miserere* (Psalm 50), and the verse
that Dante evokes here is the following: "Open my lips, O Lord, and my mouth shall
proclaim your praises."

I do not think that wretched Erysichthon
    had come to such a state of skin and bones,
    not even when he feared starvation most.   27

And I said to myself, "Look at those souls!
    They could be those who lost Jerusalem,
    when Miriam sunk her beak into her son."   30

The sockets of their eyes were gemless rings;
    one who reads *omo* in the face of men,
    could easily have recognized the *m*.   33

Who would believe, ignorant of the cause,
    that nothing but the smell of fruit or spring
    could bring them to this withered greediness?   36

I was still marveling at their famishing,
    since I did not yet understand what caused
    their leanness and their scabby shriveling,   39

when suddenly a shadow turned his eyes
    toward me and stared from deep within his skull,
    then cried: "What grace has been bestowed on me!"   42

I never would have known him by his looks,
    but in his voice I clearly recognized
    the features that his starving face disguised.   45

25. Son of King Triopas, Erysichthon committed an outrage against the goddess
Ceres by cutting trees in her sacred grove. Ceres then afflicted him with a ravenous
hunger, which drove him to sell his own daughter for food and, finally, to devour
his own flesh.

30. Josephus reports (in *The Jewish War* VI, 3) that during the Roman siege of
Jerusalem (A.D. 70), a certain Miriam, driven by hunger, killed and ate her own infant
son. Dante describes her as sinking "her beak into her son," as though she were some
horrible bird of prey.

32. The word *omo* (Latin *homo*, "man") can be "read" on the face of a man, if the
eyes are the *o*'s and the *m* is formed by the nose, eyebrows, and cheekbones. It was
believed in the Middle Ages that God had thus signed and identified his creation.

This spark rekindled in my memory
   the image of those features now so changed,
   and I could see again Forese's face.   48

"Oh, please forget about the crusty scurf
   discoloring my sickly skin," he begged,
   "pay no attention to my shriveled flesh;   51

tell me about yourself. And those two with you,
   tell me who they are too. Please answer me,
   do not withhold from me what I desire!"   54

"When death was on your face, I wept," I said,
   "and now the grief I feel is just as great,
   seeing your face so piteously disfigured.   57

In God's name tell me what strips you so bare.
   Do not ask me to speak, I am benumbed!
   And one speaks ill whose thoughts are somewhere else."   60

And he: "From the Eternal Mind a power
   descends into the water and the tree
   that you just passed: this is what makes me lean.   63

All of us here who sing while we lament
   for having stuffed our mouths too lovingly,
   make ourselves pure, thirsting and hungering.   66

The fragrance of the fruit and of the spray
   that trickles down the leaves stirs up in us
   a hungering desire for food and drink—   69

and not just once: as we go running round
   this road, our pain is constantly renewed.
   Did I say pain? Solace is what I mean!   72

For that same will that leads us to the tree
   led Christ to cry out joyously, 'Eli,'
   when he delivered us with His own blood."   75

48. Forese is Dante's friend, Forese Donati, also known as Bicci Novello, who engaged with him in a facetious poetical correspondence consisting of six sonnets.

74. Christ cried out to Eli in Matthew 27:46: "But about the ninth hour Jesus cried out with a loud voice, saying 'Eli, Eli, lema sabachthani,' that is, 'My God, my God, why has thou forsaken me?' "

And I: "Forese; since that day when you
   abandoned our world for a better life,
   less than five years from your last day have passed!   78

If, when you knew that moment of sweet grief
   that weds the soul to God again, you were
   close to your death, able to sin no more—   81

how have you climbed so high up on the mount?
   I thought, surely, to find you down below
   where souls who wasted time must pay with time."   84

"It was my Nella with her flowing tears,"
   he answered me, "who brought me here so soon
   to let me drink the sweet wormwood of pain.   87

It was her pious prayers and her laments
   that raised me from the slope where souls must wait,
   and set me free from all the other rounds.   90

All the more dear and pleasing to the Lord
   is my sweet widow that I greatly loved,
   the more she is unique in doing good;   93

for the Barbagia of Sardinia counts
   among its women many far more chaste
   than those in the Barbagia where she lives.   96

My dear brother, how can I tell you this:
   I see a future time—it won't be long—
   in which bans from the pulpit shall clamp down   99

on those ladies of Florence who, bold-faced,
   now walk our city streets as they parade
   their bosom to the tits! What barbarous girl,   102

what female Saracen, had to be taught
   spiritual discipline, or anything,
   to keep her body decently concealed?   105

85. Nella was Forese's virtuous wife, Giovanella.

94. The Barbagia was the wild, mountainous region of Sardinia inhabited by the
Barbacini, a clan of bandits said to have descended from a settlement of prisoners
established by the Vandals.

But if these shameless creatures only knew
   what the swift heavens have in store for them,
   they would by now be screaming their heads off!   108

For if our foresight here does not deceive,
   they shall have cause to grieve before the cheeks
   of those now soothed by lullabies grow beards.   111

My brother, now tell me about yourself.
   You see how everyone, including me,
   is staring there where you block out the sun."   114

I answered him: "Whenever you recall
   what we were like together, you and I,
   the memory of those days must torture you.   117

From that life I was called away by him
   who leads me here—just a few days ago,
   when his sister (I pointed to the sun)   120

was shining full. Still wearing this true flesh
   I came into and through the darkest night
   of the true dead with this soul as my guide;   123

from there, sustained by him, I came up here
   climbing and ever circling round this mount
   which straightens in you what the world has bent.   126

He says that I shall have his company
   until I am where Beatrice is—
   and from then on, without him I must go.   129

Virgil (I pointed to him) told me this.
   The other spirit standing over there
   is he for whom this mountain's terraces   132

trembled just now, releasing him to Heaven."

---

121. The Pilgrim is referring to the full moon that was shining on the night of Holy
Thursday, when he entered the Dark Wood, in the opening canto of the *Comedy*.

CANTO XXIV

THE PILGRIM AND Forese continue their conversation. Forese says that his sister, Piccarda, has already been taken up into Heaven, and then he points out a number of the souls of the Gluttonous, among them Bonagiunta Orbicciani of Lucca, Pope Martin V of Tours, Ubaldino della Pila, Boniface de' Fieschi, archbishop of Ravenna, and the Marchese degli Orgoliosi of Forlì. The Pilgrim chooses to speak to the shade of Bonagiunta, who seems particularly anxious to approach him. Bonagiunta prophesies that a woman named Gentucca will someday make the Pilgrim appreciate the city of Lucca. He then asks Dante if he is the author of the poem "Ladies who have intelligence of Love," and a brief discussion of the "dolce stil nuovo" ensues. As this discussion comes to an end, the souls of the Gluttonous turn and speed away. Only Forese remains behind to converse further with the Pilgrim, and he prophesies the ignominious death of his brother, Corso Donati. When Forese has departed, the Pilgrim encounters a second tree, from whose branches a voice shouts exempla of Gluttony; these include the drunken centaurs at the wedding feast of Theseus and the unworthy soldiers of Gideon's band, who drank greedily, putting their faces in the water. Finally the angel of Abstinence shows the three poets the way to the next terrace.

Talking did not slow down our walk, nor did
   walking our talk: conversing, on we sped
   like ships enjoying favorable winds.   3

And all those shades, looking like things twice dead,
   absorbed the miracle through caved-in eyes:
   this was a living man which they beheld!   6

And I, continuing where I left off,
   said: "He is climbing at a slower pace
   because of his companion, I suppose.   9

If you can, tell me where Piccarda is.
   And, are there any here that I should know
   among these shades that stare at me like this?"   12

10. Piccarda was the sister of Forese Donati, whom Dante later meets in Paradise (*Paradise* III, 34–123).

"My sister, who was just as virtuous
  as she was lovely, is in triumph now
  on High Olympus, joyful in her crown."   15

This he said first, and then: "No reason why
  I should not tell their names—especially
  since abstinence has milked our features dry.   18

There"—and he pointed—"Bonagiunta goes,
  the Luccan Bonagiunta; the one behind—
  see that face withered more than all the rest—   21

once held within his arms the Holy Church:
  he was from Tours, and here he fasts to purge
  Bolsena's eels cooked in Vernaccia wine."   24

Then, many others he named, one by one,
  and all seemed quite content at being named—
  no one, at least, gave him an angry look.   27

I saw two souls for hunger chewing air:
  Ubaldino della Pila, Boniface,
  who with his crook led multitudes to graze.   30

I saw Milord Marchese. He, in Forlì,
  drank endlessly and with less thirst than here—
  yet no one ever saw him satisfied.   33

15. High Olympus is Heaven.

19. Bonagiunta Orbicciani of Lucca was a poet, many of whose verses survive, as
well as an orator of some repute. He was born around 1220.

21. The face is that of Simon de Brie of Tours, who served as Pope Martin IV from
1281 to 1285.

29. Ubaldino degli Ubaldini della Pila was a great feaster and entertainer, who de-
voted much care to the preparation of meals.

29. Boniface (Bonifazio de' Fieschi of Genoa), archbishop of Ravenna from 1274 to
1294, was very wealthy and served as an arbitrator and ambassador, bringing about
a reconciliation between Alfonso III of Aragon and Philip the Fair, and negotiating
the release of Charles II of Naples.

31. Milord Marchese was a member of the Argogliosi family of Forlì and podestà
of Faenza in 1296. A great wine drinker, when told that people thought he did
nothing but drink, he replied that they should instead think of him as being always
thirsty.

Often a face will stand out in a crowd;
   this happened here: I singled out the shade
   from Lucca, who seemed interested in me.   36

He mumbled something—something like "Gentucca"
   I heard come from his lips, where he felt most
   emaciating Justice strip him bare.   39

"O, soul," I said, "you seem so much to want
   to talk to me; speak up so I can hear;
   that way your words can satisfy us both."   42

"A woman has been born," he said, "and she
   is still unmarried, who will give you cause
   to love my city, which all men revile.   45

Remember well this prophecy of mine,
   and if the words I muttered are not clear,
   future events will clarify their sense.   48

But, tell me, do I not see standing here
   him who brought forth the new poems that begin:
   'Ladies who have intelligence of Love.' "   51

I said to him, "I am one who, when Love
   inspires me, takes careful note and then,
   gives form to what he dictates in my heart."   54

---

37. Though nothing regarding Gentucca is known with certainty, she was probably one who befriended Dante during his exile.

45. This city that "all men revile" is Lucca, which had the reputation of being a hotbed of political corruption.

51. This is the opening verse of the first *canzone* of the *Vita nuova*.

52–54. This is a description of Dante's new poetic method: he follows the dictates of love, of the selfless, nonerotic love of which he learned in the *Vita nuova*, and of love as the desire for the highest good (love as explained at length in the *Purgatory* by Virgil in Cantos XVII–XVIII).

"My brother, now I see," he said, "the knot
    that held Guittone and the Notary
    and me back from the sweet new style I hear!   57

Now, I see very clearly how your wings
    fly straight behind the dictates of that Love—
    this, certainly, could not be said of ours;   60

and no one who examines the two styles
    can clarify the difference more than I."
    Then, pleased with what he said, he said no more.   63

As birds that winter down along the Nile
    take flight massed close together in the air,
    then, gaining speed, will fly in single file—   66

just so that mass of spirits lined up straight,
    and then, light with their leanness and desire,
    all of a sudden, sped away from us.   69

And as a weary racer slows his pace,
    allowing all the rest to pass him by,
    until the heaving of his chest subsides,   72

so did Forese let that holy flock
    rush by him while he still kept step with me
    as he inquired: "When shall we meet again?"   75

"How long my life will last I do not know,"
    I said, "but even if I come back soon,
    my heart already will have reached the shore,   78

because the place where I was born to live
    is being stripped of virtue, day by day,
    doomed, or disposed, to rip itself to ruin."   81

56. Guittone d'Arezzo, born ca. 1230 at Santa Firmina, seems to have been responsible for establishing the Sicilian mode of poetry in Tuscany.

56. The Notary was Giacomo da Lentino (or Lentini), a judge at the court of Frederick II, who was the major figure of the Sicilian school of poetry that flourished during the first half of the thirteenth century and that established the poetry of courtly love in Italy.

He said, "Take heart. The guiltiest of them all
   I see dragged to his death at a beast's tail
   down to the pit that never pardons sin.   84

The beast with every stride increases speed,
   faster and faster, till it suddenly
   kicks free the body, hideously mangled.   87

Those spheres," and he looked up into the heavens,
   "will not revolve for long before my words,
   which I have left obscure, will be made clear.   90

Now I must leave you. I have lost much time,
   walking along with you at your own pace,
   and time is precious to us in this realm."   93

As sometimes from a troop riding to war
   a horseman at a gallop will rush out
   to win the honor of attacking first—   96

so he strode faster leaving me to go
   my way, accompanied by those two shades
   who were such mighty marshals of the world.   99

When he had raced so far ahead of us
   my eyes could follow him no better than
   my mind could understand what his words meant,   102

I took my eyes from him—and, suddenly,
   there in the road in front of me, appeared
   another tree with verdant, laden boughs.   105

Beneath the tree I saw shades, arms outstretched,
   crying out something up into the leaves,
   like greedy children begging foolishly   108

---

82. The "guiltiest of them all" was Corso Donati, brother of Forese. He was the leader of the Black faction in Florence and persuaded Boniface VIII to send Charles of Valois to Florence.

to someone who will not answer their plea
    but who, instead, tempting them all the more,
    holds in full view the things they cannot reach.   111

At last, the souls gave up and went away.
    Then we drew close to that imposing tree,
    which was impervious to prayers and tears.   114

"Pass on. Do not come closer. Higher up,
    there is a tree which gave its fruit to Eve,
    and this plant is an offshoot of its root."   117

Thus spoke a voice from somewhere in the leaves.
    So we moved on, Virgil, Statius, and I,
    close to each other as we hugged the cliff.   120

"Recall," the voice went on, "those wicked ones,
    born of a cloud who, in their drunkenness,
    fought double-breast to breast with Theseus.   123

Recall those Hebrews drinking at their ease,
    whom Gideon, then, refused to take along
    as comrades down the hills to Midian."   126

So, walking close to one side of the road,
    we listened to accounts of Gluttony
    and learned the wages that these sinners earned.   129

Then, walking freely on the open way,
    each of us silent, deeply lost in thought,
    we had gone more than a full thousand steps,   132

when, suddenly, a voice called out: "You there,
    you three alone, what occupies your mind?"
    I gave a start like some shy beast in panic.   135

I raised my head to see who just now spoke;
    and never in a furnace was there seen
    metal or glass so radiantly red   138

125. In the campaign of the Jews against the Midianites, Gideon was instructed by the Lord to observe how his ten thousand men, when they arrived thirsty at a river, drank. Rejecting those who abandoned caution and put their faces to the water, Gideon led three hundred more prudent soldiers to victory.

as was the being who said to me: "If you
   are looking for the way to climb, turn here:
   here is the path for those who search for peace."   141

Though blinded by the brilliance of his look,
   I turned around and groped behind my guides,
   letting the words just heard direct my feet.   144

Soft as the early morning breeze of May,
   which heralds dawn, rich with the grass and flowers,
   spreading in waves their breathing fragrances,   147

I felt a breeze strike soft upon my brow:
   I felt a wing caress it, I am sure,
   I sensed the sweetness of ambrosia.   150

I heard the words: "Blessed are those in whom
   grace shines so copiously that love of food
   does not arouse excessive appetite,   153

but lets them hunger after righteousness."

CANTO XXV

As THEY CLIMB, *the Pilgrim asks how the Gluttonous could be so lean,
since they are shades and have no need of food. After a short, meta-
phorical introduction to the problem, Virgil calls upon Statius, who
delivers a lengthy discourse on the relationship of the soul to the body,
touching on the generation of the body, on the soul breathed into the
embryo by the Creator, and finally on the nature and formation of
the diaphanous body. When he has finished, the three have arrived at
the seventh and last terrace, where they discover a wall of flame that
shoots out and up from the inner bank of the cliff, forcing them to walk
at the extreme outer edge of the ledge. From within the flames, the
Pilgrim hears the hymn* Summae Deus clementiae, *and he sees the spirits*

151–154. These lines are a lengthy paraphrase of the beatitude of Temperance.

of the Lustful. After singing the hymn through, they recite together an
exemplum of the chastity of the Virgin Mary. Softly they begin the hymn
again and conclude with another exemplum: the tenacious virginity of
the goddess Diana. After the third singing of the hymn, shouts of praise
are heard for the wives and husbands who observe the laws of virtuous
wedlock.

Now was the time to climb without delay,
    for Taurus held the sun's meridian,
    and night had left its own to Scorpio.   3

Even as a man spurred by necessity
    can never be deterred no matter what,
    but goes straight on his way until the end,   6

so did we make our entrance through the gap
    and, separated by that narrow space,
    in single file, we started climbing stairs.   9

And as a little stork that longs to fly
    will lift a wing, then, still not bold enough
    to leave the nest, will let it drop again—   12

just so was I: my longing to inquire,
    first bold, then weak; all I did was attempt
    to speak, and then I quickly changed my mind.   15

My gentle father, though our pace was swift,
    encouraged me to talk: "Release your bow
    of speech, I see it drawn right to the tip."   18

Then, moved by confidence, I spoke to him,
    asking: "How could they have become so lean
    since, anyway, they have no need for food?"   21

"If you recall how Meleager burned
    as simultaneously the brand burned through,
    this should not be too hard to understand.   24

22. Ovid (*Metamorphoses* VIII, 445–632) tells the story of Meleager, whose fate it
was to live only as long as a piece of wood burning on his mother's hearth remained
unconsumed.

Or think how, when you stand before a glass
   at every move you make your image moves.
   Does this not make things clearer than they were?   27

But now to set your anxious mind at ease,
   we have here Statius: I shall call on him
   to be the doctor for your open wound."   30

"If, in your presence, I explain to him,"
   Statius replied, "God's view of things, it is
   because I can deny no wish of yours."   33

Then he began: "Son, let your mind take in
   and ponder carefully these words of mine,
   they will explain the 'how' that troubles you.   36

The perfect blood—the blood that's never drunk
   by thirsty veins (like food left on the table
   still unconsumed) but is preserved entire—   39

acquires, within the heart, formative powers
   to build the members of the human shape
   (as does the blood that serves to nourish them),   42

then, purified again, flows down into
   the part best left unmentioned; thence, it sprays
   in nature's vessel on another's blood,   45

and there the two bloods blend. Each is designed
   to play a passive or an active role,
   due to its perfect place of origin;   48

this joined to that begins to work on it:
   first it clots, then it quickens what it made
   compact to serve as working matter now.   51

The active force, having become a soul
   (like a plant's soul, except that this has reached
   its goal—the active force has just begun),   54

reaches the stage, then, of a jellyfish:
   it moves and feels. Then organs start to form
   for faculties of which it is the seed.   57

It keeps on swelling, spreading out, my son,
    this force that comes from the begetter's heart,
    where nature plans for all the body's parts.   60

But how, from animal, this thing becomes
    a child, you cannot see yet—and this point
    has led astray a mind wiser than yours,   63

for in his teaching he would separate
    possible intellect from soul, because
    he found no organ for that faculty.   66

Open your heart to what I now reveal:
    when the articulation of the brain
    has been perfected in the embryo,   69

then the First Mover turns to it, with joy
    over such art in Nature, and He breathes
    a spirit into it, new, and with power   72

to assimilate what it finds active there,
    so that one single soul is formed complete,
    that lives and feels and contemplates itself.   75

(And if you find what I have said is strange,
    consider the sun's heat that turns to wine
    when it joins forces with the juice that flows.)   78

Then, when Lachesis has run out of flax,
    the soul is freed of flesh and takes with it,
    in essence, both the human and divine;   81

its lower faculties no longer thrive,
    but memory, intelligence, and will
    are active and far keener than before.   84

By its own weight it falls, immediately,
    marvelously, on one or the other shore,
    and there it learns its course for the first time.   87

Then, once the soul is there, contained in space,
    the informing power radiates around
    to reshape what the body had before.   90

And as the air, after a heavy rain,
   adorns itself with different, fragile hues
   born of the outer rays reflected there,   93

just so, the air enveloping the soul
   where it has fallen must assume the form
   imprinted on it by the soul's own powers;   96

as flame inevitably goes with fire,
   following it wherever it may shift,
   so the new form accompanies the soul.   99

Since air around it makes it visible,
   it's called a 'shade'; and out of air it forms
   organs for every sense, including sight.   102

And we can speak, we shades, and we can laugh,
   and we can shed those tears and breathe those sighs
   which you may well have heard here on the mount.   105

The shade takes on the form of our desire,
   it changes with the feelings we may have:
   this, then, is what amazed you earlier."   108

We had, by now, arrived at the last round
   and, having made our usual right turn,
   our minds became absorbed by something else: 111

there, from the inner bank, flames flashed out straight,
   while, from the ledge, a blast of air shot up,
   bending them back, leaving a narrow path   114

along the edge where we were forced to walk
   in single file; and I was terrified—
   there was the fire, and *here* I could fall off!   117

"In such a place as this," my leader said,
   "be sure to keep your eyes straight on the course,
   for one could slip here easily and fall."   120

Summae Deus clementiae, I heard then,
   sung in the very heart of the great heat;
   this made me want to look there all the more.   123

And I saw spirits walking in the flames;
   I watched them, but I also watched my steps,
   caught between fear and curiosity.   126

When they had sung that hymn through to the end,
   they cried out loudly: *Virum non cognosco,*
   then, softly, they began the hymn again.   129

When it was finished, they cried out, "Diana
   kept to the woods and chased out Helice,
   whose blood had felt the poison lust of Venus."   132

Then came the hymn again; then came their shouts
   praising those married pairs who had been chaste,
   as virtue and the marriage laws require.   135

And this I think, they do continuously
   as long as they must burn within the fire:
   the cure of flames, the diet of the hymns—   138

with these the last of all their wounds is healed.

121. *"Summae Deus clementiae"* ("God of Supreme Clemency") is the hymn of the Lustful, which asks God to banish Lust and every sinful instinct from their hearts, and to cleanse them with His healing fire. In the liturgy the hymn was traditionally sung at Matins on Saturday.

128. *"Virum non cognosco"* is the first example of the virtue of Chastity: "I know no man," taken, as always, from the life of the Virgin Mary. The incident referred to is the Annunciation.

130–131. The second example of Chastity is taken from classical myth. To preserve her virginity, Diana took refuge in the woods as a huntress. When one of her attendants, the nymph Helice, fell prey to the "poison of Venus" and was seduced by Jove, Diana dismissed her. Helice gave birth to Arcas but was later transformed into a she-bear by Jove's wife, Juno. Jove then placed her in the sky as the constellation Ursa Major.

CANTO XXVI

ONE OF THE *souls in the flames asks the Pilgrim, whose body has at-*
tracted a good deal of attention, to stop and speak, but as he is about
to do so, they are interrupted by another group of souls rushing from
the opposite direction. The members of the two groups greet each other
quickly and then, before separating, shout out exempla of Lust. One
group cites Sodom and Gomorrah, and the other, the shameful lust of
Pasiphaë for the bull. When the commotion has died down, the Pilgrim
sets forth the purpose of his journey, and the same soul who had ques-
tioned him earlier speaks again. He explains that the souls who had
rushed on and off so hurriedly are the Sodomites, and thus they cry
"Sodom" in self-reproach. The others are those whose sins have been
heterosexual (or hermaphroditic, as Dante puts it), but since they have
not acted like human beings, they cry out, to their shame, the animal
lust of Pasiphaë. After these clarifications, the speaker identifies himself
as Guido Guinizelli, and the Pilgrim demonstrates a profound affection
for the Bolognese poet. But Guido protests that there is a far greater
poet among them, and yields his place to Arnaut Daniel. Arnaut is the
only (non-Italian) figure in the Divine Comedy *to speak in his native*
tongue, Provençal.

While we were walking at the ledge's edge
   in single file—my good guide telling me
   from time to time: "I warn you now, take heed!"—   3

the sun shone on my shoulder from the right,
   and now, the azure of the western sky
   was slowly turning pale beneath its rays;   6

my shadow made the flames a deeper red,
   and even this slight evidence, I saw,
   caused many souls to wonder as they passed.   9

And this was the occasion for those souls
   to speculate about me. I heard said:
   "He seems to have a body of real flesh!"   12

Then some of them toward me began to strain,
    coming as close to me as they could come,
    most careful not to step out of the fire.   15

"O you who walk behind the other two,
    surely, as sign of your deep reverence,
    stop, speak to me whom thirst and fire burn.   18

I'm not the only one—all of us here
    are thirsty for your words, much thirstier
    than Ethiopes or Indians for cool drink.   21

Tell us, how is it possible for you
    to block the sun as if you were a wall,
    as if you had escaped the net of death?"   24

So said a voice to me. I would have tried
    already to explain, if something else
    unusual had not just caught my eye: 27

straight down the middle of the blazing road
    facing this group, another band of souls
    was on its way. I stopped to stare, amazed,   30

for I saw shades on either side make haste
    to kiss each other without lingering,
    and each with this brief greeting satisfied.   33

The ants in their black ranks do this: they rush
    to nose each other, as if to inquire
    which way to go or how their luck has been.   36

As soon as friendly greetings are exchanged,
    before taking the first step to depart,
    each one tries to outshout the other's cry;   39

25. The voice, as we learn later (92), is that of Guido Guinizelli.

29. The group that moves in a direction contrary to the first group and the three travellers is that of the Lustful who practiced homosexuality. This sin will be suggested in line 40 and will be made explicit by Guinizelli in lines 76–81.

the group that just arrived: "Sodom, Gomorrah!"
   The rest: "Pasiphaë enters the cow
   so that the bull may rush to mount her lust!"   42

Imagine cranes forming two flocks: one flies
   off toward the Riphean heights, one toward the sands,
   one to escape the frost, and one the sun—   45

so, here, two groups went their opposing ways,
   and all, in tears, took up once more their chants,
   with cries that fit each of their penances.   48

Then those same shades who had first questioned me
   drew close to me as they had done before,
   intent on listening, their faces glowed.   51

And I, who twice now knew their eager wish,
   began: "O souls assured of entering
   beatitude whenever it may be,   54

I did not leave my body, green or ripe,
   below on earth: I have it with me here;
   it is real flesh, complete with blood and bones.   57

I climb to cure my blindness, for above
   a lady has won grace for me, that I
   may bear my mortal burden through your world.   60

But please—so may what you desire most
   be quickly yours, and Heaven's greatest sphere
   shelter you in its loving spaciousness—   63

40. The newly arrived group shouts "Sodom, Gomorrah!" in self-reproach. The city of Sodom gave its name to the sin of sodomy.

41. Pasiphaë was the wife of King Minos of Crete, to whom Poseidon sent a black bull to be offered up as a sacrifice. Minos put it in his herd and Poseidon, out of revenge, caused Pasiphaë to lust after the bull. She had Daedalus, the craftsman, make a wooden structure in the shape of a cow, which was covered with a cowhide. Pasiphaë entered the cow and was possessed by the bull. The result of this union was the birth of the Minotaur, a creature half bull, half human (see *Inferno* XII, 12–18).

62. The sphere is the Empyrean, the place from which Beatrice descended to Limbo in order to help her lover.

tell me, who are you? Who are those that run
   away behind us in the other group?
   I shall record your answers in my book."   66

No less dumbfounded than a mountaineer,
   who, speechless, gapes at everything he sees,
   when, rude and rustic, he comes down to town,   69

were all those shades there judging from their looks;
   but when they had recovered from surprise
   (which in a noble heart lasts but a while),   72

the same soul who had earlier questioned me
   began: "Blessed are you, who from our shores
   can ship experience back for a better death!   75

The shades that do not move with us were marked
   by that same sin for which Caesar as he
   passed in triumph heard himself called a 'Queen';   78

and that is why you heard 'Sodom!' cried out
   in self-reproach, as they ran off from us;
   they use their shame to intensify the flames.   81

And ours was an hermaphroditic sin,
   but since we did not act like human beings,
   yielding instead, like animals, to lust,   84

when we pass by the other group, we shout
   to our own shame the shameful name of her
   who bestialized herself in beast-shaped wood.   87

Now you know what our guilt is. Should you want
   to know our names, I do not know them all,
   and if I did, there still would not be time.   90

As for my name, I can fulfill your wish:
   I am Guido Guinizelli—here so soon,
   for I repented long before I died."   93

82. By "hermaphroditic" Dante means heterosexual, male with female.

86. The "shameful name" is Pasiphaë (see note at 41).

As King Lycurgus raged with grief, two sons
    discovered their lost mother and rejoiced—
    I felt the same (though more restrained) to hear   96

that spirit name himself—father of me
    and father of my betters, all who wrote
    a sweet and graceful poetry of love.   99

I heard no more, I did not speak, I walked
    deep in my thoughts, my eyes fixed on his shade;
    the flames kept me from coming close to him.   102

At last my eyes were satisfied. And then
    I spoke, convincing him of my deep wish
    to serve him in whatever way I could.   105

He answered me: "What I just heard you say
    has made a deep impression on my mind,
    which even Lethe cannot wash away.   108

But if what you have told me is the truth,
    now tell me what it is that makes you show
    in words and looks this love you have for me?"   111

And I to him: "Those graceful poems of yours,
    which, for as long as our tongue serves for verse,
    will render precious even the ink you used."   114

"My brother, I can show you now," he said
    (he pointed to a spirit up ahead),
    "a better craftsman of his mother tongue.   117

94–95. The sons' mother is Hypsipyle, wife of Jason, to whom she had borne two sons; she was captured by pirates and sold to Lycurgus, king of Nemea, who appointed her nurse of his infant son.

108. Lethe is the traditional river of oblivion, which we are soon to see at the summit of the mountain of Purgatory.

117. The craftsman is the Provençal poet Arnaut Daniel, who flourished between 1180 and ca. 1210. He is credited with the invention of the sestina, which Dante adopted, and he wrote in the obscure style of the *trobar clus*. He is also the author of some of the most pornographic poetry in Provençal literature.

Poets of love, writers of tales in prose—
    better than all of them he was! They're fools
    who think him of Limoges a greater poet!   120

They judge by reputation, not by truth,
    their minds made up before they know the rules
    of reason and the principles of art.   123

Guittone was judged this way in the past;
    many praised him and him alone—though, now,
    most men have been won over to the truth.   126

But now, if that high privilege be yours
    of climbing to the cloister, there where Christ
    is Abbot of the holy college, then,   129

please say a *Paternoster* for me there—
    at least the part appropriate for us,
    who are by now delivered from all evil."   132

Then, to make room for someone else, perhaps,
    he disappeared into the depths of fire
    the way fish seeking deeper waters fade.   135

I moved up toward the shade just pointed out,
    and told him my desire had prepared
    a gracious place of welcome for his name.   138

He readily and graciously replied:
    "Tan m'abellis vostre cortes deman,
    Qu'ieu no me puesc no voill a vos cobrire.   141

120. The poet of Limoges is Guiraut de Bornellh (1175–1220), another famous Provençal poet, with a far simpler style than Arnaut Daniel's.

133. Guinizelli, who has been on stage since line 16, now retreats farther into the flame.

140–147. "Your elegant request so pleases me, / I could not possibly conceal my name. / I am Arnaut, singing now through my tears, / regretfully recalling my past follies, / and joyfully anticipating joy. / I beg you, in the name of that great power / guiding you to the summit of the stairs, / remember, in good times, my suffering here."

Ieu sui Arnaut, que plor e vau cantan;
   consiros vei la passada folor,
   e vei jausen lo joi qu'esper, denan.   144

Ara vos prec, per aquella valor
   que vos guida al som de l'escalina,
   sovenha vos a temps de ma dolor!"   147

Then in the purifying flames he hid.

CANTO XXVII

*THE SUN IS near setting when the poets leave the souls of the Lustful
and encounter the angel of Chastity, singing the beatitude "Blessed are
the Pure of Heart." The angel tells them that they can go no farther
without passing through the flames, but, numbed with fear, the Pilgrim
hesitates for a long time. Finally Virgil prevails upon him and they make
the crossing through the excruciating heat. As they emerge on the other
side, they hear the invitation "Come O ye blessed of my Father," and
an angel exhorts them to climb as long as there is still daylight. But
soon the sun sets and the poets are overcome by sleep. Toward morning
the Pilgrim dreams of Leah and Rachel, who represent the active and
contemplative lives, respectively. When he awakes, he is refreshed and
eager and races up the remaining steps. In the last few lines Virgil de-
scribes the moral development achieved by the Pilgrim—such that he
no longer needs his guidance. These are the last words that Virgil will
speak in the poem.*

It was the hour the sun's first rays shine down
   upon the land where its Creator shed
   his own life's blood, the hour the Ebro flows   3

1–6. The hour is six o'clock in the morning at Jerusalem, midnight at Spain (where
the Ebro River is located), noon at India (through which the Ganges flows), and six
o'clock in the evening at Purgatory.

beneath high Scales, and Ganges' waters boil
   in noonday heat: so day was fading, then,
   when God's angel of joy appeared to us.   6

Upon the bank beyond the fire's reach
   he stood, singing *Beati mundo corde!*
   The living beauty of his voice rang clear.   9

Then: "Holy souls, no farther can you go
   without first suffering fire. So, enter now,
   and be not deaf to what is sung beyond,"   12

he said to us as we came up to him.
   I, when I heard these words, felt like a man
   who is about to be entombed alive.   15

Gripping my hands together, I leaned forward
   and, staring at the fire, I recalled
   what human bodies look like burned to death.   18

Both of my friendly guides turned toward me then,
   and Virgil said to me: "O my dear son,
   there may be pain here, but there is no death.   21

Remember all your memories! If I
   took care of you when we rode Geryon,
   shall I do less when we are nearer God?   24

Believe me when I say that if you spent
   a thousand years within the fire's heart,
   it would not singe a single hair of yours;   27

and if you still cannot believe my words,
   approach the fire and test it for yourself
   on your own robe: just touch it with the hem.   30

It's time, high time, to put away your fears;
   turn towards me, come, and enter without fear!"
   But I stood there, immobile—and ashamed.   33

8. "*Beati mundo corde*" begins the last beatitude (Matthew 5:8), "Blessed are the pure of heart, for they shall see God."

He said, somewhat annoyed to see me fixed
  and stubborn there, "Now, don't you see, my son:
  only this wall keeps you from Beatrice."   36

As Pyramus, about to die, heard Thisbe
  utter her name, he raised his eyes and saw
  her there, the day mulberries turned blood red—   39

just so, my stubbornness melted away:
  hearing the name which blooms eternally
  within my mind, I turned to my wise guide.   42

He shook his head and smiled, as at a child
  won over by an apple, as he said:
  "Well, then, what are we doing on this side?"   45

And, entering the flames ahead of me,
  he asked of Statius, who, for some time now
  had walked between us two, that he come last.   48

Once in the fire, I would have gladly jumped
  into the depths of boiling glass to find
  relief from that intensity of heat.   51

My loving father tried to comfort me,
  talking of Beatrice as we moved:
  "Already I can see her eyes, it seems!"   54

From somewhere else there came to us a voice,
  singing to guide us; listening to this,
  we emerged at last where the ascent begins.   57

Venite, benedicti Patris mei,
  came pouring from a radiance so bright,
  I was compelled to turn away my eyes.   60

Then, the voice said: "The sun is setting now
  and night is near; do not lose time, make haste
  before the west has given up its light."   63

The passageway cut straight up through the rock,
  at such an angle that my body blocked
  the sun's last rays that fell upon my back.   66

We had not climbed up many steps when I
   and my two guides knew that the sun had set
   because my shadow had just disappeared.   69

Before the colors of the vast expanse
   of the horizon melted into one,
   and Night was in possession of the sky,   72

each of us chose a step to make his bed:
   the nature of the mountain took from us
   as much the power as the desire to climb.   75

Like goats first fast and frisky on the mount,
   before they stop their play to crop the grass,
   then settling down in ruminating calm,   78

quiet in the shade, free from the burning sun,
   watched by the shepherd leaning on his staff,
   protecting their repose; or yet again,   81

a herdsman who beds down beneath the sky,
   watching beside his peaceful flock all night,
   lest they be scattered by some beast of prey—   84

so were the three of us there on the stair:
   I was the goat, and they the shepherds, all
   shut in by walls of stone, this side and that.   87

Beyond that height little was visible,
   but through that little I could see the stars,
   larger, brighter than they appear to us.   90

While meditating, staring up at them,
   sleep overcame me—sleep, which often brings
   the knowledge of events before the fact.   93

At just about the hour when Cytherea,
   who always seems to burn with love's own flames,
   first sent her eastern rays down on the mount,   96

I dreamed I saw a young and lovely girl
   walking within a meadow picking flowers;
   and, as she moved along, she sang these words: 99

"If anyone should want to know my name,
    I am called Leah. And I spend all my time
    weaving garlands of flowers with my fair hands,   102

to please me when I stand before my mirror;
    my sister Rachel sits all the day long
    before her own and never moves away.   105

She loves to contemplate her lovely eyes;
    I love to use my hands to adorn myself:
    her joy is in reflection, mine in act."   108

And now, before the splendor of the dawn
    (more welcomed by the homebound pilgrim now,
    the closer he awakes to home each day),   111

night's shadows disappeared on every side;
    my sleep fled with them: I rose to my feet,
    for my great teachers were already up.   114

"That precious fruit which all men eagerly
    go searching for on many different boughs
    will give, today, peace to your hungry soul."   117

These were the words that Virgil spoke to me,
    and never was a more auspicious gift
    received, or given, with more joyfulness.   120

Growing desire, desire to be up there,
    was rising in me: with every step I took
    I felt my wings were growing for the flight.   123

Once the stairs, swiftly climbed, were all behind
    and we were standing on the topmost step,
    Virgil addressed me, fixing his eyes on mine: 126

100–108. The story of Leah and Rachel, the two daughters of Laban, is found in
the Old Testament (Genesis 29:10–31). Leah was Jacob's first wife. The fathers of
the Church took the two women as symbols of the active and the contemplative life,
respectively.

115. The fruit, which grows on many different branches, is the ideal happiness that
mankind seeks in various ways.

"You now have seen, my son, the temporal
    and the eternal fire, you've reached the place
    where my discernment now has reached its end. 129

I led you here with skill and intellect;
    from here on, let your pleasure be your guide:
    the narrow ways, the steep, are far below. 132

Behold the sun shining upon your brow,
    behold the tender grass, the flowers, the trees,
    which, here, the earth produces of itself. 135

Until those lovely eyes rejoicing come,
    which, tearful, once urged me to come to you,
    you may sit here, or wander, as you please. 138

Expect no longer words or signs from me.
    Now is your will upright, wholesome and free,
    and not to heed its pleasure would be wrong: 141

I crown and miter you lord of yourself!"

CANTO XXVIII

THE PILGRIM WANDERS *in the heavenly forest until his path is blocked by a stream. On the other side of the stream he sees a lady singing and gathering flowers. At the Pilgrim's request, she approaches him, and, smiling from the opposite bank, tells him that this forest is the Earthly Paradise, the Garden of Eden, whence sprang the human race. She explains that the constantly moving gentle breeze is due to the earth's rotation, and she discusses the dissemination of plant life from the garden, carried on the moving air to all the lands of the earth. She further speaks of the two inexhaustible streams of the garden, Lethe and Eunoë, of which the former washes away all memory of sin and the latter re-*

127–128. The temporal fire is the fire of Purgatory: the purifying punishments of the mountain, including the wall of fire on the Seventh Terrace, which will disappear on the Judgment Day. The eternal fire is the fire of Hell.

stores the memory of good deeds. This lady, who, as yet, has not been named, concludes by telling the Pilgrim that the poets who sang of the Golden Age and of Parnassus perhaps had this place in mind.

Now eager to explore on every side
   the heavenly forest thick with living green,
   which made the bright new morning light more soft,   3

without delay I left the bank behind
   and slowly made my way across the plain,
   whose soil gave its own fragrance to the air.   6

My forehead felt the stirring of sweet air,
   whose flowing rhythm always stayed the same,
   and struck no harder than the gentlest breeze;   9

and, in the constant, moving air, each branch
   with trembling leaves was bending to one side
   toward where the holy mount first casts its shade;   12

they did not curve so sharply toward the ground
   that little birds among the topmost leaves
   could not continue practicing their art: 15

they welcomed in full-throated joyful sound
   the day's beginning to their leafy boughs
   whose soughing sound accompanied their song—   18

that sound we hear passed on from branch to branch,
   in the pine forest on the shore of Chiassi
   when Aeolus sets free Sirocco winds.   21

By now, although my steps were slow, I found
   myself so deep within the ancient wood
   I could not see the place where I came in;   24

then suddenly, I saw blocking my way
   a stream whose little waves kept pushing back,
   leftwards, the grass that grew along its bank.   27

26. The stream is Lethe, which in classical mythology was a river of Hades from which the souls of the dead drank forgetfulness of their first existence.

The clearest of all waters on our earth
   would seem to have, somehow, a cloudy tinge
   compared to this flowing transparency— 30

transparent though it flows dark, very dark
   beneath an everlasting shade, which will
   never admit a ray of sun or moon. 33

I had to stop, but with my eyes I crossed
   beyond the rivulet to contemplate
   the many-colored splendors of the boughs, 36

and there appeared—as sometimes will appear
   an unexpected sight so marvelous,
   all other thoughts are driven from the mind— 39

a solitary lady wandering there,
   and she was singing as she gathered flowers
   from the abundance painted on her path. 42

"Oh, lovely lady, glowing with the warmth
   and strength of Love's own rays—if I may trust
   your look, which should bear witness of the heart— 45

be kind enough," I said to her, "to come
   a little nearer to the river's bank,
   that I may understand the words you sing. 48

You bring to mind what Proserpine was like,
   and where she was, that day her mother lost her,
   and she, in her turn, lost eternal Spring." 51

Just as a lady in the dance will turn,
   keeping her feet together on the ground,
   and one before the other hardly moves, 54

40. The lady is Matelda, whose name is mentioned, and then quite casually, only in the closing canto (XXXIII, 119). Because she is given a name, much controversy has arisen over attempts to identify her with a historical figure.

   As to what this lady is supposed to symbolize, she must represent, among other things, the active life, as she is clearly reminiscent of the Leah of the Pilgrim's final dream in the preceding canto.

so she, among the red and yellow flowers,
  turned round toward me, her virgin modesty
  enjoining her to look with downcast eyes,   57

and, satisfying my desire, she started
  moving toward me and, with the melody,
  there came to me the sweetness of the words.   60

When she had come to where the tender grass
  is barely touched by ripples from that stream,
  she graciously did raise her eyes to mine.   63

The eyes of Venus surely were not lit
  so radiantly that day her loving son
  quite innocently pierced her with his dart.   66

Smiling, she stood there on the other bank,
  arranging in her hands the many colors
  that grew from no seeds planted on that height.   69

The stream kept us only three feet apart,
  but Hellespont, where it was crossed by Xerxes
  (whose fate should be a lesson to the proud),   72

hurling its waves from Sestos to Abydos,
  was hated by Leander less than I
  hated this one: it would not open up!   75

"This place is new to each of you," she said,
  "it could be that you find yourself amazed,
  perplexed to see me smiling in this place   78

once chosen as the cradle of mankind;
  but let the *Delectasti me* shed light
  and clear away the mist that clouds your minds.   81

And you who are in front and spoke to me,
  if there is something more you want to know,
  I came prepared to tell you what you wish."   84

80. With the *Delectasti me*, Matelda is referring to the ninety-first psalm, and surely
the lines she has in mind are "Thou didst delight me, Lord, in Thy work / and in the
works of Thy hands, I will rejoice. / How praiseworthy are Thy works, O Lord."

"The flowing water and the woodland sounds
　　seem to be inconsistent," I began,
　　"with what I have been told about the mount." 87

She said, "I shall explain the logical
　　necessity of what perplexes you,
　　and thus remove what has obscured your mind. 90

That Highest Good, Himself pleasing Himself,
　　made Adam good, to do good, then gave
　　this place as earnest of eternal peace. 93

Because he sinned, he could not stay here long;
　　because he sinned, he changed his childlike mirth,
　　his playful joy, for anguish and for toil. 96

In order that the storms that form below
　　(caused by the vapors from the earth and sea
　　as they are drawn upwards to solar heat) 99

should not disturb the garden's peacefulness,
　　this mount was made to rise so high toward Heaven
　　that past the gate no storm is possible. 102

Now, since the air is moving constantly,
　　moving as primal revolution moves
　　(unless its circulation is disturbed), 105

here on the mountain's height, completely free
　　in the encircling air, this movement strikes
　　and makes the dense leaves of the forest sing; 108

and every smitten plant begins to make
　　the pure air pregnant with its special power,
　　which, then, the whirling scatters everywhere; 111

all lands elsewhere conceive and bring to flower
　　the different plants endowed with different powers,
　　according to the climate and the soil. 114

If they knew down on earth what you know now,
   no one would be surprised to see a plant
   start growing where no seed was sown before.   117

And know, the holy land you stand on now
   is rich in every species and brings forth
   fruit that no man has ever plucked on earth.   120

The water here does not spring from a source
   that needs to be restored by changing mists,
   like streams on earth that lose, then gain, their force: 123

it issues from a spring of constant flow,
   immutable, which, by the will of God,
   regains what it pours forth on either side.   126

The water here on this side flows with power
   to erase sin's memory; and on that side
   the memory of good deeds is restored;   129

it is called Lethe here, Eunoë there
   beyond, and if one does not first drink here,
   he will not come to know its powers there—   132

the sweet taste of its waters has no peer.
   And even though your thirst may now be quenched
   by what you know already of this place,   135

I offer you a corollary gift:
   I think you will not cherish my words less
   if you learn more than I first promised you.   138

Perhaps those poets of long ago who sang
   the Age of Gold, its pristine happiness,
   were dreaming on Parnassus of this place.   141

The root of mankind's tree was guiltless here;
   here, in an endless Spring, was every fruit,
   such is the nectar praised by all these poets.''   144

130. The waters of the first miraculous stream (Lethe) "erase sin's memory" (128),
while those of the second (and same) stream (Eunoë) restore "the memory of good
deeds" (129).

As she said this, I quickly turned around
    to my two poets: I saw, still lingering,
    the smile her final words brought to their lips.   147

Then I turned back to face her loveliness.

CANTO XXIX

WHEN THE LADY has finished speaking, she sings and begins to walk
upstream, the Pilgrim keeping pace with her on the opposite bank. They
have not gone far when the lady stops and instructs the Pilgrim to be
attentive. A burst of incandescence lights up the air, and the Pilgrim
sees the approach of the heavenly pageant. It is led by seven golden
candlesticks, which emit a stream of multicolored light that extends over
the procession that follows them. Next come twenty-four elders, two
by two, and behind them, four creatures. Within a square determined
by the positions of these four comes a chariot drawn by a griffin. To
the right of the chariot are three ladies, one red, one white, and one
green; to the left are four ladies clad in purple. Behind them come two
aged men, then four more men of humble aspect, and finally one old
man alone. When the chariot has reached a point directly opposite the
Pilgrim, a thunderclap resounds, bringing the entire procession to a sud-
den halt.

Then, like a lady moved by love, she sang
    (her revelations now come to an end):
    Beati quorum tecta sunt peccata!   3

And like those nymphs that used to stroll alone
    through shaded woodlands, one seeking the sun,
    another trying to avoid its light,   6

---

3. Matelda is quoting an abbreviated version of Psalm 32:1: "Happy are they whose faults are taken away, whose sins are covered."

so she began to walk along the bank,
    moving upstream, and I kept pace with her,
    matching on my side her small, graceful steps.   9

Not a hundred steps between us had we gone,
    when the two river banks curved perfectly
    parallel—and I faced the east again;   12

when we had gone a little farther on,
    the lady stopped and, turning to me, said:
    "My brother, look and listen." Suddenly,   15

a burst of incandescence cut the air,
    with one quick flash it lit up all the woods—
    at first I thought it was a lightning flash.   18

But lightning goes as quickly as it comes;
    what I saw stayed, its radiance increased.
    "What can this be?" I thought, and as I did,   21

a gentle melody was drifting through
    the luminous atmosphere. Then righteous zeal
    made me curse the presumptuousness of Eve: 24

to think that, while all earth and Heaven obeyed
    His will, a single woman, newly made,
    would dare strip off the veil imposed by Him!   27

Had she remained submissive to His will,
    I could on these ineffable delights
    have feasted sooner and for much more time.   30

As I was moving in a blissful trance
    among these first fruits of eternal joy,
    yearning for still more happiness to come,   33

the air, beneath green boughs, became transformed
    before our eyes into a blazing light,
    and the sweet sound had now become a chant.   36

Most holy Virgins, if because of you
    hunger or cold or vigils I endured,
    allow me now to ask for my reward: 39

let Helicon pour forth its streams for me,
    and let Urania help me with her choir
    to put in verse things difficult to grasp.   42

A little farther on, I saw what seemed
    to be seven trees of gold—a false effect
    caused by the distance separating us;   45

but when I had come close enough to them
    that distance could no longer hide detail,
    and what had tricked my senses now was clear,   48

that power which feeds the process of our thought
    identified the shapes as candlesticks
    and heard the word *Hosanna* in the chant.   51

Above the splendid gold—a brilliant light,
    brighter than moonlight in a cloudless sky
    at midnight shining in her bright mid-month!   54

Full of bewilderment, I turned around
    to my good Virgil. His answer was a glance
    charged with no less amazement than I felt.   57

Then I turned back to gaze at those high things
    moving toward us as though they did not move—
    more slowly than a modest, newmade bride.   60

The lady cried: "Why are you so intent
    on looking only at those living lights?
    Have you no wish to see what comes behind?"   63

Then I saw people following the glow,
    as if they were attendants; all were clothed
    in garments supernaturally white.   66

The waters on my left received the light,
    and when I looked into this shining glass,
    my left side was reflected clearly there.   69

When I had reached the point along my bank
    where only water separated us,
    I stopped to watch the scene more carefully: 72

I saw the slender flames as they advanced,
   leaving the air behind them color-streaked—
   so many streaming pennants overhead!   75

And thus the sky became a painted flow
   of seven bands of light, all the same shades
   as Delia's cincture or Apollo's bow.   78

These bands extended farther back than eyes
   could see and, all together, I would say,
   they measured, side by side, a good ten strides.   81

And under that magnificence of Heaven
   came four-and-twenty elders, two by two,
   all of them wearing crowns of fleur-de-lis.   84

They sang as they moved on: "*Benedicta* thou
   of all of Adam's daughters, blessed be
   thy beauty throughout all eternity!"   87

When once the group of God's elect had passed
   (the flowers and the tender grass that grew
   along the other bank once more in view),   90

as groups of stars will replace other stars
   high in the heavens, following them there came
   four creatures wearing crowns of forest green.   93

Each had six wings with feathers that were all
   covered with eyes; were Argus still alive,
   his eyes would be exactly like all those.   96

Reader, I cannot spend more verses now
   describing them, for I have other needs
   constraining me—here I must spare my words;   99

---

84. The fleur-de-lis garlands of the elders represent the lily of purity, which accords
with the supernatural whiteness of their garments (66).

85. It is to the Virgin that this blessing is offered, and it is most significant that it is
uttered by the representatives of the Old Testament—a witness to the prophetic na-
ture of those Scriptures. (See Luke 1:28.)

but you can read Ezekiel's account:
    he saw them once approaching from the north
    borne on the wind, moving in cloud and fire,   102

and as he pictured them, so were they here,
    except that, in the matter of their wings,
    Saint John agrees with me and not with him.   105

The four of them were corners for a space
    filled by a triumphal two-wheeled chariot
    drawn by a griffin, harnessed to its neck.   108

He kept both wings raised high, and each one flanked
    the mid-banner between the three and three:
    so perfectly that neither one was cut.   111

His wings rose higher than my sight could rise;
    the parts of him that were a bird were gold
    and all the rest was white, with deep red marks.   114

An Africanus or Augustus never
    had such a splendid chariot from their Rome;
    indeed, that of the Sun could not compare—   117

that of the Sun which strayed and was destroyed
    at the devout petition of the Earth,
    when Jove in his mysterious way was just.   120

There were three ladies circling in a dance
    near the right wheel, and one was red, so red
    she hardly would be visible in fire;   123

the second looked as if her flesh and bones
    were fashioned out of emerald; the third
    had all the whiteness of new-fallen snow;   126

at times the white one led the dance, at times,
    the red, and from the song the red one sang
    the others took the tempo of their dance.   129

118. The reference is to Phaëton's tragic attempt to drive the chariot of the sun, referred to earlier in *Purgatory* IV, 71–72, and in *Inferno* XVII, 107.

122. Of the three colors represented by the three ladies, red is the sign of Charity, green of Hope, and white of Faith.

Beside the left wheel, dancing festively,
    were four more ladies—dressed in purple robes
    and led by one with three eyes in her head.   132

Behind the dancing figures, three and four,
    there came two aged men, differently dressed,
    but similar in bearing, staid and grave.   135

One wore the garments of a follower
    of great Hippocrates, whom Nature made
    to heal those creatures that she loved the most;   138

the other seemed to be his counterpart:
    he bore a sword, so sharp, gleaming so bright,
    that I, though on the other bank, felt fear.   141

Then I saw coming four of humble mien,
    and, last of all, an old man, by himself,
    who moved in his own dream, his face inspired.   144

130–131. The left side is a lesser position than the right—which is to give more importance to the ladies dancing near the right wheel (121), representing the three theological virtues, than to these four ladies "dancing festively" to the left, who represent the four moral or cardinal virtues: Prudence, Temperance, Justice, and Fortitude. These natural virtues are essential to the happiness or blessedness of this life, for they are the ones that govern or regulate human conduct. And because they are the basis of imperial authority, without which there can be no Earthly Paradise, these four ladies are dressed in purple, the color of Empire.

132. The leading lady among the four cardinal virtues is Prudence, whose function is to apply the restraints of reason to all aspects of our earthly life. Her three eyes indicate her ability to see the past, present, and future.

136. The follower is Luke, the physician of the soul (see Col. 4:14, where he is described as "the beloved physician"), and author of Acts.

139–140. The old man with the sharp, gleaming sword represents the various Epistles of St. Paul.

142. The approaching four represent the minor Epistles of James, Peter, John, and Jude.

144. This line is a reminder of John's vision, his dream of the Apocalypse and Second Coming, which inspired him to write Revelation—a book so different from the others of the New Testament that it is most fitting that this figure be presented as moving alone.

And these last seven, just like the group up front,
    were clad in white, except the wreaths that crowned
    their heads were not entwined with lily blooms,   147

but roses and other flowers that are red.
    Had I been farther off, I would have sworn
    a crown of flames encircled every head.   150

And when the chariot was opposite me,
    thunder was heard! The exalted creatures, then,
    as though forbidden to move on, stopped short,   153

as did the flaming ensigns at the front.

CANTO XXX

*AS THE PROCESSION comes to a halt, the twenty-four elders turn to face
the chariot. One of them sings, "Come, O bride, from Lebanon." One
hundred singing angels appear in the sky overhead; they fill the air with
a rain of flowers. Through the flowers, Beatrice appears. The Pilgrim
turns to Virgil to confess his overpowering emotions, only to find that
Virgil has disappeared! Beatrice speaks sternly to Dante, calling him by
name and reprimanding him for having wasted his God-given talents,
wandering from the path that leads to Truth. So hopeless, in fact, was
his case, to such depths did he sink, that the journey to see the souls of
the Damned in Hell was the only way left of setting him back on the
road to salvation.*

145–146. The last seven figures, who represent the New Testament, are dressed in
garments the same color as those representing the Old Testament. But the wreaths
the former wear are not white but red—the color of the first of the three theological
virtues: Charity.

When the Septentrion of the First Heaven
   (which never sets nor rises nor has known
   any cloud other than the veil of sin),   3

which showed to everyone his duty there
   (just as our lower constellation guides
   the helmsman on his way to port on earth),   6

stopped short, that group of prophets of the truth
   who were between the griffin and those lights
   turned to the car as to their source of peace;   9

then, one of them, as sent from Heaven, sang
   Veni, sponsa, de Libano, three times,
   and all the other voices followed his.   12

As at the Final Summons all the blest
   will rise out of their graves, ready to raise
   new-bodied voices singing 'Hallelujah!'   15

just so rose up above the heavenly cart
   a hundred spirits *ad vocem tanti senis,*
   eternal heralds, ministers of God,   18

all shouting: *Benedictus qui venis!* then,
   tossing a rain of flowers in the air,
   Manibus, O, date lilia plenis!   21

1. The constellation sometimes called Septentrion is probably the Little Dipper (Ursa Minor), which contains seven stars, including the North Star. Thus the "Septentrion of the First Heaven" (the Empyrean) must be the seven blazing candlesticks that direct the procession.

11. "*Veni, sponsa, de Libano*" ("Come, bride, from Lebanon") is taken from the Song of Solomon (4:8), where the bride is interpreted as the soul wedded to Christ. Here the song has to do with the advent of Beatrice, one of whose allegorical meanings is Sapientia, or the wisdom of God.

17. "*Ad vocem tanti senis*" translates as "At the voice of so great an elder."

19. "*Benedictus qui venis*" ("Blessed are Thou that comest") is a slightly modified version of Matthew 21:9, *Benedictus qui venit* ("Blessed is He who cometh"). Note that while Dante felt free to shift from the third to the second person in quoting this line, he left intact *Benedictus,* with its masculine form. In this way the word, though applied to Beatrice, who is about to appear, retains its original reference to Christ.

Sometimes, as day approaches, I have seen
    all of the eastern sky a glow of rose,
    the rest of heaven beautifully clear,   24

the sun's face rising in a misty veil
    of tempering vapors that allow the eye
    to look straight at it for a longer time: 27

even so, within a nebula of flowers
    that flowed upward from angels' hands and then
    poured down, covering all the chariot,   30

appeared a lady—over her white veil
    an olive crown and, under her green cloak,
    her gown, the color of eternal flame.   33

And instantly—though many years had passed
    since last I stood trembling before her eyes,
    captured by adoration, stunned by awe—   36

my soul, that could not see her perfectly,
    still felt, succumbing to her mystery
    and power, the strength of its enduring love.   39

No sooner were my eyes struck by the force
    of the high, piercing virtue I had known
    before I quit my boyhood years, than I   42

turned to the left—with all the confidence
    that makes a child run to its mother's arms,
    when he is frightened or needs comforting—   45

---

21. "O give us lilies with full hands." This quotation from the *Aeneid* (VI, 883) is surely intended as high tribute to Virgil, the Pilgrim's guide, since his words are placed on the same level as verses from the Bible.

31–33. The lady is Beatrice, and the colors she wears are those of the three theological virtues: Faith, Hope, and Charity.

to say to Virgil: "Not one drop of blood
    is left inside my veins that does not throb:
    I recognize signs of the ancient flame."   48

But Virgil was not there. We found ourselves
    without Virgil, sweet father, Virgil to whom
    for my salvation I gave up my soul.   51

All the delights around me, which were lost
    by our first mother, could not keep my cheeks,
    once washed with dew, from being stained with tears.   54

"Dante, though Virgil leaves you, do not weep,
    not yet, that is, for you shall have to weep
    from yet another wound. Do not weep yet."   57

Just as an admiral, from bow or stern,
    watches his men at work on other ships,
    encouraging their earnest labors—so,   60

rising above the chariot's left rail
    (when I turned round, hearing my name called out,
    which of necessity I here record),   63

I saw the lady who had first appeared
    beneath the angelic festival of flowers
    gazing upon me from beyond the stream.   66

Although the veil that flowed down from her head,
    fixed by the crown made of Minerva's leaves,
    still kept me from a perfect view of her,   69

I sensed the regal sternness of her face,
    as she continued in the tone of one
    who saves the sharpest words until the end: 72

"Yes, look at me! Yes, I am Beatrice!
    So, you at last have deigned to climb the mount?
    You learned at last that here lies human bliss?"   75

55. This is the first time that the Pilgrim hears his own name during his journey.

I lowered my head and looked down at the stream,
    but, filled with shame at my reflection there,
    I quickly fixed my eyes upon the grass.   78

I was the guilty child facing his mother,
    abject before her harshness: harsh, indeed,
    is unripe pity not yet merciful.   81

As she stopped speaking, all the angels rushed
    into the psalm *In te, Domine, speravi,*
    but did not sing beyond *pedes meos.*   84

As snow upon the spine of Italy,
    frozen among the living rafters there,
    blown and packed hard by wintry northeast winds,   87

will then dissolve, dripping into itself,
    when, from the land that knows no noonday shade,
    there comes a wind like flame melting down wax;   90

so tears and sighs were frozen hard in me,
    until I heard the song of those attuned
    forever to the music of the spheres;   93

but when I sensed in their sweet notes the pity
    they felt for me (it was as if they said:
    "Lady, why do you shame him so?"), the bonds   96

of ice packed tight around my heart dissolved,
    becoming breath and water: from my breast,
    through mouth and eyes, anguish came pouring forth.   99

Still on the same side of the chariot
    she stood immobile; then she turned her words
    to that compassionate array of beings: 102

83–84. The angels are singing the first part of the thirty-first psalm, which begins,
"In Thee, O lord, have I put my trust." They continue through line 8 (*pedes meos*),
"Thou hast set my feet in a spacious place"—which is precisely the place where the
Pilgrim is standing at this moment.

89. The land is equatorial Africa, where the sun is often directly overhead, sending
its rays straight down so that objects cast no shadow.

"With your eyes fixed on the eternal day,
    darkness of night or sleep cannot conceal
    from you a single act performed on earth;   105

and though I speak to you, my purpose is
    to make the one who weeps on that far bank
    perceive the truth and match his guilt with grief.   108

Not only through the working of the spheres,
    which brings each seed to its appropriate end
    according as the stars keep company,   111

but also through the bounty of God's grace,
    raining from vapors born so high above
    they cannot be discerned by human sight,   114

was this man so endowed, potentially,
    in early youth—had he allowed his gifts
    to bloom, he would have reaped abundantly.   117

But the more vigorous and rich the soil,
    the wilder and the weedier it grows
    when left untilled, its bad seeds flourishing.   120

There was a time my countenance sufficed,
    as I let him look into my young eyes
    for guidance on the straight path to his goal;   123

but when I passed into my second age
    and changed my life for Life, that man you see
    strayed after others and abandoned me;   126

when I had risen from the flesh to spirit,
    become more beautiful, more virtuous,
    he found less pleasure in me, loved me less,   129

and wandered from the path that leads to truth,
    pursuing simulacra of the good,
    which promise more than they can ever give.   132

I prayed that inspiration come to him
    through dreams and other means: in vain I tried
    to call him back, so little did he care.   135

To such depths did he sink that, finally,
　　there was no other way to save his soul
　　except to have him see the Damned in Hell.   138

That this might be, I visited the Dead,
　　and offered my petition and my tears
　　to him who until now has been his guide.   141

The highest laws of God would be annulled
　　if he crossed Lethe, drinking its sweet flow,
　　without having to pay at least some scot   144

of penitence poured forth in guilty tears."

CANTO XXXI

BEATRICE CONTINUES TO *upbraid Dante, who, nearly incapable of
speech, weeping and sighing, finally confesses his guilt; then, overcome
by remorse, he faints. Upon regaining consciousness he discovers that
Matelda has drawn him into the stream of Lethe up to his neck. She
carries him across and dips his head beneath the surface that he might
drink of the waters. Then she leads him, now pure, into the dance of
the four lovely maidens who flank Beatrice's chariot. They bring him in
turn to Beatrice, and as he stares into her eyes, he sees the reflection of
the griffin, manifested now in its one nature, now in the other. Finally
the other three attendant ladies induce Beatrice to unveil her mouth to
her "faithful one."*

"You, standing there, beyond the sacred stream,"
　　she cried, not pausing in her eloquence
　　and turning now the sword point of her words   3

toward me, who had already felt its blade,
　　"speak now, is this not true? Speak! You must seal
　　with your confession this grave charge I make!"   6

I stood before her paralyzed, confused;
    I moved my lips, my throat striving to speak,
    but not a single breath of speech escaped.   9

She hardly paused: "What are you thinking of?
    Answer me, now! Your bitter memories
    have not as yet been purged within this stream."   12

My fear and deep chagrin, between them, forced
    out of my mouth a miserable "yes"—
    only by ears with eyes could it be heard.   15

A crossbow, drawn with too much tension, snaps,
    bowstring and bow together, and the shaft
    will strike the target with diminished force;   18

so I was shattered by the intensity
    of my emotions: tears and sighs burst forth,
    as I released my voice about to fail.   21

She: "In your journey of desire for me,
    leading you toward that Good beyond which naught
    exists to which a man's heart may aspire,   24

what pitfalls did you find, what chains stretched out
    across your path, that you felt you were forced
    to abandon every hope of going on?   27

And what appealed to you, what did you find
    so promising in all those other things
    that made you feel obliged to spend your time   30

in courting them?" I heaved a bitter sigh,
    and barely found the voice to answer her;
    my lips, with difficulty, shaped the words.   33

Weeping, I said: "Those things with their false joys,
    offered me by the world, led me astray
    when I no longer saw your countenance."   36

And she: "Had you kept silent or denied
    what you have just confessed, your guilt would still
    be clear to the great Judge who knows all things.   39

But when the condemnation of his sin
    bursts from the sinner's lips, here in our Court,
    the grindstone is turned back against the blade.   42

Still, so that you may truly feel the shame
    of all your sins—so that, another time,
    you will be stronger when the Sirens sing—   45

master your feelings, listen to my words,
    and you shall learn just how my buried flesh
    was meant to guide you in another way.   48

You never saw in Nature or in Art
    a beauty like the beauty of my form,
    which clothed me once and now is turned to dust;   51

and if that perfect beauty disappeared
    when I departed from the world, how could
    another mortal object lure your love?   54

When you first felt deception's arrow sting,
    you should have rushed to rise and follow me,
    as soon as I lost my deceptive flesh.   57

No pretty girl or any other brief
    attraction should have weighed down your wings,
    and left you waiting for another blow.   60

The fledgling waits a second time, a third,
    but not the full-fledged bird: before his eyes
    in vain the net is spread, the arrow shot."   63

As children scolded into silence stand
    ashamed, with head bowed staring at the ground,
    acknowledging their fault and penitent—   66

so I stood there. Then she: "If listening
    can cause you so much grief, now raise your beard
    and look at me and suffer greater grief."   69

41. The court is both the heavenly court, where Beatrice and the angels dwell in the presence of God, and the divine tribunal, before which every man will one day be judged.

42. Here the grindstone symbolizes mercy as it is "turned back against" or used to blunt the blade of the sword of justice.

With less resistance is the sturdy oak
    uprooted by the winds of storms at home
    in Europe or by those that Iarbas blows,   72

than my soul offered to her curt command
    that I look up at her: she called my face
    my "beard"! I felt the venom in her words.   75

And when I raised my head, I did not look
    at her, but at those first-created ones:
    they had already ceased their rain of flowers.   78

Then when I turned my unsure eyes once more,
    I saw that Beatrice faced the beast
    who in two natures is one single being.   81

Though she was veiled and on the other shore,
    lovelier now, she seemed, than when alive
    on earth, when she was loveliest of all.   84

I felt the stabbing pain of my remorse:
    what I had loved the most of all the things
    that were not she, I hated now the most.   87

The recognition of my guilt so stunned
    my heart, I fainted. What happened then is known
    only to her who was the cause of it.   90

When I revived, that lady I first saw
    strolling alone was now bent over me,
    saying: "Hold on to me, hold tight." She had   93

led me into the stream up to my neck;
    now drawing me along she glided light,
    and with a shuttle's ease, across the stream.   96

Before I reached the sacred bank I heard
    Asperges me—so sweetly sung, my mind
    cannot recall, far less my words retell.   99

98. "*Asperges me*" ("Cleanse me of sin") is from Psalm 51:7 (Vulgate 50:9):
"Cleanse me of sin with hyssop, that I may be purified; wash me, and I shall be
whiter than snow." The *Asperges* is sung at the beginning of the Mass, when the
priest sprinkles the people with holy water.

The lovely lady, opening her arms,
   embraced my head and dipped it in the stream
   just deep enough to let me drink of it.   102

She took me from those waters, cleansed, and led
   me to the dance of the four lovely ones,
   who raised their arms to join hands over me.   105

"Here we are nymphs and in the heavens, stars;
   before Beatrice came into the world
   we were ordained her handmaids. It is for us   108

to lead you to her eyes. The other three,
   who see more deeply, will instruct your sight,
   as you bathe in her gaze of joyful light,"   111

they sang to me; then they accompanied me
   up to the griffin's breast, while Beatrice
   now faced us from the center of the cart.   114

"Look deeply, look with all your sight," they said,
   "for now you stand before those emeralds
   from which Love once shot loving darts at you."   117

A thousand yearning flames of my desire
   held my eyes fixed upon those brilliant eyes
   that held the griffin fixed within their range.   120

Like sunlight in a mirror, shining back,
   I saw the twofold creature in her eyes,
   reflecting its two natures, separately.   123

Imagine, reader, how amazed I was
   to see the creature standing there unchanged,
   yet, in its image, changing constantly,   126

And while my soul, delighted and amazed,
   was tasting of that food which satisfies
   and, at the same time, makes one hungrier,   129

116. The emeralds are Beatrice's eyes, which are green, symbolizing Hope.

128–129. Dante is paraphrasing the words of Sapientia in Ecclesiastes 24:21: "They that eat me shall yet be hungry, and they that drink me shall yet be thirsty."

the other three, revealing in their mien
   their more exalted rank, came dancing forth
   accompanied by angelic melody.   132

"Turn, Beatrice, turn your sacred eyes,"
   they sang, "and look upon your faithful one
   who came so very far to look at you!   135

Of your own grace grant us this grace: unveil
   your mouth for him, allow him to behold
   that second beauty which you hide from him."   138

O splendor of the eternal living light!
   Who, having drunk at the Parnassian well,
   or become pale within that mountain's shade,   141

could find with all of his poetic gifts
   those words that might describe the way you looked,
   with that harmonious heaven your only veil,   144

when you unveiled yourself to me at last?

CANTO XXXII

FOR THE FIRST *time in ten years, Dante the Pilgrim stares into the face
of Beatrice. Looking away, he is left temporarily blinded, and when he
recovers his sight, it is to discover that the pageant is now moving off.
He and Statius, along with the lovely lady, follow the procession, which
stops in front of a tree, where Beatrice descends. This is the tree of the
knowledge of good and evil, but it is stripped bare of leaf and fruit. The
griffin takes the pole of the chariot he has been pulling and attaches it
to the tree, which immediately bursts into bloom. As the company be-
gins to chant an unidentifiable hymn, the Pilgrim falls asleep. He is
awakened by the lovely lady to find that the pageant has departed and
that Beatrice, with her seven handmaidens, is left alone, seated beneath
the tree. She directs the Pilgrim to fix his eyes on the chariot. As he
watches, an eagle swoops down through the tree, tearing off the new-*

*born leaves, and strikes the chariot with full force. Then a fox leaps up
into the cart but is driven off by Beatrice. Again the eagle comes, but
this time it perches on the chariot and sheds some of its golden feathers
there. Suddenly the ground beneath the chariot opens, and a dragon
drives its tail up through the floor of the cart. Withdrawing its stinger,
it takes a portion of the floor with it. What is left of the chariot now
grows a rich cover of feathers and then sprouts seven heads. Seated now
upon the chariot is an ungirt whore, who flirts lasciviously with a giant
standing nearby. When the whore turns her lustful eyes toward the Pil-
grim, the giant beats her and drags the chariot off into the woods.*

I fixed my eyes on her; they were intent
　　on quenching their ten years of thirst at last—
　　I was bereft of every other sense. 3

My eyes, walled in by barriers of high
　　indifference, were drawn to her holy smile—
　　they were entranced by her familiar spell. 6

But, suddenly, my gaze was forced away
　　to where those goddesses stood at my left.
　　"He should not look so hard!" I heard them say. 9

I was like one who had just strained his eyes
　　by looking straight into the sun too long;
　　indeed, I was left blinded for a while. 12

When I had grown accustomed to dim light—
　　dim light, I mean, compared to that effulgence
　　from which I had been forced to turn away— 15

the glorious host, I saw, had wheeled about
　　on its right flank and now was moving back,
　　facing the seven torches and the sun. 18

When squadrons under shields start to retreat,
　　it is the front-line troops, bearing their colors,
　　who turn before the others can begin— 21

just so, those soldiers who were in the front
　　of the blest host had all marched past our post
　　before the chariot had turned its pole. 24

The ladies took their place beside the wheels:
    the griffin moved, pulling his sacred charge,
    without a single feather being ruffled.   27

Statius and I, along with the fair maid
    who had towed me across the stream, now moved
    behind the wheel which made the smaller arc.   30

As we walked through that high wood, empty now
    because of her who listened to the snake,
    our steps kept time to strains of heavenly notes.   33

We had already walked perhaps three times
    the distance any arrow shot full strength
    could reach, when Beatrice left the cart.   36

I heard them all murmuring Adam's name;
    and then they formed a circle 'round a tree
    whose every branch was stripped of leaf and fruit.   39

A tree like this in India's wooded lands
    would seem a very miracle of height:
    the more it rose, the wider spread its boughs.   42

"Blessed art thou, Griffin. Thy sacred beak
    tears not a shred of this tree's savory bark,
    which makes the belly writhe in deadly pain!"   45

These words were sung by all the others there
    around the tree. And the two-natured beast:
    "Thus is preserved the seed of righteousness."   48

Then, turning to the pole which he had pulled,
    he brought it up against the widowed tree,
    returning to it what it once brought forth.   51

---

40. Towering so high, this tree represents the Holy Roman Empire, the foundation
of the highest earthly law.

48. The words are spoken by the griffin; it is the only time the creature speaks. The
"seed of righteousness" firmly identifies the tree as the allegorical representation of
Justice, the Justice of God, which includes in its design the justice of human institu-
tions (empire) as well.

Just as the trees on earth in early spring—
    when the strong rays fall, mingled with the light
    that glows behind the heaven of the Fish—   54

begin to swell, burst into bloom, renew
    the color that was theirs, before the sun
    hitches his steeds beneath some other stars,   57

just so, that tree whose boughs had been so bare,
    renewed itself, and bloomed with color not quite
    roselike but brighter than a violet.   60

I did not recognize the hymn that group
    began to sing—it is not sung on earth,
    and then, I did not listen to the end.   63

Could I describe how those insistent eyes
    were lulled to sleep by the sad tale of Syrinx—
    the eyes that paid so dear for their long watch—   66

as painter painting from his model, I
    would try to show you how I fell asleep.
    But let whoever can paint sleep, paint sleep!   69

So, I shall tell you only how I woke:
    a splendor rent the veil of sleep, a voice
    was calling me: "What are you doing? Rise!"   72

When they were led to see that apple tree
    whose blossoms give the fruit that angels crave,
    providing an eternal marriage-feast,   75

59–60. Purple could signify the passion and death of Christ; hence, it is his sacrificial blood that infuses the tree with its color. The four cardinal virtues of the procession also wear purple, signifying their accessibility to mankind after the shedding of Christ's blood. Without these virtues no righteous government is possible.

72. The words are those of the "sympathetic lady" (83), who has not as yet been identified as Matelda. Similar words were used by Christ at the Transfiguration (cf. Matthew 17:7).

74. The "apple tree" (73) is Christ (Apocrypha 18:14). When in full bloom it represents Christ's promise to mankind that what will follow is the fruit of eternal bliss, enjoyed now by the angels living in perpetual union with Christ in Heaven.

Peter and John and James were overpowered
    by sleep, and then brought back to consciousness
    by that same word that broke a deeper sleep;   78

they saw their company had been reduced,
    for Moses and Elijah were not there;
    they saw their Master's robe changed back again.   81

Just so, I woke to see, bent over me,
    the sympathetic lady who, before,
    had been my guide along the riverbank.   84

Fearful, I cried: "Oh, where is Beatrice?"
    The lady said: "See, she is sitting there
    on the tree's roots beneath the newborn leaves;   87

behold the company surrounding her.
    The rest go with the griffin up to Heaven
    to sweeter music and to deeper strains."   90

I do not know if she said more than this,
    for now I was allowed to see again
    the one who reigned completely in my mind.   93

She sat there on the bare earth, left alone
    to guard the chariot that I had seen
    bound to the tree by the two-natured beast.   96

The circle of the seven nymphs now formed
    a cloister for the lady; in their hands
    they held those lights no wind on earth could quench.   99

"A short time you shall dwell outside the walls;
    then you, with me, shall live eternally,
    citizen of that Rome where Christ is Roman.   102

Now, for the good of sinners in your world,
    observe the chariot well, and what you see,
    put into writing, when you have returned."   105

Thus Beatrice. I obediently,
    devoutly, at the feet of her commands,
    gave mind and eye to satisfying her.   108

No bolt of lightning flashing through dense cloud,
    shot from the farthest region of the sky,
    has ever struck with such velocity   111

as moved the bird of Jove who then swooped down
    and through the tree, tearing off newborn leaves,
    rending the bark, destroying all the blooms;   114

with his full force he struck the chariot,
    which staggered like a ship caught in a storm,
    careened by waves, tilting starboard and port.   117

Into the cradle of the glorious car
    I saw a fox leap up, so lean it seemed
    the food it fed on had no nourishment.   120

My lady made it turn and run away,
    as fast as its weak skin and bones could go,
    accusing it of foul abominations.   123

Once more the eagle swooped down through the tree:
    this time into the framework of the car,
    to shed some of its golden feathers there;   126

like sorrow pouring from a grieving heart
    a voice from Heaven was heard: "My little ship,
    O what ill-fated cargo you must bear!"   129

109–117. The tableau signifies the persecutions of the early Church under the Roman emperors from Nero (A.D. 54–68) to Diocletian (A.D. 284–305). The "bird of Jove" is the eagle, the standard of the empire, here acting as a bird of prey, "tearing," "rending," and "destroying." Dante compares the assaulted chariot, the Church, to "a ship caught in a storm." The ship is a traditional symbol of the Church (cf. Dante's reference to Peter's ship in *Paradise* XI, 119–120).

118–123. The second tableau represents the internal heresies that threatened the early Church, particularly the heresy of Gnosticism.

124–129. The third catastrophe, again initiated by action of the eagle, is a tableau representing the Church's acquisition of temporal wealth and power through what came to be renowned as the "Donation of Constantine," the alleged gift of the Western Empire to the papacy, the "ill-fated cargo" of line 129.

And then I saw the ground between the wheels
    opening up: a dragon issued forth,
    driving its tail up through the chariot;   132

then, as a wasp withdraws its sting, that thing
    drew back its poison tail, tearing away
    part of the floor—gloating, it wandered off;   135

the rest, like fertile soil left for thick weeds
    to thrive on, grew a rich cover of plumes
    granted with good intentions, it would seem,   138

and all the chariot, with both its wheels
    and pole as well, was overgrown with them
    in less time than it takes to heave a sigh.   141

Thus changed, the holy shrine began to sprout
    heads from all parts: three on the chariot's pole
    and one from each of its four corners grew.   144

The three were horned like oxen, but the four
    had but one horn upon each of their heads.
    No one has ever seen a monster like it!   147

Seated thereon, securely, like a fort
    high on a hill, I saw an ungirt whore
    casting bold, sluttish glances all around.   150

130–135. The meaning of the fourth catastrophe is less certain. The dragon is a traditional representation of Satan (cf. Revelation 12:9), here issuing up from below to rend the floor of the chariot (i.e., the foundation of the Church). Historically, the tableau probably represents one of the schisms that divided the early Church, perhaps Mohammedanism, which rose to threaten her in the seventh century.

136–141. The tableau of the fifth catastrophe shows the Church's further acquisitions of temporal wealth and power.

148–159. The seventh catastrophe brings us to the period of history close to Dante's own time. The whore represents the corrupted papacy, which had been prostituting itself by forming lucrative alliances with the kings of France. The jealous "giant" (152) is most probably Philip the Fair (Philip III, 1285–1314) of France, and his kissing the whore "from time to time" (153) represents the mutual interests of king and pope served by their temporal alliances. Again, the imagery is apocalyptic. When the whore (at this point representing Pope Boniface VIII) casts her eyes on the Pilgrim, she is beaten by the jealous giant, who then removes both whore and transformed cart "far off into the woods" (159). The exact significance of the Pilgrim's participation here is uncertain.

Acting as if someone might take her from him,
  a giant, I saw, standing there by her side;
  from time to time the two of them would kiss.   153

But when she turned her roving, lustful eyes
  on me, her lover in a fit of rage
  beat her ferociously from head to foot.   156

Then, furious with jealousy, the giant
  ripped loose the monster, dragging it away
  far off into the woods, until the trees   159

blocked from my sight the whore and that strange beast.

CANTO XXXIII

THE SEVEN LADIES sing, weeping over the sorrowful fate of the chariot, and Beatrice grieves. But soon they set off, the seven in front of Beatrice, and the Pilgrim, Matelda, and Statius behind her. As they walk, Beatrice, in a very obscurely worded prophecy, predicts the eventual deliverance of the church and commands the Pilgrim to note her words and to repeat them exactly when he writes, in order to teach the living. The Pilgrim asks her why her words fly so high above his power to understand, and she answers that it is to teach him the difference between divine and earthly ways. They come to the source from which the two rivers of Lethe and Eunoë spring, and Matelda, on Beatrice's orders, leads the Pilgrim to drink of the restoring waters of Eunoë. The Poet protests that he would describe this inestimable pleasure at length, but that he has already filled the pages allotted for the second canticle. And so he says only that he came away from that holy water refreshed, eager to rise, and ready for the stars.

160. With the seventh catastrophe (the removal of the papacy to Avignon in 1305), we have moved into prophetic or future time, with respect to the fictional date of the journey (1300). Thus the Pilgrim is unable to see the further activities of the whore, the jealous giant, and the cart-turned-monster.

Deus venerunt gentes, sang the nymphs
  chanting in tears the dulcet psalmody,
  their voices alternating, three, then four,   3

and Beatrice listened to their song,
  sighing and sorrowful—hardly more grief
  showed in the face of Mary at the cross.   6

But when among those virgins silence reigned,
  yielding to her response, she stood up then
  and glowing like a flame, announced to them: 9

"*Modicum et non videbitis me;
  et iterum,* sisters so dear to me,
  modicum et vos videbitis me."   12

Then, having placed the seven in front of her,
  she had us move behind with just a nod
  to me and to the lady and the poet.   15

So she moved forward, and she had not gone
  ten steps into the wood when, suddenly,
  she turned to fix her eyes on mine, and said,   18

looking at me serenely: "Make more haste,
  so that, if I should wish to speak with you,
  you would be close enough to hear my words."   21

I did as I was told. Once I was close,
  she said: "Why, brother, do you hesitate
  to question me, now that you are with me?"   24

Like those who feel a paralyzing awe
  when in the presence of superiors
  and scarcely can find breath enough to speak—   27

---

1. The seven virtues begin to sing Psalm 78 [79], a lamentation for the destruction
of the temple of Jerusalem, which begins, "O God, the nations have come into your
inheritance; / they have defiled your holy temple, they have laid / Jerusalem in ruins."

10–12. Beatrice speaks the words of Christ to his disciples: "A little while and you
shall not see me; and again, a little while and you shall see me because I go to the
Father" (John 16:16).

I, too, could utter, indistinctly though,
   the words: "My lady, you know all my needs,
   and how to satisfy them perfectly."   30

Then she to me: "It is my wish that you
   from now on free yourself from fear and shame,
   and cease to speak like someone in a dream.   33

Know that the vessel which the serpent broke
   was, and is not. Let him who bears the blame
   learn that God's vengeance has no fear of sops.   36

The eagle that shed feathers on the car
   that would become a monster, then a prey,
   will not remain forever without heirs;   39

I tell you this because I clearly see
   those stars, already near, that will bring in
   a time—its advent nothing can prevent—   42

in which five hundred, ten, and five shall be
   God's emissary, born to kill the giant
   and the usurping whore with whom he sins.   45

Perhaps my prophecy with its dark words,
   obscure as those of Themis or the Sphinx,
   has not convinced you but confused your mind;   48

but soon events themselves shall be the Naiads
   that will untie this riddle's complex knot—
   with no destruction of the sheep or grain.   51

Note well my words: what I have said to you,
   you will repeat, as you teach those who live
   that life which is merely a race to death.   54

35. He "who bears the blame" is, collectively, Pope Clement and Philip the Fair.

43. Beatrice is prophesying the coming of such an heir to the Caesars: "God's emissary" (44) to Italy. Exactly whom Beatrice had in mind is a question that continues to puzzle readers of the poem.

47. Both Themis and the Sphinx are associated in classical mythology with "dark words" and obscure riddles.

And when you write, be sure that you describe
   the sad condition of the tree you saw
   despoiled, not once but twice, here on this spot.   57

Whoever robs this tree or breaks its limbs
   sins against God, blasphemes in deeds, for He
   created it to serve His Holy Self.   60

Because God's first soul tasted of this tree,
   more than five thousand years in pain he yearned
   for Him Who paid the penalty Himself.   63

Your mind's asleep if you do not perceive
   the special reason for the tree's great height
   and why it grows inverted toward the top.   66

If your vain thoughts had not been to your mind
   waters of Elsa, and your joy in them
   a Pyramus to your mulberry, then   69

from the tree's two strange attributes alone,
   you would have recognized its moral sense,
   and seen God's justice in the interdict.   72

But since I see your mind has turned to stone
   and, like a stone, is dark and, being dark,
   cannot endure the clear light of my words,   75

it is my wish you carry back with you
   if not my words themselves, at least some trace,
   as pilgrims bring their staves back wreathed with palm."   78

And I to her: "As wax stamped by the seal
   will never lose the outline of the print,
   so, your seal is imprinted on my mind.   81

But your desired words, why do they fly
   so high above my mind? The more I try
   to follow them, the more they soar from sight."   84

68. The Elsa is a river that flows into the Arno between Florence and Pisa; at certain
locations (especially near Colle) it had the property of "petrifying" objects immersed
and left in its waters.

She said: "Why do they? So that you may come
    truly to know that school which you have followed,
    and see how well its doctrine follows mine—   87

also, that you may see that mankind's ways
    are just as far away from those divine
    as earth is from the highest spinning sphere."   90

To that I answered: "I cannot recall
    ever having estranged myself from you:
    I have no guilty conscience on that score."   93

"You say that you do not remember it?"
    smiling, she said. "But, surely, you recall
    drinking of Lethe's waters just today;   96

and even as fire can be inferred from smoke,
    your lack of memory is patent proof
    that your estrangement from me was a sin.   99

But from now on, I promise you, my words
    will be as plain as they will have to be
    for your uneducated mind to grasp."   102

And blazing brighter, moving slower now,
    the sun was riding its meridian ring,
    whose point in space depends upon the viewer,   105

when—just as someone who escorts a group
    stops short if something very strange appears
    in front of him—those seven ladies stopped   108

as they approached the margin of a shade,
    pale as a mountain's shadow on cool streams
    flowing beneath green foliage and dark boughs.   111

Ahead of them I saw spring from one source
    what might have been the Tigris and Euphrates!
    Then, like close friends, they slowly drew apart.   114

103–105. It is now noon in Purgatory, and at noontime the sun appears to be moving
slower.

"O light, O glory of the human race,
    what is this water pouring from one source,
    and then dividing self from self?" I asked.   117

She answered: "Ask Matelda to explain."
    And then the lovely lady spoke, as though
    she felt she had to free herself from blame: 120

"I have already made this clear to him,
    this and much more; and Lethe, I am sure,
    could not have washed away the memory."   123

Then Beatrice: "A more important thing,
    perhaps, weighs on his mind, depriving him
    of memory and clouding his mind's eye.   126

But here before us is the stream Eunoë:
    now, lead him there and, as it is your wont,
    revive his weakened powers in its flow."   129

Then, gracious as she was, without demur,
    submitting her own will to another's will,
    once this was made apparent by a sign,   132

the lovely lady took me by the hand,
    and said to Statius as she moved ahead
    with queenly modesty: "And you come too."   135

Reader, if I had space to write more words,
    I'd sing, at least in part, of that sweet draught
    which never could have satisfied my thirst;   138

---

115. The Pilgrim addresses Beatrice in her allegorical role of Wisdom.

118. Matelda, the "lovely lady" who brought the Pilgrim across the river to Beatrice, is at last named.

129. By drinking of the waters of Eunoë, the memory of good deeds done in the past is restored.

but now I have completed every page
    planned for my poem's second canticle—
    I am checked by the bridle of my art!   141

From those holiest waters I returned
    to her reborn, a tree renewed, in bloom
    with newborn foliage, immaculate,   144

eager to rise, now ready for the stars.

THE DIVINE COMEDY: PARADISE

CANTO I

AFTER STATING THAT God's glory shines throughout the universe, Dante informs us that he has been to Paradise, and has seen things so extraordinary that he cannot possibly hope to tell about them. Nevertheless, he determines to make this final song his crowning achievement as a poet, and he calls on both the Muses and Apollo for inspiration as he focuses on his journey heavenward. At noon on the spring equinox, Dante, still in the Earthly Paradise, sees Beatrice gazing into the sun, and he imitates her gaze. In so doing, he becomes aware of an extraordinary brightness, as though God had placed in the heavens a second sun, and feels himself being "transhumanized" in preparation for his experience of Paradise. He then finds himself soaring heavenward through God's grace, although he is uncertain whether it is his soul or his corporeal self that rises. As Dante and Beatrice pass out of the earth's atmosphere into the sphere of fire that lies above it, Dante hears the music of the spheres. This music fills him with wonderment and perplexity, but before he can question Beatrice about it, she explains to him the teleological order of the universe, and how it is only natural that, having been purified, he should now rise heavenward.

The glory of the One Who moves all things
    penetrates all the universe, reflecting
    in one part more and in another less.   3

I have been in His brightest shining heaven
    and seen such things that no man, once returned
    from there, has wit or skill to tell about;   6

for when our intellect draws near its goal
    and fathoms to the depths of its desire,
    the memory is powerless to follow;   9

2–3. The light of God shines more in one part and less in another according to the greater or lesser capacity of each thing to contain it.

4. "His brightest shining heaven" is the Empyrean, the uppermost sphere and the abode of God and all the Blest.

but still, as much of Heaven's holy realm
   as I could store and treasure in my mind
   shall now become the subject of my song.   12

O great Apollo, for this final task,
   make me a vessel worthy to receive
   your genius and the longed-for laurel crown.   15

Thus far I have addressed my prayers to one
   peak of Parnassus; now I need them both
   to move into this heavenly arena.   18

Enter my breast, breathe into me as high
   a strain as that which vanquished Marsyas
   the time you drew him from his body's sheath.   21

O Power Divine, but lend me of yourself
   so much as will make clear at least the shadow
   of that high realm imprinted on my mind,   24

and you shall see me at your chosen tree,
   crowning myself with those green leaves of which
   my theme and you yourself will make me worthy.   27

So seldom, Father, are they plucked to crown
   the triumph of a Caesar or a Poet
   (the shame, the fault of mortal man's desires!)   30

that when a man yearns to achieve that goal,
   then the Peneian frond should surely breed
   a new joy in the joyous Delphic god.   33

From one small spark can come a mighty blaze:
   so after me, perhaps, a better voice
   may rise in prayer and win Cyrrha's response.   36

The lamp that lights the world rises for man
   at different points, but from the place which joins
   four circles with three crosses, it ascends   39

upon a happier course with happier stars
   conjoined, and in this way it warms and seals
   the earthly wax closer to its own likeness.   42

This glad union had made it morning there
   and evening here: our hemisphere was dark,
   while all the mountain bathed in white, when I   45

saw Beatrice turned round, facing left,
   her eyes raised to the sun—no eagle ever
   could stare so fixed and straight into such light!   48

As one descending ray of light will cause
   a second one to rise back up again,
   just as a pilgrim yearns to go back home,   51

so, like a ray, her act poured through my eyes
   into my mind and gave rise to my own:
   I stared straight at the sun as no man could.   53

In that place first created for mankind
   much more is granted to the human senses
   than ever was allowed them here on earth.   57

I could not look for long, but my eyes saw
   the sun enclosed in blazing sparks of light
   like molten iron as it pours from the fire.   60

And suddenly it was as if one day
   shone on the next—as if the One Who Could
   had decked the heavens with a second sun.   63

And Beatrice stood there, her eyes fixed
   on the eternal spheres, entranced, and now
   my eyes, withdrawn from high, were fixed on her.   66

43–44. "Evening here" refers to the hemisphere of land, the place to which the Poet
has returned following his journey to Paradise—it is the place of ignorance, sin, and
worldly cares from which he now writes. The Pilgrim's journey through Hell begins
in the evening, while that of Purgatory takes place at dawn. Now we know that the
journey through Paradise will start at high noon.

Gazing at her, I felt myself becoming
   what Glaucus had become tasting the herb
   that made him like the other sea-gods there.   69

"Transhumanize"—it cannot be explained
   per verba, so let this example serve
   until God's grace grants the experience.   72

Whether it was the last created part
   of me alone that rose, O Sovereign Love,
   You know Whose light it was that lifted me.   75

When the great sphere that spins, yearning for You
   eternally, captured my mind with strains
   of harmony tempered and tuned by You,   78

I saw a great expanse of heaven ablaze
   with the sun's flames: not all the rains and rivers
   on earth could ever make a lake so wide.   81

The revelation of this light, this sound,
   inflamed me with such eagerness to learn
   their cause, as I had never felt before;   84

and she who saw me as I saw myself,
   ready to calm my agitated mind,
   began to speak before I asked my question: 87

"You have yourself to blame for burdening
   your mind with misconceptions that prevent
   from seeing clearly what you might have seen.   90

67–69. Glaucus, a fisherman, noticed that his catch revived and jumped back into
the sea after being placed upon a certain herb. He ate some of the herb and was
transformed into a sea-god, as Ovid relates (*Metamorphoses* XIII, 898–968). The
Pilgrim is being compared to Glaucus, for, as he looks at Beatrice, who still gazes
toward the sun, he too begins to undergo a transformation—the miraculous inner
transformation that will prepare him to approach Paradise.

70. Dante the Pilgrim becomes "transhumanized" and enters a state beyond mortal
explication, a state that cannot be explained with words (*per verba*).

76–78. The "great sphere" here is the Primum Mobile, the outermost and swiftest
of all the revolving heavens and boundary of the material universe.

You may think you are still on earth, but lightning
   never sped downward from its home as quick
   as you are now ascending to your own."   93

As easily did these few and smiling words
   release me from my first perplexity
   than was my mind ensnared by yet another,   96

and I said: "Though I rest content concerning
   one great wonder of mine, I wonder now
   how I can rise through these light bodies here."   99

She sighed with pity when she heard my question
   and looked at me the way a mother might
   hearing her child in his delirium: 102

"Among all things, however disparate,
   there reigns an order, and this gives the form
   that makes the universe resemble God,"   105

she said; "therein God's higher creatures see
   the imprint of Eternal Excellence—
   that goal for which the system is created,   108

and in this order all created things,
   according to their bent, maintain their place,
   disposed in proper distance from their Source;   111

therefore, they move, all to a different port,
   across the vast ocean of being, and each
   endowed with its own instinct as its guide.   114

This is what carries fire toward the moon,
   this is the moving force in mortal hearts,
   this is what binds the earth and makes it one.   117

Not only living creatures void of reason
   prove the impelling strength of instinct's bow,
   but also those with intellect and love.   120

106. "Therein" refers to being within "the form" (104) that is the governing principle "that makes the universe resemble God" (105). "God's higher creatures" are all those rational and intellectual beings, including mankind, the angels, and the spirits of the Blest.

109. Even inanimate things are included in the system, not only men and angels.

The Providence that regulates the whole
    becalms forever with its radiance
    the heaven wherein revolves the swiftest sphere;   123

to there, to that predestined place, we soar,
    propelled there by the power of that bow
    which always shoots straight to its Happy Mark.   126

But, it is true that just as form sometimes
    may not reflect the artist's true intent,
    the matter being deaf to the appeal,   129

just so, God's creature, even though impelled
    toward the true goal, having the power to swerve,
    may sometimes go astray along his course;   132

and just as fire can be seen as falling
    down from a cloud, so too man's primal drive,
    twisted by false desire, may bring him down.   135

You should, in all truth, be no more amazed
    at your flight up than at the sight of water
    that rushes down a mountain to its base.   138

If you, free as you are of every weight,
    had stayed below, then that would be as strange
    as living flame on earth remaining still.   141

And then she turned her gaze up toward the heavens.

CANTO II

NOW ON THE threshold of the first heavenly sphere, that of the moon,
Dante warns all those who have followed him as far as this stage in his
account of the eternal realms that they must either be prepared, spiri-
tually and intellectually, to learn of the delights of Paradise, or they

123. The Primum Mobile is the heavenly sphere that spins the fastest and gives the
other spheres contained within it their respective motions.

should turn back. Having invoked Minerva, Apollo, and the nine Muses,
and having begun to prepare himself for anticipated wonders, Dante
ascends with Beatrice toward Paradise. When they reach the first of the
heavenly bodies, the sphere of the moon, and are "taken" into it, Dante
asks Beatrice what causes the markings on the moon that are visible
from earth. After asking Dante to tell what he believes to be the cause
of the spots on the moon, and then demonstrating the errors in his
reasoning, Beatrice finally explains the true cause to him, and in doing
so illuminates the nature of Divine Power, and of the heavens.

All you who in your wish to hear my words
    have followed thus far in your little boat
    behind my ship that singing sails these waters,   3

go back now while you still can see your shores;
    do not attempt the deep: it well could be
    that losing me, you would be lost yourselves.   6

I set my course for waters never travelled;
    Minerva fills my sails, Apollo steers,
    and all nine Muses point the Bears to me.   9

Those few of you who from your youth have raised
    your eager mouths in search of angels' bread
    on which man feeds here, always hungering,   12

you may, indeed, allow your boat to sail
    the high seas in the furrow of my wake
    ahead of parted waters that flow back.   15

Those heroes who once crossed the deep to Colchis,
    and saw their Jason put behind a plow,
    were not amazed as much as you will be.   18

8–9. Dante is guided by Minerva, Goddess of Wisdom, Apollo, God of Poetry, and
all nine Muses. The Bears are the constellations Ursa Major and Ursa Minor (the Big
Bear and the Little Bear) by which sailors steered.

11. The bread of angels is the knowledge of God, or wisdom.

16–18. The heroes are the Argonauts, who journeyed with Jason, their leader, to
obtain the Golden Fleece from King Æetes of Colchis.

By that innate and never-ending thirst
  for God's own realm we sped up just as fast
  as human eyes can rise to meet the skies.   21

My gaze on Beatrice, hers on Heaven,
  in less time than an arrow strikes the mark,
  flies through the air, loosed from its catch, I found   24

myself in some place where a wondrous thing
  absorbed all of my mind, and then my lady,
  from whom I could not keep my thirst to know,   27

turned toward me as joyful as her beauty:
  "Direct your mind and gratitude," she said,
  "to God, who raised us up to His first star."   30

We seemed to be enveloped in a cloud
  as brilliant, hard, and polished as a diamond
  struck by a ray of sunlight. That eternal,   33

celestial pearl took us into itself,
  receiving us as water takes in light,
  its indivisibility intact.   36

If I was body (on earth we cannot think,
  in terms of solid form within a solid,
  as we must here, since body enters body),   39

then so much more should longing burn in us
  to see that Being in Whom we can behold
  the union of God's nature with our own.   42

Once there we shall behold what we hold true
  through faith, not proven but self-evident:
  a primal truth, incontrovertible.   45

I said, "My lady, all my adoration,
  all my humility is gratitude
  to Him Who raised me from the mortal world.   48

---

30. The "first star" is the moon. It is the closest "star" or "planet" (for Dante these terms are interchangeable) to the earth and the first approached by the traveler and Beatrice as they rise toward Paradise.

But tell me what the dark spots are which, seen
   from earth along the surface of this body,
   lead men to make up stories about Cain?"   51

She smiled a little, then she answered me:
   "That human judgment must reach false conclusions
   when no key is provided by our senses,   54

this surely should be no surprise to you,
   since, as you know, even when the senses guide,
   reason's wing-span sometimes can be short.   57

But tell me what you think the cause might be."
   And I: "The differences we see from earth,
   I think, are caused by different densities."   60

She said, then: "I am certain you shall see
   that your beliefs are deeply steeped in error.
   Now listen to my counter-arguments: 63

Heaven's eighth sphere is lit by many lamps
   all of which shine with great diversity
   both in their quality and quantity.   66

If rare and dense alone produced all this,
   one single virtue would be in them all
   in more or less or equal distribution;   69

but these show different qualities, the fruits
   of diverse active principles of which
   your reasoning would demolish all but one.   72

Moreover, if the cause of those dark marks
   were density alone, this planet's substance
   would either be in certain parts translucent,   75

64. The eighth sphere is that of fixed stars in which the different constellations are
found. It is located between the Primum Mobile (the ninth sphere) and the sphere of
Saturn (the seventh sphere).

65–69. The fixed stars, like the substance of the moon, show varying degrees of
brilliance. These variations are not just a matter of relative intensity; they derive also
from the very nature, or quality, of the light shed.

or else there would be simple alternation
    of dense and rare like lean and fat in meat,
    or, in a book, as pages alternate.   78

Yet if the first were true, the moon could not
    fully block out the sun: in an eclipse
    some light would shine through the transparencies—   81

but it does not. So now let us examine
    the second case, and if I prove it wrong,
    then your opinion will be falsified.   84

Well, then, if this rare matter does not spread
    all the way through, this means there is a point
    at which some denser matter blocks its way,   87

and it would be from there that the sun's rays
    would be bent back, as color is reflected
    back from a glass concealing lead behind it.   90

Now, you could say that though there is reflection,
    the ray is dimmer there than other spots,
    since it reflects across a greater reach.   93

But you can rid yourself of this objection,
    if you are willing, by experiment,
    the source which fills the rivers of man's art: 96

Set up three mirrors so that two of them
    are equidistant from you, and the third
    between them, farther out in front of you;   99

as you stand facing them, have someone place
    a light behind you which strikes all of them
    and which reflects from them back to your sight.   102

Although the light seen farthest off is not
    as great in size as are the other two,
    you will observe its brilliance is the same.   105

Now, as the substance of the snow gives up
    the whiteness and the coldness it once had,
    beneath the piercing rays of a bright sun,   108

so is your intellect stripped clear, and I
   will now reveal a truth so radiant
   that it will sparkle for you like a star.   111

Within the highest Heaven of God's peace
   revolves a body in whose power lies
   the essence of all things contained therein.   114

The next sphere which is lit with myriad eyes
   divides this essence into many types,
   distinct from it and yet contained in it.   117

The other spheres, by various differences
   direct their own distinctive qualities
   to their own ends and fruitful operations.   120

These universal organs, you now see,
   proceed from grade to grade, receiving power
   from those above, acting on those below.   123

And now, mark well the path that I take up
   to reach the truth you seek, so that henceforth
   you will know how to take the ford alone.   126

The power and motion of the sacred spheres
   must by the blessèd movers be inspired
   just as the hammer's art is by the smith.   129

115–117. This is the next sphere down, contained within the Primum Mobile, that of the fixed stars. In this sphere occurs the first stage of differentiating and distributing the essence or "quality" that derives from God. Though distinct from Him, the differentiated "quality" nevertheless is contained in God because He envelops all of creation and exists everywhere in it.

118–120. The "other spheres" are the planetary spheres that lie within and beneath the Primum Mobile and the sphere of the fixed stars. The various secondary causes and effects within each sphere are determined by its own powers and operations, the primary cause of each having been derived from the distribution and differentiation of that "quality," essence, or "power" derived from God.

That heaven whose beauty shines with countless lamps
    from the deep mind that turns it takes its stamp
    and of that image makes itself the seal;   132

and as the soul within your living dust
    diffuses through your body's different parts,
    adapted to its various faculties,   135

just so does this Intelligence unfold
    its bounty which the stars have multiplied
    while turning ever in its unity.   138

Different virtues mingle differently
    with each rich stellar body that they quicken,
    even as the soul within you blends with you.   141

True to the glad nature from which it flows,
    this blended virtue shines throughout that body,
    as happiness shines forth through living eyes,   144

and from this virtue, not from dense and rare,
    derive those differences of light we see:
    this is the formal principle that gives,   147

according to its virtue, dark and light."

130–132. Beatrice's speech now returns to the sphere of the fixed stars (the "myriad
eyes" of line 115) with which her argument began. In the same way that the soul
distributes its power throughout the body, where it becomes differentiated according
to the nature of the receiving part or faculty, the undifferentiated power of God,
when it is distributed through the spheres, becomes differentiated in the stars and
planets as it combines with the qualities inherent in them. This produces a "blended
virtue" (143) that causes each body to emit light in accordance with its individual
qualities and its degree of excellence. It is the power of the Divine and Angelic In-
telligences, therefore, in conjunction with the stars that produces the dark and light
markings on the moon.

CANTO III

DANTE, NOW REALIZING *the folly of his ideas about the markings on the moon and appreciating Beatrice's wisdom, is about to acknowledge his errors when he sees before him pale, nebulous faces. Thinking them to be reflections, he turns around, but sees nothing. Beatrice, smiling at his mistake, informs Dante that the faces belong to those who made vows to God and broke them. Although they have a place with God in His realm, the Empyrean, these souls occupy the lowest position in the hierarchy of Paradise, and they appear to Dante in the lowest of the heavenly spheres, that of the moon. Beatrice urges Dante to speak with them and listen well to what they have to say, as they are filled, to the extent of their capacity, with the light of God. One of the souls, Piccarda Donati, explains that she was forced to leave the convent and marry, thus breaking her religious vows. In response to Dante's question about the desire of souls to attain a higher place in the hierarchy of Paradise, Piccarda talks about the perfected volition possessed by the Blest, and about the teleological order inherent in Paradise. Piccarda points out the soul of the Empress Constance, and recounts the circumstances of Constance's life on earth. As Piccarda finishes speaking, the faces begin to recede, growing fainter and fainter, and Dante turns his eyes back to the brilliance of Beatrice.*

The sun that once warmed my young heart with love
   had now revealed with proofs and arguments
   the beauty in the face of what is true,   3

and I, to show that I had understood
   my error and her wisdom, raised my head
   just high enough to meet her eyes and speak,   6

when there, before my eyes, appeared a vision,
   absorbing my attention so completely
   that all thoughts of confessing left my mind.   9

1–3. The sun is Beatrice.

As faint an image as comes back to us
   of our own face reflected in a smooth
   transparent pane of glass or in a clear   12

and tranquil pool whose shallow still remains
   in sight—so pale, our pupils could as soon
   make out a pearl upon a milk-white brow—   15

such faces I saw there, eager to speak;
   I had made the opposite mistake to that
   which kindled love in one man for his pool.   18

The moment I became aware of them,
   believing that they were reflected forms,
   I turned around to find out whose they were,   21

and saw no one. I looked around again
   into the radiance of my sweet guide
   whose sacred eyes were glowing as she smiled.   24

"You should not be surprised to see me smile
   at your naive reaction," she announced,
   "you do not trust the evidence you see;   27

you turn away to stare at emptiness:
   these are real substances that you behold,
   appearing here because they broke their vows.   30

Speak to them, listen, trust in what they say,
   for they are filled with the true light of God
   that gives them peace and does not let them err."   33

I turned, then, to that shade who seemed to be
   the most intent to speak, and I began,
   moved by an overwhelming urge, to say   36

"O well-created soul who, in the rays
   of endless life, enjoy that sweetness which,
   till truly tasted, never can be known,   39

how happy it would make me if you were
   so gracious as to tell me who you are
   and of your fate." Gladly, with smiling eyes,   42

she said: "The love in us no more rejects
   a just request than does the love in Him
   Who wills His court to be like Love Himself.   45

I was a virgin sister in the world;
   if you search deep into your memory,
   you will remember me—though now I am   48

more beautiful by far—I am Piccarda.
   You see me here among these other blest,
   blest, all of us, within the slowest sphere.   51

Our own desires that are stirred alone
   in the desires of the Holy Ghost
   rejoice conforming to His ordering.   54

Our station which appears so lowly here
   has been assigned because we failed our vows
   to some degree and gave less than we pledged."   57

I said: "Your faces shine so wondrously
   with something undescribably divine,
   transforming them beyond the memory,   60

and so I was not quick remembering;
   but now with what your words have just revealed,
   I find it easy to recall your face.   63

But tell me: all you souls so happy here,
   do you yearn for a higher post in Heaven,
   to see more, to become more loved by Him?"   66

She gently smiled, as did the other shades;
   then came her words so full of happiness,
   she seemed to glow with the first fire of love: 69

---

49. The soul is Piccarda Donati, kinswoman of Dante's wife, sister of Dante's friend
Forese (see *Purgatory* XXIII, 48) and of Corso, the infamous war leader and con-
tributor to Dante's banishment.

51. The sphere of the moon, being the innermost of the nine concentric spheres, and
the farthest from the Empyrean, moves the slowest, since the speed of each sphere is
in direct proportion to its proximity to God. Speed, like intensity and quality of lights,
is an indication of a sphere's share of Divine Love.

"Brother, the virtue of our heavenly love,
    tempers our will and makes us want no more
    than what we have—we thirst for this alone.   72

If we desired to be higher up,
    then our desires would not be in accord
    with His will Who assigns us to this sphere;   75

think carefully what love is and you'll see
    such discord has no place within these rounds,
    since to be here is to exist in Love.   78

Indeed, the essence of this blessèd state
    is to dwell here within His holy will,
    so that there is no will but one with His;   81

the order of our rank from height to height
    throughout this realm is pleasing to the realm,
    as to that King Who wills us to His will.   84

In His will is our peace—it is the sea
    in which all things are drawn that it itself
    creates or which the work of Nature makes."   87

Then it was clear to me that every where
    of Heaven is Paradise, though there the light
    of Grace Supreme does not shine equally.   90

As happens when we find we've had our fill
    of one food but still crave another kind,
    while giving thanks for this, we ask for that,   93

so did my words and gestures beg to know
    about the cloth through which she had not drawn
    the shuttle of her incompleted vow.   96

70–78. As Beatrice stated in Canto II, each heaven takes in an amount of Divine Light that is in proportion to its capacity to receive it. In the same way, each individual soul enjoys the bliss of the highest realm, in accordance with its capacity. Thus, the Blest are all content, wherever they are in the hierarchy of Paradise. For Piccarda to desire to be elsewhere would be impossible, since such a desire would spring from an imperfect will and a lack of knowledge of the teleological character of the Divine Order.

"A perfect life, great virtue have enshrined
   a lady high above," she said, "whose rule
   decides the cloak and veil of some on earth,   99

who wish, till death, to wake and sleep beside
   that Bridegroom Who accepts all vows of love
   conforming to his pleasure. From the world   102

I fled, as a young girl, to follow her,
   and in her habit's rule I closed myself,
   and pledged to always follow in her practice.   105

Then men, acquainted less with love than hate,
   took me by force away from that sweet fold,
   and God, alone, knows what my life became!   108

This other radiance, here to my right,
   who shows herself to you as she shines full
   with all the light of our low sphere, well knows   111

from her own life what my own words can mean.
   She was a sister, too; from her head, too,
   they ripped the shadow of our holy veil.   114

But even when forced back into the world
   against her will, against her sacred vows,
   she always wore the veil over her heart.   117

98. The lady is St. Clare, founder of the Franciscan Order of the Poor Clares, who inspired Piccarda to enter the religious life.

106–108. This is an allusion to Piccarda's brother, Corso Donati (see note 49).

109. Piccarda refers to another face (the "radiance" who will be named in line 118), that of the Empress Constance (1154–1198). Herself heiress to the Norman house of Tancred, and thus to the crown of Naples and Sicily, she was the wife of Henry VI, son of the Emperor Frederick Barbarossa, and the mother of Frederick II. It was thought in Dante's time that she had once been a nun, and had been forcibly taken from her convent to wed Henry VI.

She is the light of the great Empress Constance
   who, wed to Swabia's second gust of wind,
     bore him the third and final gust of power.   120

These words she spoke, and then she started "*Ave,*
   Maria" to sing and, singing, disappeared
     as something sinking in deep waters fades,   123

and I, who had been fixed upon her form
   until she vanished, turned and set my eyes
     upon the greater mark of my desire—   126

in Beatrice I was all absorbed—
   but her light flashed so deep into my eyes
     I could not bear the sight, and so at first   129

I found it difficult to question her.

CANTO IV

HAVING LISTENED TO Piccarda talk about herself and the Empress Constance, the Pilgrim becomes plagued with two doubts and is unable to decide which question to ask first. His dilemma is solved by Beatrice, who knows his thoughts and poses the questions for him. Teacher and guide that she is, she answers first the more "poisonous" (theologically speaking) of the questions—whether or not Plato was correct in believing that each soul returns to the star from which it came. Then, in turning to the second question, why Divine Justice lessened the degree of merit of the souls in this sphere, she discourses on the nature of the Will, by distinguishing between the Absolute Will, which always longs for God, and the Conditioned Will, which bends according to circum-

---

119–120. Dante refers to three Swabian princes and calls them "gusts" of wind, perhaps because of the violence and brevity of their rule. The first "gust" was Frederick Barbarossa, father-in-law of the Empress Constance; the second was Henry VI, Constance's husband; the third and final "gust" was Constance's son, Frederick II, last of the line and, according to Dante (*Convivio* IV, iii, 6), last of the Roman emperors.

stances. Piccarda and Constance are assigned to the sphere of the moon, not for corruption of the Absolute Will, but for that Will which bowed to external circumstances. Apparently still in sympathy with those who have broken their vows, Dante wishes to know if it is possible to compensate for this transgression in some way. The answer is found in the next canto.

Between two equal equidistant foods
    a man, though free to choose, would starve to death
      before he put his teeth in either one.   3

So would a lamb between the ravenings
    of two fierce wolves be caught in fear of both,
      so would a dog stand fixed between two does.   6

If, then, I stood there mute, drawn equally
    by my two doubts, I merit neither blame
      nor praise—the victim of necessity.   9

I did not speak, but written on my face
    was my desire, all of my questioning
      more vividly than words could have expressed.   12

Then Beatrice did what Daniel did
    when he appeased Nebuchadnezzar's wrath
      that drove him to such unjust cruelty.   15

She said: "I see how you are torn between
    your two desires, so that your eagerness
      is choking itself into speechlessness.   18

You think: 'But if my will for good remains
    unchanged, how can another's violent act
      lessen the measure of my just deserts?'   21

There is a second doubt that gives you pause:
    that after death all souls seem to return
      each to his star, as Plato's word affirms.   24

These are the questions that have equal weight,
    contending with your will to know; I first
      shall treat the one that is more poisonous.   27

Not the most Godlike of the Seraphim,
 not Moses, Samuel, whichever John
 you choose—I tell you—not Mary herself   30

has been assigned to any other heaven
 than that of these shades you have just seen here,
 and each one's bliss is equally eternal;   33

all lend their beauty to the Highest Sphere,
 sharing one same sweet life to the degree
 that they feel the eternal breath of God.   36

These souls appeared here not because this sphere
 has been allotted them, but as a sign
 of their less great degree of blessedness.   39

I speak as one must speak to minds like yours
 which apprehend only from sense perception
 what later it makes fit for intellection.   42

For this same reason Scripture condescends
 to your intelligence, attributing
 with other meaning, hands and feet to God;   45

and Holy Church presents to you archangels
 with human features: Gabriel and Michael
 and that one who made Tobit see again.   48

If what Timaeus says about the souls
 in Heaven is to be taken literally,
 it contradicts the truth we witness here: 51

37–39. The soul in Paradise appears in a particular level or station according to its degree of blessedness and not because of any platonic affinity between the soul and the sphere.

48. The unnamed archangel is Raphael, who instructed Tobit's son Tobias to cover his father's eyes with a certain substance, saying that when he peeled it off, Tobit's sight would be restored (Tobit 11:1–15).

he says the soul returns to its own star
    from which, he thinks, it once had been cut off
    when Nature sent it to substantial form.   54

Perhaps his words were not meant to be heard
    exactly as they sound, but make a claim
    deserving the respect of every man.   57

If he means that the honor and the blame
    of each sphere's influence returns to it,
    his arrow, then, has hit upon some truth.   60

This principle, misunderstood, once led
    the world astray when they bestowed on planets
    such names as Jove and Mercury and Mars.   63

The other doubt that still perturbs your mind
    is not as poisonous, for all its malice
    could never make you wander from my side.   66

That in the eyes of mortal men our justice
    appears to be unjust is proof of faith,
    not of heretical iniquity.   69

But since this truth is such that your own powers
    can understand its meaning easily,
    I shall explain it to you, as you wish.   72

Now, if the one who suffers violence
    contributes nothing to the violent act,
    he cannot be excused on that account;   75

for will, if it will not, cannot be quenched
    but does as nature does within a flame,
    though violence force it down a thousand times.   78

The will abets the force when it gives in
    even a little bit; this their will did,
    for they could have gone back into the cloister.   81

Had they been able to maintain their will
    intact, like that of Lawrence on the grid,
    and Mucius cruel to his own hand in fire—   84

it would have forced them back, once they were free,
    back to the path from which they had been drawn.
    But such firm will as this is seldom found.   87

If you have truly taken in my words,
    you see how they have quashed the argument
    that never would have ceased to plague your mind.   90

But now another pass that must be crossed
    opens before your eyes, and by yourself
    you would collapse before you could get through.   93

I certainly have led you to believe
    that these souls cannot lie, for they exist
    forever in the sight of Primal Truth;   96

but then you heard Piccarda say that Constance
    had never lost devotion to the veil;
    this must have seemed to contradict my words.   99

Often, my brother, it occurs that men
    against their will, to avoid a greater risk,
    have done that which should never have been done;   102

83. St. Lawrence, a supposed native of Huesca in Spain, was a deacon of the Church of Rome at the time of Valerian. He was grilled alive on an iron grid in 258 for his refusal to disclose the hiding place of Church treasures entrusted to him by Pope Sixtus II.

84. Gaius Mucius Scaevola ("left-handed") was a Roman citizen who attempted to kill the Etruscan King Porsena during the latter's siege of Rome in the late sixth century B.C. When he stabbed Porsena's secretary by mistake, Mucius was condemned to be burned alive. He thereupon stuck his right hand into a nearby sacrificial fire, and held it there without flinching. Porsena was so impressed by this display of fortitude that he spared Mucius's life.

so Alcmeon, moved by his father's prayer,
  killed his own mother: so as not to fail
  in piety, he was pitilessly cruel.   105

You understand, when things like this occur,
  how will and violence can mix to cause
  offenses that can never be condoned.   108

Absolute Will does not consent to wrong,
  but it consents in so far as it fears,
  if it draw back, to fall into worse trouble.   111

And so, Piccarda, in her explanation
  was speaking of Absolute Will, and I
  about the other; both of us spoke truth."   114

Such was the flowing of the holy stream
  that pours down from the Fountain of All Truth
  that it now laid both of my doubts to rest.   117

"Beloved of the First Love, lady divine,"
  I said then, "you whose words bathe me in warmth,
  wakening me to life again, the depth   120

of my deep love is not profound enough
  to find the thanks your graciousness deserves—
  may He Who knows and sees all be my answer.   123

I see man's mind cannot be satisfied
  unless it be illumined by that Truth
  beyond which there exists no other truth.   126

103–105. *Alcmeon* was the son of Amphiaraus the seer and Eriphyle. Amphiaraus foresaw that he would die during the Theban expedition, and hid so as not to have to join it. Eriphyle betrayed him. Before he died, he demanded that Alcmeon avenge him by slaying Eriphyle. Thus, out of obligation to and pity for his father, he killed his mother. Alcmeon's act here is presented as an example of Conditioned Will, will consenting reluctantly to evil out of a sense of fear or false obligation. (See also *Purgatory* XII, 49–51.)

109–111. Will in the absolute sense (Absolute Will) never consents to doing wrong; it is only in a relative sense that it consents (Conditioned Will); that is, it gives in or draws back in fear that if it does not it will be in greater danger ("fall into worse trouble").

Within that Truth, once man's mind reaches it,
   it rests like a wild beast within its den.
   And it can reach it—if not, all desire   129

is vain! So at the foot of truth, like shoots,
   our doubts spring up; this is a natural force
   urging us to the top from height to height.   132

And this gives me the courage that I need,
   my lady, in all reverence, to ask
   about a truth that is not clear to me: 135

would it be possible for those who break
   their vows to compensate with such good deeds
   that they would not weigh short upon your scales?"   138

Then Beatrice looked at me, her eyes
   sparkling with love and burning so divine,
   my strength of sight surrendered to her power—   141

with eyes cast down, I was about to faint.

CANTO V

Beatrice explains to the Pilgrim that a vow is a freely made sacrifice of one's own free will to God, and since free will was God's most precious gift to His creatures, what could possibly be substituted for it? But since the Church from time to time does free the individual from his vow, she finds it necessary to explain further. While a person can never take back from God the sacrifice he has made to Him of his free will, he can change the substance of his vow on two conditions: that he have the consent of the Church and that the substitution made be of greater value than the original promise. Beatrice then addresses all mankind, warning them not to take their vows lightly, to think carefully

129–130. It was a basic concept of scholastic philosophy that nothing in the universe is without a goal or purpose. Man's innate desire to know God must be satisfied, for God would never have put such a desire in man's mind if it could not be satisfied.

before making them, and to use the Scriptures and ecclesiastical au-
thority as guides. Then, in silence, she turns her eyes on high, and the
Pilgrim, still with questions to ask, dares not speak. In the meantime
they ascend with great speed to the second sphere, the heaven of Mer-
cury, which shines more brightly with the happiness of Beatrice as she
enters the planet. Countless lights appear to the Pilgrim, one of whom
he asks two questions: who it is and why it is in this particular heaven.
The light of this soul closed tightly in its own light answers, as the
closing verse of this canto says, "the way in which the following canto
chants."

"If, in the warmth of love, you see me glow
  with light the world below has never seen,
  stunning the power of your mortal sight,   3

you should not be amazed, for it proceeds
  from perfect vision which, the more it sees,
  the more it moves to reach the good perceived.   6

I can see how into your mind already
  there shines Eternal Light which, of Itself,
  once it is seen, forever kindles love;   9

and should some other thing seduce man's love,
  it can be only some trace of this Light,
  misapprehended, shining through that thing.   12

You wish to know if for a broken vow
  one can make compensation of the kind
  that makes the soul secure from litigation."   15

These were the words with which my Beatrice
  began this canto, then without delay
  continued with her sacred explication: 18

"The greatest gift that our bounteous Lord
  bestowed as the Creator, in creating,
  the gift He cherishes the most, the one   21

7–9. As Dante's journey progresses, his understanding and his ability to know God
increase.

most like Himself, was freedom of the will.
   All creatures with intelligence, and they
   alone, were so endowed both then and now.   24

Such reasoning as this should make it clear
   how sacred is the vow when it is made
   with God consenting to your own consent;   27

when, therefore, God and man have sealed the pact,
   this treasure, then, of which I speak becomes
   the sacrifice the free will wills itself.   30

What compensation can you offer, then?
   Can you use well what is no longer yours?
   You cannot do good works with ill-got gains.   33

So far, the main point should be clear to you,
   but since the Church grants dispensations here,
   which seems to contradict the truth I spoke,   36

you must sit at the table yet awhile
   because the food that you have taken in
   is tough and takes time to assimilate.   39

Open your mind to what I shall reveal
   and seal it in, for to have understood
   and not retained, as knowledge does not count.   42

The essence of this sacrifice depends
   on two things: first, the promised act itself,
   and next, the solemn nature of the pact.   45

The latter cannot be annulled except
   by its fulfillment; and it was of this
   I spoke in such precise terms earlier.   48

43–48. Two things are involved in the taking of a vow, whereby an individual offers
his free will to God. The first of these is the substance of the vow (e.g., virginity,
abstinence, poverty), or that which the individual promises to accomplish. The second
is the nature of the vow, or the fact that the individual has abdicated his free will
and contracted to keep faith with God. This second component cannot be discharged
save through complete fulfillment, and cannot be declared void without obliteration
of the pact and eventual revocation of one's gift to God.

Thus, it was mandatory for the Jews
   to sacrifice, but they could, as you know,
   substitute one offering for another.   51

This may be called the substance of the vow,
   and may be such that no real fault occur
   if the one substance take the other's place.   54

But let no one assume by his own choice
   responsibility for substitution;
   be sure the white and yellow keys have turned.   57

And any change must be considered vain
   if the new matter not contain the old,
   as six exceeds and holds the number four.   60

There are, however, certain things once sworn
   that by their value can tip every scale:
   for these no substitution can be made.   63

Let no man take his vow too lightly. Keep
   your word! But, do not make a blind, rash oath
   as Jephthah did in his first offering—   66

better if he had said, 'My vow was wrong,'
   than do far worse by keeping it. No less
   insensate was that great war-chief, the Greek   69

whose Iphigenia mourned her loveliness,
   and made the wise as well as simple weep
   to hear the tale of such a grievous rite.   72

Christians, beware of rushing into vows.
   Do not be like a feather in the wind,
   or think that every water washes clean!   75

You have the Testaments, the Old and New;
   as guide you have the Shepherd of the church:
   they should be all you need to save your soul.   78

76–78. A Christian is not obligated to make vows in order to ensure his salvation.
He has Scriptural precedent to guide him, as well as the Church; he has only to resist
faulty motivation, which leads to hasty decisions.

If evil greed incites you otherwise,
   be men, not senseless sheep, lest any Jew
   among you point his finger out of scorn!   81

Do not be like the lamb who turns away
   from its own mother's milk, capriciously
   playing a silly game to its own harm!"   84

As I have written, so spoke Beatrice.
   Then full of yearning she turned to that height
   where all the universe is quickened most.   87

Her stillness, her transfigured countenance
   imposed silence upon my eager mind,
   already stirred with new questions to ask;   90

and like an arrow that has struck the mark
   before the bow-string stops its quivering,
   we soared into the second realm, and there,   93

I saw my lady so caught up in joy
   as she went into that new heaven's glow,
   the planet shone with more than its own light.   96

And if the star changed then and seemed to smile,
   imagine what took place in me, a man
   whose nature is transmutability.   99

As in the clear, still water of a pond
   the fish are lured toward something fallen in,
   as if they knew it was their food—so, here,   102

I saw more than a thousand splendors move
   toward us, and in each one I heard the cry:
   "Behold one more who will increase our love."   105

And as they came nearer to us, the joy
   of each soul there was rendered visible
   in the clear luminance with which it shone.   108

Imagine, Reader, if I were to stop
   right here without describing what came next,
   how keenly you would crave to hear the rest—   111

and you will surely understand how keen
   I was to learn from them all they could tell
   about themselves as soon as they appeared.   114

"O bliss-born soul, to whom God grants the grace
   to see the thrones of the eternal triumph
   before abandoning the war of life,   117

the light of God that shines throughout the heavens
   is lit in us, and so, if you desire
   enlightenment, ask to your heart's content."   120

So spoke one holy soul, and Beatrice
   was quick to urge me: "Speak, and have no fear,
   confide in them, as if they were all gods!"   123

"I see how you have made yourself a nest
   of your own light and how those rays of light
   pour from your eyes that dazzle when you smile,   126

but who you are, I do not know, or why,
   O worthy soul, you are assigned this sphere
   which with another's rays is veiled to man."   129

These were the words I spoke into the glow
   that had addressed me; whereupon it shone,
   this time with light far brighter than before.   132

Just as the sun, when its increasing rays
   have broken through dense vapors, hides itself
   within the very excess of its light—   135

even so, in its own glowing jubilance
   that holy figure hid itself from me,
   and so enraptured wrapt, it answered me   138

the way in which the following canto chants.

128–129. The sphere "veiled to man" is Mercury, which is so close to the sun that it is usually obscured by it and thus seldom visible from earth.

CANTO VI

THIS SOUL, IN answer to the Pilgrim's first question, identifies himself as Justinian, Emperor of the Eastern Roman Empire in the sixth century, famous for his compilation of Roman law which became known as the Justinian Code. He then states that the very nature of his answer, in which he made mention of the Roman Eagle, necessitates a digression, and begins to give the long history of the Empire in terms of its "sacred standard," so worthy of reverence. The story of the Eagle starts with the first kings of Rome and the Republic, continuing through to the age of the Empire. He concludes his historical digression with an invective against the Guelphs and the Ghibellines, accusing both parties of defiling the Eagle in different ways. Now ready to answer the Pilgrim's second question, Justinian says that in the sphere of Mercury are those souls of the Blest who were too concerned with their own fame and earthly glory which, as a result, lessened their degree of beatitude. Nonetheless, they are perfectly happy with their degree of blessedness because they know that their reward is in perfect accord with their merit. The light of Justinian speaks from beginning to end of this canto without interruption. He concludes by making reference to a certain Romeo of Villeneuve, who proves to be a figure similar to Dante the Poet in a number of ways.

"Once Constantine reversed the eagle's flight,
    against the course of Heaven which it pursued
    behind that warrior who wed Lavinia,   3

1. The Emperor Constantine (born ca. A.D. 288) ruled from 306 to 337. He was supposedly converted to Christianity in 312, but was not actually baptized until shortly before his death in 337. In 324, he moved the seat of the Roman Empire from Rome to Byzantium. The city was renamed Constantinople, and in 330 was formally dedicated as the new Christian Rome. Thus the Imperial Eagle, standard and symbol of the Empire, was moved eastward to the new capital, in a direction counter to the westward course of the sun in the heavens.

3. The warrior is Aeneas, who married Lavinia, daughter of the Latian king (see *Inferno* IV, 125–126), and in so doing founded the line of the Roman Empire. Lavinia, then, is the mother of the Roman race.

one hundred and one hundred years and more
   the bird of God remained on Europe's edge
   close to the mountains whence it first arose;   6

there, shadowed by its sacred wings, it ruled
   over the world, passing from hand to hand,
   and changing thus, alighted on my own.   9

Caesar I was, Justinian I remain
   who, by the will of the First Love I feel,
   purged all the laws of excess and of shame.   12

Before I had assumed this task I thought
   that Christ had but one nature and no more,
   and I was satisfied with this belief;   15

but blessed Agapetus, he who was
   supreme shepherd of God, directed me
   with his enlightened words to the true faith;   18

I trusted him, and what he knew by faith
   I now see clear, as clear as you can see
   all contradictions are both true and false.   21

And once I was in step with Holy Church,
   God in his grace inspired me to assume
   that task to which I gave all of myself: 24

To my Belisarius I gave my arms,
   for God's right hand so guided his, I knew
   it was a sign for me to rest from war.   27

10. Justinian, born at Illyricum in A.D. 483, was emperor of Constantinople from 527 to 565 and the renowned codifier of Roman law.

12. Soon after Justinian became emperor, he organized a commission of jurists to collect all the valid edicts of the Roman emperors since Hadrian.

25. Belisarius (ca. A.D. 505–565), a general under Justinian, was responsible for the overthrow of the Vandals in North Africa and for the conquering of the Ostrogoths. The latter victory restored Italy to the Empire and enabled Justinian to establish himself in Ravenna.

With this your first question is answered now,
    but I have answered it in such a way
    that I am forced to add on something more   30

to make it plain to you how little cause
    have those who move against the sacred standard,
    be it the ones who claim it or disdain it.   33

Behold what courage consecrated it,
    the courage which began with that first hour
    when Pallas died to give it its first realm.   36

You know that for three hundred years and more
    it stayed in Alba Longa till, at last,
    the three fought with the three to make it theirs.   39

And you know what it did through seven kings,
    from Sabine rape up to Lucretia's woe,
    as it grew conquering its neighbor's lands,   42

and you know what it did, borne by the illustrious
    Romans against Brennus, against King Pyrrhus,
    against many a prince and government.   45

36. Pallas was the son of Evander, a Greek who had established a kingdom at La-
tium, the present site of Rome. Evander and Pallas joined Aeneas in his fight against
Turnus, and in Aeneas's victory Pallas was killed.

37–39. Aeneas established the Eagle in Latium, but after his death, his son Ascanius
moved it to Alba Longa. There it remained until, during the reign of Tullus Hostilius
(670–638 B.C.), the three Curiatii of Alba fought with the three Roman Horatii to
determine which city would claim it. In the end, the city of Alba Longa was destroyed,
never to be rebuilt, and the Imperial Eagle was restored to Rome.

40–42. After being expelled from Alba, Romulus established a base on one of the
seven hills (the Palatine) and recruited a band to raid the Sabines so as to obtain
wives. From the resulting settlement, the kingdom of Rome grew through a succession
of seven kings who regularly annexed the lands of their neighbors. After this, Sextus,
son of the last king, Tarquinius Superbus, violated Lucretia, who subsequently killed
herself. The Roman people then overthrew Sextus and established the Republic in
510 B.C.

Torquatus, then, and Quintius (so named
    for his rough curls), the Decii and the Fabii,
    all, won the glory I am glad to honor.   48

It brought low all of that Arabian pride
    that followed Hannibal across the Alps
    from which you, River Po, make your descent.   51

Under the eagle triumphed in their youth
    Scipio and Pompey, and it showed its wrath
    against that hill beneath which you were born.   54

Then, when the time came that all Heaven willed
    to bring the world to its own harmony
    Caesar, at Rome's behest, laid hold of it.   57

46. Titus Manlius Torquatus was dictator twice (in 353 and 349 B.C.) and consul three times (in 347, 344, and 340 B.C.) and led numerous Roman victories. Lucius Quintius Cincinnatus (whose surname, from the Latin *cincinnus,* means "curly" or "shaggy-haired") was summoned from his farm to become dictator and lead the Roman army against the Aequians in 458 B.C.

47. The Decii were a famous Roman family whose leaders died in the service of Rome for three successive generations (father, son, and grandson, all called Publius Decius Mus). The Fabii, another prominent family, produced a number of well-known Romans, including Fabius Maximus Cunctator ("Delayer"), who was consul five times (233–209 B.C.), and famous for the strategy of delay that he employed in a losing effort against Hannibal at the battle of Lake Trasimene.

49. The "Arabian pride" was the Carthaginians, whose territory was occupied by the Arabs in Dante's time.

50. The famous Carthaginian general Hannibal (247–ca. 183 B.C.) campaigned in Spain during the Second Punic War and then crossed the Alps into Italy in 218 B.C. After four years of successful fighting there, he moved into Africa, where, in 202 B.C., he was defeated at Zama by Scipio Africanus the Elder.

53. The great Roman general Scipio Africanus the Elder (ca. 235–ca. 183 B.C.) won fame by saving his father's life in battle against Hannibal at Ticinus in 218 B.C. Scipio was at that time about seventeen years old. Pompey-Gnaeus Pompeius Magnus (206–148 B.C.) was one of Sulla's most effective generals. He was responsible for victories in the African campaign against the faction led by Marius.

54. The hill is Fiesole, which overlooks Florence.

What it did, then, from Var to Rhine, the Seine,
   Isère and Loire beheld and every vale
   whose waters flow to fill the river Rhone.   60

Then what it wrought, when from Ravenna's shore
   it soared the Rubicon, was such a flight
   no tongue can tell or pen can write about.   63

It turned to lead its armies into Spain;
   then toward Dyrrachium, and struck Pharsalia
   so fiercely that the hot Nile felt the blow.   66

Antandros and Simois, whence it first soared,
   it saw again, and Hector's grave, and then,
   again it sprang to flight—the worse for Ptolemy.   69

On Juba, next, it struck like lightning, then,
   again it turned round to attack your West
   in answer to the blast of Pompey's horn.   72

And what it did with its succeeding chief,
   Brutus and Cassius wail about in Hell;
   it made Modena and Perugia grieve.   75

For that, still weeps the tragic Cleopatra,
   who, fleeing from its conquest, finally clasped
   the black and sudden viper to her breast.   78

58–60. These lines refer to campaigns of Julius Caesar during the Gallic Wars.

67. Antandros is a coastal town near Troy, and the Simois is a nearby river. When he brought the Eagle to Latium, Aeneas sailed from Antandros. After Pompey's death Caesar visited Troy, thus occasioning a symbolic visit of the Eagle to its homeland.

68. Hector, the great Trojan hero, who was slain by Achilles, was buried at Troy after the siege.

69. Ptolemy XII was king of Egypt from 51–47 B.C.

70–72. In 46 B.C., Caesar conquered Juba, king of Numidia (in North Africa) and ally of Pompey.

73–75. After Caesar's murder, his nephew Augustus became emperor, the second bearer (the "succeeding chief") of the standard.

With him it reached the shore of the Red Sea;
  with him it ushered in a world-wide peace
  that kept the gates of Janus' temple locked.   81

But what this banner, the cause of my words,
  had done before and what it yet would do
  throughout the realm it conquered—all of this   84

appear as dim and paltry deeds, if we
  but see it with clear eyes and honest heart
  as it appears in the third Caesar's hand,   87

because the living Justice that inspires me
  granted it, in the hand of whom I speak,
  the glory of the vengeance of His wrath.   90

Now marvel at what I shall add to this:
  later, it sped with Titus to avenge
  the vengeance taken for the ancient sin;   93

Lombard fangs bit into Holy Church,
  and under those same wings came marching forth
  victorious Charlemagne to rescue her.   96

Now you can judge those men that I accused
  when speaking earlier, and judge their crimes
  which are the cause of all your present woes.   99

79–81. After Antony's death, Augustus ruled all the way to the Red Sea, and the empire was at peace. As the gates to the temple of Janus (god of beginnings, porter of heaven, and guardian of all earthly doors and gates) were open continually during wartime, they could now be closed (for only the third time in the history of the empire).

87–90. Tiberius was the third Caesar or bearer of the standard, and during his reign Christ was crucified. This marked the zenith of the Eagle's flight as an instrument of God's will, for by the Crucifixion the sin of Adam was expiated. At the same time, the death of Christ was also a sin for which Divine Justice sought vengeance.

92–93. Titus, son and successor of Vespasian, was emperor from A.D. 79 to 81. In A.D. 70, while his father was emperor, Titus destroyed Jerusalem.

94–96. Dante now moves forward seven hundred years and refers to Charlemagne's defense of the Church against King Desiderius, the Lombard, whom he dethroned in A.D. 774.

97–98. The men are the Guelphs and the Ghibellines alluded to earlier in lines 31–33.

Against the public standard one group sets
    the yellow lilies; one claims it for its
    own party flag—and who knows which is worse?   102

Let them, those Ghibellines, let them connive
    under some other sign, for those who sever
    justice from it are not true followers!   105

Let not the new Charles trust his Guelphs to tear
    the banner down! But let him fear those claws
    that ripped the hides off mightier lions than he.   108

Many a time a father's sinful deeds
    are wept for by his sons: let Charles not think
    his lilies can replace the bird of God.   111

This little star is made more beautiful
    by valiant souls whose zealous deeds on earth
    were prompted by desire for lasting fame: 114

the more desire tending toward that goal
    thus deviating from true love, the less
    intensely burn the rays that rise toward heaven.   117

To see the perfect balance we have here
    between reward and merit gives us joy:
    for we see each commensurate with each.   120

And thus, we feel the sweetness of True Justice
    so much alive in us our will cannot
    be warped and made to turn to bitterness.   123

Disparate voices blend into sweet tones;
    so, in our heavenly life, the disparate ranks
    produce sweet harmony among these spheres.   126

100–105. The Guelphs supported France, whose standard is the golden lily (fleur-de-lys), against the Eagle. The Ghibellines used the standard of the Eagle as their own sign and for their own purposes.

106. This is Charles II (1248–1309), count of Anjou and Provence, king of Naples and leader of the Guelphs, who were supporters of the Church, as opposed to the Ghibellines, who supported the empire.

Within this pearl there also radiates
    the radiance of Romeo who accomplished
    fair, noble deeds that went unrecompensed;   129

those Provençals who worked against him, though,
    will not laugh last: he who resents the good
    done by another, walks an evil road.   132

Four daughters had Count Raymond Berenger,
    each one of them a queen, thanks to Romeo,
    this man of lowly birth, this pilgrim-soul;   135

but when those envious tongues convinced his lord
    that he should call this just man to account,
    this man who had rendered him twelve for ten,   138

Romeo, proudly, old and poor, departed.
    And could the world know what was in his heart
    as he went begging, door to door, his bread—   141

though praised today, he would be praised still more."

CANTO VII

HAVING FINISHED HIS discourse, Justinian begins to sing a Latin hymn; then he and the other souls speed off into the distance like shooting sparks. Beatrice, reading the Pilgrim's mind, sees that he has a question: how can a just vengeance be justly avenged? She offers to explain. Since mankind sinned through Adam, Christ's death on the Cross was just punishment insofar as Christ's human nature is concerned; as far as His Divinity is concerned, the punishment was sacrilegious and unjust. Beatrice sees that her ward has another unexpressed question: why did God choose this particular way to redeem mankind? Because it was the most worthy way, Beatrice says, and explains why: there were two ways in which God could accomplish man's redemption—by means of His

128. This is thought to be Romeo di Villeneuve (1170–1250), a minister of Raymond Berenger IV, the last of the counts of Provence.

Mercy or by means of His Justice. God decided to employ both means,
showing His Mercy by taking on the flesh and His Justice by His suf-
fering and death on the Cross. Beatrice then formulates an objection
the Pilgrim might have: how can the primary elements created directly
by God be corruptible? This would seem to contradict something she
had said earlier. She explains that God created only the material, but
that the form given to that material is determined by secondary causes,
and it is for this reason that they are perishable. Both the human soul
and the human body were created directly by God; the fact that the
soul is immortal necessitates the resurrection of the body following the
Last Judgment.

"Hosanna, sanctus Deus sabaoth
    superillustrans claritate tua
    felices ignes horum malacoth"   3

—singing these words, I saw him start to whirl
    to his own melody, this soul by twin
    lights fused, en-two-ed into one aureole,   6

and all the others joined him in the dance,
    and then like shooting sparks they instantly
    went disappearing into sudden space.   9

I stood there hesitant: "Speak, speak to her!"
    I told myself: "Speak to your lovely lady
    who slakes your thirst with her sweet drops of truth."   12

But the great awe that dominates my being,
    even at the mention of just *BE* or *ICE,*
    made me lower my head, like someone dozing.   15

Not long did Beatrice let me suffer
    before announcing with a glowing smile
    that would rejoice a man condemned to burn: 18

"My intuition which is never wrong
    informs me that you do not understand
    how just vengeance can justly be avenged;   21

1–3. "Hosanna, holy God of hosts, who illumines with your brightness the blessed
fires of these realms."

but I can quickly free your mind from doubt.
   Now listen well, for what I have to say
   contains the doctrine of important truths. 24

Because for his own good, he would not let
   his will be curbed, the man who knew no birth,
   damning himself, damned all his progeny; 27

therefore, the human race lay sick below
   within their error for long centuries,
   until the Word of God chose to descend: 30

there, moved by His unselfish Love alone,
   He took unto Himself, in His Own Being,
   that nature which had wandered from its maker. 33

Now listen to my reasoning: once joined
   with its First Cause, this nature was (as it
   had been when first created) pure and good; 36

but by itself alone, by its own act,
   having abandoned truth and the true life,
   out of God's holy garden it was chased. 39

Then, if the Crucifixion can be judged
   as punishment of that nature assumed,
   no penalty could bite with greater justice, 42

just as none could be judged as more unjust,
   considering the Person who endured it
   with whom that other nature was combined. 45

Thus, one event produced different effects:
   God and the Jews both pleased by this one death
   for which earth shook and Heaven opened wide. 48

Now it should not be difficult for you
   to understand the concept of just vengeance
   being avenged in time by just decree. 51

26. The man is Adam, who was created by God directly.

50–51. Even though they actually carried out God's will in crucifying Christ, the Jews sinned, for their motives were evil. The "just decree" of Titus resulted in revenge on the Jews for their sin, through the destruction of Jerusalem.

But now I see your mind is all entangled
    with one thought and another, and you wait
    with eagerness for me to loose the knot.   54

You say: 'I clearly understand your words,
    but why God did not choose some other way
    for our redemption still remains unclear.'   57

The reason, brother, for that choice lies buried
    from all men's eyes until their inner sight
    has grown to ripeness in the warmth of love;   60

nevertheless, since men have always aimed
    their arrows at this mark they rarely strike,
    I shall explain why this choice was the best.   63

Divine Goodness, which from Itself rejects
    all envy, sparkles so, that It reveals
    the eternal beauties burning in Itself.   66

That which derives directly from His Being
    from then on is eternal, for His seal,
    once it is stamped, can never be effaced.   69

That which derives directly from His Being
    is wholly free, not subject to the law
    of secondary things. Created thus,   72

it most resembles Him, most pleases Him;
    the Sacred Flame which lights all of creation
    burns brightest in what is most like Himself.   75

These are the gifts with which humanity
    was privileged; and if it fails in one
    of these, it must fall from its noble state.   78

Sin is the only power that takes away
    man's freedom and his likeness to True Good,
    and makes him shine less brightly in Its light;   81

75. The love of God shines in all things, but it shines the most in what is most like Himself: i.e., men and angels.

76–84. These "gifts" given to the human soul are immortality and freedom of the will, both of which bring man closer to the likeness of God. Sin deprives the soul of its gifts, and only through individual virtue and God's grace can the soul be redeemed.

nor can he win back his lost dignity
    unless the void left by that sin be filled
    by just amends paid for illicit joy.   84

Your nature, when it sinned once and for all
    in its first root, was exiled from these honors,
    as it was dispossessed of Paradise;   87

nor could mankind recover what was lost,
    as you will see if you think carefully,
    except by crossing one of these two fords: 90

either that God, simply through clemency,
    should give remission, or that man himself,
    to pay his debt of folly, should atone.   93

Now fix your eyes on the infinity
    of the Eternal Counsel; listen well,
    as well as you are able, to my words.   96

Given his limits, man could never make
    amends: never in his humility
    could man, obedient too late, descend   99

as far as once, in disobedience,
    he tried to climb, and this is why mankind
    alone could not make his amends to God.   102

Thus, it remained for God, in His own ways
    (his ways, I mean, in one of them or both),
    to bring man back to his integrity: 105

But since the deed gratifies more the doer,
    the more it manifests the innate goodness
    of the good heart from which it springs—so, then,   108

that Everlasting Goodness which has set
    its imprint on the world was pleased to use
    all of Its means to raise you up once more.   111

Between the final night and the first day
   no act so lofty, so magnificent
   was there, or shall there be, by either way,   114

for God, Who gave Himself, gave even more
   so that mankind might raise itself again,
   than if He simply had annulled the debt;   117

and any other means would have been less
   than Justice, if God's only Son had not
   humbled Himself to take on mortal flesh.   120

But now, to satisfy all your desires
   I go back to explain a certain point
   so that you may perceive it as I do.   123

You think: 'I see that fire, I see that air,
   that water, earth, and all which they compose
   last but a little while, and then decay;   126

and yet all of these are of God's creation,
   and so if what you said before is true,
   should they not be secure against decay?   129

The angels, brother, and all this pure space
   around us, were created—all agree—
   just as they are, unchanging and entire;   132

the elements, however, that you named
   and all those things produced from them are given
   their form by powers that are themselves created.   135

Created was the matter they contain,
   created, too, was the informing power
   within the constellations circling them.   138

The soul of every animal and plant
   is drawn from a potentiated complex
   by the stars' rays and by their sacred motion,   141

but the Supreme Beneficence breathes forth
   your life directly, filling it with love
   for Him Whom it desires evermore.   144

From what I have just said you may infer
   your resurrection, if you will recall
     how human flesh first came into its being,   147

when our first parents came into the world."

CANTO VIII

THE CANTO OPENS with an explanation for the origin of the name of the planet Venus. Without realizing it, the Pilgrim has been ascending with his guide to the sphere of Venus, and he knows that he has arrived there only because he sees that Beatrice has grown more beautiful. Joyful lights appear to welcome the traveller. The soul who addresses the Pilgrim is Charles Martel of the renowned Anjou family, though he never mentions himself by name. What interests the Pilgrim who listens to Martel's account of the line of rulers in Naples is the doctrine of heredity implied therein. It is not clear to the Pilgrim how good seed can produce bad. Martel explains that it is not a matter of heredity or lineage but rather the workings of Nature through the influence of the stars upon each individual, influencing the formation of his own character without taking into consideration the ancestors of that particular individual. Martel concludes by telling the Pilgrim that the reason many men have gone astray is that they have not been encouraged to follow their inherent character or nature.

The world once dangerously believed the lovely
   Cyprian, whirling in third epicycle,
     rayed down her frenzied beams of love on man,   3

1–2. The Cyprian is the goddess Venus, believed to have risen from the sea off Cyprus.

2. According to Ptolemaic astronomy, the planets possessed three kinds of motion: that of their diurnal cycles, that of their periodic orbits, and that of the turns of their epicycles. It was thought that each planet had a small sphere attached to it, at some point on this circumference, that "carried" the planet. This small sphere was the planet's epicycle.

so that the ancients in their ancient error
   offered their sacrifice and votive cries
   to honor her and not just her alone: 6

Dione too they honored, as her mother,
   and Cupid as her son who they believed
   had nestled once in Dido's loving lap.   9

And from that goddess who begins my canto
   they took the name and gave it to the star
   which woos the sun at both its nape and brow.   12

I was not conscious of ascending there,
   but that I was within the sphere, I knew,
   for now my lady was more beautiful.   15

Even as sparks are visible in fire,
   and as within a voice a voice is heard,
   one note sustained, while others rise and fall,   18

so I saw lights revolving in that light,
   their movements slow or swift, each, I suppose,
   according to how clearly it sees God.   21

From chilly clouds no seen or unseen winds
   ever shot down to earth with such rapidity
   as not to seem slow-motioned, cumbersome,   24

to any one who saw those holy lights
   approaching us, abandoning the dance
   begun among the lofty Seraphim;   27

and from the foremost ranks of light I heard
   "Hosanna" sung in tones so marvelous,
   my soul still yearns to hear that sound again.   30

7. Dione was the daughter of Oceanus and Tethys and mother of Venus by Jupiter.
Venus herself is sometimes referred to as Dionaea or even Dione.

8. Cupid was the son of Venus. Like Dione and Venus he was worshipped as a god
of love.

12–22. This is a reference to the motion of the planet Venus with relation to the sun.
The physical references to "nape" and "brow" are suggestive of the carnal love that
Venus was thought to inspire.

Then one came closer and announced to us:
   "We all are ready here to do your pleasure;
   we want you to have fullest joy of us. 33

We circle in one orbit, with one rhythm,
   in one desire with those heavenly Princes
   whom once you called upon from down on earth: 36

'*O you whose intellect spins Heaven's third sphere,*'
   We are so full of love that, if you wish,
   we happily will stop awhile for you." 39

I raised my eyes with reverence to meet
   my lady's light, who with her eyes bestowed
   on me all her assurance and her joy; 42

then to that light who had so generously
   offered himself, I turned again: "Who are you?"
   I said, my voice vibrant with tenderness. 45

How that light glowed and grew more beautiful
   from those few words of mine as it took on
   new happiness upon its happiness! 48

Radiant, it spoke: "The time I spent on earth
   was very brief; if my life had been longer,
   much evil that will be would not have been. 51

My happiness which wraps me in its glow
   conceals me from you: I am swathed in bliss
   just like the worm that spins itself in silk. 54

You loved me greatly once, you had good cause;
   had I not died so soon, you would have seen
   more than the first leaves of my love for you. 57

31. The soul who speaks to the Pilgrim in these lines never identifies himself by name, but we know from what he says that he is Charles Martel (1271–1295), first son of Charles II of Anjou and Mary, daughter of the king of Hungary. Charles Martel married Clemence of Hapsburg in 1291 and had three children before he died of cholera at the young age of twenty-four. Dante probably met Charles the year before he died (1294) while he was on a visit to Florence, where he was warmly received.

37. This is the first verse of one of Dante's famous *canzoni* which is the subject of a commentary in the second book of his *Convivio*.

The left bank, washed by waters of the Rhone
    when this has mingled with the River Sorgue,
    was waiting for me to become its lord;   60

as did the region of Ausonia's horn,
    bound by Catona, Bari, and Gaeta
    whence Tronto and the Verde turn to sea.   63

Already was reflected on my brow
    the bright crown of the land the Danube bathes
    once it has left behind the German shores.   66

And on the gulf most plagued by the Sirocco
    lying between Pachymus and Pelorus
    darkened by sulphur fumes, not by what some   69

believe to be the monster Typhoeus,
    beautiful Sicily would still have looked
    to have its kings through me from Charles and Rudolph,   72

if evil rule, which always alienates
    those subject to it, had not moved Palermo
    to cry out in its streets, 'Death, death to them!'   75

58–60. The land indicated here is Provence, whose west boundary was marked by the Sorgue and Rhone rivers.

61–63. Ausonia is the name the Latin poets used for Italy. These lines refer to the kingdom of Naples and Apulia to which Charles Martel was also heir.

65. This land is Hungary, of which Charles Martel became king in 1290.

67–69. This is the gulf of Catania in Sicily, where the prevailing wind is the stormy southeast Sirocco. Pachymus (now called Cape Passero) is the promontory at the southeastern tip of Sicily, and Pelorus (now called Cape Faro) is the promontory at the extreme northeast.

70. Typhoeus, or Typhon, a hundred-headed giant who attempted to rule gods and men, was conquered by Jupiter and buried under Mount Aetna. According to Ovid (*Metamorphoses* V, 346–56), the volcanic eruptions of this mountain were caused by Typhoeus's attempts to free himself.

72. Charles is Charles I of Anjou, grandfather of Charles Martel. Rudolph is Rudolph of Hapsburg, father of Clemence, Charles Martel's wife.

73–75. Charles Martel refers here to the rebellion against French tyranny known as the Sicilian Vespers, which took place on March 30, 1282. The French were killed by the Sicilians, and the crown of Sicily was passed from the house of Anjou (to which Charles Martel belonged) to the house of Aragon.

And could my brother have foreseen the facts,
   he would shun all the greedy poverty
   of Catalans before he is disgraced;   78

for clearly some provision must be made
   by him or someone else, lest on his ship,
   already weighted down, more weight be laid.   81

His stingy nature, that derived from one
   more generous, would have required men
   who cared for more than filling chests with gold."   84

"Oh Sire, I know that the deep joy your words
   have given me is clear to you, as clear
   as to myself, there where all good begins   87

and ends—so this deep joy is dearer still,
   and still more precious to me is the fact
   that you discern it as you look in God.   90

You made me happy, now make me as wise;
   your words have raised a question in my mind:
   how can sweet seed produce such sour fruit?"   93

I said. And then he said, "If I can make
   just one truth plain to you, then you will see
   what is behind your back in front of you.   96

The Good that moves and satisfies the realm
   that you now climb, endows these mighty orbs
   with all the power of His own providence;   99

and in that One Mind perfect in Itself
   there is foreseen not only every type
   of nature but the proper goal for each,   102

and thus, when this bow bends, the arrow shot
   speeds ready to a predetermined end:
   a shaft expertly aimed to strike its mark.   105

Were it not so, the heavens you climb through
   would fashion their effects in such a way
   that chaos would result, not works of art;   108

this cannot be, unless the Intellects
    that move these stars are flawed, and also flawed
    the First One Who created them with flaws.   111

Would you like me to make this truth more clear?"
    And I: "Oh no, there is no need—I see
    that Nature cannot fail in what must be."   114

And he, once more: "Tell me, would it be worse
    for man on earth were there no social order?"
    "Of course," I said, "and here I seek no proof."   117

"And can this be, unless men had on earth
    different natures, serving different ends?
    Not so, if what your master writes is true."   120

By reasoning step by step he reached this point
    and then concluded: "So, the very roots
    of man's activities must be diverse: 123

one man is born a Solon, one a Xerxes,
    one a Melchizedek, another he
    whose flight cost him the life of his own son.   126

For Nature in its circling stamps its seal
    on mortal wax, perfecting her fine art,
    with no concern about man's lineage.   129

So Esau, once conceived, differed from Jacob;
    and Romulus sprang from so base a sire,
    that men imagined him the son of Mars.   132

120. Aristotle, as referred to by Dante in the *Inferno* (IV, 131), is "the master sage of those who know."

122–123. The roots are the different dispositions or tendencies inspired by the heavens.

124–125. One man is born to be a lawgiver, another a general, and still another a priest.

126. This refers to Daedalus, the mythical artificer whose son, Icarus, plunged into the sea after flying too near the sun with wax wings fashioned by his father.

130–132. Though Jacob and Esau were twins (and therefore presumably similar in every way), they were different in character, even in the womb. Because Romulus (or Quirinus) was so great a man, his peers refused to believe that he was of lowly birth and therefore believed his father to be Mars.

The procreated being would always walk
   the procreator's path, if it were not
   for Holy Providence that overrules.   135

Now, you can see what was behind your back.
   The great joy you give me urges me now
   to wrap you in this corollary-gift: 138

Should natural disposition find itself
   not in accord with Fortune, then it must
   fail as a seed in alien soil must die.   141

If men on earth were to pay greater heed
   to the foundation Nature has laid down,
   and build on that, they would build better men.   144

But those men bent to wear the sword you twist
   into the priesthood, and you make a king
   out of a man whose calling was to preach: 147

you find yourselves on roads not meant for you."

CANTO IX

CHARLES MARTEL HAS *made some tragic predictions about his own suc-
cessors to the Pilgrim, but Dante, in an address to Martel's wife, Clem-
ence, tells her that Charles forbade him to reveal them to anyone. The
light of Martel has disappeared by this time and another soul appears
and reveals herself to be Cunizza da Romano, sister of the infamous
tyrant Ezzelino. Cunizza, after pointing out the light of another soul
nearby (without naming him) and remarking on the good reputation he
left behind on earth, goes on to make a prediction concerning the in-
habitants of the Marches and confirms the truth of her words with her
very vision of God. Cunizza returns to her heavenly dance, and the soul
whom she had pointed out earlier now addresses the Pilgrim, telling
him how he was influenced by the sphere of Venus. He is the light of
Folquet of Marseilles, who, after repenting for his worldly loves, entered
a religious order and later became Bishop of Toulouse. Folquet, reading*

the Pilgrim's mind and seeing that he wishes to know the identity of a
certain soul nearby, tells him that it is Rahab, the Whore of Jericho,
and he explains why she is with them in Venus. Folquet makes some
bitter remarks about the Pilgrim's city and the Church in general and
closes the canto by predicting that Divine Providence will eventually
liberate the Church from its adulterous state.

Fair Clemence, once your Charles had said these words
 for my enlightenment, he then informed me
 of future plots against his progeny,   3

but said, "Say nothing, let the years go by,"
 and for this reason I can only say
 that those who do you wrong will pay with tears.   6

By now the life within that holy light
 was turned to face once more the sun that fills it,
 as to the Good sufficient for all things.   9

Ah, souls deceived, devoid of piety,
 who turn your hearts away from the True Good,
 raising your haughty heads toward empty things!   12

And then! Another of those radiant lights
 drew near to me; its eagerness to please
 was shining through the splendor of its glow.   15

The eyes of Beatrice fixed on me
 now gave me full assurance, as before,
 that my desire met with her consent.   18

"O blessèd soul," I said, "grant me at once
 fulfillment of my wish, and prove to me
 that you can be a mirror for my thoughts."   21

1. Dante seems to be addressing Clemence of Hapsburg, widow of Charles Martel,
not in fact, but in memory, in a kind of apostrophe.

19. Here Dante addresses the soul that has approached him. It is that of Cunizza da
Romano (ca. 1198–1279), sister of the tyrant Ezzelino III da Romano. Cunizza had
during her life four husbands and two lovers.

Whereat the light of that still unknown soul,
   out of its depths from which it sang, now answered,
   like one whose joy is giving joyously: 24

"There in that part of sinful Italy
   which lies between Rialto's shores and where
   the Piave and the Brenta rivers spring, 27

rises a hill of no great height from which,
   some years ago, there plunged a flaming torch,
   who laid waste all the countryside around. 30

Both he and I were born from the same root:
   Cunizza was my name, and I shine here
   for I was overcome by this star's light; 33

but gladly I myself forgive in me
   what caused my fate, it grieves me not at all—
   which might seem strange, indeed, to earthly minds. 36

This precious and resplendent jewel that shines
   here, closest to me, in our heaven has left
   behind great fame, fame that will live as long 39

as this centennial year shall be five-timed—
   you see how man should strive for excellence
   so that a second life survive the first! 42

And this means nothing to that crowd that lives
   between the Tagliamento and the Adige,
   nor does the scourge of war make them repent. 45

But it will come to pass that Paduan blood,
   and soon, will stain the waters of Vincenza
   because the people shunned their duty there; 48

29. The "flaming torch" (an allusion to the belief that his mother before giving birth to him dreamed she gave birth to a torch or firebrand) is Ezzelino III da Romano (1194–1259), brother of Cunizza. He was placed by Dante with the tyrants in the first round of Circle Seven of the Inferno, in the river of boiling blood (*Inferno* XII, 110). As ruler of the March of Treviso, Ezzelino was exceedingly bloodthirsty, and was rumored to have committed all manner of atrocities.

and where Cagnano and the Sile join
   a man lords over it with lofty head
   for whom the nets already have been spread;   51

Feltre shall mourn her godless shepherd's crime,
   and no man yet was ever sent to Malta
   for treachery as foul as his shall be.   54

Immense, indeed, would have to be the vat
   to hold Ferrara's blood, and weary the man
   who would weigh ounce by ounce that bloody flood,   57

blood that this generous priest will sacrifice,
   to prove his party loyalty—but then,
   such gifts become that country's way of life!   60

Above us there are mirrors you call 'Thrones'
   through which God shines his judgments down on us—
   this justifies the harshness of our words."   63

Then she was silent, and it seemed her thoughts
   were drawn to something else, for she had joined
   the dancing wheel where she had been before.   66

That other joy which she had just described
   as something precious, now appeared to me
   like an exquisite ruby struck by sun.   69

Up there joy gives those souls a brighter light,
   as here it makes us smile, while down below
   souls darken to reveal their sullen minds.   72

49. The Sile and Cagnano rivers join at Treviso.

50–51. The reference is to Riccardo da Cammino, a son of the "good Gherardo" (*Purgatory* XVI, 124), who took his father's place as lord of Treviso and ruled like a tyrant.

53–54. For the ancient commentators, Malta was the clerical prison of Lake Bolsena.

59. The bishop was of the Guelph party.

60. The "gifts" refers to the "blood" (58) that the bishop was so happy to donate for his party's cause (59).

61–63. Cunizza is referring to the angels that move and direct the seventh heaven or the sphere of Saturn.

"God can see all, and your sight sees in Him,"
    I said, "O holy spirit, so no thought
    of mine can hide itself from your true sight.   75

Your voice, then, which eternally charms Heaven,
    in harmony with those adoring flames
    that make themselves a cowl of their six wings,   78

why does it leave my longing unfulfilled?
    I would not wait for you to ask of me
    were I to inyou as you now inme."   81

"The greatest valley into which there flows,"
    with these words he began to answer me,
    "the water of that world-encircling sea   84

runs on so far between opposing shores
    against the sun, that finally it makes
    meridian where it first made horizon.   87

I dwelt upon that valley's shores between
    the Ebro and the Magra whose short course
    divides the Tuscans from the Genoese.   90

Almost the same sunset and dawn are shared
    by Bougie and the city I came from,
    which with its own blood warmed its harbor once.   93

77–78. The flames are the Seraphim, ministers of Divine Love. In Isaiah (6:2) these
angels are said to have six wings.

81. Dante constructed the reflexive verbs "in you" and "in me" in order to convey
the notion of interpenetration of minds. He is saying that if he were capable of
knowing the question to be directed to him, as the soul is, he would answer it without
delay.

91–93. Marseilles and Bougie, on the coast of Africa, have longitudinal proximity.
In 49 B.C., during the Civil War, Caesar conquered Marseilles after a bloody victory
at sea against Pompey's supporters.

To those who knew it Folquet was my name;
    this sphere of heaven bears my imprint now
    as from my day of birth I bore its own.   96

Dido, Belus' child, did not burn more,
    wronging Sichaeus and Creusa, too,
    than I burned loving till my hair turned grey;   99

nor she of Rhodope who was betrayed
    by her Demophoön, nor Hercules
    when he enclosed Iole in his heart.   102

But we do not repent, we smile instead:
    not at the sin—this does not come to mind—
    but at the Power that orders and provides.   105

From here we gaze upon that art which works
    with such effective love; we see the Good
    by which the world below returns above.   108

But now that I may fully satisfy
    all of your wishes born within this sphere,
    let me proceed. It is your wish to know   111

who this one is within the luminance
    you see in all its splendor next to me
    like crystal water struck by rays of light.   114

94. Folquet of Marseilles (born ca. 1160) was a troubadour and poet. The son of a rich merchant of Genoa, Folquet devoted much of his life to pleasure and was well known for his amorous affairs. Later, however, he became a Cistercian monk and rose to become abbot of Torronet in 1201 and bishop of Toulouse in 1205. He died in 1231.

100–102. Rhodope is a mountain in Thrace. Phyllis, daughter of King Sithon of Thrace, was to marry Demophoön. When he did not appear on the wedding day, she hanged herself and was changed into an almond tree. Hercules loved Iole, daughter of Eurytus, king of Thessalian Oechalia, and abducted her after killing her father. His wife, Deianira, in order to recover his love, sent Hercules a shirt bathed in the blood of the centaur Nessus, believing that blood to carry a love potion. The centaur had tricked her, however, and Hercules was poisoned. In despair and grief, she killed herself.

Know, then, that there within Rahab has peace,
 and once joined with our order, she impressed
 her seal upon it at the highest rank.   117

To this sphere where the shadow of your earth
 comes to an end, she was the first to rise
 among the souls redeemed in Christ's great triumph.   120

It was most fitting that she be received
 and left in one of our spheres as a palm
 of that great victory won by those two palms,   123

for it was Rahab who made possible
 Joshua's first glory in the Holy Land—
 which seems to matter little to the Pope.   126

Your city—which was planted by the one,
 the first to turn against his Maker's power,
 and whose fierce envy brought the world such woe—   129

creates and circulates the wicked flower
 that turns the shepherds into ravening wolves
 and breaks the fold and lets the lambs run wild.   132

---

115. This is Rahab, the Whore of Jericho. When Joshua sent spies to scout that city prior to battle, Rahab hid them from the king's men, and aided their escape. Because she thus helped the people of Israel to regain the promised land, her soul rose from Limbo to Heaven immediately after the Crucifixion.

118–119. According to Ptolomy and Alfraganus, the Arabic astrologer, the shadow of the earth extended in a kind of cone shape with its point reaching no farther than the sphere of Venus. Metaphorically, these verses suggest that Venus is the last of the spheres containing souls that once were marked by an excess of earthly inclination.

120. Christ's "great triumph" was the harrowing of Hell.

122–123. The "palm" is the symbol of victory over Hell by means of the crucifixion. The "two palms" are those of Christ which were willingly extended and nailed to the Cross for the redemption of mankind.

127–129. Lucifer, the first to fall away from God, envied the happiness of Adam and Eve and made them sin, the result of which was Original Sin and the world's grief.

The Gospel and the fathers of the Church
  lie gathering dust, and Canon Law alone
  is studied, as the margins testify.   135

The Pope and Cardinals heed nothing else;
  their thoughts do not go out to Nazareth
  where Gabriel once opened wide his wings.   138

But Vatican and every sacred place
  in Rome which marked the burial-ground of saints
  who fought in Peter's army to the death,   141

shall soon be free of this adultery."

CANTO X

PRAISING THE CREATED order *which reflects its Creator, Dante the Poet
marvels at the exactitude of the structure and workings of the universe.
The Pilgrim, unaware of rising there, discovers himself in the sphere of
the sun, surrounded by spirits of such brilliance that their lights are
distinct from the light of the sun. Dancing and singing in their joy, the
spirits form a circle, making Dante and his guide their center, but they
soon pause in their movement to provide an answer to Dante's evident,
though unexpressed, desire to have the souls identified. Thomas Aquinas
steps forward to introduce his fellow spirits, all known for their wisdom
and learning. The spirits then resume their song and motion, singing
and turning with such harmony that they resemble the workings of a
clock which calls the faithful to prayer.*

Looking upon His Son with all that love
  which each of them breathes forth eternally,
  that uncreated, ineffable first One,   3

134-135. The books of Canon Law (the decretals) are the papal decrees or epistles,
usually composed in reply to a question of ecclesiastical law, and forming the foun-
dation of a large part of general Church law.

137-138. It was at Nazareth in the Holy Land that the Annunciation took place and
the angel Gabriel "opened wide his wings" in homage to Mary.

has fashioned all that moves in mind and space
    in such sublime proportions that no one
    can see it and not feel His Presence there.   6

Look up now, Reader, with me to the spheres;
    look straight to that point of the lofty wheels
    where the one motion and the other cross,   9

and there begin to revel in the work
    of that great Artist who so loves His art,
    His gaze is fixed on it perpetually.   12

Consider how the wheel the planets ride
    branches from there obliquely; this it does
    to satisfy the earth that calls on them;   15

for if their track had not been set aslant,
    then the great powers of Heaven would be vain
    and Earth's potentialities stillborn;   18

and if its deviation from the straight
    were greater than it is, or less, disorder
    would come about in both our hemispheres.   21

Now, Reader, do not leave the table yet,
    reflect upon what you have only tasted,
    if you would dine on joy before you tire.   24

I put the food out; now you feed yourself,
    because the theme which makes of me its scribe
    demands all of my concentration now.   27

The most sublime of Nature's ministers,
    which stamps the plan of Heaven on the world
    and with its light measures the time for us,   30

now being in conjunction with that place
    I pointed out, was wheeling through the spirals
    in which we see it earlier each day;   33

---

28. The "most sublime" is the sun. As the symbol of intellectual power and illumination, it represents the Creator Himself.

and I was in the sun, no more aware
  of my ascent than one can be aware
  of how a thought will come before it comes.   36

She it is, Beatrice, guides our climb
  from good to better instantaneously—
  her action has no measurement in time.   39

How brilliant in its essence must have been
  what shone within the sun, where I had come,
  not with its color but with light on light!   42

Even if I called on genius, art, and skill,
  I could not make this live before your eyes—
  a man must trust and long to see it there.   45

If our imagination cannot rise
  to such a height, no need to be surprised.
  No eye has known light brighter than the sun's;   48

So, there within, shone God's fourth family
  whom the High Father keeps in constant bliss
  showing them how He breathes, how He begets.   51

Then Beatrice said: "And now give thanks,
  thanks to the Sun of Angels by whose grace
  you have ascended to this sun of sense."   54

No mortal heart was ever more disposed
  to do devotion and to yield itself
  to God so fully and so readily   57

than mine was at her words. So totally
  did I direct all of my love to Him,
  that Beatrice, eclipsed, had left my mind.   60

But this did not displease her, and she smiled
  so that the splendor of her laughing eyes
  broke my mind's spell. Again I was aware   63

49–51. These souls found in the fourth sphere of the heavens are those who were
endowed with great wisdom: the theologians and philosophers and other great and
wise thinkers.

of many things: flashes of living light
    made us a center and themselves a crown—
    their voices sweeter than their aspect bright: 66

the way Latona's daughter sometimes seems,
    girt by her halo when the pregnant air
    catches the threads of moonlight in her belt.   69

In heaven's court from where I have returned
    there are some jewels too precious and too rich
    to be brought back to Earth from out that realm,   72

and one such gem—the song those splendors sang:
    who does not grow the wings to fly up there,
    awaits these tidings from the tongueless here.   75

When singing, circling, all those blazing suns
    had wheeled around the two of us three times
    like stars that circle close to the fixed poles,   78

they stopped like ladies still in dancing mood,
    who pause in silence listening to catch
    the rhythm of the new notes of the dance.   81

Then from within its light a voice spoke: "Since
    the ray of grace by which true love is kindled
    and then grows lovingly the more it loves,   84

shines forth in you so greatly magnified
    that it allows you to ascend these stairs
    which none descends except to mount again—   87

one could no more deny your thirsty soul
    wine from his flask than could a moving stream
    refuse to keep on flowing to the sea.   90

It is your wish to know what kinds of flowers
    make up this crown which lovingly surrounds
    the lovely lady who strengthens you for Heaven.   93

67–69. Latona's daughter is Diana or the moon. The circle of light, made up of the souls of the wise, within which Dante and Beatrice are girdled is compared here to a vaporous "halo" around the moon.

83. This *"true Love"* is the love of God.

I was one of the sacred flock of lambs
   led by Saint Dominic along the road
   where all may fatten if they do not stray.   96

This spirit close by, at my right, was brother
   and master to me: Albert of Cologne
   he was, and I am Thomas of Aquino.   99

If you would like to learn about the rest,
   let your eyes follow where my words shall lead
   all the way round this blessèd wreath of souls.   102

The next flame is the light of Gratian's smile,
   who served so well in the two courts of law
   that Heaven finds great joy in having him.   105

The next one who illuminates our choir
   was that same Peter who, like the poor widow,
   offered his modest treasure to the Church.   108

The fifth light, the most beautiful of all,
   breathes from a love so passionate that men
   still hunger down on earth to know his fate;   111

94. The speaker here is Thomas Aquinas (1225?–1274), referred to in his time as the Angelic Doctor, the most famous of Catholic theologians, although he does not identify himself until line 99. Born of a noble family (his father was the Count of Aquino), he was educated by the Benedictines; he then entered the Dominican order and studied under Albertus Magnus in Cologne.

98. Albert of Cologne was Albertus Magnus (1193?–1280), also from a noble family, a fellow Dominican and teacher of Thomas Aquinas. He studied philosophy at Paris, Padua, and Bologna and was known as the Universal Doctor because of his vast learning.

103–105. Gratian, a Benedictine monk, was born around the end of the eleventh century at Chiusi in Tuscany and was the originator of the science of canon law.

106–108. Peter Lombard, born in Novara (ca. 1100–ca. 1160)—known as the "Master of the Sentences" from the title of his *Sententiarum libri quatuor*—studied at Bologna and Paris, where he held a chair in theology.

109–114. Solomon, son of David and King of Israel, appears here as the only Old Testament figure, and he is honored as the "most beautiful," apparently for his superior wisdom and the fact that he is the author of the Canticle of Canticles which came to be interpreted as the mystical marriage of Christ and the Church. Besides being credited as the author of *Proverbs* and the *Book of Wisdom*, Solomon was singled out by God to receive a unique gift of wisdom.

his flame contains that lofty mind instilled
   with wisdom so profound—if truth speak truth—
   there never arose a second with such vision. 114

Look at the burning candle next to him
   who, in the flesh, on earth saw to the depths
   of what an angel is and what it does. 117

And next, inside this tiny light, there smiles
   the great defender of the Christian Age
   whose words in Latin Augustine employed. 120

If your mind's eye has moved from light to light
   behind my words of praise, you must be eager
   to know what spirit shines in the eighth flame. 123

Wrapped in the vision of all good, rejoices
   the sainted soul who makes most manifest
   the world's deceit to one who reads him well. 126

The body that was torn from him below
   Cieldauro now possesses; to this peace
   he came from exile and from martyrdom. 129

115–117. The burning candle is the soul of Dionysius the Areopagite, the Athenian who was converted by St. Paul (Acts 17:34). He was credited in Dante's day with having written *The Celestial Hierarchy*, a treatise explaining the angelic orders, their nature and function.

118–120. The majority of the commentators believe this to be Paulus Orosius, a fifth-century Spanish priest and disciple of Augustine whose *Seven Books of History against the Pagans* was intended to prove through historical evidence that, contrary to pagan belief, the world had not deteriorated since the adoption of Christianity.

120. Augustine made use of Orosius's Latin treatise *Historiarum libri*, which was written at the suggestion of the saint, as a means of historical confirmation for his own *City of God*.

125–129. This is the soul of Boethius (born in Rome ca. 480 and died at Pavia in 524), a Roman patrician, statesman, and philosopher, and author of the celebrated *Consolation of Philosophy*, which he wrote while in prison in Pavia. In 510 he became the consul of Theodoric the Ostrogoth, but was later imprisoned by him on false charges of treason and magic, and was finally executed.

128. Cieldauro refers to the Church of St. Peter in Ciel d'Oro in Pavia, where Boethius was buried.

See those next flames: they are the fervent breath
    of Isidore, of Bede, and of that Richard
    whose contemplations made him more than man.   132

This light from which your eyes return to me
    shines from a soul once given to grave thoughts,
    who mourned that death should be so slow to come: 135

this is the endless radiance of Siger,
    who lectured on the Street of Straw, exposing
    invidiously logical beliefs."   138

Then, as the tower-clock calls us to come
    at the hour when God's Bride is roused from bed
    to woo with matin song her Bridegroom's love,   141

with one part pulling thrusting in the other,
    chiming, *ting-ting,* music so sweet the soul,
    ready for love, swells with anticipation;   144

so I was witness to that glorious wheel
    moving and playing voice on voice in concord
    with sweetness, harmony unknown, save there   147

where joy becomes one with eternity.

131. The Spaniard St. Isidore of Seville (ca. 570–636), one of the most influential writers of the early Middle Ages, was a distinguished ecclesiastic and the author of an important and much-used encyclopedia of scientific knowledge of the time (*Etymologiarum Libri XX* or *Origines*). He was made archbishop of Seville in 600.
    The Venerable Bede (ca. 673–735), an English monk known as the father of English history, was the author of the five-volume *Ecclesiastical History of the English Nation.* He also wrote hagiography, homilies, hymns, works on grammar and chronology, and commentaries on the Old and New Testaments.

131–132. This is Richard of St. Victor, who was thought to have been born in Scotland (d. 1173). He was known as the Great Contemplator after his treatise *De Contemplatione.* He was a celebrated twelfth-century mystic, theologian, and scholastic philosopher who studied at the University of Paris and then became a canon-regular at the Augustinian monastery at St. Victor.

136–138. This is the soul of Siger of Brabant (1226?–1284?), a distinguished Averroist philosopher who taught at the University of Paris, which was located in the Rue de Fouarre or "Street of Straw." His belief that the world had existed from eternity and doubt in the immortality of the soul involved him in a lengthy dispute with his colleague Thomas Aquinas and eventually led to charges of heresy.

CANTO XI

Dante's position in the sun, among the Wise who sought Heaven's truth, gives him the opportunity to admonish mortals who seek earthly satisfaction, while he, in Paradise, stands effortlessly with Beatrice, having risen through no merit of his own to the realms of the Blest. The souls of the Wise once again cease their circling and singing in order that St. Thomas may respond to the Pilgrim's puzzlement. In the previous canto Thomas had referred to the flock of Dominic as that in which the sheep "may fatten if they do not stray" and had pointed out the soul of Solomon, saying, "there never arose a second with such vision." It is the first of these two statements which is now to be explained (the second will be dealt with in Canto XIII), but by way of explanation, Thomas, as a courtesy to the companion order of St. Dominic, relates first the love story of St. Francis and Lady Poverty. Thomas then returns to the contemporary state of his own order, the Dominicans, to condemn their degeneracy and thereby elucidate the meaning of the statement "where all may fatten if they do not stray."

(Insensate strivings of mortality—
   how useless are those reasonings of yours
   that make you beat your wings in downward flight!   3

Men bent on law, some on the *Aphorisms*,
   some on the priesthood, others in pursuit
   of governing by means of force or fraud,   6

some planning theft, others affairs of state,
   some tangled in the pleasures of the flesh,
   some merely given up to indolence,   9

and I, relieved of all such vanities,
   was there with Beatrice in high Heaven,
   magnificently, gloriously welcomed.)   12

When each light on the circle had returned
   to where it was before the dance began,
   they stopped as still as candles in a stand.   15

4. Attributed to Hippocrates, the *Aphorisms* served as a medical textbook.

And from within the splendid radiance
    that had already spoken came more words,
    and as it smiled, a more effulgent light: 18

"Just as I shine reflecting His own rays,
    so, as I gaze into the endless light,
    I understand the reason for your thoughts.   21

You are perplexed and want me to explain
    in simple terms, with clear, explicit words,
    on your mind's level, what I meant to say   24

when I said earlier: 'where all may fatten,'
    and 'never arose a second with such vision,'
    indeed, a clear distinction must be made.   27

The Providence that governs all the world
    with wisdom so profound none of His creatures
    can ever hope to see into Its depths,   30

in order that the Bride of that sweet Groom,
    who crying loud espoused her with His blood,
    might go to her Beloved made more secure   33

within herself, more faithful to her Spouse,
    ordained two noble princes to assist her
    on either side, each serving as a guide.   36

One of the two shone with seraphic love,
    the other through his wisdom was on earth
    a splendor of cherubic radiance.   39

Now I shall speak of only one, for praise
    of one, no matter which, is praise of both,
    for both their labors served a single end.   42

Between the Topine and the stream that flows
    down from that hill the blest Ubaldo chose,
    a fertile slope hangs from a lofty mountain   45

37–42. Francis is characterized by his "seraphic love," the Seraphim being the highest order of angels and symbolic of the greatest love for God. Dominic, known for his learning, is associated with the Cherubim, the second order of angels and those acknowledged as the wisest.

which sends Perugia gusts of cold and heat
    through Porta Sole, and behind it Gualdo
    grieves with Nocera for their heavy yoke.   48

Born on this slope where steepness breaks the most,
    a sun rose to the world as radiantly
    as this sun here does sometimes from the Ganges;   51

thus, when this town is named let none call it
    Ascesi, for the word would not suffice—
    much more precise a word is *Orient*.   54

Only a few years after he had risen
    did his invigorating powers begin
    to penetrate the earth with a new strength: 57

while still a youth he braved his father's wrath,
    because he loved a lady to whom all
    would bar their door as if to death itself.   60

Before the bishop's court *et coram patre*
    he took this lady as his lawful wife;
    from day to day he loved her more and more.   63

Bereft of her first spouse, despised, ignored
    she waited eleven hundred years and more,
    living without a lover till he came,   66

alone, though it was known that she was found
    with Amyclas secure against the voice
    which had the power to terrify the world;   69

49–54. St. Francis, himself a "sun," rose on the world in the manner of the real sun (the Ganges River marking the easternmost point of the habitable world). St. Francis was born Giovanni Francesco Bernardone, son of a wool merchant, in 1181 or 1182, at Assisi. As a young man he pursued a life of pleasure but changed his ways after a series of hardships (including two illnesses) befell him. He resolved to renounce the worldly life and devote himself to poverty, which he called his bride.

61–63. "*Et coram patre*" ("In the presence of his father"), and before the bishop of Assisi, in the spring of 1207, Francis gave up his inheritance and took his vow of poverty.

67–69. This story tells how Amyclas, a poor fisherman, because he possessed absolutely no worldly goods remained tranquil, unafraid, and unimpressed when Caesar, who had been waging war in his area, appeared at the door of his shack and asked to be ferried across the Adriatic.

alone, though known was her fierce constancy
   that time she climbed the cross to be
   with Christ, while Mary stayed below alone.   72

Enough of such allusions. In plain words
   take Francis, now, and Poverty to be
   the lovers in the story I have told.   75

Their sweet accord, their faces spread with bliss,
   the love, the mystery, their tender looks
   gave rise in others' hearts to holy thoughts;   78

The venerable Bernard was the first
   to cast aside his shoes and run, and running
   toward such great peace, it seemed to him he lagged.   81

O unsuspected wealth! O fruitful good!
   Giles throws his shoes off, then Sylvester too—
   they love the bride so much, they seek the groom.   84

And then this father, this good lord, set out
   with his dear lady and that family
   that now was girded with the humble cord.   87

It mattered not that he was born the son
   of Bernardone, nor did he feel shame
   when people mocked him for his shabbiness;   90

but he announced, the way a king might do,
   his hard intent to Innocent who gave
   the seal establishing his holy Order.   93

The souls who followed him in poverty
   grew more and more, and then this archimandrite—
   whose wonder-working life were better sung   96

79–81. Bernard is Bernardo da Quintavalle, a wealthy merchant of Assisi, who was the first follower of St. Francis.

83. Giles was the third disciple of St. Francis. He preached in the Holy Land and in Tunisia and died in 1262. Sylvester was another early follower of St. Francis.

95. "Archimandrite" is a Greek Church term meaning "head of the fold," or one who supervises convents.

by Heaven's highest angels—saw his work
    crowned once again, now by Honorius
    through inspiration of the Holy Spirit.   99

Then in the haughty presence of the Sultan,
    urged by a burning thirst for martyrdom,
    he preached Christ and his blessèd followers,   102

but, finding no one ripe for harvest there,
    and loath to waste his labors, he returned
    to reap a crop in the Italian fields;   105

then on bare rock between Arno and Tiber
    he took upon himself Christ's holy wounds,
    and for two years he wore this final seal.   108

When it pleased Him who had ordained that soul
    for such great good to call him to Himself,
    rewarding him on high for lowliness,   111

he, to his brothers, as to rightful heirs,
    commended his most deeply cherished lady,
    commanding them to love her faithfully;   114

and in the lap of poverty he chose
    to die, wanting no other bier—from there
    that pristine soul returned to its own realm.   117

Think now what kind of man were fit to be
    his fellow helmsman on Saint Peter's boat,
    keeping it straight on course in the high sea—   120

and such a steersman was our Patriarch;
    and those who follow his command will see
    the richness of the cargo in their hold.   123

97–98. Pope Honorius III now officially ("once again") approved the Franciscan Order in 1223.

115–117. Francis requested that after his death his body lie naked on the bare ground.

118–119. St. Dominic is Francis's "fellow helmsman."

119. St. Peter's "boat" is the Church.

121. The "Patriarch" is St. Dominic, the founder of St. Thomas's order, whose life is described in the next canto.

But his own flock is growing greedy now
   for richer food, and in their hungry search
   they stray to alien pastures carelessly;   126

the farther off his sheep go wandering
   from him in all directions, the less milk
   they bring back when they come back to the fold.   129

True, there are some who, fearing loss, will keep
   close to their shepherd, but so few are these
   it would not take much cloth to make their cowls.   132

Now, if my speech has not been too obscure,
   and if you have been listening carefully,
   and if you will recall my former words,   135

your wish will have been satisfied in part,
   for you will have seen how the tree is chipped
   and why I made the qualifying statement: 138

'where all may fatten if they do not stray.' "

CANTO XII

ST. THOMAS HAVING *completed his discourse, the ring of souls now resumes its circling and is joined by another circle which forms around it. The two move with such harmony that the outer seems an echo of the inner one, and their beauty is such that they resemble concentric rainbows or a double garland of roses. The double rings cease their singing and motion, and Bonaventure, a spirit from that new circle and himself a Franciscan, steps forward to return the compliment made to his leader by St. Thomas. In relating the story of Dominic, Bonaventure follows the pattern set up in Thomas' story of St. Francis, so that, just as the two rings of souls are twin garlands, the stories of the mendicant leaders are nearly line-by-line parallels. After finishing the story of Dom-*

126. The Dominican Order, having become greedy for worldly honors and favors, has deviated from the principles governing the order.

inic, Bonaventure comments, as did Thomas, on the present state of his
own order: the Franciscans have been divided by those who would mis-
read his rule. Then, turning from these concerns, Bonaventure intro-
duces himself and the other spirits in this outer circle to Dante.

The very moment that the blessèd flame
   had come to speak its final word, the holy
   millstone began revolving once again;   3

before it could complete its first full round
   a second circle was enclosing it:
   motion with motion, matching song with song—   6

song that in those sweet instruments surpassed
   the best our Sirens or our Muses sing,
   as source of light outshines what it reflects.   9

As two concentric arcs of equal hue,
   are seen as they bend through the misty clouds
   when Juno tells her handmaid to appear—   12

the outer from the inner one an echo,
   like to the longing voice of her whom love
   consumed as morning sun consumes the dew—   15

and reassure the people here below
   that by the covenant God made with Noah,
   they have no need to fear another Flood—   18

even so those sempiternal roses wreathed
   twin garlands round us as the outer one
   was lovingly responding to the inner.   21

1. The "blessèd flame" is the spirit of St. Thomas, who had been speaking up to this
point.

2–3. The "millstone" is the circle of spirits.

12. Juno's handmaiden is Iris, goddess of the rainbow and messenger of the gods.

14–15. Because Narcissus failed to return her love, Echo faded away until only her
voice remained.

17–18. The appearance of the rainbow was a promise to Noah that God would never
again destroy the earth by water (Genesis 9:8–17).

When dancing and sublime festivity
  and all the singing, all the gleaming flames
  (a loving jubilee of light with light),   24

with one accord, at the same instant, ceased
  (as our two eyes responding to our will,
  together have to open and to close),   27

then, from the heart of one of those new lights
  there came a voice that drew me to itself
  (I was the needle pointing to the star);   30

it spoke: "The love that makes me beautiful
  moves me to speak about that other guide,
  the cause of such high praise concerning mine.   33

We should not mention one without the other,
  since both did battle for a single cause,
  so let their fame shine gloriously as one.   36

The troops of Christ, rearmed at such great cost,
  with tardy pace were following their standard,
  fearful and few, divided in their ranks,   39

when the Emperor who reigns eternally,
  of His own grace (for they were not deserving)
  provided for his soldiers in their peril—   42

and, as you have been told, He sent His bride
  two champions who through their words and deeds
  helped reunite the scattered company.   45

Within that region where the sweet west wind
  comes blowing, opening up the fresh new leaves
  with which all Europe is about to bloom,   48

29. The voice is that of St. Bonaventure (Giovanni di Fidanza), born 1221 at Bagnoregio near Orvieto, a Franciscan monk who became general of the Franciscan Order in 1255 or 1256.

32. The other leader is St. Dominic.

37. Christ's troops, or humanity, were "rearmed" with the blood of Christ, through His sacrifice on the Cross.

46. The region is Spain, near the Bay of Biscay, which is the area nearest the source of the west wind, or Zephyr.

not far from where the waves break on the shore
    behind which, when its longest course is done,
    the sun, at times, will hide from every man,   51

lies Calaroga, fortune-favored town,
    protected by the mighty shield that bears
    two lions: one as subject, one as sovereign.   54

There the staunch lover of the Christian faith
    was born into the world: God's holy athlete,
    kind to his own and ruthless to his foes.   57

His mind, the instant God created it,
    possessed extraordinary power: within
    his mother's womb he made her prophesy.   60

The day that he was wed to Christian Faith
    at the baptismal font, when each of them
    promised the other mutual salvation,   63

the lady who had answered for him there
    saw in a dream the marvelous rich fruit
    that he and all his heirs were to produce,   66

and that he might be known for what he was,
    a spirit sent from Heaven named the child
    with His possessive, Whose alone he was: 69

Dominic he was named. I see in him
    the husbandman, the one chosen by Christ
    to help Him in the garden of His Church.   72

52–54. The village blessed by Fortune (because Dominic was born there) is Caleruega in Old Castile, which was ruled by kings whose arms consisted of quartered castles and lions, one lion below a castle and one above, thus "one as subject, one as sovereign."

55. The "staunch lover" is Dominic, who was born between 1170 and 1175, supposedly into the noble family of Guzmán, and studied theology, beginning at the age of fourteen, at the University of Valencia.

56. Dominic was "*God's holy athlete*" in the sense of defender of the Faith.

69. The name Dominic means "the Lord's" in Latin.

Close servant and true messenger of Christ,
    he made it manifest that his first love
    was love for the first counsel given by Christ.   75

Often his nurse would find him out of bed,
    awake and silent, lying on the ground,
    as if to say, "For this end was I sent."   78

O father Felix, felicitously named!
    O mother called Giovanna, 'grace of God!'
    And these names truly mean what they express.   81

Not like those men who toil for worldly gain,
    studying Thaddeus and the Ostian,
    but for the love of the eternal bread,   84

he soon became a mighty theologian,
    a diligent inspector of the vineyard,
    where the vine withers if the keeper fails.   87

And from the See which once was so benign
    to its deserving poor (but now corrupt,
    not in itself but in its occupant)   90

no right to pay out two or three for six,
    nor first choice of some fat and vacant post,
    nor *decimas quae sunt pauperum Dei,*   93

did he request, but just the right to fight
    the sinful world for that true seed whence sprang
    the four and twenty plants surrounding you.   96

75. The first counsel is the first of the Beatitudes: "Blessed are the poor in spirit" (Matthew 5:3); that is, love of poverty.

79–81. Names were believed to derive from the quality of the things named.

83. This is probably Thaddeus of Alderotto (ca. 1235–1295), a well-known physician and the presumed founder of the school of medicine at the University of Bologna, who wrote commentaries on the works of Galen and Hippocrates. Enrico da Susa, "the Ostian" (from the village of Ostia about twenty miles southwest of Rome), was a theologian who taught canon law in Paris and Bologna and was famous for his commentary on the decretals or papal decrees on ecclesiastical law.

84. The "eternal bread" is true knowledge, or "the bread of angels," as opposed to that learned for material gain.

Then, armed with doctrine and a zealous will
  with apostolic sanction, he burst forth
   —a mighty torrent gushing from on high;   99

sending its crushing force against the barren
  thickets of heresy, and where they were
  toughest, it struck with greatest violence.   102

And from him many other streams branched off
  to give their waters to the Catholic fields
  so that its saplings might have greener life.   105

If such was one wheel of the chariot
  that Holy Church used to defend herself
  and conquer on the field of civil strife,   108

you cannot fail to see how excellent
  the other must have been, about whom Thomas,
  before I came, spoke with such courtesy.   111

But now the track made by the topmost part
  of that great wheel's circumference is gone,
  and there is only mold where once was crust.   114

His family, which once walked straight ahead
  in his own footprints, now are so turned round
  they walk along by putting toe to heel.   117

Soon comes the harvest time and we shall see
  how bad the tillage was: the tares will mourn
  that access to the storehouse is denied.   120

I will admit that if you search our book
  page after page you might find one that reads:
  'I still am now what I have always been,'   123

98. Dominic's order was officially sanctioned in 1216 by Pope Honorius III.

101–102. In Provence the Albigensians had their strongest foothold.

but such cannot be said of those who come
    from Acquasparta or Casal and read
    our rule too loosely or too narrowly.   126

I am the living soul of Bonaventure
    from Bagnoregio; temporal concerns
    always came last when I was in command.   129

Illuminato and Augustine are here,
    they were the first of God's barefooted poor
    who wore the cord to show they were His friends.   132

Hugh of St. Victor is among them too,
    with Peter Mangiador, and Peter of Spain
    who in twelve books illumines men below,   135

125. Matthew of Acquasparta was appointed general of the Franciscan order in the year 1287. As general he introduced relaxations in the Franciscan rule, which unfortunately paved the way for abuses. Casal (a town in northern Italy thirty miles east of Turin) specifically refers in this case to Ubertino of Casal, leader of the Franciscan "Spirituals," who opposed the relaxations and preferred a more literal adherence to the rule.

130. Bonaventure begins his introduction of the spirits in the outer circle with these two early followers of St. Francis. Both men joined the saint in 1210. Illuminato, from a noble family of Rieti, went with Francis on his mission to the Orient. He died ca. 1280, late enough to have witnessed the corruption already present in his Order. Augustine, like St. Francis, was from Assisi. He became head of the Franciscan Order in Campania (1216) and was said to have died on the same day and at the same hour as his leader, St. Francis.

133. Hugh of St. Victor, born in Flanders around 1097, was a famous theologian and mystic of the early twelfth century who wrote numerous works characterized by great learning.

134. Peter Mangiador, also known as Petrus Comestor, was born in Troyes, France. His best-known work, the *Historia scholastica,* is a compilation of the historical books of the Bible accompanied by a commentary. Peter of Spain, born in Lisbon (ca. 1226), became Pope John XXI. His reign lasted only eight months; he was killed when a ceiling collapsed in one of the rooms in his palace at Viterbo. His *Summulae logicales,* a manual of logic, was divided into twelve parts and expanded the traditional logic of the Scholastics.

Nathan the prophet, and the Patriarch
    Chrysostom, Anselm, and Donatus who
    devoted all his thought to the first art.   138

Rabanus, too, is here, and at my side
    shines the Calabrian Abbot Joachim
    who had received the gift of prophecy.   141

The glowing courtesy of Brother Thomas,
    his modesty of words, have prompted me
    to praise this paladin as I have done   144

and moved this fellowship to join with me."

CANTO XIII

DANTE, IN ATTEMPTING *to convey the grandeur of the two encircling wreaths of illustrious souls, opens the canto with a grandiose image of the heavenly contellations. Once the singing ceases, St. Thomas begins to speak again, explaining to the Pilgrim what he meant when he said earlier in regard to Solomon: "there never arose a second with such*

136. Nathan was the Hebrew prophet who rebuked King David for having caused the death of Uriah the Hittite in order to marry Bathsheba (2 Samuel 12:1–15).

127–138. St. John Chrysostom, fourth-century patriarch of Constantinople, was noted for his preaching. Anselm, eleventh-century archbishop of Canterbury, was author of *Cur Deus Homo,* a treatise on the Atonement which attempts to prove the necessity of the Incarnation. Donatus, a fourth-century Roman rhetorician, was author of commentaries on Virgil and Terence but was best known for his widely used Latin grammar text *Ars grammatica.*

139. Archbishop of Mainz from 847 until his death in 856, Rabanus Maurus Magnentius (born ca. 776) was considered one of the most learned men of his time.

140. Joachim, preacher and prophet, born 1145 in Calabria, originated the doctrine that the dispensation of the Father (Old Testament) and of the Son (New Testament) would be followed by the dispensation of the Holy Spirit, a period of perfection and peace.

144. The "paladin" is St. Dominic, God's athlete and warrior.

*vision" (X, 114). After demonstrating that the greatest amount of wis-
dom was that which God gave Adam and Christ when he created them
(they were direct products of the Creator and therefore perfect), St.
Thomas explains that what he meant when he used the phrase in rela-
tion to Solomon was that God had given Solomon the greatest amount
of wisdom that He ever gave to a king, not a man. So, then, it was in
the context of kingly prudence or perfection that Solomon had no equal.
St. Thomas uses this occasion to warn the Pilgrim about drawing rash
conclusions and making quick judgments, and he mentions a number
of ancient philosophers and heretics as examples of those who fell into
error precisely because they did not examine all the circumstances and
make clear distinctions. He concludes by saying that one must be es-
pecially prudent when it comes to second-guessing the Almighty: just
because we see one man steal and another make offerings does not
necessarily mean that the thief will be damned and the do-gooder saved
by God.*

Imagine, you who wish to visualize
   what I saw next (and while I speak hold hard
   as rock in your mind's eye this image),   3

the fifteen brightest stars in all of heaven,
   the ones whose light is of such magnitude
   that it can penetrate the thickest mist;   6

imagine next the turnings of the Wain
   through night and day and all contained within
   the spacious vault of heaven's hemisphere;   9

imagine, too, the bell-mouth of that Horn
   whose tip is marked by that bright star which serves
   as axis for the Primum Mobile—   12

all joined into a double constellation
   (like that one which the daughter of Minos
   left in the sky when stricken by Death's chill),   15

13–15. When the daughter of Minos, Ariadne, died, the wreath she wore at her
wedding to Bacchus was transformed into a constellation called Ariadne's crown, or
the Corona Borealis.

one's rays within the other shining forth,
   and both of them revolving, synchronized
   at different speeds but moving light with light—   18

and you will have some shadowy idea
   of the true nature of that constellation
   and of the double dance encircling me,   21

for these things far exceed our cognizance,
   as far as movement of the swiftest sphere
   outspeeds the current of Chiana's flow.   24

No Bacchic hymn or Paean did they sing,
   but of three Persons in one God they sang
   and in One Person human and Divine.   27

When song and circling reached the final note,
   those holy lights then turned to wait on us,
   rejoicing as they moved from task to task.   30

The hush of that concordant group of souls
   was broken by that light from which had poured
   the wondrous story of God's pauper-saint;   33

and he said: "Now that one sheaf has been threshed
   and all its grain is garnered, God's sweet love
   invites me now to thresh the other one.   36

Into that breast, you think, from which was drawn
   the rib that was to form the lovely face
   whose palate was to cost mankind so dear,   39

and into That One Who pierced by the lance
   gave satisfaction for future and past,
   such that it outweighed all of mankind's guilt,   42

24. The Chiana is a river in Tuscany that was nearly stagnant in Dante's day.

32. The "light" is St. Thomas.

37. The "breast" is Adam's.

39. The "lovely face" is Eve's.

40. The "One" is Christ.

as much of wisdom's radiance as is given
   to human nature was infused by Him
   whose power created their humanity;   45

and so, you must have been surprised to hear
   what I said earlier of our fifth light:
   that he possessed a wisdom without equal.   48

Open your eyes to what I now reveal,
   and you will see your thoughts and my words join
   as one truth at the center of the round.   51

All that which dies and all that cannot die
   reflect the radiance of that Idea
   which God the Father through His love begets: 54

that Living Light, which from its radiant Source
   streams forth Its light but never parts from It
   nor from the Love which tri-unites with them,   57

of Its own grace sends down its rays, as if
   reflected, through the nine subsistencies,
   remaining sempiternally Itself.   60

Then it descends to the last potencies,
   from act to act, becoming so diminished,
   it brings forth only brief contingencies;   63

and by this term I mean things generated,
   things which the moving heavens produce from seed
   or not from seed. The wax of things like these   66

is more or less receptive, and the power
   that shapes it, more or less effective—stamped
   with the idea, it shines accordingly.   69

59. These are the nine orders of angels that reflect the "Living Light" (55) of God within Whom rests the plan of the universe.

61–62. The "Living Light" (55) of God finally reaches the sublunar world, having been transmitted from sphere to sphere.

63–66. The result of this filtering down of God's light is the creation of things that do not have a lasting existence.

So trees of the same species may produce
   dissimilar fruit, some better and some worse;
   so men are born with diverse natural gifts.   72

And if the wax were perfectly disposed,
   and if the heavens were at their highest power,
   the brilliance of the seal would shine forth full;   75

but Nature never can transmit this light
   in its full force—much like the artisan
   who knows his craft but has a trembling hand.   78

But if the Fervent Love moves the Clear Vision
   of the First Power and makes of that its seal,
   the thing it stamps is perfect in all ways.   81

And this is how the dust of earth was once
   made fit to form the perfect living being
   and how the Virgin came to be with child.   84

And so you see how right you are to think
   that human nature never has been since,
   nor ever will be such, as in those two.   87

Now, if I were to end my discourse here,
   you would be quick to ask: 'Then, how can you
   say that the other was without an equal?'   90

To clearly understand what seems unclear,
   consider who he was and his request
   that time God said to him, 'Ask what you will.'   93

My words were meant to bring back to your mind
   the fact he was a king, and asked his Lord
   for wisdom to suffice a worthy king;   96

he did not ask to know so that he might
   count angels here, or know whether *necesse*
   with a conditioned premise yields *necesse;*   99

75. The "seal" is God's Divine Plan.

76. Here "Nature" means the entire operation of the heavens.

nor *si est dare primum motum esse,*
    nor if without right angles, triangles
    in semicircles can be made to fit.   102

So, when I talked of unmatched wisdom then,
    royal prudence was the wisdom upon which
    I had my arrow of intention drawn.   105

If you recall the word I used, 'arose,'
    it should be clear that only kings were meant,
    of which there are full many, but few good.   108

And if my words are taken in this sense,
    they will not contradict what you believe
    of our first father and of our High Bliss.   111

Let this be leaden weight upon your feet
    to make you move slow as a weary man
    both to the 'yes' or 'no' you do not see,   114

for he ranks low, indeed, among the fools,
    who rushes to affirm or to deny,
    no matter which, without distinguishing.   117

Opinions formed in haste will oftentimes
    lead in a wrong direction, and man's pride
    then intervenes to bind his intellect.   120

Worse than useless it is to leave the shore
    to fish for truth unless you have the skill;
    you will return worse off than when you left.   123

Of this Parmenides offers clear proof
    and Bryson and Melissus and the rest
    who went their way but knew not where to go;   126

111. The "High Bliss" is Christ.

124. A Greek philosopher born at Elea in Italy (ca. 513 B.C.), Parmenides was the founder of the Eleatic school of philosophy, in which he was succeeded by Zeno.

125. Bryson, a Greek philosopher, is mentioned by Aristotle as having attempted to square the circle by using dishonest nongeometrical methods. Melissus, a philosopher of Samos, was a follower of Parmenides.

so did Sabellius and Arius
    and all those fools who were to Holy Scripture
    swordblades distorting images of truth.   129

Nor should one be too quick to trust his judgment;
    be not like him who walks his field and counts
    the ears of corn before the time is ripe,   132

for I have seen brier all winter long
    showing its tough and prickly stem, and then
    eventually produce a lovely rose,   135

and I have seen a ship sail straight and swift
    over the sea through all its course, and then,
    about to enter in the harbor, sink.   138

No Mr. or Miss Know-It-All should think,
    when they see one man steal and one give alms
    that they are seeing them through God's own eyes,   141

for one may yet rise up, the other fall."

CANTO XIV

CONCENTRIC RINGS OPEN *this canto as well, this time with an image of water rippling in a round container, as Beatrice speaks from the center of the rings of lights. The Pilgrim has another question for these lights, and Beatrice expresses it for him: will the brilliant light of these souls remain with them after the resurrection of the body and, if so, how will their reacquired sight resist such splendor? The souls dance and sing with delight at being able to answer the Pilgrim's question. Then from the inner circle Solomon reassures the Pilgrim that the light surrounding them will last eternally and always in proportion to the vision they have of God. And since they will be more perfect once they have their bodies back, their vision will be strong enough to support their great brilliance. Suddenly a third ring of bright lights begins to surround the other two concentric rings, but their intensity is too much for the eyes of the Pilgrim. Then, looking into Beatrice's eyes, he finds himself rising, without*

realizing it, to the next sphere. Because of the red glow of this planet
he knows that he is on Mars. Two enormous bands of light form, upon
which for a brief moment flashes the image of Christ, and within the
transparent arms of this cross specks of souls, like dust in shafts of light,
move in all directions as a hymn is sung in praise of Christ. Never
before, he says, has the Pilgrim been so overwhelmed by something as
beautiful as this, and then he apologizes for making this remark since,
he admits, he has yet to gaze into his lady's eyes since arriving here!

The water in a round container moves
    center to rim rippling or rim to center,
        when struck first from within, then from without: 3

this image suddenly occurred to me
    the moment that the glorious, living light
        of Thomas had concluded its remarks   6

because of the resemblance that was born
    between his flow of words and Beatrice's,
        she being moved to speak once he had spoken: 9

"This man, though he cannot express his need,
    and has not even thought the thought as yet,
        must dig the roots of yet another truth.   12

Explain to him about the radiance
    with which your substance blooms. Will it remain
        eternally, just as it shines forth now?   15

And if it does remain, explain to him
    how, once your sight has been restored, you can
        endure the brilliance of each other's form."   18

As partners in a dance whirl in their reel,
    caught in a sudden surge of joy, will often
        quicken their steps and raise their voices high,   21

so at her eager and devout request
    the holy circles showed new happiness
        through their miraculous music and their dance.   24

Those who regret that we die here on earth
    to live above, have never known the freshening
        downpour of God's eternal grace up here.   27

That One and Two and Three which never ends
   and ever reigns in Three and Two and One,
   uncircumscribed and circumscribing all,   30

three separate times was sung by all those spirits,
   and unbelievably melodious
   it sounded—Heaven's consummate reward.   33

Then, from the brightest of the lights I heard
   come from the inner round a modest tone
   as was the angel's voice that Mary heard: 36

"Long as the joyous feast of Paradise
   shall last," it said, "so long our burning love
   shall clothe us in this radiance you see.   39

Our brilliance is in ratio to our love,
   our ardor to our vision, and our vision
   to the degree of grace vouchsafed to us.   42

When our flesh, sanctified and glorious
   shall clothe our souls once more, our person then
   will be more pleasing since it is complete;   45

wherefore, the light, generously bestowed
   on us by the Supreme Good, is increased—
   the light of glory that shows Him to us.   48

It follows, then, that vision must increase,
   as must the ardor kindled by the vision,
   as must the radiance the ardor gives.   51

But as a coal burns white in its own fire
   whose inner glow outshines its outer flame
   so that its form is clearly visible,   54

so this effulgence that contains us now
   will be surpassed in brilliance by the flesh
   that for so long has lain beneath the ground;   57

34. This is the light of Solomon (see *Paradise* X, 109–114), author of the Canticle
of Canticles, which celebrates the union of the human and the divine as well as the
resurrection of the body.

nor will such light be difficult to bear,
    the organs of our bodies will be strengthened
    and ready for whatever gives us joy."   60

So quick and eager to cry out "Amen!"
    were both those choirs that it was very clear
    how much they yearned to have their bodies back— 63

not for themselves as much as for their mothers,
    their fathers, and for all those they held dear
    before they turned into eternal flame.   66

And suddenly! around us was a light
    growing as bright as all the light it circled,
    like an horizon brightening with the dawn.   69

Just as at twilight all across the heavens
    new things appear—the faint appearances
    of what we see or what we seem to see,   72

so I began to see, it seemed, new shapes
    of spirits forming there, making a ring
    around the other two circumferences.   75

Oh sparks of truth that are the Holy Spirit!
    How quick, how bright the brilliance of that light
    grew for my eyes, now overwhelmed by glory!   78

But Beatrice showed herself to me
    smiling so radiantly, it must be left
    among those sights the mind cannot retrace.   81

It gave me strength to raise my eyes again,
    and looking up I saw myself translated,
    alone with her, to more exalted bliss.   84

I was aware of having risen higher
    because I saw the star's candescent smile
    glow redder than it ever had before.   87

Then in the language common to all men,
    with all my heart, I made an offering
    unto the Lord befitting His fresh grace. 90

Nor had the sacrifice within my breast
    ceased burning when I knew my prayer of thanks
    had been accepted, and propitiously, 93

for with such mighty sheen, such ruby glow,
    within twin rays, such splendor came to me,
    I cried: "O Helios, who adorns them so!" 96

Just as the Milky Way adorned with stars,
    some large, some small, gleams white between the Poles,
    baffling the wisest of astrologers, 99

so, constellated in the depths of Mars,
    these rays of light crossed in the holy sign
    which quadrants make when joining in a circle; 102

but here my memory defeats my art:
    I see that cross as it flames forth with Christ,
    yet cannot find the words that will describe it. 105

But who takes up his cross and follows Christ
    will pardon me for what I leave unsaid
    beholding Heaven's whiteness glow with Christ. 108

From top to base, across from arm to arm
    bright lights were moving, sparkling brilliantly
    as they would meet and pass each other's glow. 111

So, here on earth, along a shaft of light
    that sometimes streaks the shade that men devise
    by means of arts and crafts for their protection, 114

our eyes see particles of matter move
    straight or aslant, some swift, some floating slow—
    an ever-changing scene of shapes and patterns. 117

And as the viol and harp, their many strings

88–90. This is the unspoken language of the heart, expressing devotion and gratitude
through silent prayer and thanksgiving.

96. Here "Helios" is God.

tuned into harmony, will ring out sweetly
   even for the one who does not catch the tune,   120

so from the spread of lights along the cross
   there gathered in the air a melody
   that held me in a trance, though I could not   123

tell what the hymn was—only that it sang
   of highest praise: I heard "Arise" and "Conquer"
   as one who hears but does not understand.   126

This music raised my soul to heights of love:
   until that moment nothing had existed
   that ever bound my soul in such sweet chains—   129

but this, perhaps, may seem too rash a statement,
   forgetting, as it were, those lovely eyes,
   the source of bliss in which my gaze finds rest,   132

but since those vivid crowning beauties grow
   in strength the higher they ascend, and since
   I had not turned to look at them as yet,   135

one must excuse me for what I accuse
   myself of to excuse myself, and see
   the truth: that sacred joy is not excluded,   138

since it grows in perfection as we rise.

CANTO XV

*As the souls of the cross conclude their hymn, the Pilgrim perceives
what he imagines to be a star falling from the right arm of the cross
down to its base without leaving the arms of the cross. Then this light
glowing like fire behind alabaster addresses him in Latin. At first the*

133. The "vivid crowning beauties" are Beatrice's eyes, which increase in brilliance
as she and the Pilgrim rise from one heaven to the next.

Pilgrim has difficulty comprehending the soul's words, but gradually the language descends to his level of understanding. The light says that he understands why the Pilgrim does not ask him who he is or why he appears so joyful to him, because he rightly believes that souls in Paradise know the thoughts of mortals through the mirror of God's love, but he asks the Pilgrim to be bold and speak just the same, since his answer is already decreed. With the approval of Beatrice he asks the light its name. The soul replies that he is Dante's great-great-grandfather Cacciaguida and that Dante's great-grandfather is on the first terrace of the mountain of Purgatory. He exhorts Dante to pray for his great-grandfather and then begins a description of the Florence of his day, his birth, his marriage to a woman of the Alighieri line, and his death during the crusade led by Conrad.

The magnanimity in which true love
    always resolves itself (as does that other,
    self-seeking love into iniquity)   3

silenced the notes of that sweet-sounding harp
    and hushed the music of those holy strings
    tuned tight or loose by Heaven's hand itself.   6

How could such beings be deaf to righteous prayers,
    those beings who to encourage my desire
    to beg of them fell silent, all of them?   9

And right it is that he forever mourn
    who out of love for what does not endure
    loses that other love eternally.   12

As now and then through calm and cloudless skies
    a sudden streak of fire cuts the dark,
    catching the eye that watches listlessly,   15

as if a star were changing places there
    (except that from the place where it flared up
    no star is missing, and the blaze dies down),   18

so, from the right arm of the cross a star
    belonging to that brilliant constellation
    sped to the center, then, down to the foot,   21

and as it coursed along the radial lines,
    this gem contained within its setting seemed
    like fire behind an alabaster screen.   24

With like affection did Anchises' shade
    rush forth, if we may trust our greatest Muse,
    when in Elysium he beheld his son.   27

"O sanguis meus, o superinfusa
    gratïa Deï, sicut tibi, cui
    bis unquam celi ianüa reclusa?"   30

So spoke that brilliance, and I stared at him.
    Then I turned round to see my lady's face;
    I stood amazed between the two of them,   33

for such a smile was glowing in her eyes,
    it seemed that with my own I touched the depths
    of my beatitude, my paradise.   36

And then this light of joy to eye and ear
    began to add to his first words such things
    I could not grasp, his speech was so profound.   39

It did not hide its thought deliberately;
    there was no other choice: its argument
    soared far beyond the target of man's mind.   42

Then once the bow of his affection had
    released its love, allowing what he said
    to hit the mark of human intellect,   45

the first words that I comprehended were:
    "Blessèd be Thou, Three Persons in One Being,
    Who showest such great favor to my seed!"   48

Then he went on: "A long-felt, welcome thirst
    born from perusal of that mighty book
    whose black and white will never altered be,   51

25–27. Anchises, the father of Aeneas, joyously greeted his son when Aeneas visited the Elysian Fields. (See *Aeneid* VI, 684–688.)

you have assuaged, my son, within this flame
   from which I speak to you, thanks be to her
   who gave you wings to make this lofty flight.   54

Since you believe your thought flows forth to me
   from Primal thought, as five and six from one,
   if understood, ray forth from unity,   57

therefore, you do not ask me who I am
   or why I show more joy in seeing you
   than any other in this joyful throng.   60

What you believe is right. We in this life,
   greatest or least alike, gaze in that Mirror
   where thoughts are thought before they are expressed.   63

Yet, that the Sacred Love in which I gaze
   eternally on God, and which creates
   sweet thirstiness in me, be best fulfilled,   66

let your own voice, confident, bold, and joyous,
   express your will, express your heart's desire—
   my answer has already been decreed."   69

I turned to Beatrice who had heard
   my words before I spoke, and with her smile
   she gave strength to the wings of my desire.   72

Then I began: "Love and intelligence
   achieved their equipoise in each of you
   once you saw plain the First Equality,   75

because the sun that warmed and lighted you
   with heat and light is poised so perfectly
   that all comparisons fall short of it.   78

But utterance and feeling among mortals
   for reasons which are evident to you,
   have different feathers making up their wings.   81

54. As his guide, Beatrice in her role of Revelation gives Dante the ability to ascend.

55–57. Dante's thoughts, as all things, are reflected in God; in the same way, numbers have their source in unity.

I, too, as man feel this disparity
    deeply, so only with my heart can I
    give thanks for your paternal welcome here.   84

I beg of you, rich topaz, living gem
    within the setting of this precious jewel,
    to satisfy my wish to know your name."   87

"Branch of my tree, the mere expectancy
    of whose arrival here gave me delight,
    I was your root"—this was his preface, then   90

he said: "He after whom your family
    was named, whose soul a hundred years and more
    still circles the first terrace of the Mount,   93

father of your grandfather, was my son.
    And meet it were that you offer your prayers
    to shorten the long sentence of his weight.   96

Florence, enclosed within her ancient walls
    from which she still hears terce and nones ring out,
    once lived in peace, a pure and temperate town: 99

no necklace or tiara did she wear,
    no lavish gowns or fancy belts that were
    more striking than the woman they adorned.   102

In those days fathers had no cause to fear
    a daughter's birth: the marriageable age
    was not too low, the dowry not too high.   105

Houses too large to live in were not built,
    and Sardanapalus had not yet come
    to show to what use bedrooms can be put.   108

---

90. The speaker is Dante's great-great-grandfather. All that is definitely known of
him comes from Dante's account in these cantos. It is not until line 135 that he
identifies himself as Cacciaguida.

98. Near the old walls of the city stood the abbey of Badia, whose bells, even in
Dante's day, rang the canonical hours. Terce is the third hour (9:00 A.M.) and nones
is the ninth (3:00 P.M.).

107–108. Sardanapalus was the last king of Assyria, who was famous for his wan-
tonness and effeminacy.

Not yet had your Uccellatoi surpassed
    Rome's Montemalo, which in its ascent
    being surpassed, will be so in its fall.   111

Bellincion Berti I have seen walk by
    belted in leather and bone, and his good wife
    come from her mirror with unpainted face;   114

de'Nerli I have seen, del Vecchio too,
    content to wear plain leather, and their wives
    to handle flax and spindle all day long.   117

O happy wives! Each one of them was sure
    of her last resting place—none of them yet
    lay lonely in her bed because of France.   120

One watching tenderly above the cradle,
    soothing her infant in that idiom
    which all new parents love to use at first;   123

another, working at her spinning-wheel
    surrounded by her children, would tell tales
    about the Trojans, Rome, and Fiesole.   126

A Lapo Salterello, a Cianghella
    would have amazed them then as much as now
    a Cincinnatus or Cornelia would.   129

109–111. At the time of which Cacciaguida speaks, Florence had not yet surpassed
the pride and splendor of Rome; later she would outdo Rome both in her magnifi-
cence and her decline. Approaching Florence from Bologna, the traveler first views
the city from Mount Uccellatoio; one approaching Rome from the north first sees
that city from Montemalo.

112. Bellincion Berti, a distinguished Florentine citizen and member of the honorable
Ravignani family, lived in the late twelfth century and was father of the "good Guald-
rada" (see *Inferno* XVI, 37).

115. De'Nerli and del Vecchio were the names of noble Florentine families.

127–129. Cianghella, a contemporary of Dante, was a Florentine woman of ques-
tionable reputation and loose and profligate lifestyle. Lapo Salterello, a prominent
Florentine citizen belonging to the Bianchi faction, was a corrupt lawyer and judge.
In the period of the Roman republic, Cincinnatus was called from the plough to be
dictator, during which time he conquered the Aequians (458 B.C.). Cornelia, daughter
of the elder Scipio Africanus, was mother of Tiberius and Gaius Gracchi, Roman
tribunes who died attempting to preserve the republic.

To this serene, this lovely state of being
  within this comity of citizens,
    joined in good faith, this dwelling-place so sweet,   132

Mary, besought by pains of birth, gave me;
  and then within your ancient Baptistry
    a Christian I became, and Cacciaguida.   135

Eliseo and Moronto were my brothers;
  my wife came from the valley of the Po
    and brought with her the surname that you bear.   138

And then I served Conrad the Emperor
  who later dubbed me knight among his host,
    so pleased was he by all my gallant deeds.   141

Along with him I fought against the evil
  of that false faith whose followers usurp—
    only because your Shepherds sin—your rights.   144

There the vile Saracen delivered me
  from the entanglements of your vain world,
    the love of which corrupts so many souls—   147

from martyrdom I came to this, my peace."

CANTO XVI

THE PILGRIM TELLS *the reader that he can no longer wonder at those*
on earth who glory in their family lineage, since he himself in Paradise,
where wills are perfect, gloried in it too. When Cacciaguida finishes
*speaking, Dante addresses him with the formal "you" (*voi *in Italian),*
at which Beatrice smiles. At Dante's request, Cacciaguida gives an ac-
count of the family history and goes on to describe his Florence, in
contrast to the corrupt Florence of Dante's time, discoursing on the

136. Nothing at all is known about Cacciaguida's brothers, Eliseo and Moronto.

139. Conrad III (1093–1152) was the son of Frederick, the duke of Swabia.

changing fortunes of the city and her old families and lamenting the
loss of the peace and glory of the earlier period.

Ah, trivial thing, our pride in noble blood!
    That you can make men glory in you here
    on earth where our affections are weak-willed,   3

will never again amaze me, for up there
    where appetite is always in the right,
    in Heaven itself, I gloried in my blood!   6

Nobility, a mantle quick to shrink!
    Unless we add to it from day to day,
    time with its shears will trim off more and more.   9

I spoke again addressing him as "*voi*"
    (a form the Romans were the first to use,
    though now her children make less use of it),   12

and Beatrice, not too far from us,
    smiling, reminded me of her who coughed
    to caution Guinevere at her first sign   15

of weakness. I began: "You are my sire.
    You give me confidence to speak. You raise
    my heart so high that I am more than I.   18

My soul is overflowing with the joy
    that pours from many streams, and it rejoices
    that it endures and does not burst inside.   21

Tell me, then, cherished source from which I spring,
    about your own forefathers, who they were;
    what years made history when you were young?   24

Tell me about the sheepfold of St. John,
    how large it was and who among the folk
    were worthiest to hold the highest seats?"   27

25. The Florentines are the "sheepfold" of St. John the Baptist, the patron saint of
Florence.

As glowing coals in a quick breath of air
    burst into flame, just so I saw that light
    grow brighter when it heard my loving words,   30

and as his beauty grew before my eyes,
    so, in a voice sweeter and more refined
    (so different from our modern Florentine),   33

his light said: "From the day 'Ave' was said
    to that on which my mother, now a saint,
    heavy with child, gave birth to me, her son,   36

to its own Lion this fiery star returned
    five hundred fifty times and thirty more
    to be rekindled underneath his paw.   39

The house where I and all of mine were born
    stands at the place the last ward is first reached
    by all those running in your annual games.   42

About my forefathers, let this suffice,
    for what their names were and from where they came
    is better left unsaid than boasted of.   45

All those who lived at that time fit for arms
    between Mars and the Baptist were no more
    than just one fifth of those who live there now;   48

The population then, polluted now
    by Campi, and Certaldo and Fighine,
    was pure down to the humblest artisan.   51

34–39. From the time of the Annunciation (Luke 1:28) to the time of Cacciaguida's birth, the planet Mars had revolved 580 times, returning to its position in the constellation Leo. One revolution of Mars was estimated to take 687 days; by multiplying 580 by 687 and dividing by 365, we can calculate that Cacciaguida's birth year was 1091.

47–48. These landmarks, the statue of Mars (on the north side of the Ponte Vecchio) and the Baptistery of St. John, mark the southern and northern boundaries, respectively, of the old city.

50. Campi, Certaldo, and Fighine are small towns near Florence whose inhabitants, according to Cacciaguida, polluted the purity of Florentine blood by moving to the city.

Oh how much better it would be if they
    were still your neighbors and your boundaries
    Galluzzo and Trespiano as they were,   54

than have such folk within and bear the stench
    of Aguglione's churl and him from Signa,
    already with a sharp eye out for swindling!   57

If that group of the world's most despicable
    had not played a stepmother's role to Caesar,
    but been a loving mother to her son,   60

a certain nouveau-Florentine who trucks
    and trades would now be back in Semifonte
    where once his own grandfather begged his bread,   63

and Montemurlo would still have its Counts,
    the parish of Acone have its Cerchi,
    and Valdigreve still its Buondelmonti.   66

A mingled strain of men has always been
    the source of city decadence, as when
    men stuff their stomachs sick with food on food;   69

54. Galluzzo is an ancient Tuscan village two miles south of Florence on the road to Siena. Trespiano lies three miles to the north of Florence on the Bologna road.

56. Baldo d'Aguglione, a prominent Guelph political leader, became prior of Florence in 1298. "Him from Signa" is probably a reference to Fazio de' Morubaldini da Signa (a town ten miles west of Florence). He was prior of Florence several times and was sent in 1310 as ambassador to Pope Clement V to aid in organizing opposition to Emperor Henry VII's coming into Italy.

64. The Conti Guidi, unable to defend the castle of Montemurlo against the Pistoians, were forced to sell it to Florence.

65. According to Cacciaguida, among the many results of the feud between the Church and the Empire was the emigration of the Cerchi family from the small town of Acone to Florence where a feud with the noble Donati family resulted in much civil disturbance. Originally of low birth, the Cerchi rose to wealth and political prominence in Florence.

66. When their castle in the valley of the Greve was destroyed to permit Florence to expand its borders, the Buondelmonti family moved in 1135 to that city. The Buondelmonti became leaders of the Guelph party in Florence.

a bull gone blind is more likely to fall
    than a blind lamb; often a single sword
    will cut more efficaciously than five.   72

If you consider Luni and Urbisaglia,
    how they have perished, how Sinigaglia
    and Chiusi too now follow them to ruin,   75

you should not find it hard to understand
    or strange to hear that families dwindle out
    when even cities pass away in time.   78

All of your works must die, as you must too,
    but they conceal this fact since they endure
    a longer time, and your life is so short.   81

And as the turning of the lunar sphere
    covers and then uncovers ceaselessly
    the shore, so Fortune does with Florence now;   84

and so, you should not be surprised to hear
    me talk about the noble Florentines
    whose fame has disappeared, concealed by time.   87

I knew the Ughi and the Catellini,
    Greci, Filippi, Alberichi, Ormanni,
    illustrious citizens even in decline;   90

I also knew, as great as they were old,
    the families dell'Arca and Sannella,
    the Soldanieri, Ardinghi, and Bostichi.   93

---

73. Luni, an ancient Etruscan city, on the border between Etruria and Liguria, decayed during the Roman period and was eventually destroyed. "Urbisaglia," the ancient Urbs Salvia, in the region of the Marches, had once been an important town, but by Dante's time it had fallen to ruin.

74. "Sinigaglia," now Senigallia, was the ancient city of Sena Gallica. This city on the Adriatic was ruined in the thirteenth century during the wars between the Guelphs and Ghibellines.

75. "Chiusi," the ancient Clusium, located halfway between Florence and Rome, had once been one of the twelve great Etruscan cities.

88–93. The families mentioned in these verses were noble Florentine families that were extinct by Dante's time.

Close to the gate now laden with the weight
    of unbelievable iniquity,
    a cargo that will soon submerge the ship,   96

once lived the Ravignani from whom came
    Guido the Count and all of those who took
    as theirs the noble Bellincione name.   99

The della Pressa were already versed
    in governing as one should, and Galigaio
    already had his hilt and pommel gilded.   102

Already great the pale of vair, the Galli,
    Sacchetti, Giuochi, Fifanti, and Barucci
    and those who blush now for the stave affair.   105

The stock from which sprang the Calfucci branch
    already had grown great, the Arrigucci,
    the Sizii occupied high seats of offices.   108

97–99. The Ravignani were another noble family extinct in Dante's day.

100. The della Pressa were a prominent Ghibelline family who were among those driven out of Florence in 1258.

101. Like the della Pressa, the Galigai ("Galigaio") were exiled with other Ghibellines in 1258.

102. A gilded sword hilt and pommel were a sign of nobility.

103–104. A representation of a strip of ermine ("vair") longitudinally bisected the escutcheon of the Pigli family arms. The Galli were a family of Ghibellines whose houses in Florence, like those of the Galigai, were destroyed in 1293. The Sacchetti were Guelphs and among those who fled Florence after the Ghibelline victory at Montaperti. The Giuochi, the Fifanti, and the Barucci were Ghibelline families; the Barucci were extinct by Dante's time.

105. Durante de' Chiaramontesi, as head of the Salt Import Department of Florence, had reduced the size of a bushel-measure by one stave, appropriating the balance.

106–108. An ancient Guelph family extinct in Dante's time, the Calfucci were ancestors of the Donati. The Arrigucci and the Sizii held public offices during Cacciaguida's time and as Guelphs were among those who fled Florence in 1260 after the Ghibelline victory at Montaperti.

How great I saw them once who now are ruined
    by their own pride! And how those balls of gold
    shone bright as Florence flowered in great deeds!   111

Such were the fathers of those who today
    prolong some vacant office in the Church
    and grow fat sitting in consistory.   114

That insolent, presumptuous clan that plays
    the dragon to all those who flee, the lamb
    to anyone who shows his teeth—or purse—   117

was on the rise, though still of such low class
    that Ubertin Donato was not pleased
    when his father-in-law made him their kin.   120

By then, the Caponsacchi had come down
    from Fiesole to the marketplace; the Giudi
    and Infangati were good citizens.   123

Here is a fact incredible but true:
    one entered the small circle by a gate
    named for the della Pera family.   126

109–110. Here Dante refers to the Uberti, a Ghibelline family of Germanic origin, who had come to Florence in the tenth century.

110–111. The Lamberti, whose arms bore golden balls on a field of blue, were of Germanic origin. The infamous Mosca, a member of their family, was responsible for inciting the Amidei to murder Buondelmonte, the act that began the Guelph-Ghibelline feud. (See note to lines 136–137).

112–114. The Visdomini and the Tosinghi families administered episcopal revenues of the Florentine bishopric whenever the See was vacant.

115–120. This "clan" is the Adimari family, who were Guelphs and as such were expelled from Florence in 1248.

121. Originally from Fiesole, the Caponsacchi were among the first Ghibelline families in Florence.

122–123. The Guidi and Infangati were two ancient Ghibelline families.

All those who bear the handsome quarterings
   of the great Baron Hugh whose name and worth
   are celebrated on Saint Thomas' Day,   129

received from him knighthood and privilege,
   though he who decks that coat of arms with fringe
   today has taken up the people's cause.   132

The Gualterrotti and the Importuni
   existed then; their Borgo would have been
   a quieter place had they been spared new neighbors.   135

The House that was the source of all your tears,
   whose just resentment was the death of you
   and put an end to all your joy of life,   138

was highly honored as were all its clan.
   O Buondelmonte, wrong you were to flee
   the nuptials at the promptings of another!   141

Many who now are sad would have been pleased
   if God had let the Ema drown you when
   you started for our city the first time.   144

127–132. The Marquis Hugh of Brandenburg, vicar of Emperor Otto III, conferred knighthood upon six Florentine families (the Giandonati, the Pulci, the Nerli, the Gangalandi, the Alepri, and the della Bella) who adopted variations of this coat of arms as their own. Giano della Bella, whose family had decked "that coat of arms with fringe," introduced strict reforms against the nobles in 1293; he was banished in 1295.

133–135. The Gualterrotti and the Importuni were ancient Guelph families who lived in the Borgo Santi Apostoli quarter. The "new neighbors," the Buondelmonti, came to live in the Borgo when their castle in Montebuono was destroyed in 1135.

136–137. The "House" was that of the Amidei family. Buondelmonte de' Buondelmonti, betrothed to a daughter of the Amidei, forsook her on their wedding day at the instigation of Gualdrada Donati, whose daughter he later married. This was a serious insult, and members of the indignant Amidei family murdered Buondelmonte, thereby beginning the feud that caused civil unrest in Florence for many years.

139. The "clan" included the Ucellini and Gherandini.

142–144. Cacciaguida laments all the tragedy brought to his city as a result of the arrival of the Buondelmonti family. The Ema river lies between Florence and the castle of Montebuono, the former home of this family.

How fitting for Florence to sacrifice
   a victim to the mutilated stone
     that guards her bridge to mark the end of peace!   147

With these and other men who ruled like them
   I saw a Florence prospering in peace
     with no cause, then, to grieve as she has now.   150

With families like these in charge I saw
   the glory and the justice of her people:
     never the lily on the staff reversed,   153

nor through dissension changed from white to red."

CANTO XVII

WHEN CACCIAGUIDA *finishes speaking, Beatrice encourages Dante to ask his ancestor what he wishes to know concerning the grave future that souls during his journey have predicted for him. Cacciaguida clarifies the prophecies by revealing to Dante that he will be exiled from Florence and that his place of refuge will be first with the great Lombard whose coat of arms is the ladder and the eagle and then with the younger one whose greatness is not yet known. Cacciaguida adds that Dante should not envy his neighbors, because his life will continue long after their perfidies are punished. Having heard the prophecy, Dante is troubled on the one hand by the bitterness of his fate and on the other by the fact that he may be too timid to reveal what he has seen and heard during his journey. His illustrious ancestor, however, urges him to tell the whole truth and assures him that while his* Comedy *and the criticism it levels against great and important men may at first seem harsh, it is bound to nourish mankind, and this honor should be a consolation. The fact that Dante has been introduced only to famous souls as examples of conduct in Hell, Purgatory, and Paradise will give*

153–154. After the expulsion of the Ghibellines in 1251, the Guelphs reversed the Florentine standard from a white lily in a red field to a red lily in a white field (cf. *Chronicles* VI, 43).

his work an enduring fame, because it is through the example of illus-
trious men that mankind can best learn.

Like him who came to Clymene to learn
　　the truth of those things said against him, he
　　who still makes fathers chary of their sons,　　　　　　　　　3

was I, and just so was I felt to be
　　by Beatrice and that holy light
　　who for my sake had moved from where he was.　　　　　　　6

Wherefore my lady said: "Release the flame
　　of your consuming wish; let it come forth
　　marked clearly with the stamp of your desire,　　　　　　　　9

not that your words would add to what we know,
　　but that you better learn to speak your thirst
　　in order that your cup be filled for you."　　　　　　　　　12

"O my own cherished root, so highly raised
　　that, as men see no triangle contains
　　among its angles two that are obtuse,　　　　　　　　　　15

you see, gazing upon the final Point
　　where time is timeless, those contingent things
　　before they ever come into true being.　　　　　　　　　18

While I was still in Virgil's company,
　　climbing the mountain where the souls are healed,
　　descending through the kingdom of the dead,　　　　　　21

ominous words about my future life
　　were said to me—the truth is that I feel
　　my soul foursquare against the blows of chance;　　　　24

and so, it is my keenest wish to know
　　whatever fortune has in store for me:
　　fate's arrow, when expected, travels slow."　　　　　　　27

1. On hearing that he was not Apollo's son as he had always believed, Phaëthon
went to his mother, Clymene, for the truth. She swore that, indeed, he was and urged
him to ask for himself. Phaëthon did so, and at that interview he persuaded his father
to let him drive the chariot of the Sun, an action that proved fatal to him (see *Met-
amorphoses* I, 750–761).

These were the words I spoke to that same light
   who spoke to me before, and so my wish,
   as Beatrice wished, was now confessed.   30

Not with dark oracles that once ensnared
   the foolish folk before the Lamb of God,
   Who takes away all sins, was crucified,   33

but in plain words, with clarity of thought,
   did that paternal love respond to me,
   both hidden and revealed by his own smile: 36

"Contingency, which in no way extends
   beyond the pages of your world of matter,
   is all depicted in the eternal sight;   39

but this no more confers necessity
   than does the movement of a boat downstream
   depend upon the eyes that mirror it.   42

As organ music sweetly strikes the ear,
   so from this Vision there comes to my eyes
   the shape of things the future holds for you.   45

As Hippolytus was forced to flee from Athens
   by his devious and merciless stepmother,
   just so you too shall have to leave your Florence. 48

So it is willed, so it is being planned,
   and shall be done soon by the one who plots
   it there where daily Christ is up for sale.   51

The public will, as always, blame the party
   that has been wronged; vengeance that Truth demands,
   although, shall yet bear witness to the truth.   54

37–42. Contingent things (i.e., things derived from secondary causes) do not exist
beyond the material world, as contingency has no place in eternity. The fact that
these things can be seen within God does not mean that His foreknowledge neces-
sitates events any more than the eyes, seeing a boat move downstream, determine the
course of the vessel.

46–48. When Phaedra, Hippolytus's stepmother, fell in love with him, Hippolytus
rejected her advances and was forced to flee Athens when she subsequently accused
him of attempting to dishonor her (see *Metamorphoses* XV, 497–505).

You shall be forced to leave behind those things
    you love most dearly, and this is the first
    arrow the bow of your exile will shoot.   57

And you will know how salty is the taste
    of others' bread, how hard the road that takes
    you down and up the stairs of others' homes.   60

But what will weigh you down the most will be
    the despicable, senseless company
    whom you shall have to bear in that sad vale;   63

and all ungrateful, all completely mad
    and vicious, they shall turn on you, but soon
    their cheeks, not yours, will have to blush from shame.   66

Proof of their bestiality will show
    through their own deeds! It will be to your honor
    to have become a party of your own.   69

Your first abode, your first refuge, will be
    the courtesy of the great Lombard lord
    who bears the sacred bird upon the ladder,   72

and he will hold you in such high regard
    that in your give and take relationship
    the one will give before the other asks.   75

With him you shall see one who at his birth
    was stamped so hard with this star's seal that all
    of his achievements will win great renown.   78

62–69. The "company" is that of the Bianchi, or White Guelphs, who were exiled
with Dante. After the exile in 1302, they made several attempts to march on Florence.
Dante did not participate in the last attempt in 1304, and about this time he broke
from the party. Specific reasons for this severance are unknown.

70–72. The "great Lombard lord" is believed to be a member of the Scalinger family,
Bartolommeo della Scala of Verona, whose arms consisted of the Imperial eagle
perched upon a golden ladder. Dante took refuge with him in Verona immediately
after separating from the other exiled members of his party.

76–78. The young man is Can Grande della Scala, younger brother of Bartolommeo,
who was born in 1291. Can Grande is said to have been "stamped so hard with this
star's seal" (77) in the sense that, born under the influence of Mars, his great achieve-
ments would be in the field of the martial arts.

The world has not yet taken note of him;
     he is still very young, for Heaven's wheels
     have circled round him now for just nine years.   81

But even before the Gascon tricks proud Henry,
     this one will show some of his mettle's sparks
     by scorning wealth and making light of toil.   84

Knowledge of his munificence will yet
     be spread abroad: even his enemies
     will not be able to deny his worth.   87

Look you to him, expect from him good things.
     Through him the fate of many men shall change,
     rich men and beggars changing their estate.   90

Now write this in your mind but do not tell
     the world"—and he said things concerning him
     incredible even to those who see   93

them all come true. Then he said: "Son, you have
     my gloss of what was told you. Now you see
     the snares that hide behind a few years' time!   96

No envy toward your neighbors should you bear,
     for you will have a future that endures
     far longer than their crime and punishment."   99

When, by his silence, that blest soul revealed
     that he had ceased weaving the woof across
     the warp that I had set in readiness,   102

I said, as one who is in doubt and longs
     to have the guidance of a soul who sees
     the truth and knows of virtue and has love: 105

82. Before 1312, Pope Clement V, the Gascon, had supported Emperor Henry VII
and invited him to Italy; however, Clement apparently changed his mind, withdrew
support, and even fostered opposition to Henry.

91–94. Dante the Poet cannot tell the world (only the Pilgrim knows) because these
things that Can Grande did still have to be done. We must remember that the time
of the Poem is 1300, and Can Grande is only nine years of age.

95. The "gloss" is Cacciaguida's clarification of the many predictions Dante heard
during his journey through the Inferno and Purgatory.

"Father, well do I see how time attacks,
   spurring toward me to deal me such a blow
   as falls the hardest on the least prepared;   108

so, it is good that foresight lend me arms;
   thus, should the place most dear to me be lost,
   my verse, at least, shall not lose me all others.   111

Down through the world of endless bitterness
   and on the mountain from whose lovely crown
   I was raised upward by my lady's eyes,   114

then through the heavens, rising from light to light—
   I learned things that, were they to be retold,
   would leave a bitter taste in many mouths;   117

yet, if I am a timid friend to truth,
   I fear my name may not live on with those
   who will look back at these as the old days."   120

The light that was resplendent in the treasure
   I had found there began to flash more light,
   just like a golden mirror in the sun,   123

and then replied: "The conscience that is dark
   with shame for his own deeds or for another's,
   may well, indeed, feel harshness in your words;   126

nevertheless, do not resort to lies,
   let what you write reveal all you have seen,
   and let those men who itch scratch where it hurts.   129

Though when your words are taken in at first
   they may taste bitter, but once well-digested
   they will become a vital nutriment.   132

110. The "place most dear" is Florence.

112. The "world of endless bitterness" is Hell.

113. The mountain is that of Purgatory.

Your cry of words will do as does the wind
    striking the hardest at the highest peaks,
        and this will be for honor no small grounds;   135

and so you have been shown, here in these spheres,
    down on the Mount and in the pain-filled valley
        only those souls whose names are known to fame,   138

because the listener's mind will never trust
    or have faith in the kind of illustration
        based on the unfamiliar and obscure—   141

or demonstration that is not outstanding."

CANTO XVIII

WHILE DANTE AND Cacciaguida are rapt in thought, Beatrice calls to
the Pilgrim to look into her eyes that are filled with Divine Love, the
love that releases him from all other desires. Beatrice breaks his rapture
by telling him to turn and listen once more to his ancestor, because
Paradise is not only in her eyes. Then Cacciaguida introduces Dante to
a number of famous soldier-souls who appear in the cross flashing like
lightning at the mention of their names. Dante turns to Beatrice and is
again lost in her gaze when suddenly he realizes that he has been trans-
ported from the rosy glow of the fifth sphere of Mars to the silvery sixth
sphere of Jupiter. In this sphere the shining souls group together to form,
one at a time, the letters of the first verse of the Book of Wisdom:
DILIGITE IUSTITIAM QUI IUDICATIS TERRAM, appearing as
gold against silver. Having formed the final letter M, the souls stop.
More lights descend singing on the summit of the M and then suddenly

134. The "highest peaks" refer to the powerful and eminent men such as popes and
politicians who will hear his words.

135. Striking at "the highest peaks" takes much courage.

136–142. Only by using well-known persons as examples can the Comedy be effi-
cacious; Dante can convince no one by citing unknown examples or proof drawn
from obscure facts.

shoot up to form the neck and head of an eagle. The souls of the M now move to fill out the rest of the design of the eagle. Moved by this vision of Justice Dante, in a bitter apostrophe against the Pope, accuses him of having forgotten the example of his predecessors Peter and Paul who died for the Church he is now in the process of ruining.

That holy mirror was rejoicing now
   in his own thoughts, and I was left to taste
   and temper mine, the bitter with the sweet.   3

Then she who was my guide to God said: "Stop,
   think other thoughts. Think that I dwell with Him
   Who lifts the weight of every wrong man suffers."   6

Those loving words made me turn round to face
   my Solace. What love within her holy eyes
   I saw just then—too much to be retold;   9

not only do I fear my words may fail,
   but to such heights my mind cannot return
   unless Another guides it from above.   12

I can recall just this about that moment:
   as I was gazing at her there, I know
   my heart was freed of every other longing,   15

for the Eternal Joy was shining straight
   into my Beatrice's face, and back
   came its reflection filling me with joy;   18

then, with a smile whose radiance dazzled me,
   she said: "Now turn around and listen well,
   not in my eyes alone is Paradise."   21

As here on earth the eyes sometimes reveal
   their deepest wish, if it is wished with force
   enough to captivate all of the soul,   24

1. The "holy mirror" is Cicciaguida, whose soul reflects the light of God, as do the souls of all the Blest.

2–3. Dante's thoughts focus on the predictions, good and bad, which he has heard concerning his future.

8. Cf. Virgil's role in *Purgatory* III, 22; IX, 43, where he is addressed with the same words, *mio conforto,* as is Beatrice here ("my Solace").

so, in the flaring of the sacred fire
   to which I turned, I recognized his wish:
   I saw that he had something more to say.   27

He spoke: "Upon the fifth tier of the tree
   whose life comes from its crown and which bears fruit
   in every season, never shedding leaves,   30

blest spirits dwell whose fame below on earth,
   before they came to Heaven, was so widespread
   that any poet would be enriched by them.   33

Now look up and observe the cross's arms,
   each soul that I shall name there you will see
   flash quick as lightning flashes through a cloud."   36

I saw, as he pronounced the name of Joshua,
   a streak of light flashing across the cross—
   no sooner was it said than it was done.   39

And at the name of the great Maccabees
   I saw another whirling light flash through—
   the cord that spun that top was its own joy!   42

Then came the names Roland and Charlemagne,
   and eagerly I followed these two lights,
   as hunters watch their falcons on the wing.   45

William of Orange, then, and Renouard
   and the Duke Godfrey drew my sight with them
   along the cross; then came Robert Guiscard.   48

40. Maccabees was Judas Maccabaeus, the great warrior who succeeded in resisting the attempts of the kings of Syria to destroy the Jewish religion.

43. Charlemagne (742–814), king of the Franks and Holy Roman emperor, and Roland, his nephew and greatest warrior, are presented here for their efforts against the Saracens.

46. William, count of Orange, is the hero of a group of Old French epics, the *Aliscans* being the best known.

47. Godfrey of Bouillon, leader of the First Crusade (1096), became the first Christian king of Jerusalem.

48. In the latter half of the eleventh century, the Norman warrior Robert Guiscard took southern Italy and Sicily from the Saracens. He died in Salerno in 1085.

The light who spoke to me now moved away
  to mix with other lights and let me hear
  the artist that he was in Heaven's choir.   51

I turned to Beatrice at my right
  to learn from her by word or by a sign
  what she thought I should do, and I beheld   54

new brilliance in her eyes, such purity,
  such ecstasy, her countenance was now
  more beautiful than it had ever been.   57

And as a man feeling from day to day
  more joy in doing good, becomes aware
  thereby that virtue grows in him, just so,   60

seeing that miracle grow lovelier,
  I noticed that my circling with the heavens
  had taken on a greater arc of space.   63

And such a transformation as is seen
  upon a fair-skinned lady's face when shame
  recedes, and blushes vanish instantly,   66

I saw when I turned round: before my eyes
  there was the pure white of the temperate star,
  the sixth, that had received me in its glow;   69

I saw within that Jovial torch the light
  of all the sparkling love rejoicing there
  and forming words of speech before my eyes.   72

As birds just risen from the water's edge,
  as if in celebration for their food,
  flock now in circles, now in drawn-out lines,   75

so there, within those lights the blessèd beings
  were circling as they sang, turning themselves
  first to a *D*, then *I*, then into *L*.   78

49–51. Just as the Cacciaguida episode opened with the notes of the hymn "Arise"
and "Conquer" (*Paradise* XIV, 125), so here in line 51 it comes to its close with the
old warrior returning to the glowing choir of the cross and to the singing of the same
hymn. Dante dedicates 550 lines to his illustrious ancestor, which is the most given
to any character (with the exception of Virgil and Beatrice) in the *Comedy*.

They first flew, singing, to their music's rhythm,
    then having made a letter of themselves,
    they held their form and stopped their song a while.   81

O sacred Muse of Pegasus who gives
    glory to men of genius and long life,
    as they, through you, give it to realms and towns—   84

let your light shine on me that I may show
    these letter-shapes of souls fixed in my mind;
    let your power show through these few lines of mine!   87

They showed themselves to me in five times seven
    vowels and consonants, and I was able
    to understand the written words they formed.   90

The first words of the message, verb and noun:
    DILIGITE IUSTITIAM; then came
    QUI IUDICATIS TERRAM after them.   93

And in the final letter, in the *M*
    of the fifth word they stayed aligned—and Jove's
    silver became the background of their gold.   96

I saw more lights descend, and they alighted
    upon the *M*, and from its peak they sang,
    I think, about the Good that summons them.   99

Just as one sees innumerable sparks
    go flying up when smoldering logs are poked
    (which once encouraged fools to prophesy),   102

so, there I seemed to see more than a thousand
    lights rising up, mounting to different heights,
    as chosen by the Sun that kindles them;   105

and once each spark had found its place of rest,
    I saw the crest and neck of a great eagle
    now patterned in the fire of those sparks.   108

91–93. The message, "Love justice, you who judge the earth," comes from the first
verse of the Book of Wisdom of Solomon in the Apocrypha. The souls in Jupiter are
those of the just, and justice is the project of this sphere.

(The One who paints there has no one to guide
   his hand. He guides Himself. It is from Him
   that skill in birds to build their nests is born.)   111

The other blessèd ones who seemed at first
   content to lilify themselves into the *M*
   with a slight shift completed the design.   114

O lovely star, how many and what jewels
   shone there declaring that justice on earth
   comes from that Heaven which you yourself begem.   117

Therefore, I pray the Mind—for there begins
   your movement and your power—to examine
   the place whence comes the smoke that dims your rays,   120

so that its wrath descend upon, once more,
   all those who buy and sell within the temple
   whose walls were built with miracles and martyrs.   123

O Heaven's army to whom my mind returns,
   pray for those souls on earth who are misled
   by bad example and have gone astray.   126

It used to be that wars were waged with swords,
   but now one fights withholding here and there
   the bread our Father's love denies to none.   129

And you who write only to nullify,
   remember that Peter and Paul, who died
   to save the vineyard you despoil, still live.   132

But you will answer: "I, who have my heart
   so set on him who chose to live alone
   and for a martyr's crown was danced away,   135

know nothing of your Fisherman or Paul."

120. The avarice of the popes is the smoke that blocks imperial authority and prevents the clear administration of justice on earth.

130–132. Pope John XXII was supposed to have issued and rescinded many orders of excommunication. The cancellation of excommunications was a source of revenue for the papacy.

CANTO XIX

THE EAGLE NOW *appears to the Pilgrim with open wings and as if composed of countless sparkling rubies. The lights of the souls who form the beak of the eagle move, and a voice that speaks for all of those composing the sacred emblem informs the Pilgrim that it is exalted in this sphere as the symbol for Divine Justice, and that, although its memory is preserved on earth, its example is not followed. He then asks the eagle to elucidate the meaning of Divine Justice and to help him to resolve a doubt he has had for some time: what justice is there in damning a good soul who, through no fault of his own, has not heard of Christ and has not been baptized? Before he has the chance to express this doubt the eagle goes into a long discourse on the unfathomable nature of God and the inability of His creatures to understand His infinite wisdom. The eagle, showing displeasure, circles above Dante as its souls sing an incomprehensible song which the eagle likens to the mystery of Eternal Judgment which cannot be understood by mortals. Finally, the eagle condemns all those rulers of the times who governed without justice.*

And there before my eyes with wings spread wide
    that splendid image shone, shaped by the souls
    rejoicing in their interwoven joy.   3

They were set there like splendid rubies lit
    each of them by a gleaming ray of sun
    which was reflected straight into my eyes.   6

And what I have to tell you here and now
    no tongue has told or ink has written down,
    nor any fantasy imagined it,   9

for I could hear the beak and see it move;
    I heard its voice use words like *I* and *Mine*
    when in conception it was *We* and *Ours.*   12

11–12. The eagle, representing Justice, is composed of a multitude of souls, but it speaks with one voice and as one being.

"Because of my justice and piety,"
    it said, "I have been raised up to this glory,
    the highest our desires can conceive,   15

and I have left on earth a memory
    which even wicked men are wont to praise,
    though they refuse to follow in my course."   18

Just as from many burning coals will come
    one glow of heat, so from that image came
    a single sound composed of many loves.   21

And I exclaimed: "O everlasting flowers
    of the eternal bliss who concentrate
    all of your many fragrances in one,   24

breathe forth your words now, breaking at long last
    the fasting that has kept me hungering
    for food that I could never find on earth.   27

I know that though God's justice is beheld
    within some other mirror in these spheres,
    your kingdom apprehends its light unveiled.   30

You know my eagerness to hear you speak,
    you also know the nature of the question
    whose answer I have hungered for so long."   33

Then as the falcon, now freed from its hood,
    stretches its neck and starts to beat its wings,
    and preens itself—to show its eagerness—   36

so moved the ensign made of woven voices
    in exaltation of God's grace with song
    known only to the souls who dwell in bliss.   39

Then it said: "He Who with His compass drew
    the limits of the world and out of chaos
    brought order to things hidden and revealed,   42

28-30. The "other mirror" is the sacred mirror of God's justice. The angelic order
of Thrones, which guides the sphere of Saturn, is the order that reflects Divine
judgments.

could not impress his quality so much
    upon the universe but that His Word
    should not remain in infinite excess.   45

The proof of this is in that first proud one,
    the highest of all creatures, who plunged down
    unripe because he would not wait for light;   48

hence, clearly, every lesser nature is
    too small a vessel to contain that Good
    which knows no bounds, whose measure is Itself.   51

Therefore, our vision which can only be
    one of the rays that come from that prime Mind
    which penetrates every created thing,   54

cannot of its own nature be so weak
    as not to see that its own Principle
    is far beyond what our eyes can perceive.   57

And so the vision granted to your world
    can no more fathom Justice Everlasting
    than eyes can see down to the ocean floor: 60

while you can see the bottom near the shore,
    you cannot out at sea; but nonetheless
    it is still there, concealed by depths too deep.   63

There is no light except from that clear sky
    forever cloudless—darkness is the rest,
    the shadow or the poison of the flesh.   66

Now you can see what hiding place it was
    concealed from you the truth of living Justice
    concerning which you were so plagued with doubts;   69

for you would say: 'Consider that man born
    along the Indus where you will not find
    a soul who speaks or reads or writes of Christ,   72

and all of his desires, all his acts
    are good, as far as human reason sees;
    not ever having sinned in deed or word,   75

he dies unbaptized, dies without the faith.
    What is this justice that condemns his soul?
    What is his guilt if he does not believe?' 78

Now who are you to sit in judgment's seat
    and pass on things a thousand miles away,
    when you can hardly see beyond your nose? 81

The man who would argue fine points with me,
    if holy Scripture were not there to guide us,
    surely would have serious grounds for doubt. 84

O earthbound creatures! O thick-headed men!
    The Primal Will, which of Itself is good,
    never moves from Itself, the Good Supreme. 87

Only that which accords with it is just.
    It is not drawn to any finite good,
    but sending forth its rays creates that good." 90

Just as the stork once it has fed its young
    will fly around the nest, and as the chick
    she fed will raise its head to look at her, 93

so did that sacred image circle me,
    those many wills joined there to move its wings,
    and so did I lift up my head to it. 96

Circling, it sang, then spoke: "Even as my notes
    are too high for your mind to comprehend,
    so is Eternal Judgment for mankind." 99

Those blazing fires of the Holy Spirit
    stopped still, and then still in that ensign shape
    which had brought Rome the reverence of the world, 102

it raised its voice again: "And to this realm
    none ever rose who had not faith in Christ,
    before or after he was crucified. 105

But then there are all those who cry, 'Christ, Christ!'
   and at the Judgment Day will be less close
   to Him than will be those who know not Christ.   108

Such Christians shall the Ethiop condemn
   the Day those two assemblies separate,
   one rich, the other poor forevermore.   111

What will the Persians say, then, to your kings
   when they shall see God's open Book and read
   what has been written of their infamies?   114

There they will read, where Albert's deeds are found,
   that act already trembling on the pen,
   which shall lay waste to all the realm of Prague.   117

There they will read about the Seine's distress
   provoked by that debaser of the coin
   whose death will wear the hide of a wild boar;   120

there they will read about the thirsting pride
   by which the Scot and Englishman are maddened,
   neither content to stay within his bounds.   123

The book will show the lecherous, soft life
   of him of Spain, and the Bohemian
   who knew no valor nor had wish to know;   126

109–111. The Ethiop (i.e., heathens in general) will condemn these "Christians" on Judgment Day, when the saved ("rich") and the damned ("poor") shall be separated. (Cf. Matthew 25:31–46; also 8:11–12.)

112. Like "Ethiop" in line 107, "Persians" here stands for heathens in general.

113. The book is that of God's judgment.

118. The "Seine's distress" is the grief that the French people were made to suffer. The Seine River stands for all of France.

119–120. The "debaser of the coin" is Philip the Fair, who, to pay for the wars against Flanders, inflated French currency, resulting in economic ruin for many.

121–123. In the early fourteenth century Edward I and Edward II were at war with Scotland under Wallace and Bruce. The "thirsting pride" is their desire for dominion.

125. Ferdinand IV, king of Castile and Leon (1295–1312), is "him of Spain." The king of Bohemia is Wenceslaus IV (1270–1305).

the book will mark an *I* for all the good
   the Cripple of Jerusalem has done,
   and *M* for all of his perversities;   129

the book will show the cowardice and greed
   of him who guards the island of the fire
   on which Anchises ended his long life,   132

and just to show how little he was worth,
   he will be written up in bits of words
   which will say much in very little space;   135

and clear to all will be the filthy deeds
   of his brother and uncle, who cuckold
   a splendid lineage, a double crown;   138

and Norway's king and Portugal's shall be
   recorded there, and Rascia's, who debased
   the coin of Venice and disgraced himself.   141

127–129. The "Cripple" is Charles II of Naples, titular king of Jerusalem. Charles is characterized here as having one (*I*) virtue as opposed to one thousand (*M*) vices. His one good quality was said to have been his liberality.

131. Frederick II of Sicily had at one time supported the Imperial cause, but on the death of Emperor Henry VII, he abandoned it. Sicily is "the island of the fire."

132. The father of Aeneas, Anchises died in Sicily after the arrival of the Trojans.

137. Frederick's brother was James II of Aragon. His uncle was James, king of the Balearic Islands.

138. The "double crown" refers to the kingdoms of Aragon and Mallorca.

139. Norway's king was Haakon V (1270–1319), who engaged in wars with Denmark. Diniz (or Dionysius), the king of Portugal (1279–1325), is thought to have been one of the better rulers of the time. The reason for his inclusion here is unclear.

140. The capital of Serbia, Rascia, was commonly used to refer to that country. Stephen Urosh II (1275–1321), Rascia's king, counterfeited the Venetian coinage by issuing coins of debased metal in imitation of the Venetian grosso.

Oh happy Hungary, if she escapes
    further abuse! Happy Navarre if she
    but make a rampart of her mountain-chain!   144

In proof of this let everyone pay heed
    to Nicosia's and Famagosta's lot
    whose own beast makes them wail and shriek as he   147

keeps pace with all the others in this pack."

CANTO XX

WHEN THE INDIVIDUAL souls composing the eagle have finished singing,
the eagle tells the Pilgrim to watch its eye closely as it points out six
famous souls who were champions of justice on earth. First the eagle
introduces King David, who is the pupil of the eye, after which come
the five lights that form the eyebrow of the great bird: the Emperor
Trajan, who is the soul closest to the eagle's beak, then Hezekiah fol-
lowed by the Emperor Constantine, then King William II of Naples and
Sicily, and last the Trojan Ripheus. The Pilgrim is puzzled by the pres-
ence of the two pagans, Trajan and Ripheus, and he asks why they are
here. The eagle explains that they were Christians when they died
through the power of Divine Grace and that the workings of predesti-
nation are even beyond the understanding of the souls in Paradise. As
the eagle speaks the two lights of Trajan and Ripheus flash in accom-
paniment.

142–143. The throne of Hungary, which had belonged to Charles Martel (see *Par-
adise* VIII, 64–66), was usurped by Andrew III.

143–144. The kingdom of Navarre, if she could use the Western Pyrenees Mountains
to protect her from French annexation, might remain happy as she is.

145–148. Navarre (and any who are at peace) should take the examples of Nicosia
and Famagosta as representative of the evils that may befall them. These towns of
Cyprus were suffering under the corruption of the rule of Henry II of Lusignan, a
Frenchman.

When he who floods the whole world with his light
    has sunk so far beneath our hemisphere
    that day on every side has disappeared, 3

the sky which he, the sun, alone had lit
    before, now suddenly is lit again
    by many lights, reflections of the one; 6

I was reminded of this heavenly change
    the moment that the emblem of the world
    and of its lords was silent in its beak, 9

for all those living lights were now ablaze
    with brighter light as they began their songs,
    whose fleeting sweetness fades from memory. 12

O sweetest love which wraps you in its smiles,
    how ardent was your music from those flutes
    played with the breath of holy thoughts alone! 15

And when those precious, light-reflecting jewels
    with which I saw the sixth planet begemmed
    imposed silence upon their angel tones, 18

I seemed to hear the murmur of a stream
    as its clear waters flow from rock to rock
    revealing the abundance of its source. 21

And as at the lute's neck the sound of notes
    take form, as does the breath that fills a flute
    escape as music through an opening, 24

just so without a moment of delay,
    the murmur of the eagle seemed to climb
    up through its neck, as through a hollow space, 27

where it became a voice, and from the beak
    emerged the words which I had longed to hear
    and which are now inscribed upon my heart. 30

"That part of me which in a mortal eagle
    sees and endures the sun," it said to me,
    "I want you now to fix your gaze upon. 33

Of all the fire-souls which give me form
    the ones that give the eye within my head
    its brilliant lustre are the worthiest.   36

He at the center as the pupil's spark
    wrote songs inspired by the Holy Spirit
    and once conveyed the ark from town to town,   39

and now he knows the value of his psalms
    so far as his own gifts contributed,
    for his bliss is commensurate to it.   42

Of those five souls that form my eyebrow's arch
    the one who shines the closest to my beak
    consoled the widow who had lost her son,   45

and now he knows from living this sweet life,
    and having lived its opposite, how dear
    it costs a man to fail to follow Christ.   48

He who comes next on the same curving line
    along the upper arch of which I speak
    delayed his death by his true penitence,   51

and now he knows that God's eternal laws
    are not changed when a worthy prayer from earth
    delays today's events until tomorrow.   54

The next light went to Greece bearing the laws
    and me to let the Shepherd take his place—
    his good intentions bore the worst of fruits;   57

37–39. King David, whose psalms were inspired by the Holy Spirit, had the ark of
the covenant moved to Jerusalem (2 Kings 6:2–17; cf. also *Purgatory* X, 55–64). He
forms the pupil of the eagle's eye.

44–48. The "one who shines" is the Roman emperor Trajan (who lived in Christian
times but was a pagan at his death). He was said to have granted a widow's request
for compensation for the death of her son.

49–54. Hezekiah, king of Judah, when told of his impending death, prayed that God
remember his faithful service, and he was rewarded with fifteen more years of life
(see 2 Kings 20:1–6).

55–60. The emperor Constantine, who occupies the highest point on the arch of the
eagle's eyebrow, moved the capital of the Roman Empire to Byzantium, thereby leav-
ing Rome to the popes.

and now he knows that all the evil sprung
   from his good action does not harm his soul,
   though, thereby, all the world has been destroyed.   60

And at the down sweep of the arch you see
   that William, mourned for by the land which now
   deplores the fact that Charles and Frederick live;   63

and now he knows how much is loved in Heaven
   a righteous king, and splendidly he makes
   this clear to all through his effulgence here.   66

Who in your erring world would have believed
   that Ripheus of Troy was here, the fifth
   in this half-circle made of holy lights?   69

And now he knows much more about God's grace
   than anyone on earth and sees more deeply,
   though even *his* eye cannot probe God's depths."   72

Then like the lark that soars in spacious skies,
   singing at first, then silent, satisfied,
   rapt by the last sweet notes of its own song,   75

so seemed the emblem satisfied with that
   reflection of God's pleasure, by Whose will
   all things become that which they truly are.   78

Though my perplexity must have shown through,
   as color shows clear through a piece of glass,
   I could no longer bear to hide my doubt—   81

it burst forth from my lips: "How can this be?"—
   such was the pressure of its weight—at which
   I saw a festival of flashing lights.   84

61–62. These lines refer to William II, "the Good," king of Naples and Sicily (1166–1189), a just ruler whose death was mourned by his people.

63. Charles and Frederick were the kings of Naples and Sicily, respectively. (See *Paradise* XIX, 127–135, where they are reproached.)

68. Ripheus of Troy was one of several Trojan heroes who fell during the sack of Troy and whom Virgil points out as "foremost in justice and zealous for the right" (*Aeneid* II, 426–427). The presence of this relatively obscure pagan in Paradise is a further proof of the incomprehensible nature of Divine Justice.

And then, its eye more radiant than ever,
   the blessèd emblem answered me at once
   rather than keep me wondering in suspense: 87

"I see that you believe these things are true
   because I say them, but you see not how;
   thus, though they are believed, their truth is hid.   90

You do as one who apprehends a thing
   by name, but cannot see its quiddity
   unless someone explains it for his sake.   93

Regnum celorum suffers violence
   gladly from fervent love, from vibrant hope
   —only these powers can defeat God's will: 96

not in the way one man conquers another,
   for That will wills its own defeat, and so
   defeated it defeats through its own mercy.   99

The first soul of the eyebrow and the fifth
   cause you to wonder as you see this realm
   of the angelic host adorned with them.   102

They did not leave their bodies, as you think,
   as pagans, but as Christians with firm faith
   in feet that suffered and in feet that would.   105

One came from Hell (where there is no return
   to righteous will) back to his flesh and bones,
   and this was the reward for living hope;   108

the living hope that fortified the prayer
   made unto God that he be brought to life
   so that his will might be set free to choose.   111

94. The kingdom of heaven willingly endures the assault of love or of hope. Either of these has the power to "defeat God's will" (96), which allows itself to be defeated ("for That will wills its own defeat," 98).

106–108. The one who "came from Hell" is Trajan, whose soul had been in Limbo. "Righteous will" (107) was not enough to lift the soul of Trajan out of Limbo: he needed God's sanctifying grace for his salvation, a grace that is granted only to the living.

This glorious soul, having regained the flesh
   in which it dwelt but a short space of time,
   believed in Him Who had the power to save;   114

and his belief kindled in him such fire
   of the true love that at his second death
   he was allowed to join our festival.   117

The other soul, by means of grace that wells
   up from a spring so deep that no man's eye
   has ever plumbed the bottom of its source,   120

devoted all his love to righteousness,
   and God, with grace on grace, opened his eyes
   to our redemption and he saw the light,   123

and he believed in this; from that time on
   he could not bear the stench of pagan creed,
   and warned all its perverse practitioners.   126

He was baptized more than a thousand years
   before baptism was—and those three ladies
   you saw at the right wheel were his baptism.   129

Predestination! Oh, how deeply hid
   your roots are from the vision of all those
   who cannot see the Primal Cause entire!   132

You men who live on earth, be slow to judge,
   for even we who see God face to face
   still do not know the list of His elect,   135

but we find this defect of ours a joy,
   since in this good perfected is our good;
   for whatsoever God wills we will too."   138

118. The "other soul" is Ripheus.

122–123. God bestowed special grace on Ripheus, enabling him by means of implicit faith, comparable to that which God had given those who were harrowed from Hell, to believe in Christ before His coming.

128. The "three ladies" are the theological virtues of Faith, Hope, and Charity.

Thus, with these words did the supernal sign
   administer to me sweet medicine
   to remedy the shortness of my sight.   141

And as a good lute-player will accord
   his quivering strings to a good singer's voice
   making his song all the more beautiful,   144

so, as the eagle spoke, I can recall
   seeing the holy lights of those two souls
   (as if two blinking eyes were synchronized)   147

quiver in perfect timing with the words.

CANTO XXI

BEATRICE AND THE Pilgrim *have now reached the sphere of Saturn, and Beatrice tells him that she cannot smile here; her beauty is now so great that if it were to shine forth in her smile, the Pilgrim's mortal eyes could not withstand it. Countless lights descend and circle about a golden ladder rising up beyond his sight. A soul approaches; the Pilgrim asks why it has come to him and why there is no music in this sphere. The soul explains: there is no music here for the same reason that Beatrice does not smile; and he has simply come to welcome him as a gesture of love. In an attempt to understand the nature of predestination the Pilgrim insists on asking why it was he and not another who was chosen to welcome him. The soul whirls about, and then it says that not even the highest order of angels could answer that question, and that the Pilgrim should warn mankind, once he has returned to earth, not to presume to know more than the Blest themselves can understand. Humbled, the Pilgrim only asks who the soul was on earth. He identifies himself as Peter Damian, and, after describing his simple life as a contemplative, with bitter sarcasm he criticizes the self-indulgence of the present-day leaders of the Church. At his final words the other lights descend and group around him, raising such a strange and thunderous shout that the Pilgrim is completely overwhelmed.*

By now I had my eyes fixed once again
  upon my lady's face, and with my eyes,
  my mind, which was oblivious of all else.   3

She was not smiling, but, "Were I to smile,"
  she said to me, "what Semele became
  you would become, burned to a heap of ashes: 6

my beauty, as you have already seen,
  becomes more radiant with every step
  of the eternal palace that we climb,   9

and if it were not tempered, such effulgence
  would strike your sight the way a bolt of lightning
  shatters the leafy branches of a tree.   12

We have ascended to the Seventh Light
  which underneath the Lion's blazing breast
  sheds down its radiance mingled with his might.   15

Now back your eyes with an attentive mind;
  make of them perfect mirrors for the shape
  that in this mirror shall appear to you."   18

If one could understand with what delight
  my eyes were feeding on that blessèd face
  when I, at her command, turned them away,   21

then he would know how much joy it gave me
  to be obedient to my heavenly guide,
  were he to weigh one joy against the other.   24

Within the crystal which still bears the name,
  as it goes round the world, of that dear king
  under whose rule all evil was extinct,   27

5–6. At the instigation of Jupiter's jealous wife, Juno, Semele asked to see Jupiter, her lover, in his full splendor. The god's radiance was so great that Semele was burned to ashes (*Metamorphoses* III, 253–315).

26–27. The king was Saturn, the father of Jupiter, who was said to have ruled during a Golden Age of peace and harmony.

I saw—color of gold as it reflects
    the sun—a ladder gleaming in the sky,
    stretching beyond the reaches of my sight.   30

And I saw coming down the golden rungs
    so many splendors that I thought the heavens
    were pouring out the light of every star.   33

As crows, obedient to instinctive ways,
    will flock together at the break of day
    to warm their frigid feathers in the sky,   36

some flying far away not to return,
    some coming back to where they started from,
    some staying where they were, wheeling about,   39

just such a rush of movement happened here,
    with all that sparkling having flocked as one,
    and then alighted on a chosen rung.   42

A splendor from the sparkling nearest us
    became so bright that I said to myself,
    "I see the love for me with which you glow,   45

but she, who teaches me the how and when
    to speak and not to speak, keeps still, so I,
    against my will, do well not asking now."   48

Then she who saw my silence in the sight
    of Him whose vision can behold all things
    said to me: "Satisfy your deep desire."   51

"I know I am not worthy in myself
    to have an answer from you," I began,
    "but for the sake of her who gives me leave   54

to speak, O blessèd life, hidden within
    your happiness, I pray you, let me know,
    what is it made you come so close to me,   57

and tell me why Heaven's sweet symphony
    is silent here in this sphere while below
    in all the rest its pious strains resound."   60

29. The ladder is a symbol of contemplation.

"Your hearing is but mortal like your sight,"
   he said. "There is no singing here just as
   there is no smile on Beatrice's face.   63

Only to welcome you with words and light
   with which my soul is mantled do I come
   this far down on the sacred ladder's steps;   66

nor was it greater love that prompted me:
   as much and even more love burns above—
   you see it in the flaming lights up there.   69

But that deep charity which urges us
   to serve the wisdom governing the world
   assigns each soul his task, as you can see."   72

"O holy lamp," I said, "I clearly see
   how in this court a love entirely free
   gladly obeys Eternal Providence;   75

what I find hard to understand is this:
   why you alone among your fellow souls
   have been predestined for this special task."   78

I had not finished speaking when the light
   just like a millstone at full speed began
   to spin around its inner luminance;   81

and then the love that was inside it said:
   "A ray of God's light focuses on me
   and penetrates the light enwombing me,   84

whose force once joined to that of my own sight
   lifts me above myself until I see
   the Primal Source from which such might is milked. 87

From this derives the joy with which I burn;
   the clearness of my flame will ever match
   my clarity of spiritual vision.   90

Yet even heaven's most illumined soul,
   that Seraph who sees God with keenest eye,
   could not explain what you have asked to know. 93

70. The "deep charity" is God's love.

The truth you seek to fathom lies so deep
   in the abyss of the eternal law,
   it is cut off from every creature's sight.   96

And tell the mortal world when you return
   what I told you, so that no man presume
   to try to reach a goal as high as this.   99

The mind that shines here smolders down on earth;
   how, then, can it accomplish down below
   what it cannot even once it reaches heaven?"   102

I put aside that question which his words
   had so proscribed me from and only dared,
   with humble voice, to ask him who he was.   105

"Between two shores of Italy, not far
   from your own birthplace, rise great crags so high
   that thunder sounds from far below their peaks;   108

they form a humpback ridge called Catria
   below which stands a holy hermitage
   once dedicated to God's praise alone."   111

Thus he began his third address to me,
   and then went on to say: "There I became
   so steadfast in God's service that I lived   114

on nothing but plain foods in olive oil,
   suffering gladly heat and cold all year,
   content in only thoughts contemplative.   117

That cloister once produced for all these heavens
   harvests of souls, but now it is so barren,
   and soon its decadence must be exposed.   120

There I was known as Peter Damian—
   Peter the Sinner in Our Lady's house
   that lies along the Adriatic shore.   123

109. Monte Catria is in the Apennines on the border of Umbria and the Marches.

110. The "holy hermitage" is the monastery of Santa Croce di Fonte Avellana.

121–123. Peter Damian was known also as "Peter the Sinner in Our Lady's house,"
that is, in the monastery of Santa Maria in Porto near Ravenna.

Little of mortal life remained to me
    when I was called and forced to wear the Hat
    which seems to pass only from bad to worse.   126

Lean and barefooted Cephas came, and came
    the mighty vessel of the Holy Spirit,
    both taking food wherever it was offered.   129

Your modern pastors need all kinds of help:
    one here, one there, to lead, to prop and hold
    up their behinds—they are so full of food;   132

their flowing cloaks cover the horse they ride:
    two beasts beneath one hide appear to move!
    O Heaven's Patience, what you must endure!"   135

As he spoke these last words, I saw more flames
    descending, whirling rung to rung, and they
    grew lovelier with every whirl they made.   138

Around this light they came to rest, and then,
    in one voice all those lights let out a cry
    the sound of which no one on earth has heard—   141

nor could I hear their words for all the thunder.

CANTO XXII

THE PILGRIM, STUNNED *by the deafening shout at the close of the last canto, turns for comfort to Beatrice. Like a mother consoling her child, she tells him to remember that he is in Heaven where everything is done for the good; had he understood the words that he heard shouted, he would know the just vengeance that is to befall the corrupt clergy in his own lifetime. The bright light of another soul, St. Benedict, now approaches and speaks. After the saint gives a brief account of his life, the Pilgrim asks the saint if it would be possible to see him without his veil of light. St. Benedict explains that this will be possible only in the highest of heavens where there is perfection and all desires are satisfied.*

St. Benedict hoped that his order would climb the ladder that reaches this highest heaven, but men no longer climb and the monastic orders have relaxed their original spiritual discipline. Having said this the saint, together with his companions, rises in the form of a whirlwind up the ladder, and the Pilgrim and his guide swiftly follow them up into the next heaven: the sphere of the fixed stars. There they enter the constellation of Gemini, the sign under which the Poet was born. In order to put the world in its proper perspective Beatrice suggests that the Pilgrim look back down through the seven celestial spheres. He sees the earth and smiles at its puny insignificance. Then turning to Beatrice, he fixes his eyes on her great beauty.

Shocked, in amazement, like a little boy
 who always runs back to the one in whom
 he trusts the most, so I turned to my guide;   3

and she, just like a mother quick to help
 her pale and breathless son by giving him
 her voice whose calmness always reassures,   6

said, "Don't you know that you are up in Heaven,
 and don't you know that all is holy here
 and every act here springs from righteous zeal?   9

Imagine had they sung or had I smiled,
 what would have happened to you then, if now
 you are so shaken by a single cry?   12

If you had heard the prayer within their shout
 you now would know the vengeance yet to come,
 though you will witness it before you die.   15

The sword of Here on High cuts not in haste
 nor is it slow—except as it appears
 to those who wait for it in hope or fear.   18

But now turn your attention to the rest;
 if you allow my words to guide your eyes,
 many illustrious spirits you will see."   21

As she directed me I turned my eyes
 and saw hundreds of little globes of fire
 growing in beauty through each other's light. 24

I stood there like the anxious man restrained,
    forced to hold back the thrust of his desire,
    longing to ask while fearing to offend;   27

and then the largest and the brightest one
    among those pearls came forward to fulfill
    my silent longing to know who he was.   30

Then from inside it I heard words: "If you
    could see, as I do, with what love we burn,
    you would have shared your silent thought with us.   33

But rather than to cause you some delay
    in reaching your high goal, I shall reply
    directly to the question you hold back.   36

The summit of that mountain on whose slope
    Cassino lies was once inhabited
    by people with perverse and false beliefs;   39

I was the first to carry up to them
    the name of Him Who brought down to the earth
    that truth which gives mankind the strength to rise;   42

such grace shone down on me that I reclaimed
    all the surrounding towns, converting them
    from pagan worship that seduced the world.   45

These other flames were all contemplatives,
    men who were kindled by the warmth that breeds
    the flowers and the fruits of holiness.   48

28. The "largest and the brightest one" is the spirit of St. Benedict, founder of monasticism in the Western Church.

37–39. Monte Cassino, which overlooks the Liri Valley, is approximately halfway between Naples and Rome. The town of Cassino is located at the mountain's base.

Here is Macarius and Romuald,
    here are my brothers who kept to the cloisters,
    and, never roaming, kept a steadfast heart."   51

And I to him: "The love you have shown me
    in speaking this way and the good intentions
    I truly see glowing in all your fire   54

allow my confidence to open wide:
    it grows, unfolding petals like a rose
    warmed by the sun, till now it is full blown: 57

therefore, I pray you father, please tell me,
    assure me: do I have sufficient grace
    to see the unveiled image of your face?"   60

Whereon he said: "Brother, your high desire
    shall be fulfilled in the last sphere, for there
    not only mine but every wish comes true;   63

for there, and only there, is every wish
    become a perfect, ripe, entire one,
    there where each part is always where it was: 66

that sphere is in no space, it has no pole,
    and since our ladder reaches to that height,
    its full extent is stolen from your sight.   69

It was the patriarch Jacob who saw
    our ladder stretch to touch the final height,
    the time he dreamed of it so thronged with angels.   72

49. Several saints are known by the name Macarius, the two most famous being St. Macarius the Elder (301–391), also called the Egyptian, and St. Macarius the Younger of Alexandria (d. 404). Both were disciples of St. Anthony. St. Macarius the Younger directed the activities of five thousand monks, and is known as the founder of Eastern monasticism. As such, he can be viewed as the counterpart of St. Benedict, and is probably the saint to which Dante refers in this sphere. Born ca. 950 in Ravenna of the Onesti family, Romuald founded the Order of Camaldoli, or reformed Benedictines.

70–72. Jacob "dreamed that a ladder was set upon the ground with its top reaching to heaven; angels of God were ascending and descending on it" (Genesis 28:12).

But now no man will lift a foot from earth
    and try to climb it, and my Rule is worth
    the wasted parchment it is written on.   75

The walls that used to be our abbey cells
    are dens for beasts now, and the cowls monks wear
    are just so many sacks of rotting meal.   78

The greed of usury, however gross,
    offends God less than does that holy fruit
    which drives the hungry hearts of monks insane;   81

for what the Church has in its keeping should
    be for the poor who ask it in God's name,
    not for the families of monks—or worse.   84

The flesh of mortals is so weak: on earth
    a good beginning does not last as long
    as the oak's springing to the acorn's birth.   87

Peter built his without silver or gold,
    and I constructed mine with prayer and fast
    while Francis, his convent, with humbleness;   90

if you examine each one's origins,
    then look again at what became of it,
    you see the white has withered into dark.   93

Yet Jordan's waters at the will of God
    flowed backward and the Sea fled—miracles
    far greater than if God now helped His Church."   96

These were his words to me; then he drew back
    into his company whose flames closed in,
    and like a whirlwind, they were swept on high.   99

With a mere gesture my sweet lady sped
    me up behind them, up the ladder's rungs,
    my nature conquered by her greater power.   102

Down here on earth where men go up or down
    by natural means, there never was a speed
    to match the motion of my wings up here.   105

Reader, as I hope ever to return
    here to this holy triumph for whose sake,
    I weep my sins and beat my breast—no quicker   108

could you have pulled your finger from a flame
    and thrust it in, than I caught sight and was
    already in the sign that follows Taurus.   111

O glorious constellation! O mighty stars
    pregnant with holy power which is the source
    of all of whatever genius may be mine,   114

in company with you there rose and set
    He who is father of all mortal life
    when I drew my first breath of Tuscan air;   117

and then, when that grace was bestowed on me
    to enter the great sphere that makes you turn,
    to your own zone of stars I was assigned!   120

To you devoutly my soul breathes its prayer
    to grant it strength enough for what is now
    the hardest phase to reach the journey's end.   123

"You are so close to final blessedness,"
    said Beatrice, "that you now must keep
    your eyes unclouded and your vision keen;   126

and so, before insiding further here,
    look down and see how vast a universe
    I have already put beneath your feet,   129

so that your heart, knowing the utmost joy,
    may greet that host of the Triumphant
    who come in joy through this ethereal round.   132

My vision travelled back through all the spheres,
    through seven heavens, and then I saw our globe;
    it made me smile, it looked so paltry there.   135

115–116. The sun was rising and setting in Gemini (May 21–June 21) when Dante
was born in 1265. The precise day of Dante's birth, however, is not known.

I hold that mind as best that holds our world
    for least, and I consider truly wise
    the man who turns his thoughts to other things. 138

I saw Latona's daughter glowing full
    without those shadows which had led me once
    to think that she was rare and dense in parts. 141

On your son's face, Hyperion, my eyes
    could gaze, and I saw, circling close to him,
    how Maia and Dione's children move; 144

From there I saw the tempering of Jove
    between his son and sire—and it was clear
    how they could change position in their course. 147

All seven at one time were visible:
    I saw how vast they were, how swift they spun,
    and all the distances between the spheres; 150

as for the puny threshing-ground that drives
    us mad—I, turning with the timeless Twins,
    saw all of it, from hilltops to its shores. 153

Then, to the eyes of beauty my eyes turned.

139–141. Latona's daughter is the moon, or Diana, sired by Jupiter.

142–143. Hyperion, one of the Titans, was father of Helios, the Sun god in earliest Greek mythology (called Sol by the Romans). For the first time in the poem the Pilgrim can bear to look into the sun, an indication of his growth in vision and understanding.

144. Maia, the daughter of Atlas, produced Mercury by Jupiter. Dione's child was Venus. All of these references are to the parents of gods for whom heavenly bodies were named.

145–147. Jove's son was Mars and his sire Saturn. Jove (Jupiter) is referred to as "tempering" because of its location in the planetary system: It is between the heat of Mars and the cold of Saturn.

CANTO XXIII

Now in the sphere of the fixed stars Beatrice is anxiously waiting for
something to appear. Before long the sky begins to lighten and Beatrice
announces the arrival of the Church Triumphant. Looking up, the Pil-
grim sees the light of Christ shining on the whole assembly, and he is
so transfixed and transported by the sight of Him that he can no longer
remember what he did at that point. The Pilgrim can now look upon
the smiling face of Beatrice, and when he does, he is forced to admit
that her beauty defies description. Beatrice tells him to look again at
the Triumph of Christ. By this time Christ has ascended, but His splen-
did light shines down on everyone from above as the Pilgrim fixes his
eyes on the brightest of the remaining lights, the Virgin Mary, who is
crowned by a torch borne by an angel who circles the Virgin summoning
her to follow her Son to the highest sphere. They ascend while all the
souls of the Church, their arms stretched towards the heavens, begin to
sing with unforgettable beauty the hymn Regina celi.

As a bird quiet among the leaves she loves
    sits on the nest of her belovèd young
    all through the night that hides things from our sight,   3

anxious to look upon her longed-for ones,
    eager to go in search of food for them
    (her heavy labors she performs with joy),   6

foretelling daybreak from an open bough,
    she waits there for the sun with glowing love,
    her gaze fixed on the birth of a new day—   9

just so my lady waited, vigilant,
    intense, as she looked at that part of Heaven
    beneath which the sun's movement seems so slow;   12

then I, who saw her poised in longing there,
    became like one who wishes he had more
    and lets his hope feed on anticipation.   15

But time between the *when* was quick to pass—
   I mean the *when* of waiting and beholding
   the heavens growing bright and brighter still.   18

And Beatrice said: "Behold the hosts
   of Christ in triumph, and see all the fruit
   harvested from the turning of these spheres."   21

I saw her face aflame with so much light,
   her eyes so bright with holy happiness,
   that I shall have to leave it undescribed.   24

As in the clearness of a fullmooned sky
   Trivia smiles among eternal nymphs
   who paint the depths of Heaven everywhere,   27

I saw, above a myriad of lights,
   one Sun that lit them all, even as our sun
   illuminates the stars of his domain;   30

and through its living light there poured the glow
   of its translucent substance, bright, so bright
   that my poor eyes could not endure the sight.   33

O Beatrice, loving guide, sweet one!
   She answered: "That which overcomes you now
   is strength against which nothing has defense.   36

Within it dwell the wisdom and the power
   that opened between Heaven and earth the road
   mankind for ages longed for ardently."   39

As fire when it expands within a cloud
   must soon explode because it has no space,
   and, though against its nature, crash to earth,   42

so my mind there amid so rich a feast
   began to swell until it broke its bounds,
   and what became of it, it does not know.   45

"Open your eyes, look straight into my face!
   Such things have you been witness to that now
   you have the power to endure my smile."   48

25–27. Trivia is another name for Diana, the goddess of the moon.

As one just shaken from a dreamy sleep
  who having dreamed has now forgotten all
  and strives in vain to bring it back to mind,   51

so I was hearing her self-offering,
  an invitation that can never be
  erased within the book of my past life.   54

If at this moment all the tongues of verse,
  which Polyhymnia and her sisters nourished
  with their sweet milk, sang to assist my art,   57

their singing would not come to one one-thousandth
  part of the truth about her sacred smile
  nor how it set her holy face aglow;   60

so I find that my consecrated poem
  describing Paradise will have to make
  a leap, like one who finds his road is blocked.   63

Now bear in mind the weight of my poem's theme,
  think of the mortal shoulders it rests on,
  and do not blame me if I stagger here: 66

this stretch of sea my vessel's prow now dares
  to cut is no place for a little boat
  nor for a captain who would spare himself.   69

"Why are you so enamored of my face
  that you do not turn to the lovely garden
  flowering in the radiance of Christ?   72

There is the Rose in which the Word of God
  took on the flesh, and there the lilies are
  whose fragrance led mankind down the good path."   75

Thus Beatrice. And I, eager to serve
  her every wish, surrendered once again
  my frail eyes to the battle of the light.   78

___

56. Polyhymnia is the Muse of songs to the gods, and her "sisters" are all the other Muses.

Sometimes on cloudy days my eyes have seen
   a ray of pure sunlight come streaming through
   the broken clouds and light a field of flowers, 81

just so I saw there hosts of countless splendors
   struck from above by ardent rays of love,
   but could not see the source of such a blaze. 84

O Mighty Force that seals them with such light,
   You raised yourself on high so that my eyes,
   powerless in your presence, might perceive. 87

The sound of that sweet flower's name, the one
   I pray to night and day, drew all my soul
   into the vision of that flame of flames; 90

and when both of my eyes revealed to me
   how rich and glorious was that living star
   that reigns in Heaven, as it had reigned on Earth, 93

down from Heaven's height there came a flaming torch
   shaped in a ring, as if it were a crown,
   that spun around the glory of her light. 96

The sweetest sounding notes enrapturing
   a man's soul here below would sound just like
   a clap of thunder crashing from a cloud 99

compared to the melodious tones that poured
   from the sweet lyre crowning the lovely sapphire
   whose grace ensapphires the heaven's brightest sphere: 102

"I am angelic love encompassing
   the joy supreme who breathed from out the womb
   which was the place where our Desire dwelt, 105

92. The "living star" is Mary, who in the liturgy of the Church is referred to as the "Morning Star" as well as the "Star of the Sea."

94–96. The "flaming torch" is probably the loving flame of the Angel Gabriel. His shaping of a ring in the form of a crown around the "glory of her light" is symbolic of the Annunciation.

105. Here Desire is Christ.

and I shall circle you, Heavenly Lady
    while you follow your Son, to highest heaven
    and with your presence make it more divine."   108

With this the circling melody was sealed,
    and all the other lights within that sphere
    sang out the Blessèd Virgin Mary's name.   111

The regal mantle folding itself round
    the turning spheres, and nearest to the breath
    and ways of God it burns and quickens most,   114

was curving round us with its inner shore
    at such a distance that from where I stood
    as yet there was no sign that it was there;   117

and so my mortal eyes did not have strength
    enough to see the crowned flame as it rose,
    higher and higher, following her son.   120

And as an infant after it has suckled
    will raise its arms up searching for its mother,
    expressing all the love with which it glows,   123

so I saw all those radiances stretch
    their flame on high, thus making clear to me
    how deep their love, how much they cherished Mary.   126

There they remained suspended in my sight
    singing "*Regina celi*" in tones so sweet,
    the joy of it will never leave my mind.   129

O what abundant grace is stored up here
    inside those richest coffers who below
    in our world sowed the land with their good seed!   132

Herein they truly live and they enjoy
    the wealth their tears had won for them while they
    in Babylonian exile scorned all gold.   135

128. "*Regina celi*" is a Church hymn sung at Easter in praise of the virgin Mary,
the "Queen of Heaven."

135. "Babylonian exile" is a reference from the Old Testament that came to signify
the earthly life.

And here, victorious, beneath the Son
  of God and Mary and amid the good
    souls of the Old and the New Covenant   138

triumphs the one who holds the keys to glory.

CANTO XXIV

BEATRICE SOLEMNLY REQUESTS that the Pilgrim be allowed to partake in some way of the Divine Knowledge of the souls in this sphere. From the brightest group of spinning lights the brightest light of St. Peter comes forth in answer to Beatrice's request and circles her three times. Beatrice asks St. Peter to test her ward on his faith, not that there is any question about it but rather so that he may have the opportunity to glorify it here in this heaven. St. Peter first asks the Pilgrim to define Faith, then he asks him if he possesses it, and finally he inquires about the source of his faith and how he knows that the source is valid. As a sign of their approval of his answers, all the souls there sing out "Te Deum laudamus." Then the great saint asks the Pilgrim to confess to him what he personally believes and to tell how it was made known to him. Because the Pilgrim has answered so well, St. Peter joyfully blesses him, and singing, he circles him three times.

"O fellowship of those chosen to feast
  at the great supper of the Lamb of God
    Who feeds you, satisfying all your needs,   3

if by the grace of God this man foretaste
  of what falls from the table of the Blest
    before the hour death prescribes for him,   6

consider his immeasurable thirst;
  bedew him with a few drops, for you drink
    forever from the Source of this man's thoughts."   9

Thus Beatrice. Then those blissful souls
  started to spin in circles on fixed poles,
    each looking like a comet flaming bright.   12

As wheels in clocks are synchronized to move,
    one slowly, looked at closely, almost still—
    the other seems to fly compared to it,   15

just so those whirling wheels by different-
    ly dancing, through their movement, fast or slow,
    revealed to me the measure of their bliss.   18

From one that spun the richest light I saw
    emerge a flame so radiant with joy,
    no greater brightness danced within the sphere;   21

three times it circled Beatrice's soul
    accompanied by music so divine
    my memory cannot recapture it,   24

and so, my pen skips over such detail—
    not fantasy nor words are good enough
    to paint the subtle folds of Heaven's light.   27

"O holy sister mine, the burning love
    that glows within your earnest prayer to us
    releases me to you from my bright sphere."   30

That sacred fire, once it stopped circling her,
    breathed forth his words directly to my lady,
    saying precisely what I said above.   33

And she: "Eternal light of the great man
    to whom Our Lord brought down and did bequeath
    the keys to this, our paradise of joy,   36

now test this man on questions grave or light,
    as pleases you, pertaining to that faith
    by means of which you once walked on the sea.   39

If love and hope and faith he truly has,
    you will know, for your eyes are fixed upon
    the place where everything that is is seen.   42

But since this realm was won by citizens
    of the true faith, fitting it is for him
    to glorify it by discussing it."   45

42. The "place" is God.

Just as a bachelor arms his mind with thought
   in silence till his master sets the question
   to be discussed but not decided on,   48

so did I arm myself with arguments
   while she was speaking, that I be prepared
   for such a questioner and such a creed.   51

"Speak up, good Christian, and declare yourself!
   Faith, what is Faith?" At which I raised my eyes
   to look upon the light that breathed these words;   54

and then I turned to look at Beatrice
   whose glance was urging me to let pour forth
   the waters welling up within my soul.   57

"May the same Grace that grants me to profess
   my faith before the great centurion,"
   I said, "grant that my thoughts be well expressed."   60

And I went on: "As the veracious pen,
   father, of your dear brother, who with you
   set Rome upon the path of true faith, wrote: 63

Faith is the substance of those hoped-for things
   and argument for things we have not seen.
   And this I take to be its quiddity."   66

Next I heard: "You are right but only if
   you understand why Faith is classified
   as *substance* first and then as *argument*."   69

I answered: "The deep mysteries of Heaven
   that generously reveal themselves to me
   are so concealed from man's eyes down on earth   72

that they exist there only in belief;
   on such a base is high hope built—it is
   substant by its own nature, one could say.   75

And since from this belief we must construct
   logical proofs for what cannot be seen,
   by nature, this partakes of *argument*."   78

62. The "dear brother" is St. Paul.

Then I heard: "If, on earth, all that is learned
   by mortal minds is so well understood,
   there would be no place for the sophist's wit."   81

That burning love breathed forth these words, and then
   he added: "Now that you have thoroughly
   examined both this coin's alloy and weight,   84

tell me, do you have such coin in your purse?"
   I answered: "Yes I do, so bright and round,
   I have no doubt as to its quality."   87

Then from the depths of that light's radiance
   poured the words: "This inestimable gem
   upon which every other virtue sets,   90

where did you get it?" I: "The bountiful
   rain of the Holy Spirit showering
   the parchments, Old and New, is to my mind   93

unquestionable certainty of Faith,
   so accurate that any other proof
   compared to it would sound most unconvincing."   96

I heard: "These premises, the Old and New,
   which you believe to be conclusive proof,
   how do you know they are God's holy word?"   99

And I: "The proof that what I read is true
   is in the works that followed: Nature's hand
   could never heat or forge that kind of iron."   102

Then the reply: "Tell me, how do you know
   that these works ever were? You use as proof,
   and nothing more, what still needs to be proved."   105

"If the world turned to Christ without the help
   of miracles," I said, "then that would be
   a miracle far greater than them all,   108

for you, hungry and poor, entered the field
   to sow the good plant of the faith that once
   grew as a vine and now is but a thorn."   111

89. The "inestimable gem" is Faith.

I said this, and the high and holy choir
   let ring "*Te Deum laudamus*" through the spheres
   in strains of music heard only in Heaven.   114

That Baron who had led me branch by branch,
   examining my faith, to where we now
   were getting closer to the topmost leaves,   117

spoke out again: "The Grace that lovingly
   speaks with your mind, parting your lips, till now
   has let them speak the way they should, and I   120

approve of what I heard come from your mouth.
   But now you must declare your creed to me,
   and then tell me the source of your belief."   123

"O holy father, spirit who now sees
   that faith confirmed that led him to the tomb,
   though younger feet than his arrived there first,"   126

I answered him, "you want me to reveal
   the form of my unhesitating faith,
   and you have asked the reason for its being.   129

I tell you: I believe in one, sole God
   eternal Who, unmoved, moves all the heavens
   that spin in His love and in His desire;   132

and for such faith as mine I have the proofs
   not only of physics and metaphysics,
   but of that truth which rains down from this realm   135

through Moses, through the Prophets, through the Psalms,
   and through the Gospel and through you who wrote
   once kindled by the Holy Spirit's tongue;   138

and I believe in three eternal Beings,
   an Essence that is One as well as Three
   where *is* and *are* describe it equally.   141

Concerning this profound and holy state
    of which I speak, the teachings of the Gospel,
    in many places, has made up my mind.   144

This is the source, this is the very spark
    which then ignites into a living flame
    and like a star in Heaven lights my mind."   147

Then, as a lord delighted with the message
    delivered by his page embraces him,
    rejoicing in the happy news he bears,   150

thus, singing benedictions over me,
    the apostolic light that bid me speak,
    when I was silent, circled me three times,   153

so much delight my words had given him.

CANTO XXV

*THE CANTO OPENS with an expression of the Poet's hope to be able to
return by means of his poetic endeavors to Florence, and there at the
site of his baptism into the faith receive the poet's crown. Then Beatrice
points out St. James, who has just approached and greeted St. Peter.
Beatrice initiates the second examination by asking St. James to make
Hope heard in this sphere. Encouragingly, the saint tells the Pilgrim to
look up and have confidence, and then poses the following questions:
What is Hope? What is its source? What does it promise? When he
answers the questions correctly, all the souls from above sing, "Sperent
in te." Then a third light, whom Beatrice identifies as St. John, joins
Peter and James in their dance. Intent on seeing with his own eyes if
the legend concerning St. John's body being taken to Heaven with his
soul was true, the Pilgrim stares fixedly at the glowing saint, who per-
ceives the Pilgrim's curiosity and replies that his body has turned to dust
on earth and that until the Day of Judgment only Christ and the Virgin
Mary possess both body and soul. As the Pilgrim listens and looks at*

the light of St. John he loses his sight and is troubled that he can no longer see his guide, Beatrice.

If ever it happen that this sacred poem
    to which both Heaven and Earth have set their hand,
    and made me lean from laboring so long,   3

wins over those cruel hearts that exile me
    from my sweet fold where I grew up a lamb,
    foe to the wolves that war upon it now,   6

with a changed voice and with another fleece,
    I shall return, a poet, and at my own
    baptismal font assume the laurel wreath,   9

for it was there I entered in the faith
    that counts God's souls for Him, the faith for which
    Peter just turned himself into my crown.   12

And then a light began to move toward us
    out of the sphere which had produced that rare
    first fruit of Christ's own vicarage on earth;   15

whereat, my lady, radiant with joy,
    said to me: "Look, look there! You see the Baron
    who draws souls to Galicia down on earth."   18

As when a dove alights beside its mate,
    and it begins to coo and circle round
    the other in expression of its love,   21

even so did I behold one glorious
    and great lord greet the other as the two
    sang praises for the feast that Heaven serves.   24

Then, once the joyful greetings were exchanged
    they stopped and stood in silence *coram me*—
    their brilliance was too powerful for sight.   27

17–18. The Baron is St. James the Apostle (the same term is applied to St. Peter in Canto XXIV, 115). James was the son of the fisherman Zebedee and Salome, and the brother of John the Apostle and Evangelist.

23. The "two" are St. Peter and St. James.

26. *Coram me* is Latin, meaning "in front of me."

And then my Beatrice, smiling, said:
  "Illustrious life, the one chosen to write
  of the largesse of our celestial Court,   30

make hope resound throughout this heaven's height:
  you can, you were its symbol all those times
  Jesus bestowed more light upon His three."   33

"Lift up your head and reassure yourself,
  for all that rises from the mortal world
  must ripen here in our own radiance."   36

These words of strength came from the second flame,
  whereby, up to those hills I raised my eyes,
  which had been lowered by excessive brilliance,   39

"Since of His grace our Emperor has willed
  that you before your death come face to face
  with His own Counts in His most secret hall,   42

that, having seen the truth of our Court here,
  you, in yourself and others, may give strength
  to Hope which makes men love the good on earth,   45

now tell me what is Hope, how much of it
  thrives in your mind, and where your Hope comes from."
  So spoke the second light a second time.   48

And that devout one who on my high flight
  had guided every feather of my wings
  anticipated my reply, and said: 51

"There is no son of the Church Militant
  with greater hope than his, as you can read
  in Him whose radiance lights all our host;   54

and this is why he is allowed to come
  from Egypt to behold Jerusalem
  before his fighting days on earth are done.   57

42. The "Counts" are the saints (cf. feudal terminology in 17 and 40); the "most secret hall" is the Empyrean.

56. Egypt represents life on earth (see Psalm 113:1), and it makes allusion to the slavery of the Jews in Egypt (see *Purgatory* II, 46), while Jerusalem stands for the City of God (see Hebrews 12:22).

The two remaining questions you have asked
   not for your sake, but that he may report
   to men on earth how much you cherish Hope— 60

I leave to him: they are not difficult
   nor is self-praise involved. So let him speak,
   and may he answer with the grace of God." 63

As pupil answering his teacher would,
   ready and willing to display his worth,
   so well-versed in his subject, I said, "Hope 66

is sure expectancy of future bliss
   to be inherited—the holy fruit
   of God's own grace and man's precedent worth. 69

From many stars this light comes to my mind,
   but he who first instilled it in my heart
   was highest singer of the Highest Lord. 72

'Let them have hope in Thee who know Thy name,'
   so sings his sacred song. And who does not
   know of That Name if he has faith like mine? 75

And in your own epistle you instilled
   me with his dew, till now I overflow
   and pour again your shower upon others." 78

While I was saying this, within that living
   bosom of luminescence flashed a flame,
   repeating quick and bright as lightning strikes. 81

It breathed: "The love that always burns in me
   for Hope, that followed me even to the palm
   and the departure from the battlefield, 84

moves me to speak again to you who loves
   this virtue: give me joy by telling me
   what promise does your Hope make to your soul." 87

And I: "The Old and the New Testaments
   define the goal—which points me to the promise—
   of those souls that Our Lord has made His friends. 90

71–72. He "who first instilled" is David, the Psalmist.

Isaiah testifies that every man
　　in his homeland shall wear a double raiment,
　　and his homeland is this sweet life of bliss.   93

There is also your brother, where he writes
　　about the white robes—he makes manifest
　　this revelation more explicitly."   96

And, on the sound of my last word I heard
　　ring out "*Sperent in te*" above my head,
　　and all the dancing spheres gave their response.   99

Then, one among those lights became so bright
　　that if the Crab possessed just one such star,
　　winter would have one month of one long day.   102

As a young girl rises and in her joy
　　rushes to dance in honor of the bride
　　without a thought of showing off herself,   105

so did I see that brilliant splendor rush
　　to reach the two circles that whirled in dance
　　whose rhythm was in tune with their great love.   108

It joined them in their dance and in their song;
　　and all the while my lady, like a bride,
　　stood gazing at them, motionless and quiet.   111

"This is the one who lay upon the breast
　　of our own Pelican; he is the one
　　who from the Cross assumed the great bequest."   114

These were the words my lady said to me,
　　but no more after than before she spoke
　　did she once take her eyes away from them.   117

As one who squints and strains his eyes to see
　　a little of the sun in its eclipse,
　　and who through looking can no longer look,   120

91–93. The "double raiment" is the union of body and soul in Heaven. (See Isaiah
61:7.)

so did I stare at that last blaze of light
    until I heard the words: "Why blind yourself
    by looking for what has no place up here?"   123

My body is in earth as earth, and there
    it lies with others till our number is
    the predetermined total set by God.   126

Two Lights and no more, were allowed to rise
    straight to our cloister clad in double robes—
    explain this to your world when you go back."   129

His voice had stopped the flaming circle's dance,
    and with it stopped the mingling of sweet sound
    breathed by that triune breath in harmony,   132

as oars, driven through water at a pace,
    stop all together when a whistle blows,
    to signal danger or prevent fatigue.   135

Ah, the strange feeling running through my mind
    when I turned then to look at Beatrice
    only to find I could not see, and she   138

so close to me, and we in Paradise!

CANTO XXVI

ST. JOHN BEGINS *the third and final examination on Love by asking the Pilgrim what the final goal of his love is, assuring him in the meantime that Beatrice has the power to restore his sight. The Pilgrim answers that the beginning and end of his love is God. Having satisfactorily answered this question, the Pilgrim is required to tell precisely how and why he is drawn to right love. When he answers correctly, the whole assembly together with Beatrice sings "Holy, Holy, Holy" and the Pil-*

127–129. The "Two Lights" are Christ and the Virgin Mary, who were the only ones allowed to rise to Heaven in the body.

grim regains his sight. He is surprised to see that another light has joined
the three there beside him. It is Adam, who immediately discerns the
Pilgrim's questions in the mind of God and tells the Pilgrim so. He has
four questions for Adam: how long ago was he created, how much time
did he spend in the Earthly Paradise, what did he do to provoke God's
wrath, and what language did he speak.

While I stood there confounded by my blindness,
    from out the effulgent flame that took my sight,
    there came a breath of voice that made me heed   3

its words: "Until you have regained the sense
    of sight which your eyes have consumed in me,
    let discourse be a means of recompense.   6

Begin then, tell what is it that your soul
    is set upon—and you may rest assured
    your sight is only dazzled not destroyed: 9

the lady who guides you through the Divine
    spheres has that power in a single glance
    that rested in the hand of Ananias."   12

I said: "At her own pleasure, soon or late,
    let her restore my eyes that were the gates
    she entered with the fire that burns me still.   15

The Good, that full contentment of this Court,
    is Alpha and Omega of all texts
    Love reads to me in soft or louder tones."   18

The same voice that had just now calmed the fear
    I felt in sudden blind bewilderment
    once more encouraged me to speak. It said: 21

"But certainly, you need a finer sieve
    to sift this matter through: you must explain
    who made you aim your bow at such a mark?"   24

I said: "Through philosophic arguments
    and through authority which comes from here
    such love as this has stamped me with its seal;   27

for good perceived as good enkindles love,
    and makes that love more bright the more that we
    can comprehend the good which it contains.   30

So, toward that Essence where such goodness rests
    that any goodness found outside of It
    is only a reflection of its ray,   33

the mind of man, in love, is bound to move
    more than toward any other, once it sees
    the truth on which this loving proof is based.   36

Such truth is made plain to my mind by him
    who demonstrates to me the primal love
    of each and every endless entity.   39

Plain it was made by the True Author's voice
    when He said, speaking of Himself, to Moses:
    "I shall show you all of my goodness now."   42

Made plain it also is from the first words
    of your great Gospel which cries out to men,
    loudest of all, the mysteries of Heaven."   45

And then I heard: "As human reason proves
    and revelation which concurs with it,
    of all your loves the highest looks to God.   48

But tell me, are there other ties you feel
    that draw you to Him? Let your words explain
    the many teeth with which your love can bite."   51

The sacred purpose in the questioning
    of Christ's own eagle here was clear to me—
    I knew which way my answer had to go.   54

I spoke again: "All of those teeth with strength
    to move the heart of any man to God
    have bitten my heart into loving Him.   57

The being of the world and my own being,
    the death He died so that my soul might live,
    the hope of all the faithful, and mine too,   60

joined with the living truth mentioned before,
    from that deep sea of false love rescued me
    and set me on the right shore of true Love.   63

I love each leaf with which enleaved is all
    the garden of the Eternal Gardener
    in measure of the light he sheds on each."   66

The instant I stopped speaking all of Heaven
    filled with sweet singing, as my lady joined
    the others chanting: "Holy! Holy! Holy!"   69

As sleep is broken by a flash of light,
    the visual spirit rushing to the gleam
    which penetrates the eyes from lid to lid,   72

and the roused sleeper shrinks from what he sees,
    confounded by his sudden wakening,
    until his judgment comes to aid his sight,   75

so Beatrice drove out every speck
    clouding my vision with her splendid eyes
    whose radiance spread a thousand miles and more;   78

so I could see much better than before,
    and then, surprised with my new sight, I asked
    about a fourth light that was with us now.   81

My lady said: "Within that blaze of rays,
    in loving contemplation of his maker,
    is the first soul the First Power first made."   84

As tops of trees will bow to sweeping gusts
    of wind, only to straighten up again
    by force of their own natural resilience,   87

so I, amazed, was bent the while she spoke;
    but then I found my confidence restored,
    and burning with the wish to speak again,   90

I spoke these words: "O one and only fruit
    who was created ripe, first, oldest sire,
    father and father-in-law of every bride,   93

I beg of you devoutly, I implore
    you, speak to me. You see right through my wish;
    to hear you speak the sooner, I speak less." 96

Sometimes an animal will tremble in its skin
    and thus reveal its feelings from within
    as he moves his own cover from inside; 99

so, that first soul of souls revealed to me,
    stirring transparently in his own glow,
    how joyously it moved to bring me joy. 102

And then it breathed: "Without your telling me,
    I know your wish much better than you know
    whatever seems most evident to you; 105

I see it in that Mirror of the Truth,
    Itself perfect reflector of all things,
    yet no thing can reflect It perfectly. 108

You wish to know how long ago it was
    God placed me in the Earthly Paradise
    where she prepared you for this long ascent, 111

and how long did my eyes delight in it;
    and the true reason for the wrath of God;
    the language which I spoke and formed myself. 114

Know now, my son, the tasting of the tree
    was not itself the cause of such long exile,
    but only the transgression of God's bounds. 117

Four thousand three hundred and two full suns
    I longed for this assembly from that place
    your lady summoned Virgil to your aid; 120

I saw the sun return to run the course
    of all its stars nine hundred thirty times
    while I was living as a man on earth. 123

118–119. Adam spent 4,302 solar years in Limbo, the place whence Virgil came to the Pilgrim's aid, before Christ rescued him.

121–123. Adam lived 930 years on earth before he died (see Genesis 5:5). Added to the number of years he spent in Limbo (4,302), this gives a total of 5,232 years between the creation of Adam and the Crucifixion.

The language that I spoke was long extinct
   before that unaccomplishable task
   entered the minds of Nimrod's followers;   126

no product of the human mind can last
   eternally for, as all things in Nature,
   man's inclination varies with the stars.   129

That man should speak is only natural,
   but how he speaks, in this way or in that,
   Nature allows you to do as you please.   132

Till I descended to the pains of Hell,
   I was He called on earth That Highest Good
   Who swathes me in this brilliance of His bliss;   135

and then He was called *El:* for naturally
   man's habits, like the leaves upon the branch,
   change as they fall and others take their place.   138

Atop that mountain highest from the sea
   my time of innocence until disgrace
   was from my first day's hour until the hour,   141

as sun shifts quadrant, following the sixth."

CANTO XXVII

*ALL THE SOULS of the Blest sing "Gloria" to the Trinity with such
sweetness that the Pilgrim thinks of his experience in terms of the uni-
verse smiling. Suddenly the light of St. Peter begins to take on a reddish
glow; the moment the souls have stopped their singing, he begins a bitter
invective against his successors and the corruption of the Church. Now
all the souls, including Beatrice, have turned red, and Dante compares
the change to the eclipse that took place at the death of Christ. St. Peter
closes his invective with a vague prediction of a coming reform and
invites Dante to reveal all he has heard once he has returned to earth.
All the souls in the sphere of the fixed stars now ascend to the Empy-*

rean; the Pilgrim watches them until they are out of sight. Beatrice
instructs her ward to look down and through all the space he has trav-
eled. Then, once again, he looks back to Beatrice whose miraculous eyes
transport him to the ninth sphere of the Primum Mobile. Beatrice ex-
plains the function of this sphere, which is moved directly by God and
which gives all the other spheres their movement. She then proceeds to
lament the greed of mankind and blames the general disorder of things
on earth on the fact that there is no one to govern below, concluding
with an announcement that it will not be long before mankind changes
its course.

"To Father and to Son and Holy Spirit,"
   all Heaven with one voice cried, "Glory be!"
   inebriating me with such sweet sound.   3

I seemed to see all of the universe
   turn to a smile; thus, through my eyes and ears
   I drank into divine inebriation.   6

O joy! O ecstasy ineffable!
   O life complete, perfect in love and peace!
   O wealth unfailing, that can never want!   9

Before my eyes those four torches kept blazing;
   and then the first light who had come to me
   started to grow more brilliant than the rest,   12

and he took on the glow which Jupiter
   would take, if he and Mars were like two birds
   that could exchange their feathers with each other.   15

That Providence assigning Heaven's souls
   each to his turn and function now imposed
   silence on all the choirs of the blessèd,   18

and I heard: "Do not marvel at my change
   of color, for you are about to see
   all of these souls change color as I speak.   21

He who on earth usurps that place of mine,
   that place of mine, that place of mine which now
   stands vacant in the eyes of Christ, God's Son,   24

has turned my sepulchre into a sewer
    of blood and filth, at which the Evil One
    who fell from here takes great delight down there."   27

The color which paints clouds at break of day,
    or in the evening when they face the sun—
    that same tint I saw spread throughout that Heaven.   30

And as a modest lady, self-secure
    in her own virtue, will at the mere mention
    of someone else's failings blush with shame,   33

so did the face of Beatrice change—
    the heavens saw the same eclipse, I think,
    when the Almighty suffered for our sins.   36

Then he continued speaking, but the tone
    his voice now had was no more different
    than was the difference in the way he looked: 39

"The bride of Christ was not nourished on blood
    that came from me, from Linus and from Cletus,
    only that she be wooed for love of gold;   42

it was for love of this delightful life
    that Sixtus, Pius, Calixtus, and Urban,
    after the tears of torment, spilled their blood.   45

Never did we intend for Christendom
    to be divided, some to take their stand
    on this side or on that of our successors,   48

not that the keys which were consigned to me
    become the emblem for a battleflag
    warring against the baptized of the land,   51

42. St. Linus succeeded Peter as pope in either A.D. 64 or 67. Then St. Cletus suc-
ceeded St. Linus as pope from ca. 79 to ca. 90. He suffered martyrdom under
Domitian.

44. Sixtus I was pope under Hadrian (ca. 115–125). Pius I was bishop of Rome under
Emperor Antonius Pius from ca. 140 to ca. 155. Calixtus I was pope from 217 to
222, followed by Urban I (222–230). All were known as early martyrs.

nor that my head become the seal to stamp
   those lying privileges bought and sold.
     I burn with rage and shame to think of it!   54

From here we see down there in all your fields
   rapacious wolves who dress in shepherd's clothes.
     O power of God, why do You still hold back?   57

Sons of Cahors and Gascony prepare
   to drink our blood: O sanctified beginning,
     to what foul ending are you doomed to sink!   60

But that high Providence which saved for Rome
   the glory of the world through Scipio's hand,
     will once again, and soon, lend aid, I know;   63

and you, my son, whose mortal weight must bring
   you back to earth again, open your mouth down there
     and do not hide what I hide not from you!"   66

As frozen vapors flake and start to snow
   down through our air during the time of year
     the horn of heaven's goat touches the sun,   69

so I saw all of Heaven's ether glow
   with rising snowflakes of triumphant souls
     of all those who had sojourned with us there.   72

My eyes followed their shapes up into space
   and I kept watching them until the height
     was too much for my eyes to penetrate.   75

My lady then, who saw that I was freed
   from gazing upward, said, "Lower your sight,
     look down and see how far you have revolved."   78

Since the last time that I had looked below
   I saw that I had moved through the whole arc
     which the first climate makes from mid to end: 81

58. John XXII, pope from 1316 to 1334, was from Cahors, capital of the province of Quercy in southern France. It was reputed to harbor usurers. John's successor, Clement V, was a native of Gascony, whose inhabitants were reputed to be greedy. During his pontificate the papacy was transferred to Avignon.

I saw beyond Cadiz to the mad route
   Ulysses took, and nearly to the shore
   Europa left as a sweet godly burden.   84

More of this puny threshing-ground of ours
   I would have seen, had not the sun moved on
   beneath my feet a sign and more away.   87

My mind in love, yearning eternally
   to court its lady, now was burning more
   than ever to behold the sight of her.   90

And all that art and nature can contrive
   to lure the eye and thus possess the mind,
   be it in living flesh or portraiture   93

combined, would seem like nothing when compared
   to the Divine delight with which I glowed
   when once more I beheld her smiling face.   96

The power which her gaze bestowed on me
   snatched me from Leda's lovely nest, and up
   it thrust me into Heaven's swiftest sphere.   99

The parts of this, the quickest, highest heaven,
   are all so equal that I cannot tell
   where Beatrice chose for me to stay,   102

but she, who knew my wish, began to speak,
   such happiness reflecting in her smile,
   the joy of God, it seemed, was on her face: 105

"The nature of the universe, which stills
   its center while it makes all else revolve,
   moves from this heaven as from its starting-point;   108

no other 'Where' than in the Mind of God
   contains this heaven, because in that Mind burns
   the love that turns it and the power it rains.   111

By circling light and love it is contained
   as it contains the rest; and only He
   Who bound them comprehends how they were bound.   114

98. "Leda's lovely nest" is the constellation of Gemini.

It takes its motion from no other sphere,
   and all the others measure theirs by this,
   as ten is product of the two and five.   117

How time can hide its roots in this sphere's vase
   and show its leaves stemming through all the rest,
   should now be clear to your intelligence.   120

O Greed, so quick to plunge the human race
   into your depths that no man has the strength
   to keep his head above your raging waters!   123

The blossom of man's will is always good,
   but then the drenchings of incessant rain
   turn sound plums into weak and rotten ones.   126

Only in little children can we find
   true innocence and faith, and both are gone
   before their cheeks show the first signs of hair.   129

While still a lisper, one observes fast-days,
   but once he's free to speak, he stuffs his mouth
   with all he can at any time of year;   132

one still in lisping childhood loves and heeds
   his mother's words, but soon in grown-up language,
   he'd rather like to see her dead and buried;   135

thus, the white skin of innocence turns black
   at first exposure to the tempting daughter
   of him who brings the morn and leaves the night.   138

My words should not surprise you when you think
   there is no one on earth to govern you
   and so the human family goes astray.   141

Before all January is unwintered—
   because of every hundred years' odd day
   which men neglect—these lofty spheres shall shine   144

a light that brings the long-awaited storm
   to whirl the fleet about from prow to stern,
   and set it sailing a straight course again.   147

Then from the blossom shall good fruit come forth."

CANTO XXVIII

WHEN BEATRICE FINISHES *speaking, the Pilgrim notices an unusually bright light reflected in her eyes. He turns around and sees a brilliant point around which are nine glowing circles, all spinning at a rate of speed lesser in proportion to their distance from the central point. Beatrice explains that this point is the source of all the heavens and all of Nature. Puzzled, the Pilgrim wishes to know why the visible order of the universe (the physical picture) does not conform to the order he is presently observing in the model before him (the ideal picture). Beatrice tells him he must not judge by the size of the sphere he sees but rather by the power of the angelic order governing that sphere; since the Seraphic order of the angels who govern the Primum Mobile—the sphere closest to God—is the most powerful order, and since there is perfect correspondence between the heavenly spheres and the angelic orders governing them, the correspondence only seems to be in inverse order. (What the Pilgrim is seeing now is the physical universe from the spiritual point of view—from God's eye, as it were—with God at the center.) As the Pilgrim expresses his delight at having understood Beatrice's explanation, the nine fiery circles begin to emit countless singing sparks: the nine orders of angels that govern the nine spheres. Beatrice names the orders of angels, explains their functions, and tells him that Dionysius was right and St. Gregory wrong in his ordering of the angelic hierarchies, and that he should not marvel at the fact that Dionysius was privileged to such secret information since, after all, it was St. Paul in person who told him!*

Then once the adverse truth of mankind's present
    miserable state was clearly brought to light
    by her who holds my mind imparadised,   3

as one who in a mirror catches sight
    of candlelight aglow behind his back
    before he sees it or expects to see it,   6

and, turning from the looking-glass to test
    the truth of it, he sees that glass and flame
    are in accord as notes to music's beat;   9

just so do I remember doing then,
    as I stood gazing at the lovely eyes,
    those lures which Love had used to capture me,   12

for, when I turned around, my eyes were met
    by what takes place here in this whirling sphere
    whenever one looks deep into its motion.   15

I saw a point that radiated light
    so piercing that the eyes its brightness strikes
    are forced to shut from such intensity.   18

That star which seems the smallest seen from here
    if set beside that point, like star by star
    appearing in the heavens, would seem a moon.   21

Perhaps the distance of a halo's glow
    around the brilliant source that colors it
    when vapors hold it in their density,   24

as close as that a ring of fire whirled
    around this point at speed that would surpass
    the sphere that spins the swiftest round the world;   27

this one was circled by a second one,
    second by third, and third by yet a fourth,
    the fifth the fourth, and then the sixth the fifth;   30

the seventh followed spreading out so wide
    that Juno's messenger, if made complete,
    could not contain it in her circle-bow.   33

So came the eighth, the ninth; and each of them
    revolved more slowly according as it was
    in number farther from the central one   36

16. The point is God, an infinitesimal yet brilliant point of light representing the indivisible center of all of Heaven's brightness.

19. "Here" is earth, where the Poet is writing.

22. The "halo's glow" is the kind of misty light that at times is seen surrounding the moon or the sun.

27. This sphere is the ninth heaven, or the Primum Mobile, where the Pilgrim is at present.

whose radiance was clearest of them all
    for, circling nearest the Pure Spark of Being,
    I think it shares the fullest in Its Truth.   39

My lady, who observed my eagerness
    and my bewilderment, said: "On that Point
    depend all nature and all of the heavens.   42

Observe the circle nearest it, and know
    the reason for its spinning at such speed
    is that Love's fire burns it into motion."   45

And I to her: "If all the universe
    were ordered in the way these wheels are here,
    I would be satisfied with what I see,   48

but from our world of sense we can observe
    the turning of the spheres are more God's own,
    the further from its center they revolve.   51

Now, if my wish to know is to be granted
    here in this wondrous and angelic shrine,
    whose only boundaries are love and light,   54

it still has to be made clear to me why
    the model and the copy are at odds,
    for on my own I fail to understand."   57

"If your weak fingers find it difficult
    to loosen such a knot, it is no wonder,
    for it is tight from never being tried!"   60

So spoke my lady. Then she said: "If you
    wish to be satisfied, listen to what
    I tell you, then, sharpen your wits on it.   63

The course of the material spheres is wide
    or narrow in accord with more or less
    of virtue that infuses each throughout.   66

The greater goodness makes for greater bliss;
    a greater bliss calls for a greater body,
    if it is perfect in all of its parts;   69

therefore, this sphere which sweeps all of the world
 along with it must correspond to this,
  the inner ring, that loves and knows the most.   72

And so, if you will take your measurements
 not by circumference but by the power
  inherent in these beings that look like rings,   75

you will observe a marvelous congruence
 of greater power to more, lesser to small,
  in every heaven with its Intelligence."   78

As splendid clearness and tranquillity
 will overcome the airy hemisphere
  when Boreas blows from his milder cheek   81

a breeze which purifies the air and clears
 all the obscuring mist so heaven smiles
  its loveliness from all its dioceses,   84

so was my mind, as soon as I received
 my lady's brilliant answer, and I saw
  the truth shine like a clear star in the heavens.   87

When she had spoken her last word, there came
 showers of light from all the fiery rings,
  like molten iron in fire spurting sparks,   90

and each spark kept to its own ring of fire—
 the number of them thousand into more
  than any doubling of the chessboard yields.   93

I heard them sing "Hosanna," choir on choir,
 to the Fixed Point that holds each to his *ubi*,
  the place they were and will forever be.   96

And she, who looked into my mind and saw
 I was confused, told me: "The first two rings
  show you the Seraphim and Cherubim.   99

They spin so swiftly speeding in their bonds
 to grow as much like that Point as they can,
  and they can in proportion to their sight.   102

Those loves that circle round the other two
    are called the Thrones of the Eternal Aspect;
    they close the first triad of God's own world;   105

And know that all of them delight in bliss
    according to how deep their vision delves
    into the Truth in which all minds find rest.   108

And so, you understand, their state of bliss
    is based upon the act of seeing God,
    not loving Him which is the second step.   111

The measure of their vision is their worth,
    born of His grace and of their own good will:
    for this their ranks proceed from grade to grade.   114

The second triad in full blossom here
    in this spring of eternity whose buds
    no nightly frost of Aries can despoil,   117

warbling 'Hosanna!' sempiternally,
    sing winter out in threefold melody,
    that sounds through triple ranks of trinity.   120

This hierarchy of divinities
    consists of the Dominions first, and next
    the Virtues, and the third are called the Powers.   123

In the next to last of the last dancing trio
    whirl Principalities, and then Archangels;
    the festive Angels fill the last with play.   126

And all of the angelic ranks gaze upward,
    as downward they prevail upon the rest,
    so while each draws the next, all draw toward God.   129

103–105. The Thrones form the bottom of the first triad of the highest set of angelic orders.

109–111. Vision belongs to the intellect, which precedes love, which is an act of the will. The question of which comes first, knowledge of God or love of Him, was much discussed by the theologians of Dante's day.

Dionysius set his mind to contemplate
    these ranks with so much holy zeal for truth,
    he named and ordered them the way I do;   132

Gregory, later, disagreed with him,
    but when he died to waken in this heaven
    he saw the truth, and laughed at his mistake.   135

And that such secrets were revealed by one
    still living on the earth, you need not wonder:
    the one who saw it here told him this truth   138

and many other truths about these rings."

CANTO XXIX

AFTER A BRIEF *silence Beatrice sees in the mind of God that the Pilgrim
has a question, and so she explains to him that the creation of the angels
by God was an act of pure love that took place in the Empyrean before
time began. She goes on to explain why some angels rebelled against
God and others remained faithful to Him. Since, according to Beatrice,
there is so much confusion on earth concerning the different qualities
of the angels, she wishes to make some further clarifications. Those who
insist that the angels possess memory are wrong. Angels have no need
of memory, because they see everything through God. She reprehends
those men who go around teaching and showing off new and exotic
theories that twist the truth of the ultimate authority of the Scriptures.
Christ, she says, expected his Apostles to spread truth and not garbage.
But these ambitious preachers are fattening themselves on the lies they
feed their parishoners. After this digression Beatrice returns to the sub-*

130. Dionysius the Areopagite (mentioned in *Paradise* X, 116–117) was a famous
Athenian who was converted to Christianity by the preaching of Paul (see Acts 17:
34). He is believed to have been the first bishop of Athens and was martyred there
ca. A.D. 95.

133. Gregory is Pope Gregory I, "the Great" (590–604), who discussed the angelic
orders in his *Homilies on the Gospel* (XXIII, 48).

*ject of angels, explaining that they are so many in number that the
human mind could not possibly think in such terms. The light of God
shines upon this multitude of angels, all of whom receive His light in
as many different ways as there are celestial intelligences. Think, then,
how great God is, Who can divide His light among all these loving and
reflecting angelic mirrors and remain Himself forever One and Whole!*

When the twin children of Latona share
    the belt of the horizon and are crowned
    one by the Ram, the other by the Scales,   3

no longer than the zenith holds them poised
    in balance till their weights begin to shift,
    as each moves to a different hemisphere,   6

for just so long, her face a radiant smile,
    was Beatrice silent, her eyes fixed
    upon the Point whose light I could not bear.   9

She said: "I tell you, without asking you,
    what you would hear, for I see your desire
    where every *where* and every *when* is centered.   12

Not to increase His good, which cannot be,
    but rather that His own reflected glory
    in its resplendence might proclaim *I am*   15

in His eternity, beyond all time,
    beyond all comprehension, as pleased Him,
    new loves blossomed from the Eternal Love.   18

Nor did He lie in idleness before,
    for neither 'after' nor 'before' preceded
    the going forth of God upon these waters.   21

Pure form, pure matter, form and matter mixed
    came forth into a perfect state of being
    shot like three arrows from a three-stringed bow.   24

As in crystal or in amber or in glass
    a shaft of light diffuses through the whole,
    its ray reflected instantaneously,   27

1. The twin children are Apollo and Diana, the sun and the moon.

so the threefold creation of the Lord
   was rayed into existence all at once,
   without beginning, with no interval.   30

With every essence there was co-created
   its order: at the summit of the world
   the ones created of pure act were set;   33

and pure potential held the lowest place;
   and in between, potential-to-act was tied
   so tight that they can never be untied.   36

Jerome left word with you about the stretch
   of centuries that angels had existed
   before the rest of God's world came to be,   39

but this truth is declared in many texts
   by writers of the Holy Spirit's word,
   and you will find it if you look with care;   42

reason itself can almost understand:
   it could not grant that the angelic powers
   remain short of perfection for so long.   45

So now you know the where and when and how
   these loves came into being, and so already
   three flames of your desire are now quenched.   48

Nor could you count from one as high as twenty
   faster than part of the angelic group
   shook the foundation of your elements.   51

The rest remained and started practicing
   their art, as you can see, with such delight
   they take no time to pause, but whirl forever.   54

The reason for the Fall was the accursed
   presumption of the one you saw below
   crushed by the weight of all the universe.   57

These others you see here were humbly prompt
   to recognize their great intelligence
   as coming from the Goodness of their Lord,   60

whereby their vision was raised to such heights
    by God's enlightening grace and their own worth
    that now their will was steadfast and entire;   63

and should you doubt, I would have you believe
    that the receipt of grace implies one's worth
    in measure as love opens up to it.   66

By now, if you have understood my words,
    you should be able to conclude much more
    about this sacred place without more help.   69

But since on earth you still teach in your schools
    that the angelic nature is possessed
    of understanding, memory, and will,   72

I shall say more and show you the pure truth
    of what on earth has now become confused
    by equivocations in their arguments.   75

From the first moment these beings found their bliss
    within God's face in which all is revealed,
    they never turned their eyes away from It;   78

hence, no new object interrupts their sight,
    and hence, they have no need of memory
    since they do not possess divided thought;   81

and so on earth men dream their waking dreams,
    some speaking in good faith, some unbelieving—
    to these belong the greater guilt and shame.   84

You mortals do not keep to one true path
    philosophizing: so carried away
    you are by putting on a show of wits!   87

Yet even this provokes the wrath of Heaven
    far less than when the Holy Word of God
    is set aside or misconstrued by you.   90

Men do not care what blood it cost to sow
    the Word throughout the land, nor how pleasing
    he is who humbly takes Scripture to heart.   93

To make a good impression they contrive
    their own unfounded truths which then are furbished
    by preachers—of the Gospel not a word!   96

Some say that during Christ's Passion the moon
    reversed its course intruding on the sun
    whose light, then, could not reach as far as earth—   99

such preachers lie! For that light hid itself,
    and men in Spain as well as India
    shared this eclipse the same time as the Jew.   102

Fables like these are shouted right and left,
    pouring from pulpits—more in just one year
    than all the Lapi and Bindi found in Florence!   105

So the poor sheep, who know no better, come
    from pasture fed on air—the fact that they
    are ignorant does not excuse their guilt.   108

Christ did not say to his first company:
    'Go forth and preach garbage unto the world,'
    but gave them, rather, truth to build upon.   111

With only His word sounding on their lips
    they went to war to keep the faith aflame;
    the Gospel was their only sword and shield.   114

Now men go forth to preach wisecracks and jokes,
    and just so long as they can get a laugh
    to puff their cowls with pride—that's all they want;   117

But if the crowd could see the bird that nestles
    in tips of hoods like these, they soon would see
    what kind of pardons they are trusting in.   120

105. Lapo and Bindo (diminutives of Iacopo and Ildobrando) were very common boys' names in Florence.

110. This line is a parody of Christ's word to His Apostles (cf. Mark 16:15): "Go throughout the world and preach the gospel to every creature."

118–119. The bird is the Devil.

120. The pardons are absolution and indulgences in general.

What folly in mankind's credulity:
    no need of proof or testimonials,
    men rush at any promise just the same!   123

On this Saint Anthony fattens his pig,
    and bigger pigs than his get fatter too,
    paying their bills with forged indulgences.   126

We have digressed enough. Turn your mind's eye
    back to the road of truth; we must adjust
    discussion to what time is left us here.   129

The angelic nature goes so far beyond
    the scale of mortal numbers that there is
    no word or concept that can reach that far.   132

Look in the Book of Daniel; you will see
    that when he speaks of thousands of these beings,
    no fixed or finite number is revealed.   135

The primal Light shines down through all of them
    and penetrates them in as many ways
    as there are splendors with which It may mate.   138

And since the visual act always precedes
    the act of loving, bliss of love in each
    burns differently: some glow while others blaze.   141

And now you see the height, you see the breadth
    of Eternal Goodness that divides Itself
    into these countless mirrors that reflect   144

Itself, remaining One, as It was always."

---

124. St. Anthony the Great, the hermit of Egypt, was born ca. 250 and lived to the age of 105. He is considered the founder of monasticism, as those disciples who followed him into the desert drew together and formed an order of sorts.

133. "Thousands of thousands ministered to him, and ten thousand times a hundred thousand stood before Him" (Dan. 7:10).

CANTO XXX

THE NINE CIRCLES *with their central point of light slowly fade from sight and the Pilgrim looks again at Beatrice, whose beauty he can no longer find words to describe. Beatrice tells the Pilgrim that they are now in the Empyrean, and he finds himself wrapped in a veil of intense light that momentarily blinds him, but then he feels his powers of sight grow stronger. He sees a river of light flowing between two banks laden with flowers and an exchange of countless sparks between the river and the flowers. Beatrice tells him to keep his eyes fixed on the river, warning him, however, that what he sees is only a preface to the truth. As the Pilgrim bends down and takes the river in with his eyes, its linear form becomes round like a vast lake of light, and what had appeared to be flowers are now the souls of the Elect, seated in tiers of petals that grow in circumference the higher they rise, opening up like an immense rose, all parts of which are equally clear to the Pilgrim since the laws of nature do not apply here. The sparks, meanwhile, have taken the shape of angels ceaselessly flying between God and the Elect. Beatrice leads the Pilgrim into the center of the Rose, and after showing him how few seats still remain to be filled, she points to the one soon to be occupied by the soul of Henry VII who will have tried, but in vain, to help cure Italy of its ills, and blames Henry's failure on the Pope (Clement V) who she predicts will be damned to Hell, stuffing his predecessor (Boniface VIII) deeper down into his hole of simony.*

About six thousand miles away high noon
   is blazing, and the shadow of our world
   already slopes into a level bed,   3

when in the midst of heaven, so deep above,
   a change begins, and one star here and there
   starts fading from our sight at such a depth;   6

and as the brightest handmaid of the sun
   comes closer, and the heavens start to close
   light after light, until the fairest fades,   9

just so the Triumph that forever plays
    its round around the Point of dazzling light
    that seems contained by what Itself contains,   12

little by little faded from my sight;
    and seeing it no more, my love constrained
    my eyes to look again at Beatrice.   15

If all I said of her up to this time
    were gathered in a single poem of praise,
    it would be but a scanty comment now.   18

The beauty I saw there goes far beyond
    all mortal reach; I think that only He
    Who made it knows the full joy of its being.   21

At this point I admit to my defeat:
    no poet, comic or tragic, ever was
    more outdone by his theme than I am now;   24

for, as sunlight does to the weakest eyes,
    so did the mere thought of her lovely smile
    strike every recognition from my mind.   27

From the first day that I beheld her face
    in this life till the vision of her now,
    I could trust in my poems to sing her praise,   30

but now I must stop trying to pursue
    her beauty in my verse, for I have done
    as much as any artist at his best.   33

As such I leave her to the heralding
    of greater clarion than mine, which starts
    to draw its arduous theme now to a close.   36

She, with the tone and gesture of a guide
    whose task is done, said: "We have gone beyond—
    from greatest sphere to heaven of pure light,   39

light of the intellect, light full of love,
    love of the true good, full of ecstasy,
    ecstasy that transcends the sweetest joy.   42

37–39. Beatrice's role as guide is now finished.

Here you shall see the twofold soldiery
   of Paradise, and one host you will see
   as you will see them on the Final Day."
           45

Just as a sudden flash of lightning strikes
   the visual spirits and so stuns the eyes,
   that even the clearest object fades from sight,
           48

so glorious living light encompassed me,
   enfolding me so tightly in its veil
   of luminence that I saw only light.
           51

"The Love that calms this heaven forever greets
   all those who enter with such salutation,
   so is the candle for Its flame prepared."
           54

No sooner had these brief, assuring words
   entered my ears than I was full aware
   my senses now were raised beyond their powers;
           57

the power of new sight lit up my eyes
   so that no light, however bright it were,
   would be too brilliant for my eyes to bear.
           60

And I saw light that was a flowing stream,
   blazing in splendid sparks between two banks
   painted by spring in miracles of color.
           63

Out of this stream the sparks of living light
   were shooting up and settling on the flowers:
   they looked like rubies set in rings of gold;
           66

then as if all that fragrance made them drunk,
   they poured back into that miraculous flood,
   and as one plunged, another took to flight.
           69

"The deep desire burning, urging you
   to seek the answers to what you have seen,
   pleases me more, the more I see it surge;
           72

but you must first drink of these waters here
   before such thirst as yours is satisfied,"
   —so did she speak, that sunlight of my eyes;
           75

and then she said: "The stream, the jewels you see
    leap in and out of it, the smiling blooms,
    are all prefigurations of their truth.   78

These things are not imperfect in themselves;
    the defect, rather, lies within your sight,
    as yet not strong enough to reach such heights."   81

No baby, having slept too long, and now
    awakened late, could rush to turn his face
    more eagerly to seek his mother's milk   84

than I bent down my face to make my eyes
    more lucid mirrors there within that stream
    which pours its light for their embetterment;   87

no sooner had the eaves of my eyes drunk
    within those waters, than the river turned
    from its straight course to a circumference.   90

And then, as people at a masquerade
    take off the masks which have until that time
    been hiding their true selves—so, then and there,   93

before my eyes the sparks and flowers changed
    into a greater festival: I saw
    both courts of Heaven in their reality.   96

O splendid grace of God through which I saw
    the one true kingdom's triumph, grant me now
    the power to find the words for what I saw!   99

There is a light above whose glory makes
    Creator visible to his creations
    whose only peace is in beholding Him;   102

in figure of a circle this light spreads,
    and is so vast that its circumference
    would be too loose a belt to bind the sun.   105

96. "Both courts of Heaven" and the "twofold soldiery" (see line 43 above) refer to
the angels and the human souls.

And its expanse comes from a single ray
   striking the summit of the First Moved Sphere
   from which it takes its vital force and power. 108

And as a hillside rich in grass and flowers
   looks down into a lake as if it were
   admiring the reflection of its wealth, 111

so, mirrored, tier on tier, within that light,
   more than a thousand were reflected there,
   I saw all those of us who won return. 114

And if the lowest tier alone can hold
   so great a brilliance, then how vast the space
   of this Rose to its outer petals' reach! 117

And yet, by such enormous breadth and height
   my eyes were not confused; they took in all
   in number and in quality of bliss. 120

There, near and far nor adds nor takes away,
   for where God rules directly without agents,
   the laws of Nature in no way apply. 123

Into the gold of the eternal Rose,
   whose ranks of petals fragrantly unfold
   praise to the Sun of everlasting spring, 126

in silence—though I longed to speak—was I
   taken by Beatrice who said: "Look
   how vast is our white-robed consistory. 129

Look at our city, see its vast expanse.
   You see our seats so filled, only a few
   remain for souls that Heaven still desires. 132

In that great chair, already set with crown
   above it and which draws your eyes to it,
   before your summons to this nuptial feast, 135

shall sit the soul, predestined emperor,
of that Great Henry who one day will come
to set straight Italy before her time.   138

You are bewitched by blind cupidity
that makes you starve to death like a poor child
who has a nurse but pushes her away.   141

And at that time the prefect of God's Court
will be a man who publicly agrees
to tread his path, but not so secretly.   144

But God will not permit him to stay long
in Holy Office: he shall be thrust down,
where Simon Magus pays his guilt, and he   147

shall stuff the Alagnese deeper down!"

CANTO XXXI

THE PILGRIM BEHOLDS *the Elect in the form of a pure white rose and the angels like bees continuously flying from God to the Elect and back, transporting His love. Never, however, in spite of their countless numbers, do they block the Divine Light from the Pilgrim's sight. He compares his amazement to that of a barbarian from the far north seeing the splendors of Rome for the first time, and his joy to that of a pilgrim who has reached his final goal. After examining the general formation of Paradise he turns to ask Beatrice a question but finds that a venerable old man has taken her place. The old man explains that Beatrice has asked him to lead her ward to his final goal, and he points to where*

136–137. This is Henry, count of Luxembourg (b. ca. 1275), who became Emperor Henry VII.

142–144. Clement V was pope (or "prefect") at the time of Henry's death.

148. The Alagnese is Clement's predecessor in simony, Boniface VIII, Dante's personal archenemy, who was born in the town of Alagna, or Alagni. Beatrice here confirms the prophecy made in *Inferno* XIX, 73–75.

she is seated in the third from the highest tier of the Rose. The Pilgrim,
looking up, sees his lady clearly and offers up to her a tender prayer of
gratitude for all she has done on his behalf, expressing his hope that
with her help he may someday return to her there as pure as he is at
that moment. Beatrice smiles at him and then returns her gaze to God.
The old man reveals himself as St. Bernard and urges the Pilgrim to
shift his focus even higher to the Virgin Mary on whom his spiritual
progress now depends.

So now, appearing to me in the form
   of a white rose was Heaven's sacred host,
   those whom with His own blood Christ made His bride,   3

while the other host—that soaring see and sing
   the glory of the One who stirs their love,
   the goodness which made them great as they are,   6

like bees that in a single motion swarm
   and dip into the flowers, then return
   to heaven's hive where their toil turns to joy—   9

descended all at once on that great bloom
   of precious petals, and then flew back up
   to where its source of love forever dwells.   12

Their faces showed the glow of living flame,
   their wings of gold, and all the rest of them
   whiter than any snow that falls to earth.   15

As they entered the flower, tier to tier,
   each spread the peace and ardor of the love
   they gathered with their wings in flight to Him.   18

Nor did this screen of flying plenitude
   between the flower and what reigned above
   impede the vision of His glorious light;   21

for God's light penetrates the universe
   according to the merits of each part,
   and there is nothing that can block its way.   24

This unimperiled kingdom of all joy
   abounding with those saints, both old and new,
   had look and love fixed all upon one goal.   27

O Triune Light which sparkles in one star
    upon their sight, Fulfiller of full joy!
    look down upon us in our tempest here!   30

If the barbarians (coming from such parts
    as every day are spanned by Helice,
    travelling the sky with her belovèd son)   33

when they saw Rome, her mighty monuments
    (the days the Lateran, built high, outsoared
    all mortal art), were so struck with amazement,   36

then I—coming to Heaven from mortal earth,
    from man's time to Divine eternity,
    from Florence to a people just and sane—   39

with what amazement must I have been struck!
    Truly, between my stupor and my joy,
    it was a pleasure not to hear or speak.   42

And as a pilgrim now refreshed with joy
    surveys the temple of his vow, and wonders
    how to describe it when he is back home,   45

so through the living light I let my eyes
    go wandering among the ranks of Blest,
    now up, now down, now searching all around.   48

I saw love-dedicated faces there,
    adorned in borrowed light and by their smiles
    and gestures graced with chastest dignity.   51

By now, my eyes had quickly taken in
    a general plan of all of Paradise
    but had not fixed themselves on any part;   54

32. Helice, also known as Callisto, was one of Diana's nymphs, who was banished after she had been seduced by Jupiter and had borne him a son, Arcas.

35. In Dante's time the Lateran palace in Rome was the residence of the pope.

and with new-kindled eagerness to know,
   I turned around to ask my lady things
   that to my mind were still not clear enough.   57

What I expected was not what I saw!
   I thought to see Beatrice there but saw
   an elder in the robes of Heaven's saints.   60

His eyes, his cheeks, were filled with the divine
   joy of the blest, his attitude with love
   that every tender-hearted father knows.   63

And "She, where is she?" instantly I asked.
   He answered: "I was urged by Beatrice
   to leave my place and end all your desire;   66

you will behold her, if you raise your eyes
   to the third circle from the highest tier,
   enthroned where her own merit destined her."   69

I did not say a word but raised my eyes
   and saw her there in all her glory crowned
   by the reflections of eternal light   72

Not from that place where highest thunder roars
   down to the very bottom of the sea,
   is any mortal's sight so far away   75

as my eyes were from Beatrice there;
   but distance made no difference, for her image
   came down to me unblurred by anything.   78

"O lady in whom all my hope takes strength,
   and who for my salvation did endure
   to leave her footprints on the floor of Hell,   81

---

60. As we are told in line 102, this elder is St. Bernard, abbot of Clairvaux and the force behind the Second Crusade.

through your own power, through your own excellence
    I recognize the grace and the effect
    of all those things I have seen with my eyes.   84

From bondage into freedom you led me
    by all those paths, by using all those means
    which were within the limits of your power.   87

Preserve in me your great munificence,
    so that my soul which you have healed may be
    pleasing to you when it slips from the flesh."   90

Such was my prayer. And she, so far away,
    or so it seemed, looked down at me and smiled;
    then to Eternal Light she turned once more.   93

The holy elder spoke: "That you may reach
    your journey's perfect consummation now,
    I have been sent by sacred love and prayer;   96

fly through this heavenly garden with your eyes,
    for gazing at it will prepare your sight
    to rise into the vision of God's Ray.   99

The Queen of Heaven, for whom I constantly
    burn with love's fire, will grant us every grace,
    because I am her faithful one, Bernard."   102

As one who comes from someplace like Croatia—
    to gaze on our Veronica, so long
    craved for, he now cannot look long enough,   105

and while it is displayed, he says in thought:
    "O Jesus Christ, my Lord, the One true God,
    is this what your face truly looked like then?"—   108

just so did I while gazing at the living
    love of the one who living in the world,
    through contemplation, tasted of that peace.   111

---

94. The "holy elder," St. Bernard, now undertakes to prepare the Pilgrim for the final stage of his journey.

100. The "Queen of Heaven" is the Virgin Mary.

"My son of grace," he spoke again, "this state
   of blissful being will not be known to you
   as long as you keep your eyes fixed down here;   114

look up into the circles, to the highest
   until your eyes behold, enthroned, the Queen
   who holds as subject this devoted realm."   117

I raised my eyes. And as at break of day
   the eastern parts of the horizon shine
   brighter than at the point the sun goes down,   120

so I saw, as my eyes still climbed from vale
   to mountain-top, there at the highest point,
   a light outshining all that splendorous rim.   123

And as our sky, where we expect to see
   the ill-starred shaft of Phaëthon's chariot,
   burns brightest dimming all the light around,   126

so there, on high, that oriflame of peace
   lit up its center while on either side
   its glow was equally diminishing;   129

and all around that center, wings outstretched,
   I saw more than a thousand festive angels,
   each one distinct in brilliance and in art.   132

And there, smiling upon their games and song
   I saw a beauty that reflected bliss
   within the eyes of all the other saints;   135

and even if I were as rich in words
   as in remembering, I would not dare
   describe the least part of such beauty's bliss.   138

Bernard, when he saw that my eyes were fixed
   devotedly upon his passion's passion,
   his own he turned to her with so much love   141

that he made mine more ardent in their gaze.

CANTO XXXII

St. Bernard now reveals the order of the division of the arena of the Rose. A line of souls bisects the Rose vertically, separating those who believed in Christ before His coming from those who believed afterwards. The Virgin is in the highest seat and heads the half of the line containing Hebrew women (Christ to come); St. John the Baptist heads the half comprised of male saints (Christ already come). When St. Bernard instructs the Pilgrim to focus his gaze on the Virgin in order to acquire sufficient strength to contemplate Christ, he sees the angel Gabriel hail her with outspread wings, and all the souls respond with song. Then St. Bernard points out the position of other prominent souls: Adam and Moses; St. Peter and St. John the Evangelist; St. Anne, the mother of the Virgin; and St. Lucy, who, by inviting Beatrice to come to the aid of her lover, set the Divine Comedy *in motion. Having indicated that little time remains to complete the journey, St. Bernard instructs the Pilgrim to direct his sight to God, and begins his prayer to the Virgin that she may provide the grace necessary to complete the final stage of the journey.*

Rapt in love's Bliss, that contemplative soul
    generously assumed the role of guide
    as he began to speak these holy words: 3

"The wound which Mary was to close and heal
    she there, who sits so lovely at her feet,
    would open wider then and prick the flesh.   6

And sitting there directly under her
    among the thrones of the third tier is Rachel,
    and, there, see Beatrice by her side.   9

4–6. When Mary gave birth to Christ she provided the means of healing the wound of original sin. She "who sits so lovely at her feet" (5) is Eve, who disobeyed God and surrendered to the serpent.

Sarah, Rebecca, Judith, and then she,
  who was the great-grandmother of the singer
  who cried for his sin: '*Miserere mei*,'   12

you see them all as I go down from tier
  to tier and name them in their order,
  petal by petal, downward through the Rose.   15

Down from the seventh row, as up to it,
  was a descending line of Hebrew women
  that parted all the petals of the Rose;   18

according to the ways in which the faith
  viewed Christ, these women constitute the wall
  dividing these ranks down the sacred stairs.   21

On this side where the flower is full bloomed
  to its last petal, sit the souls of those
  who placed their faith upon Christ yet to come;   24

on that side where all of the semi-circles
  are broken by the empty seats, sit those
  who turned their face to Christ already come.   27

And just as on this side the glorious throne
  of Heaven's lady with the other seats
  below it form this great dividing wall,   30

so, facing her, the throne of the great John
  who, ever holy, suffered through the desert,
  and martyrdom, then Hell for two more years,   33

and under him, chosen to mark the line,
  Francis, Benedict, Augustine and others
  descend from round to round as far as here.   36

---

10. Sarah was Abraham's wife and the mother of Isaac. Rebecca was the daughter of Bethuel and the sister of Laban. She was married to Isaac and bore Esau and Jacob. Judith was the daughter of Meraris. She murdered Holofernes (Nebuchadnezzar's general) while he slept and thus saved Bethulia, which was under siege by the Assyrians. After the Assyrians fled the city Judith was celebrated by the Jews as their deliverer.

11–12. Ruth was the wife of Boaz and great-grandmother of David (the "singer"), author of the psalm of penitence, the *Miserere mei* ("have mercy on me," Psalm 51).

Now marvel at the greatness of God's plan:
  this garden shall be full in equal number
  of this and that aspect of the one faith.   39

And know that downward from the center row
  which cuts the two dividing walls midway,
  no soul through his own merit earned his seat,   42

but through another's, under fixed conditions,
  for all these spirits were absolved of sin
  before they reached the age to make free choice.   45

You need only to look upon their faces
  and listen to the young sound of their voices
  to see and hear this clearly for yourself.   48

But you have doubts, doubts you do not reveal,
  so now I will untie the tangled knot
  in which your searching thoughts have bound you tight.   51

Within the vastness of this great domain
  no particle of chance can find a place—
  no more than sorrow, thirst, or hunger can—   54

for all that you see here has been ordained
  by the eternal law with such precision
  that ring and finger are a perfect fit.   57

And, therefore, all these souls of hurried comers
  to the true life are not ranked *sine causa*
  some high, some low, according to their merit.   60

The King, through whom this kingdom is at rest
  in so much love and in so much delight
  that no will dares to wish for any more,   63

creating all minds in His own mind's bliss,
  endows each with as much grace as He wishes,
  at His own pleasure—let this fact suffice.   66

59. *Sine causa* is a Latin legal expression meaning "without cause."

And Holy Scriptures set this down for you
   clear and expressly, speaking of those twins
   whose anger flared while in their mother's womb; 69

so, it is fitting that God's lofty light
   crown them with grace, as much as each one merits,
   according to the color of their hair. 72

Thus, through no merit of their own good works
   are they ranked differently; the difference is
   only in God's gift of original grace. 75

During mankind's first centuries on earth
   for innocent children to achieve salvation,
   only the faith of parents was required; 78

but then, when man's first age came to an end,
   all males had to be circumcised to give
   innocent wings the strength to fly to Heaven; 81

but when the age of grace came down to man,
   then, without perfect baptism in Christ,
   such innocence to Limbo was confined. 84

Now look at that face which resembles Christ
   the most, for only in its radiance
   will you be made ready to look at Christ." 87

I saw such bliss rain down upon her face,
   bestowed on it by all those sacred minds
   created to fly through those holy heights, 90

that of all things I witnessed to this point
   nothing had held me more spellbound than this,
   nor shown a greater likeness unto God; 93

and that love which had once before descended
   now sang, *Ave, Maria, gratïa plena*,
   before her presence there with wings spread wide. 96

68–69. Jacob and Esau were the twin sons of Rebecca and Isaac (see Genesis 25:21–34). St. Bernard mentions them as an example of the mystery of Divine Grace.

79. Man's "first age" is from the time of Abraham until the birth of Christ.

Response came to this holy prayer of praise
   from all directions of the Court of Bliss
   and every face grew brighter with that joy.   99

"O holy father, who for my sake deigns
   to stand down here, so far from the sweet throne
   destined for you throughout eternity,   102

who is that angel who so joyously
   looks straight into the eyes of Heaven's Queen,
   so much in love he seems to burn like fire?"   105

Thus, I turned for instruction once again
   to that one who in Mary's beauty glowed
   as does the morning star in fresh sunlight.   108

And he: "All loving pride and gracious joy,
   as much as soul or angel can possess,
   is all in him, and we would have it so,   111

for he it is who bore the palm below
   to Mary when the Son of God had willed
   to bear the weight of man's flesh on Himself.   114

Now let your eyes follow my words as I
   explain to you, and note the great patricians
   of this most just and pious of all realms.   117

Those two who sit most blest in their high thrones
   because they are the closest to the Empress
   are, as it were, the two roots of our Rose: 120

he, sitting on her left side, is that father,
   the one through whose presumptuous appetite
   mankind still tastes the bitterness of shame;   123

and on her right, you see the venerable
   Father of Holy Church to whom Christ gave
   the keys to this beautiful Rose of joy.   126

---

108. Reference to the morning star, Venus, is made in the litany to the Blessed Virgin.

120. Adam is one root of the Rose because from him sprung those who believed in Christ to come; St. Peter is the other because from him sprung those who believed in Christ who had already come.

And he who prophesied before he died
   the sad days destined for the lovely Bride
   whom Christ won for himself with lance and nails   129

sits at his side. Beside the other sits
   the leader of those nurtured on God's manna,
   who were a fickle, ingrate, stubborn lot.   132

Across from Peter, see there, Anna sits,
   so happy to be looking at her daughter,
   she does not move an eye singing Hosanna;   135

facing the head of mankind's family
   sits Lucy, who first sent your lady to you
   when you were bent, headlong, on your own ruin.   138

But since the time left for your journey's vision
   grows short, let us stop here—like the good tailor
   who cuts the gown according to his cloth,   141

and turn our eyes upon the Primal Love
   so that, looking toward Him, you penetrate
   His radiance as deep as possible.   144

But lest you fall backwards beating your wings,
   believing to ascend on your own power,
   we must offer a prayer requesting grace,   147

grace from the one who has power to help you.
   Now, follow me, with all of your devotion,
   and do not let your heart stray from my words."   150

And he began to say this holy prayer:

127–130. St. John the Evangelist, author of the *Apocalypse*, foretold the adversity
that would befall the Church. (Cf. *Purgatory* XXIX, 143–144.) The "lance and nails"
(129) refers to the Crucifixion.

130. The "other" is Adam.

CANTO XXXIII

ST. BERNARD LOVINGLY praises the Virgin Mary and then recounts the Pilgrim's journey through Hell, Purgatory, and the celestial spheres, entreating the Virgin to clear away the obstacles from the Pilgrim's eyes so that he may behold God's glory. Bernard then signals the Pilgrim to look upward, but he has already done so, spurred on by his clearer sight. He sees the multiform world bound in a single unity with love. Then, as he gazes into the Divine Light, he sees three rings of three different colors all of which share and are bound by one and the same circumference. The first ring of color reflects the second; both reflect the third: the miracle of the Trinity. Again the poet's words begin to fail him. He fixes his eyes on the second ring of reflected light and perceives God in the image of man, but he is unable to grasp how the forms coincide. Then with a sudden flash the Pilgrim's mind is illuminated by the Truth and he feels, now that the ultimate vision has been granted him, his desire and will turning in harmony with Divine Love, "the Love that moves the sun and the other stars."

"Oh Virgin Mother, daughter of your son,
   most humble, most exalted of all creatures
   chosen of God in His eternal plan,   3

you are the one who ennobled human nature
   to the extent that He did not disdain,
   Who was its Maker, to make Himself man.   6

Within your womb rekindled was the love
   that gave the warmth that did allow this flower
   to come to bloom within this timeless peace.   9

For all up here you are the noonday torch
   of charity, and down on earth, for men,
   the living spring of their eternal hope.   12

Lady, you are so great, so powerful,
   that who seeks grace without recourse to you
   would have his wish fly upward without wings.   15

Not only does your loving kindness rush
   to those who ask for it, but often times
   it flows spontaneously before the plea.   18

In you is tenderness, in you is pity,
   in you munificence—in you unites
   all that is good in God's created beings.   21

This is a man who from the deepest pit
   of all the universe up to this height
   has witnessed, one by one, the lives of souls,   24

who begs you that you grant him through your grace
   the power to raise his vision higher still
   to penetrate the final blessedness.   27

And I who never burned for my own vision
   more than I burn for his, with all my prayers
   I pray you—and I pray they are enough—   30

that you through your own prayers dispel the mist
   of his mortality, that he may have
   the Sum of Joy revealed before his eyes.   33

I pray you also, Queen who can achieve
   your every wish, keep his affections sound
   once he has had the vision and returns.   36

Protect him from the stirrings of the flesh:
   you see, with Beatrice, all the Blest,
   hands clasped in prayer, are praying for my prayer."   39

Those eyes so loved and reverenced by God,
   now fixed on him who prayed, made clear to us
   how precious true devotion is to her;   42

then she looked into the Eternal Light,
   into whose being, we must believe, no eyes
   of other creatures pierce with such insight.   45

And I who was approaching now the end
   of all man's yearning, strained with all the force
   in me to raise my burning longing high.   48

Bernard then gestured to me with a smile
    that I look up, but I already was
    instinctively what he would have me be: 51

for now my vision as it grew more clear
    was penetrating more and more the Ray
    of that exalted Light of Truth Itself.   54

And from then on my vision rose to heights
    higher than words, which fail before such sight,
    and memory fails, too, at such extremes.   57

As he who sees things in a dream and wakes
    to feel the passion of the dream still there
    although no part of it remains in mind,   60

just such am I: my vision fades and all
    but ceases, yet the sweetness born of it
    I still can feel distilling in my heart: 63

so imprints on the snow fade in the sun,
    and thus the Sibyl's oracle of leaves
    was swept away and lost into the wind.   66

O Light Supreme, so far beyond the reach
    of mortal understanding, to my mind
    relend now some small part of Your own Self,   69

and give to my tongue eloquence enough
    to capture just one spark of all Your glory
    that I may leave for future generations;   72

for, by returning briefly to my mind
    and sounding, even faintly, in my verse,
    more of Your might will be revealed to men.   75

If I had turned my eyes away, I think,
    from the sharp brilliance of the living Ray
    which they endured, I would have lost my senses.   78

And this, as I recall, gave me more strength
   to keep on gazing till I could unite
   my vision with the Infinite Worth I saw.   81

O grace abounding and allowing me to dare
   to fix my gaze on the Eternal Light,
   so deep my vision was consumed in It!   84

I saw how it contains within its depths
   all things bound in a single book by love
   of which creation is the scattered leaves: 87

how substance, accident, and their relation
   were fused in such a way that what I now
   describe is but a glimmer of that Light.   90

I know I saw the universal form,
   the fusion of all things, for I can feel,
   while speaking now, my heart leap up in joy.   93

One instant brings me more forgetfulness
   than five and twenty centuries brought the quest
   that stunned Neptune when he saw Argo's keel.   96

And so my mind was totally entranced
   in gazing deeply, motionless, intent;
   the more it saw the more it burned to see.   99

And one is so transformed within that Light
   that it would be impossible to think
   of ever turning one's eyes from that sight,   102

because the good which is the goal of will
   is all collected there, and outside it
   all is defective that is perfect there.   105

Now, even in the things I do recall
   my words have no more strength than does a babe
   wetting its tongue, still at its mother's breast.   108

91–93. The conjoining of substance and accident in God and the union of the temporal and the eternal is what Dante saw at that moment.

Not that within the Living Light there was
    more than a sole aspect of the Divine
    which always is what It has always been,   111

yet as I learned to see more, and the power
    of vision grew in me, that single aspect
    as I changed, seemed to me to change Itself.   114

Within Its depthless clarity of substance
    I saw the Great Light shine into three circles
    in three clear colors bound in one same space;   117

the first seemed to reflect the next like rainbow
    on rainbow, and the third was like a flame
    equally breathed forth by the other two.   120

How my weak words fall short of my conception,
    which is itself so far from what I saw
    that "weak" is much too weak a word to use!   123

O Light Eternal fixed in Self alone,
    known only to Yourself, and knowing Self,
    You love and glow, knowing and being known!   126

That circling which, as I conceived it, shone
    in You as Your own first reflected light
    when I had looked deep into It a while,   129

seemed in Itself and in Its own Self-color
    to be depicted with man's very image.
    My eyes were totally absorbed in It.   132

As the geometer who tries so hard
    to square the circle, but cannot discover,
    think as he may, the principle involved,   135

so did I strive with this new mystery:
    I yearned to know how could our image fit
    into that circle, how could it conform;   138

but my own wings could not take me so high—
    then a great flash of understanding struck
    my mind, and suddenly its wish was granted.   141

At this point power failed high fantasy
    but, like a wheel in perfect balance turning,
    I felt my will and my desire impelled   144

by the Love that moves the sun and the other stars.

VITA NUOVA

I

In my Book of Memory, in the early part where there is little to be read, there comes a chapter with the rubric: *Incipit vita nova*.[1] It is my intention to copy into this little book the words I find written under that heading—if not all of them, at least the essence of their meaning.

I I

Nine times already since my birth the heaven of light[2] had circled back to almost the same point, when there appeared before my eyes the now glorious lady of my mind, who was called Beatrice even by those who did not know what her name was. She had been in this life long enough for the heaven of the fixed stars to be able to move a twelfth of a degree[3] to the East in her time; that is, she appeared to me at about the beginning of her ninth year, and I first saw her near the end of my ninth year. She appeared dressed in the most patrician of colors, a subdued and decorous crimson, her robe bound round and adorned in a style suitable to her years. At that very moment, and I speak the truth, the vital spirit,[4] the one that dwells in the most secret chamber of the heart, began to tremble so violently that even the most minute veins of my body were strangely affected; and trembling, it spoke these words: *Ecce deus fortior me, qui veniens dominabitur michi*.[5] At that point the an-

1. Latin for "The new life begins."

2. The Sun; the fourth heaven of the Universe in the Ptolemaic system. Radiating in concentric circles from the center Earth were the Moon, Mercury, Venus, Sun, Mars, Jupiter, Saturn, the Fixed Stars, the Primum Mobile, and the Empyrean.

3. The Fixed Stars (the eighth heaven) was believed to move from west to east one degree in 100 years (or one-twelfth of a degree in eight years and 4 months), a phenomenon known now as precession of the equinoxes.

4. In this passage Dante mentions the three physiological spirits, the vital, the animal, and the natural, taking his categories from Albertus Magnus (*De Spiritu et Respiratione*). These spirits had substance; the vital originating in the heart, becoming natural in the liver, and animal in the brain. They were all three ruled by the soul.

5. Latin for "Here is a God stronger than I who comes to rule over me."

imal spirit, the one abiding in the high chamber to which all the senses bring their perceptions, was stricken with amazement and, speaking directly to the spirits of sight,[6] said these words: *Apparuit iam beatitudo vestra.*[7] At that point the natural spirit, the one dwelling in that part where our food is digested, began to weep, and weeping said these words: *Heu miser, quia frequenter impeditus ero deinceps!*[8] Let me say that, from that time on, Love governed my soul, which became immediately devoted to him, and he reigned over me with such assurance and lordship, given him by the power of my imagination, that I could only dedicate myself to fulfilling his every pleasure. Often he commanded me to go and look for this youngest of angels; so, during those early years I often went in search of her, and I found her to be of such natural dignity and worthy of such admiration that the words of the poet Homer suited her perfectly: "She seemed to be the daughter not of a mortal, but of a god."[9] And though her image, which remained constantly with me, was Love's assurance of holding me, it was of such a pure quality that it never allowed me to be ruled by Love without the faithful counsel of reason, in all those things where such advice might be profitable. Since to dwell on my passions and actions when I was so young might seem like recounting fantasies, I shall put them aside and, omitting many things that could be copied from the text which is the source of my present words, I shall turn to those written in my memory under more important headings.

III

After so many days had passed that precisely nine years were ending since the appearance, just described, of this most gracious lady, it happened that on the last one of those days the miraculous lady appeared,

6. One of the *spiriti sensitivi*, emanations of the *spirito animale* that act as vehicles for the senses. The spirits of sight traveled to the object and back to the eyes, carrying the image.

7. Latin for "Now your bliss has appeared."

8. Latin for "Alas, wretch, for I shall be disturbed often from now on!"

9. These words appear not in Latin but in Italian; an allusion to the *Iliad*, XXIV 258–259 (regarding Hector), which Dante knew from his reading of Aristotle. Homer had not yet been translated into Latin, and Dante did not know Greek.

dressed in purest white, between two ladies of noble bearing both older than she was; and passing along a certain street, she turned her eyes to where I was standing faint-hearted and, with that indescribable graciousness for which today she is rewarded in the eternal life, she greeted me so miraculously that I seemed at that moment to behold the entire range of possible bliss. It was precisely the ninth hour of that day,[10] three o'clock in the afternoon, when her sweet greeting came to me. Since this was the first time her words had ever been directed to me, I became so ecstatic that, like a drunken man, I turned away from everyone and I sought the loneliness of my room, where I began thinking of this most gracious lady and, thinking of her, I fell into a sweet sleep, and a marvelous vision[11] appeared to me. I seemed to see a cloud the color of fire and, in that cloud, a lordly man, frightening to behold, yet he seemed also to be wondrously filled with joy. He spoke and said many things, of which I understood only a few; one was *Ego dominus tuus*.[12] I seemed to see in his arms a sleeping figure, naked but lightly wrapped in a crimson cloth; looking intently at this figure, I recognized the lady of the greeting, the lady who earlier in the day had deigned to greet me. In one hand he seemed to be holding something that was all in flames, and it seemed to me that he said these words: *Vide cor tuum*.[13] And after some time had passed, he seemed to awaken the one who slept, and he forced her cunningly to eat of that burning object in his hand; she ate of it timidly. A short time after this, his happiness gave way to bitterest weeping, and weeping he folded his arms around this lady, and together they seemed to ascend toward the heavens. At that point my drowsy sleep could not bear the anguish that I felt; it was broken and I awoke. At once I began to reflect, and I discovered that the hour at which that vision had appeared to me was the fourth hour of the night;[14] that is, it was exactly the first of the last nine hours of the night. Thinking about what I had seen, I decided to make it known to many of the famous poets[15] of that time. Since just recently I had

---

10. The canonical hours of the day began at six in the morning.

11. The first of three visions in the *Vita nuova*. (Cf. *Ezekiel* 1–3.)

12. Latin for "I am your master."

13. Latin for "Behold your heart."

14. The hours of the night began at six P.M. It was between nine and ten P.M.

15. Lyric poets accustomed to debate problems of love in verse.

taught myself the art of writing poetry, I decided to compose a sonnet addressed to all of Love's faithful subjects; and, requesting them to interpret my vision, I would write them what I had seen in my sleep. And then I began to write this sonnet,[16] which begins: *To every captive soul.*

> To every captive soul and loving heart
>   to whom these words I have composed are sent
>   for your elucidation in reply,
>   greetings I bring for your sweet lord's sake, Love.
> The first three hours, the hours of the time
>   of shining stars, were coming to an end,
>   when suddenly Love appeared before me
>   (to remember how he really was appalls me).
> Joyous, Love seemed to me, holding my heart
>   within his hand, and in his arms he had
>   my lady, loosely wrapped in folds, asleep.
> He woke her then, and gently fed to her
>   the burning heart; she ate it, terrified.
> And then I saw him disappear in tears.

This sonnet is divided into two parts. In the first part I extend greetings and ask for a response, while in the second I describe what it is that requires the response. The second part begins: *The first three hours.*

This sonnet was answered by many, who offered a variety of interpretations; among those who answered was the one I call my best friend,[17] who responded with a sonnet beginning: *I think that you beheld all worth.* This exchange of sonnets marked the beginning of our friendship. The true meaning of the dream I described was not perceived by anyone then, but now it is completely clear even to the least sophisticated.

---

16. The Italian troubadours invented the sonnet form, still a mode of debate in which the problem is set forth in a *proposta*, inviting a *risposta* (using the same rhymes) from another poet. Together the two sonnets formed a *tenzone*.

17. The poet Guido Cavalcanti (1259?–1300), who died in exile after banishment by Dante's own party and with his consent. Cf. *Inferno* X, 58–111; *Purgatory* XI, 97.

I V

After that vision my natural spirit was interfered with in its functioning, because my soul had become wholly absorbed in thinking about this most gracious lady; and in a short time I became so weak and frail that many of my friends were worried about the way I looked; others, full of malicious curiosity, were doing their best to discover things about me, which, above all, I wished to keep secret[18] from everyone. I was aware of the maliciousness of their questioning and, guided by Love who commanded me according to the counsel of reason, I would answer that it was Love who had conquered me. I said that it was Love because there were so many of his signs clearly marked on my face that they were impossible to conceal. And when people would ask: "Who is the person for whom you are so destroyed by Love?" I would look at them and smile and say nothing.

V

It happened one day that this most gracious of ladies was sitting in a place where words about the Queen of Glory[19] were being spoken, and I was where I could behold my bliss. Halfway between her and me, in a direct line of vision, sat a gentlewoman of a very pleasing appearance, who glanced at me frequently as if bewildered by my gaze, which seemed to be directed at her. And many began to notice her glances in my direction, and paid close attention to them and, as I left this place, I heard someone near me say: "See what a devastating effect that lady has had on that man." And, when her name was mentioned, I realized that the lady referred to was the one whose place had been half-way along the direct line which extended from the most gracious Beatrice, ending in my eyes. Then I was greatly relieved, feeling sure that my glances had not revealed my secret to others that day. At once I thought

18. The identity of his beloved.

19. The Virgin Mary.

of making this lovely lady a screen[20] to hide the truth, and so well did I play my part that in a short time the many people who talked about me were sure they knew my secret. Thanks to this lady I concealed the truth about myself for several years and months, and in order to encourage people's false belief, I wrote certain trifles for her in rhyme which I do not intend to include unless they could serve as a pretext to treat of that most gracious Beatrice; therefore, I will omit them all except for what is clearly in praise of her.

VI

Let me say that during the time that this lady acted as a screen for so great a love on my part, I was seized by a desire to record the name of my most gracious lady and to accompany it with the names of many others, and especially with the name of this gentlewoman. I chose the names of sixty of the most beautiful ladies of the city in which my lady had been placed by the Almighty, and composed a *serventese*[21] in the form of an epistle which I shall not include here—in fact, I would not have mentioned it if it were not that, while I was composing it, miraculously it happened that the name of my lady appeared as the ninth among the names of those ladies, as if refusing to appear under any other number.

VII

The lady I had used for so long to conceal my true feelings found it necessary to leave the aforementioned city and to journey to a distant town; and I, bewildered by the fact that my ideal defense had failed me, became extremely dejected, more so than even I would previously have believed possible. And realizing that if I should not lament somewhat

20. This pretended devotion to another woman was a common device of the troubadour poets.

21. The *sirventes* in Provençal poetry was a political poem; in Italy it became narrative, often characterizing individuals in a critical or satiric manner. No trace of Dante's *serventese* has been found.

her departure, people would soon become aware of my secret, I decided to write a few grieving words in the form of a sonnet (this I shall include here because my lady was the direct cause for certain words contained in the sonnet, as will be evident to one who understands). And then I wrote this sonnet[22] which begins: *O you who travel.*

> O you who travel on the road of Love,
> pause here and look about
> for any man whose grief surpasses mine.
> I ask this only: hear me out, then judge
> if I am not indeed
> the host and the abode of every torment.
> Love—surely not for my slight worth, but moved
> by his own nobleness—
> once gave me so serene and sweet a life
> that many times I heard it said of me:
> "God, what great qualities
> give this man's heart the riches of such joy?"
> Now all is spent of that first wealth of joy
> that had its source in Love's bright treasury;
> I know Love's destitution
> and have no heart to put into my verse.
> And so I try to imitate the man
> who covers up his poverty for shame:
> I wear the clothes of joy,
> but in my heart I weep and waste away.

This sonnet has two main parts. In the first I mean to call upon Love's faithful with the words of the prophet Jeremiah: *O vos omnes qui transitis per viam, attendite et videte si est dolor sicut dolor meus,*[23] and to beg that they deign to hear me; in the second part I tell of the condition in which Love had placed me, with a meaning other than that contained in the beginning and the ending of the sonnet, and I tell what I have lost. The second part begins: *Love—surely not.*

22. This is a *sonetto doppio* (or *rinterzato*) in which six seven-syllable lines are inserted among the usual eleven-syllable lines, each rhyming with the line preceding. Another *sonetto doppio* appears in chapter VIII.

23. Quoted in Latin from the *Lamentations of Jeremiah* 1:12: "All ye that pass by behold and see if there be any sorrow like unto my sorrow."

VIII

After the departure of this gentlewoman it pleased the Lord of the angels to call to His glory a young and very beautiful lady, who was known in the aforementioned city for her exceeding charm. I saw her body without the soul, lying in the midst of many ladies who were weeping most pitifully; then, remembering that I had seen her several times in the company of that most gracious one, I could not hold back my tears and, weeping, I resolved to say something about her death, in recognition of having seen her several times in the company of my lady. (And I suggest something of this toward the end of the words I wrote about her, as will be evident to the discerning reader.) I composed, then, these two sonnets, the first beginning: *If Love himself,* and the second: *Villianous death.*

> If Love himself weep, shall not lovers weep,
>   learning for what sad cause he pours his tears?
> Love hears his ladies crying their distress,
>   showing forth bitter sorrow through their eyes
> because villainous Death has worked its cruel
>   destructive art upon a gentle heart,
> and laid waste all that earth can find to praise
>   in a gracious lady, save her chastity.[24]
> Hear then how Love paid homage to this lady:
>   I saw him weeping there in human form,
>   observing the stilled image of her grace;
> and more than once he raised his eyes toward Heaven,
>   where that sweet soul already had its home,
>   which once, on earth, had worn enchanting flesh.

This sonnet is divided into three parts. In the first part I call upon Love's faithful, imploring them to weep, and I say that their lord himself weeps and that they, learning the reason for his tears, should be more disposed to hear me. In the second part I give the reason. In the third part I speak of a certain honor that Love bestowed upon this lady. The second part begins: *learning for what,* the third: *Hear then how.*

24. Her honor preserved in the minds of men.

Villainous Death, at war with tenderness,
  timeless mother of woe,
  judgment severe and incontestable,
  source of sick grief within my heart—a grief
  I constantly must bear—
  my tongue wears itself out in cursing you!
  And if I want to make you beg for mercy,
  I need only reveal
  your felonies, your guilt of every guilt;
  not that you are unknown for what you are,
  but rather to enrage
  whoever hopes for sustenance in love.
You have bereft the world of gentlest grace,
  of all that in sweet ladies merits praise;
  in youth's gay tender years
  you have destroyed all love's lightheartedness.
  There is no need to name this gracious lady,
  because her qualities tell who she was.
  Who merits not salvation,
  let him not hope to share her company.

This sonnet is divided into four parts. In the first part I address
Death with certain names appropriate to it; in the second I tell it
why I curse it; in the third I revile it; in the fourth I allude to some un-
specified person who, yet, is very clear to my mind. The second part
begins: *source of sick grief,* the third: *And if I want,* the fourth: *Who
merits not.*

IX

Not long after the death of this lady something happened that made it
necessary for me to leave the aforementioned city and go in the direction
of (but not all the way to) the place where the lady who had formerly
served as my screen was now staying. Though I was in the company of
many others it was as if I were alone: the journey so irked me, because
I was going farther away from my bliss, that my sighs could not relieve
the anguish in my heart. Therefore his very sweet lordship, who ruled

over me through the power of that most gracious lady, took the shape in my mind of a pilgrim[25] scantily and poorly dressed. He seemed distressed; he stared continually at the ground except for the times his eyes seemed to turn toward a beautiful river, swift and very clear, flowing by the side of the road I was traveling. It seemed that Love called me and spoke these words: "I come from that lady who has been your shield for so long a time; I know that she will not return soon to your city, and so, that heart which I made you leave with her I now have with me, and I am carrying it to a lady who will now be your defense, just as the other lady was." He named her, and she was a lady I knew well. "If you should, however, repeat any of the things I have told you, do so in a way that will not reveal the insincerity of the love you showed for the first lady, and which you must now show for another." Having said these words, his image suddenly vanished from my mind, because Love had become so great a part of me; and as if transformed in my appearance, I rode on that day deep in thought, with my sighs for company. The next day I began writing a sonnet about all this, which begins: *As I rode out.*

> As I rode out one day not long ago,
>   by narrow roads, and heavy with the thought
>   of what compelled my going, I met Love
>   in pilgrim's rags, coming the other way.
> All his appearance told the shabby story
>   of a once-great ruler since bereft of power;
>   and ever sighing, bent with thought, he moved,
>   his eyes averted from the passers-by.
> But he saw me and called me by my name,
>   and said: "I come from that place far away
>   where I had sent your heart to serve my will;
>   I bring it back to court a new delight."
>   Then he began to fuse with me so strangely,
>   he disappeared before I knew he had.

This sonnet has three parts. In the first part I tell how I encountered Love and how he looked; in the second I relate what he told me—only

25. A traveler who has left his proper home behind.

in part, however, for fear of revealing my secret; in the third part I tell how he disappeared from me. The second part begins: *But he saw me,* the third: *Then he began.*

X

After returning from my journey I sought out that lady whom my lord had named to me on the road of sighs, and, to be brief, I shall say that in a short time I made her so completely my defense that many people commented on it more than courtesy would have permitted; this often caused me grave concern. And for this reason, that is, the exaggerated rumors which made me out to be a vicious person, my most gracious lady, scourge of all vices and queen of the virtues, passing along a certain way, denied me her most sweet greeting in which lay all my bliss. Now I should like to depart a little from the present subject in order to make clear the miraculous effect her greeting had on me.

XI

I must tell you that whenever and wherever she appeared, I, in anticipation of her miraculous greeting, could not have considered any man my enemy; on the contrary, a flame of charity was lit within me and made me forgive whoever had offended me. And if, at this moment, anyone had asked me about anything, I could only have answered, my face all kindness: "Love." And when she was about to greet me, one of Love's spirits, annihilating all the others of the senses, would drive out the feeble spirits[26] of sight, saying to them, "Go and pay homage to your mistress," and Love would take their place. And if anyone had wished to know Love, he might have done so by looking at my glistening eyes. And when this most gracious one greeted me, Love was no medium capable of tempering my unbearable bliss, but rather, as if

26. For these spirits, see notes to II.

possessed of an excess of sweetness, he became so powerful that my body, which was completely under his rule, often moved like a heavy, inanimate object. By now it should be most evident that in her salutation dwelt my bliss, a bliss which often exceeded my capacity to contain it.

XII

Now, returning to my subject, let me say that no sooner was my bliss denied me than I was so stricken with anguish that, withdrawing from all company, I went to a solitary place to bathe the earth with bitterest tears. After my sobbing had quieted down somewhat, I went to my bedroom where I could lament without being heard; and there, begging pity of the lady of courtesy,[27] and saying, "Love, help your faithful one," I fell asleep like a little boy crying from a spanking. About half-way through my sleep I seemed to see in my room a young man sitting near the bed dressed in the whitest of garments and, from his expression, he seemed to be deep in thought, watching me where I lay; after looking at me for some time, he seemed to sigh and to call to me, saying these words: *Fili mi, tempus est ut pretermictantur simulacra nostra.*[28] Then I seemed to know who he was, for he was calling me in the same way that many times before in my sleep he had called me; and as I watched him, it seemed to me that he was weeping piteously, and he seemed to be waiting for me to say something to him; so, gathering courage, I began to address him, saying: "Lord of all virtues, why do you weep?" And he said these words to me: *Ego tanquam centrum circuli, cui simili modo se habent circumferentie partes; tu autem non sic.*[29] Then, as I thought over his words, it seemed to me that he had spoken very obscurely, so that I decided, reluctantly, to speak, and I said these words to him: "Why is it, my Lord, that you speak so obscurely?" And this time he spoke in Italian, saying: "Do not ask more than is useful to you." And so, I began telling him about the greeting that had been denied me, and when I asked him for the reason why, he answered me

27. The Virgin Mary.

28. Latin for "My son, it is time to do away with our false ideals."

29. Latin for "I am like the center of a circle equidisdant from all points on the circumference; you, however, are not."

in this way: "Our Beatrice heard from certain people who were talking about you that your attentions to the lady I named to you on the road of sighs were doing her some harm; this is the reason why the most gracious one, who is the opposite of anything harmful, did not deign to greet you, fearing your person might prove harmful to her. Since she has really been more or less aware of your secret for quite some time, I want you to write a certain poem, in which you make clear the power I have over you through her, explaining that ever since you were a boy you have belonged to her; and, concerning this, call as witness him who knows, and say that you are begging him to testify on your behalf; and I, who am that witness, will gladly explain it to her, and from this she will understand your true feelings and, understanding them, she will also set the proper value on the words of those people who were mistaken. Let your words themselves be, as it were, an intermediary, whereby you will not be speaking directly to her, for this would not be fitting; and unless these words are accompanied by me, do not send them anywhere she could hear them; also be sure to adorn them with sweet music where I shall be present whenever this is necessary." Having said these words he disappeared, and my sleep was broken. Then I, thinking back, discovered that this vision had appeared to me during the ninth hour of the day; before I left my room I decided to write a ballad following the instructions that my Lord had given me, and later on I composed this ballad[30] which begins: *I want you to go, ballad.*

> I want you to go, ballad, to seek out Love
> and present yourself with him before my lady,
> so that my exculpation, which you sing
> may be explained to her by Love, my lord.
>
> Ballad, you move along so gracefully,
> you need no company
> to venture boldly anywhere you like,
> but if you want to go with full assurance,
> first make a friend of Love;
> perhaps to go alone would not be wise,
> because the lady you are meant to speak to
> is angry with me now (or so I think),

30. The *ballata* was poetry set to music, meant to be sung during dance. It begins with a *ripresa* to be repeated as a refrain, followed by one or more stanzas whose last lines rhyme with one of the lines of the *ripresa*.

and if you were to go your way without him,
she might, perhaps, refuse to take you in.

But sweetly singing, in Love's company,
start with these words (but only
after you have begged her for compassion):
"My lady, the one who sends me here to you
hopes it will be your pleasure
to hear me out and judge if he is guilty.
I come with Love who, through your beauty's power,
can make your lover's whole appearance change;
now can you see why Love made him look elsewhere?
Remember, though, his heart has never strayed."

And say to her: "That heart of his, my lady,
has been so firmly faithful
that every thought keeps him a slave to you;
it was early yours, and never changed allegiance."
If she should not believe you,
tell her to question Love, who knows the truth;
and end by offering this humble prayer:
if granting me forgiveness would offend her,
then may her answer sentence me to death,
and she will see a faithful slave's obedience.

And tell Love, who is all compassion's key,
before you take your leave,
tell Love, who will know how to plead my case,
thanks to the strains of my sweet melody:
"Stay here awhile with her,
talk to her of your servant as you will;
and if your prayer should win for him reprieve,
let her clear smile announce that peace is made."
My gracious ballad, when it please you, go,
win yourself honor when the time is ripe.

This ballad is divided into three parts. In the first I tell it where to
go and encourage it so that it will go with more assurance, and I tell it
whom it should have for company if it wishes to go securely and free
from any danger; in the second I tell it what it is supposed to make
known; in the third I give it permission to depart whenever it pleases,

commending its journey to the arms of fortune. The second part begins: *But sweetly singing,* the third: *My gracious ballad.*

Here one might make the objection that no one can know to whom my words in the second person are addressed, since the ballad is nothing more than the words I myself speak; and so let me say that I intend to explain and discuss this uncertainty in an even more difficult section of this little book; and if anyone may have been in doubt here, perhaps wishing to offer the objection mentioned above, let him understand,[31] there, the explanation to apply here as well.

XIII

After this last vision, when I had already written what Love commanded me to write, many and diverse thoughts began to assail and try me, against which I was defenseless; among these thoughts were four that seemed to disturb most my peace of mind. The first was this: the lordship of Love is good since he keeps the mind of his faithful servant away from all evil things. The next was this: the lordship of Love is not good because the more fidelity his faithful one shows him, the heavier and more painful are the moments he must live through. Another was this: the name of Love is so sweet to hear that it seems impossible to me that the effect itself should be in most things other than sweet, since, as has often been said, names are the consequences of the things they name: *Nomina sunt consequentia rerum.*[32] The fourth was this: the lady through whom Love makes you suffer so is not like other ladies, whose hearts can be easily moved to change their attitudes.

And each one of these thoughts attacked me so forcefully that it made me feel like one who does not know what direction to take, who wants to start and does not know which way to go. And as for the idea of trying to find a common road for all of them, that is, one where all might come together, this was completely alien to me: namely, appealing to Pity and throwing myself into her arms. While I was in this mood,

31. He invites the reader to hold this passage in mind until he comes to the explanation in XXV. Cf. *Convivio* III 9.

32. Latin for "Names are the consequences of things": a common gloss on civil law. Cf. *Genesis* 2:19–20.

the desire to write some poetry about it came to me, and so I wrote this
sonnet which begins: *All my thoughts.*

> All my thoughts speak to me concerning Love;
>   they have in them such great diversity
>   that one thought makes me welcome all Love's power,
>   another judges such a lordship folly,
>   another, with its hope, brings me delight,
>   another very often makes me weep;
>   only in craving pity all agree
>   as they tremble with the fear that grips my heart.
> I do not know from which to take my theme;
>   I want to speak, but what is there to say?
>   Thus do I wander in a maze of Love!
>   And if I want to harmonize them all,
>   I am forced to call upon my enemy,
>   Lady Pity, to come to my defense.

This sonnet can be divided into four parts. In the first I say and
submit that all my thoughts are about Love; in the second I say that
they are different, and I talk about their differences; in the third I tell
what they all seem to have in common; in the fourth I say that, wishing
to speak of Love, I do not know where to begin, and if I wish to take
my theme from all my thoughts, I would be forced to call upon my
enemy, my Lady Pity—and I use the term "my lady" rather scornfully.
The second part begins: *they have in them;* the third: *only in craving;*
the fourth: *I do not know.*

XIV

After the battle[33] of the conflicting thoughts it happened that my most
gracious lady was present where many gentlewomen were gathered. I
was taken there by a friend who thought I would be delighted to go to
a place where so many beautiful ladies were. I was not sure why I was
being taken there but, trusting in the person who had led his friend to

---

33. Another military term, common to the troubadour lyric. Cf. "foe" and "defense"
in XIII.

the threshold of death, I asked him: "Why have we come to see these ladies?" He answered: "So that they may be fittingly attended." The fact is that they were gathered there to be with a certain lovely lady who had been married that day, for according to the custom of the afore-mentioned city[34] they were supposed to keep her company during the first meal at the home of her bridegroom. So I, thinking to please my friend, decided to remain with him in attendance upon the ladies. No sooner had I reached this decision than I seemed to feel a strange throbbing which began in the left side of my breast and immediately spread to all parts of my body. Then, pretending to act naturally, I leaned for support against a painted surface that extended along the walls of the house and, fearing that people might have become aware of my trembling, I raised my eyes and, looking at the ladies, I saw among them the most gracious Beatrice. Then my spirits were so disrupted[35] by the strength Love acquired when he saw himself this close to the most gracious lady, that none survived except the spirits of sight; and even these were driven forth, because Love desired to occupy their enviable post in order to behold the marvelous lady. And even though I was not quite myself, I was still very sorry for these little spirits who bitterly protested, saying: "If this one had not thrust us from our place like a bolt of lightning, we could have stayed to see the wonders of this lady as all our peers are doing." Now many of the ladies present, noticing the transformation I had undergone, were amazed and began to talk about it, joking about me with that most gracious one. My friend, who had made a mistake in good faith, took me by the hand and, leading me out of the sight of the ladies, asked me what was wrong. Then I, somewhat restored, for my dead spirits were coming back to life, and the ones ejected were returning to their rightful domain, said these words to my friend: "I have just set foot on that boundary of life beyond which[36] no one can go, hoping to return." And leaving him, I went back to my room of tears where, weeping in humiliation, I said to myself: "If this lady were aware of my condition, I do not believe she would ridicule my appearance but, on the contrary, would feel pity."

34. Weddings were regulated by the city of Florence, whose rules allowed an invited guest to bring a friend.

35. Cf. II, XI. He was unable to see Beatrice except through the eyes of Love.

36. On the verge of the Unknown. Cf. *Inferno* XXVI, 90–142, Ulysses's account of going to his death beyond the gates of Hercules; *Hamlet,* III, 1: "The undiscovered country from whose bourn no traveller returns."

In the midst of my tears I thought of writing a few words addressed to her, explaining the reason for the change in my appearance and saying that I was well aware that no one knew the reason and that, if it were known, I believed it would arouse everyone's compassion; I decided to write this in the hope that my words by chance would reach her. Then I composed this sonnet which begins: *You join with other ladies.*

> You join with other ladies to make sport
>   of the way I look, my lady, and do not ask
>   what makes me cut so laughable a figure
>   when I am in the presence of your beauty.
> If only you knew why, I am sure that Pity
>   would drop her arms and make her peace with me;
>   for Love, when he discovers me near you,
>   takes on a cruel, bold new confidence
> and puts my frightened senses to the sword,
>   by slaying this one, driving that one out,
>   till only he is left to look at you.
> Thus, by the changeling Love, I have been changed,
>   but not so much that I cannot still hear
>   my outcast senses mourning in their pain.

I do not divide this sonnet into parts, since this is done only to help reveal the meaning of the thing divided; and since what has been said about its occasion is sufficiently clear, there is no need for division. True, among the words with which I relate the occasion for this sonnet, there occur certain expressions difficult to understand, as when I say that Love slays all my spirits and the spirits of sight remain alive, though driven outside their organs. But it is impossible to make this clear to anyone who is not as faithful a follower of Love as I; to those who are, the solution to the difficulty is already obvious. Therefore, there is no need for me to clear up such difficulties, for my words of clarification would be either meaningless or superfluous.

XV

After that strange transformation a certain thought began to oppress my mind; it seldom left me but rather continually nagged at me, and it took form in this way: "Since you become so ridiculous-looking whenever you are near this lady, why do you keep trying to see her? Now assume that she were to ask you this, and that all your faculties were free to answer her, what would your answer be?" And to this another thought replied, saying modestly, "If I did not lose my wits and felt able to answer her, I would tell her that as soon as I call to mind the miraculous image of her beauty, then the desire to see her overcomes me, a desire so powerful that it kills, it destroys anything in my memory that might have been able to restrain it; and that is why what I have suffered in the past does not keep me from trying to see her." Moved by such thoughts, I decided to write a few words in which I would acquit myself of the accusation suggested by the first thought, and also describe what happens to me whenever I am near her. Then I wrote this sonnet which begins: *Whatever might restrain me.*

> Whatever might restrain me when I'm drawn
> to see you, my heart's bliss, dies from my mind.
> When I come close to you, I hear Love's warning:
> "Unless you want to die now, run away!"
> My blanching face reveals my fainting heart
> which weakly seeks support from where it may,
> and as I tremble in this drunken state
> the stones in the wall I lean on shout back: "Die!"
> He sins who witnesses my transformation
> and will not comfort my tormented soul,
> at least by showing that he shares my grief
> for pity's sake—which by your mocking dies,
> once it is brought to life by my dying face,
> whose yearning eyes beg death to take me now.

This sonnet is divided into two parts. In the first I explain why I do not keep myself from seeking this lady's company; in the second I tell what happens to me when I go near her, and this part begins: *When I come close.* This second part can be further divided into five sections, according to five different themes. In the first I tell what Love, counseled by reason, says to me whenever I am near her; in the second I describe the condition of my heart by reference to my face; in the third I tell how all assurance grows faint in me; in the fourth I say that he sins who does not show pity, which might be of some comfort to me; in the last part I tell why others should have pity, namely, because of the piteous look which fills my eyes. But this piteous look is wasted; it is never really seen by anyone, all because of the mockery of this lady who causes others, who perhaps might have noticed this piteousness, to do as she does. The second part begins: *My blanching face;* the third: *and as I tremble;* the fourth: *He sins;* the fifth: *for pity's sake.*

XVI

Soon after completing this sonnet I was moved by a desire to write more poetry, in which I would mention four more things concerning my condition which, it seemed to me, I had not yet made clear. The first of these is that many times I suffered when my memory excited my imagination to re-evoke the transformations that Love worked in me. The second is that Love, frequently and without warning, attacked me so violently that no part of me remained alive except one thought that spoke of this lady. The third is that when this battle of Love raged within me so, I would go, pale and haggard, to look upon this lady, believing that the sight of her would defend me in this battle,[37] forgetting what happened to me whenever I approached such graciousness. The fourth is that not only did the sight of her not defend me: it ultimately annihilated the little life I had left. And so I wrote this sonnet which begins: *Time and again.*

> Time and again the thought comes to my mind
>   of the dark condition Love imparts to me;
>   then the pity of it strikes me, and I ask:
>   "Could ever anyone have felt the same?"
>   For Love's attack is so precipitous
>   that life itself all but abandons me:
>   nothing survives except one lonely spirit,
>   allowed to live because it speaks of you.
> With hope of help to come I gather courage,
>   and deathly languid, drained of all defenses,
>   I come to you expecting to be healed;
>   and if I raise my eyes to look at you,

---

37. This passage is notable for its terms of warfare, a convention for the lover being tested in his loyalty.

within my heart a tremor starts to spread,
driving out life, stopping my pulses' beat.

This sonnet is divided into four parts according to the four things it treats, and since these are explained above, I concern myself only with indicating the parts by their beginnings; accordingly, the second part begins: *For Love's attack;* the third: *With hope of help;* the fourth: *and if I raise.*

XVII

After I had written these three sonnets addressed to this lady, in which little concerning my condition was left unsaid, believing I should be silent and say no more about this even at the cost of never again writing to her, since it seemed to me that I had talked about myself enough, I felt forced to find a new theme, one nobler than the last. Because I think the occasion for my new theme is a story pleasant to hear, I shall tell it, and as briefly as possible.

XVIII

Because of my appearance many people had learned the secret of my heart, and certain ladies who had seen me swoon at one time or another, and who knew my heart very well, happened to be gathered together one day, enjoying each other's company, when I, as if guided by fortune, passed near them and heard one of these gentlewomen call to me. The lady who addressed me had a very lively way of speaking, and so, when I had come up to them and saw that my most gracious lady was not with them, gaining confidence, I greeted them and asked what I could do to please them. There were many ladies present: several were laughing together; others were looking at me as if waiting for me to say something; there were others talking among themselves—one of whom, turning her eyes toward me and calling me by name, said: "Why do you love this lady of yours, if you are unable to endure the sight of her? Tell us, for surely the goal of such a love must be strange indeed." After she had said these words, not only she but all the others showed by their expression that they were waiting for my answer. I said: "Ladies, the goal of my love once consisted in receiving the greeting of this lady to whom you are, perhaps, referring, and in this greeting rested the bliss which was the goal of all my desires. But since it pleased her to deny it to me, my lord, Love, through his grace, has placed all my bliss in something that cannot fail me." With this the ladies began to speak among themselves and, just as sometimes the rain can be seen falling mingled with beautiful flakes of snow, so did I seem to hear their words issuing forth mingled with sighs. After they had spoken to each other for awhile, the one who had first addressed me spoke to me again, saying: "We beg you to tell us where this bliss of yours now rests." And I answered her: "In those words that praise my lady." And the one who had asked me the question said: "If you are telling us the truth, then those words you addressed to her describing your condition must have been written with some other intention." Then I, shamed by her words, departed from these ladies, saying to myself: "Since there is so much bliss in words that praise my lady, why have I ever written in any other way?" Therefore, I resolved that from then on I would always choose as the theme of my poetry whatever would be in praise of this most gracious one. Then, reflecting more on this, it seemed to me that I had undertaken a theme too lofty for myself, so that I did not dare to begin writing, and I remained for several days with the desire to write and the fear of beginning.

XIX

Then it happened that while walking down a path along which ran a very clear stream, I suddenly felt a great desire to write a poem, and I began to think how I would go about it. It seemed to me that to speak of my lady would not be becoming unless I were to address my words to ladies, and not just to any ladies, but only to those who are worthy, not merely to women. Then, I must tell you, my tongue, as if moved of its own accord, spoke and said: *Ladies who have intelligence of love.* With great delight I decided to keep these words in mind and to use them as the beginning of my poem. Later, after returning to the afore-mentioned city and reflecting for several days, I began writing a *can-*

zone,[38] using this beginning, and I constructed it in a way that will appear below in its divisions. The *canzone* begins: *Ladies who have.*

> Ladies who have intelligence of love,
>   I wish to speak to you about my lady,
>   not thinking to complete her litany,
>   but to talk in order to relieve my heart.
>   I tell you, when I think of her perfection,
>   Love lets me feel the sweetness of his presence,
>   and if at that point I could still feel bold,
>   my words could make all mankind fall in love.
>   I do not want to choose a tone too lofty,
>   for fear that such ambition make me timid;
>   instead I shall discuss her graciousness,
>   defectively, to measure by her merit,
>   with you, ladies and maidens whom Love knows,
>   for such a theme is only fit for you.
>
> The mind of God receives an angel's prayer:
>   "My Lord, there appears to be upon your earth
>   a living miracle, proceeding from
>   a radiant soul whose light reaches us here."
>   Heaven, that lacks its full perfection only
>   in lacking her, pleads for her to the Lord,
>   and every saint is begging for this favor.
>   Compassion for His creatures still remains,
>   for God, who knows they are speaking of my lady,
>   says: "Chosen ones, now suffer happily
>   that she, your hope, live her appointed time
>   for the sake of one down there who fears her loss,
>   and who shall say unto the damned in Hell:[39]
>   'I have beheld the hope of Heaven's blest.' "

38. A poem of Provençal origin consisting of a number of stanzas identically structured. Dante considered it the noblest form of poetry and wrote of it in detail in his *De vulgari eloquentia* (II). It was later diversified and perfected by Petrarch. This canzone ("*Donne ch'avete intelletto d'amore*") is Dante's most famous because of its mention in *Purgatory* XXIV, 49–63, as a model of the "*dolce stil novo.*"

39. Several interpretations of this controversial line are offered: He expects not to be saved; he anticipates the death of Beatrice and his subsequent languishing in a hell on earth without her; he anticipates his descent into hell in a future work of imagination, like the *Divine Comedy.*

My lady is desired in highest Heaven.
    Now let me tell you something of her power.
    A lady who aspires to graciousness
    should seek her company, for where she goes
    Love drives a killing frost into vile hearts
    that freezes and destroys what they are thinking;
    should such a one insist on looking at her,
    he is changed to something noble or he dies.
    And if she finds one worthy to behold her,
    that man will feel her power for salvation
    when she accords to him her salutation,
    which humbles him till he forgets all wrongs.
    And God has graced her with a greater gift:
    whoever speaks with her shall speak with Him.

Love says of her: "How can a mortal body
    achieve such beauty and such purity?"
    He looks again and swears it must be true:
    God does have something new in mind for earth.
    Her color is the pallor of the pearl,[40]
    a paleness perfect for a gracious lady;
    she is the best that Nature can achieve
    and by her mold all beauty tests itself;
    her eyes, wherever she may choose to look,
    send forth their spirits radiant with love
    to strike the eyes of anyone they meet,
    and penetrate until they find the heart.
    You will see Love depicted on her face,
    there where no one dares hold his gaze too long.

My song, I know that you will go and speak
    to many ladies when I bid you leave,
    and since I brought you up as Love's true child,
    ingenuous and plain, let me advise you
    to beg of anybody you may meet:
    "Please help me find my way; I have been sent
    to the lady with whose praise I am adorned."
    And so that you may not have gone in vain,
    do not waste time with any vulgar people;

40. The color of dawn, denoting ideal perfection in a philosophic sense.

do what you can to show your meaning only
to ladies, or to men who may be worthy;
they will direct you by the quickest path.
You will find Love and with him find our lady.
Speak well of me to Love, it is your duty.

In order that this *canzone* may be better understood I shall divide it more carefully than the previous poems. I first divide it into three parts: the first part is an introduction to the words that follow; the second continues the theme treated; the third is, as it were, a servant to the words that precede it. The second part begins: *The mind of God*, the third: *My song, I know*. Now the first part falls into four subdivisions. In the first I tell to whom I wish to write; in the second I tell about the condition in which I find myself whenever I think of her perfection, and how I would write if I did not lose courage; in the third I mention the way in which I intend to write about her in order not to be intimidated; in the fourth, referring again to those to whom I mean to write, I give the reason why I have chosen them. The second begins: *I tell you*; the third: *I do not want*; the fourth: *with you, ladies*.

Then, when I say: *The mind of God*, I begin to talk about my lady, and this part falls into two subdivisions. In the first I tell how she is thought of in Heaven; in the second I tell how she is thought of on earth: *My lady is desired*. This second part, in turn, is divided into two. In the first I describe the nobility of her soul, telling about the effective powers that proceed from it; in the second I describe the nobility of her body, telling about some of its beautiful qualities: *Love says of her*. The second part is in turn divided into two. In the first I speak of certain beautiful qualities involving particular parts of her body: *her eyes, wherever*. This is again divided in two. First I speak of her eyes, which are the initiators of love; then I speak of her mouth,[41] which is the supreme desire of my love. So that here and now any perverse thought may be dispelled, let him who reads this remember what has been previously said about this lady's greeting, which was an action of her mouth, and which was the goal of all my desires so long as I was allowed to receive it.

Then when I say, *My song, I know that you,* I am adding a stanza

41. The flame of desire is struck in the eyes; its goal is the mouth from which issues the greeting of the lady. Cf. *Convivio* III 8.

as a sort of handmaiden[42] to the others. In this stanza I tell what I want my song to do; because this last part is easy to understand, I do not bother to divide it further. Certainly, to make the meaning of this *canzone* still clearer, I should have to make the divisions even more minute; however, if anyone is not intelligent enough to understand[43] it from the divisions already made, I would not mind in the least if he would simply leave my poem alone. As it is, I am afraid I may have shared its meaning with too many readers because of these divisions I have already made —if it should happen that many would bother to read them.

X X

After this *canzone* had become rather well known, one of my friends who had heard it was moved to ask me[44] to write about the nature of Love, having perhaps, from reading my poem, acquired more confidence in me than I deserved. So, thinking that after my treatment of the previous theme it would be good to treat the theme of Love and, feeling that I owed this to my friend, I decided to compose a poem dealing with Love. And I wrote this sonnet, which begins: *Love and the gracious heart.*

> Love and the gracious heart are a single thing,
>   as that wise poet tells us in his poem:[45]
>   and one can no more be without the other

---

42. The final stanza serves as messenger, technically named an *envoi, congedo,* or *commiato.*

43. Professing to aim to a select audience was a common stance in troubadour poetry.

44. Dante here echoes the first line of Cavalcanti's most famous canzone, "*Donna mi prega.*"

45. Guido Guinizzelli, the forerunner of Dante, who formulated the doctrine of the gracious heart in his most famous *canzone* "*Al cor gentil ripara sempre Amore.*" Guinizzelli like Dante changed his style from describing conventionally the sensual effects of love to exploring the intellectual aspects of it originating in nobility of character. Dante refers to Guinizzelli in *De Vulgari Eloquentia* I, 15; *Convivio* IV, 20; *Purgatory* XXVI, 97–99; he echoes this *canzone* again in *Inferno* V, 100.

than can the reasoning mind without its reason.
Nature, when in a loving mood, creates them:
Love to be king, the heart to be his home,
a place for Love to rest while he is sleeping,
perhaps for just a while, or for much longer.
And then the beauty of a virtuous lady
appears, to please the eyes, and in the heart
desire for the pleasing thing is born;
and this desire may linger in the heart
until Love's spirit is aroused from sleep.
A man of worth has the same effect on ladies.

This sonnet is divided into two parts. In the first I speak of Love as a potential force;[46] in the second I speak of him as potentiality realized in action. The second part begins: *And then the beauty*. The first part is again divided into two: first, I tell in what kind of substance this potentiality resides; secondly, I tell how this substance and this potentiality are brought into being, and how the one is related to the other as matter is to form.[47] The second subdivision begins: *Nature, when*. Then when I say: *And then the beauty,* I explain how this potentiality is realized in action: first, how it is realized in a man, then how it is realized in a lady, beginning: *A man of worth*.

XXI

After having dealt with Love in the last sonnet, I felt a desire to write more, this time in praise of that most gracious lady, showing how, through her, this Love is awakened, and how she not only awakens him there where he sleeps but also, how she, miraculously working, brings him into existence there where he does not potentially exist. And so I wrote this sonnet which begins: *The power of Love*.

46. Of *Idea*—eternal form. Cf. *Convivio* II, 1 and III, 7.

47. Cf. the Aristotelian principle of causation from *De anima* II, 2: The perfection of the thing is its realization in nature (entelechy) in virtue of which it attains its fullest function. According to Guinizzelli's poem, the phenomenon is like a bird finding its home and renewing itself in the greenness of the woods.

The power of Love borne in my lady's eyes
    imparts its grace to all she looks upon.
All turn to gaze at her when she walks by,
and when she greets a man his heart beats fast,
the color leaves his face, he bows his head
and sighs to think of all his imperfections.
Anger and pride are forced to flee from her.
Help me to honor her, most gracious ladies.
Humility and every sweet conception
    bloom in the heart of those who hear her speak.
(Praise to the one who first saw what she was!)
The image of her when she starts to smile
dissolves within the mind and melts away,
a miracle too rich and strange to hold.

This sonnet has three parts. In the first I tell how this lady actualizes this potentiality by means of her most gracious eyes; in the third I tell how she does the same by means of her most gracious mouth; and between these two parts is a very small part, which is like a beggar asking for help from the preceding and following parts, and it begins: *Help me to honor her*. The third begins: *Humility*. The first part divides into three. In the first I tell how she miraculously makes gracious whatever she looks upon, and this is as much as to say that she brings Love into potential existence there where he does not exist; in the second I tell how she activates Love in the hearts of all those whom she sees; in the third I tell of what she miraculously effects in their hearts. The second part begins: *Men turn to gaze*, and the third: *and when she greets*. Then when I say: *Help me to honor*, I indicate to whom I wish to speak, calling upon ladies for their assistance in honoring my lady. Then when I say: *Humility*, I repeat what I said in the first part, using, this time, two actions of her mouth: the first is her sweet manner of speaking, the second is her miraculous smile. I do not mention the effect of the latter on people's hearts, since the memory is not capable of retaining a smile like hers or its effects.

XXII

Not many days after this, according to the will of the Lord of Glory (who Himself accepted death), he who had been the father[48] of such a miraculous being as this most gracious Beatrice clearly was, departed from this life, passing most certainly into eternal glory. Since such a departure is sorrowful to those who remain and who have been friends of the deceased; and since there is no friendship more intimate than that of a good father for a good child, or of a good child for a good father; and since this lady possessed the highest degree of goodness; and since her father, as is believed by many, and is the truth, was exceedingly good—then it is clear that this lady was filled with bitterest sorrow. And since it was the custom of this city for ladies to gather with ladies and men with men on such occasions, many ladies were assembled in that place where Beatrice wept piteously. I saw several of them returning from her house and heard them talking about this most gracious one and how she mourned; among their words I heard: "She grieves so that anyone who sees her would surely die of pity." Then these ladies passed by me, and I was left in such a sad state that tears kept running down my face so that I often had to cover my eyes with my hands. I would have hidden myself as soon as I felt the tears coming, but I hoped to hear more about her, since I was standing where most of those ladies would pass by me after taking leave of her. And so, while I stayed in the same place, more ladies passed by me talking to each other, saying: "Who of us can ever be happy again after hearing this lady grieve so piteously?" After these, other ladies passed, saying as they came: "This man here is weeping exactly as if he had seen her, as we have." Then came others who said: "Look at him! He is so changed, he doesn't seem to be the same person." And so, as the ladies passed, I heard their words about her and about me, as I have just related. After reflecting awhile, I decided, since I had such an excellent theme, to write a poem in which I would include everything I had heard these ladies say. And since I would have been glad to question them, if I had not thought it would be indiscreet, I presented my theme as if I had asked them questions

48. The father of Beatrice, usually identified as Folco Portinari, who died in 1289 leaving six daughters and five sons, all of whom were mentioned in his will, including Beatrice.

and they had answered me.[49] I composed two sonnets: in the first I ask those questions which I had wanted to ask; in the other I give the ladies' answer, using what I had heard them say and presenting it as if they had said it in reply to me. The first sonnet begins: *O you who bear,* and the other: *Are you the one.*

> O you who bear a look of resignation,
>   moving with eyes downcast to show your grief,
>   where are you coming from? Your coloring
>   appears to be the hue of grief itself.
>   Is it our gracious lady you have seen
>   bathing with tears Love's image in her face?
>   O ladies, tell me what my heart tells me:
>   I see her grace in every step you take.
> And if you come from so profound a grief,
>   may it please you to stay with me awhile
>   and tell me truly what you know of her.
>   I see your eyes, I see how they have wept,
>   and how you come retreating all undone;
>   my heart is touched and shaken at the sight.

This sonnet divides into two parts. In the first I address these ladies and ask them if they come from my lady, telling them that I believe they do, since they come back as if made more gracious; in the second I ask them to talk to me about her. The second part begins: *And if you come.*

Here follows the other sonnet, composed in the way explained previously:

> Are you the one that often spoke to us
>   about our lady, and to us alone?
>   Your tone of voice, indeed, resembles his,
>   but in your face we find another look.
>   Why do you weep so bitterly? Pity
>   would melt the heart of anyone who sees you.
>   Have you seen her weep, too, and now cannot
>   conceal from us the sorrow in your heart?
> Leave grief to us; the path of tears is ours

49. The two sonnets together, question and answer, form a *contrasto.*

> (to try to comfort us would be a sin),
> we are the ones who heard her sobbing words.
> Her face proclaims the agony she feels;
> if anyone dared look into her eyes,
> he would have died, drowned in his tears of grief.

This sonnet has four parts according to the four responses of the ladies for whom I speak, and since they are made evident enough in the sonnet, I do not bother to explain the meaning of the parts: I merely indicate where they occur. The second begins: *Why do you weep,* the third: *Leave grief to us,* the fourth: *Her face proclaims.*

XXIII

A few days after this it happened that my body was afflicted by a painful disease which made me suffer intense anguish continuously for nine days; I became so weak that I was forced to lie in bed like a person paralyzed. Now, on the ninth day, when the pain was almost unbearable, a thought came to me which was about my lady. After thinking about her awhile, I returned to thoughts of my feeble condition and, realizing how short life is, even if one is healthy, I began to weep silently about the misery of life. Then, sighing deeply, I said to myself: "It is bound to happen that one day the most gracious Beatrice will die." At that, such a frenzy seized me that I closed my eyes and, agitated like one in delirium, began to imagine things: as my mind started wandering, there appeared to me certain faces of ladies with dishevelled hair, and they were saying to me: "You are going to die." And then after these ladies there appeared to me other faces strange and horrible to look at, who were saying: "You are dead." While my imagination was wandering like this, I came to the point that I no longer knew where I was. And I seemed to see ladies preternaturally sad, their hair dishevelled, weeping as they made their way down a street. And I seemed to see the sun grow dark, giving the stars a color that would have made me swear that they were weeping. And it seemed to me that the birds flying through the air fell to earth dead, and there were violent earthquakes.[50]

50. These phenomena are reminiscent of events that accompanied the death of Christ (Matthew 27:51–54; Luke 23:44), and of Revelation 6:12–14.

Bewildered as I dreamed, and terrified, I imagined that a friend of mine came to tell me: "Then you don't know? Your miraculous lady has departed from this world." At that I began to weep most piteously, and I wept not only in my dream, I wept with my eyes, wet with real tears. I imagined that I looked up at the sky, and I seemed to see a multitude of angels returning above, and they had before them a little pure-white cloud. It seemed to me that these angels were singing in glory, and the words of their song seemed to be: *Osanna in excelsis;*[51] the rest I could not seem to hear. Then it seemed that my heart, which was so full of love, said to me: "It is true, our lady lies dead." And hearing that, it seemed to me I went to see the body in which that most noble and blessed soul had dwelt, and in the intensity of my hallucination I saw this lady dead. And it seemed that ladies were covering her head with a white veil, and her face seemed to have an expression of such joyous acceptance that it said to me: "I am contemplating the fountainhead of peace." At the sight of her in this dream I felt such a serenity that I called upon Death and said: "Sweet Death, come to me. Do not be unkind to me: you should be gracious, considering where you have just been. So, come to me, for I earnestly desire you, and you can see that I do, for I already wear your color." And when I had witnessed the administering of the sorrowful rites customarily performed on the bodies of the dead, it seemed I returned to my room and from there looked toward Heaven, and so vivid was my dream that, weeping, I began to speak aloud: "O most beautiful soul, how blessed is he who beholds you!"

As I was saying these words in a spasm of tears, calling upon Death to come to me, a young and gracious lady,[52] who had been at my bedside, thought that my tears and words were caused by the pain of my illness, and greatly frightened began to weep. Then other ladies who were about the room became aware of my weeping because of her reaction to me. After sending away this lady, who was most closely related to me, they drew near to wake me, thinking that I was having a dream, and said to me: "You must wake up" and "Do not be afraid." And with these words of theirs my wild imaginings were cut off just when I was about to say: "Oh, Beatrice, blessed art thou," and I had already said: "Oh, Beatrice," when I opened my eyes with a start and realized

51. Latin for "Hosanna in the highest," the greeting given to Christ when he entered Jerusalem. Cf. Mark 11:10; Matthew 21:9; *Purgatory* XI, 11; XX, 136.

52. Said below to be a "close relative," perhaps a younger sister.

that it had been only a dream. Although I had called out this name, my voice was so broken by my sobbing that I think these ladies were not able to understand what I said. Even though I was very much ashamed, still, somehow prompted by Love, I turned my face toward them. And when they saw me, they began saying: "He looks as if he were dead!" And they said to each other: "Let us try to comfort him." And so they said many things to comfort me, and then they asked me what it was that had frightened me. Being somewhat comforted, aware that nothing was true of what I had imagined, I answered them: "I will tell you what happened to me." Then I began at the beginning and continued to the end, telling them what I had seen but without mentioning the name of the most gracious one.

After I had recovered from my illness, I decided to write about what had happened to me, since it seemed to me this would be something fascinating to hear about. And so I composed the *canzone*[53] which begins: *A lady of tender years;* it is constructed in a manner made clear in the divisions that follow it.

> A lady of tender years, compassionate
>   and richly graced with human gentleness,
>   was standing near and heard me call on Death;
>   she saw the piteous weeping of my eyes
>   and heard the wild confusing words I spoke;
>   she was so struck with fear she wept aloud.
>   Then other ladies, made aware of me
>   by the weeping figure standing by my bed,
>   sent her away from there;
>   and they drew near to rouse me from my sleep.
>   One of them said: "Wake up!"
>   Another asked: "Why are you so distressed?"
>   With this I left my world of dreams and woke,
>   Calling aloud the name of my sweet lady.
>
> I called to her in a voice so weak with pain,
>   so broken by my tears and anguished sobs,
>   that only my heart heard her name pronounced.

53. The longest poem in the *Vita nuova*, this is the centerpiece of the work; i.e., it is preceded by fifteen poems and followed by fifteen and is separated from the other two *canzoni* by four poems each. The six stanzas each have fourteen lines, lines 9 and 11 being settenary. There is no *commiato*.

In spite of my deep-felt humiliation
which showed itself most plainly on my face,
Love made me turn and look up at these ladies.
The pallor of my skin amazed them so
they could not help but start to speak of death.
"Oh, let us comfort him,"
implored one lady sweetly of another;
and more than once they asked:
"What did you see that took away your strength?"
When I felt comforted somewhat, I said:
"Ladies, now you shall know what I have seen:

While I was brooding on my languid life,
and sensed how fleeting is our little day,
Love wept within my heart, which is his home;
then my bewildered soul went numb with fear,
and sighing deep within myself, I said:
'My lady someday surely has to die.'
Then I surrendered to my anguished thoughts,
and closed my heavy wept-out tired eyes,
and all my body's spirits
went drifting off, each fainting in despair.
And then, drifting and dreaming,
with consciousness and truth left far behind,
I saw the looks of ladies wild with wrath,
chanting together: 'Die, you are going to die.'

Now captured by my false imaginings
and somehow in a place unknown to me,
I was the witness of unnatural things:
of ladies passing with dishevelled hair,
some weeping, others wailing their laments
that pierced the air like arrows tipped in flame.
And then it seemed to me I saw the sun
grow slowly darker, and a star appear,
and sun and star did weep;
birds flying through the air fell dead to earth;
the earth began to quake.
A man appeared, pale, and his voice was weak
as he said to me: 'You have not heard the news?
Your lady, once so lovely, now lies dead.'

I raised my weeping eyes to look above
  and saw what seemed to be a rain of manna:
  angels who were returning to their home;
  in front of them they had a little cloud
  and sang 'Hosanna' as they rose with it
  (had there been other words, I would have told you).
  Then I heard Love: 'I shall no longer hide
  the truth from you. Come where our lady lies.'
  My wild imaginings
  led me to see my lady lying dead;
  I looked at her, and then
  I saw ladies covering her with a veil.
  She had an air of joyful resignation;
  it was as if she said: 'I am in peace.'

Then I became so humble in my sorrow,
  seeing, in her, humility incarnate,
  that I could say: 'O, Death, I hold you dear;
  from now on you should put on graciousness
  and change your scorn to sympathy for me,
  since in my lady you have been at home.
  See how I yearn to be one of your own:
  I even look the way you would, alive.
  Come, for my heart implores you!'
  When the last rites were done, I left that place,
  and when I was alone,
  I raised my eyes toward Heaven, and declared:
  'Blessed is he who sees you, lovely soul!'
  You called to me just then, and I am grateful."

This *canzone* has two sections. In the first, speaking to some uniden-
tified person, I tell how I was aroused from a delirious dream by certain
ladies, and how I promised to relate it to them; in the second I report
what I told them. The second begins: *While I was brooding.* The first
section divides into two parts: in the first I tell what certain ladies, and
one particular lady, moved by my delirious state, said and did before I
had returned to full consciousness; in the second I report what these
ladies said to me after I had come out of my frenzy, and this part
begins: *I called to her.* Then when I say: *While I was brooding,* I relate
what I told them about my dream. And this section has two parts: in

the first I describe the dream from beginning to end; in the second I tell at what point I was called by these ladies and, choosing my words discreetly, I thank them for waking me. And this part begins: *You called to me.*

XXIV

After this wild dream I happened one day to be sitting in a certain place deep in thought, when I felt a tremor begin in my heart, as if I were in the presence of my lady. Then a vision of Love came to me, and I seemed to see him coming from that place where my lady dwelt, and he seemed to say joyously from within my heart: "See that you bless the day that I took you captive; it is your duty to do so." And it truly seemed to me that my heart was happy, so happy that it did not seem to be my heart because of this change. Shortly after my heart had said these words, speaking with the tongue of Love, I saw coming toward me a gentle-woman, noted for her beauty, who had been the much-loved lady of my best friend.[54] Her name was Giovanna, but because of her beauty (as many believed) she had been given the name of Primavera, meaning Spring, and so she came to be called. And, looking behind her, I saw coming the miraculous Beatrice. These ladies passed close by me, one of them following the other, and it seemed that Love spoke in my heart and said: "The one in front is called Primavera only because of the way she comes today; for I inspired the giver of her name to call her Primavera, meaning 'she will come first' (*prima verrà*) on the day that Beatrice shows herself after the dream of her faithful one. And if you will also consider her real name, you will see that this too means 'she will come first,' since the name Joan (*Giovanna*) comes from the name of that John (*Giovanni*) who preceded the True Light, saying: *Ego vox clamantis in deserto: parate viam Domini.*[55] After this, Love seemed to speak again and say these words: "Anyone of subtle discernment would call Beatrice Love, because she so greatly resembles me." Later, thinking

54. Guido Cavalcanti; cf. III and XXX. No Joan (Giovanna) has been found in the poems of Cavalcanti, although a *ballata* begins "*Fresca rosa novella, piacente Primavera.*"

55. Latin for "I am the voice crying in the wilderness; prepare ye the way of the Lord." Cf. Matthew 3:3; Mark 1:3; Luke 3:4; John 1:23.

this over, I decided to write a poem to my best friend (not mentioning certain things which I thought should not be revealed), whose heart, I believed, still admired the beauty of the radiant Primavera. And I wrote this sonnet which begins: *I felt a sleeping spirit.*

> I felt a sleeping spirit in my heart
>   awake to Love. And then from far away
> I saw the Lord of love approaching me,
>   and hardly recognized him through his joy.
> "Think now of nothing but to honor me,"
> I heard him say, and each word was a smile;
> and as my master stayed awhile with me,
> I looked along the way that he had come
> and saw there Lady Joan and Lady Bice[56]
>   coming toward the place where I was standing:
>   a miracle that led a miracle.
> And, as my memory recalls the scene,
> Love said to me: "The first to come is Spring;
>   the one who is my image is called Love."

This sonnet has many parts. The first tells how I felt the familiar tremor awaken in my heart, and how it seemed that Love, joyful, coming from a far-away place, revealed himself to me in my heart; the second records what Love seemed to say to me in my heart, and how he looked; the third tells how, after he had remained awhile with me, I saw and heard certain things. The second part begins: *Think now,* the third: *and as my master.* The third part divides into two: in the first I tell what I saw, in the second I tell what I heard. The second part begins: *Love said to me.*

XXV

At this point it may be that someone worthy of having every doubt cleared up could be puzzled at my speaking of Love as if it were a thing

---

56. The familiar name of Beatrice. This is the only time Dante names her while she is alive. A fictitious name to conceal the identity of the lady was called a *senhal* in troubadour poetry.

in itself,[57] as if it were not only an intellectual substance, but also a bodily substance. This is patently false, for Love does not exist in itself as a substance, but is an accident in a substance. And that I speak of Love as if it possessed a body, further still, as if it were a human being, is shown by three things I say about it. I say that I saw it coming; and since "to come" implies locomotion, and since, according to the Philosopher,[58] only a body may move from place to place by its own power, it is obvious that I assume Love to be a body. I also say that it laughed and even that it spoke—acts that would seem characteristic of a human being, especially that of laughing; and so it is clear that I assume love to be human. To clarify this matter suitably for my purpose, I shall begin by saying that, formerly, there were no love poets[59] writing in the vernacular, the only love poets were those writing in Latin: among us (and this probably happened in other nations as it still happens in the case of Greece) it was not vernacular poets but learned poets who wrote about love. It is only recently that the first poets appeared who wrote in the vernacular; I call them "poets" for to compose rhymed verse in the vernacular is more or less the same as to compose poetry in Latin using classical meters.[60]

And proof that it is but a short time since these poets first appeared is the fact that if we look into the Provençal and the Italian literatures,[61] we shall not find any poems written more than a hundred and fifty years ago. The reason why a few ungifted poets acquired the fame of knowing how to compose is that they were the first who wrote poetry in the

---

57. He speaks also of Beatrice, just identified as Love. This passage is extremely important as an example of early literary criticism.

58. Aristotle, known to Dante through Latin translations and the writings of St. Thomas Aquinas.

59. Didactic poets who disseminated their ideas through the medium of love poetry, writing in the learned tongue.

60. Dante argues from a Scholastic position for poetic license in the formation of vernacular verse, composed within certain limitations (*secundam aliquam proportionem*). Unless writing in Latin grammar and meter, a poet technically was not called a poet.

61. '*In lingua d'oco e in quella di sì*,' referring to Languedoc and the Italian vernacular. Dante understood Provençal (Languedoc) to be that language spoken in southern Europe, which used the Latin *hoc* for the word "yes." Old French (*langue d'oïl*), spoken in northern France, used *oïl* (*hoc* + *ille*). Italian used *sì* from the Latin *sic*. Cf. *Inferno* XXXIII, 80.

Italian language. The first poet to begin writing in the vernacular was moved to do so by a desire to make his words understandable to ladies who found Latin verses difficult to comprehend. And this is an argument against those who compose in the vernacular on a subject other than love,[62] since composition in the vernacular was from the beginning intended for treating of love.

Since, in Latin, greater license is conceded to the poet than to the prose writer, and since these Italian writers are simply poets writing in the vernacular, we can conclude that it is fitting and reasonable that greater license be granted them than to other writers in the vernacular; therefore, if any image or coloring of words is conceded to the Latin poet, it should be conceded to the Italian poet. So, if we find that the Latin poets addressed inanimate objects in their writings, as if these objects had sense and reason, or made them address each other, and that they did this not only with real things but also with unreal things (that is: they have said, concerning things that do not exist, that they speak, and they have said that many an accident in substance speaks as if it were a substance and human), then it is fitting that the vernacular poet do the same—not, of course, without some reason, but with a motive that later can be explained in prose. That the Latin poets have written in the way I have just described can be seen in the case of Virgil, who says that Juno, a goddess hostile to the Trojans, spoke to Aeolus, god of the winds, in the first book of the *Aeneid*: *Eole, nanque tibi,*[63] and that this god answered her: *Tuus, o regina, quid optes explorare labor; michi iussa capessere fas est.*[64] This same poet has an inanimate thing speak to animate beings in the third book of the *Aeneid*: *Dardanide duri.*[65] In Lucan the animate being speaks to the inanimate object: *Multum, Roma, tamen debes civilibus armis.*[66] In Horace a man speaks to his own inspiration as if to another person, and not only are the

---

62. Dante later expanded his categories to include the defense of the community, virtue, and morality. Cf. *De Vulgaris Eloquentia* II, 2.

63. Latin for "Aeolus, for to you."

64. Latin for "Yours, O queen, is the task of determining your wishes; mine is the right to obey orders," speaking of Juno (*Aeneid* I, 65, 76–77).

65. Latin for "You hardy Trojans" (*Aeneid* III, 94); Phoebus is speaking in his role as the sun.

66. Latin for "Much, Rome, do you owe, nevertheless, to the civil war" (*Pharsalia* I, 44); addressed in the original to the emperor.

words those of Horace but he gives them as if quoting from the good Homer, in this passage of his *Poetics: Dic michi, Musa, virum.*[67] In Ovid, Love speaks as if it were a human being, in the beginning of the book called *The Remedy of Love: Bella michi, video, bella parantur, ait.*[68]

From what has been said above, anyone who experiences difficulties in certain parts of this, my little book, can find a solution for them. So that some ungifted person may not be encouraged by my words to go too far, let me add that just as the Latin poets did not write in the way they did without a reason, so vernacular poets should not write in the same way without having some reason for writing as they do. For, if any one should dress his poem in images and rhetorical coloring and then, being asked to strip his poem of such dress in order to reveal its true meaning,[69] would not be able to do so—this would be a veritable cause for shame. And my best friend and I are well acquainted with some who compose so clumsily.

XXVI

This most gracious lady of whom I have spoken in the preceding poems came into such widespread favor that, when she walked down the street, people ran to see her. This made me wonderfully happy. And when she passed by someone, such modesty filled his heart that he did not dare to raise his eyes or to return her greeting (many people, who have experienced this, could testify to it if anyone should not believe me). Crowned and clothed with humility, she would go her way, taking no glory from what she heard and saw. Many would say after she had passed: "This is no woman, this is one of the most beautiful angels of Heaven." And others would say: "She is a miracle! Blessed be the Lord

---

67. Latin for "Tell me, Muse, of the man" (*Ars Poetica* 141–142). In this passage, Horace translates the first two verses of Homer's *Odyssey,* making his memory of Homer's words the object of his speech.

68. Latin for "Wars against me I see, wars are preparing, he says" (*Remedia Amoris* 2). For a mention of all four of these poets together, see *Inferno* IV, 79–90.

69. Dante invites us to find this meaning not only in his own figures or personifications but in the way they link with the figures of the four poets cited.

who can work so wondrously." Let me say that she showed such decorum and was possessed of such charming qualities that those who looked at her experienced a pure and sweet delight, such that they were unable to describe it; and there was no one who could look at her without immediately sighing. These and still more marvelous things were the result of her powers. Thinking about this, and wishing to take up again the theme of her praise, I decided to write something which would describe her magnificent and beneficent efficacy, so that not only those who could see her with their own eyes, but others, as well, might know of her whatever can be said in words. And so I wrote this sonnet which begins: *Such sweet decorum.*[70]

> Such sweet decorum and such gentle grace
>   attend my lady's greeting to mankind
>   that lips can only tremble into silence,
>   and eyes dare not attempt to gaze at her.
>   Untouched by all the praise along her way,
>   she moves in goodness, clothed in humbleness,
>   and seems a creature come from Heaven to earth,
>   a miracle manifest in reality.
> Miraculously gracious to behold,
>   her sweetness, through the eyes reaches the heart
>   (who has not felt this cannot understand),
>   and from her lips there seems to move a spirit
>   tender, so deeply loving that it glides
>   into the souls of men and whispers: "Sigh!"

This sonnet is so easy to understand from what has preceded that it has no need of divisions. And so, leaving it aside, let me say that my lady[71] came into such high favor that not only she was honored and praised, but also many other ladies were honored and praised because of her. Having observed this and wishing to make it evident to those who had not seen it, I decided to compose something else in which this would be brought out. I then wrote this next sonnet, which begins: *He*

70. *"Tanto gentile e tanto onesta pare,"* Dante's most famous sonnet, in which Love's personification in Beatrice brings out her miraculous curative powers. Cf. *Convivio* III, 7.

71. Some editions begin a new chapter here, adding one more to the total.

sees an affluence, telling how her virtuous power affected other ladies, as appears in the divisions.

> He sees an affluence of joy ideal
>   who sees my lady, in the midst of other ladies;
>   those ladies who accompany her are moved
>   to thank God for this sweet gift of His grace.
> Her beauty has the power of such magic,
>   it never rouses other ladies' envy,
>   instead, it makes them want to be like her:
>   clothed in love and faith and graciousness.
> The sight of her creates humility;
>   and not only is she splendid in her beauty,
>   but every lady near her shares her praise.
> So gracious is her every act in essence
>   that there is no one can recall her to his mind
>   and not sigh in an ecstasy of love.

This sonnet has three parts. In the first I tell in whose company this lady seemed most admirable; in the second I tell how desirable it was to be in her company; in the third I speak of those things which she miraculously brought about in others. The second part begins: *those ladies who;* the third: *Her beauty.* This last part divides into three. In the first part I tell what she brought about in ladies, that was known only to them; in the second I tell what she did for them as seen by others; in the third I say that she miraculously affected not only ladies but all persons, and not only while they were in her presence but also when they recalled her to mind. The second begins: *The sight of her;* the third: *Her every act.*

XXVII

After this I began one day thinking over what I had said about my lady in these last two sonnets and, realizing that I had not said anything about the effect she had on me at the present time, it seemed to me that I had spoken insufficiently. And so I decided to write a poem telling how I seemed to be disposed to her influence, and how her miraculous power worked in me; and believing I would not be able to describe this within the limits of a sonnet, I immediately started to write a *canzone*[72] which begins: *So long a time.*

> So long a time has Love kept me a slave
>   and in his lordship fully seasoned me,
>   that even though at first I felt him harsh,
>   now tender is his power in my heart.
>   But when he takes my strength away from me
>   so that my spirits seem to wander off,
>   my fainting soul is overcome with sweetness,
>   and the color of my face begins to fade.
> Then Love starts working in me with such power
>   he turns my spirits into ranting beggars,
>   and, rushing out, they call
>   upon my lady, pleading in vain for kindness.
>   This happens every time she looks at me,
>   yet she herself is kind beyond belief.

XXVIII

Quomodo sedet sola civitas plena populo! facta est quasi vidua domina gentium![73] I was still engaged in composing this *canzone,* in fact I had completed only the stanza written above, when the God of Justice called this most gracious one to glory under the banner of that blessèd Queen, the Virgin Mary, whose name was always uttered with the greatest reverence by the blessèd Beatrice. And even though the reader might expect me to say something now about her departure from us, it is not my intention to do so here for three reasons. The first is that such a discussion does not fit into the plan of this little book, if we consider the preface which precedes it; the second is that, even if this had been my intention, the language at my command would not yet suffice to deal

72. But for one seven-syllable line (11), this poem could be a sonnet, being made up of one stanza of fourteen verses. According to the *Vita nuova*'s symmetrical scheme, a sonnet is called for in this position.

73. Latin for "How doth the city sit solitary that was full of people! How has she become a widow, she that was great among the nations!" from the Lamentations to Jeremiah 1:1.

with the theme as it deserves; the third is that even supposing that the first two reasons did not exist, it still would not be proper for me to treat the theme since this would entail praising myself—which is the most reprehensible thing one can do. Therefore, I leave this subject to some other commentator.

But since the number nine has appeared many times in what I have already written (which clearly could not happen without a reason), and since in her departure this number seemed to play an important part, it is fitting that I say something here concerning this, inasmuch as it seems to fit in with my plan. And so I shall first speak of the part it played in her departure, and then I shall give some reasons why this number was so close to her.

XXIX

Let me begin by saying that if one counts in the Arabian way,[74] her most noble soul departed this life during the first hour of the ninth day of the month, and if one counts the way they do in Syria, she departed in the ninth month of the year, the first month there being Tixryn the First,[75] which for us is October. And, according to our own way of reckoning, she departed in that year of our Christian era (that is in the year of Our Lord) in which the perfect number had been completed nine times[76] in that century in which she had been placed in this world: she was a Christian of the Thirteenth Century. One reason why this number was in such harmony with her might be this: since, according to Ptolemy and according to Christian truth, there are nine heavens that move, and

74. In order to make a connection between Beatrice's death and the number nine, Dante used his knowledge of the Ptolemaic-based work *Elementa Astronomica* by Alfraganus (cf. *Convivio* II, 5), which revealed that for Arabs, day began at sunset rather than sunrise. Beatrice died on June 8, 1290; according to the Arabian system the first hour of the night in Italy was the first hour of day June 9.

75. June would be the ninth month in the Syrian system, Tixryn, a two-month period the first part of which corresponded to the Roman October.

76. No foreign calendar was required to make the connection between 1290 and the number nine. It had been reached ten times (ten being the perfect number according to St. Thomas) in the thirteenth century of the Christian era.

since, according to widespread astrological opinion, these heavens[77] affect the earth below according to the relations they have to one another, this number was in harmony with her to make it understood that at her birth all nine of the moving heavens were in perfect relationship[78] to one another. But this is just one reason. If anyone thinks more subtly and according to infallible truth, it will be clear that this number was she herself—that is, by analogy. What I mean to say is this: the number three is the root of nine for, without any other number, multiplied by itself, it gives nine: it is quite clear that three times three is nine. Therefore, if three is the sole factor of nine, and the sole factor of miracles is three, that is, Father, Son, and Holy Spirit, who are Three in One, then this lady was accompanied by the number nine so that it might be understood that she was a nine, or a miracle, whose root, namely that of the miracle, is the miraculous Trinity itself. Perhaps someone more subtle than I could find a still more subtle explanation, but this is the one which I see and which pleases me the most.

XXX

After she had departed from this world, the aforementioned city[79] was left as if a widow, stripped of all dignity, and I, still weeping in this barren city, wrote to the princes of the land describing its condition, taking my opening words from the prophet Jeremiah where he says: *Quomodo sedet sola civitas.*[80] And I mention this quotation now so that everyone will understand why I cited these words earlier: it was to serve as a heading for the new material that follows. And if someone should wish to reproach me for not including the rest of the letter, my excuse is this: since it was my intention from the beginning to write in the

77. Cf. *Convivio* II, 3. In Ptolemy's system the ninth heaven is the *primum mobile.* The tenth heaven (corresponding to the perfect number) is the motionless Empyrean.

78. As they were at the birth of Christ. Cf. *Paradise* VI, 55–56.

79. Florence. By "princes of the land" Dante may mean Florentines or he may have been addressing a wider audience. A 1314 letter addressed to the Italian cardinals meeting in Carpentras uses the same quotation from Jeremiah.

80. Latin for "How doth the city sit solitary."

vernacular, and since the words which follow those just quoted are all in Latin,[81] it would be contrary to my intention if I were to include them. And I know that my best friend,[82] for whom I write this book, shares my opinion: that it be written entirely in the vernacular.

XXXI

After my eyes had wept for some time and were so wept out that they could no longer relieve my sadness, I thought of trying to relieve it with some sorrowful words; and I decided to compose a *canzone* in which, lamenting, I would speak of her who was the cause of the grief that was destroying my soul. Then I started writing a *canzone* which begins: *The eyes grieving.* And in order that this *canzone* may seem to remain all the more widowed after it has come to an end, I shall divide it before I copy it. And from now on I shall follow this method.

Let me say that this sad little song has three parts. The first is an introduction; in the second I speak of her; in the third I sadly address the *canzone* itself. The second part begins: *Beatrice has gone,* the third: *Now go your way.* The first part divides further into three: in the first I say why I am moved to speak; in the second I tell who it is I wish to speak to; in the third I tell who it is I wish to speak about. The second begins: *Since I remember;* the third: *My words will be.* Then when I say: *Beatrice has gone,* I am speaking about her, and of this I make two parts: first I tell the reason why she was taken from us; then I tell how someone laments her departure, and I begin this part with the words: *And once withdrawn.* This part further divides into three: in the first I tell who it is that does not mourn her; in the second I tell who it is that does mourn her; in the third I speak of my own condition. The second begins: *But grief,* the third: *Weeping and pain.* Then when I say: *Now go your way,* I am speaking to this *canzone,* designating the ladies to whom it is to go and with whom it is to stay.

81. Dante's letter, the first part of which is quoted in the Latin of the Vulgate (from Lamentations of Jeremiah) was all in Latin.

82. Guido Cavalcanti. Cf. III, XXIV. Dante implies that it was Cavalcanti who encouraged him to turn to the vernacular Italian for literary purposes.

The eyes grieving out of pity for the heart,
    while weeping, have endured great suffering,
    so that they are defeated, tearless eyes.
    And now, if I should want to vent that grief,
    which gradually leads me to my death,
    I must express myself in anguished words.
    Since I remember how I loved to speak
    about my lady when she was alive,
    addressing, gracious ladies, you alone,
    I will not speak to others,
    but only to a lady's tender heart.
    My words will be a dirge, for they tell how
    she suddenly ascended into Heaven,
    and how she left Love here to grieve with me.

Beatrice has gone home to highest Heaven,
    into the peaceful realm where angels live;
    she is with them; she has left you, ladies, here.
    No quality of heat or cold took her
    away from us, as is the fate of others;
    it was her great unselfishness alone;
    because the light of her humility
    shone through the heavens with such radiance,
    it even made the Lord Eternal marvel;
    and then a sweet desire
    moved Him to summon up such blessedness;
    and from down here He had her come to Him,
    because He knew this wretched life on earth
    did not deserve to have her gracious presence.

And once withdrawn from her enchanting form,
    the tender soul, perfectly full of grace,[83]
    now lives with glory in her rightful place.
    Who speaks of her and does not speak in tears
    has a vile heart, insensitive as stone
    which never can be visited by love.
    No evil heart could have sufficient wit
    to conceive in any way what she was like,

83. An attribute of the Virgin Mary. Cf. *Luke* 1:28; Petrarch, *canzone* 366, 40–42.

and so it has no urge to weep from grief.
But grief comes and the wish
to sigh and then to die a death of tears
(and consolation is denied forever)
to anyone who pictures in his thoughts
that which she was and how she went from us.

I breathe deep sighs of anguished desolation
when memory brings to my weary mind
the image of that one who split my heart;
and many times, while contemplating death,
so sweet a longing for it comes to me,
it drains away the color from my face.
When this imagining has hold of me,
bitter affliction binds me on all sides,
and I begin to tremble from the pain.
I am not what I am,
and so my shame drives me away from others;
and then I weep alone in my lamenting,
calling to Beatrice: "Can you be dead?"
And just to call her name restores my soul.

Weeping and pain and many anguished sighs
torment my heart each time I am alone,
and if some one should hear me, he would suffer;
just what my life has been like since the hour
my lady passed into the timeless realm,
there is not any tongue could tell of it.
And so, my ladies, even if I tried,
I could not tell you what I have become;
my bitter life is constant suffering,
a life so much abased
that every man who sees my deathly face
seems to be telling me: "I cast you out!"
But what I have become my lady knows;
I still have hope that she will show me grace.

Now go your way in tears, sad little song,
and find once more the ladies and the maidens
to whom your sister poems[84]

---

84. The other *canzoni*.

were sent as messengers of happiness;
and you who are the daughter of despair,
go look for them, wearing my misery.

XXXII

After this *canzone* was composed, a person came to see me who, according to degrees of friendship, was second after my best friend.[85] And he was so closely related to this glorious lady that no one else was more so. After we had talked together for a while, he begged me to write something for him about a lady who had died, disguising his motives so as to appear to be speaking of a different one who had recently died. I, being quite aware that he was speaking only about that blessèd one, told him I would do as he asked. Then, thinking it over, I decided to compose a sonnet, to be sent to this friend of mine, in which I would express my sorrow in such a way that it would seem to be his.

And so I wrote this sonnet which begins: *Now come to me*. It consists of two parts: in the first I call upon Love's faithful to listen to me, in the second I speak of my wretched condition. The second part begins: *the sighs that issue*.

Now come to me and listen to my sighs,
    O gracious hearts (it is the wish of Pity),
    the sighs that issue in despondency.
    But for their help I would have died of grief,
    because my eyes would be in debt to me,
    owing much more than they could hope to pay
    by weeping so profusely for my lady
    that, mourning her, my heart might be relieved.
And sighs of mine shall ceaselessly be heard
    calling upon my lady (who is gone
    to dwell where worth like hers is merited),
    or breathing their contempt for this our life,
    as if they were the mournful soul itself
    abandoned by its hope of happiness.

85. Believed to be the brother of Beatrice (cf. XXXIII: "grieves as a brother").

XXXIII

After I had composed this sonnet, I realized, thinking more about the person to whom I intended to give it as an expression of his own feelings, that the poem might seem a poor and empty favor for anyone so closely related to my lady now in glory. So, before giving him the sonnet included above, I wrote two stanzas of a *canzone,* one of them truly in behalf of my friend and the other for myself, although to an unobservant reader they would both appear to speak for the same person. Anyone who examines them closely, however, sees clearly that different persons are speaking, since one does not call her his lady while the other does, as the reader may see for himself. I gave him this *canzone* and the sonnet included above, telling him that it was all written for him alone.

This *canzone* begins: *Each time,* and it has two parts. In one of them, in the first stanza, it is this good friend of mine and close relative of hers who laments; in the second I myself lament, that is, in the other stanza which begins: *Then there is blended.* And so it is clear that two people are lamenting in this *canzone,* one of whom grieves as a brother, the other as Love's servant.

> Each time the painful thought comes to my mind
> that I shall nevermore
> behold the lady I will always mourn,
> my grieving memory summons up such grief
> swelling within my heart,
> that I must say: "Why linger here, my soul?
> The torments you will be subjected to
> in this life which already you detest,
> weigh heavily upon my fearful mind."
> Then calling upon Death,
> as I would call on lovely, soothing Peace,
> I say with yearning love: "Please come to me."
> And I am jealous of whoever dies.
>
> Then there is blended out of all my sighs
> a chorus of beseeching,
> begging continuously for Death to come.
> All my desires have centered on this wish
> since that day when my lady

was taken from me by Death's cruelty.
This is because the beauty of her grace,
withdrawing from the sight of men forever,
became transformed to beauty of the soul,
diffusing through the heavens
a light of love that greets the angels there,
moving their subtle, lofty intellects
to marvel at this miracle of grace.

XXXIV

On the day which completed a year since that lady had become a citizen of the Eternal Life, I was sitting in a place where, thinking of her, I was drawing an angel on some panels.[86] And while I was drawing, I looked up and saw around me some men to whom all consideration was due. They were watching what I was doing and, as I was then told, they had already been there some time before I became aware of their presence. When I saw them, I stood up and, greeting them, I said: "Someone was with me just now; that is why I was so deep in thought." After they left, I returned to my work of drawing figures of angels and, while I was doing this, the idea came to me to write some poetry, in the nature of an anniversary poem, and to address it to those men who had just been with me. And so I wrote this sonnet which begins: *Into my mind,* and which has two beginnings; for this reason I divide it first according to the one, and then according to the other.

Now, according to the first beginning, this sonnet has three parts. In the first I say that this lady was already in my memory; in the second I tell what Love, therefore, did to me; in the third I speak of the effects of Love. The second begins: *Love, who perceived,* the third: *Lamenting.* This last part divides into two: in the first I say that all my sighs came forth speaking; in the second I state that some spoke different words from the others. The second begins: *but those.* According to the other beginning this sonnet divides in the same way, except that in the first part I tell when it was that this lady came into my memory, while in the first beginning I do not.

---

86. Cennino Cennini in *Il libro dell'arte* described these *tavolette* as wooden or parchment, six inches square, used by beginners for exercises in drawing.

First beginning

Into my mind had come the gracious image
    of the lady who because of her great worth
    was called by His most lofty Majesty
    to the calm realm of Heaven where Mary reigns.

Second beginning

Into my mind had come the gracious image
    of the lady for whom Love still sheds his tears,
    just when you were attracted by her power
    to come and see what I was doing there.
    Love, who perceived her presence in my mind,
    and was aroused within my ravaged heart,
    commanded all my sighs: "Go forth from here!"
    And each one started on his grieving way.
Lamenting, they came pouring from my heart,
    together in a single voice (that often
    brings painful tears into my grieving eyes);
    but those that poured forth with the greatest pain
    were saying: "This day, O intellect sublime,
    completes a year since you rose heavenward."

XXXV

Sometime afterward, when I happened to be in a place which recalled past times, I was in a very pensive mood, and I was moved by such painful thoughts that I must have had a frightening expression of distress on my face. Becoming aware of my terrible condition, I looked around to see if anyone were watching me. And I saw at a window a gracious lady,[87] young and exceedingly beautiful, who was looking

87. The events recounted in XXXV–XXXIX are further treated in *Convivio* II and in the *canzone* "*Voi che 'ntendendo il terzo ciel movete*." In *Convivio* II, 12, Dante gives an "allegorical and true exposition" of this compassionate lady as a symbol of Philosophy. In the light of this interpretation (which follows Dante's demonstration of her "literal" coming into his life) controversy has arisen about the existence of both Beatrice and this *donna gentile* as real women. The *Convivio* presumably was written some years after the *Vita nuova* when Dante sought poetic ways to universalize his real experience, finding hidden reasons for what happened.

down at me so compassionately, to judge from her appearance, that all pity seemed to be concentrated in her. And because whenever an unhappy person sees someone take pity on him, he is all the more easily moved to tears, as if taking pity on himself, so I immediately felt the tears start to come. Fearing that I was revealing all the wretchedness in my life, I turned away from her eyes and left that place. And later I said to myself: "It must surely be true that with that compassionate lady there is present most noble Love."

And so I decided to write a sonnet which I would address to her and in which I would include everything that has been narrated in this account.[88] And since, because of this account, its meaning is sufficiently clear, I shall not divide it. The sonnet begins: *With my own eyes.*

> With my own eyes I saw how much compassion
>   there was in the expression of your face,
>   when you saw how I looked and how I acted
>   (it is my grief that forces me to this).
>   Then I became aware that you had seen
>   into the nature of my darkened life,
>   and this aroused a fear within my heart
>   of showing in my eyes my wretched state.
> I fled, then, from your presence as I felt
>   the tears begin to overflow my heart
>   that was exalted at the sight of you.
>   Later, within my anguished soul, I said:
>   "There must dwell with that lady that same Love
>   that makes me go about like this in tears."

XXXVI

After that, it always happened that whenever this lady saw me, her face would become compassionate and turn a pale color almost like that of love, so that many times I was reminded of my most noble lady who

---

88. In Provençal poetry such a prose account was called "*razo*," perhaps given orally when the poem or song was recited. Boethius also alternated prose and verse in his *Consolation of Philosophy*, a work Dante cites in *Convivio* II as his first investigation into philosophy.

always had a similar coloring. And many times when I was unable to vent my sadness by weeping, I used to go to see this compassionate lady whose expression alone was able to bring tears to my eyes. And so the urge came to me to write some other poetry addressed to her, and I composed this sonnet which begins: *Color of love.* And because of what has just been said, it is clear without analysis.

> Color of love, expression of compassion,
>   have never so miraculously come
>   to the face of any lady when she gazed
>   at eyes susceptible of anguished tears,
>   as they came to your face whenever I
>   stood in your presence with my grieving face;
>   and something comes to mind because of you:
>   a thought that makes me fear my heart will split.
> I cannot keep my devastated eyes
>   from looking ever and again at you
>   because of the desire they have to weep;
>   and you intensify their longing so
>   that they consume themselves in helpless yearning,
>   for, in your presence, they cannot weep tears.

XXXVII

The sight of this lady had now brought me to the point that my eyes began to enjoy the sight of her too much; I often became angry at myself because of it, and I felt I was very contemptible. So, many times I would curse the wantonness of my eyes, and in my thoughts I would say to them: "You used to make anyone weep who saw your sad state, and now it seems you want to forget about all that because of this lady who gazes at you, who gazes at you only because of her grief for the glorious lady whom you used to mourn. Do whatever you will, but I shall remind you of her many times, damned eyes, for never, before death comes, should your tears have ceased." And after I had said this to myself, addressing my eyes, I was overcome by sighs, deep and anguished. I felt that this conflict which I was having with myself should not remain known solely to the wretch that experienced it, so I decided to compose a sonnet describing this terrible condition.

I wrote the sonnet which begins: *The bitter tears*. It has two parts: in the first I tell my eyes what my heart was saying to me; in the second I prevent any confusion by explaining who is speaking this way, and this part begins: *This is what my heart*. The sonnet could very well be analyzed further, but this would be superfluous, as the preceding account makes its meaning quite clear.

> "The bitter tears that you once used to shed,
>   you eyes of mine, and for so long a time,
>   have made the tears of other persons flow
>   for pity's sake, as you yourselves have seen.
>   And now it seems to me you would forget,
>   if for my part I could be so disloyal
>   as to give you any chance, by not forever
>   reminding you of her whom once you mourned.
> I think about your infidelity,
>   and I am frightened; I have come to dread
>   the lady's face that often looks at you.
>   Until death kills your sight, never should you
>   forget your gracious lady who is dead."
> My heart proclaims these words—and then it sighs.

XXXVIII

When, once again, I returned to see this lady, the sight of her had such a strange effect on me that often I thought of her as someone I liked too much. I thought of her in this way: "This is a gracious, beautiful, young, and discreet lady, and perhaps through the will of Love she has appeared in order that my life may find peace." Often I thought in still more loving terms, so much so that the heart consented to it, that is to the loving feeling. And when I had consented to this, I reconsidered, as if moved by reason, and I said to myself: "God, what kind of thought is this that tries to console me so basely and scarcely allows me to think about anything else?" Then another thought arose and said to me: "Since you have endured so many tribulations, why do you not try to escape further bitter suffering? You see that this is an inspiration of Love, which brings amorous desires into our presence, and it proceeds from so gracious a source as the eyes of the lady who has shown us so much compassion." Finally, having battled like this within myself many times, I wished to write more poetry about it, and since in the battle of the thoughts those won which spoke in the lady's favor, it seemed right that I address myself to her. And I wrote this sonnet which begins: *A thought, gracious;* and I say "gracious" in so far as it involved a gracious lady, for in all other respects it was most base.

In this sonnet I divide myself into two parts according to the way my thoughts were divided. One part I call *heart,* that is desire; the other, *soul,* that is reason; and I tell what one says to the other. That it is justifiable to call desire *heart* and reason *soul* is certainly clear to those persons that I wish my procedure to be clear to. It is true that in the preceding sonnet I take the part of the heart against the eyes, and this seems contrary to what I say in this sonnet. So let me state that in the preceding sonnet, too, the heart stands for desire, since my greatest desire was still that of remembering my most gracious lady rather than of gazing at this one—even though I did have some desire for her then; but it seemed slight. And so it is evident that the one interpretation is not contrary to the other.

This sonnet has three parts. In the first I tell this lady how my desire turns completely toward her; in the second I tell how the soul, that is reason, speaks to the heart, that is desire; in the third I tell how the heart replies. The second part begins: *The soul says,* the third: *The heart replies.*

> A thought, gracious because it speaks of you,
>   comes frequently to dwell awhile with me,
>   and so melodiously speaks of love,
>   it talks the heart into surrendering.
>   The soul says to the heart: "Who is this one
>   that comes with consolation for our mind,
>   possessing such outrageous strength that he
>   will not let other thoughts remain with us?"
> The heart replies: "O reasonable soul,
>   this is a spirit of Love, tender and new,
>   who brings all his desires here to me;
>   all his intensity, his very life,
>   have come from that compassionate one's eyes
>   who was distressed about our martyrdom."

XXXIX

One day, about the ninth hour,[89] there arose in me against this adversary of reason a powerful vision, in which I seemed to see that glorious Beatrice clothed in those crimson garments with which she first appeared to my eyes, and she seemed young, of the same age as when I first saw her. Then I began to think about her and, remembering her in the sequence of past times, my heart began to repent painfully of the desire by which it so basely let itself be possessed for some time, contrary to the constancy of reason; and once I had discarded this evil desire, all my thoughts turned back to their most gracious Beatrice.

Let me say that, from then on, I began to think of her so deeply with my whole shameful heart that my many sighs were proof of it, for all of them on issuing forth would repeat what my heart was saying, that is, the name of that most gracious one and how she departed from us. And many times it happened that some thoughts were so filled with anguish that I would forget what I was thinking and where I was. By this rekindling of sighs, the tears which had subsided began to flow again, so that my eyes seemed to be two objects whose only desire was to weep. And often it occurred that after continuous weeping a purplish color encircled my eyes, as often appears in one who has endured affliction. In this way they were justly rewarded for their inconstancy, and from then on they could not look at any person who might look back at them in such a way as to encourage again a similar inclination. And in order for it to be known that such an evil desire and foolish temptation had been destroyed, so that the poetry I had written before would raise no question, I decided to write a sonnet which should contain the essence of what I have just related. And I wrote: *Alas! By the full force,* and I said "Alas!" because I was ashamed of the fact that my eyes had been so faithless.

I do not divide this sonnet because its reason for existence makes it clear enough.

> Alas! By the full force of countless sighs
> born of the thoughts that overflow my heart,
> the eyes are vanquished, and they do not dare

89. Ecclesiastically the period between noon and 3 P.M. (the 7th, 8th, and 9th hours of the day). Cf. III and XII.

to return the glance of anyone who sees them.
They have become twin symbols of my yearning,
to show, by shedding tears, how much I suffer;
and many times they mourn so much that Love
encircles them with martyrdom's red crown.[90]

These meditations and the sighs I breathe
become so anguishing within the heart
that Love, who dwells there, faints, he is so tortured;
for on those thoughts and sighs of lamentation
the sweet name of my lady is inscribed,
with many words relating to her death.

X L

After this period of distress,[91] during the season when many people go to see the blessed image that Jesus Christ left us[92] as a visible sign of his most beautiful countenance (which my lady beholds in glory), it happened that some pilgrims were going down a street which runs through the center of the city where[93] the most gracious lady was born, lived and died. These pilgrims, it seemed to me, were very pensive as they moved along and I, thinking about them, said to myself: "These pilgrims seem to come from distant parts, and I do not believe that they have ever heard this lady mentioned; they know nothing about her—in fact, their thoughts are centered on other things than what surrounds them; perhaps they are thinking of their friends far away whom we cannot know." Then I said to myself: "I know that, if they were from a neighboring town, they would in some way appear distressed as they

90. In the prose account, "a purple color."

91. The exact time of the event described here is not clear, and some commentators have considered the chapter to be out of order, more appropriately occurring soon after the death of Beatrice than after the battle between his heart and his reason. Others date it much later, for example in the Jubilee year 1300.

92. The cloth called Veronica, imprinted with the likeness of Christ's features when he wiped his face with it while carrying the Cross to Calvary, preserved at St. Peter's in Rome and displayed to the faithful from time to time. Cf. *Paradise* XXXI 103–108; Petrarch, sonnet 16.

93. Florence, although never named in the *Vita nuova*.

passed through the center of the desolated city." Again I said to myself: "If I could detain them for awhile, I know I could make them weep before they left this city, for I would speak words that would make anyone weep who heard them." After they had passed from my sight, I decided to compose a sonnet in which I would reveal what I had said to myself.

And, to make the effect more pathetic, I decided to write it as if I were speaking to them, and I composed this sonnet which begins: *Ah, pilgrims*. And I used the word "pilgrims" in its general sense, for the term can be understood in two ways, one general and the other specific. In the general sense a pilgrim is one who is traveling outside of his own country; in a specific sense "pilgrim" means only one who travels to or returns from the house of St. James.[94] And it is to be known further that there are three ways that those who travel in the service of the Most High may be accurately designated. They are called "palmers" who cross the sea to the Holy Land and often bring back palms; they are called "pilgrims" who travel to the house of Galicia, because the tomb of St. James is farther away from his own country than that of any other apostle; they are called "Romers" who travel to Rome, where those whom I call "pilgrims" were going.

I will not divide this sonnet since its reason for existence makes it clear enough.

> Ah, pilgrims, moving pensively along,
>   thinking, perhaps, of things at home you miss,
>   could the land you come from be so far away
>   (as anyone might guess from your appearance)
>   that you show no signs of grief as you pass through
>   the middle of the desolated city,
>   like people who seem not to understand
>   the grievous weight of woe it has to bear?
> If you would stop to listen to me speak,
>   I know, from what my sighing heart tells me,
>   you would be weeping when you leave this place:

94. After his death at the order of Herod (cf. *Acts* 12:2) the body of the apostle James was said to have been transported miraculously to Galicia in northwestern Spain. The burial place at Santiago de Compostela—pointed out by a star in the ninth century—was a frequent destination for pilgrims in the Middle Ages. Cf. *Paradise* XXV, 17–18; *Convivio* II, 14.

> lost is the city's source of blessedness,
> and I know words that could be said of her
> with power to humble any man to tears.

XLI

Some time afterward, two gentlewomen sent word to me requesting that I send them some of my poetry. Taking into consideration their noble station, I decided not only to let them have some of my poems but also to write something new to go along with those words—in this way doing their request more honor. So I wrote a sonnet which tells of my condition and sent it to them accompanied by the preceding sonnet and by the one which begins: *Now come to me and listen to my sighs.*[95]

The new sonnet I wrote begins: *Beyond the sphere,*[96] and contains five parts. In the first I tell where my thought is going, naming it after one of its effects. In the second I tell why it goes up there, that is, who causes it to go. In the third I tell what it saw, that is, a lady being honored up there, and I call it a "pilgrim spirit" because it makes the journey upward spiritually and, once there, is like a pilgrim far from home. In the fourth I tell how it sees her to be such, that is of such a nature, that I cannot understand it: that is to say that my thought ascends into the nature of this lady to such a degree that my mind cannot grasp it, for our minds function in relation to those blessèd souls as the weak eye does in relation to the sun, and this the Philosopher tells us in the second book of the *Metaphysics.*[97] In the fifth part I say that, even though I cannot understand what my thought has taken me to see, that is her miraculous nature, at least I understand this much: this thought of mine is entirely about my lady, for many times when it comes to my mind, I hear her name. At the end of this fifth part I say: "dear ladies," so that it be understood that it is to ladies that I speak. The second part begins: *a new intelligence,* the third: *Once arrived,* the fourth: *But when it tries,* the fifth: *This much.* It could be divided and

---

95. This sonnet appears in XXXII.

96. To the Empyrean where Beatrice dwells.

97. Aristotle's work, which Dante knew from reading St. Thomas Aquinas. The analogy of the eye and the sun is St. Thomas's.

explained more subtly, but since it can pass with this analysis, I do not concern myself with further division.

> Beyond the sphere that makes the widest round,
>   passes the sigh arisen from my heart;
>   a new intelligence that Love in tears
>   endowed it with is urging it on high.
>   Once having reached the place of its desiring
>   it sees a lady held in reverence,
>   splendid in light; and through her radiance
>   the pilgrim spirit looks upon her being.
> But when it tries to tell me what it saw,
>   I cannot understand the subtle words
>   it speaks to the sad heart that makes it speak.
>   I know it tells of that most gracious one,
>   for I often hear the name of Beatrice.
>   This much, at least, is clear to me, dear ladies.

XLII

After I wrote this sonnet there came to me a miraculous vision in which I saw things that made me resolve to say no more about this blessèd one until I would be capable of writing about her in a nobler way. To achieve this I am striving as hard as I can, and this she truly knows. Accordingly, if it be the pleasure of Him through whom all things live that my life continue for a few more years, I hope to write of her[98] that which has never been written of any other woman. And then may it please the One who is the Lord of graciousness that my soul ascend to behold the glory of its lady, that is, of that blessèd Beatrice, who in glory contemplates the countenance of the One *qui est per omnia secula benedictus.*[99]

---

98. After a period of intense study to write of his vision of Beatrice in a more worthy manner; i.e., in the *Divine Comedy*. Cf. *Convivio* II.

99. Latin for "who is through all ages blessed."

SELECTED BIBLIOGRAPHY

THE NEWEST AND MOST AUTHORITATIVE Italian edition of Dante's *Comedy* is by Giorgio Petrocchi (*La Commedia secondo l'antica vulgata* in 4 vols., Milano: Mondadori, 1966–67). For the text of the *Vita nuova* see the edition by Domenico De Robertis (*Vita nuova*, Milano-Napoli: Ricciardi, 1980).

Among the most useful general introductory studies on Dante are those by Thomas Bergin (*Dante*, Westport, Conn., 1976), Francis Fergusson (*Dante*, London and New York, 1966), Michele Barbi (*Life of Dante*, Berkeley, Calif., 1954; London, 1955).

Of the many prose translations of the *Commedia* the two outstanding ones are the Modern Library edition by Carlyle-Wickstead and the John Sinclair version (New York, 1961) which is straightforward and faithful to the original.

Important reference and bibliographical sources include Umberto Bosco (*Handbook to Dante Studies*, Oxford, 1950); the journal *Dante Studies* with a thorough, descriptive bibliography of Dante scholarship in the United States (edited by Anthony L. Pellegrini for many years and now by Christopher Kleinhenz, published by the State University of New York at Binghamton); Charles Dinsmore (*Aids to the Study of Dante*, New York: Houghton Mifflin, 1903); the *Enciclopedia Dantesca* edited by Umberto Bosco (6 volumes, Rome, 1970); the most useful bibliographical reference book in Italian is by Enzo Esposito (*Bibliografia analitica degli scritti su Dante*, 1950–70, Firenze: Olschki, 1990); Edmund Gardner (*Dante*, London, 1985); Paget Toynbee (*A Dictionary of Proper Names and Notable Matters in the Works of Dante*, revised by Charles S. Singleton, Oxford, 1968); and E. H. Wilkins, T. G. Bergin, et al. (*A Concordance to the Divine Comedy of Dante Alighieri*, London and Cambridge, Mass., 1965).

DIVINE COMEDY

Auerbach, Erich. *Dante: Poet of the Secular World*. Translated by Ralph Manheim. Chicago University Press, 1961.

———. *Mimesis*. Princeton University Press, 1953.

Barolini, Teodolinda. *Dante's Poets, Textuality and Truth in the "Comedy."* Princeton University Press, 1984.

———. *The Undivine "Comedy," Detheologizing Dante*. Princeton University Press, 1992.

Boyde, Patrick. *Dante Philomythes and Philosopher: Man in the Cosmos*. Cambridge University Press, 1981.

Brandeis, Irma. *The Ladder of Vision: A Study of Dante's Comedy*. New York University Press, 1961.

Comparetti, Domenico. *Virgil in the Middle Ages*. Translated by E. F. M. Benecke. New York, 1895.

Davis, Charles Till. *Dante and the Idea of Rome*. Oxford University Press, 1957.

Demaray, John I. *The Invention of Dante's "Commedia."* New Haven, Conn. Yale University Press, 1974.

d'Entrèves, Passerini. *Dante as a Political Thinker*. Oxford University Press, 1952.

Dunbar, H. Flanders. *Symbolism in Medieval Thought and Its Culmination in the Divine Comedy*. New York University Press, 1961.

Fergusson, Francis. *Dante's Drama of the Mind, A Modern Reading of the "Purgatorio."* Princeton University Press, 1952.

Ferrante, Joan. *The Political Vision of the "Divine Comedy."* Princeton University Press, 1986.

Fletcher, Jefferson Butler. *Dante*. Notre Dame University Press, 1965.

Foster, Kenelm. *The Two Dantes and Other Studies*. Berkeley and Los Angeles: University of California Press, 1977.

Freccero, John. *Dante: The Poetics of Conversion*. Edited by R. Jacoff. Cambridge, Mass.: Harvard University Press, 1986.

Grandgent, Charles H. *Companion to the "Divine Comedy."* Edited by Charles Singleton. Cambridge, Mass.: Harvard University Press, 1975.

Haskins, Charles Homer. *The Renaissance of the Twelfth Century*. Cambridge, Mass.: Harvard University Press, 1927.

Hollander, Robert. *Allegory in Dante's "Commedia."* Princeton University Press, 1969.

Lansing, Richard H. *From Image to Idea: A Study of the Simile in Dante's Commedia*. Ravenna: Longo Editore, 1977.

Masciandaro, Franco. *Dante as Dramatist*. Philadelphia: University of Pennsylvania Press, 1991.

Mazzeo, Joseph Anthony. *Structure and Thought in the "Paradiso."* Ithaca, N.Y.: Cornell University Press, 1958.

———. *Medieval Cultural Tradition in Dante's "Divine Comedy."* Ithaca, N.Y.: Cornell University Press, 1960.

Mazzotta, Guiseppe. *Dante's Vision and the Circle of Knowledge*. Princeton University Press, 1992.

———. *Dante, Poet of the Desert*. Princeton University Press, 1979.

Musa, Mark. *Advent at the Gates: Dante's Comedy*. Bloomington: Indiana University Press, 1974.

———. *Essays on Dante*. Bloomington: Indiana University Press, 1964.

Nolan, David, ed. *Dante Commentaries*. New Jersey, 1977.

Orr, M. A. *Dante and the Early Astronomers*. Rev. ed. London, 1956.

Ruggiers, Paul R. *Florence in the Age of Dante*. Norman: University of Oklahoma Press, 1964.

Sayers, Dorothy. *Introductory Papers on Dante*. New York, 1959.

———. *Further Papers on Dante*. New York, 1957.

Schnapp, Jeffrey. *The Transfiguration of History at the Center of Dante's "Paradise."* Princeton University Press, 1986.

Seznec, Jean. *The Survival of the Pagan Gods: The Mythological Tradition and Its Place in Renaissance Humanism and Art*. Translated by B. Sessions. Princeton University Press, 1953.

Singleton, Charles S. *Dante Studies I*. Cambridge, Mass.: Harvard University Press, 1954.

Sowell, Madison, ed. *Dante and Ovid, Essays in Intertextuality*. Binghamton, N.Y., 1991.

Stambler, Bernard. *Dante's Other World*. New York University Press, 1957.

Thompson, David. *Dante's Epic Journeys*. Baltimore, Md.: The Johns Hopkins University Press, 1974.

Vossler, Karl. *Medieval Culture*. Translated by W. C. Lauxton. New York, 1929.

VITA NUOVA

Barber, Joseph A. "The Role of the Other in Dante's *Vita nuova*." *Studies in Philology* 78 (1981): 128–137.

Bigongiari, Dino. "Dante's *Vita nuova*." In *Essays on Dante and Medieval Culture*, 65–76. Firenze: Olschki, 1964.

Carruthers, M. *The Book of Memory: A Study of Memory in Medieval Culture*. Cambridge University Press, 1990.

Corsi, Sergio. *Il "modus digressivus" nella "Divina Commedia."* Potomac, Md.: Scripta Humanistica, 1987.

Cro, Stelio. "*Vita nuova* figura *Comoediae*: Dante tra la Villana Morte e Matelda." *Italian Culture* 6 (1985): 13–30.

D'Andrea, Antonio. "La struttura della *Vita nuova*: le divisioni delle rime." *Yearbook of Italian Studies* 4 (1980): 13–40.

De Bonfils Templer, Margherita. *Itinerario di Amore: dialettica di Amore e Morte nella* Vita nuova. Chapel Hill: University of North Carolina Studies in Romance Languages and Literatures, 1973.

Elata-Aster, Gerda. "Gathering the Leaves and Squaring the Circle: *Recording, Reading* and *Writing* in Dante's *Vita nuova* and *Divina Commedia*." *Italian Quarterly* 24.92 (1983): 5–26.

Fletcher, Jefferson Butler. "The 'True Meaning' of Dante's *Vita nuova*." *Romanic Review* 11 (1920): 95–148.

Guzzardo, John. "Number Symbolism in the *Vita nuova*." *Canadian Journal of Italian Studies* 8:30 (1985): 12–31.

Hainsworth, P. "Cavalcanti in the *Vita nuova*." *Modern Language Review* 83 (1988), 586–90.

Harrison, Robert Pogue. *The Body of Beatrice*. Baltimore, Md.: The Johns Hopkins University Press, 1988.

Hollander, Robert. "*Vita nuova*: Dante's Perceptions of Beatrice." *Dante Studies* 92 (1974): 1–18.

Holloway, Julia Bolton. "The *Vita nuova*: Paradigms of Pilgrimage." *Dante Studies* 103 (1985): 103–24.

Howe, Kay. "Dante's Beatrice: the Nine and the Ten." *Italica* 52 (1975): 364–71.

Kleiner, J. "Finding the Center: Revelation and Reticence in the *Vita nuova*." *Texas Studies in Literature and Language* 32:1 (1990), 85–100.

Klemp, P. J. "The Women in the Middle: Layers of Love in Dante's *Vita nuova*." *Italica* 61:3 (1984): 185–194.

Mazzaro, Jerome. *The Figure of Dante: An Essay on the "Vita nuova."* Princeton University Press, 1981.

Mazzotta, Giuseppe. "The Language of Poetry in the *Vita nuova*." *Rivista di studi italiani* 1:1 (1983): 3–14.

McKenzie, Kenneth. "The Symbolic Structure of Dante's *Vita nuova*." *PMLA* 18 (1903): 341–55.

Musa, Mark. *Dante's "Vita nuova": A Translation and an Essay.* Bloomington: Indiana University Press, 1973.

Nolan, Barbara. "The *Vita nuova*: Dante's Book of Revelation." *Dante Studies* 88 (1970): 51–77.

Norton, Charles Eliot. *The New Life of Dante Alighieri.* Boston and New York: Houghton-Mifflin, 1895.

Pipa, Arshi. "Personaggi della *Vita nuova*: Dante, Cavalcanti e la famiglia Portinari." *Italica* 62:2 (1985): 99–115.

Scott, J. A. "Dante's 'Sweet New Style' and the *Vita nuova*." *Italica* 42 (1965): 98–107.

Shaw, J. E. *Essay on the "Vita nuova."* Princeton University Press, 1929.

Singleton, Charles S. *An Essay on the "Vita nuova."* 1949. Cambridge, Mass.: Harvard University Press, 1958.

Smarr, Janet Levarie. "Celestial Patterns and Symmetries in the *Vita nuova*," *Dante Studies* 98 (1980): 145–50.

Sturm-Maddox, Sarah. "The Pattern of Witness: Narrative Design in the *Vita nuova*," *Forum Italicum* 12:2 (1978): 216–32.

Trovato, Mario. "Il capitolo xii della *Vita nuova*." *Forum Italicum* 16:1–2 (1982), 19–32.

Valency, M. *In Praise of Love: An Introduction to the Love Poetry of the Renaissance.* New York: Macmillan, 1958.

Vincent, E. R. "The Crisis in the *Vita nuova*." In *Century Essays on Dante by Members of the Oxford Dante Society*, 132–42. Oxford: The Clarendon Press, 1965.

Viegnes, Michel J. "Space and Love in the *Vita nuova*." *Lectura Dantis* 4 (1989): 78–85.

FOR THE BEST IN PAPERBACKS, LOOK FOR THE

In every corner of the world, on every subject under the sun, Penguin represents quality and variety—the very best in publishing today.

For complete information about books available from Penguin—including Penguin Classics, Penguin Compass, and Puffins—and how to order them, write to us at the appropriate address below. Please note that for copyright reasons the selection of books varies from country to country.

In the United States: Please write to *Penguin Group (USA), P.O. Box 12289 Dept. B, Newark, New Jersey 07101-5289* or call 1-800-788-6262.

In the United Kingdom: Please write to *Dept. EP, Penguin Books Ltd, Bath Road, Harmondsworth, West Drayton, Middlesex UB7 0DA.*

In Canada: Please write to *Penguin Books Canada Ltd, 10 Alcorn Avenue, Suite 300, Toronto, Ontario M4V 3B2.*

In Australia: Please write to *Penguin Books Australia Ltd, P.O. Box 257, Ringwood, Victoria 3134.*

In New Zealand: Please write to *Penguin Books (NZ) Ltd, Private Bag 102902, North Shore Mail Centre, Auckland 10.*

In India: Please write to *Penguin Books India Pvt Ltd, 11 Panchsheel Shopping Centre, Panchsheel Park, New Delhi 110 017.*

In the Netherlands: Please write to *Penguin Books Netherlands bv, Postbus 3507, NL-1001 AH Amsterdam.*

In Germany: Please write to *Penguin Books Deutschland GmbH, Metzlerstrasse 26, 60594 Frankfurt am Main.*

In Spain: Please write to *Penguin Books S. A., Bravo Murillo 19, 1° B, 28015 Madrid.*

In Italy: Please write to *Penguin Italia s.r.l., Via Benedetto Croce 2, 20094 Corsico, Milano.*

In France: Please write to *Penguin France, Le Carré Wilson, 62 rue Benjamin Baillaud, 31500 Toulouse.*

In Japan: Please write to *Penguin Books Japan Ltd, Kaneko Building, 2-3-25 Koraku, Bunkyo-Ku, Tokyo 112.*

In South Africa: Please write to *Penguin Books South Africa (Pty) Ltd, Private Bag X14, Parkview, 2122 Johannesburg.*

Orlando Furioso
Ludovico Ariosto
Translated with an Introduction by Barbara Reynolds
A dazzling kaleidoscope of adventures, ogres, monsters, barbaric splendor, and romance, this epic poem stands as one of the greatest works of the Italian Renaissance.   *Part I: ISBN 0-14-044311-8*
Part II: ISBN 0-14-044310-X

The Decameron
Giovanni Boccaccio
Translated with an Introduction and Notes by G. H. McWilliam
Read as a social document of medieval times, as an earthly counterpart of Dante's *Divine Comedy*, or even as an early manifestation of the dawning spirit of the Renaissance, *The Decameron* is a masterpiece of imaginative narrative whose background is the Florentine plague of 1348.
ISBN 0-14-044930-2

The Travels
Marco Polo
Translated with an Introduction by Ronald Latham
Despite piracy, shipwreck, brigandage, and wild beasts, Polo moved in a world of highly organized commerce. This chronicle of his travels through Asia, whether read as fact or fiction, is alive with adventures, geographical information, and descriptions of natural phenomena.
ISBN 0-14-044057-7

The Story of My Life
Giovanni Giacomo Casanova
Translated by Stephen Sartarelli and Sophie Hawkins
Edited with an Introduction by Gilberto Pizzamiglio
Seducer, gambler, necromancer, swashbuckler, spy, self-made gentleman, entrepreneur, and general bon vivant, Casanova lived a life richer and stranger than most fiction. The first new translation since the 1960s, this edition provides the highlights from his twelve volumes in one beautiful, unique volume   *ISBN 0-14-043915-3*

The Book of the Courtier
Baldesar Castiglone
Translated with an Introduction by George Bull
Discretion, decorum, nonchalance, and gracefulness are qualities of the complete and perfect Italian Renaissance courtier that are outlined in this series of imaginary conversations between the principal members of the court of Urbino in 1507.   *ISBN 0-14-044192-1*

Autobiography
Benvenuto Cellini
Translated with an Introduction and Notes by George Bull
With enviable powers of invective and an irrepressible sense of humor, Cellini provides an unrivaled portrait of the manners and morals of the Italy of Michelangelo and Medici. *ISBN 0-14-044718-0*

The Portable Machiavelli
Niccolò Machiavelli
Edited by Peter Bonanella and Mark Musa
This essential collection of Machiavelli's writings brings together the complete texts of *The Prince*, *Belfagor*, and *Castruccio Castracani*, as wells as an abridged version of *The Discourses*, private letters, and selections from his *The Art of War*. *ISBN 0-14-015092-7*

The Discourses
Niccolò Machiavelli
Edited with an Introduction by Bernard Crick
with Revisions by Brian Richardson
Translated by Leslie J. Walker
Machiavelli examines the glorious republican past of Rome. In contrast with *The Prince*, this unfinished work upholds the Republic as the best and most enduring style of government. *ISBN 0-14-044428-9*

The Prince
Niccolò Machiavelli
Revised Translation by George Bull
Introduction by Anthony Grafton
Machiavelli's famous portrait of the prince still "retains its power to fascinate, frighten and to instruct." Rejecting the traditional values of political theory, Machiavelli drew upon his own experiences of office under the turbulent Florentine republic when he wrote his celebrated treatise on statecraft. The tough realities of Machiavelli's Italian are well preserved in the clear, unambiguous English of George Bull's translation.
ISBN 0-14-044915-9

Letters to Father
Suor Maria Celeste to Galileo, 1623–1633
S. M. Celeste Galilei
Translated and Annotated by Dava Sobel
Placed in a convent at the age of thirteen (where she was renamed Suor Maria Celeste), Virginia Galilei, Galileo's eldest daughter, wrote to her father continually. The letters span a dramatic decade that included the Thirty Years' War, the bubonic plague, and the development of Galileo's

own universe-changing discoveries, but though they touch on these events, the letters mostly focus on the details of everyday life that connect this fascinating father and daughter. All 124 surviving letters are here translated into English.   *ISBN 0-14-243715-8*

Lives of the Artists
Volume 1
Giorgio Vasari
Translated and Edited with an Introduction by George Bull
Vasari offers insights into the lives and techniques of twenty artists, from Cimabue, Giotto, and Leonardo to Michelangelo and Titian.
                                              ISBN 0-14-044500-5

Lives of the Artists
Volume 2
Translated and Edited with an Introduction by George Bull
and Notes on the Artists by Peter Murray
Vasari's knowledge was based on his own experience as an early Renaissance painter and architect. Volume 2 explores the lives of twenty-five artists, from Perugino to Giovanni Pisano.   *ISBN 0-14-044460-2*

New Science
Giambattista Vico
Translated by David Marsh with an Introduction by Anthony Grafton
This astonishingly ambitious attempt to provide a comprehensive science of all human society by decoding the history, mythology, and law of the ancient world marked a turning-point in humanist thinking as significant as Newton's contemporary revolution in physics.   *ISBN 0-14-043569-7*

The Betrothed
Alessandro Manzoni
(I promessi sposi)
Translated with an Introduction by Bruce Penman
Manzoni chronicles the perils of two lovers caught in the turbulence of seventeenth-century Italy.   *ISBN 0-14-044274-X*

Cavalleria Rusticana and Other Stories
Giovanni Verga
Translated with an Introduction by G. H. McWilliam
Giovanni Verga's brilliant stories of love, adultery, and honor are set against the scorched landscapes of the slopes of Mount Etna and the Plain of Catalan. This edition contains the first major English translations since those of D. H. Lawrence in the 1920s.   *ISBN 0-14-044741-5*

FOR THE BEST IN CLASSICS LOOK FOR THE

Epic of Gilgamesh
Translated with an Introduction by N. K. Sandars
Fifteen centuries before Homer, this Mesopotamian cycle of poems tells of Gilgamesh, the great King, Uruk, and his long and arduous journey to the spring of youth in search of immortality.   *ISBN 0-14-044919-1*

The Odyssey
Homer
Translated by E. V. Rieu with a Revised Translation by D. C. H. Rieu and a New Introduction by Peter Jones
Odysseus's perilous ten-year voyage from Troy to his home in Ithaca is recounted in a revised translation that captures the swiftness, drama, and worldview of the Greek original.   *ISBN 0-14-044556-0*

Confessions
Saint Augustine
Translated with an Introduction by R. S. Pine-Coffin
This autobiography is both an explanation of Augustine's own conversion to Christianity and an attempt to convince the reader that it is the one true faith.   *ISBN 0-14-044114-X*

The Ramayana
R. K. Narayan
This shortened modern prose version of the Indian epic—parts of which date from 500 B.C.—was composed by one of today's supreme storytellers.   *ISBN 0-14-018700-6*

Beowulf
Anonymous
Edited with an Introduction, Notes, and Glossary by Michael Alexander
This edition presents Anglo-Saxon verse text on the left-hand page, faced by a page on which almost every word is glossed. Succinct footnotes clarify historical and cultural matters.   *ISBN 0-14-043377-5*

Sir Gawain and the Green Knight
Edited by J. A. Burrow
Dating from the latter part of the fourteenth century, this subtle and accomplished poem is roughly contemporary with *The Canterbury Tales*, though written in a more provincial dialect. This edition is accessible to modern readers while retaining the integrity of the original.
    ISBN 0-14-042295-1